A
Kingsley
AMIS
Omnibus

JAKE'S THING
–
STANLEY AND THE WOMEN
–
THE OLD DEVILS

A Kingsley AMIS Omnibus

JAKE'S THING

–

STANLEY AND THE WOMEN

–

THE OLD DEVILS

Hutchinson
London

JAKE'S THING
© Kingsley Amis 1978

STANLEY AND THE WOMEN
© Kingsley Amis 1984

THE OLD DEVILS
© Kingsley Amis 1986

The right of Kingsley Amis to be
identified as Author of this work has been asserted
by Kingsley Amis in accordance with the
Copyright, Designs and Patents Act, 1988

This omnibus edition first published in 1987 by
Hutchinson
Reissued 1992

Random Century Group Ltd
20 Vauxhall Bridge Road, London SW1V 2SA

Random Century Australia (Pty) Ltd
20 Alfred Street, Milsons Point, Sydney, NSW 2061, Australia

Random Century New Zealand Ltd
PO Box 40–086, Glenfield, Auckland 10, New Zealand

Random Century South Africa (Pty) Ltd
PO Box 337, Bergvlei, 2012, South Africa

British Library Cataloguing-in-Publication Data
Amis, Kingsley
  A Kingsley Amis omnibus.
  I. Title
  823.914[F]

Printed and bound in Great Britain by
Clays Ltd, Bungay Suffolk

ISBN: 0 09 172719 7

JAKE'S THING

Contents

1   This Is It

'When did you first notice something was wrong?'

'Well, notice, it must be five or six weeks, I could give you the date if I had to. But then as soon as I did notice I realised something had been wrong much further back than that.'

'How much further back?'

'Oh . . . A year? Year and a half?'

'About the time your other trouble started to become acute, in fact.'

'Yes. There must be a link.'

By way of answer the doctor gave a quiet sigh. His patient, a round-faced bespectacled man called Jake Richardson, was left to wonder whether this meant that the link was all too grimly real, that only a fool would suppose one existed or that the task of explanation seemed altogether daunting. Jake didn't wonder for long. To have gone on doing so would have been to concede the doctor (Curnow by name) too much importance. When asked why he persistently went to a man he had so little time for, Jake would say that disliking your GP was a good insurance against getting dependent on him.

Now Dr Curnow shook his head a few times and swallowed. In the end he said, 'There's nothing I can do for you.'

'Oh, but surely you must have a – '

'No. The only way is for me to send you to someone.'

'That was rather what I – '

'Excuse me a second, would you please?'

Funny how it's got ruder to say please than not, Jake thought to himself as the doctor began to turn slowly through a small leather-bound book on his desk. He seemed to find its contents of unusual interest, even novelty. One page in particular absorbed his attention for longer than would have been necessary if he had been doing no more than reading the whole of it with care. After this interval he lifted his head abruptly and looked Jake straight in the eye for a quarter of a minute or so. Then he returned his gaze to the book before him, keeping it fixed there while he reached for his telephone. It had buttons instead of a dial.

'Dr Rosenberg? Dr Curnow here.' This information was enough to provoke a considerable speech from the other end, though Jake couldn't make out anything of what was said. 'I have a patient you might be able to do something for,' said Curnow at last. 'I have him here in the room with me. Name of Richardson, J. C. Richardson. . . . Well, you'll remember the Mr Pickering I sent to you last autumn. . . . Oh did he, I'm sorry to hear that. . . . Yes, I'm afraid so. . . .' What Curnow heard next made him stare at Jake again but more consideringly, look him over rather than look at him. 'Certainly not. No question of anything like that. . . .' Curnow's face changed, except for the direction and quality of his stare, and he started nodding emphatically. 'Oh *yes*, very much so. . . . Yes, the perfect description. . . . Oh really? You will? . . . I'll ask him.' Curnow arranged an appointment for the following week, listened with a grave, responsible expression to a final passage of words from far (from not all that far, actually, just a couple of hundred yards up Harley Street) and rang off.

'A very able man, Dr Rosenberg. Very able.'

'Good,' said Jake. 'Rosenberg. Presumably he's some sort of –'

'Would you excuse me a second, please?' Curnow lifted a switch on what he no doubt called his intercom, which had started to hum hoarsely. 'Yes, what is it?'

'Sheikh Qarmat bin Ezzat el Sha'ket is here,' said a version of a girl's voice.

'Bring him in thirty seconds precisely and cash as he leaves of course,' said Curnow, getting up. 'Well, Mr Richardson, you'll be letting me know how things go. Insides behaving themselves?'

'Oh, mustn't complain.'

'That's right. No pain in the abdomen?'

'Just a twinge or so, nothing out of the way.'

'Urine satisfactorily pale?'

'Yes thank you.'

'Faeces satisfactorily dark?'

'Yes.'

'What about the haemorrhoids?'

'You mean piles. I haven't got piles,' said Jake truthfully. 'I don't have them.'

The doctor chuckled and shrugged his shoulders, tolerant of his patient's nervous or whimsical avoidance of the topic. 'Getting plenty of exercise?'

'I thought I was suppose to take it easy.'

'Mild exercise. Walking. Gardening. Didn't you say you gardened?'

'Yes I did. I do.'

'Keep on with it. It can't fail to do you good. Whatever's wrong with you.'

'Thank you, Dr Curnow.'

In the hall the man of the East, clad quite as if he had just arrived from there, without even time to freshen up after the journey, was approaching across a carpet that looked as if it had once taken a similar course: no doubt the gift of some grateful emir or caliph. The receptionist, a girl of twenty or twenty-five, was in attendance. Jake noticed that her breasts were either remarkably large or got up to seem so by a professional. He tried to reckon the chances of Curnow's knowing which and felt downcast for a moment, because any chance at all was too much. But almost at once he cheered up again: between the front door and that of the waiting-room there moved a fellow-patient he had seen at least once before under this roof, moved with new and extreme labour, one leg straight and stiff, the other bent and stiff. Teach him, thought Jake. Not me yet, he also thought.

As one who did what doctors said while still rather looking down on them, he decided to walk to Warren Street and catch a 127 bus instead of taking a taxi. That in any case wouldn't have been as easy as winking in this area. No sooner had one black, brown or yellow person, or group of such, been set down on the pavement than Americans, Germans, Spaniards were taken up and vice versa. It was just after four o'clock on a fine afternoon early in April. Jake lengthened his stride and crossed the road in front of a double-parked car, large, black and with CD plates. An unmistakable witch-doctor, in equally manifest need of outside help, was doing his best to alight from it. Portland Place turned out to be easily as full of north-bound vehicles, most of them cars, as might have been expected at this hour on Wednesday in Holy Week, no less so than it would doubtless turn out to be on 23rd December or, this year, more likely 22nd. Despite their intermittent and slow progress, Jake waited for the lights to change before he left the kerb. He had made this a rule ever since a momentously near miss by a motor-bike the previous year. The traffic going the other way was much lighter but no faster, thanks to some extensive road-works with nobody working on them.

By contrast, though not altogether by contrast, Euston Road resembled a motor-racing track, or a network of such. Jake felt some relief at reaching the northern side undamaged. He waved and smiled cheerily at an old friend he couldn't have named for the moment and the old friend, who had just come out of Thames Television House, waved and smiled cheerily back a couple of seconds before Jake realised he wasn't an old friend but the chap who played the superintendent in that police series. Oh Christ, thought Jake; still, the bugger must get a lot of that.

Half an hour later, having been carried up through Camden Town, Chalk Farm and Hampstead, Jake got off the 127 at the stop outside the Orris Park National Westminster Bank. He was about to start the five-minute walk to his house when his eye fell on the window of Winesteals Ltd and an all-written notice that nevertheless clearly proclaimed Crazy Cuts: 10p in the £ off everything this week only. He hesitated only a moment. He had brought himself to go and see his doctor, he had responsibly taken a bit of exercise, he had saved something like £1.20 by not taking a taxi home, and he was fed up with Tunisian Full-Bodied Red Table Wine (Dry) every night of his life. Into the shop he darted and over to the French

corner. Côtes de Nuits Villages 1971 at £2.05 less presumably 20½p?
Beaune Clos de la Mousse 1972 at. . . . To hell with it: Château Talbot
1967 at £4.09 less whatever the fuck. On his way to what people probably
meant by the check-out he noticed a pile of boxes of liqueur chocolates
and hesitated again, longer this time. £2.17, but that wasn't what was at
stake. In the end he took a box.

Ahead of him at the till stood a customer in very dirty whitish overalls
smoking a cigar and chatting to the senior of the two shopmen present
while the junior cast up what he was buying.

'Is it worth it?' he asked a couple of times. 'This is it. If it isn't, I don't
want to know. If it isn't, I'm not interested. If it is, then this is it. I mean,
this is it. Right?'

'Right.'

'And it is. It bloody is. Like everything else.' As he talked the overalled
man took a roll of £20 notes from his side pocket and counted some out;
Jake thought five but wasn't sure. 'It bloody is. Twelve-year-old's better
than eight-year-old and '61's going to be better than '62. I mean, you
know, this is it. Ever tried Jack Daniel's Green Label?'

'No.'

'Worth trying.' Change was handed over, not much. 'Ta. Yeah, worth
trying. Shows you the Black's worth it. Green's good, though. Well, cheers.'

'Cheers.'

Jake moved along, put his two items down on the stub of counter and
set himself to see which buttons on his machine the junior shopman would
prod. 3, then one he missed, so he gave up and waited for the receipt slip
to be torn off and wordlessly handed to him. He screwed up his eyes.
003.69, 002.17, 006.86. He went on looking while the senior shopman
drew in air through his nose.

'Er, the. . . . You've charged the full price for the chocolates.'

'Right.'

'But your notice says 10p in the pound off everything.'

'Everything bar chocolates and smokes.'

'But it says everything.'

'It means everything bar chocolates and smokes.'

'But. . . .'

'You want them, do you, squire?'

' . . . Yes.'

'Right.'

After a short pause, during which he took a blow on the kneecap from
the corner of a wire basket in the hand of a man in a blue boiler-suit, Jake
paid, picked up his goods and left, remembering he should have said Cheers
just as the exit door swung shut after him. Out in the street he noticed that
away from the sunlight the air was chilly: the spring had begun late and
wet. There were still a few dead leaves half beaten into the triangular patch
of bare earth bounded by concrete, probably due to become a communal

flower-bed any day, at the corner of the High Street and Burgess Avenue. The near end of the latter consisted of two longish brick terraces put up a hundred years before to house the workers at some vanished local industry and these days much in demand among recently married couples, pairs of homosexuals and older persons whose children had left or never existed. Jake had bought no. 47 in 1969; he couldn't have afforded to now.

2   The Farting Ploughboy

The house stood out among its neighbours by not having had anything done to its outside: no stucco, no curious chimneys, no colourful shutters, no trailing ferns in wire baskets, front door and window-frames and drain-pipes not painted cinnabar or orpiment or minium or light mushroom, and garden neither turned into a tiny thicket nor altogether removed to accommodate a car. Having no car had made it comparatively easy for Jake to prevent that last option but some of the others had taken toll of his powers of resistance. He opened and then shut the gate, which was not of wrought iron or imitation bronze, walked up the eight yards of gravel path and let himself in.

A great deal had managed to get itself done to the inside of no. 47 because so much of it was in items small in themselves and capable of being introduced a bit at a time. He was also at the mercy of the view that whatever rights a man might have over the exterior of his dwelling lapse by definition once its threshold is crossed. The place was full of things. It had to be admitted that some of these weren't as small as all that, like the heavy-duty cheval-glass near the front door and the giant's-coffin-sized Dutch (or some such) clock in the alcove by the sitting-room fireplace, but a lot were. No flat surface except the ceiling and parts of the floor was free of ashtrays bearing quotations from poem and song, serious souvenir mugs and antique paper-weights, and screens supplemented the walls for the hanging of small pictures enclosed in large mounts and photographs of dead strangers. It was hard to find a square foot that hadn't been made nice.

The person who had brought all this about was Jake's fat wife Brenda, who stood up, brushing cake-crumbs off her knee-length fisherman's-knit cardigan, to be kissed on the cheek by him. He went over and greeted similarly her old friend Alcestis Mabbott, who was fat too, not as fat as Brenda but short with it. And then Alcestis's hair stood away from her head in a stiff dun froth while Brenda's, though no more vivid, was smooth and abundant, so that almost anybody would have decided that Brenda had the better of things between the two of them.

'Hallo, Allie dear,' said Jake. 'What a nice surprise.'

'I told you she was coming,' said Brenda.

'Did you, darling? I must have forgotten.'

One way or the other the presence of Alcestis was certainly a surprise to Jake. If it hadn't been he wouldn't have come carting his recent purchases into the sitting-room like a boy back from the fair. It was on them, as he could have predicted without the least trouble, that Alcestis's round-eyed gaze instantly fell.

'Been shopping, have we?' she asked gruffly. It wasn't a tone or vocal quality adopted for the occasion. On their first meeting, round about ten years earlier at a dinner-party in some cultural crapper south of the river, Jake had come really close to congratulating her on a marvellous imitation, unasked-for though it was, of the way retired colonels were supposed to talk. All that had deterred him was puzzlement about why she thought it went well with the detailed account she was giving him of how she had made the unpleasant dress she had on. Then, soon after she had switched the focus of attention to the new wallpaper she was going to have in her dining-room and kept her voice the same, he had got it. Whenever he considered he had done something particularly foolish, which wasn't often, he would cheer himself up by remembering that at least he'd never made a pass at Alcestis ('Smudger' to him in his thoughts).

He answered her question, or anyhow spoke while looking at her. 'Just one or two odd things.'

'One of them looks to me like a very odd thing indeed.' She meant the bottle which, though wrapped in brown paper, was obviously either a bottle or an object shaped just like a bottle.

Forewarned of he knew not quite what, Jake put it down on a tiled coffee-table slightly to his rear and said to his wife, 'Got you a little something.'

'Ooh. . . .' Brenda moved her spectacles from the top of her head to the region of her nose and uncovered the liqueur chocolates. 'Oh, darling, you really shouldn't.'

'Nonsense, everybody deserves a bit of a – '

'I mean you *shouldn't*, darling,' said Brenda. Her eyes, unlike her friend's, were long from corner to corner and also bright, both in the intensity of their greenish colour and in the shining of their surfaces even through glass. Jake had never forgotten the first time they had been turned full on him: not where or when, just how they had looked. 'You know, this is exactly what I'm not supposed to have because they're sugar and booze and I can't resist them. It's very sweet of you but honestly.'

'You haven't got to dispose of the whole – '

'I'm sure good old Jake'll give you a hand if you're well and truly stuck. Always ready to help out, our Jake, eh, what?' Alcestis didn't actually utter the last two words but they were there in the way she rocked her long head to and fro and pushed her lips up afterwards.

'I should jolly well hope so, I can tell you,' said Jake, and saw Brenda give him a sharp glance over the top of her glasses. He added hastily, 'I mean that's right, I can always – '

'What absolutely fills me with the most burning curiosity is the question of what's inside the other parcel, the chappie over there.'

'Well, it's a . . . a *bottle* actually of all things, Allie. With drink corked up inside it.'

'Absolutely agog.'

The two women waited. Jake reached out and snatched up the bottle and tore the paper off it as fast as he could. In wine-waiter style he displayed the label to Alcestis, who nodded several times and gave a grunt or so of approval. There was another pause.

'I wonder. . . .' said Alcestis. 'Of course it is a bit on the early side.'

'Would you like a glass?' asked Brenda.

'Well, I must say, I don't normally, I – '

'Come on, do you good, why not, fill your boots, great stuff, that's the spirit.' It wasn't (Jake saw) that Alcestis had guessed he had been going to give himself a treat which she had maliciously decided to impair, nor that she had simply fancied a glass of wine: she had sensed, without realising that she had sensed, that he hoped she wouldn't ask him for one and so naturally had asked him for one, or better still had got herself asked to have one. 'Shan't be a jiffy.'

Along in the kitchen he got going fast. Off with the vile plastic foil they put round the necks of bottles these days and out with the cork; same treatment for a bottle of Tunisian Full-Bodied Red Table Wine (Dry). Now a jug, or rather pair of jugs.

'I remember as if it were yesterday,' he said as he worked. 'Jerry had given our lads a fearful pasting round St Quentin and Compiègne and most of us thought that when the big push came in the spring we'd be done for. Not a word of a lie. Literally. I said done for and I meant done for.' He raised his voice. 'Where's the bloody corkscrew? Oh, here it is – all right – got it.'

By this time he had the two wines in jugs of their own and was pouring the Château Talbot into the Tunisian bottle. A jet aircraft came into earshot.

'There were men in my battalion who'd gawn six months without sleep and the average life of a subaltern in the front line was thirty seconds. Absolute gospel. Literally. Then one day in the shithouse at Division I ran into old Bugger Cockface who I'd known at Eton and Sandhurst and in the Crimea and at Spion Kop.' The jet was almost overhead. 'And I said to him, I said, "Are we done for, Bugger?" and he said, "By George not yet, Smudger," and I thought, damn fine soldier, damn fine Englishman, damn fine feller, what? What? *What?*'

'I said what on earth are you doing? You've been simply ages.'

Brenda had spoken. Alcestis was at her side. The two must have stolen up on him under the noise of the aircraft, which had begun to recede. Jake hoped he hadn't turned round too abruptly. There stood near him the two bottles each filled with what had been in the other and the jugs not noticeable. He said,

'Just. . . . It took me a while to find the – '

'Two bottles,' said Alcestis. 'I say, are we having a piss-up?'

'That one's for dinner-time. These cheap plonks, if you take the cork out a couple of hours before you – '

'Tunisian Full-Bodied. . . . This is good enough for me.'

'No really, it won't have – '

'Suit me down to the ground. I'm not a connoisseur chappie like you.'

'No, the other one's much – '

'No, you have that with your dinner. Able to appreciate it, mm?'

'I'd far rather – '

It was no good: she had noticed, again unconsciously, that he now wanted her to have what a minute earlier he hadn't wanted her to have, and maintained the appropriate reaction. (She must have grasped too that something was going on in the kitchen because he hadn't been out there that long.) Back in the sitting-room she took a sip and raised her unabundant eyebrows.

'I think this is awfully good, Jake. What did you pay for it you don't mind my asking?'

He took a gulp. Although he much preferred drink with food he was fucked if he was going to, etc. 'I don't know,' he said a little wildly. 'One twenty-five . . . ten. . . .'

'Where? No don't tell me, no point, memory like a sieve. Of course, I suppose with your experience and your palate, easy. Brenda love, aren't you drinking?'

'No, I'm cutting down,' said Brenda. She went to the tea-tray, poured herself a cup and added milk and three lumps of sugar.

'But you're . . .' said Jake and stopped.

'I'm what?'

'You're . . . entitled to break the rules once in a way.' He was acting on the principle that every drop of claret outside Alcestis was a drop saved. 'Let me get you a glass.'

'No thank you.' She spoke sharply.

'What have you been up to today, Jake?'

Distracted by Brenda's tone, which had led him to start reviewing his words and actions in the short time since he'd entered the house, he answered Alcestis without thinking. 'Seeing the doctor.'

'Oh.' She drew him down to sit beside her on the padded bamboo settee. 'Anything . . . troublesome?'

'Not really,' said Jake, who had recovered his wits enough to try to spread a little embarrassment. 'What you might call a man's thing.'

'I see.'

'I don't expect to die of it exactly.'

'Good,' she said, laying her hand on his shoulder for a moment. 'Do you care for Curnow terribly?'

'No, but I trust his judgement.'

'Neither do I, but Geoffrey swears by him.' She referred to her husband. 'He's Cornish, Curnow, you know. Like Michael Foot.'

'Is he?'

'Oh *yes* my dear, in fact his name's Cornish for Cornish. Worse than the Welsh. Oh yes.'

'Ah.'

'Can I finish my story now, Brenda love?'

'Oh yes Allie, do.' this time Brenda's tone was warm but the warmth was firmly vectored on her friend.

'I was just getting into it when you turned up, Jake.'

'Sorry.'

'Well, just to put you in the picture very briefly, Brenda's probably told you about the trouble we had with our drains last year. Well, the plumber was simply charming. Young fellow, very good-looking, extremely intelligent, all that. Now I can't quite explain it, but he rather fell for old Geoffrey and me. Nothing was too much trouble any hour of the day or night, brought us some little cake affairs his wife had made – cookies, brought *her* along one evening, said she'd been making his life a misery, always on at him to take her to see the people he'd told her so much about. Anyway, some time in the summer he said he'd had enough, of this country that is: no freedom, take all your money off you, won't let you work harder and better yourself. If you want to put it crudely, he felt his initiative was being strangled. Well, to cut a long story short he got a job in Nigeria and went off there with wife and two young kids for good. Emigrated. Out. Gone. Bang. This was last October, that's nearly . . . six months . . . ago.'

Alcestis paused, put the palms of her hands together and rested her chin on her thumbs. Jake asked himself which way it was going to go: Minister of Plumbing, uranium strike, massive diamond find, fleet of Cadillacs, gold bed? Surely not, and preferably not too in the case of a moron and pervert on the present scale: wild-life reserve trip, safari camp, freedom fighters, tribal ritual, cut off his, forced to eat. . . .

'And then, just last week, we had some news. A letter. I knew straight away who it was from by the stamp. I mean we don't know anyone else out there. I just opened it without thinking, as one would. No idea what was in it. Geoffrey was with me. And what it said, quite simply and straightforwardly, was this. Everything had gone fine, they have a lovely house, got on splendidly with all the people there, job's evidently exactly what he wanted, the whole thing. Now don't you think that's marvellous?'

'*Oh* how exciting,' said Brenda.

Jake was close to tears. In that moment he saw the world in its true light, as a place where nothing had ever been any good and nothing of significance done: no art worth a second look, no philosophy of the slightest appositeness, no law but served the state, no history that gave an inkling of how it had been and what had happened. And no love, only egotism, infatuation and lust. He was glad when, two or twenty-two minutes later, Geoffrey Mabbott turned up, and not just because the fellow's purpose was to take Alcestis away; he was actually glad to see Geoffrey himself, even offered him wine. By now this seemed almost natural, unimportant: Jake's feelings of self-identification with Graham Greene's whisky priest, who sat helplessly by while greedy berks drank the wine he had meant to use at a communion, had reached their peak when old Smudger, what there was of her eyebrows again raised, silently held out her glass for a second dose after bringing her plumber story to its climax.

Rotten bastards might have said that Geoffrey was Alcestis's third husband just as Brenda was Jake's third wife, but they would have been getting the just-as part all wrong. Just as was just as it wasn't. Jake had had two unsatisfactory former wives, or so he would have put it; Alcestis had exercised a mysterious attraction and then an unmysterious repulsion on two former husbands, the second of whom had had to resort to fatal coronary disease to get away from her. It was to be presumed that Geoffrey was in some uncertain intermediate state. That would at any rate be typical: he was in uncertain states of one sort or another far more than not. One of his specialities was the inverted pyramid of piss, a great parcel of attitudes, rules and catch-words resting on one tiny (if you looked long and hard enough) point. Thus it was established beyond any real doubt that his settled antipathy to all things Indian, from books and films about the Raj to Mrs Gandhi, whom by a presumably related crotchet he took to be a daughter-in-law of the Mahatma, was rooted in Alcestis's second husband's mild fondness for curries. His preference for Holland's gin over the London and Plymouth varieties, often-mentioned partiality for cream cakes and habit of flying by KLM had been less certainly connected with his possession of a sketch by Van Dyck, whom on a good day he might very well have supposed to have been a Dutchman. How he managed to be a buyer for a firm of chutney-manufacturers, or indeed be paid for doing anything, was an enigma, a riddle. His taste in clothes was odd too.

He frowned, as he so often did, when he looked at the wine-bottle, and said nothing at first. Jake waited expectantly, running his eye over Geoffrey's conventional dark-grey suit, self-striped orange shirt, pink bow-tie and thick-heeled white shoes: what far-distant event, rumour or surmise was plodding on its way to decide the issue for him?

'It's frightfully good, darling,' said his wife.

'Mm.' Then all at once his brow cleared and he spoke with his usual liveliness. 'First-rate notion. Thanks, I'd love some. You know, these Middle East wines are about the best value there is these days. Algerian, of course. And some very, very decent Moroccan red I had the other day.' (He must have remembered being annoyed by a Jew, or meeting or seeing one, thought Jake as he handed him his glass.) 'Oh, thanks most awfully.

Mm. Well, it's no vintage claret, but it's a good honest drink. Better than tequila, anyway.'

'It's certainly that,' said Jake. 'But aren't they rather different types of drink?'

'Aren't which?'

'Wine and tequila.'

'Well of course they are, that's what I'm saying. Wine comes from grapes and tequila comes from cactuses.'

'Well actually it's a – '

'Vile stuff. Make it in the Argentine, don't they?'

'Mexico, I think.'

'Really? Ever been there?'

'No, never,' said Jake lightly, and added even more lightly, 'You, er . . . you been there, Geoffrey?'

'Me? But . . . Why should I have been there?' Geoffrey's frown was turning his forehead white in patches. 'I've never even been to the States, let alone South America.'

'Actually Mexico's in – '

It must have been that Alcestis felt she had done enough in the way of holding her mouth open in a smile and blinking her eyes quickly to show how bowled over she still was by her husband even after all these (five? seven?) years. Certainly she changed her expression to one of a kind of urgency and said, 'Some of this modern architecture they've got in Mexico City, finest in the world you know, especially the museums and the university. *And* some of the blocks of flats and offices. Something to do with the use of materials. Just nothing like it anywhere.'

She ended up looking at Jake, so he said, 'How did you er . . . ?'

'Common knowledge.'

'Oh I see.'

'How are you, Brenda dear?' Geoffrey spoke as if in greeting, but the two had exchanged warm hugs and several words on his arrival; it was just that he hadn't noticed her since then.

'Fat,' said Brenda, and everyone laughed; Jake saw that Alcestis put her head back further than usual, to show that she knew what had been said was a *joke*. Brenda went on to ask Geoffrey how he was.

'About the same, thanks. Yes, very much the same. Well, no, actually, not really. All right if I have a slice of this? One of my weaknesses, this sort of stuff.'

On Brenda's nod he picked up a large slice of cream cake and ate it carefully, his eyes fixed straight ahead of him. He was concentrating either on what to say next or on the cake, a small problem cleared up when he swallowed finally, said 'Quite delicious' and emptied his glass.

'In what way aren't you the same?' asked Brenda.

'Not what?'

'You said you weren't – '

'Oh, that's right. Well, that's a jolly good instance. Physically no problem, just getting older as who isn't. It's concentration. You know the sort of thing I mean – you go up to your bedroom to get a clean handkerchief and when you get there you've forgotten why you've come and have to go back downstairs to where you started. Quite normal up to a point. But with me, I've got to the stage where I take a cup over to the stove to pour some tea into it and find there's one there already, from . . . half a minute before. And then I have to taste it to see if I've put sugar in. Now that's still just annoying. As I say, it just adds on a few seconds to some of the things I do. But . . . er . . . the . . . silliest part is what I'm thinking about instead of what I'm doing. It's me I'm thinking about, and that's not a very interesting subject. I mean, if a chap's thinking about his, er, his mathematics instead of his teacup, or his . . . symphony, then that's all right, that's reasonable. It's in proportion. But me – I ask you!'

Geoffrey had not departed from his cheerful tone. The two women laughed affectionately. Jake held up the wine bottle, which still held about a glassful, but Geoffrey smiled and shook his head and went on as before.

'And the stupidest thing of the lot is, I don't think poor old me, or poor old me in the financial sense, though I jolly well could like everybody else these days, and certainly not *brilliant* old me. Just, just me. It's not enough, you know.'

'It certainly is not by a long chalk,' said Alcestis, going up to her husband and putting her arm through his. 'I only married you because you were the most boring chap I knew so nobody but me could stand you. Now I'm going to take you home, or rather you're going to take me home and we'll leave these good people in peace.'

'Why don't you stay to supper?' asked Brenda. 'There's nothing very much but I'm sure you and I could knock something up, Allie.'

' . . . Yes, do,' said Jake.

'No, sweet of you, but we've tried your patience long enough already.' Alcestis embraced Jake briefly. 'Come along Mabbott, let's hit the trail.'

By custom Brenda saw thhe visitors out while Jake stayed behind in the sitting-room. Normally at such a time he could count on a good five minutes to himself, but today it was only a few seconds before he heard the front door slam and his wife approach along the passage.

3   Domestic Interior

'When the bishop farted we were amused to hear about it,' said Jake. 'Should the ploughboy find treasure we must be told. But when the ploughboy farts . . . er . . . keep it to yourself.'

Brenda had started putting the tea things together, not very loudly. With her back turned she said in her clear soprano, 'Did you make that up?'

'Free translation of one of Martial's epigrams.'

'Quite good, I suppose.'

'It enshrines a principle poor old Allie would do well to – '

A saucer whizzed into the empty fireplace and broke. 'You leave Allie alone! You did quite enough when she was here!'

'What? I didn't do anything at all.'

'Much! I know you can't be expected to like my friends, that isn't reasonable, why should you, we can't all be the same, I don't necessarily like your friends.' Brenda was talking very fast, though not for the moment quite at the pitch to be expected from someone who had reached the crockery-throwing stage. Now she paused and bit her lower lip and gave a shaky sigh. 'But I don't see why you feel you have to make your low opinion of my friends so devastatingly crystal-clear!'

Jake heard the last part with annoyance and some self-reproof. He had thought his behaviour to the Mabbotts a show-piece of hypocritical cordiality. And now he came to think of it, hadn't Brenda said something of this sort the last time they had seen Alcestis, or the time before? 'I haven't got a low opinion of Allie,' he said with an air of slight surprise, 'I just find her a bit of a – '

'She knows exactly what you find her, she's not a fool whatever you may think, though even a fool could tell. The way you imitate her and take the mickey out of her and the way your face goes when she tells a story and the way you *sit*, I didn't think it was a very terrific story either but she wouldn't have told it if you hadn't shut her up and absolutely sat on her about the doctor and brought the whole conversation to an absolute full stop. You used to quite like her, I can't understand it.'

'I didn't want to discuss the doctor with her, obviously.' Jake poured out the last of the wine. He longed for a smoke but had given it up four years previously and was determined to stick to that. There were no cigarettes in the house anyway.

'You still had no need to sit on her and be crushing,' said Brenda in about the same tone as before. Although she was standing above him she talked with her chin raised, a mannerism that had stood her in good stead since she began to put on weight. 'And I don't know what she thought when she finished her story and you just *sat* there as if you hadn't heard a word, or rather I *do*.'

'I didn't realise it was over at first. I honestly thought that couldn't be the end. And what do you mean she wouldn't have told it if I hadn't shut her up about the doctor? She'd already started to tell it to you before I got back, that was quite clear.'

'I meant she wouldn't have gone on with it. She'd been telling it to me because it was a tiny little thing in her life that she thought might interest me for about five seconds. That's what old friends do when there's just the two of them together, or didn't you know that? I tell her the same sort of thing all the time. We don't go on swapping translations of epigrams by Martial hour after hour.'

'No of course you don't, I quite see,' said Jake mildly, as opposed to saying harshly that that would be all right if the story didn't take fifty times as long as it was supposed to be interesting for.

Brenda's expression softened in response but a moment later it had hardened again. 'And the way you treat poor old Geoffrey, as if he's off his head or something.'

'I think he is a bit off his head, always has been as long as I've known him. Look at those bloody silly clothes he — '

'That's no excuse for treating him like that. You should have seen the way you were looking at him.'

'When?'

'*When?* Whenever he said anything or was getting ready to say anything, when he said he'd like some wine. . . . And what was all that about the wine in the kitchen? What were you up to?'

'Nothing, just opening it. The other bottle was. . . .'

'No, you were up to something but I know it's no use going on about it. When he said something about Mexico and when he said he was absent-minded, Allie saw the way you were looking at him, and then when I asked them to stay and after about five minutes you said what a good idea as if it was your own funeral. You should have heard yourself.'

She paused. Jake looked up at his wife. Her breasts were about as large as Curnow's receptionist's but her hips were large too. And, partly concealed by the loose-fitting cardigan, one of her favourite forms of dress over the last couple of years, her waist, her thighs and her upper arms were also large and her paunch was fairly large. But her face, as he had recently noticed from a photograph, had hardly changed in ten years: it was still the face of a woman anxious not to miss anything good or happy that might come her way in the future. That anxiety in it had been the second thing he had observed about her, after her eyes. She turned their glance on him now. He reached out his hand and she took it; he considered getting up and putting his arms round her but somehow decided not to. Without hostility she soon withdrew her hand.

'I'm sorry,' he said. 'I'll try to do better next time.' Of course he meant do and nothing more: how could anyone change his attitude to a pair like the Mabbotts? But next time was going to have to include next time they came up in conversation as well as in person, and that meant fewer of those jocular little sallies about them which had so often cheered up his half of the breakfast or lunch table. A few moments earlier he had thought of telling Brenda that in fact the idea of those two having noticed anything in the least objectionable was a load of rubbish and that she was cross with him for what she knew he felt about them, not for how he had behaved to them, but that too he decided against.

She had moved to the fireplace, he now saw, and was carefully picking up the pieces of china. 'How did it go with the doctor, darling? I should have asked you before.'

'That's all right. Oh, he . . . asked me the sort of questions one might have expected and said *he* couldn't do anything and fixed up an appointment for me with some fellow who might be able to do something.'

'When? I mean when's the appointment?'

'Tuesday. Right after Easter.'

'Good,' said Brenda, going back to the tea-tray. 'Anybody interesting at the club?'

The club was a long way from St James's in more than the geographical sense and existed for the benefit of unprosperous middle-aged and elderly men of professional standing. In order to survive it had recently had to sell half of itself, of its premises that is, to a man who had constructed a massage parlour there. 'Just the usual crowd,' said Jake, accurately enough.

'I see. Ooh, the Thomsons have asked us round for drinks one evening next week,' she said, mentioning one of the comparatively few couples in Orris Park who didn't go on about their cars or their children the whole time. 'I've put it in the diary.'

'Well done.'

'You know, we ought to give a party some time. We can't go on just taking other people's hospitality.'

'I quite agree, but it's so bloody expensive. Everybody drinks Scotch or vodka these days.'

'They can't do much about it if you just offer them wine.'

'I suppose not.'

'I was thinking.' Brenda stood with the tray held in front of her stomach. 'I thought we might give that new Greek place a try.'

'Tonight?'

'I just thought. . . .'

'I don't really like Greek food. I always think Greek food is bad Turkish food and Turkish food isn't up to much.'

'What about Sandro's? We haven't been there for ages.'

'They charge the earth and they never seem to change their menu. Isn't there anything in the house?'

'Only the rest of that chicken.'

'Sounds fine. You could fix up a salad, couldn't you?'

'I suppose so. . . . Then we could go to a film.'

'There's nothing very marvellous on, I looked at the *Standard* yesterday. Oh, apart from that thing about Moloch turning up in the crypt of a San Francisco church and having children fed to him alive, *The Immolation*, that's it, I wouldn't mind seeing that.'

'Well I would.'

'You are funny, I keep telling you it's all pretend. Look love, I vote we pull up the drawbridge tonight. I know it's selfish of me but I don't honestly feel quite up to stirring out and that probably means I shouldn't, don't you think? Let's be absolute devils and have the heating on and huddle round the telly.'

So when the time came, Brenda went and sliced the chicken and made a salad and a dressing and got out the rather swarthy Brie that needed eating up and put it all on trays and brought them into the sitting-room. The TV was a colour set, small but all right for two. On it she and Jake watched episode 4 of *Henry Esmond*, the News, including film of a minor air disaster in which a good half of those involved hadn't even been hurt, International Snooker, with a commentary that laid great stress on the desire of each player to score more points than the other and so win the match, World Outlook, which consisted largely of an interviewer in a spotted bow tie being very rude to a politician about some aspect of nuclear energy and the politician not giving a shit, and Rendezvous with Terror: *The Brass Golem*. Or rather Jake watched that far; Brenda gave up at the first soccer result and opened her Simon Raven paperback. At the start of the col-legno violin passage advertising the approach of the rendezvous just alluded to, she got up from the sofa which she had herself covered with crimson velvet.

'You off, darling?' asked Jake. 'These things are always innocuous ballocks, you know. About as frightening as Donald Duck.'

'No, I'll be off anyway. Still the spare room?'

'I think while we're still sleeping badly.'

'Mm. Ooh, I'm sorry I didn't thank you properly for the chocolates.'

'The. . . . Oh yes. Oh, I thought you did.'

'If the scales aren't too bad in the morning I might treat myself to one tomorrow night. Well. . . .'

'Good night, love.'

She bent and kissed him on the cheek and was gone. Jake washed down his Mogadon with some of his second glass of what was supposed to be claret. He was sorry now that he hadn't done what impulse and habit had suggested and told Brenda about the abortive wine-switch. Done properly the tale would have amused her, its confessional aspect given her pleasure, the row over the Mabbotts been prevented or disposed of, not merely broken off. But to have done it properly would have meant taking trouble, not much, true, but more than he had on the whole felt like taking at the time. Well there it is, he thought.

Despite everything the background bass clarinet could do, and it did indeed get a lot done in quantity, terror as expected failed altogether to turn up at the prearranged spot. Summoned by an ancient curse but otherwise unaccounted for, the metalloid protagonist ran his course in twenty minutes less commercials. His most mysterious endowment was the least remarked: that of always coming upon his quarry alone, out of sight and hearing of everyone else, in a blind alley, in a virtually endless tunnel, in a room with only one door and no usable window, etc. He ground to a halt finally through gross overheating of the lubricants in the Turkish bath where Providence, in the form of total chance, had led his last intended victim to take refuge. Very neat.

As he went round the room turning everything off, Jake reconstructed the brief script conference att which the creative producer had outlined the story to his colleagues. 'Right,' he snarled, stabbing at the air with an invisible cigar to point the turns in his argument, 'got this guy made of like brass, see, buried somewheres for a coon's age, okay, comes like an earthquake or explosion or whatever, right, anyways he done get gotten dug up, see, this old like parchment says any motherfucker digs me up gets to done get gotten fucked up good, okay, he fucks up three-four guys around, right, chases the last guy into somewhere fucking hot, see, now the brass guy done gotten oil like instead of blood, okay, so *he* gets to done get gotten fucked up, right, Zeke and Zack get on it right away, see, they don't get to done get gotten done it by tomorrow, they lose their asses, okay, and any number of cunts all over the world who know a bloody sight better will watch the bloody thing. Right.'

Upstairs, Jake unhurriedly cleaned his teeth and peed, feeling a comfortable drowsiness at the edge of his mind. Light showed under Brenda's door: she liked to read for a time before settling off, which he didn't. He went into the spare room and undressed. There were pictures in here no less than everywhere else, most of them non-modern black-and-white unoriginals; in almost every case he could have said whether or not a given one belonged to the house but he would never have missed any of them. He put on his pyjamas, turned off the light and was about to get into bed, then changed his mind and went to the window.

Looking out, he remembered with no great vividness doing the same thing one night some shortish time after Brenda and he had come to live here. Then as now there had been plenty to see, mainly by the street-lamp that stood no more than twenty yards off: houses, trees, bushes, parked cars, the bird-table in the garden diagonally opposite. Then, too, some of the windows must have been illuminated and it was quite possible that, as now, the only sounds had been faint voices and distant footsteps. After some effort he remembered further his feelings of curiosity, almost of expectation, as if he might find himself seeing a link between that moment and things that had happened earlier in his life. He remembered, or thought he did; there was no question of his re-experiencing those feelings, nor of his wishing he could. What was before him left him cold, and he didn't mind.

4 Thunderball

The next Tuesday morning when Jake set off down Burgess Avenue it was raining, but not very hard. Even if it had been very hard he would have more or less had to set off just the same. Four or five years ago there had been a taxi-rank at the end of the High Street by St Winifred's Hospital and a telephone-call fetched one to the front door within a few minutes in any weather. The sign and the shelter were still there but they served only to trap the occasional stranger into a fruitless wait. Minicabs either didn't come or had drivers you had to pilot street by street to places like Piccadilly Circus. And there was the expense. And the Underground was only worth while for long journeys, over the river or out to Chelsea: Jake had established that 47 Burgess Avenue NW16 was about as equidistant as anywhere could be from the stations at Golders Green, East Finchley, Highgate and Hampstead. He had several times read, though not recently, of plans to extend one or other branch of the Northern Line to a contemplated Kenwood Station in the 1980s.

Every 6–7 mins was how often 127s were supposed to turn up at the stop by the Orris Park Woolworths, so to be given the choice of two after only 10–11 was rather grand and certainly welcome in the increasing rain and squirts of cold wind. Jake got on to the second bus, one of the newish sort distinguished by a separate entrance and exit. The doors closed after him with a swish of compressed air that resembled to what was almost a worrying degree the sound of the off-licence bugger and his overalled customer saying Cheers to each other. The conductor too was one of the newish sort, which in this case meant that he chucked you off if you hadn't got the exact money. But Jake made a great point of not being caught out by things like that.

Whenever he could he liked to sit at the back on the offside, where there was a niche just wide enough for an umbrella between the emergency door and the arm of the seat, but someone from Asia was there that morning so he took the corresponding position upstairs. Among the people he had a good or fair view of, there was none he remembered having seen before. They were divided, as well they might have been, into those older than him, round about his age and younger than him. In different ways all three groups got him down a bit. Only one child seemed to be about the place but it was making a lot of noise, talking whenever it felt like it and at any volume it fancied. Far from admonishing or stifling it, its mother joined in, talked back to it. Like a fool he had forgotten to bring anything to read.

Although there was no shortage of his fellow human beings on the pavements and in and out of shops, other places and spaces were altogether free of them, so recurrently that his mind was crossed by thoughts of a selective public holiday or lightning semi-general strike. A railway bridge revealed two or three acres of empty tracks and sidings; large pieces of machinery and piles of bricks stood unattended on a rather smaller stretch of mud; no one was in sight among the strange apparatuses in what might have been a playground for young Martians; a house that had stayed half-demolished since about 1970 overlooked a straightforward bomb-site of World War II; nearer the centre, the stone face of a university building was spattered with rust-stains from scaffolding on which Jake had never seen anybody at work. Even Gr nville Co rt, Collin woo C urt and the others, angular but lofty structures of turd-coloured brick resting on squat stilts, seemed to be deserted. Even or especially.

Warren Street was at hand; he climbed warily down the stairs, holding on with all his strength when a deeper cavity than usual in the road-surface lifted him heel and toe into the air. He got off by Kevin's Kebab, crossed over and fought his way westward against a soaking wind that blew now with fatuous indignation. 878 Harley Street. Proinsias Rosenberg MD, MA (Dip. Psych). The door opened in his face and an Englishman came out and stepped past him and was away. A small woman in a white housecoat showed Jake into a room where folk from many lands and of nearly as many creeds sat in chintz-covered armchairs reading *Punch* and *Private Eye*. But it was no more than ten minutes before she came back, took him along a corridor to another room and shut him in.

Jake found himself closeted with a person he took to be a boy of about seventeen, most likely a servant of some kind, in a stooped position doing something to an electric fire. 'I'm looking for Dr Rosenberg,' he said.

It was never to cut the least ice with him that the other did not in fact reply, 'Ah now me tharlun man, de thop a de mornun thoo yiz' – he might fully as well have done by the effect. ('Good morning' was what he did say.)

'Dr Rosenberg?' said Jake again, a little flustered. He saw now that the youth was a couple of years older than he had supposed at first, short-haired and clean-shaven, wearing a sort of dark tunic-suit with a high collar that gave something between a military and a clerical air.

'Rosenberg it is. How do you do, Dr Richardson.' Jake got a hearty handshake and a brown-eyed gaze of what looked like keen personal admiration but in the circumstances could hardly have been the genuine article. 'Do come and sit down. I hope this room'll be warm enough – such a wretchedly cold spring we've been having so far, isn't it?'

When he failed to add what Jake was in a way expecting and would certainly have accepted, that his master or father if not grandfather would be down in a minute, things eased quite quickly. 'I'm sorry, I'm afraid I. . . .'

'You're not the first by a very long chalk indeed, Dr Richardson, I can assure you of that.' He who must after all be conceded to be Dr Rosenberg didn't really talk like an O'Casey peasant, his articulation was too precise for that, but he did talk like a real Irishman with a largely unreconstructed accent, even at this stage seemed no more than twenty-one or- two and had shown himself, between finishing with the fire and sitting down behind his desk, to be about two foot high. He said in an oddly flat tone, 'I understand very well how strange it must be to hear my style of talk coming out of a man with a name straight from Germany.'

'Or Austria.' Which would be rather more to the point, thought Jake, and thought too that he had conveyed that meaning in his inflection.

'Or Austria.' The doctor spoke as one allowing a genuine if rather unimmediate alternative.

Jake went back to being flustered. No sooner had he managed to bring himself to have this tiny Emerald Isler palmed off on him instead of the bottled-at-the-place-of-origin Freudian anybody just hearing the name would have expected than he was being asked to believe in a student of the mind who didn't know where Freud had come from. He said quickly, 'Dublin man, are you?'

'Correct, Dr Richardson,' said Dr Rosenberg, in *his* inflection awarding his new patient a mark or two for knowing that many Irishmen were Dubliners and virtually all Dubliners Irishmen. 'Perhaps it might be of interest,' he went on, though not as if he had any very high hopes of this, 'if I were to explain that an ancestor of mine was a German consular official who liked the look of the old place, married a local girl, and no doubt you'll be able to fill in the rest of the story for yourself. I charge seventeen pounds fifty a session – is that acceptable?'

'Yes,' said Jake. Christ, he thought.

'Good. Now Dr Curnow has sent me a report on you.' The psychologist's manner had changed and he opened a file with an alacrity that would have been quite uncharacteristic of his colleague. 'There's just one point I'd like to have clearly understood before we get down to business. You do realise that in our work together I shall be asking you a number of questions.'

'Yes.'

'And you have no objection.'

'No,' said Jake, suppressing a different and longer answer.

'Good. First question then. What is your full name?'

'Jaques [Jakes] Cecil Richardson.' Jake spelt out the Jaques. And I reckon I got seventy-five per cent on that, he thought, in mind of a comic monologue a decade or two old.

'Jaques. Now that's an uncommon name for an Englishman.'

'Yes. *My* ancestor came over from Paris in 1848.'

'1848! You must have made a close study of your family history.'

'Oh, I wouldn't say that. After all, 1848 was 1848.'

'Just so, but the date would seem to have lodged in your memory.'

'Well, they did have a spot of bother there in that year, if you – '

'Ah, when did they not the horrible men? Do you know, Dr Richardson, I think those French fellows must have caused *nearly* as much trouble in the world as we Irish?' Rosenberg gave a deep-toned laugh, showing numerous very small white teeth. 'Oh dear. Your age.'

'Fifty-nine.'

'Sixty,' said Rosenberg as he wrote.

'Well, it is actually fifty-nine, not that there's a lot of difference, I agree.'

'We always enter the age next birthday. We find it makes for simplicity.'

'Oh I see.'

'Your profession.'

'I teach at a university.'

'Any particular one?'

'Yes. Oxford. I'm Reader in Early Mediterranean History there and a Fellow of Comyns College. And by the way I have got a doctorate but I don't normally use the title.'

'So it's *Mr* Richardson. Now your trouble is that your libido [lib-eedo] has declined.'

'My what?' asked Jake, though he had understood all right.

'Your libido, your sexual drive.'

'I'm sorry, I'd be inclined to pronounce it lib-ighdo, on the basis that we're talking English, not Italian or Spanish, but I suppose it'll make for simplicity if I go along with you. So yes, my lib-eedo has declined.'

'Are you married?'

'Yes.'

'How much does your wife weigh?'

'*What?* No I beg your pardon, I heard what you said. How much . . . I don't know. But you're right. I mean she weighs a lot. She's quite tall but she weighs a lot. Fourteen stone? I don't know. How did you know?'

'Oh, it's just one of the most statistically common reasons why men lose sexual interest in their wives. I couldn't say I knew.'

'All right. I mean I see. But it isn't that, or rather it may well be that too, or *there* may well be that too but it's general, I simply don't – '

'Your wife's age?'

'Forty seven.'

'Does she know you've come to see me today?'

'Good God yes, of course. We're still, well, on close terms.'

'It's important she starts losing weight as fast as it's safe to do so. May I telephone her?'

'No, don't do that. Write her a letter, but leave it a couple of days. Not that I can see it having much effect.'

'Ah, one never knows, one can but try.' The doctor hurried on; the conversation about weight, however necessary, had been an obvious check to his interest. 'You were saying you'd suffered a general loss of drive.'

'That's right. I don't fancy anyone, not even girls I can see are very attractive. And it wasn't always like that, I promise you.'

'I think Mr Richardson, before we go any further you might tell me when you first – '

'Let's see, I first noticed something was wrong,' began Jake, and went on to talk about the year or more he had spent in continual, at times severe gastric pain being treated by Curnow for an ulcer, drinking almost nothing, watching his diet, taking the antacid mixture prescribed him and telling himself that pain, discomfort, general below-parness had temporarily reduced his desires to some unestablished low level. In the end he had developed jaundice, had had diagnosed a stone in the common duct (that into which the canals from the liver and the gall-bladder unite) and had had this removed by surgery, another set of experiences decidedly not associated with satyriasis. Out of hospital his recovery had been steady but slow, marked by periods of fatigue and weakness, a third period in which it seemed to him natural to postpone sexual dealings with his wife, let alone going in pursuit of other ladies. He had still somehow not got round to either branch of activity, though admittedly beginning to feel rested and fit, when there came that fatal Saturday in late February – the night of *Thunderball*.

There was no point in telling Rosenberg the full story, but Jake remembered it with great vividness. Brenda had gone to stay with her grand cousins in Northumberland, one of the places where by tradition he didn't go with her. She had left on the Thursday; she was due back on the Monday evening; she had actually telephoned that lunchtime to ask him to find and read over to her a recipe for quenelles she had meant to take with her. Given ten years of his precept and example in the matter of each being kept informed of where the other was at all times, her dislike of changes of plan, the non-existence of anything likely to bring her back prematurely which he wasn't bound to hear of first, she couldn't have been away in a more armour-plated, hull-down, missile-intercepting fashion. Arriving back from Oxford on the Thursday night he had found her already well gone, had spent most of Friday self-indulgently and yet dutifully writing to some of the old friends and ex-pupils who had fled from the England of the 1970s and had made Saturday a remorseless build-up to the time at which, an avocado pear with prawns, a trout with almonds supported by Brussels sprouts and chestnuts and a bottle of his beloved Pouilly Fumé (£1.99 while stocks last) before him, he would settle down to watch the film of *Thunderball* on television.

When, twenty minutes before the off, the telephone brought him hurrying from the bog he had felt no premonitory stirrings: Brenda most likely, checking that it was indeed six pinches of powdered baboon's balls in the sauce, and if not, even Alcestis could hardly talk him out in Brenda's de luxe absence. A female voice he at once recognised but couldn't at once name had asked him if he was there.

'Speaking.'

'Jake! You stinker. This is good old Marge. Remember me?'

Christ yes, as what seven years earlier had been a bosomy thirty-five-year-old from Baltimore, the source of a strenuous and reprehensible couple of months before some now-forgotten necessity had plucked her away across the ocean. He had gone on to say enough to show he did remember her.

'You sound as if you're alone.'

'I am.'

'Completely?'

'Yes.'

'Oh, that being so, why don't I just grab a cab and come toddling up to your place and we could get along with kind of renewing our acquaintance if you've nothing better to do?'

'Fuck me wept!' he had cried, regressing to an oath of his Army days; he had clapped his hand over the mouthpiece in the nick of time. 'Shit!' he had added. And then he had been filled with alarm and horror.

'You're telling me it was a failure, is that right?' asked Dr Rosenberg.

'Not in the sense you probably mean, no. I . . . performed. Not with any distinction, but adequately. No worse than many a time in the past. No, the striking thing was afterwards, immediately afterwards. I kept thinking about the trout and whether we could – '

'Hunger is a normal reaction on completion of sexual intercourse.'

'I'm not talking about hunger, I was thinking about missing my dinner or it being spoilt or there not being enough for the two of us, no, it was more there being enough for me if she had some too and what else could she have. In fact the evening as I'd planned it for myself, very much including what was left of *Thunderball*. I reckoned that if – '

'I wonder if you'd kindly explain about this thunderball thing you've been constantly referring to. I don't believe I – '

'Well, you know, *Thunderball*. Film, didn't I say? Sean Connery. James Bond. Ian Fleming. Barbara something, was it?'

'Ah to be sure, James Bond,' said Dr Rosenberg without producing much conviction in Jake. 'Do you want to tell me what happened later?'

'I will. We lay around for a bit, not very long, and then she said brightly she was hungry and what about dinner, and I said we could eat at home, and she said if I didn't mind what she felt like was a long lazy rather greedy evening somewhere with a lot of pasta and a lot of vino, and so that's what we did, and it was quite good fun really, and we said good night in the restaurant. She was marvellous, she did it very well. The only thing she couldn't do was make me think she didn't know. Of course she couldn't.

They always know things like that, not that much acumen was called for in this case. Yes. She knew I knew she knew I knew she knew.'

Rosenberg seemed to think this last part was important; at any rate he went in for a good deal of writing while Jake's memory fastened against his will on the hours he had lain awake that night and on how he had spent most of the next day: unable to read, unable to attend to radio or television, eating almost nothing, staring into space, hardly thinking, trying not so much to accept what had happened to him as just to take it in. To distract his mind from this he glanced round the small and by now slightly overheated room with artificial interest. He saw a couch of a height inconvenient for anyone much under eight foot (to use it himself the doctor would pretty well need a rope ladder), a green filing-cabinet, no books beyond diaries and directories and, on a fluted wooden pedestal, a life-sized human head in some shiny yellowish material with the surface of the skull divided into numbered sections. That distracted his mind like mad.

'Right,' said Rosenberg at last, 'I think I have that clear. And you've had no intercourse at all since then. Have you masturbated?'

It took Jake a little while to get the final participle because the Irishman had stressed it on its third syllable, but he did get it. 'Er . . . yes. Well, a couple of times.'

'Do you have early-morning erections?'

This time Jake responded at once, with a desire to tell the bugger to mind his own business. Then he saw that that sort of wouldn't do and said, 'Yes. Usually anyway.'

'Do you have fantasies?'

'Sexual fantasies. A bit. Not much.'

'Have you over these last weeks used written or pictorial pornography or visited a sex movie?'

'No to the lot. I haven't read any pornography for years and I've never been to a, a sex movie.'

'I see. Going back now to before your illness, how was your libido in those days?'

'Well, not what it was when I was a youngster, obviously, but my wife and I were having a – performing sexual intercourse at least once a week and more at special times like holidays, and I worked out that in '74 I had two affairs, one of them only a couple of, er, occasions but the other lasting several months on and off.'

'And longer ago, how active were you sexually in your forties and thirties?'

'Just put it this way, in my time I've been to bed with well over a hundred women.'

Rosenberg had made some notes of the answers to all his questions until this last one, at which to Jake's distinct annoyance he merely nodded. More questions followed and more notes were taken. Parents, characters of, probable sex-life of, attitude to; knowledge of sex, how acquired; masturbation, frequency of (high); homosexual activities (none); first sexual experience, to what degree a success (bloody marvellous, thanks very much); then, at a less leisurely pace, subsequent sexual experience, marriages, divorces, causes of, present wife, relationship with, sexual and non-sexual. As far as he knew Jake kept nothing back here, but he had the feeling that a series of negatives was all that was established; still, necessary work, no doubt. At last the scientist of mental phenomena looked at his watch and said,

'Ah now, just one or two final points. What is your height, Mr Richardson?'

'Five foot eleven.'

'And your weight?'

'Twelve stone six' – noted by Jake only the previous week to be exactly right for his height and age, according to whatever chart it had been.

Rosenberg gave a small frown. 'Is that all?'

'Yes, that's all.'

'Mm. Well I think all the same you'd do well to lose a few pounds. Try to get down to twelve stone. Cut down on starchy foods and take more exercise. And of course, how much do you drink?'

'Sometimes a glass of beer with lunch, sometimes a glass of sherry before dinner, three or four glasses of wine with dinner rising to a whole bottle on special occasions, say once every three or four weeks.' This was the exact truth.

Rosenberg frowned more deeply. 'No more than that? No spirits?'

'I haven't drunk any spirits for over thirty years. I found they didn't agree with me.'

'Try not to go beyond three glasses of wine in future.'

'All right.'

'Would you care to make a note of those points? There'll be more to come.'

'Okay.' Jake scribbled on the back of his cheque-book in his shameful handwriting. 'Starch. Exercise. Wine.'

'Good. Now Mr Richardson, there is a certain programme of tasks that you have to work through with me. We call it inceptive regrouping. Is this time next week convenient? Very well. Between now and then I want you to do the following. Buy some pictorial pornographic material and study it on at least three occasions for a minimum of fifteen minutes at a time. See that this leads to masturbation at least once, preferably twice. Write out a sexual fantasy in not less than six hundred and not more than a thousand words. Oh, and fill this in – there we are – making sure you give only one answer to each question. I'm not going too fast for you, I hope? Good. I also want you to have a non-genital sensate focusing session with your wife. You understand what I mean by non-genital?'

'Yes, I understand that.'

'In a non-genital sensate focusing session the couple lie down together in the nude and touch and stroke and massage the non-genital areas of each other's bodies in turns of two or three minutes at a time for a period of up to half an hour. They don't perform sexual intercourse. That's exceedingly important: sexual intercourse is strictly forbidden at this stage. You'll find it all set out here.' He handed over a second sheet of sleek paper. 'Now we come to the use of the nocturnal mensurator. If you'd just step over here, Mr Richardson.'

Dr Rosenberg turned and took from a narrow table behind him an object Jake had not noticed before, a heavy wooden box outwardly of much the sort women keep sewing or embroidery in. When the lid was raised it could be seen that a black composition panel covered most of the inside. On the panel were a brass turntable with a short thick spindle, an arm on the gramophone principle with a stub of pencil in place of the needle, a two-point socket, two electric switches and two lengths of double flex with various attachments at each end.

'If you'll pay attention,' said the doctor, 'you'll find this is quite straight-forward. Mains here.' He put the plug at one end of the fatter length of flex into a socket in the side of the box and the plug at the other end into a socket in the wall behind him. 'Mains on.' He snapped one of the switches. 'This in here.' He put the much smaller plug at one end of the thinner length of flex into the socket on the panel and showed that attached to the other end was a broken hoop of light plastic an inch and a half or so across and apparently stiffened with wire. Then, neatly enough but with rather more force than might have been expected, he tore off a corner of paper, pushed a ballpoint pen through it and fastened it by way of the hole just made to the spindle. 'You'll be wanting to run up nice neat little discs like gramophone records for your own use but this'll show the general idea. Now we lower the pencil on to the paper so, press the other switch so, and the turntable is now revolving, too slowly for you to see, but you can take it from me it is. Now: this fellow here' – he held up the plastic loop – 'is what they call a circuit-breaker. At the moment the wires in it are touching and so the circuit is closed. Now watch the pencil when I pull the wires apart and break the circuit.' The pencil together with its arm moved an undramatic but definite tenth of an inch inwards, towards the centre of rotation. 'Close.' The pencil moved back. 'Break. Close. And so on. So: when you go to bed you fasten the ring round the root of your penis, you go to sleep, the turntable revolves maybe half an inch, you get an erection, which pushes the wires apart and breaks the circuit and bingo! the pencil moves and stays in the same position until the erection passes. And so on. And in the morning, there we have a complete record of your nocturnal erections. Ingenious, don't you think?'

'Very. What use is it?'

'It's of use, or I wouldn't be asking you to go through all this riddle-me-ree, now would I? Every night, please, until further notice. Bring the discs with you when you come next week. Oh, and be sure to keep a note of the times you go to bed and wake up. Erections when you're awake don't count. And don't forget to turn off *both* switches when you get out of bed.'

While he talked the doctor had been swiftly dismantling the nocturnal mensurator. He shut the lid and put the box into a Harrod's plastic carrier, explaining with a smile that Jake wouldn't be wanting to have people in the Tube or wherever ask to see his tape recorder. On request, Jake supplied his address and telephone number, taking a visiting-card in exchange.

'Proinsias. Is that a German name?'

'Irish. It's pronounced Francis. The correct Gaelic spelling. I take it you've no objection to exposing your genitals in public?'

'I hadn't really – '

'It's only semi-public. All qualified personnel. We have a first-rate sex laboratory at the McDougall Hospital in Colliers Wood. I venture to say it's the finest in the world at this time. Professor Trefusis runs a splendid team. We'll be running the rule over you.'

'Will you?'

'I will, I'll be there too. It'll take a few days to fix it up – I'll let you know. And I'll write to your wife.'

'Just one question, doctor, if I may. Can I take it that there is a connection between my illness, convalescence and so on and my loss of, er, lib-eedo?'

'We don't generally find it helpful to talk in those terms.'

'Perhaps you'd talk in them this once just to please me. Connection?'

'Physical pain and fatigue do not in general inhibit libido.'

'Thank you.'

5   Business-Head and Carter-Face

It was almost with eagerness that Jake embarked on his programme of inceptive regrouping. A kind of savour attached to the official, by-order-in-council doing of things often thought inappropriate, even unseemly, in those past their first youth. To the idea of doing them, at least. But first there was the Brenda side of the question to be settled. How much, if anything, was she to be told of the bits that didn't directly involve her? With the nocturnal mensurator his mind was made up for him by the impossibility of concealing it about his person on arrival back home, nor could he think of a plausible false description of it. And what after all did it matter? No accountability could be apportioned anywhere for how his tool behaved, or failed to behave, while he slept.

Its conduct in waking hours was a horse of another colour. Any woman, even the most severely rational in intention, a category that excluded Brenda, must feel slighted to some degree when the one she regarded as her own property was turned to a different sexual use, not by any means least in cases where her successful rival existed only on paper, so to speak, or in the mind. And he felt sure that all the talk he could devise about the entire point of it being the restoration of their sex-life, however well argued, however carefully listened to, would only end up with her asking him to promise to try not to enjoy it. Besides, sneaking off on the quiet with some pictorial pornographic material would be like old times.

The next morning looked like giving him as good a chance as he was likely to get: Brenda had gone off early with Alcestis to probe a new kickshaw-mart in New King's Road, an operation any male could have polished off in three hours at the most, bus there and back, but was going to last those two, travelling in the Mabbott's Peugeot though they were, most of the day with lunch thrown in, no doubt at one of those places where they really worked on you to get you to have a glass of wine with your food. (Alcestis: he had whimpered and gone all shaky for a while at the thought – unentertained the previous day – of what would have happened without fail if she'd been at no. 47 when he got back from Rosenberg: him – Jake – flat on his back on the bamboo settee ballock-naked with the plastic whatsit round his john thomas and the other end of the flex plugged into the plugged-in nocturnal bloody mensurator in one minute flat.)

Once a keen buyer of tit-magazines, he realised as he left the house that he hadn't even glanced at one for what felt like about three years but was probably a bit more. He did know, though, that the old order, of Venus Films Ltd and Visart Dept 100 of *Kamera, Pagan, Zoom, QT* and *Solo* no. 3 (featuring Rosa Domaille) sold alongside science fiction in the little shop in Newport Court, had yielded place to the open and widespread sale of large glossy journals that went further and also elsewhere, in the sense that they included supposedly serious or at least non-ruttish short stories and articles on probably cars and clothes. However widespread, their sale could hardly be universal; better make for the Blake Street end of Orris Park, by tradition the cheaper and nastier end. At first glance this wasn't apparent: the buildings were no grimier, the proportion of derelict shops with corrugated iron in the window-frames no higher, the amount and variety of litter underfoot no greater. Then he saw the hand-done poster on the door of the Duke of Marlborough – Pub Live Family Entertainment with Bridie on drums, The Cowboy Himself, Mick on Duovox – and reflected that not all distinctions had been effaced.

The shop was on a corner next to a place with a lot of corroded refrigerators and rusty gas and electric cookers on the pavement outside it. Jake pretended to peer at one of these while he spied out the land. Confectionery counter – kid's toys and things – greeting-card stand – the stuff. In he went and started trying not to read what it said on the cards and looking the stuff over. Not easy: it was arranged in an overlapping row so that only the one at the end was fully visible. In Newport Court, under the headmistressy yet motherly eye of the white-coated lady in charge, limited browsing had been the rule, half-a-crown's worth of purchase per five or six minutes. Here there were no other customers to give guidance, though some was provided by the look of the bloke behind the confectionery, just the kind of squat bald forty-year-old to jump at the chance of asking Jake menacingly if he could help him. So one fell swoop would have to do it. *Mezzanine* – hadn't they seized a couple of issues of that in Australia recently? The rest of the lettering wasn't encouraging: The Gay Lib Game, Through the Insurance Maze, Exclusive – Britain's Secret Police Network. The picture was different. It showed a girl with the kind of angular good looks that suggested a sound business head and the kind of clothes, though in some disarray, that real girls wore. In one hand she held a tipped cigarette, but what counted for much more, especially on a cover, was where the other wasn't quite. One, thought Jake. Further along he caught sight of the fragment *sington* and took it to be part of *Kensington*, the name of a periodical recently described by its proprietor (in what connection Jake had forgotten) as entirely educational in character. Two. Directly to the side he caught a glimpse of half an outsize bare breast and decided that had better be three and the lot before the bald bugger asked him if he wasn't tiring his eyes with all that reading.

As it turned out he had been hard on this man, who politely didn't smile or leer when he saw Jake's selection, named a cash sum once and said Cheers five times, the first time when he noticed the approach of his customer, again when handed the magazines, again when he took money, again when he gave change and the last time when bidden good-bye. Better than arseholes to you, thought Jake.

He set off home with quite a spring in his step. Dirty girls approached and passed him, overtook him, moved across his front. When he observed this it occured to him to take stock of them and so lend some background and depth to the study he would shortly be making of the relevant portions of *Mezzanine, Kensington* and whatever the other one was called – he hadn't liked to look and was carrying the things rolled up and back outwards. So, as the creatures cruised about him on the split and loosened paving-stones, advanced and receded between skips full of rubble at the kerb and fat black plastic bags full of rubbish against or near the shop-fronts, he took a bit of stock of them.

They differed from the ones he had used to know within quite a wide range and yet unmistakably, as a random bunch of passers-by in Prague would have differed from the Brussels equivalent. Apart from their dirtiness, which was often no more extreme than a look of entire neglect as in a hermit or castaway, they tended to have in common smallness of frame that wasn't quite slimness, smallness of feature that went with roundness of head, dark-blonde colouring and nothing to shout about in the way of tits, so much not so that the odd one here and there was probably a boy: anyhow, there were enough such to point to a large secret migration from (as it might have been) Schleswig-Holstein. The favoured attire suggested a lightning raid on the dressing-up chest or actual deprivation of clothing as normally thought of. They were wearing curtains, bed-spreads, blankets, tablecloths, loose covers off armchairs and sofas. A sideboard-runner hung round one neck in the manner of a stole, a doubled-over loop of carpet round another in that of an academic hood. And somebody's fucking them, thought Jake.

The pageant continued unabated throughout the walk back to Burgess Avenue, so there had been no malign Blake Street influence at work. Perhaps there was one which embraced Orris Park in general and even, it could be, surrounding territories too; he must keep his eyes open on his travels and compare. Turning in at his gate he realised there was one thing shared by the whole crowd, the larger as well as the smaller, the ones in clothes no less than the ones in household textiles, the black and the white and the khaki: they had all not looked at him.

Jake wielded his latchkey and opened the front door slowly, cautiously. As soon as he had created an aperture wide enough for it to do so, a human head came into view at about the level of his knee and no more than a few inches from it. The eyes caught his and showed astonishment. He wanted to kick the head, which ascended and receded as part of a move from a crouching to a standing posture. It belonged to Mrs Sharp, the woman who came in three mornings a week to clean the house. He had told her about three-quarters of an hour earlier that he was going out for about three-quarters of an hour, so it was no more than natural that after about forty minutes she should have settled down (as he now saw) to polish the brass frame round the mat immediately inside the front door, nor that astonishment should have visited her to find him of all people entering the house at such a time and by such a route. It was sensing enough of this that must have led him to open the door in the way he had.

He had had plenty of practice at that kind of thing in the four years Mrs Sharp had been working here. Obviously she had been recommended by Alcestis and might even have worked for her at some stage. He was unsure about this and likely to remain so, since he had asked Brenda and forgotten the answer too many times. What he was sure of was that she (Mrs Sharp) bore marks of being Alcestis-trained or alternatively was Alcestis continued by other means. A round-shouldered woman of about forty with prominent but otherwise rather good teeth and a trick of murmuring indistinguishably in tones of self-reproach or mild alarm, Mrs Sharp was always in the way, his way at least. On the stairs, on the thresholds of rooms, in the narrow bit of passage from between the foot of the stairs and the dining-room door to the kitchen door (especially there), dead in front of whichever part of whichever shelf held the book he wanted – always, always. She monitored his shits, managing to be on reconnaissance patrol past the lavatory door or standing patrol in sight of it whenever he went in and out; he couldn't have said why he minded this as he did. Keeping at him in this way meant so much to her that she took 10p an hour less than the going rate and so, in these thin times, rendered herself virtually unsackable.

Today offered her special opportunities. The first of course concerned the nocturnal mensurator. Debarred from what would have been old Smudger's approach – direct questioning for as long as necessary – Mrs Sharp would if she could have led with something like 'I'm afraid I may have broken your record player or whatever it is, Mr Richardson, look. Would you see if it's still working, then I can get it repaired if it isn't.' At the moment the apparatus was in Jake's study, which he was able to keep locked on the vague grounds that it contained some rare books and without this precaution, supposedly, the milkman would rush up and pinch them. (In fact the rarest book there was a copy of his own early work on the first Greek settlements in Asia Minor: most of the small only edition had been pulped in the post-war paper shortage.) A locked door wasn't anything like a hundred-per-cent protection against Mrs Sharp – he wouldn't have been much more astonished than she just now if he had found her on the roof setting fire to petrol-soaked rags and dropping them down the study chimney – but it was a hell of a sight better than nothing.

On his entry she had flattened herself against the wall to allow him, and any twenty-stone friends he might have brought with him, to pass. He got out of range of her, so that if she fell over at this point she wouldn't be able to knock the magazines out of his hand in the process, and said weightily,

'I'm going up to my study now, Mrs Sharp.'

'Yes, Mr Richardson.' (Already a most unusual exchange: it was her habit never to speak except while she was being spoken to.)

'I've got some very important work to do.'

'Yes, Mr Richardson.'

'I don't want to be disturbed for the next hour.'

'No, Mr Richardson.'

Somebody who knew her less well than he did might have thought that this would put ideas into her head. Perhaps, but they would have come of their own accord, born of that mysterious power, shared with Alcestis, of *unconsciously* sensing how and when and where to be obstructive and acting on it. He had said what he had said merely to forearm himself against whatever way she might rise to her second special opportunity of the day, for rise to it she would: the readiness was all. The same somebody as before might have deferred matters till the afternoon or next day: no good: she would have stayed on to make up for hours not worked last week, come tomorrow so as not to have to come on Friday when her daughter, etc. *And* he was fucked if he was going to, etc. He knew the Alcestis-Mrs Sharp gang counted a lot on that reaction but sod it.

As he went upstairs he sang under his breath a ditty learned in those Army days of his:

Get older this . . .
Get older that . . .
When there isn't a girl about
Yer feel so lonely,
When there isn't a girl about
Yer on yer only . . .
Get older this (bash! bash!)
Get older that (boom! boom!) . . .

It certainly didn't take him back. Locking himself in with a load of new-bought wankery, on the other hand, did, as predicted, but the distance was far smaller in the second case. He settled down comfortably in his handsome brass-studded red-leather armchair, a present from Brenda on his fiftieth birthday, and opened *Kensington*.

After looking through it at colour-supplement speed he put it aside. It was full of chaps and parts of chaps, or rather of course it was full of girls but with chaps very much in the picture. *Zoom* and its contemporaries had occasionally included the odd chap dressed as a policeman or rustic, only he had been dressed, and the point of him had been the mistaken though innocuous one of something like comic relief, and you could usually get rid of him or most of him by folding the page. No amount of ingenuity of that order would have got rid of the chaps here.

The journal he had picked up in the shop almost at random turned out to be called *Agora*, and the breast he had spied on its cover turned out to be part of a drawing, more precisely part of a drawing-within-a-drawing that a chap in the outer drawing was drawing. He was the only visible chap throughout *Agora*, but there were dozens of his sex in the letterpress of which, apart from small or smallish advertisements and some more non-erotic drawings, it entirely consisted. The range was from she ran her dainty fingers up and down my, by way of the other night my girl-friend took hold of my, to can anything be done to straighten out my. Some of it wasn't supposed to be true and some of it was.

Lastly and with renewed expectation he came to *Mezzanine*. It was about the size of the Liverpool telephone directory but was printed on much nicer paper. As part of the fun-delaying ritual that was itself part of the fun, he began at the beginning. Car. Cigarette. Soft drink. Hard drink. Mezzanine Platform – this was some more on the lines of said she'd never seen anything like my. Cigarette. Car. Article on speedboats. Article on Loire wines. He was over halfway through this, finding it sound enough if rather jocosely written, when he so to speak remembered where he was. Guiltily he flipped over the page and came upon a small photograph and a large photograph, both a bit misty on purpose, of a very pretty girl who at the same time looked like President Carter, in the sense that her face looked like his face, and who had almost no clothes on without giving much away. Over the next page, three more photographs, arty angles, unlikely poses. Over the *next* page, well this is it folks. Wham. And (there being two such) bam. And thank you most awfully mam.

Jake stared, though without amazement. Tit- was not what this magazine was. In one sense he was on very familiar territory, even if the familiarity was slightly dated; in another he'd never been here before. His mind searched slowly. It was all a matter of how you looked at it, in two senses again if not more. In itself it was a bit. . . . And for some reason you found you had to consider it in itself, even though most of the rest of her was there, including her face. In itself it had an exotic appearance, like the inside of a giraffe's ear or a tropical fruit not much prized even by the locals. He turned on and found more of the same, on again and found more art, again and came to an article on hair-pieces. Men's. To put on their heads.

In the days of *Zoom* – when, that is, *Zoom*-style had been as far as you could easily, safely and not expensively go – he had believed that to come across, by some stupendous accident, one of his favourite *Zoom* girls, Anne Austin, June Palmer or Rosa herself, in a pose such as he had just seen would have constituted the summit of human (or at least male) felicity. Well, *then* no doubt it would have done. That had been *then*.

He turned on yet again through various commemorations of the unfree good things in life until he came to the expected series of photographs with the girl on the cover as model. There was quite a lot of stuff alongside about her personal habits, including a clear statement in large letters and between quotation marks of what she regarded as the best thing in *her* life. Jake found this slightly offensive; her holding such a view was at least unobjectionable but he would have preferred to reach that conclusion about her under his own steam. In some of the accompanying pictorial pornographic material her hand was quite where it hadn't been quite on its cover and her mouth was open and her eyes shut. Right. Now that should have been just what the doctor ordered. Why wasn't it? What made it, to a very small degree but unmistakably, off-putting? Before he could get his censor out of bed the thought popped up in his mind that she was no lady. By Gad sir, he said to himself, country's going to the dogs, time and place for everything, but without squashing that thought, which even attained the clarification that while what this girl was up to or at any rate was trying to be mistaken for being up to lay well within the scope of a lady, being so photographed didn't. But, he reminded himself, the girls he imagined to himself got up to things that were much more, more – come on, out with it: more degrading than this. Yes, but that was him. And those girls did what they did because, however perversely, they enjoyed it, not because they were getting paid. He had imagined better than he knew when he credited this one with a sound business head. All rationalisation and self-deception, he said to himself; you wouldn't have thought of any of that *then*. Ah, but supposing it had been *then* that you. . . .

Jake did a mental about-turn. He had decided that the only picture of business-head that he really liked was one of her shopping (fully clothed) in a vegetable-market and was about to junk the whole project when he remembered with a start what the flesh-and-blood doctor had ordered. Fifteen minutes had he said? Oh Christ. Well, knock off five for time already put in. He set himself to pore grimly over business-head and Carter-face in alternate bouts of two minutes each, fighting off as best he could the distractions of the possibly-Roman ring worn by the one, the pleasant-ness of the rural scene in which the other wallowed, the uncertainly identifiable ornament or utensil in the shadows behind the one, and so forth. After a while, this way or that he was getting interested. Then the dead silence was broken by a tremendous rattling of the lock on the door.

That fairly hurtled him back not far off fifty years. He went into a kind of throe and made wild self-defensive motions. 'What is it?' he asked. He had to ask most of it twice or more.

No answer, further rattling, but the door itself did seem to be holding for the moment.

'What do you want? Mrs Sharp?' This was louder and steadier. 'I told you I didn't want to be – '

' – thought your knob looked as if it could do with a polish.' No no, *of course* she didn't say that, couldn't have done; she must have been talking about th' door-knob or y' door-knob, but it had sort of come through to him different.

'Oh I see. I mean it probably does, still surely there's no need for you to start on it – '

' – come back and finish it later if I'm disturbing you.'

'Yes do. No don't.' It would be anything from two to a hundred and two minutes later. 'No, finish it now you've – '

' – easily come back after I've – '

'No. No. Finish it *now*, Mrs Sharp.'

'Well . . . if that's what you really want, Mr Richardson.'

The buffeting resumed and went on for a minute or so, then stopped. Moving only his eyes, and them not much, Jake sat and waited for another half-minute. At the end of that time he executed a playful lunge, a feint. Instantly the buffeting re-resumed. He rocked triumphantly in his chair. 'Gotcha!' he hissed. 'Now try and tell me it's all imagination.'

But the funny part came when the polishing was well and truly over and he could go on where he had left off, or rather more or less where he had begun. As if acting on orders committed to memory and carried out many times in rehearsal he went to the top drawer of his desk, took out an unused long envelope, turned to the picture of Carter-face that he liked most of best, put the envelope so that it covered the less endearing part of her and went on from there.

Later he said out loud, 'And that's only the beginning. No. It's a start.'

6   Focusing Session

'What does it mean?' asked Brenda.

'Well, sensate ought to mean endowed with sense or senses, as dentate if it occurs must mean endowed with teeth, but I don't see how any sort of focusing can be endowed with any sort of sense. I think they wanted an adjective from sense and noticed or someone told them sensuous and sensual were used up and they noticed or someone told them a lot of words ended in -ate. Makes it sound scientific too. Like nitrate. And focusing, well. Homing in on? No? Concentrating? Something like that.'

'I see. But what does it mean?'

'Christ, love, I don't know. Getting you, getting one interested in the other person physically, something like that I should think. Anyway, we know what we're supposed to do.'

'Yes. Darling, you're not to be cross but I must ring Elspeth before we start. She said she'd ring me today or tomorrow and I *know* it'll be while we're doing our focusing if I don't get in first. You know.'

'Check.' As just disclosed, Elspeth was of the Alcetis-Mrs Sharp sorority though, living as she did on the far side of London at Roehampton, less to be feared. 'You take as long as you have to. I'll be in the study.'

Jake finished putting the lunch plates in the rack on the metal draining-board and went where he had said. The study had been made out of what had been not much more than a spacious box-room and the kneehole desk, the celebrated red-leather armchair and a pair of Queen Anne bookcases left little space for anything else, but even he could see that the turquoise carpet was a pretty shade and went well with the wallpaper and Madras cotton curtains.

With the intention not so much of getting in the mood as of keeping up the good work he glanced at a couple of papers that lay on the desk, had been lying there in perfect security since the previous Thursday, even though it was now Monday and Mrs Sharp had by standing arrangement attended the house on the Friday and that very morning. For both times Brenda had been at home and, as in many a (or many another) case of hypernormal powers, Mrs Sharp's were severely curtailed or even curbed altogether by the presence of a third party. Jake picked up one of the papers.

M27 (he read) I find the thought of sexual intercourse with a willing female somewhat under the age of consent, say 14–15 yrs

1 very pleasant
2 fairly pleasant
3 a little unpleasant
4 very unpleasant

In so far as he could make himself address his mind to the problem, he found he thought all four. The age thing didn't come into it: the attractiveness of any willing female past puberty depended for him on her attractiveness, though as far as he knew he had in practice confined himself to those of 16 yrs and over. What counted was the immediacy or lack of it. Some time or other in Hawaii or somewhere, very pleasant; on his next trip to Italy, fairly pleasant, by the end of next month in Orris Park, a little unpleasant; here and now, very unpleasant. Even that wasn't quite right because of the difference between the thought of sexual intercourse and the thought of the thought of it. If he could snap his fingers and poof, there he was in mid-job, very pleasant; if she were really actually in fact standing a yard away on the precise point of starting to show how willing she was, very unpleasant. Not unpleasant, either, just as much as his old man needed to set it trying to haul itself up into his abdomen. But he couldn't write all this down, especially since the question was obviously nothing to do with any of it. Like the good examinee he had always been (best classical scholarship of his year at Charterhouse, First in Mods, best First of his year in Greats) he asked himself what was expected here, what was being looked for. A means of sorting out the child-molesters from the gerontophiles, why yes, and no doubt of making the finer distinction between the inhibited who welcomed any accepted restriction and the robust sturdy husky hardy hearty etc. He ticked 2 and picked up the other paper.

A fantastically beautiful girl with an unbelievable figure wearing a skin-tight dress cut as low as it possibly could be is looking at me with eyes blazing with uncontrollable passion (he read). With lazy languorous movements she peels off the dress and reveals herself as completely stark naked and utterly nude. Her breasts are so enormous that there is hardly room for them on her thorax. They are rising and falling with irresistible desire as with her shapely hips swaying lazily she glides over and stands insolently before me with her hands on her curving hips and her colossal breasts jutting 100 words out at me. I tear off all my clothes and she gives a tremendous gasp of astonishment and admiration and awe. She lies down on a bed which is there.

There was more, but he was still 73 words short of the 600 minimum set by Rosenberg and had already been compelled to introduce two additional girls, the first with immense breasts, the second with gigantic ones, for the sake of variety. He felt that this must violate some important canon of the genre but could find no other alternative to direct repetition. It was not that he had been idle; this was the fourth draft. The first, which had said all he really wanted to say on the matter, had consisted only of nouns, verbs, prepositions, pronouns and articles and been 113 words long; gamma minus at best. Well, he had to find those 73 somewhere before setting off for Harley Street the next morning. What about a black girl? With Brobdingnagian breasts? No no, with gleaming ebony skin. Mm. . . . The trouble was that being white himself he tended to think about white girls when he thought about girls at all.

Brenda tapped softly at the open door. 'All right?'

'Right.'

He followed her across the small landing, where a Bengal rug lay, and into their bedroom. Here, in a drill they had been through many times together, they lifted off, folded and laid down on an ottoman the patchwork quilt she had expertly made. Again by tradition, lapsed in this case, she slipped off to the bathroom and he quickly undressed and got into bed. He felt calm and yet uneasy, quite resolved to carry out orders but unable not to wish that something harmless in itself would prevent what was in prospect. After a minute he turned over so that he would have his back to Brenda when she reappeared. She had treated with exemplary seriousness Rosenberg's letter about her need to lose weight, had joined the local group of Guzzlers Anonymous at the first opportunity and had already taken off six ounces, but that wasn't going to be enough to make her feel all right about being seen naked, which she had avoided for the past year or more, he supposed.

There was a patter of arrival behind him (she moved lightly for so large a woman) and she got in and snuggled up to him with wincing and puffing noises.

'Ooh! It's freezing. It's supposed to be the middle of April and it's like January.'

'Would you like to turn the other way?'

'No, this is fine for me. Had you heard of comfort eating before?'

'What?'

'Comfort eating. What Dr Thing said I'd been going in for because of feeling sexually inadequate. Had you heard of it?'

'I think so, anyway it's clear enough what it's supposed to mean, which is all balls. If there's anybody who feels sexually inadequate it's me and I haven't started eating my head off. Just another example of thinking that if you name something you've explained it. Like . . . like permissive society.'

'I don't think you're always meant to go in for comfort eating when you feel sexually inadequate. And in any case what makes you think you're the one who feels it so terrifically you leave everybody else standing, how adequate do you think *I* feel when I think about things and look back, that's what I'd like to. . . .'

Brenda, who had started talking at some speed, stopped altogether because a jet was passing and even at this range she would have to shout rather and she was bad at shouting. A part of the window-frame buzzed for a short time as it always did on these occasions. Eventually Jake said,

'My fault. I just got fed up and guilty and ashamed. Of course you must feel inadequate if we have to use the word, but I can tell you there's no need for you to, it's all me, we went into that.'

'I know we went into it, but we decided it must be me as well as you.'

'You may have thought so, but it wasn't what we decided.'

'Well *I* think it was. And of course it is, it's obvious. Anyway I'm warm enough now. Hadn't we better get on with it?'

'All right.' Grunting, Jake turned over so as to face his wife. They intertwined their legs in a friendly way.

'Tell me again what we're meant to do.'

'We take it in turns to stroke and massage each other anywhere but what you used to call down below.'

'Did I? Anyway I bags you start.'

'Okay. Lift up. . . . Put your arm. . . . That's right.'

He started stroking the back of her neck and her left shoulder and upper arm. She sighed and settled herself more comfortably, moving her head about on the pillow. A minute or so went by.

'Is that nice?' he asked.

'Yes. Are we meant to talk?'

'He didn't say we weren't to, the doctor, so I suppose it's all right.'

'Good.'

But neither did any more talking for the moment. With his glasses off, Brenda's face was a bit of a blur to Jake but he could see her eyes were shut. By his reckoning, the second minute was just about up when she said,

'Did the doctor say we weren't to have a kiss?'

'No.'

'Let's have one then.'

He couldn't have said how long it had been since they had kissed each other on the mouth, probably less than twenty-four hours, but it was longer since he had noticed them doing that. Their mouths stayed together for a time, again showing friendliness, this time roughly of the sort that, on his side, he would have shown an amiable acquaintance in public at a New Year's party. He thought Brenda was putting about the same into it. The kiss ended by common agreement.

'Well, that was all right . . .' he said.

' . . . as far as it went. We'll get better, darling. Lots of ground to be made up.'

'Yes – your turn now.'

'To what?'

'Stroke me the way I was stroking you.'

'Oh yes. Will the same sort of place suit you? Round here?'

'Fine.'

'I'm sorry I'm so fat,' said Brenda after a moment.

'That's all right, I mean you couldn't help it and you've started doing something about it.'

'Yes. Do you think I ought to do something about my hair?'

'What's the matter with it?'

'Matter with it? It's all grey, or hadn't you noticed?'

'Of course I'd noticed. It's a very nice grey. A, an interesting sort of grey.'

'Wow, you make it sound terrific. I could have it dyed back to something like what it used to be. They do jolly good dyes these days.'

'Oh but you can always tell.'

'Not if it's done properly. And supposing you can tell, what about it, what's wrong with that?'

'Well, it looks a bit. . . .'

'A bit what? A bit off? A bit bad taste? A bit not quite the thing? A bit mutton dressed up as lamb?'

'Of course not. Well yes, a bit, but that's not really what I . . . I just think it looks ugly. Because it's unnatural.'

'So's make-up unnatural. So's shaving armpits. So's you shaving.'

'All right, just ugly then.'

'I wasn't going to have it bright red or bright yellow or bright purple, just something like what it used to be like, which was brownish mouse if you remember. No *I* think you think it's sort of out of place.'

'I doubt if we're supposed to talk as much as this.'

'Not that you care.'

Jake looked mildly startled. 'What do you mean?'

'You're not enjoying this are you, me stroking you? Your face went all resigned when I started. Are you?'

'I'm not disenjoying it.'

'Thanks a *lot*,' said Brenda, stopping stroking.

'No don't. What else could I have said? You knew anyway. And it isn't you. With this it really isn't you. You said we'd got a lot of ground to make up. We've only just started.'

'All right, but I reckon it's your turn again now.'

'Fair enough.'

'Did the doctor say you weren't to stroke my tits?'

'No.'

'Well, you can stroke them then, can't you?'

'I suppose so.'

'Only suppose so? They aren't down below are they?'

'No, but they're sort of on the way there. Put it like this, if down below's red and your arm's green, that makes your tits amber.'

'Yes, I see. Perhaps we'd better be on the safe side and not.'

'On the other hand of course, it'd be a natural mistake to make, so if it is, if it would be a mistake you'd think he'd have made sure of saying so, you know, oh and by the way non-genital includes tits, excludes them rather, I should say breasts. No, mammary areas.'

'You mean we can?'

'I don't see what harm it could do, do you?'

'Fire away.'

He fired away for a full two minutes. She stayed quite passive, eyes again shut, breathing slowly and steadily, giving an occasional contented groan. No doubt what he was doing, or how he was doing it, bore a close resemblance to its counterpart of a couple of years before, but there was no means of comparison because he had felt so different then, in particular felt more. What he felt now was an increasing but still never more than mild desire to stop doing what he was doing. In itself each motion he made was unequivocally if only by a little on the pleasant side of the pleasant/unpleasant borderline; the snag was there were so many of them. Patting a favourite child on the head or indeed stroking a beloved animal (to single out two activities he had never felt much drawn to) became unnatural if continued beyond a certain short time, however willing child or animal might be to let things go on. My God, another twenty-five minutes of this? – it was a good job he was such a faithful doer of what doctors told him to do. Hadn't Rosenberg told him to carry on with this bleeding sensate-focusing carry-on for *up to* half an hour? Twenty minutes was that, wasn't it? So was ten. And five. But to argue so was to use advertiser's mathematics. Amazing reductions at Poofter's, up to twenty per cent on all furnishings. Daily brushing with Bullshitter's fleweridated toothpaste reduces cavities by up to thirty per cent, in the case you happen to be looking at by only point-nought-one of one per cent but what of it, and also of course helps fight (not helps *to* fight) tooth decay, alongside drinking things and not eating toffee all day long. Daily brushing with candlewax or boot-polish would also reduce cavities by up to something or other and help fight tooth decay. There were enough laws already but surely there ought to be one about up to, restricting it to, oh, between the figure given and half of it. Helping fight things would be rather more of a –

'Isn't it about time for my turn?' asked Brenda.

'Oh, er . . . yes I suppose it is. I sort of lost count of time.'

'Carried away. No I don't mean that darling, forget I said it, I was just being frightfully silly. Now on this round I think we might. . . .'

'Hey!'

'What's the matter?'

'Supposed to be non-genital.'

'That's non isn't it, there?'

'Well yes, but only – '

'Genital's genital and non's non.'

'But the spirit of the – '

'Sod the spirit. And even the spirit doesn't say you're not supposed to enjoy it.'

'I don't think we ought to – '

'Shut up.'

After a little while, Jake began to breathe more deeply, then to flex and unflex his muscles. Forgotten feelings, located in some mysterious region that seemed neither body nor mind, likewise began to possess him. Brenda sighed shakily. He pressed himself against her and at once, try as he would, the more irresistibly for his trying, which was like the efforts of a man with no arms to pick up a pound note off the pavement, the flow reversed itself. In a few more seconds he relaxed.

'Oh well, that's that,' he said.

'No it isn't. Only for now. It shows there's something. What do you expect at this stage?'

'What I expect at *this* stage, and what I shall no doubt get, is about twenty more minutes of an experience I wasn't looking forward to and which has turned out to justify such . . . mild forebodings. It isn't you, it's me.'

'Don't think you're the only one, mate. It isn't you, it's me cuts both ways, you know. You're not blaming me, that's how you mean it, but you're not taking me into consideration either. What about that?'

'Yes. Yes, you're right.'

'If you had – been considering me, you might have wondered what I was doing telephoning Elspeth when all I needed to do to make sure we weren't interrupted was take the receiver off. That's right. Putting off the evil hour. Giving way to mild whatnames. It wasn't you, it was me. Now you'd better start stroking again, uncongenial as it may be. The doctor said you were to.'

'It's not un*congenial*, it's just – '

'No, not there. Do my back.'

He started doing her back. 'You said it was nice before, when I was on your shoulder and arm. Was it? Is this?'

'Oh yes. Not tremendous, but nice.'

'Sexy?'

'No,' she said as if he had asked her whether she had said yes or no. 'Nice all the same. I like all that sort of thing, massages and sauna baths and whatnot. You don't, do you?'

'Never been able to see the point of it.'

'I suppose it's just how you're made. I suggest what we do now is go on for however long it is and not mind too much how we get there, talk or recite or sing as long as we put in the time.'

'Yes. The idea must be to get us used to touching each other again.'

'Start to get us used.'

7   Are You Disturbed?

That was on the Monday. On the Tuesday Jake went down to see Rosenberg again, taking his homework with him: the completed questionnaire, the sixth and final draft of his fantasy and the paper discs that recorded the doings of the nocturnal mensurator. These troubled him slightly. Each disc bore a faintly pencilled arc with, at intervals, a thicker line or perhaps a pair of contiguous ordinary lines in a radial position. They were no more than a millimetre or two long and must represent movements of the metal arm on the breaking and making of the electrical circuit. But by this time Jake had forgotten which way the thing was supposed to go when, so he didn't know whether he had had a series of virtually continuous erections, broken only by breathing-spaces in a continuous-performance dreamland orgy, or half a dozen flickers of mild interest per night.

Though he inspected the discs thoroughly, Rosenberg made no comment on this or any other point about them and Jake didn't care to ask him. He took even longer over the questionnaire, nodding as he looked through it with a slow regularity Jake began to find offensive: was he (Jake) such a predictable mess? He had only just begun to find this when the doctor suddenly raised his head and, Curnow-like, stared hard at him for God knew how long. Could this be a reaction to the breach of discipline in his answer to *M41* I think children should receive sex education 1 as soon as they can understand 2 before puberty 3 at puberty – *never* scrawled at the bottom? More likely it was his regarding (*M49*) the thought of being watched while engaged in sexual intercourse as not very pleasant nor fairly pleasant nor even a little unpleasant but very unpleasant that had produced the stare, on this view a signal much less of hostility or alarm than of wonder, of a desire to fix in the mind something to tell one's grandchildren.

It was soon clear that the fantasy was altogether on the wrong lines. Rosenberg's chubby little features filled with deep disappointment. Once or twice he screwed up his eyes and frowned as if in actual pain, whether bodily or mental. But in the end he laid aside the neatly typed sheets with a muttered promise to take a more careful look later and asked Jake a lot of questions about his childhood and adolescence, some on new topics like any dreams, wet and non-wet, he remembered from that period and how he had felt about the physical changes he had experienced then, others over already-traversed ground, his parents' relationship and suchlike, in the evident but vain hope of eliciting significant contradiction of previous responses. Together with his detailed account of the non-genital sensate focussing session, interspersed with further questions from Rosenberg which continuing to listen in silence would in most cases have rendered needless, these activities filled up the hour. Or very nearly: there was time at the end for three momentous directives. One – Jake and Brenda were to go on to practise genital sensate focusing, a term which Rosenberg explained with a wealth of well-known words derived from the classical tongues. Two – Brenda was to accompany Jake on his next visit to the consulting-room. And three – before that could come to pass, the following Thursday afternoon in ·fact, Jake was to visit the sex laboratory at the McDougall Hospital. By way of reassurance Rosenberg again asked him to say, virtually with his hand on the book, whether he had any objection to exposing his genitals in public and was given the answer no.

The nearer it got to Thursday afternoon the less that answer squared with the truth. In the past he had been very willing indeed to carry out such exposure to selected individual females in private, though not of course just like that, but in the Army, in sports changing-rooms and so on he had been one of the majority who preferred where possible to keep themselves to themselves. At the time he had followed that policy without thinking of it as a policy or as anything at all, but now it looked as if he had better start thinking of it as something. This change of approach was just part of the steady progress towards more sophisticated awareness which had come to fuck up (so it seemed to him) most kinds of human behaviour in the last however many years it was. Preferring to keep himself to himself must be allied to the quirk whereby he regarded the thought of being watched while engaged in sexual intercourse as very unpleasant. And that was going to have to do for the minute.

His bus map told him that having taken the 127 to Gower Street he could change there to a 163 and, via Chelsea, Putney Bridge and Southfields, be transported to Colliers Wood. That was what he did. On this journey he had remembered to bring the *Times* crossword puzzle but the lurching and plunging of the vehicle at the various irregularities of the highway, together with the difficulty of the clues, led him to stop it soon. He was also distracted by the very loud unsteady wailing noise to be heard whenever the driver used his brakes. The view out of the windows south of the river, after the 163 had passed under a couple of dozen railway bridges in a mile or so, was definitely less attractive than what was to be seen from the 127. Here were derelict churches covered with grime, yards of hoardings with no posters on them, dining-rooms and small draper's shops such as he hadn't seen since the '30s, waste lots big enough to accommodate a shopping complex barely to be dreamed of and, beyond them, hulking greyish towers of offices or dwellings that loomed on the smoky distance. He supposed that people who lived here might well vote for or against some-body at an election, neither of which he had bothered to do since 1945 (Liberal). The ones he saw had an archaic look too, dumpy, dark-clothed, wearing hats: the infiltrators from Schleswig-Holstein had not reached here yet.

Sitting near the front of the bus on the upper deck he became aware by degrees that a sort of altercation was going on behind him, the sort, as it soon proved, in which only one voice was to be heard, a woman's, deep and powerful, projected with that pressure of the diaphragm used by actors.

'It isn't right, is it? I mean do you think it's right? After all these years and all I been through? I said I've had enough, I done everything you told me and I've had enough, I said. I told him straight. What's in it for me, I said, yeah, what's in it for me? I've had e-bloody-nough. Now that's my rights, isn't it? I reckon that's my rights, don't you? I said don't you?'

He looked over his shoulder to see what kind of unfortunate was having to put up with this, and found that nobody and everybody was, staring hard out of the window or at a newspaper or into space. The speaker wore a dark-brown coat flecked with green and a very pale lilac-coloured silk scarf round the neck. That neck looked too slender for the job of connecting the broad-shouldered trunk to the large round head. The woman's complexion was dull, her chin pointed, her nose thin, her hair straight and dry, standing out and up from her scalp. While she continued to talk she seemed never to look directly at anyone, always between people.

'I'm not going to stay there,' she repeated several times in the same tone as before, accusing rather than angry. 'I told him so. I said, I don't mind coming along, well I do, but I will. I don't mind coming along but I'm not going to stay. I've had enough of that. Where's it got me, that's what I'd like to know. It's not fair, it's taking advantage, that's what it is. He's got me where he wants me and there's nothing I can do about it. I been given a raw deal, haven't I, a raw bloody deal. Don't anybody think I've been given a raw deal?'

Jake had turned back to face his front after one good look. The sound-quality of the last couple of dozen words told him that the woman had got up and was moving towards the top of the stairs, presumably on the way to getting off the bus. On an impulse he didn't at once understand he shifted round in his seat and said, 'Yes, I do.'

Now she did look straight at someone and he saw with unusual clarity that everything about her face was wrong. The tip of her nose was a narrow white peak above a pair of ill matched nostrils partly outlined in red; her eyes didn't so much protrude or glare as have no discernible sockets to lie in; her eyebrows were irregular streaks of bristle; her ears were set a little too far back on her skull; the borders of her lips were well marked at one corner and blurred at the other; the state of her skin showed him for the first time what it really meant to say that someone was pale and drawn. That's right, he thought to himself: they're not just mad inside their heads, they're mad to their fingertips, to the ends of their hair. And he had spoken to her to make her give him the straight look he had needed in order to see that in her.

What might have been the beginnings of a smile showed on the woman's face in the second before she stepped clumsily to one side and passed out of view down the stairs. Soon afterwards the bus stopped and from his position above the pavement he saw her walk away, swinging her arms a lot. Some distance ahead lay a small piece of park or public garden, a grassy triangle where, with a show of energy unexpected in these latitudes, a group of men in helmets and jerkins were attacking some trees. Products of their labours were strewn about them in the shape of much sound timber and vigorous foliage. The peevish wavering groan of their saws could be clearly heard through the noise of the traffic. At first idly, then with concern, Jake took in a rusty street-sign that said Trafalgar Place. Distracted by the incident of the madwoman, he was about to overshoot the stopping-point he had picked out on his de luxe *A to Z*. He toiled his way downstairs at his best speed but no kind of speed shown by him would have affected the progress of the bus, which finally dropped him a couple of hundred yards beyond the turning he wanted.

It was raining slowly but, with his umbrella and navy-blue light mackintosh, he found this no great infliction and set off with a brisk stride, a touch elated at having successfully brought off what was for him an out-of-the-way journey. There were six minutes to go before his appointment, which should be enough if the hospital was reasonably close to the main road. He had nearly reached the corner when he saw something he did find a great infliction, a figure he recognized standing on the opposite pavement and looking at him. Of course the McDougall was a psychiatric as well as a psychological joint; of course those who attended it regularly knew the nearest bus-stop to it; of course chaps who were fool enough to speak to people like that deserved all they got. And of course his first thought was of flight, but he loathed being late for anything. If he had known the district even slightly he might have risked a detour but again he didn't. So he turned the corner and quickened up to light-infantry speed.

'Excuse me!'

It was harsh and hostile and he ignored it.

'Excuse me.'

This time he thought he detected a note of appeal and found himself half-turning and slowing down so that the woman could catch him up. 'Yes?'

'I seen you on the bus, didn't I?'

'I believe so, yes.'

'You said you thought I been given a raw deal.'

'Yes, I . . .'

'Why d'you say that?' she asked merely as if she wanted to know.

'Well, I thought you seemed a bit upset and I wondered if I could cheer you up, that's all.'

'You're the first one as said I been given a raw deal for I don't know how long. They all say I get the best attention and all they want to do is take care of me but they got a funny way of showing it is what I say. I was in the hospital for five months and all they done was boss me around. The doctor just give his orders and never took a blind bit of notice of how I felt or what I thought. It's not fair, it's taking advantage.'

All this had been said in a tone that showed a sense of injury but none of the bitterness noticeable on the bus. Poor devil, thought Jake, a complete stranger throws her a kind word and she calms down immediately – these bloody doctors are all the same. Not that he had stopped looking for the hospital, of which at the moment there was no sign.

'Are you disturbed?' went on the lunatic.

He grasped at once that to her there could be no other reason for coming this way than her own. 'No, just, er, tension.'

'I been disturbed for . . . a long time. Ever since my mum died but they say it's nothing to do with that. Do you think it's to do with that?'

'I don't know. It must have something to do with it, I'd have thought.'

'You're the first one as ever said I been given a raw deal.' She turned her head towards him and smiled, showing a wide variety of teeth. 'That was real nice, that was. Real nice.'

'Oh I think most other people would have done the same,' he said, trying not to gabble it, to stay calm, to work out what to do if she pounced on him.

'I get very lonely. I'd like someone to come and see me. After I've had my tea, that's when I wouldn't mind someone, that sort of time. They don't, though, not them, no fear, they got better things to do, the lot of them. Dead selfish, the lot of them. Six weeks it's been since Harry come, and as for that June. . . .'

Just then there was a sign of the hospital in the form of a hospital sign, and the monologue on selfishness kept up satisfactorily while the two approached Reception – All Patients, stopping only at the swing doors. Inside, Jake's companion, swinging her arms in her awful way, went straight on without a word or a look while he made for the desk. A girl in a grey uniform standing behind it called over his shoulder,

'Excuse me dear, are you sure you know where to go?'

The words were delivered with unimpeachable gentleness but it was as if – no, to hell with as if: the madwoman had heard something different. She stopped dead and sent towards the desk a look of great fear and hatred. In that moment Jake recognised that, with the sole exception of the three words he had spoken on the bus, she had heard nothing of what he had said to her; he also withdrew what he had been thinking a couple of minutes earlier about bloody doctors.

'Who are you going to see, dear?'

'Holmes. Dr Holmes.'

'Good, he'll be waiting for you.' The girl blew out her cheeks as she turned to Jake. 'I'm new – they told me everyone was supposed to report here. Sorry – can I help you?'

'I was told to ask for Professor Trefusis.' He squared his jaw, took darting glances round the hall and tapped his rolled newspaper against the palm of his hand, trying to look like the vital, dynamic, thrusting head of a giant transcontinental sex consortium. 'I'm Dr Richardson.'

'Oh yes, doctor, room 35, third floor.'

In the lift, he asked himself what the hell he was doing there. Then he realised he hadn't noticed anything at all about what the girl at the desk had looked like except for her grey uniform, and told himself what.

8   Informal Basis

'Mr Richardson? Do come in. I'm Professor Trefusis.'

After the Rosenberg business no mere Yap Islander or Kalahari Bushman going under that name would have disconcerted Jake in the least, but a woman did rather, especially one that even he in his reduced state, could see was very attractive, in her middle thirties probably, with thick blonde hair parted at the side, blue eyes and a figure that would not have thrown *Zoom* into abject disgrace. Her manner was quiet and friendly. In succession she introduced him to Dr Thatch, a boyish-looking boy with mnemonically helpful abundant long hair, Dr something he missed, another boy but still distinguishable from his colleague by being nearly bald, Miss Newman, a lumpish, gloomy girl of about twenty(?), and Mr something he couldn't believe was a name, which didn't matter much because the man it referred to, tall and of dignified bearing, stood out at once from everyone else in the room by being black; he was said to be a citizen of Ghana and present only as an observer. Oh, so everyone else was going to twiddle with him, hey?

'And Dr Rosenberg of course you know.'

Seen by Jake for the first time in the company of others, the Irishman looked unexpectedly less small than on his own; he could have been as much as five foot, even perhaps an inch or two more. He shook hands and gave a cheerful smile.

'The purpose of this preliminary encounter,' said Professor Trefusis in the tones of a lecturer, but of an outstandingly good lecturer, one interested in the subject, 'is to establish amicable relations on an informal basis. We find the quickest way of doing this is for me to quote a few personal details relating to each member of the team. Now we know about you, Mr Richardson, that your first name is Jaques or Jake, that you're sixty years old, you're married, you're employed at Oxford University and you have a house in Orris Park. My first name is Rowena, I'm thirty-six years old, married to a photographer, we have two children in their teens and we live just up the road from here in Tooting. Dr Thatch is called Bill . . .'

Jake stopped listening then. He meant to switch on again to hear the bald doctor's name but forgot to. This part was easy enough; what was to come? What *sort* of thing? Before he could ask, Rowena Trefusis (Daphne du Maurier? No, more like Barbara Cartland) got there on her own.

' . . . people you're going to work with in a relaxed atmosphere. The work itself is quite straightforward. We hook you into an electric circuit – the current passed is minute, so even if everything went wrong at once you'd be in no danger even of discomfort – and then we present you with a series of sexual stimuli and measure your responses to them. It's an essentially simple process and the procedure is totally informal.'

'That's good,' said Jake, thinking it was something to be spared a totally formal procedure of measuring his responses.

'We try to use dress as a way of promoting informality. No white coats here, you'll have noticed.'

He just about had; now that he looked further he saw that the boys were wearing zipped-up jackets of imitation leather and trousers of some stuff like oakum or jute, Miss Newman the same sort of trousers and a light pullover with a Union Jack on it and the head of the team a smartly cut suit in what might have been highbrow mackintosh material. The African of course was turned out like a Japanese businessman. Jake made some approving noises.

'Well, I think we might as well – '

'Just one moment if I may, Professor Trefusis.' Rosenberg's manner had turned grave. 'You're sure, Mr Richardson, you've no objection to exposing your genitals in public?'

If you ask me that again, my little man, Jake thought to himself, I'll expose yours right here and now and your weeny bum for good measure. He said, 'Quite sure.'

'Very well, so let's be getting along to the theatre.'

'The what?' Images of operating tables and surgical masks rose in Jake's mind. 'Isn't that going to be rather . . .'

All of them except Miss Newman laughed. Professor Trefusis stopped almost at once and looked self-reproachful.

'I'm sorry, Mr Richardson, we've made that mistake before. Have no fear – you won't have to face any spotlights or rolls of drums. Dr Rosenberg meant the lecture theatre.'

'The *what*? Look, if you think I'm going to . . . expose my genitals to a whole crowd of God knows – '

'There'll be no crowd, I promise you. The number is eight, and one of those is doubtful.'

'All medical students,' said Thatch. 'Think of them as doctors, like us.'

'They won't get in anybody's way,' said Rosenberg. 'They've been carefully briefed on being as unobtrusive as possible and things are so arranged that you'll hardly know they're there.'

Jake reflected: there were six of them here; another seven or eight wouldn't make much odds, true, but it was a bit thick to be treated as mid-Victorian for not favouring a come-one-come-all admissions policy at the impending show. When he signified that on consideration this could go ahead they switched to treating him like a child just bravely out of its mopes or dumps. So, as the party trooped along a corridor that had the look of being identical to several hundred others in the place, he was not best pleased when Rosenberg moved him a little apart from the others and said,

'I found your attitude just now quite interesting.'

'Oh you did, did you?'

'You reacted somewhat violently to the notion of a large number of persons witnessing our investigations.'

'Mm.'

'Why?'

'Well, to start with, it's not inconceivable I might be recognised.'

'Would that be so disastrous?'

'Most things people object to aren't so disastrous or even disastrous, doctor. I object to somebody who knows me seeing me having this done, whatever it may be.'

'You mean the exposure itself?'

'Well – needing treatment for sexual . . . inadequacy.'

'Really now? You wouldn't object to being known to need treatment for, er, diabetes, which arises from insulin inadequacy?'

'Of course not. That's different.'

'Would you call that a mature attitude?'

'Perhaps I wouldn't and then again perhaps I would, and either way it's my attitude. Like my genitals.'

'We'll discuss this again, Mr Richardson,' said Rosenberg as they approached an unluxurious lift in which the others already stood.

The lecture-theatre was of a type familiar to Jake chiefly from American films: semi-circular tiers of seats rising up from a level space on the other side of which were blackboards and a projection-screen attached to the wall. Near the middle of the space there stood a metal framework mounted on struts and castors and with electric cables attached to several of its components; Jake assumed that what he saw was the back of the apparatus, which as he soon gathered bore dials or other measuring devices on its front. He found himself sitting on an ugly and expensive-looking straight-backed chair without his trousers and underpants. Otherwise he was neatly, almost formally dressed on the clean-linen-for-the-scaffold principle: dark-grey suit jacket, cream shirt, well-knotted regimental tie, grey socks and much-polished black shoes. The promise of immunity from spotlights given him a little earlier had been kept in the letter but not so much in the spirit: though there were several sources of light, all of them overhead or somewhere near it, their illumination was concentrated on him and the couple of dozen square yards round him; the one exception shone on the faces of Thatch and his bald colleague as they peered at their machine and clicked a switch here and there. Professor Trefusis stood near Jake at a metal table taking folders, typewritten sheets and a hardbacked file-cover of some kind out of a briefcase and arranging them on the table. Her expression was serious almost to the point of grimness, like that of an official about to announce a threat to the security of the kingdom. What was her husband like? What did he photograph? Did she do this instead of sex or was she so barmy about it that she had to spend her whole working day on this sort of substitute or semblance, keeping herself quiet, so to speak, until she could scuttle off for several uninterrupted hours of the real thing? Could anyone really tell? What about the visitor from Ghana, the only other person in plain sight? Which raised a question.

'Are your students here, Professor Trefusis?'

'Yes, all eight of them.'

'So the doubtful one made it after all; I'm so glad. Tell me, how can they see to take notes?'

'They don't have to. All the technical information and a full account of the procedure have been circulated to them already. From their point of view, this session provides an opportunity to watch the work actually being carried out under field conditions.'

'Oh I see.'

'I think we're about ready. Miss Newman?'

Miss Newman came into the light carrying a length of flex that ended in what looked to Jake like a classier version of the plastic hoop on the old nocturnal mensurator. Without looking him in the eye she hung it on him and withdrew. Was that all she did?

'Bill?'

'Okay.'

'Now Mr Richardson, I want you to try and concentrate entirely on me, on what I tell you and on what I show you. Forget about everybody else. If there's anything you don't like for any reason you're to say so immediately, and you can stop the whole session at any time simply by saying Stop. Right? Now. Shut your eyes. Have a sexual fantasy. Think of something that really turns you on.'

What Jake wanted to say immediately was that nothing really did that and if anything within reason really did then he wouldn't be there and hadn't Rosenberg told her so, but he followed doctor's orders and thought away like mad. Or tried to. Girl. Beautiful girl. Fantastically beautiful girl with an unbelievable. . . . No. *Girl.* Girl with slinky dress which she slowly draws up over the head. Underclothes and stockings. No, tights these days. Bugger these days. She slowly takes off one stocking. But he'd never been one for that kind of thing: off with the lot in short order had been his way. Off with the lot, then. Kiss. And so forth. He was well, or as well as he could manage, into the so forth when Professor Trefusis said,

'All right, Mr Richardson, hold it and relax for a moment. Bill?'

'Point-nine and thirty-three point-nine.'

Perhaps these figures displeased or disquieted the boss; anyway, she went over and joined the two at the apparatus, behind whom Jake could now make out two or three or more dim shapes. He could tell there was at least one other person to his left rear but didn't look round. Only the Ghanaian observer was now in full view; he had got in a lot of observing when Miss Newman did her bit and even now was still at it on and off. Jake wanted to tell him to pull up a prayer-mat or whatever he fancied and be his guest. He yawned and stretched. It could hardly be that he had broken the machine by overloading it – no no, here came Professor Trefusis with a satisfied expression.

'Sorry about that.' She picked up the file he had noticed and passed it to him. 'Would you read aloud what it says on the first page? I should explain that the object is to make sure you're turned off after each stimulus.'

'Ah.' He found that the thing was actually a loose-leaf book containing sheets of typescript. Clear enough. He read aloud,

Apart from the peculiar tenets of individual thinkers, there is also in the world at large an increasing inclination to stretch unduly the powers of society over the individual, both by the force of opinion and even by that of legislation; and as the tendency of all the changes taking place in the world is to strengthen society and diminish the power of the individual, this encroachment is not one of the evils which tend spontaneously to disappear, but, on the contrary, to grow more and more formidable. The disposition of mankind, whether as rulers or as fellow-citizens, to impose their own opinions and inclinations as a rule of conduct on others, is so energetically supported by some of the best and by some of the worst feelings incident to human nature that it is hardly ever kept under restraint by anything but want of power; and as the power is not declining, but growing, unless a strong barrier of moral conviction can be raised against the mischief, we must expect, in the present circumstances of the world, to see it increase.

He shut the book and handed it back, aware as he did so that no more observing was going on in his immediate neighbourhood. Whatever was next came out of one of the folders and was held up so that the group near the machine could see it. A moment later the professor was showing him a magazine photograph of one of the business-head-Carter-face sister-hood displaying her giraffe's ear.

'I don't like that,' he said.

It was out of sight in an instant. 'What don't you like about it?'

'It's ugly.'

'You find the model ugly?'

'No, not at all. I mean her . . . parts.'

'They repel you?'

'Yes. What I see there repels me.'

She hesitated and glanced momentarily to his left. That must be Rosenberg standing there, perhaps, among others, and were those questions his, put on his behalf instead of directly out of what, etiquette? Never mind: with no more said the second exhibit was exhibited after the same fashion as the first. It was much more up Jake's street, a nice-looking girl who also looked nice, possible too in the sense that you met girls like her, and arranged or shown in what might be called neo-*Zoom* style – advantage taken of some of the freedoms of the last few years without the surrender of decency.

'Better?'

'Fine.'

'Concentrate on it.' Trefusis leaned towards him, lowered her voice and said kindly, 'And remember this: by now nobody's thinking of you as an individual or a person. You're just an object.'

'Thank you.'

He concentrated and quite soon it started being rather a success, nothing to cause any wild surmising at the instrument panel, but still. This part went on for some minutes. Then he was told to forget about that and given the book open at a different page. He read aloud.

'If all mankind minus one were of one opinion, and only one person were of the contrary opinion, mankind would be no more justified in silencing that one person than he, if had the power, would be justified in silencing mankind. Were an opinion a personal possession of no value except to the owner; if to be obstructed in the enjoyment of it were simply a private injury, it would make some difference whether the injury was inflicted only on a few persons or on many. But the peculiar evil of silencing the expression of an opinion is that it is robbing the human race; posterity as well as the existing generation; those who dissent from the opinion, still more than those who hold it. If the opinion is right, they are deprived of the opportunity of exchanging error for truth; if wrong, they lose, what is almost as great a benefit, the clearer perception and livelier impression of truth, produced by its collision with error.'

The third offering showed two girls being familair with each other, no more than that, on a piece of very clean and neat garden furniture. That went down reasonably well too. Before his third bout of reading Jake said,

'May I ask a question?'

'Certainly.'

'I'd just like to make it clear' – he resisted the temptation to look over his shoulder – 'that what, well, appealed to me there wasn't what they were getting up to really, it was just the fair one, the look of her face and her breasts.'

'I'm sorry, what's your question?'

'Oh. Oh well I haven't really got one, I just wanted to say that.'

There was no reply apart from an undecided nod of the head, which he felt was quite as much as his non-question had deserved. Why had he bothered? Perhaps the same problem was exercising others: he heard whispers from the far side of the apparatus and a murmur behind him. But in a short time he was reading aloud,

'We take care that, when there is a change, it shall be for change's sake, and not from any idea of beauty or convenience; for the same idea of beauty or convenience would not strike all the world at the same moment, and be simultaneously thrown aside by all at another moment. But we are progressive as well as changeable: we continually make new inventions in mechanical things, and keep them until they are again superseded by better; we are eager for improvement in politics, in education, even in morals, though in this last our idea of improvement chiefly consists in persuading or forcing other people to be as good as ourselves. It is not progress that we object to; on the contrary, we flatter ourselves that we are the most progressive people who ever lived. It is individuality that we war against: we should think we had done wonders if we had made ourselves all alike; forgetting that the unlikeness of one person to another is generally the first thing which draws the attention of either to the imperfection of his own type, and the superiority of another, or the possibility, by combining the advantage of both, of producing something better than either. We have a warning example in China.'

The next thing was that the lovely Rowena was showing him a photograph of a girl doing what he didn't want to see any girl doing ever except to him – school of *Kensington*, in fact.

'I don't like that,' he said. 'And what I don't like about it isn't the activity itself, far from it, but being shown it going on between other people. It's not that I disapprove. Well yes actually come to think of it I do disapprove rather. Of that photograph being published I mean.'

'Fair enough,' she said, but spent the next minute or so looking through her folders, presumably in search of material that wouldn't offend his susceptibilities. At last she handed him a sheaf of seven or eight pictures and asked him to pick the two he liked best. That was easy: he chose one girl who, by the look of her, could have had no idea in the world why those men had asked her to lean against a tree wearing just a straw hat, and one with a faintly intellectual expression who reminded him of a *Zoom* favourite of his. The procedure had an end-of-session feel to it and some nuance of the professorial manner, he thought, suggested the same thing. So he was surprised and a little fed up to be told, after both girls had been disposed of, that he could take a short rest.

He put on a smile. 'Before what?'

'Before the second part of the programme. Do smoke if you want to, Mr Richardson.'

'No thanks, I've given it up.' The same thing only live? 'What happens in the second part?'

'We stimulate you artificially.'

'As opposed to – '

'With an artificial stimulator,' explained the professor.

'Oh I see.'

She went across and seemed to confer with the group by the machine. Although they were so near he couldn't hear a word of what they were saying. Rosenberg came strolling out of the shadows, followed by the Ghanaian.

'Well now, and how's it going?'

'I thought you were supposed to tell me that.'

'I meant your personal reaction in mental and emotional terms.'

'How I feel, you mean. Well, I suppose one can get used to anything. Look here, what's this stimulator?'

'Ah, there's a cunning little gadget if you like.'

'No doubt, but what is it?'

'Let's see, it's metal, and it's powered by electricity, and it . . . revolves rapidly.'

'You brave man,' interposed the observer.

Jake gave up Rosenberg and nodded appreciatively, hoping to be told what for this fellow said him brave man.

'Your ego has been subjected to a massive onslaught. Of the events in detail inducing you to set your foot on the path that has brought you here this afternoon, I know nothing; but of this I am quite sure, that they were of a sort to injure your pride most severely. So it must have gone with all the intervening events. Today, given among other factors your age and class, was the supreme test. I confess to having done a little to aggravate it; I apologize, and can plead only the excuse of scientific curiosity. I salute you, sir, and would ask you to do me the honour of allowing me to shake your hand.'

They shook; Jake had been about to get up from his chair to do so but remembered the state of his clothing, which indeed had seldom been far from his thoughts over the past half-hour and which now, for some reason, decided him against getting up. He was still most interested in the question of the artificial stimulator and was satisfied soon enough. Professor Trefusis, with Miss Newman at her side, again stood before him. She was holding up an object of yellowish metal about the size of a pepper-pot with a small protuberance at the top.

'This,' she said, 'is the artificial stimulator.'

With a neat movement she tripped a switch on the device and a thin high-pitched whine started up. To Jake it sounded like a dentist's high-speed drill and some of his reaction to the thought must have shown in his face, because Trefusis smiled and spoke reassuringly, took his hand and laid the metal protuberance, which he now saw was spinning rapidly, against it. He felt an agreeable stroking sensation, not intense, as if something between a finger-tip and a feather were being applied with super-human regularity. He nodded appreciatively again.

Part II now went ahead with businesslike dispatch. Artificial stimulator in hand, Miss Newman knelt before him. Professor Trefusis looked quickly through the contents of one of her folders and said,

'You'll now be subjected to the same stimuli as before while also being stimulated genitally. No doubt you'll appreciate that should your response come to climax the programme would have to be discontinued.'

'Yes,' said Jake, thinking this was a bit mealy-mouthed of her in the circumstances.

'So if you raise your hand the genital stimulation will cease at once.'

'Fine.'

What followed was physical pleasure in its purest form, unaccompanied, in other words, by any of the range of feelings from tenderness to triumph normally embodied with it. Even the desire for its continuance was missing, so that every minute, every dozen seconds he had to strive not to send the damned contraption flying and run for the door, no trousers or no no trousers. How can she do it? he kept asking himself, not rhetorically: what sort of woman does it take to measure what happens to chaps' willies for a living? What does your mummy do? And how can her husband cope? The she he meant was entirely the fair professor; Miss Newman never entered his thoughts. It was that, he saw afterwards, that made the whole shooting-match bearable: by luck or amazing judgement they had passed over for the artificial-stimulator-wielding spot all the impossible kinds of person, to wit males, attractive females and unattractive females, and come up with somebody as near nobody as anybody could be, somebody totally unmemorable, somebody who did nothing at all except as ordered. Or perhaps her behaviour, or absence of behaviour, was the result of her having been carefully briefed in the interests of relaxation of atmosphere and total informality.

The girl in the straw hat went back into the folder and the whine of the cunning little gadget sank in pitch and disappeared. Jake sighed and swallowed. His eyelids felt heavy; in fact so did most of the rest of him. Professor Trefusis came and muttered into his ear.

'Would you like a climax? We can give you one, not out here of course, or we can arrange for you to give yourself one in private.'

'I don't think I will, thanks very much all the same.'

When they parted a few minutes later she said to him, 'I hope to see you again soon.'

'Again? Soon?'

'After the successful completion of Dr Rosenberg's treatment.'

9   Guilt and Shame

Jake and Rosenberg went together across the hospital hall, which had a fight going on in it near one of the side walls. Two medium-sized men in white suits were struggling to hold a largish man in a fawn raincoat who seemed to be doing no more than trying to free himself from them. Not many of the people standing about or passing through bothered to watch.

'If it's been like that all the way here,' said Jake, 'those two are earning their money.'

Rosenberg smiled leniently. 'They're ward staff. The poor fellow's objection must be to being made to leave. There, you see?'

The man in the raincoat, at liberty for a moment, ran back towards the lifts where the two nurses caught him again. Jake had a last glimpse of the captive's forefinger straining to reach, and being held back from reaching, the call-button with great intensity, as if this were no call-button but, TV-style, the means of activating a bank alarm or nuclear missile. Outside it wasn't quite raining but was damp and chilly. Rosenberg looked to and fro a couple of times in a furtive sort of way, swinging his unnaturally large black briefcase about, then he said,

'How were you intending to make the return journey, Mr Richardson?'

'Bus.'

'Ah, it's not the weather for that. I have my car here, I'd be happy to give you a ride.'

'That's very kind of you.'

But the other stayed where he was a space longer, looking down at his disproportionately small feet. There was that in his manner which meant that it came as no complete surprise when he flung back his head and produced one of those stares he and Curnow went in for, had perhaps developed together as part of some research project. Jake met this one and waited. When Rosenberg spoke it was in a strained, almost querulous tone, as if he was at great moral cost dragging out a deeply overlaid memory.

'Am I quite mistaken or did you tell me you were sometimes known to take a glass of sherry before dinner?'

'I must have. It's true anyway.'

'I thought so. I thought so. And it's before dinner now. Some time before,

I grant you, but before. You see I find a small amount of alcohol at this time of day distinctly beneficial. Tell me, have you any objection to drinking in a public house?'

In its tone and much of its phraseology the last part of that so closely resembled the bugger's favourite question that Jake started to want to hit him, but he soon stopped and said, 'Not in principle.' He could have added that in practice he found the activity distasteful, especially of late; it was also true that nothing would have kept him from seeing the little psychologist in the proposed new setting.

With a peremptory sideways movement of his head Rosenberg led off at a smart pace. A minute's walk up towards the main road brought them to a pub called the Lord Nelson which Jake, occupied with his madwoman, hadn't noticed on the way down. The exterior, royal blue picked out in yellow, was promising, and the interior had no more than half a dozen youngsters in it, wearing their offensive perpetual-holiday clothes, true, but not laughing and talking above a mild shout. The noise from the fruit-machine was that of an intermittent and fairly distant automatic rifle, and even the juke-box thumped and cried away well below the threshold of pain; all in all a real find. Of course it was early yet.

Rosenberg had said they might as well look in here, but any pretence of unfamiliarity was at once undone by the whiskered tee-shirted fellow behind the bar, who greeted him as doctor and without inquiry picked up a half-pint glass tankard and began to fill it with beer. When this was done he looked at Jake with a slight frown and narrowing of the eyes, as if less interested in what he might want to drink than in what form of lunacy possessed him.

'And you'll have a sherry, will you not?' asked Rosenberg.

'Thank you, medium dry.'

'Is sherry still the great Oxford drink or is that all folklore?'

Jake made some idle answer. At the mention of Oxford any hint of misgiving or antagonism left the barman's manner; he was evidently satisfied that his customers were not doctor and patient but doctor and colleague. His underlying assumption that having to do with Oxford somehow vouched for sanity might itself be said to imply derangement, but it would be more interesting to consider what had made Rosenberg a habitué of this place. One's first assumption, that being Irish he would naturally be rushing round the corner all the time to get a lot of strong drink inside him, wasn't borne out by that modest half of bitter. Could there be a convivial side to him? It seemed unlikely, though Jake couldn't have told why.

Again taking the lead, Rosenberg moved decisively across the room and sat down with his back to the wall on a padded bench enveloped in black artificial something. Jake, always in favour of getting a good view of anybody he might be talking to, looked round for a chair, but there was none to be seen, only long- and short-legged stools. He fetched a short-legged one, finding that its top was covered with the same stuff as the bench. Apart from being so covered it was too convex to suit a normal bum like his, pleasing as that convexity might well have been to the trend-blurred eye of whatever youthful fart had designed it. He sat regardless and faced Rosenberg across a circular table made of semi-transparent amber-coloured substance. Huge photographs of Wild West people and scenes covered the walls.

'I had lunch recently with a friend of mine,' announced Rosenberg.

'Oh yes?' said Jake encouragingly, but not just encouragingly in case what he had heard had been deemed worthy of remark in itself, which he thought was possible.

'Have you ever come across a magazine called *Mezzanine?*'

'Yes, in fact – '

'This friend of mine is the editor. He's been in the job for about four years would be my guess. That's a long time in that sort of journalism, he says. The pace, you know. I doubt if he'll stick it much longer. I'll be sorry when he goes, because he and I have been fortunate enough to build up an excellent working relationship. In practice it benefits me distinctly more than him.' The doctor gave his deep laugh; the present rendering gave an effect of reluctant self-congratulation. 'Oh dear. Of course he has a very acute social conscience, which makes him anxious not to publish any material that might in any way be harmful.'

'What sort of material would that be?'

'Encouragement of anti-social fantasies involving violence chiefly but also such matters as simulated hanging which can be dangerous.'

'You mean physically dangerous.'

'I do. Death from that cause is not uncommon.'

'Mm. So what people see and read in that way does affect their actions.'

Rosenberg put down his glass, which was still nearly full. He laughed again slightly. 'Why my dear sir, of course it does. If it didn't, my work would have to take a very different form. You must realise that, even from the little we've done together.'

'I suppose I do. But going back – can't your editor pal spot what to steer clear of for himself? I mean for instance I can tell straight away that a chap whipping a girl involves violence.'

'It's not always as simple as that,' said the doctor rather peevishly, then went on in the sunniest of spirits, 'Where *I* score is having access to the unpublished *Mezzanine* correspondence, which is most valuable. They write things they'd never dare say to fellows like me.'

'For fear of bursting out laughing in your face.'

'Ah not at all, not at all. You can always spot the ones who're trying to take you for a ride.'

'Always? How?'

'Let me put it to you the way my friend put it to me. If you say when you write, if you call something warm, or soft, or firm, or moist, or hard, or anything like that then you're not serious. You don't use adjectives when you're serious. Which brings us by a long way round to the fantasy you wrote for me, Mr Richardson. But first let me get you another drink.'

'My turn. Same again?'

'No thank you, I'll just nurse this.'

Jake would have cancelled his own drink at that but he wanted a couple of minutes to reflect. Standing at the counter he decided it was dull of Rosenberg to have moved with such speed and determination from what had sounded like the start of a nice credulity-stretching story or two about *Mezzanine* to that bloody fantasy. And there had been something dull too, dull in a different sense, about the tone of voice in which he had mentioned the editor and the four years in the job and the pace and the working relationship. More than dull. In the act of ordering his sherry Jake became conscious that he had heard that very tone elsewhere in the last couple of weeks, and at the same time that Rosenberg reminded him of someone. He went on trying to think where and who until he got back to the table and saw that the typewritten pages of his fantasy were spread out on it.

'Uncontrollable passion. Irresistible desire.' Rosenberg sipped slowly at his beer. 'Colossal breasts. Quivering thighs. Delirious response. Do you know if I hadn't heard different from you I think I'd be wondering whether you'd ever performed sexual intercourse?'

At the first phrase Jake had looked hurriedly about. No one was in earshot, not yet, although the bar now held twice as many youngsters as before and an additional two, moustached and flat-chested respectively, were entering at that moment. He sat down, spreading his arms slightly to try to screen off Rosenberg and his reading-matter. 'Would you?' he said.

'I think I would. As the friend I was mentioning to you would put it, you're not serious.'

'Good God, do you imagine I'd have come to you in the first place and gone through all that . . . rigmarole this afternoon if I weren't serious?'

'Why did you come to me in the first place?'

Jake started to speak and then found he had to consider. 'I realised something that used to be a big part of my life wasn't there any more.'

'And you miss it.'

'Of course I miss it,' said Jake, instantly seeing that the next question ought to have to do with how he could be held to miss what he no longer wanted; you don't miss a friend you'd be slightly sorry to run into, do you? Can you miss wanting something?

Perhaps Rosenberg already knew the answers. 'Any other reasons?' was what he asked.

'Well, there's my wife to consider. Obviously.'

'There is, obviously. Very well. I didn't mean you weren't serious in your overall approach to your condition, I meant you weren't serious when you wrote this. You weren't in a state of sexual excitement.'

'These days I very rarely am. That was in another sense why I came to see you in the first place.'

'No doubt it was, but the state under discussion can be achieved with the aid of pictorial pornographic material, manual manipulation and so forth. You clearly omitted to use such aids. It's my view that consciously or unconsciously you avoided doing so. Because you sensed that if you did use them you'd almost certainly write something you'd have been embarrassed to let me see. You'd have used different words – none of your quivering thighs and delirious response. I'm sure you know the kind of words I mean.'

For all the Irishman's ridiculous accent, his articulation was as distinct as ever and he had not lowered his ordinary conversational volume. Another glance over his shoulder showed Jake that the moustached shag and the flat-chested bint, whose skull as he now saw was about the size of a large grapefruit, had moved away from the bar with their drinks and were now standing just near enough, given goodish hearing and less than full absorption in each other, to catch some of whatever Rosenberg might say next. 'I'm sure I do too,' mouthed Jake faintly, rolling his eyes and raising and lowering his eyebrows and pointing through himself at the couple.

For the moment it was hard to tell whether the doctor had heeded or even read these signals. 'We often find it best to avoid them in a consultation context for socio-psychological reasons,' he said at his previous pitch, 'especially in the earlier stages of therapy. But they tend to be useful in the kind of work you were doing here. I suppose I might have. . . .' He dismissed without apparent trouble the thought of whatever it was he might have done and continued, 'I strongly recommend you to use such words when you try again, which I want you to do between now and next Tuesday. They may help you to resolve your main difficulty. You see – '

With the effect of a great door bursting open the noise of the juke-box increased perhaps fourfold in mid-beat. Rosenberg's voice mounted above a swell of half-human howling and mechanical chirruping and rumbling. 'As well as what you wrote, your attitude before our investigations this afternoon commenced, you remember, and your response to some of the stimuli during them – it all suggests to me that our society's repressive attitude towards sex has engendered an unrelaxed attitude in you. You've been conditioned into acceptance of a number of rigid taboos.' Perhaps now he did notice Jake's expression, which had turned to one of impatience or weariness, because he went on to bawl, 'You're suffering from guilt and shame.'

'What?'

'I said you're – '

'I heard you. Look, can't we discuss this somewhere else?'

'Please let's finish. I know this is uncomfortable for you but that's why I brought you here. Certain states of feeling can be brought to the surface more efficaciously in this type of environment than in a consultation situation. Now just one moment if I may.'

The clamour changed somehow, perhaps became more measured or emphatic. Rosenberg opened his briefcase and fingered through its contents, taking his time in a way that once more recalled Curnow. He was getting ready, Jake knew, to say or rather shout something unsayable at the instant when the noise ceased, which it must be on the point of doing. The instant came; Rosenberg was silent, but he had taken from his case and tossed down on the table between them a coloured magazine cutting pasted on to thin cardboard. The object landed with a soft click which seemed amplified in the first moment of silence. Jake saw that it was the photograph of the girl wearing just a straw hat, apart from which and in a way partly because of which she was without doubt completely stark naked and utterly nude. Her breasts were not in any true sense gigantic but they were large enough, and the rest of her made appropriate all manner of unserious adjectives. Everything about her for some reason struck him more forcibly here in the Lord Nelson than it had in the lecture-theatre.

'That's the one you liked best,' said Rosenberg with unimprovable clarity. 'According to that clever little machine back there.'

Jake sensed there were a number of people close behind him; he heard a movement, a grunt, a giggle, a whisper without knowing whether they referred to him or the picture or something quite different and naturally without turning to see. The temperature of the skin on the back of his neck changed, though he couldn't have said in which direction. He still had his *Times* with him. In a manoeuvre that sent his sherry-glass rocking he shoved the newspaper over and round the picture and scooped it up and laid the package thus made on the floor. Then he gave a deep sigh.

'Guilt and shame.' Rosenberg's voice was so low that it could have been audible only to Jake, who acknowledged in time that the little bugger could be effective whatever you might think of the effect. But for now all he said was,

'No. There are some things that are too. . . . No, you're wrong. You've got it all wrong.'

10 Wanker!

That Saturday was the first day of the Oxford summer term. Jake had to go up there to supervise a collection, no charitable enterprise, this, but an examination set and marked by himself and intended to assess the extent to which his pupils had done the reading set them for the vacation just ended, or more practically to deter them a little by its prospect from spending every day of that period working in a supermarket and every night fornicating and smoking pot or whatever they did now. A drag, yes; all the same, satisfyingly more of a drag for them than for him and over just in time for him to be back at Burgess Avenue for Saturday Night at the Movies, of course not actually *at* the movies but in front of the television set.

The following Tuesday Jake went back to Oxford after he and Brenda had kept their appointment with Rosenberg in Harley Street and eaten something, in her case very little and in his not much more, at a place called Mother Courage's off the Marylebone Road. The food wasn't much good and they were rather nasty to you, but then it cost quite a lot. After walking part of the way in the interests of health, Jake got to Paddington a good twenty minutes before the departure of the 3.5, a train otherwise known to more than a few as the Flying Dodger for being the latest one even the most brazen and determined evader of his responsibilities would dare to catch at the 'start' of the 'working' week at the university, or 'university', and in consequence much esteemed among senior members of that institution. It was sometimes not easy to get a seat for the neglectful philologists, remiss biochemists and other lettered column-dodgers who swarmed aboard it; hence part of the reason for Jake's early arrival. He stood in a queue that by its diversity would have served quite well as model for a Family of Man photograph, laid out his fifty quid or whatever it was for a second-class ticket and went along to the bookstall. Here he searched carefully among the paperbacks and in the end came up with something called *The Hippogriff Attaché-Case* by an author unknown to him. He couldn't understand the jacket-design, which consisted chiefly of illuminated numbers and different-coloured little light-bulbs as well as a quantity of wasted space, and turned to the matter on the back of the cover.

To the heart of a vast computer complex buried miles deep in the earth's crust beneath America's Rocky Mountains come a brilliant cybernetics engineer, an international thief whose specialty is by-passing sophisticated alarm systems, a disillusioned CIA hit man and the beautiful but enigmatic daughter of a US general who has disappeared in mysterious circumstances (he read). Their mission? To extract from the computer's banks the identities of American society's most dangerous enemies with the aim of unofficially executing them. Only trouble is . . . *one* of the team of four is a psychopathic killer. . . .

Just the job, thought Jake as he handed over his few more quid: right up the street of a past-it ancient historian about to be on his way by unsophisticated train to one of England's premier seats of learning. Roll on wrist-watch television.

Time to get aboard the train; it was already filling up, with younger persons for the most part, undergraduates, junior dons, petty criminals. Jake found a lucky corner seat in one of the dozen identical uncompart-mented carriages of the type he had by now almost grown used to after years of vaguely imagining it to be a stopgap measure adopted while something less desolate was under construction. He wondered, not for the first time, about the irremovable tables between each pair of seats: what unbriefed designer, Finnish or Paraguayan, had visualized English railway travellers beguiling their journey with portable games of skill or chance, academic study, even food and drink? Well, he would beguile the first part of this one with reading, or letting his eyes run over, a *Times* article on the Soviet armed threat to Western Europe. He kept at it until the train had slid out of the station and begun to pass the rows of dreadful houses that backed on to the line and all his fellow-passengers had settled down. The chances were quite high that this particular mobile other-ranks' bun-shop held two or three people he knew well enough to talk to, and as high or higher that the moment he saw who they were he wouldn't want that. When he lowered the paper he found he was safe enough with a young couple opposite in a loose half-embrace, eyes bent on vacancy, mouths and jaws slack to a degree that suggested heavy sedation, and next to him an old bitch with a profile like a chicken's who obviously hadn't talked to anyone for years.

He opened *The Hippogriff Attaché-Case* but several things made concen-tration difficult: the small print, the sudden directionless lurches of the train, although it wasn't yet going very fast, and thoughts of the session with Rosenberg and the lunch that had followed. To get away from the last lot he started on thoughts of his job and his work, topics he seldom investigated consciously. The job side of life presented no difficulties, called merely for constant vigilance; it was perhaps the one such side he could afford to feel a tingle of complacency about. After years of effort and much nerve and resource he had got the job sewn up almost to the point of not being underpaid; one more work-shedding coup, to be mounted at an early opportunity, and for the next academic year at least he would be able to consider himself well remunerated for his efforts – not counting inflation of course.

The work, in the sense of his subject and his attitude and contributions to it, gave less grounds for satisfaction. If challenged he would have said that he tried fairly hard and with fair success to keep up with developments in his chosen sphere, Greek colonization from the first Olympiad to the fall of Athens, and did a sporadic something about the, to him, increasingly dull mass of the rest; but he hadn't revised his lectures and his seminar material except in detail, and not much of that, for how long? – well, he was going to say five years and stick to it. Learned articles? He must get that bit of nonsense about Syracuse off the ground again before too long. Stuff in the field? According to a Sunday newspaper, the kind of source he sneezed at less and less as time went by, two Dutchmen had found a pot or so near Catania and he was going to have a look in September, but since he knew there couldn't be much more to find round there and he wasn't an archaeologist anyway the look would be brief, its object far less the acquisition of knowledge than to get off tax his travelling expenses for a fortnight's holiday with Brenda. Books? Don't make him laugh: apart from the juvenile one about the sods in Asia Minor there had been three others, all solidly 'researched', all well received in the places that received them, all quite likely to be on the shelves of the sort of library concerned, all combined still bringing in enough cash to keep him in bus fares. Three or, in the eye of charity, four books were probably enough to justify Dr Jaques ('Jake') Richardson's life. They were bloody well going to have to.

That life was unlikely to run much beyond the end of the present century. Never mind. Jake's religious history was simple and compact. His parents had been Anglicans and right up to the present day the church he didn't go to had remained Anglican. As far as he could remember he had never had any belief, as opposed to inert acquiescence, in the notion of immortality, and the whole game of soldiers had been settled for him forty-five years previously, when he had come across and instantly and fully taken in the Socratic pronouncement that if death was unconsciousness it was not to be feared. Next question. It, the next question, did bother him: how to see to it that the period between now and then should be as comfortable and enjoyable as could realistically be expected. The one purpose raised the problem of retirement, the other of sex. Oh bugger and bugger. Talking of sex, the girl across the table, moving as if buried in mud, had shifted round in her seat, put her arms across the young man and given him a prolonged kiss on the side of the neck. A perceptible lifting of the eyelids on his part was evidence that he had noticed this. Jake produced a very slight gentle smile, which just went to show what a decent chap he was, not turning nasty like some oldsters when they saw youngsters who were presumably having it off, on the contrary feeling a serene, wry, amused, faintly sad benevolence. Like shit – all it just went to show was how far past caring he'd got. Nought out of ten for lack of envy in colour-blind shag's feelings about other shag's collection of Renoirs.

These and related topics, together with another uninformative glance at *The Hippogriff Attaché-Case* and a short involuntary nap, filled most of the journey. After the houses and the factories and the clumps of presumably electrical stuff standing in the open it was sometimes worth glancing out of the window. Much of what should have been green was still brown after the drought of '76, but past Reading it turned pretty decent, with the Thames running beside the track and once, for some seconds, a swan in full sight; bloody good luck to you, chum, thought Jake. Eventually the train stopped as usual outside Oxford station by the cemetery. This sight, although quite familiar enough, reminded him of his bus journey to Colliers Wood, or of that later part of it before the advent of the madwoman. He had been carried past mile after mile, probably getting on for two anyway, of ground given over to the accommodation of the departed, stretching away for hundreds of yards on one side of the road or the other, sometimes on both at once, interrupted by a horticultural place or one that sold caravans only to resume, covered with close-order ranks and files of memorial stone arranged with a regularity that yet never repeated itself, so extensive and so crowded that being dead seemed something the locals were noted for, like the inhabitants of Troy or Ur. The thought of shortly arriving in some such place himself and staying there meant little to Jake, as noted, but this afternoon there was that in what he saw which dispirited him. In the circumstances he was quite grateful for the yards of rusty galvanised iron fences, piles of rubble and of wrecked cars and, further off, square modern buildings which helped to take his mind off such matters.

The train pulled up at the platform at 4.29 on the dot, which was jolly good considering it often didn't do that till 4.39 or 49 and wasn't even supposed to before 4.17. Jake descended into the pedestrian tunnel that ran under the line to the front of the station; once, there had been an exit on this side too, but it had been discovered years ago, not long after he got his Readership, that the only people who benefited from this arrangement were passengers. An amplified voice blared something at him as he made the transit. He saw nobody he recognised in the taxi queue, not that he looked about for such. When his turn came he found himself sharing with a fat old man who said he wanted to go to Worcester College and a girl of undergraduate age who evidently made her needs known without recourse to speech. She had the other type of young female physique, the one being that of the bullet-headed shrimps he had identified on his visit to Blake Street: this genus was strongly built with long straight fair hair which, an invariable attribute, had been recently washed and, seen from the rear, hung down over not an outer garment but a sort of collarless shirt with thin vertical blue-and-white stripes. The old man shook slightly from distinction or drink or both. The driver put him down some yards short of the gate of Worcester, not, or not only, to disoblige but to avoid being inexorably committed by the city's one-way system to driving the two or three miles to Wolvercote before being permitted to turn right.

They were soon entering the north end of Turl Street and joining a line of traffic that moved forward a few seconds at a time. There were still forty or fifty yards between it and Jake's destination, the front gate of Comyns College, when the driver stuck his head out of his window and peered forward.

'Trouble there,' he said.

'What is it?' asked Jake.

'Picket or demo or whatever you like to call it.'

'Outside Comyns?'

'Right. Better if I drop you here.'

'What's going on?'

'Some crowd.' The driver pulled up. 'Better if I drop you here. Forty.'

Puzzled and annoyed, wishing he knew how to insist, Jake paid and got out. He approached cautiously, able to make out nothing at first for vehicles and passers-by and the slight curvature of the street, then caught glimpses of dull blue and straw-colour and black and white. Peering through his bifocals from a few paces nearer he made out the blue and straw colour as belonging respectively to the clothes and hair of girls resembling the one in the taxi, who as he was soon to see might indeed have doubled back after being dropped round the corner. The black and white belonged to placards, one of which was turned in his direction for a second: it said Piss Off Comyns Pigs.

Jake knew where he was at once without liking it there. Before he could think further there was a rapid movement ahead of him, a scuffle as somebody tried to enter or leave. At a brisk pace but without hurry, Jake crossed the momentarily clear road with the intention of recrossing it when opposite the gate, thus striking from an unexpected angle while attention was still diverted. This turned out to be a bad idea. With the sound and a touch of the speed of a smallish aeroplane, a motor-cycle, headlight glaring, rider got up like a riot policeman, seemed to be coming straight at him down the street, illegally too he fancied. As he hesitated the girls round the gate, their erstwhile victim dispatched or escaped, all turned and saw him, seventeen or eighteen of them, blonde and wearing blue. Shouts arose.

'Admit women as undergraduates!'

'End medieval discrimination!'

'Down with élitist chauvinism!'

'I know that bugger!'

'Fall into line with other colleges!'

'Richardson! Bloody Richardson!'

'Wanker!'

'Wanker Richardson!'

Jake lost his head, though short of running away at once and creeping back after nightfall there wasn't a lot he could have done. With his suitcase held up in front of him he charged, to be easily halted by three of four muscular female arms. The uproar continued but in a changed form, that of cries of simulated passion or ecstasy, some involving low terms. Instead of the blows he had foreseen, kisses descended, breasts were rubbed against him and his crotch was grabbed at. There was a great deal of warmth and flesh and deep breathing and some of the time he could see no more than an inch or two: My Body Is Mine But I Share, he read at close quarters, holding his glasses on with his left hand and his case with his right. He felt frightened, not of any physical harm or even of graver embarrassment, but of losing control in some unimagined way. There seemed no reason why this jollification should ever stop, but after what felt like an agreed period, probably no more than fifteen or twenty seconds, he found himself released, stumbling over the wicket in some distress of mind but no worse off physically than for a couple of smart tweaks of the hampton.

The head porter Ernie, as fat and yet as pale as ever, stood in his habitual place at the entrance of his lodge. He gave Jake a savage wink that involved the whole of one side of his face and everything but the eye itself on the other.

'Nice little lot of young gentlewomen come up to our university these days, eh sir?'

'Wonderful.' Jake put down his suitcase and straightened his tie and smoothed his hair.

'No problem to you though, I'll be baned.' Bound was what most men would have said but this one came from Oxfordshire or somewhere.

'I don't quite see why you. . . .' Oh Christ, he had forgotten again.

The porter chuckled threateningly and wagged a forefinger. 'Nay nay, Mr Richardson, you know what I'm talking abate. Plenty of people remember the way you used to weigh the girls, I can tell you. A ruddy uncraned king you were. You fancied something – pay! you got it. And I bet you still know how to mark 'em dane.'

The lodge entrance was only wide enough for one person, which was why it was Ernie's habitual place. He would vacate it at once on the approach of the Master, the Dean, some senior Fellows and luminaries like the Regius Professor of Latin, who happened to be a Comyns don, but almost anyone else could safely count on a minute or two of enforced conversation. Jake said rather slackly,

'We're all of us getting on, Ernie, you know.'

'*Aitch!* Don't remind me sir – we are indeed. And hay!'

Ernie still showed no sign of moving yet but just then the buzzer on the telephone switchboard sounded and with a grunt of something close to apology he turned on his axis, which showed a marked declination, like the Earth's, and creaked off towards the inner lodge. From behind the glass partition of this he was soon to be heard confidently declaring that someone was not in college, nor likely to be for an immeasurable time. All porters are the same porter, thought Jake as often before. By now he was at his pigeon-hole in quest of mail, driven chiefly by habit, not expecting that much or any would have arrived since his fair-sized pick-up on Saturday. But some had: the Historical Society's programme for the term, a publisher's catalogue and an oddly shaped package addressed in large light-green characters. The first two he threw away on the spot, the package he shoved unopened into his mackintosh pocket, for Ernie could bar his exit in a few strident strides. He picked up his case.

It was a hopelessly established tradition that Ernie should be licensed to chaff him about his amatory career, and in some senses a justified one. They were the same age; they had been acquainted for over forty years, since Jake's arrival at Comyns as an undergraduate to find Ernie already employed as a servant in Hall and on staircases; elevation to junior porter had come just when Jake, first marriage about to collapse, was starting out on his most ambitious round of sexual activity since youth, using his college rooms to pursue parts of it too, discreetly enough to escape notice in every quarter that mattered but of course not in the lodge, by a larger tradition the clearing-house of all internal gossip. Another bond between the two men was the similarity of their careers in the war, Jake rising in a rifle regiment to command one of its companies in France and Germany in 1944–5, Ernie becoming a warrant-officer of light infantry and picking up a decoration after Anzio. At his times of gloom, which were frequent, the ex-sergeant-major would use barrack-room catch-phrases to describe his wonder at what the world was coming to. Jake, who was feeling a bit cross, united these two themes now in a mumbled monologue as he set off across the front quad.

'Assit, lad, give her the old one-two. Take your bloody finger eight and get stuck in. Lovely bit of crackling. Shit-hot slice of kifer. Go on Joe, your mother won't know, are you a man or a mace? There you are old boy, take a good look round, and if you find anything you fancy I'll buy it for you. You've seen the mighty piston-strokes of the giants of the CPR, with the driving force of a thousand horse so you know what pistons are, or you think you do. Better than pork. I *am* the vicar. With his bloody great kidney-wiper and balls the size of three, and half a yard of. . . .'

At this stage Jake was moving towards the arch communicating with the further quad where his rooms were and was passing the gift shop in the cloisters by the chapel. This popular source of revenue offered for sale all manner of authentic stuff, tea-sets with the Comyns coat of arms on them just like the Master drank his own tea out of, Comyns beer-tankards made from genuine English pewter, Comyns paperweights, Comyns corkscrew-cum-bottle-openers, not Comyns neckties on account of some stuffed shirt had put a no on that one but Comyns head-scarves and Comyns handker-chiefs and all kinds of Comyns postal cards showing the insides of some of the buildings, including the chapel, and different parts of the campus, and then there was this extremely interesting historical one of some document in old-fashioned writing supposed to be written by was it Edward II? A number of tourists were clustered round the doorway of the shop. As Jake drew level they all looked at him, very much as the girls outside the gate had done. This time there was a short pause before the shouting started, but it started.

'Da geht ja einer!'

'En v'là un!'

'Ach, man, daar gaan een!'

'Oh där har vi en!'

'Hey, there's one of them!'

'Ha, asoko nimo iruyo!'

They began to move towards him in twos and threes, slowly at first, the men unslinging their cameras with grim professionalism, the women pleased, all agog. Jake quickened up, got to the arch, in fact more of a short tunnel under the first floor of the library, and ran like hell through it and at an angle across the lawn of the quad beyond. Behind him he heard a babel of voices, more literally such than most and gaining added force from the echo-chamber properties of the tunnel. By the time he reached the shelter of his staircase the leaders were almost upon him, but before they could actually bring him down he was safe behind his oak, that outer door with no outer handle. The windows of his sitting-room looked directly on to the quad. Through them he could see his pursuers walking or standing disconsolately about, shrugging their shoulders and shaking their heads, reslinging their cameras. All right, he thought.

He switched on his standard-lamp and moved it and a padded chair as far forward as he could, took a bottle out of the cupboard and poured a glass of what was semi-sweet sherry, not port – all one to them though. His academic cap lay where he had put it after Saturday's collection; in an instant he was wearing it, sitting in the chair, holding the glass up to the light. A muffled cheer sounded from outside and the cameras clicked and fizzed once and again, one lot, then another. He gave them a simulated in-the-act-of-drinking pose, a here's-to-you pose and a glass-out-of-sight pose for the religiously scrupulous. Then he switched off the light to signal the end of the show and acknowledged the grateful smiles, waves and thumbs-up.

'No, not at all, fuck *you*,' he said. 'Fuck you very much, ladies and gents, fucks a million. And a fisherman's fart to all at home.'

He had poured the untasted sherry back into the bottle, which was only there for visitors, and was going to hang up his raincoat when he noticed a bulge in the pocket – the thing he had collected at the lodge. He felt interest, curiosity, a nice change for one given to knowing all too well and at first sight whatever the post might have brought him. The outer cover, reinforced with sticky tape, was resistant. When at last he got it off he had come to a roughly cylindrical object wrapped in many thicknesses of purple lavatory-paper. After unwinding these he found himself holding an imitation phallus made out of some plastic material or other with the words

Try This One, Wanker! written on it in the same large green letters as the outside. Moving faster than he had done for some years Jake locked the object up in his desk, then looked briefly and without result at the wrapper, went not at all fast to his armchair by the empty fireplace, sat down and put his hand across his mouth and sighed. All he needed now was a visit from the madwoman, dropping in on her way to catch Harry or June as they came off shift at British Leyland, or more likely find them on strike.

11   Academic Study

Jake didn't know how long he sat on in the armchair. He roused himself at the sound of a light step on the stone flags of the corridor outside. Anyone coming to visit him would clear off without further ado at the sight of the shut outer door, a convention that had stood him in unimprovable stead in the days Ernie had referred to but not wanted at the moment. He hurried to open that door, looked out and saw the figure of a girl retreating.

'Miss Calvert?'

She turned back. 'I'm sorry, I thought. . . .'

'No, my fault. The door must have. . . .' He found he had started to suggest that half a hundredweight of forest giant had swung through something like a hundred and fifty degrees at a puff of wind, and changed tack. 'I had to shut it to keep some tourists out.'

'Tourists? Out?'

'Yes, they chased me from the gift shop. They wanted to photograph me. I mean not me in particular, just a don. Any don. An Oxford don. So I put my square on and let them. Photograph me, I mean. Might as well. Do sit down, Miss Calvert. Now I'll just find your essay – your collection paper.'

They had moved into the sitting-room, where his suitcase, containing Miss Calvert's collection paper and everybody else's collection paper and much else besides, stood on the otherwise empty dining-table. He went over and put his hands on the corners of the case. Should he open it in here or take it through the communicating door into his bedroom and open it in there? The first would be quicker if the scripts were at or near the top, as he was almost certain they were. Or rather the first would be quicker wherever they were, only if they weren't near the top he would have to unpack a lot of his belongings on to the table and then at some stage put them back again before finally unpacking in the bedroom. How certain was he that the scripts were near the top? Had he perhaps put them in first to make sure of not leaving them out? Realising that he must have been standing there with his back to the girl for close on half a minute, he unclicked the catches of the case and at the same instant became almost certain he had indeed put the scripts in first. Then he had better reclick the catches and do the necessary unpacking in the bedroom after all. But one of the catches, the left-hand one, was hard to fasten securely, always had been. Would the other one stand the strain if he carried the case by its handle in the normal way? – he didn't want his belongings all over the floor. So should he try to carry it held horizontally out in front of him? He could. Then he must. Quick. Now. He wriggled his forearms underneath the bugger and, no doubt looking rather like a man who risks his life to remove a bomb from a place of public resort, took himself and burden off at top speed. Thank Christ the communicating door wasn't latched.

The scripts were on top, as he could have seen earlier with little trouble. Miss Calvert's wasn't among them. Yes it was. There was something worrying about it but he took it straight back into the sitting-room, where Miss Calvert had failed to sit as requested. Although she had been his pupil for two terms he had never properly looked at her before. Now he did. He saw that her eyes were darker than most fair-complexioned girls' and that her jaw was firm, not much more than his original vague impression of generic blue-clad blondeness; he certainly made no progress in estimating whether she could be, should be, surely must be considered attractive or not. This failure wasn't the result of loss of interest, in the way that morbid failure of appetite for food might be expected to impair the palate: he had had no trouble over Professor Trefusis. That was because the comely scientist was in her middle thirties, well above the decisive age-limit. No, it wasn't an age-limit in the usual sense, because the ones just below it were getting older all the time. The whole thing was a matter of date, of year of birth: 1950 would be about right. So when he was seventy he wouldn't be able to tell whether any female under thirty-seven was attractive or not. A curious world that would be.

Enough. He tried to bring himself round. 'Ah. Of course. Miss Calvert.'
'Yes, Mr Richardson?'
The sound of his name reminded him of the last time he had heard it uttered by a female, not long ago and not far from here. Someone in the picket had known it, had recognised him, and he was an obscure person, never on TV or in the papers, in no sense an Oxford character, more or less of a stranger even to many undergraduates of his own college, one who taught a subject neither soft nor modish nor remunerative. Was it this girl who had identified him? And of course what had bothered him about her script was that it was written in green ink, like the words on the object he had locked up in his desk. He glanced at the script, saw immediately that the respective hands were quite different and even the ink was a bit different, then looked wordlessly at the girl.
'Are you all right?' she said, taking a short pace towards him.
The movement brought to mind what he must have noticed before, how slim she was, her middle hard-looking and yet flexible, more like a thick electric cable than any thin living creature. He had embraced slim girls in

his time and could remember consistently finding them more substantial then than the sight of them suggested. Perhaps fellows found the same thing today. 'Oh – yes,' he said. 'Yes, thanks. Do sit down. Been rather a hectic day one way and another. Here we are.'

He pushed the padded chair back to its usual place. It wasn't very comfortable and it certainly looked nasty but it was the second-best in the room to the battered old dining-chair at his desk, its leather scuffed by generations of academic bums. Everything else was wine- or ink-stained, fire- or water-damaged, extruding springs, possessed of legs or arms that fell off all the time, impossible to open, impossible to close and repulsive. For years he had lived here most of the week, most weeks, not only in term-time, and without meeting Brenda's standards the place had been quite decent. Since then, by ruse, hard bargaining and straightforward theft-and-substitution the Domestic Bursar had plundered it into the ground. Well, not easy to complain when you spent no more than a tenth of the year in it.

'I hope you had a pleasant vacation?'

'Yes thank you.'

'Settling down all right this term?'

'Yes.'

'Good.' He picked up a lecture-list. 'Now I presume you went to Sir Clarence Frankis yesterday and will continue to do so.'

'I didn't actually.'

'Why not?'

'Well, there's a lot to do, you know, and a lot to get through, and it isn't in my special subject, Minoan, and you said yourself it would be more detailed than I needed.' For some reason she had a deep voice.

'Yes. I did. but, er . . . Minoan . . . *civilisation* is fairly interesting, and Sir Clarence is probably the most – er, rather good. It's not really a question of need, not totally. You ought to go. Sorry, I mean try to go whenever you can. No difficulty with the others? Right. Now your collection paper, Miss Calvert. I don't quite know what to say to you about it.'

But he quite knew what he wanted to say to her about it and related matters. One, see if you can't work out some way of getting yourself just a bit ashamed and scared of not wanting to know anything about anything or to be any good at anything. Two, if that fails, at least try to spell a bit and write legibly and write a sentence now and then – you can forget, or go on never having heard, about punctuation. Three, when you see a word you recognise in a question, like Greek or Tyre or Malta, fight against trying to put down everything remotely connected with it that you may have – oh stuff it. And four, go away and leave your place at St Hugh's to someone who might conceivably – oh stuff it.

Jake didn't say any of this because he wanted Miss Calvert's benevolent neutrality at least in the coming struggle for power at his Wednesday lectures, where that little bastard from Teddy Hall seemed about to escalate his campaign of harassment into a direct bid to seize the lectern. So he said as gently as he thought he could,

'Your handwriting. You do realize, don't you, that we're allowed to ignore anything we can't read or else have it typed up and make you pay the typist?'

'Why could a typist read it if you couldn't?'

Once, he might have been able to tell if this was defiance or ingenuous inquiry. Now, he couldn't or couldn't be bothered. 'Because the typist would have you there with your script reading out to her what you'd written. With incidentally an examiner looking over your shoulder to see you didn't correct anything or put new bits in.'

'Her? Why not him? Why shouldn't a typist be a man?'

Oh for. . . . 'No reason at all. It's just that in fact the typists in this case are as far as I know all women.'

'I didn't know that. And I'm sorry, I didn't understand about the typing.'

'That's all right. You do now. Don't forget either that I know your writing pretty well by this time, but it won't always be me reading it. Now your spelling. I'm quite tolerant about that,' because a policy of being quite intolerant would multiply the failure rate by something like ten, which would never do, 'but the same thing applies. I know some of these names are difficult; even so, I think it might pay you for instance to remember that Mediterranean is spelt with one T and two Rs and not the other way round. Especially,' he went on, striving not to shake from head to foot with rage and contempt as he spoke and summoning to his aid the thought that in Oxford of the '70s plenty of his colleagues would share Miss Calvert's difficulty, 'since it appears in the actual title of the subject and is very likely to come in the wording of some of the questions – four times on this paper, in fact.' Was she listening? All right, call it the fucking Med! was what he wanted to shout, but forbore. 'I've put a wavy line under some of the other examples.

'In general, you clearly have a concentration problem,' are an idle bitch, 'and I was wondering whether there was anything in your personal life that. . . . I'm not asking you to tell me about it but you could mention it to your Moral Tutor. Or if you like I could – '

'No it's all right thanks. There isn't anything really. Except the point.'

'What point?'

'The point of going on.'

'With the subject.'

'Well. . . .'

'With Oxford?'

'All sorts of things really.'

Jake said in his firmest tone, 'I think most people feel like that from time to time. One just has to hang on and have patience and hope it'll put itself right.' He couldn't remember now why he had started to ask her; habit, something to say, show of concern to assuage possibly wounded feelings.

Yes, habit, a carry-over from the days when he might have gone on to suggest discussing her problems under more informal conditions. Oh well. 'Now you answered only two questions but I'm going to give you a beta-double-minus all the same,' like a bloody fool. 'You must try for three next time. Now which of the other questions would you have tried if you'd had longer?'

Muttering to herself, Miss Calvert studied the paper for a space. At last she said, 'I think "Culture is the most profitable export." Discuss with reference – '

'Oh yes. Well, suppose you take that as your subject for next week.' This favourite tactic not only gratified his perennial need, strangely exacerbated today, to avoid having to think up essay subjects whenever remotely possible, it also relieved him, having just marked several exam answers on the topic, from the slightest mental exertion about it till next week came, if then. He tried to turn his complacent grin into a smile of friendly dismissal, but before the process was finished felt his face stiffen at the tone of the girl's next remark.

'Mr Richardson . . . you know that article of yours in JPCH you asked us to look at? On Ionian trade-routes?'

'Yes?'

'Well, the copy in the Bodleian's all . . . well, people have been writing things on it.'

'Writing things? What sort of things?'

'Like graffiti.'

'Really.'

'I sort of thought you ought to know.'

Malice or goodwill? Those two should on the face of it be no trouble to tell apart, but not much thought was necessary to recall that in practice they mixed as readily and in as widely-varying proportions as coffee and milk, no sugar, no third element, needed. But then what of it? He would look in at the library on the way to or from his lecture the next morning; for now, he thanked Miss Calvert, gave her her script back and sent her off, noticing at the last moment that she bore a handbag like a miniature pack-saddle, all flaps and buckles. He watched out of the window to see if she tossed the script over her shoulder as she left, but she held on to it at least until after she had vanished into the tunnel. Her walk showed that their interview had entirely left her mind.

longer.

12   I Have Heard of Your Paintings Too

Jake stood at the window in thought, though not of any very purposeful description, for a couple of minutes. It took him as long to make quite sure that the locked drawer of his desk was indeed locked, secured, made fast, proof against anything short of another key or a jemmy. Then he collected himself and went into the bedroom to unpack. It was small and dark but dry and not particularly draughty, and had in it the only decent object in the set, the bed that filled about a third of it, his own property from long ago and as such safe from the Domestic Bursar's depredations. By the time he had finished in here and glanced through his notes for next day, the chapel clock, the nearest among innumerable others, was striking six. He slung his gown over his shoulder and sauntered across the grass, looking about at the buildings, which had once been attributed to Nicholas Hawksmoor; recent research, after the fashion of a lot of recent research, had disproved this without producing any certain reattribution. Never mind: they were pleasing to the eye for two sufficient reasons – someone had put them up well before 1914, and no one, out of apathy, lack of money, instinctive conservatism or sometimes even perhaps deficiency of bad taste, had laid a hand on their exterior since except to clean them. Until about a quarter of a century back, Jake had had no architectural sense that he knew of but, like every other city-dweller in the land with eyesight good enough to get about unaided, he had acquired one since all right, had one doled out to him willy-bloody-nilly. So it was no great wonder that he halted and looked about all over again before entering the staircase in the far corner.

Here, on the first floor, there lived an English don called Damon Lance-wood, like Ernie in being an almost exact contemporary of Jake's but unlike him in an incalculable number of ways. One of the fewer ways in which he was unlike Jake has already been mentioned: he lived where Jake only popped in and out. Lancewood belonged to the lonely and diminishing few who still treated college as home. It was true that he had a cottage near Dry Sandford and also true, while less well known, that he was joined there most week-ends by the owner of a small business in Abingdon, a man of fifty or so to whom he had been attached for the past twenty-two years.

Jake knocked at the door, which had a handsome brass finger-plate and other furniture on it, and obeyed the summons to come in. He saw that Lancewood had somebody with him and spoke up at once.

'I'm sorry Damon, I didn't realize you were – '

'No no no, my dear Jake, I was expecting you. I'd like you to meet a colleague of mine. . . .'

Introductions were made. Jake failed to gather or shortly forgot the Christian name and college of the visitor, a tall long-haired sod in his thirties, but caught the surname – Smith. Lancewood, himself tall but with neatly cut white hair and a bearing and manner of dress that suggested a retired general rather than a don, turned his blank-looking gaze on Jake.

'I think you could do with a glass of sherry.'

'I think so too. Thank you.'

Quite possibly it was Jake's sherry: he brought Lancewood a bottle now and then, a much nicer arrangement for everyone than returning hospitality in his own place. It came in a solid bit of glass that went with the way the room was fitted up, which in turn reflected its occupant's military style: nothing overtly martial or imperial but suggestive of bungalow here, club there, mess somewhere else, the many pictures showing horses, dogs, an occasional parrot or monkey, what could have been a troopship, what could have been a cantonment, portraits of dark-skinned persons no one had the authority to say were not sometime servants. They even included three or four water-colours of aggressively English scenes given that niggling, almost effeminate treatment characteristic of men of action.

'Thank God,' said Jake, sipping. 'I've just been closeted with a female pupil.'

Lancewood cocked his head. 'Was that such an ordeal for you?' This question Ernie would have understood perfectly, though his phrasing of it would have been quite different.

'You don't know her.' Jake was beginning to feel like an inefficient imposter, constantly putting his foot through his cover. 'Attractive enough, I . . .' – no, not suppose – 'grant you, but – well, you know the sort. A kind of celestial indifference to being seen to be, oh, lazy, stupid, ignorant, illiterate, anything you please.'

'Do you find the women worse than the men in that way?' asked Smith in an expressive adenoidal voice.

'I hadn't really thought about it,' said Jake, who if he had been strictly truthful would have gone on to say that now he had had a second and a half to think about it of course he bloody did.

'Well I bloody do,' said Smith. 'As a matter of fact we were on that very point when you turned up. Naturally Damon was taking the opposite view. He seems to have some sort of thing about women.'

'Indeed I have. Which reminds me of one of my favourite ones. How's my darling Brenda?'

'Fighting fit,' said Jake. And hay, he added silently.

'John had a rotten cold with all this vile weather but he's fine again now.'

This was of course the Abingdon chap. 'Good, give him my love,' said Jake, registering the adroit passing of the message that Smith knew about that. He (Jake) surmised that that sort of adroitness came in jolly handy for people like Lancewood, must be well worth the trouble of acquiring.

Lighting a French cigarette, Smith pursued his point. 'I mean, the levels to which they'll sink. And go on sinking because they stay the same and the problem stays the same, which is: a whole literature, six hundred years' worth, and virtually all of it written by male chauvinists. So, Wordsworth was no good because he abandoned Annette Vallon, no good as a poet that is, the Brontës and George Eliot went over to the enemy by adopting male pseudonyms so they were no good, Doll Tearsheet is the heroine of *Henry IV*, Part 2 at least, and of course the real – '

Lancewood gave a guttural sigh. 'Have a heart, she was joking.'

'Not this one,' said Smith firmly. 'The one who told her might have been, but not this one.'

'Well then somebody was or, or might have been. You really do – '

'Damon, it's nothing *in them*, it's forced on them. The men would probably be just as bad if you could find a way of making them think of themselves as men all the time, if such a way were conceivable.' Smith caught sight of Jake. 'I say, this must be rather – '

'Go on, I want to hear.'

'Well – the bright ones can't help seeing that, right, Sappho. . . .'

'Who was untypical?' said Lancewood.

'And who's mostly folk-lore anyway. Then you really come to, as far as they're concerned, the Matchless Orinda. Sorry, Katherine Philips, born in the same year as Dryden, died young, not as young as Shelley though, for instance, anyway she's quite good. Of course she is. What would you? Having taken the precaution of not being born with the digits one nine in front of her decade, but that's a. . . . Anyway, after her, let's stick to poetry for the moment, you get the Countess of Winchilsea, even more of a household name, and then you sit around for a couple of centuries waiting for Christina Rossetti, who's quite good, and that's that. If no female had ever emerged they'd have been able to put it down to male oppression but Katherine spoiled all that. Back in the middle of the seventeenth century she showed it was *possible*. As I say, it works down from the top, so that the ones who don't know what the seventeenth century was feel it as much as the others, well, insofar as they can, hence collective inferiority feelings, hence collective aggression. Admittedly with the novel it's not quite such a – '

'All this *they* talk.' Lancewood gestured with the decanter at Jake, who was all right as he was, then poured sherry for Smith and himself. 'The ones and the others. From the way you go on, most people would say you were the one with the thing about women.'

'Let's just nail that one right away. My relations with them, with women that is, have been and are normal to an unparalleled, even preternatural degree. Three-point-seven premarital affairs, the precise average, married at twenty-five-point-whatever-it-is, lived happily ever after, or since. Perhaps that's not so normal.'

'It's probably a bit early to tell,' said Jake. 'What does your wife think about poetry?'

'She's a biologist,' said Smith. He seemed puzzled at the question.

'Curious you should mention centuries,' said Lancewood. 'One of *them*, which you must admit sounds like something quite different, brought me a new interpretation of *Hamlet* yesterday. Now this, I want you to understand, is a thoroughly sweet, good-natured, charming little girl, no aggression in the wide world. As to brightness, well you shall hear. Hamlet was a woman.' He gave them both his blank look.

Smith gave a great groan but said nothing.

'Even I know that's not very new,' said Jake. 'Didn't Sarah Bernhardt play him, or her?'

'Indeed she did, and I'd said as much before I realised that of course my little girl would never have heard of her. Quite senseless to expect it. Cruel in a way. Well what could I do, great actress of the nineteenth century, quite natural she should want to play one of the greatest parts, different approach in those days, all that, but I needn't have bothered because I'd lost her, as she would have expressed herself, at the nineteenth century. Now she'd clearly heard of it, she even knew it was something to do with a tract of time but all the same there was more to it than that, just as the Age of Johnson or the Nineties, say, don't refer merely to a pair of dates. To her it was, the nineteenth century I mean was, not exactly when old people were young because there can be no such period, but awful and squalid and creepy, with all sorts of things going on – she could easily have come across figures like Dracula and Frankenstein and Jack the Ripper and Dr Arnold and realised they were nineteenth century. Well, the look she gave me, you should have seen it.' Lancewood half turned his face away, narrowed his eyes and peered out of their corners. 'Suspicion and morbid curiosity and a hint of distaste.'

'If you're doing it properly it was more like ungovernable lust,' said Smith to Jake's agreement.

'In that case I'm not. She was wondering what I used to get up to with Sarah Bernhardt, whom I must have known at least or why bring her up? Actually quite funny it should have been the great Sarah, in view of her reputed. . . . I think if one actually challenged my little girl up to the hilt, as it were, she'd say that the years beginning with nineteen were in the nineteenth century up to about 1950, after which it became the twentieth.

That would cover the years of birth of even her most senior contemporaries. One understands very well. All these references to people being dragged kicking and screaming into the twentieth century when it's agreed that that's the number of the century we're in, it must be most frightfully confusing. One does sympathise.

'Well. Her . . . her *case* was roughly that since Hamlet is far too nice and intelligent to be a man, he must be a woman because there's nothing else for him to be. I was ready to come back smartly with what about the way he treats Ophelia, male chauvinism if there ever was such a thing, but she'd thought of that – that was how all the men went on in those days, still do really, and it would have been suspicious if she, Hamlet, had behaved differently. What about old Hamlet and Gertrude? – you'd have expected them to notice. Old Hamlet had noticed, but he needed an heir, so he got Polonius to rig things, which gave Polonius the leverage he needed to be kept on at court when all he was fit for was talking balls. I liked that, quite as good as any other explanation I've come across if you think that's what he did talk. Gertrude hadn't noticed because women weren't allowed to bring up their own children then, any more than they are now really. I must say I thought that part was a little weak. Horatio guessed, naturally, but he couldn't say anything. And what did I suppose it was that had driven Ophelia mad? Obviously a sexual shock, eh?

'I shouldn't be going on like this because it'll only feed your prejudices, but, well, I said what about the whole of the play, there's nothing in it that suggests that things are any different from what they seem. She didn't know about that, she said; *she thought* Hamlet was a woman.'

'I hope you told her she needed weightier authority than that,' said Smith. 'A Radio 1 disc-jockey thinks Hamlet was a woman. An unemployed school-leaver in Wapping thinks Hamlet was a woman. A psychiatric social worker –'

'That's just sneering, my boy. What she also *thought*, in a different sense, was that Hamlet was a woman in some other . . . realer sphere than the play of Shakespeare's sources or anything that might historically have taken place at Elsinore or any other actual spot. Some third domain beyond fiction and fact. That's the terrifying thing.'

At the end of a short silence Smith said, 'I used to get that from one of my three-point-seven as it might be after films. How did they get on when they started having kids in that place? Did she come back to him in the end? Not might, assuming for fun and for the moment that it's life we're talking about. No – did.'

'Not too dull for you I hope, Jake?'

'It's exactly what they're like. I didn't know anybody else had realised, it's never been said, not in my hearing anyway. Absolutely hit it off to a T. When you get past all the poise and the knowingness and the intimacy there's a tiny alien particle that doesn't understand.' It came to Jake that he had been speaking with some warmth and he altered his tone. 'You'll have to bear with a very ancient historian who spends most of his time coping with drop-outs from Kettering Catering College. Well, what a rarity, listening to two dons discussing their subject,' and so on and so forth.

Not long afterwards Lancewood suggested that they should go over. Smith asked for a quick pee and was shown where. As soon as possible Jake said,

'Damon, what's a wanker?'

Lancewood hunched his shoulders with a jerk, showing that as well as being amused by the question he wasn't totally surprised by it. Again in a way uncharacteristic of dons, or perhaps of the popular idea of them, he spent no time on prolegomena but went straight to what was intended.

'These days a waster, a shirker, someone who's fixed himself a soft job or an exalted position by means of an undeserved reputation on which he now coasts.'

'Oh. Nothing to do with tossing off then?'

'Well, connected with it, yes, but more metaphorical than literal.'

'That's a relief. Up to a point. Well. I got called it today.'

'No really? By that pupil of yours?'

'No, by that picket of women's-lib women at the gate.'

'Oh yes of course. It's quite clever, all that, their campaign to make people feel old and senile and clapped out and impotent – that's where the literal part of wanker comes in.'

'Clever? As a means of persuading us to admit women?'

'Certainly. I can think of several colleagues of our sort of age who'd be troubled and frightened by such treatment and inclined to do what they could to put a stop to it. Can't you?'

'I suppose so.'

'Have you had anything unpleasant through the post? I gather there's been a certain amount of that.'

'Yes, today I was sent a. . . .'

Although Jake considered Lancewood one of his closest as well as oldest friends he found himself perfectly unable to tell him what he had been sent that day. Luckily Smith came back just then and the three set off. In the quad a fine drizzle was falling, so fine that it hardly had the weight to fall and wandered almost horizontally. The zenith was a weak grey but the sun showed for a moment or two. Lancewood mentioned that the question had come up of the admission of women to men's colleges.

'Oh yes, you're one of the last-ditch trio here, aren't you?' said Smith. 'Comyns, Merton and Oriel. Rather grand in a way.'

'How long have you been letting them in at your place?' asked Jake.

'Oh, we haven't let them *in*, what do you take us for? At the end of '75 we published a Declaration of Intent that declared our intent to do something or other about it some time, and since then we've been consulting away like mad, pretty well without stopping, the JCR, the porters and the rest of the staff, the other colleges in our awards group, and the women's colleges of course, bloody funny that, and it all seems to have cooled off. We might just ride it out until the next thing turns up, World War III or whatever it might be. I often think my namesake in Rhodesia could have done with a touch of the Oxford spirit.'

'What's bloody funny about the women's colleges?'

'What? Oh, just our Governing Body is about as solidly against the idea as any, nearly all for Victorian anti-feminist reasons in effect, and there they are or were in a secret alliance with the crowd who want to block it for Victorian feminist reasons. Like something out of who, Damon, C. P. Snow?'

'Or Shaw. Jake,' said Lancewood rather patiently, 'letting women into the men's colleges will damage the women's colleges for ten or twenty years, perhaps longer, because they'll only get the men and the women the men's colleges don't want. *Jake*, because no man or woman is going to go to St Anne's when he or she could go to Balliol.'

'I'm sorry, I don't seem to have been keeping up with things.'

'It's tough,' said Smith, evidently alluding to the likely state of the women's colleges, 'but overall the case in favour is unanswerable.'

'I thought you didn't care for women undergraduates, at least in your own subject,' said Jake.

'As they stand I don't.' Smith seemed slightly cross. 'That's the whole point. Living and working among the men is bound to improve them. It's the only way they'll ever forget they're women and start behaving like, I know, not students, but – '

'You make them all sound the same,' said Lancewood, seeming slightly cross himself. 'Anyway, it'll mean the end of this.'

This must have been in the first place the Senior Common Room, where they had just arrived. Considerable parts of the building that embodied it dated from the fifteenth century; the room itself had been radically reconstructed in the 1870s under the influence of a Master of advanced artistic taste, and was well known to those interested in such matters for its carved pillars, multi-coloured floor tiles, authentic Morris wallpaper and pair of stained-glass windows depicting respectively The Progress of Art and The Progress of Science. There were also some paintings from that period, a Burne-Jones, two Poynters, a Calderon, a Simeon Solomon and others and, from an earlier one, a Romney of an otherwise unnoted Fellow of the college; recent research had been at that too, though so far without managing to dislodge the reputed artist. Jake had liked the room and its furniture on sight in 1936, when his tutor had invited him up to dessert, and still did, despite certain changes he could not now have defined.

Its occupants for the moment were rather less to his taste, starting with Roger Dollymore, the Senior Tutor, and an elderly chemist called Wynn-Williams. Jake went over to them not because he much wanted to but to give Smith and Lancewood, whom he hoped to sit with in Hall, a rest from him meanwhile. Little enough was required of him by the other two, who seemed quite happy, or not significantly more unhappy than might have been expected, telling each other about the plays they had seen in London during the vacation. Jake thought briefly how he hated plays, then tried to remember how each of them stood on the women-in-or-out thing. He knew how they ought to stand if they had any sense; all he could remember about Wynn-Williams's wife was that she was impossible, but he knew Naomi Dollymore fairly well, or had done in the days when there were dinner-parties, and could have gone on for quite a long time without repeating himself about her readiness to share most details of her experience, recent or remote, with whoever she might be talking to, not in Alcestis's pseudo-sequential, fool's-anecdote style but by as free a process of association as you could hope to come across. So both husbands ought to be ready to lay down their lives for the status quo: the feminisation of college, once begun, would lead irresistibly to the taking-over of common-room and High-Table life, of college life, by the wives. Just imagine the way. . . .

'What?' said Jake. 'I'm sorry?'

'I said,' said Dollymore in his sheep's voice, the only one he had, 'where are you going.'

'What? Well at the moment I. . . .'

'Away. Abroad.' Wynn-Williams might have been a Shakespearean king or other hero encouraging his followers into the saddle but of course he wasn't really, he just sounded like an old-style actor. 'We go to Venice at the end of June.'

'Naomi and I have rather fallen out of love with Venice,' said Dollymore. His interest in Jake's holiday plans had perhaps never been deep. 'So commercialised and full of Americans. That is the perennial struggle, to find a place that isn't. Naomi and I have been moving on almost every year for . . . years. We've been driven out of one Greek island after another. It seems Nisiros is still comparatively unspoiled.' After a long pause he went on at a reduced speed, 'Though I'm sure it's very different nowadays from. . . from the time when. . . .'

Wynn-Williams came in quite quickly. 'The time when Jake's . . . Jake's. . . .'

'Jake's pals from the . . . the. . . .'

'From the long-ago were. . . .'

'There. Were there.'

'Were there, yes.'

The two laughed in simple pleasure at having jointly recollected Jake's subject and succeeded in bringing that fact to utterance. He laughed too. It was at any rate nicer over here than it could possibly have been in the larger group by The Progress of Art. They were all young, under about thirty-five anyway: the philosopher who was co-editor of a London weekly paper, the political scientist who ran a current-affairs programme on TV, the historian of drama who put on plays full of naked junior members of the university torturing one another, the writer in residence with his look of eager disdain for his surroundings, somebody's guest with his look of unearned eminence – a wanker of the future, if when the future came it tolerated any judgements of worth.

'Good evening, Master,' said Dollymore, and Wynn-Williams and Jake said something very similar.

They did this because the Master of Comyns, Marion Powle by name, had come up to them. He was fifty-five, a distinguished crystallographer, recent successor to a mad Graecist, serious, well liked even among the arts men: Jake quite liked him. Or didn't mind him. Not really. He opened his mouth with tongue against top teeth and held the pose for a few seconds, an effective way of calling for attention. Then he said,

'I must draw Jake aside briefly. I have to consult him about women.'

The other two responded like two immensely respectful and discreet versions of Ernie, if such a thing could be imagined. Jake wondered how Don Juan would have stood up to this sort of thing. He also wondered whether recent research might not have uncovered a historical prototype of that character and found him to have been a timid, anxious recluse like Isaac Newton, ending up married to his cook.

'And the desirability of admitting them to this college,' added the Master.

This time the two sighed noisily and flapped their hands, and Jake wondered what stopped them from seeing that, for good or ill, this was the most interesting matter ever likely to come their way, short of death.

'As you know, it's on tomorrow's agenda,' said the Master when he and Jake had moved off.

'Yes,' said Jake. Now he did. He had already known, though he had forgotten, that a College Meeting, i.e. of its Fellows, not of teachers and taught alike, was to take place the following afternoon.

'It's a bore, we agree, but we have to settle something before the end of the year. All I propose doing tomorrow is to announce a full discussion in two weeks' time and to nominate two Fellows to summarise the cases for and against just to set the ball rolling. A couple of minutes apiece, no more. I'm going to ask Roger Dollymore to put the anti point of view and I'd like you to put the pro. I thought of you partly because of your long experience and the fact that the small number of your pupils means you're not going to be personally affected either way. You won't have to say anything tomorrow except yes you'll do it, that's if you agree. I didn't want to spring it on you.'

Powle refrained from stating what another part of his grounds for asking Jake to do this job might have been, nor did he imply anything of the kind by his manner, which was entirely free from both jocoseness and its conscious avoidance. Jake agreed to serve.

'Good lad. Oh, you needn't bother with any fact-grubbing, state of play in other colleges and such. I'll hand that to one of the youngsters. Yes, I think probably Whitehead. He's still a bit pleased with himself over the reception of that paper of his last year. Do him good.'

Soon afterwards the members of the college and their guests went down the worn stone steps into Hall. Jake sat near the middle of the table facing the body of the room with Lancewood and Smith directly and diagonally opposite him and Dollymore beside him. Gossip started on the events leading to the premature retirement of the head of another learned foundation. Lancewood knew more than Dollymore about this and so was able to keep him almost completely quiet. Later, while host and guest conversed together, Dollymore got back by going on about rising prices in a markedly personal style, suggesting either that he was the first to have spotted the phenomenon or that the increases were being levied on him alone. Out of the idlest curiosity Jake began counting those recognisable as females on the benches before and below him, stopping before he reached ten. Bloody nice cheap trouble-free way of victualling your girl-friend between pokes, he thought to himself with tremendously unwilling respect. The food and drink at High Table were excellent as usual. Over the savoury he considered whether or not to go on to dessert back in the SCR. If Lancewood hadn't had a guest there would have been no issue; as things were there was the risk of a further dose of Dollymore and/or, worse, of Wynn-Williams, fifteen minutes of whom might be thought enough to keep any man topped up. The Feisal Room it was, then.

In this chamber, adjacent to the main SCR, the Regius Professor of Latin, the Fellow and Tutor in Oriental studies and the Principal Demonstrator of Anatomy were watching a colour-television screen on which a man with a woollen sort of mask over most of his face was using a pick-helve studded with nails to hit on the head an older man in a dark-blue uniform, or was at least feigned to be doing so. The Reader in Early Mediterranean History silently joined the audience.

About three hours later the gownsman just referred to descended the same stone steps as before but this time went out into the open. Not so many years ago at this time, the right side of midnight, the place would have been alive with activity, undergraduates fighting, vomiting, illicitly playing pianos or gramophones, setting fire to the JCR, throwing bottles of brown ale at the Dean's window, wrecking the rooms of Jews or pinioning them to the lawns with croquet-hoops. So at least it seemed to Jake. Now all was quiet. What were they doing instead? Fornicating? Taking drugs? Working? Writing poetry? He had no idea and didn't want to know.

An obstruction in his ear, catarrh or wax, clicked in not quite exact time with his footsteps on the stone. It would probably get all right left to itself. He entered his staircase and then his bedroom without having had to turn on any lights on the way, a skill acquired during some barely recalled business of fuel economy or power cut. After taking his Mogadon and putting on his pyjamas he had a thought, decided to forget it and then decided there could be no harm in just making sure. He went into the sitting-room and assured himself that nobody had burst or blown open his desk. Half a minute later he decided there could be no harm in just making sure, returned to the bedroom for his keys and opened the relevant drawer. The plastic phallus lay there snug as a bug in a rug, heart-warmingly undisturbed. Vowing to dispose of it the next day he turned off all the lights and settled down to sleep.

Time went by. Jake tried to remember some of the ladies who had shared this bed with him in the past and was quite successful in two or more cases, except that what he remembered was all a matter of their bracelets and their cigarette-lighters, the way they sneezed or asked for a drink, where they lived and how he used to get there and they here, the time he and one of them bought an evening paper or he and another of them went into Blackwell's bookshop. For a few seconds he had lying beside him some sort of image of that fair-haired South African who had worked in the University Registry, but what there was of it went before he could pretend to himself that he was even touching it. He did no better with just *a* woman or with merely considering in a general way business-head, Carter-face and the *Zoom* stable: his mind kept drifting away to other things. So then there was nothing for it but to give in and have his attention turned to what had been lined up for it ever since it had happened, Brenda's convinced but unexcited statement before Rosenberg and him, somewhat amplified over whatever they (she and he – Jake) had eaten at Mother Courage's, that she had had no pleasure or other benefit out of her marriage for a not very small number of years and only acquiesced in its continuance out of habit, laziness and dislike of upsets and, in particular, that she considered her husband to be at best indifferent to all women except as sexual pabulum. In fact she had put her point more shortly than that, adding that the biggest mistake of her life had been to understand her mother's maxim about men only wanting one thing as applying no further than to transactions with them outside marriage.

In the end he fell asleep, woke up about five and spent a couple of hours going over what Brenda had said and thinking about it, and then again fell asleep and dreamed he had to go on parade but couldn't find his boots, equipment, rifle or cap and didn't know the way to the parade ground.

13 Can I Take You out to Dinner?

Not very long afterwards Jake got up and went over to the buttery for breakfast. The cafeteria system here was most efficient and in no time he had settled himself at one of the waxed oak tables with his plastic tray. Nor did it take him long to dispose of the sausages that went to coarse powder in your mouth, electric-toaster toast charred round the edges but still bread in the middle, railway butter and jam, and coffee tasting of dog fur. When he had he went back to his rooms, dictated some letters into a cheap tape-recorder and took the spool over to the College Secretary's office, where someone would eventually type its contents. As often he looked in on the Secretary's secretary, a woman of about Brenda's age called Eve Greenstreet. Years ago she had gone to bed with him for a few weeks, something which a great many members and ex-members of the university could say for themselves. When the time came for him to move over he had felt no resentment, probably wouldn't have even if he hadn't already started on another lady, but had missed and gone on missing what he clearly remembered as her liveliness and quick common sense. Since her marriage some time in the '60s (was it?) she had supposedly turned respectable, not that she had become sedate in her manner or stopped taking care of her slim dark good looks – marvellous teeth and nice way of holding herself too.

She was on the telephone when he put his head round her door but at once she frowned theatrically and beckoned him in. 'Well, whoever seemed to think that seemed to think wrong, I can assure you: the Estates Bursar is the. . . . Yes, I can – extension 17. . . . Not a bit. Good-bye.' After ringing off she looked wonderingly at the telephone and said, 'I told the same bloody fool yesterday.' Then she jumped up and came round her desk and kissed Jake, whom she hadn't seen since before the end of the previous term. He asked after her husband and was told he was fine and she asked after Brenda.

'Fine.'

'Oh? What isn't, then?'

'How do you mean?'

'Oh, come off it, love. What's she done, flown the coop with somebody?'

'Of course not.'

'There's no of course about it the way you sounded.' Her expression changed. 'You're not ill, are you?'

'No, I'm fine. I mean really fine.'

There was an awkward silence; then Eve said abruptly, 'Sorry, I seem to have got off the mark a bit fast. I just thought you. . . .'

He spoke abruptly too, without forethought. 'Actually there is something. Could I talk to you about it?'

'Not now, I presume?'

'Can I take you out to dinner?'

They arranged to meet the following Tuesday at La Sorbonne off the High Street where the old Chinese place used to be. As Jake was going Eve said to him,

'Just one thing, my old Jayqueeze,' and went on without pissily waiting to be asked what it was, 'I'm Mrs Greenstreet now, Mr Greenstreet's wife, if you get what I mean.'

'I do.'

'Because it would be such a shame, and so on.'

He was going to trumpet something about anything like that being off the cards in a big way, but before he could thereby let out to Eve what he wanted to discuss with her a girl knocked and came in with a couple of folders, so he just declared that he thought so too and took himself off. He couldn't have stayed much longer in any case if, in order to heed the state of its copy of his JPCR article as mentioned by Miss Calvert, he was to look in at the Bodley before his lecture. With a pupil coming at twelve, he realised, there would be no time afterwards, and then there was lunch, and . . . and anyway he somehow wanted to see what was in store for him as soon as he could. When he did see, he wished he hadn't been so keen. Apart from Wanker! rather tastefully executed in orange and Prussian blue and various more familiar obscenities, there were marginalia of an altogether different order. Copied from Grossman, PAHS, vol. xlvi, p.44 – when he hadn't even heard of Grossman, let alone read his article. Not possibly before 900, unlikely before 800; see Nardini, MES, vol. xxx, p.524 – when he knew pretty well the sort of thing Nardini would be saying and had no time for it. Refuted by Silvester, RHSF July 1969 – when nobody could be expected to read everything. After a quick glance, or glare, round he ripped out the offending pages and hastened from the scene.

His lecture, delivered in a windowless room off Parks Road belonging to the Department of Criminological Endocrinology, went down like a bomb: well, he came through it with a whole skin. Even the little bastard from Teddy Hall had no very violent objection to his answer to a question about the Median legal system. When all was over for that week he walked back to Comyns through a shower of rain that stopped abruptly, like a tap being turned off, when he was a dozen yards from his staircase. The expected pupil turned up within half a minute, having followed in his wake from the lecture-room. He was a fat little fellow from Bradford who nevertheless showed both some curiosity about early Mediterranean history and some respect for Jake's standing in that subject, a combination so dazzlingly rare that Jake had come near to looking forward to their tutorials. Today discussion of the collection paper and of a single point from the lecture kept them going till they were interrupted by the chapel clock striking one. Still able to come occasionally that way, Jake thought to himself. He walked over to the SCR and ate some bright yellow soup with globules of oil on the top and a layer of farinaceous material on the bottom, two rectangles of ham of a greyish as well as pink complexion, a rudimentary salad and a segment of wrapped Camembert, and drank a tankard of beer because you couldn't get wine at lunch because that was easier for the staff. From half-way through the soup to the start of the Camembert, Roger Dollymore stood at his right rear and read out to him an article in *The Economist* about the economy. After Jake had drunk his coffee, which tasted of licorice and its own grounds more than dog fur, and glanced through the daily papers it was time to go into the Grade Room for the College Meeting. These conventions, held weekly in term, had once started at five o'clock and ended at a point which enabled the members of the college to stroll into the main SCR and drink a glass of sherry before going down to the best Hall, i.e. dinner, of the week. Now all that was changed and the thing started at two on the dot to let people bugger off as sharp as they could.

That afternoon's portion held nothing that lodged in Jake's mind after it was over except the Master's request, notified the previous evening, that he should briefly put the case for the admission of women into Comyns at the meeting to be held a fortnight on, and his saying he would. In fact the two utterances not only lodged in his mind, they weighed on it too, slightly but to a degree he couldn't put down to anything. It meant extra work, too little though to oppress even him. More likely he was not fancying the prospect of the rallying, chaffing, twitting, bantering smiles, winks, nudges and grimaces to be seen, or fancied to be seen, when he duly spoke for the ladies. There had been a touch of that this time.

He took tea in the SCR and bloody good it was as usual, one of the bits they hadn't got to yet, like the Halls: toasted bun, cucumber sandwiches and Jackson's Earl Grey. At five minutes past five he went over to his rooms, there to conduct his seminar on Lydia – the region of Asia Minor and ancient empire of that name. Doing that put him in just the right frame of mind to receive his guest for the evening at 6.30. This was an ex-pupil, a graduate student from St John's who had been short-listed for an assistant lectureship at the University College of South Wales at Cardiff, largely no doubt on the strength of the laudatory but quite fair reference provided him by Jake. For a reason that will be seen in a moment, he had fought as hard and conscientiously as he could to clobber the chap's chances by praising him with faint damns, but in vain: integrity, curse it, had triumphed as it so often had in the past, long ago condemning him, with some assistance from laziness, to the non-attainment of a professorial chair. But in this case there was still a chance of undoing its ravages. Tonight he would tell his man that while Cardiff was a thoroughly respectable place there might be better things in store for him here in Oxford. If he stayed on and – point coming – ran or helped to run Jake's seminar for a year or so, he would be in a much stronger position to walk into Jake's readership when in due course it fell vacant. Integrity was going to demand that he made it clear to the chap that he would be warmly supported for that post whether he went to Cardiff or not, but he felt he could submit to that demand with a comparatively good grace.

When it came to it the operation was painless, though the young man gave no sign of being drawn towards or away from Cardiff. Jake took him on to dessert and gave him port; to help to seem to be giving rather than plying with he took a small glass himself. Not that plying with of various sorts and intensities wasn't raging about the two of them. Far to seek was the guest invited for his company rather than for some turn he might serve – back a candidate for a college place or a university lectureship, agree to publish a book of dolled-up learned articles, endow something, withhold support from something else – or perhaps had served: Lancewood, who might have provided an exception, hadn't been in Hall. Jake wondered what was being asked of the only woman in the room, distantly known to him as a fellow-historian with interests in medieval Scandinavia. There had been senior women guests at Comyns for years now; all things considered, among them her age and general condition, the present one was most unlikely to hurl herself diagonally across the polished walnut and snatch at his winkle; nevertheless he was put out to see her there, as if she knew something about him that he would have preferred to keep hidden.

The evening ended quite agreeably: guest thanked host and said he would think things over and let him know. Jake went to bed and, aided it might have been by the port he had drunk, slept much better than the previous night. He was up early, in good time to face a string of tutorials starting at nine, or rather 9.10. During the intervals he wrote a short note to whom it might concern that said here was a copy of the Ionian-trade-routes thing for the recipient's personal use. This, together with an off-print of the article and a slip asking for 20 copies please, he took over to the Secretary's office and handed in at the place where they kept the photostat machine. Miss Calvert would probably talk around among her thick pals and the little bastard from Teddy Hall would probably whip across to the Bodley to go over the ground and hence to deduce further who must have mutilated the relevant number of JPCR and to laugh, if he ever laughed, but what of it?

Jake was between Didcot and Reading in the earliest of the three usual return Flying Dodgers (the choice was less confined than on the outward journey) when it came to him that the plastic phallus was still in his desk drawer. Unless somebody else had already taken it out, of course.

14 Sexual Act

'What exactly is it?' asked Brenda.

'It's like what we did before, only this time it's *genital* sensate focusing, so down below is all right, in fact the whole point so to speak.'

'I see. There is a thing called a feel-up, isn't there? I mean of course there is, but that is an expression, feel-up?'

'It certainly used to be. I expect it still carries on.'

'Okay. Now: how is this genital whatname different from a feel-up?'

'It's a feel-up by numbers,' said Jake in a sneering tone.

'Don't sound like that about it. What's by numbers? No I see, so many minutes each, sort of like a drill.'

'Exactly like a drill. They must think that takes the anxiety out of it, everything being predictable, no decisions to take.'

'That seems quite sensible to me, as far as it goes.'

'I don't know, perhaps it is. Well. . . .'

'And we're allowed to have sexual intercourse but not required to.'

'Yes. There goes predictability. I must have muddled it up, that part.'

Jake and Brenda got up from their seats in the sitting-room at Burgess Avenue and clasped hands with an air little different from that of a couple shaking them before going off to face some minor social ordeal like boss to dinner or speech to local society. Upstairs they put the patchwork quilt on one side, she went out to the bathroom and he started undressing. At first he tried not to think of what was in store; then he decided that was silly and thought. Thinking passed quickly and imperceptibly into feeling. What feeling? Reluctance? Yes. Revulsion? No. Fear? No. Embarrassment? No. Boredom? Er, no. Dejection? Yes, but still not the right section of the thesaurus. Disfavour? Yes, but not much further forward. *Dismay* – of a peculiar kind, one not encountered before in any of his admittedly unhabitual attempts to analyse his emotions: it was profound . . . and . . . unalloyed . . . and . . . absorbing . . . and . . . (Christ) . . . very very mild, like so much else. Well, what did he know about that?

He finished undressing and got into bed with his back towards the door. Brenda pattered in and joined him.

'Ooh! Let's get warm first, shall we?'

'Sure.'

'I've lost another five ounces. Mostly going without potatoes last night, that must be.'

'Good for you.'

'I am trying you know.'

'Of course you are. I said good for you.'

'Will you remember the programme all right, do you think?'

'I won't have to, I've got it here.'

'Oh marvellous.' After a silence, Brenda said, 'Well, shall we start?'

'Okay,' said Jake cheerfully. 'Now the first thing is five minutes each of sensate focusing, that's the non-alcoholic sort. Who's going to go first?'

'Me. Remember you're to say if I'm doing it right and what I'm not doing that you'd like me to.'

'Check.'

Brenda did it right rather than wrong and he couldn't think of anything she wasn't doing that he'd have liked her to, except for falling asleep, going to answer the telephone etc. Then he called time and took his turn. He put in a solid, conscientious performance that must have gone down quite well, because she evidently couldn't think of anything he wasn't doing that she'd have liked him to do.

'Right,' he said at last, still cheerfully, reached for the xeroxed sheet on the bedside table and put his glasses on. 'Yes – now you stimulate my nipples and breasts by stroking, tickling or gentle pinching, or the whole breast area may be gently rubbed. Off you go.'

And off she went. After a couple of minutes he said,

'Let's scrub this. It says fifty per cent of males respond sexually to such stimulation. That probably means up to fifty per cent. Anyway, I must be one of the other fifty per cent. Now it's my turn, or your turn. I'd better just. . . .' He put his glasses on again. 'Female breast area, here we are. Yes, you're supposed to explain to me just how you like it done.'

This proved to be unnecessary. Brenda plainly liked it done how he was doing it, responded perceptibly more than last time. He was glad about that: he felt pleased, though without feeling pleasure. That was to be expected: if he had been getting pleasure out of what he was at there would be no need for him to be at it, or alternatively he would have been at it anyway without ever having heard of genital sensate focusing or been near bloody Rosenberg. But to have not the slightest expectation of any pleasure whatsoever undoubtedly eased the strain. Grating a carrot or polishing a spoon would be far more tedious if you had to keep on the alert waiting for it to 'turn you on', as he had gathered it was called. Somehow, too, not talking helped. It made the whole business more serious, more like the Army. When he did say something it was out of the book.

'End of Phase I. Now with Phase II either partner can begin, so shall we swap round? It seems more. . . .'

'If you like.'

'Okay. That means I sit with my back against the head of the bed with my legs spread out and you sit between them with your back to me. Then I' – glasses – 'I use gentle tickling, stroking or kneading movements in long, even, rhythmic strokes and you, well what it boils down to is you guide me and after a bit I . . . yes, I conduct a gentle but persistent invasion . . . and mustn't be afraid to stop for rests. That sounds pretty straightforward. Shall we go?'

The first part of Phase II was completed according to instructions. At its conclusion the partners changed their positions as follows: the woman sat with her back against the head of the bed with her legs spread out and the man faced her, put his legs on either side of her and lay back with his genital region accessible to her. After a period of stimulation, beginning with gentle tickling, stroking, pinching and scratching, the man showed signs of arousal and excitement. In due course an act of intercourse took place, in the course of which both partners achieved climax and evinced various signs of relaxation in course of time.

Afterwards the male partner lay on his side in a reposeful posture, his facial area in close proximity to the facial area of the female partner and his right upper limb partially surrounding her trunk. Well, he thought to himself, that (the taking place of the act of intercourse) ought to prove something. The question was what. That he could if he would, at any rate. What more? That there was nothing organically wrong with him. But he already had Dr Curnow's word for that.

As if she sensed that he was in a questioning frame of mind, Brenda kissed him warmly on the cheek. That was nice.

'You see?' she murmured. 'All just worry and tension.'

'Was it all right for you?'

'Yes.' After a pause she added, 'Like old times.'

That was nice too, but the male partner didn't think much of it as a statement of fact, or at least of how he felt, he himself speaking personally as of then and there. What had finished a minute earlier had been pretty much like old times, physically at least and as far as he could remember – the remembering trouble having less to do with the oldness of the times than the inherent difficulty of remembering a lot about any such experiences or series of them; so at least plenty of people would say. But over the last minute, now extending itself to two or three more of the same, he could find in himself rather little, hardly enough to be worth mentioning, of the old-time mixture of peace and animation. That might be round the corner: early days yet, long way to go, walk before we can run etc.

'Would you like a cup of tea?' he asked.

'Ooh, *yes*.'

'And a slice of toast?'

'Oh *darling*,' she said as if he had added a gold chain or something to his original offer of a diamond necklace, which was agreeably far from taking things for granted but also rather convicted him of having done bugger-all for the preceding decade. Then she added immediately, 'I daren't. Guzzlers Anonymous would kill me.'

'I won't tell them.'

'I know, but still. . . .'

He tossed a coin in his mind and said sternly, 'I didn't think, I shouldn't have suggested it. Of course you mustn't have toast.'

'All right.' She put her face under the bedclothes.

The post-coital cup of tea was very much an old-time institution, with assorted origins or purposes. It satisfied Jake's need at this stage to be up and doing instead of going on lying about; its making and fetching gave Brenda the chance for a short nap; it was a small token of his appreciation; drinking it together brought a pleasant cosiness. Or rather all these things had once been the case; at a more primeval period, the interval that ended with the laying down of cups had turned out to be just right for his thoughts to start returning whither they had started turning half an hour before. No surprise was expressed or felt when that didn't happen this afternoon, or more precisely early evening. After the tea was drunk Jake went and had a bath, as usual leaving the water for Brenda so as to save fuel. Then he dressed himself with a certain care in clean pale-pink shirt, mildly vivid tie, the Marks and Spencer suit he betted would fool anyone he had much chance of running into, and the grey suede half-boots that had been all the rage in some relatively recent era like that of Hitler's rise to power. He hadn't a lot of hair left on his head but he tidied what there was with the touch of complacency this exercise always tended to arouse in him: better bald as a badger than train it over from side or back and be afraid to sneeze. That done, he went downstairs and watched Crossroads. Just as it was finishing Brenda came into the room.

'Ready,' she said in exactly the same way, eager and yet nervous, as he remembered from when he had taken her out to dinner in Oxford for the first time after they were married, at the Dollymores' house in St Margaret's Road; she had worn a sort of coppery-coloured dress of some shiny stuff and bright green slippers with gold clasps and pointed toes. Jake felt more than one kind of pang, at how time had gone by, what quantity and in what way, and at how long it had been since anything much about Brenda had struck him. He got up quickly.

'You look beautiful.'

She smiled delightedly and without reserve. 'That's good. You look all right yourself.'

'It's the tie. Brings out the blue in my eyes.'

'Off?'

'Yes.'

They were indeed off that night, not however to anyone's house but to a fairly classy Chinese restaurant called the Bamboo Bothy and situated almost round the corner from them in Vassall Crescent, easy walking distance anyway so no trouble or expense over transport. The idea – in general: the choice of premises had been left entirely open – was Rosen-berg's, indeed his instruction. Weekly until further notice, the Richardsons were to engage in interpersonal recreative sociality, in other words to 'go out together'. It had been and would remain Jake's part to initiate the enterprise, though Brenda had an equal voice in determining its nature. Since what he would have liked best, granted he had to leave the house at all, was a straight-there-and-back attendance at the most violent and/or horrific film on show in Greater London while what she would have liked best was drinks at the Ritz followed by dinner at the Connaught, things might seem to have gone her way of the two, if not by much, but he had really scored by vetoing the below-subsistence-level man's, the famine-relief-beneficiary's version of the Connaught that was all they could afford: cooling bad quasi-continental food served tardily and rudely in hot dark noisy smelly dirty crowded surroundings. 'We won't go *there* again,' Brenda would say, but they did in all but name, admittedly less often in the last year or so.

The Bothy was almost empty, to Jake's knowledge its invariable state: turning up at eight or nine o'clock, walking past at eleven showed the same three unpeopled files of immaculate white tablecloths. It must be just the lid of an arsenal for use when. The proprietor's grandson or father greeted them pleasantly and showed them to a booth or berth at one side of the room. The composition covers on the benches or banquettes made your bottom give awful snarling, farting noises as you squirmed it along, forced so to squirm it by the overhang of the lowish table. Would they like a drink? No, they would like to order, though having done so they, in the person of Jake, also ordered a bottle of stuff called Wan Fu which they had tried and liked before. Among the welter of what must be Chinese on the label it said, in English, that this wine was specially selected to accompany Chinese dishes, and added reassuring references in French to negotiants, Bordeaux and cellars. Jake pictured a negotiant, or the appointee of one, walking round a cellar in Bordeaux with his mind bent hard on spare ribs, sweet and sour prawn, fried crispy noodle and chicken with bamboo shoots and every so often suddenly and infallibly selecting. Well worth the mark-up.

'Ooh, I was going to say, the garden's in a bit of a state I thought today,' said Brenda.

'There's always rather a lot to do at the beginning of a term.' It was true that he had a little more to do then than at some other times. 'Anyway I've finished pruning the roses and I'll do the chrysanthemum fertiliser over the week-end. Weather hasn't been very inviting you must admit. Ah, thank you very much, that looks delicious.' As soon as the waiter had gone Jake said, 'Well, darling, we've got something to celebrate.'

'Something, yes.'

'Oh I agree it isn't very much, but. . . .'

'No it isn't. Well, it's just something.'

He groaned to himself. 'It's only supposed to be a start.'

'What is? What's *it* exactly?'

'Well, a . . . successful . . . what Rosenberg would call act of intercourse.'

'What's that? What's a successful one of those?'

'Just . . . one where the man gets it up and eventually comes, and the woman comes too.'

'How important is that, the woman coming too?'

'Very important, I mean it wouldn't. . . .'

'It wouldn't be Grade A without that, would it? Not strictly kosher. Not quite all present and correct. It might mean you weren't able to hold back for the number of minutes and seconds laid down in Screwing Regulations for Mature Males section fourteen sub-section D.'

'You know it's more than that,' said Jake a little absently. He was going over in his mind what he had said since leaving the house, because it must have been since then.

'Nobody would have known it from the way you asked me just after-wards if it had been all right for me. You should have heard yourself. Talk about any-complaints-carry-on.' Brenda had been looking down at the food through her spectacles, sorting out for herself the less calorie-crammed items; now her eyes met his. She had spoken and continued to speak in the same unheated tone she had used in Rosenberg's consulting-room when making similar points more generally. 'I've taken in quite a lot of that Army stuff of yours. It might have been the best time of your life.'

'If we're going to get on to that level we might as well – '

'That's not on a level, you think about it, not now, and you see if it wasn't. Anyway if it's of any interest, sorry no I know it's of interest, it was all right for me, just, what you might call technically.'

'You said it was like old times.'

'So it was. I meant it.'

Jake's spirits fell sharply. 'Gee thanks,' he said.

'Don't misunderstand me, that's better than nothing, and I wasn't thinking of the real old times, when we started together. They were – '

'But you didn't sound as if you meant it, well, disappointedly then. You sounded friendly and affectionate then.'

'That was then. Even after your any-complaints thing I wanted to make you feel as good as I could. . . .'

'Which you're losing no time in duly reversing.'

' . . . *so* that you might start showing a bit of physical affection to me, instead of which you shot out of bed and started getting some tea going.'

'You didn't sound as if you minded the tea idea, quite the contrary, and surely you remember we always used to have tea afterwards, it isn't that long ago good God, and what do you think I'd been doing before but showing you physical affection – putting you in your place socially? I think you might – '

'I was making the best of a not frightfully good job, and I fancied a cup anyway, though a large gin would have been more like it just then quite frankly,' – Brenda was warming to her theme a little now – 'and of course I remember how we used to have tea once, but that was different, and . . . what was the other thing?'

'Er. . . .' Jake looked away diagonally across the aisle of the restaurant and saw that the three youngish men he had vaguely noticed a couple of minutes earlier, men whom by their open-necked shirts and pullovers or leather jackets he had vaguely taken for a group of gasmen or dustmen on emergency call, were peering at menus. One of them was in the middle of a tremendous unshielded yawn. *Really*, the way they . . . 'Er . . . Christ . . . physical affection.'

'Oh yes. Well I don't count a poke as physical affection, I'm thinking of before that, the non-genital stimulation or whatever it's called. That's part of what that's meant to be, you realise, it's meant to be partly affectionate, or rather you don't realise, not like grooming a horse or more like pumping up a bicycle-tyre. You were like – I've never heard anybody gritting their teeth so loudly in my life, when you were doing it to me *and* when I was doing it to you. And not saying a bloody word.'

'I thought that would help us concentrate. And you didn't say anything yourself either.'

'I took my time from you to start with and then I just hung on out of curiosity to see how long you were going to keep your mouth shut.'

Jake started to speak with resentment and defiance, then checked himself. 'Now look. I know I've said it before, I'm merely reminding you, this is all me or, all right, mostly me, largely me, it starts with me, not you. I'd be the same with anybody.'

'I don't care about anybody. I'm meant to be special as far as you're concerned.'

'You are, and that's bound to make a difference but it's not going to happen all at once, we must accept that. And we have made a start. After all, biologically we've – '

'Screw biologically. We've made one sort of start, but there's another sort we haven't made,' said Brenda with an emphasis he had never heard her use before, or else had forgotten, 'and this really is you. You've got to find out whether you feel any affection for me or whether you're the sort of man who can only feel affection for women he wants to go to bed with or wouldn't mind going to bed with or thinks of in a sort of bed whatname, context. If you're not that sort, if you do feel some affection for me even though you don't want to go to bed with me you'd better start working on it and trying to show it. And remember I can tell.'

'What about your affection for me?' he asked after a silence.

'It's there but it's keeping itself to itself. It tends to watch its step a bit after the knocks it's taken.'

'When did it last take a knock?' This was playing for time while he tried to recover a memory.

'Ooh, about two hours ago, when I kissed you and tried to start talking to you and you came back with any complaints and put your arm round me as if I was an old sow you were having to keep warm till the vet arrived.'

'I didn't mean it like that.'

'I don't say you *meant* it like anything. I just might as well have been an old sow.'

'I suppose you think this is a good time to bring all this up.'

'Yes I do. Check. An excellent time. After you've taken the first step towards getting your, well, your confidence back and before you sell yourself the idea that that's all you have to do. I mean before you absolutely stop wondering what went wrong. Dr Rosenberg seemed to think they go together, you know, screwing and being affectionate, as far as I could make out what he meant, and so do a lot of other people.'

'Yes of course.' Jake had remembered, 'You believed me when I said you looked beautiful in the sitting-room just before we came out.'

'I believed something. Something nice. What made you say it?'

'Just remembering how things used to be, sort of suddenly.'

She dropped her gaze to her plate, which was now quite empty, and pushed her hand out towards him between the dishwarmer and the soy sauce. He took the hand and squeezed it, telling himself it was amazing how after all these years one went on forgetting the old truth that women meant things differently from men. They (women) spoke as they felt, which meant that you (a man) would be devastated for ever if you took them literally. (The compensation, in fact bonus on aggregate, was that they thought you operated in the same way, so that they forgave and forgot the devastating things you said to them. He had once, in the course of one of their rows about her relations, called Brenda an illiterate provincial, which had gone down at least as badly as expected at the time but had never since been thrown in his face, thank God; just think what he would have done about and with an accusation of remotely comparable nearness to the bone. And felt about it too.) So what she had said last Tuesday to Rosenberg and him, what he had lain awake going over in his mind in the medium-sized hours the following day, what had then seemed to him to write or at any rate rough-draft finis to their marriage — all that that had boiled down to was saying in bold sans-serif Great Primer italics that she was seriously fed up with him and he had bloody well better stop feeling sorry for himself and take a bit of notice of her for a change. And she had been and was absolutely right. So there they were.

'I think all this might sort itself out in the end with a bit of luck,' he said.

'So do I, darling.'

'Good. . . . We must have earned at least a beta-double-plus from Dr Rosenberg for this evening's work.'

'If not beta-alpha query.'

'If he could see us now he'd be nodding his little head in approbation.'

'Rubbing his tiny hands with satisfaction.'

'Showing all his miniature teeth in a benevolent smile.'

'Dancing on the tips of his microscopic toes.'

'Shaking his filter-passing buttocks.'

'I quite like him really.'

Jake lifted the corner of his lip and sighed. 'What's this do he's got lined up for us next week-end?'

'The Workshop?'

'Oh *Christ*, I'd forgotten it was called that, I must have censored it out of my memory.'

'What's wrong with it?'

'*Wrong* with it? If there's one word that sums up everything that's gone wrong since the War, it's Workshop. After Youth, that is.'

'Darling, you are a silly old Oxford don, it is only a word.'

'*Only* a word? – sorry. No, this whole thing is all about language.'

'Whole thing? What whole thing?'

'Well, the . . . you know, bloody Rosenberg and his jargon, and beyond that, the way nobody can be bothered to. . . . Anyway, what is this fucking Workshop? I may say that if it's a *fucking* Workshop you can all count me out. I'm buggered if I'm going to start taking part in exhibeeshes in my condition, or even trying to.'

'It's nothing like that, it's a sort of group where everyone has a different sort of problem and says what it is and the others talk back to them. It's meant to help you unburden yourself and gain insight. But Dr Rosenberg explained it to us. Weren't you listening?'

'I suppose unburdening yourself might be a good thing in some cases. No, I was too bored.'

'You must try and make it a success, you know, and take it seriously.'

'I promise you I'll try, but at this distance it does give off a distinct smack of piss.'

15   At Mr Shyster's

The following day week, Saturday, at a quarter to ten of an overcast but so far not actually wet morning, Jake and Brenda made their way on foot to a house in Maclean Terrace some five hundred yards from their own. The events of the intervening eight days may be briefly summarised. There had been two further sessions of genital sensate focusing, the first slightly, the second considerably less successful than the initial one; the consultation with Rosenberg had thrown further light on Jake's sexual behaviour and attitudes but made visible thereby nothing in particular, or so it seemed to the patient; Brenda had told Jake, this time over tandoori chicken and bindhi gosht at the Crown of India in Highgate, that if he wanted to show affection for her he must try harder and then had discussed their holiday plans for September; Eve Greenstreet had cancelled her dinner with Jake because it looked as if her mother had started dying; and Mrs Sharp had tried to break down Jake's study door in order to admit a woodworm authority while he (Jake) was deeply engaged with business-head and Carter-face. Oh, and Brenda had had lunch and been to a film about peasants with Alcestis.

The house that was to house the Workshop was a little older and, to judge by its front, a little larger than the Richardsons'. That front had also had nothing done to it but in a bigger way: parts of the stucco facing had fallen off and there was a quite interesting-looking crack running down from the corner of an upstairs window. The front garden had no flowers or shrubs in it but quite enough in the way of empty beer-tins, fag-packets and cardboard food-containers thrown over the low hedge by tidy-minded passers-by and not removed by the inmates. What were the latter going to be like? Jake, who would have had to confess unwillingly to suffering slight twinges of curiosity and expectation as well as uneasiness at what might be in store for him, felt the uneasiness start to mount and become better defined. He noted successively the broken window-pane mended with a square of linoleum, the lidless dustbin in which a thick slightly shiny off-white vest with shoulder-straps and a bottle that had held Cyprus sherry caught the eye, the bucket half full of what you hoped was just dirty water and the comfortable-looking two-legged armchair in the passage that led to the rear. Agoraphobic stockbrokers, dentists afflicted with castration anxiety, anally-fixated publicity consultants he had been prepared for; mixed-up berks from building sites or off those lorry things that pulped your rubbish were quite a different prospect. Nor was he one whit reassured by the child's bicycle propped against the side of what was doubtless known as the porch.

No knocker or bell-push was to be seen on or near the peeling front door, so Jake pounded on it with the side of his fist. In the interval that followed he and Brenda embraced, briefly and without looking at each other. Then the door opened quite normally to reveal a long-haired middle-aged man holding a glass of what looked like whisky and water which he swirled all the time.

'Yer?'

'We're looking for something called the Workshop,' said Jake.

'Doctor you wanted, was it?'

'Yes. Yes, I suppose so,'

The fellow motioned with his head, his locks flying. He said in a lowered tone, 'Second on the left down there,' stood aside and carefully shut the door behind the Richardsons. Apart from what might perhaps have been a bead curtain the interior was featureless, also rather dark; there was a faint sweetish smell, not unpleasant; in the distance an organ, probably but not certainly through one or another means of reproduction, could be heard playing something a bit religious. In the past, Jake thought to himself, this would have made quite a plausible setting for a down-market spiritualist séance, though there of course your feelings would have been rather different – more certitude of tangible benefit and so on.

The room he and Brenda went into made much the same impression, but with more emphasis on things being dirty and damp. It also had Rosenberg in it. The little psychologist slipped to the floor from the sofa-like object on which he had been perching and shook hands with the curious warmth he always showed on meeting, not quite false and yet not right, off target, appropriate to some other relationship, perhaps that of a nephew.

'And how are we now?' he asked. 'Do make yourselves comfortable.'

In the circumstances this was self-evidently out of the question but Jake and Brenda made no demur about it taking off their topcoats and throwing them across a chair that could have come from his rooms at Comyns, and then settling themselves side by side on a kind of bench that had the attraction of being not far from a tall electric fire. This gave off a hasty buzzing sound from time to time.

'Whose house is this?' asked Jake.

'It belongs to Mr Shyster,' Rosenberg seemed to say. He spoke with an air of self-satisfaction.

'Does he run the . . .' – Jake set his teeth – '. . . Workshop?'

'He does not,' said Rosenberg, shocked that anybody at all should need to be set right on this point. 'The facilitator is called Ed.'

'The what?' asked Jake delightedly, having heard quite well.

'Facilitator. We like to avoid words like organiser and leader. They have the wrong associations.'

'Whereas facilitator has exactly the right ones. I see.'

Brenda looked hard at Jake. 'Does it matter what he's called?'

'Oh indeed it does, Mrs Richardson, indeed it does. Words embody attitudes of mind.'

'I was making the very same point the other day,' said Jake with a respectful nod of the head. 'And who is Ed? Apart from being the facilitator of the Workshop, that is.'

'Well, he had a brilliant and extremely creative career in the United States and came to this country just over a year ago. He says he thinks it's his duty to stay because the need for him is greater here. They're streets ahead of us over there in this field, as you might imagine.'

Jake had subvocalised an oath. Funny how everything horrible or foolish was worse if it was also American. Modern architect – modern American architect. Woman who never stops talking – American ditto. Zany comedian. Convert to Buddhism. . . . 'Oh yes,' he said when Rosenberg paused.

'I asked you both to come a few minutes early to tell you a little about this work. First of all I take no part, I merely observe. Ed's object is to induce the participants to express their emotions, to confess what he or she thinks he or she is really like or what's wrong with him or her, or to say what he or she feels about another participant. Or the others may help him or her to a more intense experience. Things of that nature. The essential point is that the emotion should be expressed in full – no holds barred, as we say. Also it must be *emotion:* Ed'll be listening not to what you say but how you say it.'

'So it's all right if I talk nonsense,' said Jake.

'Oh indeed, Ed wants to know how you *feel.*'

'I don't think I can feel much about nonsense except that it is nonsense.'

'You were saying just now what we said was meant to be important,' said Brenda. 'Words embodying things.'

'That's the mental aspect. It's the emotions we're on to now.'

'Oh.'

'Now the purpose of Workshop activity is twofold. The first applies in equal measure to every participant. It enables him or her to achieve release and gain insight into himself or herself. The second purpose is individual and is different for every participant. It helps him or her to overcome his or her special problem. In your case, Mr Richardson, it's the overcoming of sexual guilt and shame. You'll find that by – '

'You keep saying that,' said Jake in some irritation, 'and I keep telling you I don't – '

'I keep saying it because it's true and you won't accept it. Look at yourself at the McDougall.'

'I have, and what of it? Anyone would have felt the same.'

'Wrong. As you'll come to see. You think it's disgraceful that your libido has declined. Yes you do. As you'll come to see it's no more disgraceful than catching cold. But I mustn't lay too much stress there, that's just on the surface. Deeper down you feel that the slightest little deviation from any sexual norm is cause for guilt and shame, as your fantasy showed. There are parts of your sexual make-up you still refuse to let me see.'

Jake slowed himself down. 'Look, Dr Rosenberg, if I have got any parts like that I don't know what they are. As I've explained to you before, I don't particularly object to oral sex or anal sex or the rest of the boiling, I just don't enjoy that kind of thing as much as the . . . straightforward stuff. Didn't enjoy it, I should say. No desire to be a voyeur or be at the receiving end of one. Et cetera. And what of it if I had? And I had to eke out my fantasy with adjectives and so forth because what I was imagining was too simple to run to the number of words you asked me for.'

'Please just listen. Deepest down of all you think everything about sex is unpleasant as a result of your puritanical upbringing.'

'Good . . . God.'

'Excuse me but we must get on. Mrs Richardson, your problem is inferiority feelings. You agree with that, I think.'

'You bet I do. I feel completely hopelessly – '

'Save it for the Workshop. The only other thing I have to say – well, two things. You two are the only participants with directly sexual problems, and everyone is selected with great care – vetted. Some people will try to enter this kind of work for the wrong motives: to acquire a sexual partner or just to enjoy the dramatic aspect of plain curiosity. One of the ways in which Ed is so good is he can detect those fellows as if it's by taking one look at them. Ah.'

A muffled thumping indicated a new arrival and a series of loud creaks the progress up the passage of Mr Shyster, if indeed it was he. A double series of creaks coming the other way duly followed, there was a light tap at the door and a girl of about twenty came in. She was dressed rather unfashionably (Jake decided) in a terracotta-coloured trouser-suit and frilly green shirt and carried a long umbrella with a curved handle.

'This is Kelly,' said the doctor. 'All Christian names is the rule here. Kelly, this is Jake and this is Brenda.'

'How do you do Jake, how do you do Brenda,' said the girl in a pleasant expensive-upbringing voice, shaking hands firmly and looking each of them straight in the eye. Considering her ease of manner, healthy skin and teeth and at least perfectly adequate features (good unsoft mouth), hair (reddish) and figure (far from flat-chested), he found it hard to imagine what her special problem could be.

While Rosenberg was filling in about what Jake did and where Kelly lived (just where Orris Park merged into Hampstead) another person's approach was heard. It proved to be that of Geoffrey Mabbott. He showed not the least surprise at finding the Richardsons there, a very Geoffrey-like reaction but so total that Jake's first thought, soon to be corrected, was that he had been told of their recruitment. Jake's next thought, rounded out later that day, was that he wasn't as surprised to see Geoffrey as he ought by rights to have been, and not just because after all Geoffrey was a bit touched and lived locally. No, the real reason was that Rosenberg always reminded him of Geoffrey. Since bringing to light at their first session that Rosenberg didn't know where Freud functioned, what had happened in 1848 or who James Bond was, he had established with varying degrees of certainty that Rosenberg had never heard of the *Titanic*, haggis, T. S. Eliot, plutonium, Lent, Vancouver (city, let alone island or chap), Herodotus, Sauternes, the Trooping of the Colour, the *Times Literary Supplement*, the battle of Gettysburg, Van Gogh, Sibelius, *Ulysses* – (a) good going for an Irishman (b) and no doubt Ulysses too – chlorophyll, Florence Nightingale, the Taj Mahal, pelota, lemurs, Gary Cooper and Hadrian's Wall; theoretically, on the face of it, in the strict sense there was no reason why you shouldn't never have heard of one or other or even all of that lot and still be a good psychologist; after all, he hadn't never heard of pornography, parents, marriage, erections and sex; and yet somehow.... (By the way, how had he ever got to hear of sherry-and-Oxford, even sherry and Oxford?) Geoffrey wouldn't never have heard of most of the items on the list but he would tend not to have much idea of who or what they were, scoring not very near misses with the same consistency as Rosenberg showed in not recognising the target at all. In Geoffrey's world Eliot would be a famous actor of Victorian times, Vancouver a lake in Rhodesia, chlorophyll a newish health food, Florence Nightingale a campaigner for female suffrage. These magpies of his were seldom associated with the wrong bullseye, Eliot not being taken for a female novelist nor chlorophyll for an antiquated anaesthetic; Jake would have felt easier in his mind about them and about Geoffrey if they had been.

This morning he had dressed in the dark as usual: chocolate-brown corduroy trousers, navy-blue cable-stitch pullover, black shoes and the jacket of his dark-grey suit. His manner was friendly but slightly restless, again a familiar combination. Jake lost no time in asking him whether Alcestis was expected to join them.

'Alcestis?'

'Yes. Is she joining us?'

Geoffrey frowned and shook his head. 'No,' he said with an upward inflection. 'Where did you get that idea from?'

'I didn't get – '

'I mean why should she be joining us?'

'Well, Brenda's here, and I thought – '

'I know, Jake, I know Brenda's here, I've just this moment spoken to her.' said Geoffrey, gently enough but with some triumph at having so readily diagnosed the acute senile dementia that must have caused Jake to be brought to this place.

To distract himself from restraining himself from kicking Geoffrey in the balls Jake said, 'What's whatsisname like, Ed, the fellow who runs these do's?'

First Geoffrey dilated his eyes. Then he drew in his breath in a long hiss, slowly pouting his lips as he did so. Next he clenched his fists, raised them slowly again to shoulder level, lowered his head until it was between them and pounded his cheekbones rhythmically, meanwhile slowly once more expelling his breath. After that he unclenched his hands, indeed made them quite flat, pushed them out horizontally in front of him to the length of his arms and cut the air with them a number of times. Finally he dropped them to his sides and gave Jake a nod that showed he had finished.

'Oh I *see*,' said Jake. 'My goodness, he does sound an interesting sort of chap.'

When the facilitator arrived a few minutes afterwards he was at once distinguishable as such from the two or three other men who turned up at about the same time. Jake didn't quite know what he had expected beyond somebody designed to be as offensive in his sight as possible: hairiness, uncleanliness, youthfulness, jeans, beads, hat etc. The reality was the opposite of all that without being in consequence the least bit more encouraging. Ed turned out to be in his late thirties, heavily built, dark after a Spanish or Italian fashion, wearing an oddly cut oatmeal-coloured suit that was none the less a suit, moving in a way that put you in mind of a cross between an experienced actor and a man well used to responsibility. He soon showed he had a trick of stroking his face in detail while he peered at you. When he spoke it was in a deep slightly wheedling voice.

'All right everybody, let's get to work,' he said. 'We have a couple of new participants today, Brenda and Jake. Hi Brenda, hi Jake.'

Salutations of differing amplitude came from the rest of the company, now seated in a rough square with Ed on his feet in the middle. Counting him and Rosenberg there were twelve persons present, seven men and five women.

'Now let's just introduce you around. This is Lionel, who steals things out of stores and says he can't help it, and this is Winnie, who's so shy she can't stand to talk to anybody even although she comes here every week, and this is Ivor, who's afraid of the dark and being alone and a whole raft of other things, and I have word you know Geoffrey, who gets worried because he's figured out he's an asshole, and this is Ruth, who doesn't have anything to do except cry all the time, and this is Chris, who doesn't like the human race, and this is Kelly, who can't run her life, and this is Martha, who has to look after her mother and says her mother is mean to her.'

It wasn't that Ed recited this in a lifeless or even a neutral tone, it was simply that Jake couldn't tell whether he was amused or compassionate or

bored or contemptuous or generously indignant. Those so briskly character-
ised showed no signs of surprise or resentment: Lionel, who stole things,
even blinked and pursed his lips in a self-deprecatory fashion as if he
thought Ed had in his case been somewhat over-gracious.

After a moment, Ed went smoothly on. 'What's with Jake is that he can't
get it up any more, and what's with Brenda is she thinks it's her fault for
having gotten middle-aged and fat, so she feels bad.' (Jake knew they were
all looking at him but he didn't look back at any of them.) 'Now since we
have our two new participants we'll make today a salad. For openers,
scanning pairs. Jake, Brenda, that means each of you looks another person
over and they do the same with you but no intimate physical contact. You
start with the eyes – the others'll show you. All right – Ivor, Winnie. . . .'

In due course Jake found himself standing near the window and facing
Martha, the one with the mother. Her eyes were fixed on him in an
unbroken stare. He stared back for quite a long time on the view that this
must be what was required but in the end got fed up with it and shifted
his gaze. Ed appeared at that very juncture and caught the tiny movement.

'No no no,' he said, and again he might have been feeling impatient or
sympathetic or anything else. 'Hold it at eye to eye until I give you the
word to break.'

It went on for a period that could have contained without substantial
cuts the whole of an evening's viewing from Batman to Closedown, or
strictly speaking that was how it seemed to Jake. Strange things happened
to his vision: at one stage Martha's face went two-dimensional, became a
rough disc floating against a background of dark clouds or water, at
another it receded a whole mile but grew in size proportionately so that
the space it occupied was unchanged. His mind could do nothing but
announce its distress to itself: silent recitation of Catullus or poems from
the Anthology was about as useful an idea as thinking about sex. When,
hardly looked for any longer, the word came to break it suggested at short
notice a breaking wave of relief, but as waves do this one quite soon
receded. He felt shaken up, uncoupled from the outside world. If Ed had
wanted to do that thoroughly but without resorting to shock tactics he had
succeeded to the full.

He had also, perhaps without meaning to, stated a major theme of the
Workshop's activities, namely that every single one of them without any
exception whatsoever lasted for very much longer than you would ever
have thought possible. The next stage was a first-rate case in point. It was
called free scanning, which meant in practice that you and your yoke-
fellow inspected each other's faces with a thoroughness that would have
made it possible to count the pores on them if required. Martha's was the
face of a woman of forty or so, neither pretty nor ugly. Subjecting it to
this kind of scrutiny meant that conventional details of general shape of
nose or mouth went unregarded; if Jake were to pass Martha in the street

the next day he would have been less not more likely to recognise her as a result of this experience.

The face business was not of course the end of it: Martha took and examined each of Jake's hands in turn, and he hers. Then she walked very slowly round him like an exalted tailor. He looked out of the window on to a patch of knee-high grass with things like discarded clothes-horses and oil-stoves showing here and there and said quietly,

'What does your mother – '

'No talking,' said Ed, 'there'll be plenty of time for talking in a little while.'

There was, though the bit about the little while turned out to be relative. At last Ed clapped his hands above his head and called on Chris to make the rounds.

'Make the rounds?' It came out high-pitched and querulous.

'Yeah, you know. Start with Winnie and end with Jake and Brenda.'

Chris was the one who didn't like the human race, young, pale and (happily) on the small side. He went and stood in front of Winnie, swaying backwards and forwards slightly in apparent thought. Then he got off the mark, telling her she was a bloody bitch and Christ he'd be shy if he was her and much more of the same. It was a full six minutes by Jake's watch before Chris moved on. At that rate it would be close to an hour before the rounds were finally made, and at *that* rate, not allowing for intervals, it would be close to ten hours before everybody had had or done his (or her) turn, but long before then one participant at least would have suffered irreversible brain-damage from rage and boredom. Chris's tirades were repetitive in the extreme, but of course it was the tune that mattered, not the words. By the time Chris had moved on again Jake had spotted a periodic element in that tune, a repeated decline from the expression of apparent fury to a mere ill-natured jeering. But was it jeering? More significant, was it fury? Would Ed know?

Jake's interest perked up when Chris turned his attention to Geoffrey, on the basis that even the unobservant couldn't fail to observe a few things about him that would be just right for a truculent harangue, if only his witty clothing, but there was nothing worth attention apart from an all-too-short passage of Joycean word-play about assholes towards the end. Geoffrey appeared dumb-founded at most of it, but then he would have found your visiting-card a pretty tough nut to crack. Kelly was next and Jake's interest perked back up for a different reason – what reason? Oh, just interest. She stood perfectly still with her arms folded and stared Chris in the face throughout his speech to her. The folded arms brought her bosom into prominence. It was good all right. There was something about her, perhaps starting with the clothes, that separated her from others of her age, made her the opposite of Miss Calvert, helped him to see that she was attractive. He went on looking at her after Chris had shifted to Lionel, had his eye caught and looked away. When he looked again, sidelong this time, she was giving Ivor one of the cautious bits of appraisal he had earlier noticed her sending him and Brenda. Kelly wanted to know what Ivor felt about what was taking place between Chris and Lionel. Ah.

Chris finished with Lionel and started on Ruth, who was the oldest person there and was sobbing within seconds. Jake wanted to stop it and went on wanting more and more. So did Brenda, he could see. Kelly he thought did, but wasn't sure. Nobody else showed the smallest sign. Rosenberg didn't look up from the journal he was reading; Ed was peering and squeezing his chin. Suddenly he looked at his watch and said in his usual tone.

'All right, cut it, Chris. Go to Jake.'

Chris did as he was told at once. He said nothing for much longer than he had said nothing to any of his previous victims, his small features working their way through a limited range of expressions of loathing.

'Who do you think you are, you old bastard?' he inquired finally. 'Who gave you the bloody right to be so fucking superior? You think I'm dirt, don't you? Bloody dirt. Don't you? Come on, don't you?'

Jake thought it was rather clever of Chris, considering Chris, to have worked that out but kept the view to himself. 'I haven't any particular – '

'No talk-back, Jake,' said Ed.

Without turning round Chris made a shushing gesture that told of ingratitude or preoccupation. 'Eh hevvn't ennair pahtierkyawlah ballocks. You know what you are, don't you? You want to know what you are, what you really are? You're just one big lump of shit.' After that he descended to personal abuse. So far from waning in vigour as before his displeasure mounted. Then he fell abruptly silent. When he went on it was in a tone he hadn't used before, one unmistakably (to Jake) indicating real anger and so reducing all his earlier behaviour to some kind of charade. 'If you don't take that look off your face right away.' he said slowly and quietly, 'I'm going to. . . .'

It helped Jake that he had once been quite a good tennis-player and was still pretty nimble for his age, also that he had noticed Chris glance over towards Ed for an instant; anyway, when the punch came he was almost ready for it, just managed to deflect it past his ear. Ed was there in no time and gave Chris a tremendous slap across the face so that he cried out and nearly fell. That was about when Jake saw what a good thing it was that Chris was undersized. He felt a sudden sharp twinge of total lack of pity for him.

'Bad boy,' said the facilitator blandly. 'Around here we don't play it that way, okay?'

'You didn't see the look on his face.' Chris was close to tears. 'He was looking at me as if he thought I was a lump of shit – you should have seen him, honestly.'

'Well, you called him one.' (This feat of memory, for Chris had used quite a number of other expressions, impressed Jake. He realised he hadn't seen Ed take a single note.) 'Maybe he does think you're a lump of shit. Maybe you *are* a lump of shit. Now get yourself together and go to Brenda.'

'Not going to. Not fair.' (Twenty-five if he's a day, thought Jake.)

'You are going to. In my Workshop people do as they're told.'

That was believable. Chris's resistance crumbled within ten seconds. In ten more he had gone to Brenda and rather perfunctorily set about calling her old, fat etc. She faced him with a look of open contempt; Jake's contempt had not been open, or so he believed.

The next ingredient of the salad was called Winnie in the cool seat. Each participant participated in making her feel better, more relaxed, more *wanted*. One by one they told her nice things and were allowed to stroke or hug her but not to enter the sexual area. Chris mildly surprised Jake by being no worse at this than anyone else, telling Winnie first that she was great and then that she was, you know, great. When it was Jake's turn he took her hands and said.

'The thing to remember is that a good half of the people you meet are shy too, it's just that they don't show it, or rather don't show it in front of you. There was a famous – '

'Hold it right there Jake,' said Ed. 'That's thought bullshit. You have to get away from reason and logic. No because or although or if. The only good conjunction is and.'

So Jake reproached himself for forgetting Rosenberg's warning and told Winnie a lot of things he didn't mean much because they didn't mean much and everybody else seemed satisfied. When she finally vacated the cool seat Ruth replaced her as the centre of attention, though Jake missed the official title of what she was doing or being. Not that that could have mattered: she told them in the simplest terms that she had nothing to live for and went on to explain just as simply the circumstances that had brought about this state of mind. She was seventy-one and her husband was dead and her son had been killed in an industrial accident and her daughter was in a home for the feeble-minded and she lived in one room and nobody came to see her and she couldn't afford to go out or to have television and she'd never taken to reading (Jake took this to mean she was illiterate or near enough). She wept frequently during this recital and so in varying degrees did all the other women and Lionel and Ivor. Jake found that this time he could turn his mind to Catullus and the Anthology. When Ruth had apparently got to the end Ed made her start again. This he did twice more. Then he put Ivor in the hot seat. Ivor gave an unannotated list of the things that frightened him, which besides the dark and being alone included underground railways and any other form of tunnel, lifts, buses and large buildings, and after that the others took it in turns to reprehend him as severely as they could for being cowardly, spineless, ridiculous and babyish. When Jake started on him he gave him as many furious Ernie-sized winks as he could before Ed, warned perhaps by something in Ivor's expression, moved round so that he could see Jake's. Ivor, who had looked pretty hangdog at the outset, was showing healthy signs of boredom before the end.

To limit the danger of cardiac arrest from indignation and incredulity Jake had made an agreement with himself not to look at his watch, but while Brenda was gamely trying to sound as if she despised Ivor he (Jake) looked out of the window and saw, not the Queen-Moon on her throne, but bright or brightish daylight. Soon after that Mr Shyster came in with a tray of food and Jake relaxed his rule: two minutes past one. Night must have come and gone unnoticed. A queue formed. It was soon established that Mr Shyster was supplying sardine or cheese sandwiches at 50p each Jesus Christ, cardboard cups of coffee at 25p each Jesus Christ, and a lot of whisky-vapour free. Jake and Brenda had one of each sort of sandwich each – she contriving to leave most of the bread – and agreed in due time that the sardine ones were better or less bad than the cheese ones because the nasty sardine still eluded modern science for the moment. But that agreement was not yet, for Ed accosted Jake, Ed with Rosenberg at his side, both chewing savagely as if they were a couple of those Third-Worlders you read about who earn $15 a year.

'Well, Jake, what do you think of our work so far?'

'I think it's interesting.'

'Interesting. I do like that word, don't you, Frank? It's a great word. Yes, Jake, your hostility was very evident. That happens.'

After a stage of wondering who Ed thought Rosenberg was Jake remembered that poxing stuff about Proinsias/Francis and was able to answer fairly normally.

'What happens?'

'Hostility. Happens a lot. Don't worry about it.'

'I'm not,' said Jake. It was all that training with Miss Calvert and some of his other pupils, all that not going for them with the sitting-room poker at each new display of serene apathy, which restrained him now, he would have alleged, from jumping feet first at Ed's face.

'Well anyway don't worry about it. Now I expect you've got a few questions you'd like to ask, Jake.'

'Yes, I have, but I'm not sure this is the right time and place.'

'It is. I say it is.'

'Very well. Except right at the end that fellow Chris didn't seem to me to be really . . . cross at all.'

'Hey, he got that, Frank, how about that? Very good, Jake, you're coming on. Chris is just frightened. He's small and he's not a raving beauty and he's afraid he doesn't count, so he gets his blow in first. The more I make him act aggressive the more he sees he doesn't feel it. I'm just showing him to himself. Oh and he wasn't really what you called cross at the end either. What it was, Jake, you got him a little annoyed and he tried harder, which was useful.'

All this, at any rate on immediate hearing, sounded so appallingly reasonable that when Jake spoke next it was with something less than the perfect self-possession he had been trying for. 'I suppose you were showing Ruth to herself too.'

'That's right. This is only the third time she's been along and it's going to be pretty painful for everybody for a while yet, but they're a nice gang and they'll take it. You see, Ruth is all eaten up with self-pity – okay, she has plenty to be unhappy about, though not everything she says is true, right Frank?'

'That's quite correct. People in the same house visit her now and then and Lionel has called on two occasions. The second time he found she'd been invited in to watch her landlady's TV.'

'Which isn't a hell of a lot, but . . . She needs to be shaken up and made to do things, Jake, go out and find friends, it's possible, there's plenty going on in a neighbourhood you don't have to pay for, nothing wrong with her physically, she rides free on the buses – and so on. I'm going to wait until everybody knows her story by heart and then put her in the hot seat and have the group tell her she bores the balls off them. And if you're worried about Ivor, Jake, he's ashamed of his fears, thinks he ought to face up to them like a man, pull himself together. Which is impossible. You don't know how his psychiatrist had to work on him to come here at all. He has to learn he has a troublesome but not very serious sickness which he acquired through no fault of his and which can be cured, and he can't learn that until he sees how fucking stupid it is to call him a coward or whatever. Which we just made some progress in showing him.'

Ed stopped speaking abruptly, thus exploiting his advantage over Jake, who was thoroughly taken down by his further discovery that the facilitator at least seemed to want to facilitate mental health rather than bloodshed and raving lunacy, much too thoroughly to set about questioning on the spot the practicality or wisdom of the measures taken and proposed. Trying for a loftily non-committal tone, he said, 'Thank you very much for the various explanations,' but it came out a bit lame.

'Any time, Jake.'

16   At Mr Shyster's (continued)

The afternoon session began with Lionel's round table. Ed stage-managed or rather produced it more closely than any of the morning's events, calling on Lionel himself to answer questions like whether or how far he thought stealing was wrong and one or other of the rest to comment positively (bear-oil him) or negatively (crap on him). The emotional temperature again was lower than before but without any more sense being talked as a result. Several comparatively interesting things did emerge in passing, however: that Lionel was head of a small building firm, for instance, that he was forty-three years old, that he lived with his mother, of whom he was fond, that he stole things he liked the look of, that sometimes he went weeks without stealing so much as a paperclip and then spent a couple of days stealing away like billy-ho – things like that. Jake also noticed a couple of inconsistencies in Lionel's account of himself and more than a couple of hesitations when somebody pressed him for details of when and where and the like. Nothing came up to challenge the surmise that Lionel had never contemplated theft for a moment and was probably an inactive queer in search of a like-minded companion, having picked on kleptomania for his cover as simple and unobnoxious. In that case what happened to Ed's renown as a sham-detector?

The round table was dismantled and Geoffrey's self-draining announced. Jake's curiosity flared up at once, nor did it ever burn low during what followed. Geoffrey began with some information new to Jake, and perhaps to all the others too, namely that he had been educated at home because of his elderly father's adherence to the doctrines of Charles Bradlaugh. Asked to explain the rationale of this he disappointed Jake slightly and surprised him a lot by not stating that Bradlaugh had been, say, a pioneer of vegetarianism, and then again by not classing as a freethinker an opponent of the corporate state. The home educator, by some associated twist of paternal whim, had been not a tutor but a governess (who must have taught him everything he 'knew' from T. S. Eliot's Victorian-thespian status onwards and downwards – wrong, as it was to turn out). There followed a passage in praise of women so intense, categorical and of course long that a confession of hyperactive homosexuality seemed almost boringly inevitable. Wrong straight away, or straight away by the standards of the occasion: women had one defect – they could be loved, they were there for men to love them, but they couldn't be heroes. Geoffrey gave one of his frowns at this point as some verbal or other nuance swam towards his ken and away again. Hero-worship, he now affirmed, was an integral part of any lad's growing-up but it should be worked out or through or off at the normal time and place: school. He hadn't been able to start his hero-worship till he got to Cambridge and that had been too late, in the sense that once acquired the habit had proved impossible to shake off – none of this had been clear to him at the time and for long after and he had only recently identified its consequences.

Where on earth Geoffrey's narrative would lead was quite obscure – perhaps it would bend back to buggery after all – but it was making a bit of a kind of sense in itself, at any rate enough, it might have been supposed, for Ed to have denounced it as thought bullshit; no, he held his peace and massaged the side of his neck. What, Geoffrey went on to ask, had those heroes of his in common? Strong individuality. They were unlike the mass of mankind, and also one another, in many of their opinions, their interests, their likes and dislikes, even their tastes in food and drink. A would wish the United Kingdom to apply for admission one day to the United States, B spend his week-ends studying the behaviour of social insects, C endlessly re-read *Pilgrim's Progress*, D refuse all dealings with Roman Catholics on principle, E eat only fish and fruit and F mix alcoholic cordial of cloves with his Scotch. With a humility that might have disarmed some people Geoffrey admitted he hadn't the talents to belong to the A – F class but was so vain that he wanted to seem to belong to it. He must therefore light upon some views and practices that were unusual without being too outlandish and also hadn't been pre-empted by the A – Fs. No easy task, this, and one complicated by the fact that, as he soon found, he held no views and neither practised nor hankered after practising any practices that weren't conventional to the point of banality. To create the right sort from scratch has been tough, too (for him at any rate), so he had left things to chance and kept his eyes and ears open. Almost at once – this must have been while he was still at Cambridge, or soon after – Fate had smiled on him. He had accidentally barged into a nurse in a crowded street and knocked a bag of groceries out from under her arm and she had called him a clumsy oaf. At a stroke he was in possession of a whole network of A – F-type material that had extended itself over the years from simple antagonism towards nurses and the mention or portrayal of them in print or on screen to points of view about the National Health Service, pay increases, equal opportunities, the right of those operating essential services to strike and even immigration. His biggest stroke of luck, and one of the happiest passages of his life, had come a year or two before with the success in London of a film representing unfavourably a nurse in a mental hospital;

he had felt a sense of vindication. So he had become a sort of G, the chap with the terrific thing about nurses.

(The inverted pyramid of piss exposed, confirmed, systematised! For Brenda's benefit Jake worked like a black at dissembling his fascination and glee, hoped he had started to in time, went on listening just as closely. There must be more where that came from. Perhaps there was to be a definitive pronouncement on the Hollands gin/KLM/cream cakes question.)

No such luck, though Geoffrey did let fall that his supposed admiration for the works of Dvořák, always likely to be proclaimed when music, the nineteenth century or Hungarians (*sic*) came up, rested on nothing more substantial than a pubescent crush on an American film actress of that surname. Well, that was the end, he implied, of Part I. In Part II he talked about his ignorance, a subject that could have kept them there all night and well into the next day, but he was commendably brief. About the time of his setting out to acquire simulated individuality it had dawned on him that the A – Fs, and plenty of others too, were always referring to things – places, works of art, important events – and men and women living and dead, especially though not by a big margin dead, that he'd never heard of. So he had started to read through the encyclopedia, not every word or every article but essential subjects like . . . history – English history. When after some years he was about a third of the way through he had experienced another dawn: to put it more succinctly than he did, he still knew very, very little more about Africa and the battle of Bosworth and Charlemagne and *Dombey and Son* than he did about Xenophanes, Yaksas and Zoutpansberg (and had stopped reading forthwith). Until quite recently he had put this unalleviated uninformedness down to a bad memory. That brought him to Part III.

One evening he had been extolling Dvořák in the musical context when a woman had asked him, to all appearance quite innocently, if he didn't think that the something sharp minor melody in the middle of the something movement of the, er, the New World Symphony was as fine in its way as the famous tune played by the something in the first section and that only the . . . the syncopations and the something elses in it, which made it hard for the uninitiated to sing, had stopped it being as famous. He had said quickly (and Jake could imagine with what stiffness) that in such matters he always followed the popular view and the subject had dropped. But afterwards he had started thinking and had realised that, although the existence of the New World Symphony and Dvořák's authorship of it were as firmly settled in his mind as the establishment of the principle of evolution by (steady) Darwin, he knew nothing about it, of how it might differ from its composer's old-world symphonies if any, of how the least part of it went, of how many decades had gone by since he had last heard it assuming he ever had. How then had work and musician come to hold their curious importance to him? For the first time since God knew when the lovely Ann Dvorak had returned to his mind and it was in that moment (he must have read a book or two of a sort at some point) that he understood how he had acquired what he had thitherto thought of as his opinions. All these disappeared as such instantly and reverted to what they had always been: things he said so as to seem to be someone.

'But I wasn't anyone and I'm not anyone.' said Geoffrey. 'I don't just mean I'm not important, though I'm certainly not that. I'm completely cut off. Oh I don't mean in a personal sort of way – I've got a wife whom I adore and we get on very well and I have some very nice friends.' He looked affectionately at Brenda and Jake. 'But they're all like just sort of comforts, marvellous to have around but I don't want to know anything more about them that I do already. They don't interest me. Nothing ever has – I've never wanted to know anything at all. That's why I couldn't remember what I read in the encyclopedia: I had no reason to and I wasn't concerned with knowing for the sake of knowing. It was different with my governess and exams and so on. But now I've got nothing to think about and I realise it, nothing except myself and that's very dull. There's nothing *in* me. I'm contemplating my own navel – I remember reading that or being told it, I suppose everybody has to remember some things or we couldn't read at all or even speak or function in any way – and my navel's a pretty boring subject.'

That seemed to be all for now. From the familiar lively manner of his in which he had talked of his dealings with nurses and Dvořák, a manner quite reconcilable with a keen curiosity about himself and the workings of his own mind, Geoffrey had in the last minute or so fallen with some abruptness into a hollow, lugubrious mode of speaking that matched the content of what he said. This – the tune, not the words – recaptured the attention of his audience which, apart from Jake, Brenda and Kelly, and in a different way Ed and Rosenburg, had stopped listening at about the Bradlaugh stage. Even Chris might well have noticed the change. There was a pause, during which facilitator and psychologist conferred inaudibly; then Geoffrey was thanked for his efforts rather as if he had just failed an audition by a small but distinct margin. Poor old bugger, Jake thought to himself, at least you're a cut above Miss Calvert and that lot. To them, the failure of things like knowledge to win their interest constituted a grave if not fatal defect in the thing itself.

Martha's one-to-one followed. She was herself and you were her mother and there were slanging-matches which she always won. Jake did his best when it came round to him but he was a bit distracted by wondering, and also beginning to nourish a man's-hand-size-cloud-type suspicion of, what the good Ed might have in store for him. He also wondered, not so hard but still quite a bit, what would be required of the person whose turn must intervene between Martha's and his – Kelly.

Time, plenty of it, came to the rescue here: Kelly was to engage in self-expression. In Jake's vocabulary this was a vague term applied to activities like swearing and children's art but in the present context it evidently meant something more specific. The girl at once left her chair, sat down on one of the more affluent patches of carpet and clasped her knees.

'All right, Kelly.' The note of coaxing in Ed's voice was intensified. 'Your assignment is to give us yourself. You gave us a whole lot last time but now you're going to try to give us all of it, the piece, Kelly. Whenever you're ready.'

After half a minute of inert silence she uttered the first of a great number of loud howling noises. If this was self-expression it was hard to name the part of the self being expressed, its fear, its rage, its grief, its pain, its hatred or its disappointment or some other thing. Jake had never heard the cries of a maniac, far less those of a damned soul, but he thought there might be some common ground in both cases. The girl thrashed about on the floor, arching her backbone to a degree a trained gymnast might have envied and thrusting her trunk forwards and down between her parted thighs. The movements of her head were so rapid that it was hard to catch anything interpretable in her face, though there was a moment at which he saw clearly what he had seen only once before in his life, when the small child of a colleague had fallen in a Summertown garden and cut its knee: a tear spurting from a human eye. Next to him Brenda shivered or shuddered and reached out and took his hand.

At last the howls were reduced to moans and then to long gasping breaths; Kelly wiped her cheeks with her fingers and Ed helped her to her feet and told her that maybe that wasn't quite all of it but it was damn near and congratulations. Jake was bracing himself for the fray when Mr Shyster, fetched as it now seemed by means of a bell-push beside the disfigured fireplace, came in with more refreshments. This time there were cups of tea at the everything-must-go price of 20p and biscuits Jake didn't bother with. He saw that Geoffrey was unattended and crossed over to him.

'I thought that took some doing, what you did.'

'Took some. . . . Oh. Oh, it wasn't all that difficult. Did you think it went down all right?'

'Who with?'

'Ed's in a funny mood, he didn't seem at all impressed, not even with the last bit, and that really was rather difficult, I was really trying then.'

'To express emotion, you mean.'

'But then he said hardly anything to Lionel either. It's probably just his mood. He's only human like the rest of us, after all.'

'Geoffrey, there's just one thing that – '

'Yes'

'Er, well I was just going to say there was one thing that sort of puzzled me a bit in what you said – which was all absolutely fascinating, I don't mean that. It was about . . . you not going to school because of your father's ideas, which I quite. . . .'

'No no, my father was *against* my going to school, any sort of school.

It would have been contrary to his principles for me to be taught scripture
and go to chapel. I thought I'd explained all that.'

'Oh I think I understood. But what I was going to ask you, I took you
to mean you wished your father had let you go to school, because if you
had, you'd have been able to get your hero-worshipping done while you
were still there. Surely if you had, you'd have seen through the whole thing
that much sooner and realised that much sooner, which is quite a long
time, that you only got your opinions and all that from imitating the way
your hero-worship chaps went on. Which wouldn't have been at all a good
thing, would it, because you'd have seen you were whatever you said,
nobody in particular, years, decades before you did in fact. In reality. As
it happened.'

'Jake – everything you advance as an argument is quite true,' said Geoffrey weightily. 'But with respect you seem to be missing the point. It was
because I didn't go to school that I *failed* to meet all those people. If I *had*
gone to school I'd have met them *sooner*.'

'And realised you were imitating them sooner, that was my whole – '

'No no, if you go over it in your mind you'll see I'm right.'

What Jake did see was that he had fallen into his old error, still quite
common with him even when dealing with pupils, of supposing that because
somebody used things like verbs and conjunctions he (or she) could follow
what others said. Changing tack he said, and meant it, 'Amazing how you
managed to get that much insight into yourself and not be afraid to follow
it up.'

'How do you mean?'

'Realising how you'd come by all your views and that you've got no
thoughts of your own. It took courage to face that.'

'Oh well, there we are.' Geoffrey had been frowning but now his features
relaxed and he smiled cheerfully. 'I haven't the faintest idea what you're
talking about. Just not my day.'

'How's Allie?' asked Jake to cover his renewed wonderment.

'Allie?'

'Yes. How is she?'

'She's all right. Why?'

'Nothing, pure interest.'

'She's never been better as long as I've known her. Why shouldn't she
be?'

'No reason. If you'll excuse me I must just have a word with Brenda,'
said Jake, who at that stage would have welcomed a word with Ernie, Mrs
Sharp, anybody at all. But he didn't get his word because Ed declared it
was time to be getting on, nor was the least disagreement voiced. After the
tea-things had been collected and removed, he said,

'All right, Jake, strip.'

An expected or, as in this case, not really unexpected piece of nastiness
is not thereby rendered less nasty; so at least it seemed to Jake at the time.

Another point that struck him with almost equal force at about the same moment was that a piece of nastiness that has been preceded over a period by several other roughly comparable pieces of nastiness is not thereby rendered less nasty either. He said he wouldn't (do as he was told) and was disconcerted to hear how petulant and fatuous it seemed to sound.

'Wasn't I just telling you about yourself suffering from sexual guilt and shame?' This of course was Rosenberg, his little nose lifted in triumph.

'It isn't that, it's just embarrassment. For a . . . with a female with sex in mind, that's a different matter.'

'Why so? You may have forgotten, but you once gave me an assurance that you had no objection to exposing your genitals in public.

Imprecations suggested themselves in such profusion and variety that Jake was silent quite long enough for Ed to say in his calmest tone.

'Cut the bullshit. Jake, I said take off your clothes. So take off your fucking clothes.'

He caught Brenda's eye, which stated with the utmost clarity of diction available to eyes that it would be measurably better for him if he complied with the facilitator's request. Everyone else was clearly expecting it too. So in the end he complied, marvelling a certain amount that he had had the unconscious predictive power or something to make that a clean-underclothes day. Well there he was, grey-and-white chest hair, elliptic areolas round the nipples, some broken veins on the chest, a perceptible if less than gross pot-belly, pimple-scars on the thighs, yellow toenails and all, not forgetting those parts that had once so interested him and from time to time others. For a moment it didn't feel too bad, and then it felt too bad.

Acting on Ed's orders, the nine other participants came up to him successively and stroked or squeezed various parts of him though avoiding the genital area oh I say how frightfully decent; in practice his shoulders and upper arms got most attention. While they were doing that they were supposed to tell him things like he was all right. Kelly looked and sounded sorry for him, Chris, whom he had been looking forward to least, told him that he was all right and then that he was definitely all right, and Brenda seemed pleased with him, but he didn't take much notice of any of them because he was concentrating so hard on stopping himself from trembling all over. That was a help in a way. When they had all finished and he got dressed what struck him was how much less better he felt now he had got dressed than he had expected. He had some difficulty in giving his full attention to Brenda when, complying with Ed's request to conduct a self-draining (so you could have two of the same sort of thing in the salad), talked for twenty-five minutes about how unattractive and stupid and incompetent and ignorant and unattractive and useless and silly and unattractive she felt all the time. But he got the main drift.

17 Exposing Ed

When the Workshop broke up at half-past six Brenda asked Geoffrey if he
would like to come with her and Jake for a cup of tea and a drink. He
understood her fully and at once and thanked her but said he had to be
off to his own home to change and take Alcestis to a theatre. However he
showed no disposition to be off in a hurry, hanging about in the room
they had spent so long in and near the front door (at a spot from which
another room was to be seen with only a wicker-covered carboy and a
ping-pong table in it) and asking the other two if they didn't think that
one or another part of the proceedings had been particularly good and
saying he thought it had been. This minor delay made them the last to
leave, just behind Rosenberg and Ed, who were exchanging farewells in
the 'porch'. On their conclusion Rosenberg startled Jake by wheeling away
the child's bicycle that had been parked there, mounting it at the kerb and
riding off on it – startled him till he saw that of course a child's bicycle
and a Rosenberg's bicycle would be indistinguishable for practical purposes.
And any bicycle would be quite effective in today's traffic and was much
cheaper than a car, especially one modified for a two-foot-high driver.

Geoffrey promised to be in touch soon and went, walking with his
characteristic head-down gait – because he doesn't want to see anything,
thought Jake. He said to Brenda.

'I'd give a few bob to know what he's changing into.'

'What? A suit, I imagine. Why?'

'He's got half a suit on already. For the theatre I should think he'd go
for, er . . . a safari jacket with a frilled shirt and velvet bow-tie, jeans, tartan
socks. . . .'

'What are you talking about?'

'Well you must admit he does dress extraordinarily.'

'Honestly, just because he doesn't dress like anybody else. . . .'

'You don't overstate the case. No, it's more than that. It's one of his
character-trait-substitutes like pretending to hate nurses and like Dvořák.
No . . . it's not that either, if that was what he was after it would be much
easier and less ridiculous if he just always wore white or bright red or had
a collection of outlandish ties, say. Ah, you were right after all, not dress

like *anybody* else. Perverseness! An instinct, a compulsion to get things wrong. That's why. . . .' Jake's voice tailed off; he understood now about Geoffrey's magpies, Lake Vancouver and Florence Nightingale throwing herself under the King's horse at the Grand National, results of an endless series of drawn battles between memory and the will to err, but as he felt at the moment he couldn't face explaining all that from the start. He went on fast instead, 'That's why he's such a pest to talk to, always on the look-out for chances of getting at cross-purposes with you. In fact there was the most amazing – '

'Why are you so against him?'

'Darling I'm not *against* him, I'm just interested in him. You never know, we might even be able to help him.' (It was true enough that Jake didn't consider himself to be more against Geoffrey than any reasonable man ought to be and was indeed interested in him, but the mention of helping him was pretty pure hypocrisy.) 'You saw I was talking to him in that tea-break? Well, I congratulated him on sort of seeing through himself – that's what he said he'd done if you remember, there was nothing in him, he said. Anyway, he said he couldn't make out what I was driving at. That really staggered me, because I thought, when he said that all his views and everything were just to make him seem interesting, which struck me as absolutely dead right, perhaps it was sheer chance he got it right, he didn't really mean it, all he was doing was saying another thing that was supposed to make him seem interesting.'

'Bit of a coincidence, wouldn't that be, or have I got it wrong? I expect I have. *I* just thought he was terrifically brave.'

'Perhaps he was. I told him I thought so, which can't do any harm, I suppose, though he didn't seem to take it in much.'

They were nearly home now, hurrying through the rain that had begun to fall. Two car-loads of Asians dawdled past. Brenda said hesitantly,

'What did you think of the other stuff, the other people?'

'Oh I really don't know, don't ask me yet. I'm what Ed would no doubt call too close to it.'

'All right. But you were good. Can't have been much fun.'

'Thank you darling.'

As soon as they were indoors Brenda slipped out to the kitchen and put the kettle on; Jake followed.

'You can't have tea at this time,' he told her, 'it's a quarter to seven.'

'Oh can't I, you just watch me. It's either that or gin and it had better not be gin. Not for a bit anyway.'

'What I could really do with is a cigarette.'

She gave him a glance of sympathy but said nothing. After a moment he picked up her discarded coat and head-scarf and put them with his own hat and coat in the hall cupboard, which had a floral china door-knob on it. An aeroplane went slowly by, or rather not slowly at all but staying in earshot for about three-quarters of an hour. With greater intensity than ever before he wished he still had his 'libido', because if he had he and Brenda would be on their way upstairs now to make love. Of course they would; nothing like the Workshop had ever come their way before but of course they would. The thing about you and your wife making love was that it made things all right, not often for ever but always for a time and always for longer than the actual love-making. In that it was unique: adultery could make life more interesting but it couldn't make things all right in a month of Sundays. And as for booze you must be joking – as well expect a fairly humane beating-up to do the job.

He went back into the kitchen where Brenda was spooning the Jackson's Earl Grey, one of their few indulgences, into the teapot, which was floral too.

'Look at me not making buttered toast,' she said.

'I do so, and I admire.'

'Twelve pounds I've lost in just three weeks. The Guzzlers say that's as fast as it's safe to go.'

'I'm sure they're right.'

The door-bell chimed. Jake always wished it wouldn't do that but would ring or be a buzzer instead; the trouble was it counted as being outside the house, which was his province, and he couldn't be bothered so it went on chiming. Anyway, when he opened the door he found Kelly was there, though she wasn't for long; she furled her umbrella and stepped across the threshold so promptly and confidently that he at once assumed that Brenda had invited her during one of the breaks at Mr Shyster's and for some odd reason neglected to mention it. Standing now by the cheval-glass the girl nodded and smiled inquiringly at him.

'We're in the kitchen,' he said; 'Brenda's just making a cup of tea.'

'Oh marvellous. Is it this way?'

Brenda had entered upon the very act of tea-making. The look she gave reversed Jake's understanding as fast as it had formed: the appearance of Kelly was a surprise to her, and not a particularly welcome one either. If the second half of this was noted it wasn't reacted to: Kelly walked over to the sink and stood her umbrella up in it to drain, talking eagerly the while.

'It's so kind of you both to let me just barge in on you like this, I hope you don't mind too much. You may be wondering how I found you, well I simply followed you from that frightful house. At a respectful distance, so I wasn't quite sure which gate you went in at but I got it on the second try. It's the most awful cheek on my part but I did so want to have a chat with you both.'

'What about?' asked Brenda in a colourless tone.

Kelly seemed to find this an unexpected question. 'That ghastly session and the incredible things that happened and that criminal man Ed.' When neither Richardson responded immediately she hurried on, 'Of course if you're busy or anything I quite understand, I'll take myself off in a flash, you've really only to say the word.'

Something like sixty-three and a half percent of this last bit was directed at Jake, who didn't say the word. What he did say (and when taken up later on the point by Brenda said truthfully that when he said it disinclination to chuck someone, anyone out with no decent excuse in sight came first among whatever motives he might have had) was, 'No no, we're not doing anything special, stay and have a cup of tea with us.'

'Oh thank you, you are nice. You see, the reason I've come to you two like this is there's really nobody else I can talk to. The others are all very sweet people, even poor little Chris, his bark's worse than his bite, but they're not what you'd call intellectual giants, well, Ivor's no fool and Martha's quite sensible except about her mother, but you can't sort of *talk* to them, so up till now I've had to work on my own.'

'Work at what?' asked Brenda as before.

'It may sound silly to you both but I want to expose Ed. Oh not so much Ed personally but the whole Workshop bit. So I, what do you call it, I infiltrated this one. Jolly easy it was too. I just went to my GP, who's a silly little man, and I spun him a yarn about not being able to keep a job or settle to anything and having rows with my parents, and he passed me on to that even sillier little man Rosenberg who passed by on to Ed, and there I was, simple as that. I've been going to these get-togethers for six weeks now. Oh I say what a beautiful room, it must have taken you absolute years to get it like this, Brenda, I do congratulate you.'

The room in question was naturally the sitting-room into which, Jake carrying the tea-tray, the three had now moved. General praises were followed by plenty of particular ones lavished on glass paperweight, trailing plant, some sort of candlestick, some sort of miniature and like lumber. It all went down well enough with Brenda, though it fell some way short of winning her over. Jake put up with it as long as he could before moving back towards a matter that had started to interest him, not a lot, but more than any bleeding paperweight or miniature was going to.

'This business of exposing the Workshop,' he said in a slender interval between such articles. 'You mean publicly? In court, for instance?'

Brenda, as she was apt to whenever he tried to take a conversation back to an earlier point, gave a look attributing to him either slowness on the uptake of pedantry; for her, things must run on, not back, unless of course Alcestis had a 'story' to finish. But Kelly turned eager again at once and he was touched with surprise and gratitude as the variegated awfulness and fatuity of the day sank for the moment out of sight.

'Well yes,' she said. 'Well, I don't know, I haven't found out enough yet, but how it began, a friend of mine at work went to another Workshop round Sloane Square, and it was absolutely appalling she told me, people beaten up and, you know, group sex and everything, so she stopped going. Then I heard from someone else about Ed, don't repeat this either of you because it may not be true, but this person said that after one of Ed's sessions a chap had gone straight home and killed himself with sleeping-pills. So I thought somebody had better look into it, so I joined as I said and, well, you've both just seen for yourselves.'

'Seen what?' asked Brenda.

'Well, him, Ed, encouraging Chris to be aggressive when what he needs is a damn good smack-bottom and being told not to be so boring, and poor Ruth, you're not going to tell me being made to do all that crying does any good, *made* to do it, four times over, and Lionel, after this afternoon the only thing he can be is more confused than when he started. And Ivor ought to stick to proper treatment and not. . . . And making Jake strip,' – straight to Brenda in a relaxed informal interested conversational tone – 'just to humiliate him. He did the same thing to Chris two weeks ago after he'd ticked Ed off without being told to. I noticed you talking to him when we stopped for lunch, Jake – how did you hit off with him?'

'He said it was obvious I was hostile.'

'Exactly. Getting back at you. But he doesn't really need that, even, something to set him off. It's just power, hurting and embarrassing and generally abusing everybody and all in the name of therapy and no one to stand in your way.'

Jake offered more tea and was accepted. 'I think in fairness I ought to remind you of what Rosenberg said to me when I resisted. About . . . shame and guilt. You could say there was a connection.'

'In this business everything's connected with everything else. I forgot why it was supposed to be good for Chris to strip but I could soon run up an explanation, couldn't you, either of you?'

'Another thing it might interest you to know is that during our chat in the lunch-break he told me his plan for Ruth. What she needs is a shake-up, you see, so when the time comes she'll be put in the hot seat and told what a bloody bore she is. A great help to be told that when you're old and lonely and frightened.'

'The swine. Anyway, thanks for telling me. One more bit of information.'

'He can be very plausible, though. He had me thinking it might be a good idea, and the same with Chris and Ivor.'

'Exactly.'

They looked at each other in silence for a moment, Jake on the corner of the velvet-covered sofa and Kelly sitting animatedly forward on what had used to be called a pouf or pouffe but obviously couldn't be these days; she reminded him for an instant of someone he had recently met, he had no idea who. Brenda had been standing by a carved plant-table near the window; now, announcing by her move that she would join the conversation for a strictly limited period and purpose, she perched on the arm of the chair in which she normally watched TV or read. Her voice was rather livelier than before when she said,

'Er . . .' – leaving an empty space where Kelly's name would have fitted – 'do you mind if I ask you a question?'

'No, Brenda, of course not.'

'You say you, what was it, you infiltrated the Workshop so as to show it up, so that means you faked being somebody who needed therapy, psychotherapy.'

'Yes, I went to quite a lot of trouble actually, but I needn't have bothered, it was as easy as pie, as I said.'

'So when Ed asked you to do whatever it was and you cried and writhed about and so on, you were faking that too.'

'Oh absolutely.'

'But you really were crying, real tears, I saw them. And you still look slightly weepy, as if you've been crying.'

'Do I? Oh yes, they were real tears all right, but I was faking them at the same time. What I mean is, it was a performance that included crying. I can cry at will, always have been able to. My dad says I get it from him, he's in the theatre, he says it's all a matter of being self-centred enough. I studied acting for a year until I realised I couldn't stand the people.'

'I see,' said Brenda. 'How can we help you?'

'Well really just knowing I've got the two of you on my side is a big help in itself. And you can both keep your ears open for anything you may hear, from Rosenberg and so on, and if I can't make it one Saturday I'll need someone to watch Ed for me. That sort of thing.'

'And when you've got enough information you'll decide whether you're going to sue him or not.'

'I might sue him or I might write about him in a newspaper.'

'What would you sue him for?'

'Well, I'm no legal expert, I'd have to find out about that but I'd have thought one could get him for fraud. After all he *is* a fraud isn't he?'

Brenda said nothing to that. Jake hesitated before he came in.

'An intellectual fraud certainly. All this stuff about getting away from logic and reason which he isn't even consistent about. And *of course* when a crowd of people tell you on instruction that you're nice you're not going to feel in the least less shy when you meet a crowd of other people you've never seen before. And whatever any of them may have got off their chests will all be back on their chests by now. *And* he makes a hundred and fifty quid a time out of us and God knows how many other lots he runs. But he hasn't got a contract with me, he hasn't even said he might be able to help me. So I don't really see quite how we. . . .'

'Neither of you know the first thing about it so I think it'd be better if you shut up and gave him a chance.' Brenda spoke in a livelier style than ever. 'You say you've been six times and today was our first, it seems to me perfectly ridiculous to expect any results for several months, Dr Rosenberg said we shouldn't. And there are always rumours about these sort of things which I don't think should be passed on. And I don't care what rot anybody talks if they make me feel better and I dare say you won't believe me or think it matters but I felt really better after saying my piece even if it didn't last very long.'

She got up from her chair-arm and not very quietly began putting the tea-things together. The speed with which Kelly delivered thanks and good-byes, fetched her umbrella from the kitchen, made for the door and vanished, all without appearance of hurry, impressed Jake. In the passage he had to step lively to avoid being run down by Brenda with the tea-tray before her and no eye for him.

'What's the matter?' he called after her.

'Nothing.'

'Oh Christ.'

Again he followed her out to the kitchen, where she dropped the tray on to the draining-board from a height of several inches and turned round with the speed of a wide-awake sentry. Then she slowed down.

'I suppose it's not your fault.'

'Oh bloody good, what's not?'

'What do you think she wanted? Would you like another cup?'

'Yes I would, thank you. What do you mean? To get us on her side – I don't know how serious that was. Or just to have a chat.'

'To get the pair of us, both of us, the two of us, the couple of us on her side, you mean. She overdid it there. No, it was you she was after.'

'After?'

'Some girls like old men. I'm not being nasty, you're not an old man to me but you obviously are to her. She could see you thought the Workshop was a joke at best and didn't like Ed, oh don't be ridiculous, anybody could have in five minutes, so she cooked up this story about exposing him as a fraud and wanting our help. Sod that.'

'Fancy me when she'd seen me starkers? Thanks.' They were for his fresh tea.

'That probably gave her the idea. No really darling, I should say you're pretty good for your age-group. What?'

Jake was shaking his head. 'Just. . . . You see I was thinking the other day, before this business came along, girls, women would look me over a bit, I don't mean send me an invitation but at least look *at* me. Now they don't. Literally. Well they do when they have to, when I'm talking to them, pupils and so on, but only the minimum. Obviously the normal man sends out little signals all the time, not lecherous glares, just saying he's not against the idea. So I must be sending out signals saying I am against it, and they pick them up, without realising it of course. So if you're right, why hasn't Kelly?'

'Because she's a howling neurotic with all her wires crossed. Do you honestly believe what she did back there was faked by as much as one per cent? Ed said she couldn't run her life.'

'Mm. But wouldn't she have held back a bit if she was planning to get us to believe she was faking?'

'She got carried away, or she reckoned we'd take her word for it. Or she just forgot.'

'Mm. She's so bright. Seeing that in Ed's world everything's connected with – '

'Neurotics very often are bright – Dr Rosenberg said. By the way, what happened to you being too close to it to discuss it, the Workshop? You were discussing it pretty openly with her just now.'

'I know, but that was her, she was the one who brought it up, for Christ's sake.'

'You still needn't have. Do you fancy her?'

'Darling, have I got to tell you again I don't fancy anybody?'

'Funny you brought up signals, anyway I just thought the ones she was sending you, because she was even though she was trying not to in front of me and thought she wasn't, I thought you might have picked them up and that would sort of take you back. I wouldn't mind. She'd be a dangerous girl to get involved with but that would be up to you. What I mean is you wouldn't have me to worry about. However this business ends up neither of us are going to have that kind of thing coming along much more in our lives. And if you did get interested in her it might be a way of you getting interested in me again.'

Jake put down his cup, went across the kitchen and embraced her, mouth against neck.

18   Eve's Thing

'So that's life as lived by me at this moment in time,' said Eve Greenstreet. 'No worse than that of many under late capitalism, I'm sure. Not very onerous tasks in the Secretary's office, bun-fights in Rawlinson Road attended by ladies who wear hats indoors, actually I can't remember when I last went to a bun-fight in Rawlinson Road or anywhere else but it's that *kind* of thing and in point of actual fact the percentage of ladies wearing hats indoors will probably be down to single figures by the end of the year, like inflation, or rather not like inflation, and, said she still miraculously keeping her balls in the air, being married to Syd.'

'Syd?' said Jake with a grin. 'I thought he was called – '

'Oh, he has a name for formal occasions and when I'm putting him in his place but in a non-variform-conditions situation he's Syd. Can it be that the fact has failed to penetrate you? After Sydney Greenstreet as the extremely wicked and extremely fat man in the star-studded cast of famed movie classic *The Maltese Falcon*. You remember. Upon my soul sir you are a character. Said to one-time screen idol Bogie-bogie. I'm sorry but I just can't resist calling him that. Shiddown, shweethat, and shtart shingin. That's enough. End of nostalgia bit. Syd, my Syd that is, what is Syd? Well to begin with of course he's Syd. Then he's a bank manager, no connection with the university except as customers, nothing queer about our Syd. And when you're looking at him you're looking at a bank manager. But hey there Jacob old boy, you have already received notification of this phenomenon among others. We had you and your charming wife come for dinner at our delightful Headington home one time shortly after our marriage.'

'That's right, of course.' He had completely forgotten and didn't remember anything about it now.

'Well, as I say, when you look at Syd you see a bank manager. Unless that is you happen to have cultivated one of the strange powers of the mind that man has possessed since the dawn of his days but some hidebound and blinkered scientists continue to deny. If you *had*, cultivated and so on, you'd see not just a bank manager but a bank manager with a noticeable and most efficient distinguishing organ of sex, one with an unusually low turn-around time too. You better believe it, Jayqueeze buddy, when Syd fucks you you stay fucked.'

'Really.' Jake poured wine.

In one sense he was able to do this because he and Eve were dining in a restaurant, not as planned La Sorbonne, which had been booked up when telephoned, but a perhaps rather Spanish place recently opened in the strange quarter sprung into being after most of the oldest part of the city had been gleefully hauled down a few years before. Here, where once you could have sworn there was nothing but a couple of colleges, some lodgings and an occasional newsagent or tobacconist, stood hairdressers' and clothiers' and trumpery-bazaars of a glossy meanness formerly confined to the outskirts of the large cities. Here, within these walls, were dons and undergraduates and others in statu pupillari dressed for fishing expeditions or semi-skilled work on the roads, and most of them had females with them, but Jake took no notice of any: other matters filled his attention.

It was the evening of the Tuesday after the Workshop, Eve's mother having proved not to be starting to die for the moment. They (he and Eve) had met at the restaurant at seven-thirty, and at seven-forty he had ordered a second sherry, with a third destined to follow before the arrival of the sort of paella – yes, it must be Spanish – and the bottle of red wine. Or rather the first bottle of red wine: they were now half way through the second. Three-quarters of the amount so far drunk was inside him. She had remembered his habit of moderation and asked him if he had changed his ways and he had said not in general but this evening was a special occasion.

Eve told him a little more about her husband's abilities, then dilated her eyes and clapped her hand to her forehead. 'Hold it right there,' she said in vibrant tones. 'Rewind.' She stabbed with her forefinger as at a button or switch and made high-pitched gibbering, quacking noises that were not so very much unlike those made by a tape revolving at high speed. After a time she made more finger-motions, saying, 'Clunk. Replay. Clunk,' then went on in the baritone register and in an accent Jake thought over-refined, 'Eve old girl, there's something I'd like to chat to you about. Would you do me the honour of letting me take you out to dinner? Well yes Jake that would be extremely nice of you thank you very much indeed,' the last series of words delivered in the kind of whining monotone to be loosely associated with imitations of footballers interviewed on television. The performance ended with switching-off noises and motions.

Jake gave a laugh. 'That's a new one, isn't it? Yes, I remember the scene you so vividly evoke, but there's nothing to it really. It was just an excuse to take you out to dinner after these God knows how many years.'

'Cock,' said Eve firmly. 'Uh-uh. No, as they say, way. It was a sadly shaken and deeply disturbed Jake Richardson who, that cold, rainy, windy morning in April, encountered his one-time close friend Evelyn Greenstreet at her place of work and sepulchral was the gloom wherewith he answered her polite inquiry as to the well-being or otherwise of his wife, right?'

'Well, we had had quite a nasty row, it's true, but once I'd – '

'Boom-boom-boom-boom-boom,' said Eve, this time like a tommy-gun and with appropriate arm-vibrations. You talk now or you talk later, but understand one thing, just one thing. You talk.'

And Jake did talk, though not till he had ordered cheese and a third bottle of wine. Eve demurred at the wine and asked if he was trying to get her drunk; he said he wasn't trying to do that, that these Spanish reds were very light and that they needn't drink it all.

'I'm worried about Brenda,' he eventually said. 'She goes on complaining I don't show her enough affection.'

'Are you showing her enough erect male member?'

'What?' He half turned away from her as if he had thought for a moment that somebody across the room had waved to him. 'Oh yes I think so. I don't think that's the problem.'

'You say you think.' Eve was now peering at him over phantom half-moon glasses of a forensic stamp. 'Am I to take that as indicating that there is doubt in your mind on this head?'

'No, that would be. . . . No. Of course none of us are what we were.'

'Not each and every one of us at all events. No, I asked because affection and the erect male member tend to go hand in hand, if you'll pardon the expression.'

'That's just the trouble.'

'Eh? eh?'

'I mean . . . they probably do for most people. Yes, I quite agree they do for most people. The, er, the thing is they don't seem to for me. At least that's what Brenda says. According to her I'm the type of man who hasn't really got much time for women except as creatures to go to bed with. In fact I only want one thing, always have. According to Brenda.'

Jake's demeanour now was rather that of a motorist in an unfamiliar town who, after a couple of wrong turnings and the odd near-collison, suddenly finds himself on a route that will get him there after all. If Eve saw any of this she didn't make it known, instead examining him from a wide variety of angles, at one moment with her cheek and ear almost resting on the tablecloth, at the next bolt upright with her head thrown back so that she stared at him down her cheeks. While she did this she clicked her tongue at different pitches. He used the time, which must have been getting on for a minute, to appraise more fully than before the degree to which she had kept her looks. Pretty high, he decided: the streaks of grey in her hair only witnessed to the genuine blackness of the rest, her skin still had a pale glow to it, and nothing had gone wrong with what he could see of her neck, which wasn't its entirety because of the very jolly reddish blouse or shirt she was wearing. It had gold bits on the collar and cuffs. Compiling this inventory made his eyes feel tired. They also felt hot when he closed them, or perhaps it was that his eyelids were cold. But why should they be?

Eve finished her inspection. 'I wouldn't have thought, well as you know all too thoroughly I always wouldn't have thought given half a chance, that's just poor little Evie for you, but I wouldn't have *thought*, balls in the air again, that our Brenda had very much there or thereabouts. From what various purblind and reactionary elements would no doubt regard as my somewhat discreditably wide experience I would have said, and as you know equally well I would always have *said*, that my old compeer and associate the Reader in Early Mediterranean History, how about that, woman's got a mind like a razor, was, balls yet again, and I would wager still is, one of those whose interest in womankind extends well beyond the small central area designated by that notoriously short and unattractive little word. You managed to put up with me with great good cheer when bedtime was far far away and I was in full verbal flight – oh yes, little Evie knows she makes considerable conversational as well as other more shall I say corporeal demands on her swains. So I venture to suggest, paying due regard to the interests of our partners in the European Economic Community, the provisions of Phase III of the Incomes Policy, the recommendations of the Race Relations Board and the findings of the Budleigh Salterton Tiddleywinks and Action Sculpture Committee, that on the matter at issue our trusty and well-beloved Brenda is talking through her sombrero.'

'Let's have some brandy,' said Jake.

19 That Lazy Feeling

Jake woke up suddenly in total darkness. At first he thought he was in bed in his rooms in Comyns. Certainly and more pressingly he had a severe headache, his mouth was dry, he needed a pee and he knew something awful had happened. He was also lying in an uncomfortable position and unwontedly was naked. As soon as he moved he found that the pillow under his head was thinnish where his Comyns one was fattish and the bed itself, the mattress, was slightly concave where his Comyns one was very slightly convex. He was on his right side with, as it soon proved, one edge of the bed within a few inches of his chest. What about the other edge and, more to the point, the intervening space? At the speed of a foot a minute he pushed his left hand out behind him. When the back of his middle finger touched what was probably a bare bottom he didn't do what instinct might have led him to do and recoil as from a nest of serpents, because he had already made up his mind that he could hardly be anywhere else but in Eve's bed with Eve; he drew his hand back in good order and adjusted his position as far as he could without setting off the fear that he might wake her, which wasn't at all far, hardly any distance really.

Memories, half-memories, inferences, questions, emotions, prospects, interrupted now and then by self-abandonment to passive suffering, came at him in great profusion. To methodise the inextricable, he determined that he had began to feel drunk, as opposed to merely recognising with benefit of hindsight that he must have been drunk, some time before they left the restaurant. Then they must have left the restaurant. Then he had tried to insist that they should go to a pub not only to have another drink but also to buy a bottle for later, with what success in either regard he had no idea. There had also been something about getting a bottle from the Comyns buttery instead because the pub was shut or too far or unwilling to sell bottles, or might have turned out to be one or other of these, but quite likely the thought had never attained action or even utterance. Later there had been the interior of a taxi or other vehicle of that size and general construction with him kissing Eve in it, and after that a room that also had him kissing her in it – a downstairs room, with a clock. Then he had found himself lying naked half on top of her on a bed, doubtless this bed, and doing the most extraordinary things to her with his hands and mouth. He knew he had done closely similar things to her and other women innumerable times in his life, in fact the two sets of things were virtually identical except for the recent one being so extraordinary, not seeming, being: what on earth could have possessed him? He had wondered that then and he wondered it now, on and off.

Finally, or rather 'finally', since it came circling round his mind every half-minute or so, the awful part. He knew nothing about it except how it felt, but that was quite enough. Oh, he did know it was awful in a non-new way, so he hadn't strangled Eve or pleaded with her to tie him up and whip him or pee on him. That was something, though again it didn't feel like much. Reason pointed to fiasco - plus - reproach, fiasco - plus - her - being - decent - about - it and fiasco as the most promising contenders; emotion pointed away, anywhere away from speculation about what it was. On each of its reappearances he tried vainly to assure himself he was better off in ignorance.

Actually there was one more thing he knew about the awful part: it asserted without fear of contradiction that he must do all he could to go on seeing to it that Eve stayed asleep as long as possible, till there was light enough for him to find his clothes, the door, the stairs, the kitchen at least. He wasn't going to go off without facing her but he must face her as his daytime self. A close consequence of these necessities was that any sortie for the discharge or intake of fluid, with its entailed voyage across a totally uncharted bedroom, was ruled out. O Iuppiter irrumator. O tetrakopros. Oh bugger. Wait a minute. In fact it was two or three before his inquisitive hand, moving as slowly as it could while still describable as being in motion, found a glass of something, presumably water, on something or other. Ah – but then he hesitated. To drink would alleviate one of his discomforts, but wouldn't it aggravate another? Not so's he'd notice: in his present condition the liquid would be doing fine if any of it reached his stomach, let alone his bladder. So he drank (it was water), and sure enough by the time he had settled the glass back again he could feel the first faint dryness returning to his tongue and throat. Just then his headache gave him something to think about for a change by taking a turn for the worse. From the start it had been one of the localised sort, well entrenched above the right eyebrow and the area slightly to the left of there; now it started pushing downwards into the top of his nose and the inner corner of his eye-socket. He rubbed and squeezed at the place, finding that the pain and the action together did a little to divert him from the short mental loop he was constantly tracing and retracing.

Where was Syd? Not around; that much was plain and little more seemed needed – Eve could be trusted to have seen to it that he wasn't going to cease to be not around at any sensitive stage. In fact that little more was all there was going to be: Jake never knew where Syd was that night and so likewise never knew whether his absence had been engineered or merely taken advantage of. He wondered about that for a bit till he saw it didn't make much odds. Where was here? He had forgotten anything Eve might have said to him or the taxi-driver that indicated which direction it was or how far it was from wherever they had picked up the taxi, though he could well remember having been in the taxi for at least fifteen seconds. When he listened he heard a distant vehicle, then another – no clue there. She had mentioned Headington, sure, but in a connection that implied past rather than present domicile. He wasn't approaching the problem in a spirit of pure disinterested inquiry. In the end there could presumably be expected to be a morning; when it came he would be all right if he was in Rawlinson Road, but if he was in a cottage halfway between Thame and Aylesbury he might find some difficulty in getting back to Comyns and picking up his lecture notes in time to make it to Parks Road by eleven, this on the assumption that Comyns, lecture-notes and the like still existed.

Round about this point something he hadn't bargained for happened: a light went on at the other side of the bed. He went into a distinguished underplayed imitation of a man sound asleep, breathing deeply and regularly *nearly* all the time, not being lavish with grunt, sniff and swallow. So matters seemed to rest for a couple of minutes; not having sat up or made any other detectable move she could hardly be reading. When the minutes were up she got out of bed without the flurry he had half-expected and was to be heard walking away. A swift blink showed her naked back view going out by a doorway in the far corner. He looked about: his clothes, or most of them, seemed to be on and around a chair next to a dressing-table at the window. And he now knew where the door was, but to gather up clothes and exit either instantly or later, in the dark, wasn't worth considering, so he looked about the room further. It was quite a big room with a certain amount of probably expensive furniture in it, and some pictures, paintings – he did notice them. Clever old Syd and lucky old Eve.

He heard a cistern flush and revivified the role of sound-asleep man. Quietly but audibly she came back into the room and over to the bed, this time to his side of it. Silence and stillness. What was she doing? He opened his mouth a little and shut it again. Nothing continued to happen. The moment at which he would have to scream and thrash about approached and arrived and prolonged itself. After he had given up hope she sighed, made a small wordless noise that might have indicated contempt or affection or sadness or pity or almost anything else but pleasure, went round the bed, got carefully back into it and switched off the light.

The return of darkness had the effect of informing him authoritatively that he wasn't going to sleep again that night. The soporific effect of the alcohol he had drunk had long since been dissipated, his Mogadons were far away and the bottom sheet had become strewn with little irregular patches of hot semi-adhesive sand. More than this, his recent struggles to breathe regularly had fucked up some neural mechanism or other so that he now seemed to be breathing by conscious control alone: in, hold it, out, hold it, in. He kept trying to yawn but couldn't fill his lungs to the point where he could turn the corner, get over the hump and exhale naturally. So exhale anyhow, hang about and try again. He didn't know whether to be glad or sorry that he hadn't looked at his watch while he had had the chance.

In the end he came to a state of which it could be said with more truth than of any other in his experience that it was between sleeping and waking. He had thoughts; no, there were thoughts, each one of an unmeaningness, of a neglect of any imaginable kind of order that caused him leaden wonderment, numb doubt whether he would ever be able to go back to proper thinking. They came along at a regular moderate pace, each one a dozen or twenty words or word-semblances long and lasting a few seconds before being overlaid by the next. Most of them posed as statements of remarkable fact or hitherto unformulated views and beliefs, though a few were pseudo-questions that it was out of his power to begin to try to answer; the nearest comparison was the sort of stuff they gave you to read in dreams.

They receded sharply at an abrupt clashing sound and a voice saying Tea but didn't go away altogether for the first few seconds after he opened his eyes and at once started to come back when for excellent reasons he shut his eyes again. He struggled up to a sitting position, having to take his time about it because of the way his head rolled about like a small baby's unless he concentrated hard, and concentrating at all was no light matter. The curtains had been drawn back and it was full day, in fact, as he saw when he had hauled and crammed his glasses on to his face, seven-forty. There was indeed a cup of tea on the bedside table and he got it to where he could drink from it without spilling a drop outside the saucer. The state of his bladder had become something he could live with, given his present standard of living, so he sat and sipped and felt the hot sweet brew sinking into his tissues and doing him no good at all. When he had finished he got up, put on his trousers, soon found the bathroom and thank Christ. After that he drank, by way of tap and tooth-glass, something approaching his own weight in water. There was a metal cabinet above the basin, in the mirror of which he gained a first-rate view of his face. It looked as if it had been seethed in a salt solution for a time and then given a brisk buffing with sandpaper, but it felt as if it had also been lashed with twigs. He bathed it gently, which left it none the worse. More extensive ablutions would have meant deferring the time when he should be fully clothed and that would never do.

Back in the bedroom he got trousers off, pants on, trousers back on double-quick, then slowed right down, his head pounding. The ache in it was now firmly established in the top of his nose and had even moved on to the inner end of his left eyebrow, but it had relinquished a little of its former territory on the other side of his forehead. As he started to get up after easing on his shoes a wave of giddiness pushed him forward in a sudden crouching run that, if not checked, might well have sent him out of the window. The move brought him a view of what looked very much like part of North Oxford: one fear disposed of. He tied his tie and combed his hair, thereby making his arms ache a lot, put on his jacket and went.

He found Eve in a large well-equipped kitchen reading the *Daily Telegraph*, which she lowered when she saw him. Her glance and tone were pointedly neutral.

'You look bloody awful,' she said.

'Yes.'

'How do you feel?'

'If you don't mind I think I'd rather not try to answer that question.'

'Spirits don't seem to agree with you.'

'They differed from me sharply this time.'

'Would you like some breakfast?'

'No thanks, I must be on my way.'

'Cheero then.'

'Look, I'm sorry about last night.'

'Which part of it?' When he didn't speak she went on, 'You don't remember much about it, do you? I might have known. Well, at your urgent insistence we went to bed, an act of sexual intercourse duly took place, and you immediately turned – '

'Oh really?'

'Yes really. If that's what was bothering you you can forget it – honour was satisfied. In fact considering how pissed you were you did quite well. It was what happened afterwards that you might consider feeling sorry about.'

He waited but in the end had to say, 'What was that?'

'Fuck-all. You said Good night love, turned over and went to sleep.'

'I was tired. And pissed.'

'That's when we show what we're like. You practically went on your knees to get me to play, when you'd promised not to try when you first asked me, right? and I told you twice at least I'd be breaking eight years of being faithful to Syd, yes we've been married quite a bit longer but it took me a while to give up my old ways, and then you do that. A nice man would have tried to make a girl feel it had been worth while, however tired and pissed he was. No that's not fair, a man who sees more in women than creatures to go to bed with, a man who doesn't only want one thing. So you see I've rather come round to Brenda's way of thinking. Suddenly. Before last night I couldn't have agreed with her less.'

Again he could think of nothing to say, though on a larger scale than before: he had the awful part squarely in front of him now.

'Don't worry about me.' Eve picked up the paper again. 'I'll get over it. You're the one with the problem. Turn right outside and you'll be in the Banbury road in three minutes.'

He found his raincoat in the hall and saw himself out. When he got to

the Banbury road he saw he was only about half a mile north of St Giles',
say a mile all told from Comyns. It wasn't actually raining and a walk
would do him good. It did, in that it brought about in him an additional
form of physical exhaustion to help take his mind off his other troubles.
He stepped through the wicket with what alertness he could muster: he
must not run into Ernie, be found by him entering college at a quarter to
nine in the morning. At first sight there was nobody about. He tiptoed over
to the lodge and had a peep: one of the under porters behind the glass
partition. Moving quite naturally now he went in, nodded good morning,
wished he hadn't nodded anything, went to his pigeon-hole and was turning
over a couple of pieces of mail when he heard the approach of a familiar
and dreadful creaking sound. Perhaps he could just. . . . He was still a yard
or two from the doorway when Ernie was there, filling it, well not filling
it but making it hard for any creature much larger than a rabbit to get
past.

'Morning, Ernie,' said Jake, taking a half-pace diagonally forward as if
he somehow expected the porter to make way for him.

'Morning, Mr Richardson.' Of course he didn't budge. 'You're up early.'
He looked more closely; it wasn't going to do Jake any good not to have
been actually witnessed at the gate. 'Had a night on the tain have you sir?'

'Staying with, with friends.'

'Yes, you always were a bit of a night-ale, like, but never much of a. . . .'
'If I didn't know you better I'd have said you'd been draining your sorrows.
I just hope you don't feel as lazy as you look.'

'Oh yes. No. Now if you — '

'Oh well, in for a penny, in for a bloody — ' Ernie advanced suddenly
and with loud creak, his head twisting round over his shoulder. 'Sorry sir,
I didn't know you was there.'

'Well, now you do, now you do. Morning, Jake.'

It was Roger Dollymore, looking offensively fit and spruce. The sight of
him was an instant reminder of the College Meeting to be held that afternoon and the hortations to be delivered there for and against the admission
of women. No doubt Dollymore's was already prepared. Jake's wasn't. He
stumbled off to his room to see if he could think of anything to say.

20 Girls Everywhere

He thought of something quite soon and wrote it down on the spot, and that was a good idea, because not long afterwards he was just wondering whether he could possibly feel worse, given present circumstances, in other words not given epilepsy or impending execution, when he put his mind at rest about that by starting to feel not only worse, but worse and worse. The newcomer among his sensations was anxiety. By the time he reached the lectern in Parks Road it was advanced enough to reduce his entire audience, the little bastard from Teddy Hall along with the rest, to immobile silence. They were all keyed up for the moment when he should collapse and die or start screaming and tearing off his clothes. But he disappointed them. When he had finished he cancelled his tutorial with the Bradfordian, savoured an all-too-brief moment of self-congratulation at his own sagacity and fought his way back to Comyns through a medium that seemed appreciably denser than air. In his sitting-room he ran his eyes over the print of some of *The Hippogriff Attaché-Case*. He wanted to lie down but what he didn't want was another dose of those bloody thought-substitutes.

Having (purposely) missed breakfast he decided he had better try to eat some lunch and managed to get quite a decent way through a portion of steak-and-kidney pie with cabbage and mashed potatoes. It was slow work but he left the SCR in bags of time to get over to his rooms, throw up and stroll back so as to arrive in the Grade Room on the stroke of two. Inside him there continued to lie a dissolving Mogadon, taken with the object not of inducing sleep, which your true-to-form College Meeting could do on its own, but of soothing his nerves: Curnow had said when prescribing the stuff that it was a muscle-relaxant, which surely must mean that it relaxed the muscles, and offhand he couldn't think of any muscle of his that couldn't have done with some relaxation bar his sphincter, which for the last four hours or so had notably excepted itself from the tension that possessed him.

Lancewood was already settled in his usual place, halfway down the left-hand vertical, so to speak, of the hollow square of baize-covered tables, at the top horizontal of which sat or shortly would sit the Master, the Dean, the Senior Tutor and other holders of office. Jake went round and joined Lancewood, who at first sight of him said,

'Hallo, how terrible you look.'

'Ernie was saying much the same thing this morning.'

'Even Ernie is right sometimes. I think it's your eyes mostly. No, that's too easy – it is your eyes, but it's your mouth mostly. Its shape has changed. What have you been up to?'

'Oh Christ. Are you in to Hall?'

'Yes, and at a loose end afterwards. Skip dessert and come straight over to my rooms.'

'Christ. I mean thanks.'

Very soon afterwards Marion Powle came in and took his place at the centre of the top table. He announced that the minutes of the last meeting had been circulated and asked if he might sign them as correct. Jake could find no more objection than anybody else. Then Powle recited the names of lazy bastards who had said they weren't coming. After that part the Estates Bursar was called upon to introduce Agenda Item 3. (They mean Agendum 3, thought Jake.) The item or agendum in question concerned the sale of some college property in a part of the kingdom that had until just the other day borne the name of an English county but was now known by some historically authentic title that meant as good as nothing to anyone. The price quoted ran into six figures and was immediately agreed by those assembled. It was a very different story when the next item-agendum came up. This time the focus of attention was the proposed new chairs for the library, the joint proponents of the proposition being the Domestic Bursar and the Mods don who doubled as the Librarian of the college. A prototype was brought in by a menial and examined with some closeness, several leaving their own chairs to see it better. At first it seemed to gain some approval, and when Wynn-Williams sat on it and it didn't collapse its adoption looked almost certain. But then the cost was asked for and given as £125 and all over the room there were wincing noises, rather like but in sum louder than those made by Brenda on getting into a cold bed. For a chair! they all kept saying – for a chair? Not quite all. *Of course* it seems a lot, said Jake to himself, but haven't you noticed that *everything* seems a lot these days, you fucking old fools? In the end the Domestic Bursar, after he had made it plain that it would be no use going back to the maker and trying to beat him down, was instructed to do just that.

The next topic was described simply as Stanton St Leonard Churchyard. All Jake knew about Stanton St Leonard was that it was a village to the north-west of Oxford, that the living of its church was in the gift of Comyns and that by way of consequence a part of its churchyard was set aside for the remains of Fellows of the college, an amenity not much in use for however long it was since they had been permitted to marry. Probably the local authorities wanted the place concreted over and a community centre or skateboard park built on the site.

The Master looked round the meeting with a serious expression. 'Now I'm afraid I have a rather serious matter to draw to the attention of Fellows,' he said seriously. After explaining about Stanton St Leonard for the benefit of the recently elected, he went on, 'During the vacation a certain Hoyt H. Goodchild, a citizen of the United States, was visiting relatives in the village when he suddenly died. It seems that these were his only relatives; at any rate, there was silence on the other side of the Atlantic and the family in Stanton decided to bury Mr Goodchild in the churchyard there. By a most unfortunate and grievous coincidence the rector was away at the time and the sexton ill, and evidently neither had briefed his substitute in full, because on returning to their duties they found Mr Goodchild buried at the Comyns end.'

There was a general gasp of consternation, almost of horror, in which Jake couldn't quite prevent himself joining. Funny how we all overact at these get-togethers, he thought to himself: what ought to be of mild, passing interest attracted passionate concern or a facsimile of it, ordinary care for the interests of the college came out as crusading zeal. All part of being donnish.

Powle was continuing, 'Both men have expressed their profoundest apologies but that's hardly the issue. I must have some guidance here. Senior Tutor?'

'No difficulty that I can see,' said Dollymore. 'He'll have to come up, won't he?'

Wynn-Williams and some of the other senior Fellows showed their agreement.

'I don't really think we can quite do that,' said Powle.

'*We* won't have to do anything, Master. It's up to those two in Stanton to set right their mistake.'

'There would have to be an exhumation order, which might not be easy to obtain. And there are the feelings of Mr Goodchild's relatives to be considered, surely.'

'They'll be village people, I don't expect much obstacle there. And as for the exhumation, the authorities are bound to understand our historic right not to have a total stranger, and an American at that, in our own sacred ground. Why, some of those graves go back to the time of the Civil War.'

'I think everybody here understands that, Senior Tutor, but I very much doubt if the authorities would, to the point of taking action that is. They'd be nervous of the publicity and I couldn't blame them.'

'It's out of the question, sir,' said the political scientist who ran a current-affairs programme on TV.

'Out of the question to do what is fully within our rights and in conflict with no law?'

'I'm afraid that in this case, we'll have to bow to the opinions, the prejudices if you like of . . . outsiders,' said Powle.

'Good God,' said Dollymore. 'What a world it's become.'

'You're proposing that no action be taken at all, Master?' asked Wynn-Williams.

'Not necessarily. Are there any suggestions?'

There were none for half a minute. Then a natural scientist of some sort asked where Goodchild's grave was in relation to the others and was passed a marked plan of the churchyard. On examining it he said,

'As one might have expected it's at the end of a row and it also happens to be near the yew hedge. One might be able to plant a section of hedge, or transplant one, better, so that the intruding grave is as it were segregated from the others.'

This suggestion was debated at some length; in the end it was agreed upon. But Roger Dollymore hadn't finished yet. He said defiantly,

'It'll be all very well until the autumn.'

The writer in residence, who had often declared that he had done no writing at all as yet and had no plans for doing any while in residence, and who was wearing a red-and-black upper garment the material of which had been fashioned by human ingenuity, and who had uttered a loud yelp of deprecation on hearing Dollymore's first proposal for the treatment of the offending cadaver said, 'What happens in the autumn then?'

Dollymore said as to an imbecile, 'The leaves fall.'

'And?'

'And cover the ground.'

'So?'

'So somebody has to clear them eh-way.'

'Like?'

'Like? Like?'

'I mean who, you know.'

'Oh who. Well not the sexton is what I'm suggesting.'

'Why not?'

'Because his responsibility is to us, not to Mr . . . Goodchild or his relations. He must have nothing to do with that grave and it'll be an ugly sight by Christmas.'

'I think we can probably come to some compromise arrangement there,' said the Master with a confident smile. 'Now – Garden Committee to report on the south lawn.'

So it went. Nearer and nearer came 12: Admission of Women, and step by step Jake's anxiety mounted, some of it now detaching itself and identifiable as anxiety about his anxiety. What the bugger was wrong with him? He hadn't had a hangover for thirty years but he could have sworn that today's was a radical departure. Well, thirty years were thirty years, weren't they?

Finally, by way of closed scholarships, a report from the Wine

Committee, a discussion of a vile sculptured thing some people wanted to put in the front quad and stuff like the recommendation from the historian of drama (the one who put on plays full of naked junior members of the university torturing one another) that the library should start a sexism section, 12 arrived. It opened innocuously enough with a summary of what the other colleges had done in the matter of admitting women and what their policies for the future were, as far as these could be discovered or inferred, all ably presented by young Whitehead. And it went on, if not innocuously then at any rate not leading to physical violence, with Dolly-more back in the limelight outlining what he saw as the case against admission. Quite radiant with hypocrisy he led off with the point made by Smith in Jake's hearing a couple of weeks earlier, that to let women into men's colleges reduced the status of the women's colleges. After that he mentioned the harm he thought would be done the academic performance of Comyns undergraduates by the distraction from their studies he thought they would suffer. Then he unwisely stressed the opposition of the college staff to the scheme, unwisely because it was hard to think about the college staff without thinking first and foremost of Ernie, and if there was anything that could have united that motley Governing Body it was that whatever Ernie was opposed to you were for. As his final argument he dilated on the incompatibility between a mixed college and the kind of intimate communion which members of Comyns had enjoyed for seven centuries; undergraduates came and went, but Fellows lived their lives here. 'All that,' he ended, the dramatic effect heightened rather than the reverse by his bleating tones, 'all . . . *this* . . . would be lost – for ever.'

There was a general murmur of appreciation of a case well put or at least strongly felt even if not necessarily found convincing. 'Thank you, Senior Tutor,' said the Master. 'Now I call on Mr Richardson to put the other view.'

'We are dealing here with an example of something we have all encountered more and more often over the last twenty or thirty years: a trend.' Jake spoke a little inexpressively because most of his attention was concentrated on getting the words out with their syllables in the right places. 'I would say two things about trends. One is that while many or most may be undesirable and on those grounds to be resisted, a trend is not undesirable per se. The other is that while no trend can be said to be irresistible until it is altogether dominant, there are trends to which resistance seems likely or very likely to be vain. In such cases it may be better, more advantageous, to yield at once rather than fight on. So we don't resist a policy of admission just because admission is the trend, nor do we resist it if we have no or virtually no chance of winning. In my view that chance disappeared five years ago or more if it had ever existed. I therefore appeal to the anti-admission party to yield at once, thereby giving itself the chance of doing what it would no doubt call salvaging something from the wreck rather than being finally compelled and so losing the option.

'Such is the pragmatic case, and discussion there will turn on the resistibility of the trend. But before we come to that let me briefly state the human case. I see it as divided into three. One, from what we were hearing earlier, both men and women undergraduates are overwhelmingly in favour of admission in general. As with trends, this is not sufficient grounds for resistance. Two, when they arrive here these young people still have some growing-up to do, and to be able to do it in close daily proximity to members of the opposite sex is a clear and considerable benefit.' (There was a faint stir of rallying, chaffing, etc. at this but Jake didn't notice it.) 'Three, admission to men's colleges is the only way so far devised of providing more places for women while leaving relatively intact the present collegiate and university structure.'

It was done. He found he was panting and leaned forwards over the table, head lowered, while he tried to recover his breath unnoticed. There was a handy interval before and while Dollymore asked if he might ask a question, was told he might and asked it.

'I'll take up Mr Richardson's *relatively* intact collegiate structure in a minute; for now I'd like him to tell me if he would whether he regards the provision of more places for women as a, as a clear and considerable benefit.'

'Indeed I do,' said Jake, grinding it out. 'Mr Whitehead's figures show clearly the disparity against women.'

'I take that point: women candidates are competing for a proportionately smaller number of places. What assurance have we that to increase that proportion will reveal a similar or comparable increase in the proportion of those found acceptable?'

'I'm afraid . . . I suppose. . . .'

'More fundamentally, doesn't Mr Richardson's clear and considerable benefit rest on what I will persuasively call the faith that academically acceptable women are as numerous or about as numerous as their male counterparts?'

Jake's fists were tightly clenched under the table. 'In posse if not in esse.'

'A dangerous concession, surely, but let that go. May we hear some evidence for this academic parity or approximate parity?'

'The view I'm advancing can't be supported by figures or by self-sustaining facts, only by an inadequate number of individual indications that woman is the intellectual equal of man, that her powers of observation, analysis, induction and so forth are on a level with his, and that her admittedly inferior performance numerically . . . er . . . results from a number of . . . social factors of which one is that they can't, I mean she can't get into a university as easily as a man.'

The writer in residence spoke. 'Look, are you trying to tell us – ' He checked himself at something said to him by the philosopher who was co-editor of a London weekly paper, then went on, 'Sorry, got it wrong. Is – what? – is Mr Richardson trying to tell us he believes that? About women being equal to men? Does he believe it?' He looked round the room as if pleading for enlightenment. 'I mean, you know, like really *believe* it?'

'I think – ' began the Master but Jake rode over him. He didn't know or care whether the writer in residence was trying to do more than demonstrate the impartiality of his contempt and/or simply draw attention to himself: he (Jake) saw in him a slight physical resemblance to the little bastard from Teddy Hall, who was little in worth, not size, but who by some association led him to think of Chris at the Workshop and even of Rosenberg. Rage and dizziness struck him together.

'Of course I don't believe it, you . . .' He stopped just in time to avoid technically calling the Master what he had been about to call the writer in residence. 'I was asked to put a case and I put it, that's all. No doubt they do think, the youngsters, it'd be more fun to be under the same roof, but who cares what they think? All very well for the women no doubt, it's the men who are going to be the losers – oh, it'll, it'll happen all right, no holding it up now. When the first glow has faded and it's quite normal to have girls in the same building and on the same staircase and across the landing, they'll start realising that that's exactly what they've got, girls everywhere and not a common-room, not a club, not a pub where they can get away from them. And the same thing's going to happen to us which is much more important, Roger's absolutely right, all this will go and there will be women everywhere, chattering, gossiping, telling you what they did today and what their daughter did yesterday and what their friend did last week and what somebody they heard about did last month and horrified if a chap brings up a *topic* or an *argument*. They don't mean what they say, they don't use language for discourse but for extending their personality, they take all disagreement as opposition, yes they do, even the brightest of them, and that's the end of the search for truth which is what the whole thing's supposed to be about. So let's pass a motion suggesting they bugger off back to Somerville, LMH, St Hugh's and St Hilda's where they began and stay there. It won't make any bloody difference but at least we'll have told 'em what we think of 'em.'

Only then, when he had in a sense finished, did Jake become aware of just how hard Lancewood had been squeezing his arm, of the pantomime of apology, helplessness, agreement and doubtless more that the writer in residence was putting on, and of what sort of silence had fallen. The Master thanked him with preternatural composure but Jake felt he couldn't very well stay after what he had said and how he had said it, matters on which he was already not quite clear. His headache drove and twisted at his brows. He asked to be excused, hurried out and stood in the main SCR with both hands on the back of a chair. Lancewood was only a couple of seconds behind him.

'I'll just see you over to your rooms.'

'No I'm all right, you go back.'

'Don't be silly, it'll only take a second.'

'No Damon, if you don't go back straight away they'll think there's something really wrong. Tell them, say it's side-effects of some new pills. Please, Damon.'

'If you're really sure. But we'll talk later.'

'Yes. Yes, we will. Thanks.'

As Jake approached his staircase he met Ernie coming out of it. The porter gave one of his fiercest winks.

'There you are after all, sir,' he said. 'I told your visitor you probably wouldn't be arraigned for a bit, with the College Meeting and all, but she said she'd wait if that was allayed, and I couldn't find it in my heart to say her nay. She really does you credit, Mr Richardson, at your time of life – take a bay!'

'What? Oh yes.'

He hurried into his sitting-room, unable to venture even a surmise.

'Hallo, Jake,' said a strange girl in a green trouser-suit.

21 I Can Help You

The next moment he saw it wasn't a strange girl at all but Kelly, smiling, coming up and shaking hands. It bothered him, made him think himself senile, that even with the trouser-suit clue he hadn't recognised her at first, though he tried to cover this.

'Kelly, how nice to see you. What are you doing in Oxford?'

'Paying a call on you, Jake. Actually I've been staying with an aunt in Woodstock, so I thought I'd look you up on my way back to London.'

'Jolly good idea, I could do with a bit of lively company. I've just come out of a meeting of such boredom. . . .'

'You don't look well, Jake. I know one isn't supposed to say such things, but you don't.'

'Had a rotten night. I feel as if I hadn't slept a wink.'

'Bad luck. Of course if you're used to sleeping with someone else it is that much more difficult on your own.'

'Yes,' he said, keeping to himself the fact that his troubles had come about in the opposite way. 'How did you track me down?'

She smiled again. 'Oh, I'm good at that sort of thing. Remember how I ran you to earth in Burgess Avenue?'

'Finding me here must have been a damn sight more difficult.'

'Not really, Jake. Not to me.'

'You're a clever girl.' He looked at his watch. 'We could go out and have some tea soon.'

'It's a little early, isn't it?'

'I suppose it is, but I've got to be back here at five o'clock to talk to some undergraduates.'

'Can't you put them off?'

'Not possible, I'm afraid.'

'You could ring them up,' she said coaxingly, nodding towards the telephone on his desk.

'They're not in the same place, they're all over Oxford. I couldn't hope to reach them in the time.'

'Oh, what a bore.'

'I'm sorry, but if you'd let me know you were coming. . . .'

. . . I still wouldn't have done anything about it, he finished in his mind. At her remark about the demerits of sleeping alone a little alarm-bell of uneasiness had sounded there; it continued to purr away as he came to recognise that she was talking and behaving in an entirely different style from the one she had used at Burgess Avenue the previous Saturday. No cheerful confidence or confidingness now, no long eager speeches; instead, langour with a querulous edge to it. Above all, the Kelly of Saturday would never have tried to get him to cancel his seminar, would on the contrary have offered to leave at once in case he had preparations to make. So he had been half justified in not recognising her straight away. He had meant what he had said about being glad to see her; he only hoped that the uneasiness would turn out to be misplaced, that things were going to take a turn for the better after the last twenty hours or so, that she was no more than tired or perhaps shy without Brenda's diluting presence. Ah! – Saturday-Kelly would certainly have –

'How's Brenda?'

'Oh . . . she's fine, thanks.'

'I bet she doesn't come here much, does she? No, I thought not, she wouldn't be able to stand it and quite frankly I'm surprised you can, Jake. I mean look at this, pretend you haven't seen it before and look at it properly.' Kelly indicated the padded chair she had just got up off. 'Isn't it absolutely revolting?'

'I know it's not very nice, but I don't spend much time here, so . . .'

'What happens when you entertain? – oh of course you're going to tell me you don't entertain. I can't understand how a cultivated man like you can bring himself to live in such, well I can't call it squalor because it isn't actually dirty or damp or anything but it's pretty damn slummy you have to admit. Not even a picture to take your eyes off it. And honestly these curtains, you'd have thought . . . Oh I say that really is something. How gorgeous.'

Jake joined her at the window where she was apparently admiring the buildings on the far sides of the quad. 'Yes it is pretty good, isn't it?'

'What is it, early eighteenth century?'

Christ, he thought mildly. 'Yes, about then.'

'It must make up for a lot, having that out there in front of you all the time. What's the other way?'

She turned and made for the open bedroom door, past which daylight was to be seen. He followed her.

'There's not a great deal, but. . . .'

'Do you mind?'

'No, go ahead.'

The bedroom window showed a stretch of wall and part of the rear quad of Jesus College. Kelly looked appreciatively at them for a few moments and started to back to the sitting-room, or so Jake thought till he made to follow and found she had shut the door and was facing him with her back to it.

At first he felt only mild surprise and puzzlement. 'What. . . .'

'Jake, listen to me, this is important and we don't have very much time. We haven't known each other very long but I feel we appreciate each other and I don't know about you but I can say I trust you. It's an old-fashioned expression but I wish you well, and that's good because I can do something for you, I can help you with your problem. You might not think so but I've had a lot of experience, you could almost call it training. You put yourself in my hands and it'll all work out. You just leave everything to me and I mean everything. Okay? Right, let's go.'

All this was said in such a friendly, reasonable tone that Jake couldn't believe she meant what he knew she meant until she crossed the room, a matter of no more than a couple of strides, quick ones in this case, and closed with him, her arms round his neck and what Ed and Rosenberg would call her pubic area pushing into his. Jake had had to evade or discourage amorous females before, though admittedly none as forceful as this, and without Ed and Rosenberg and all that, and in particular without Eve, he would probably have done better than do what he did do, which was to pull Kelly's arms away and thrust her from him and call on her in a frightened voice to leave him alone, leave him alone.

She showed her teeth: as he had noticed before they were good enough teeth, white and regular, but this time he saw something about the way they were set in the gums that told him beyond all doubt who it was she had reminded him of on Saturday. He was horrified and got ready to defend himself, crouching with his balls tucked between his thighs, but she didn't come at him, didn't even throw anything at him, perhaps because there wasn't a lot to throw, no ashtray, no water-jug or tumbler and again no pictures. All she did was shove the bedside lamp on to the floor, which did no more than knock the shade off its frame, and abuse him verbally. She used not only what is often called foul language in great copiousness and diversity but also foul ideas, and produced surprising variations on the themes of old age and its attendent weaknesses. After some minutes she stopped all at once in mid-incivility and seemed taken by a fit of violent shivering. By degrees she moved to the side of the bed and sat down on it with her hands on her knees. Then she started to weep.

Jake had come across lachrymose females before too, but never one like this, never one who gave such a sense of intolerable pressure within, as if what was being wept over was growing faster than it could be wept away. 'Sorry,' she said as the tears flew from her eyes, 'sorry, sorry, sorry, sorry, sorry. . . .' She must have said it a hundred times, each time if possible with a different inflection. Jake sat down next to her, though not very close to her, gave her a clean handkerchief out of his drawer, and kept telling her it was all right, and in the end she stopped saying sorry and merely sobbed continuously.

'You aren't planning to expose Ed or anything like that, are you?' he asked as soon as he thought she might be listening.

She shook her head violently.

'You're just one of his patients, and Rosenberg's, aren't you?'

This time she nodded so hard it involved her whole body.

'Were you just after me when you came to the house?'

Another nod.

'There isn't any aunt in Woodstock, is there? . . . Is it true what Ed said, that you can't run your life? . . . Have you been like that for a long time? . . . What's just happened here this afternoon, has it happened to you before? . . . Often? . . . But you have had a lot of men? . . . Have you enjoyed it? . . . Where do you live? – I mean you do live with your parents? . . . They're kind to you, are they? . . . But your father isn't in the theatre and you haven't studied acting?'

Each time he got the answer he expected. He looked at his watch: he had half an hour to get this creature fit to move and to move her before his class started to assemble. But none of it could be hurried. Meanwhile there was another question he wanted to ask, for no good reason that he could see, another yes-or-no question in form but to which he hoped for a more than yes-or-no response. When the sobbing had become intermittent he said.

'You came up from London just to see me? Just for this to happen?'

'I suppose in a way,' she said in a dazed blocked-up voice. 'But it wasn't all I did. I came up quite early and had a look round the shops and found a good place for lunch in that street where there are no cars, and then I thought I couldn't come and see you right away, so I went for a nice walk by the river first.'

He would very willingly have done without this information. 'But you did . . . expect me to turn you down?'

'In a way.' She sobbed for a little before she went on, blinking at the floor. 'I didn't use to get turned down much but now I nearly always do, but I still go on. Dr Rosenberg says that's what's wrong with me, I don't learn from experience, but I'm quite intelligent and I'm young, he says, so I might get better one day. I'm sorry I said those things, they were horrible and I'm ashamed. I didn't mean any of them.'

'I know, I could tell that. I didn't listen, I couldn't tell you what they are now.'

'I must go, I've wasted enough of your time, and with you feeling rotten after your bad night.'

'That's nothing. I'll get you a taxi.'

'No don't bother, I can walk.'

'Not in this rain. It's about a mile to the station.'

'I've got my umbrella.'

'No, listen, you come along here.' He took her slouching and subdued into the small bathroom that occupied the space of what until not at all long ago had been part of the bedroom. 'You freshen up while I telephone for a taxi.'

It sounded plausible enough; the trouble was that a telephone, a British telephone of the 1970s, came into it. Following procedure he dialled 9 and got to the exchange, then started on the number of the taxi firm he always used. After the first digit a kind of steady cooing noise sounded, which meant that according to the telephone tens of thousands of people in the Oxford area had had their line communications cut by fire, accident or flood or in consequence of mass non-payment of bills. Further attempts brought the same absence of result. He tried to raise the lodge with the idea of getting the porter to dial direct — no reply. A last go at the taxi number succeeded, granted that being told there would be a delay of twenty minutes was success. Well, he had better treat it as such: if all parties went strictly by the clock, taxi and seminarists would coincide at the lodge, but he was unlikely to be able to improve on the present offer in the time, so he said yes thank you and rang off.

Kelly didn't reappear for quite a while, which was bad because he wanted to be sure of getting shot of her, but good because he didn't want to have to talk to her or deal with her in any way before getting shot of her. He was about to go and give her a knock when she stepped quite briskly out of the bathroom, collected her long-handled umbrella from where he hadn't noticed it and came and stood in front of him.

'I'll go whenever you want me to,' she said.

He looked her over to see if she was presentable and then just looked. In general her skin was even better than at first glance, but there was some roughness near the eyes that he didn't think had arrived in the last half-hour, and he noticed a broken blood-vessel or two in her cheek.

'How old are you, Kelly?'

'Twenty, Twenty-one in September.'

It seemed a bit soon. 'Now I want you to know that when I turned you down it was nothing to do with you, it would have been the same with anybody. Ed got it wrong, it's not that I can't, I can but I don't want to. With anybody. It wasn't you, I think you're very attractive.'

'Don't worry, I shan't bother you again, I never try twice with the same person. You're quite safe.'

'That's not what I mean. If I fancied anyone I'd fancy you, believe me. I'm just old and past it. Ten years ago I wouldn't have turned you down.'

'You really haven't got to worry.'

'But. . . . Oh very well; let's be off.'

'You've no need to come, I'm perfectly okay now. I expect you'd like to have things ready for your students.'

'I just want to make sure you get the taxi all right,' and also make sure you don't go and lay about you with your umbrella in the chapel or, more important, in the gift shop.

She used it for its intended purpose as they moved across the quad, protecting him from the light drizzle as well as herself. In a way that might have been natural she took his arm.

'If only I had a bit of sense,' she said thoughtfully, 'I could have quite an enjoyable life. For instance today, when you said let's go out and have some tea I could have said yes let's, and we could have had a nice talk and perhaps we might have arranged for me to come up another day and you show me around Oxford or something, and we could have been friends, and now we can't.'

'It would have been difficult anyway,' said Jake, not knowing a hell of a lot about what he meant.

They reached the lodge and stood about outside in the dry for a minute or two. The Bradfordian, always inclined to be early, came through the wicket, saw Jake and hesitated. He didn't look at Kelly.

'Carry on, Mr Thwaites,' called Jake. 'I'll join you in just a moment.'

'You'll have to go.' She had moved some feet away and spoke without looking at him, presumably in an effort to spare him the embarrassment of being associated with her. 'I can manage, honestly I can.'

It was true he would have to go in the end, but the taxi might not come for another twenty minutes or ever, and for some reason he shrank from the thought of her walking to the station after all. At that point Ernie appeared in the lodge entrance. Jake made straight for him.

'Ernie, I want a word with you.'

The porter made a half-revolution as smartly as a guardsman and with Jake closely following retreated into the inner lodge, behind the glass partition. 'Sir?'

'The young lady is a little upset. I've ordered her a taxi. I have a class in two minutes. Would you see she gets off all right?'

'Receiving you laid and clear, Mr Richardson. Send her in here to me and I'll do the necessary, you may be sure – skate's honour, sir!'

Outside again, Jake told Kelly the porter would look after her and then hesitated.

'Thanks. Good-bye,' she said, shaking hands. Her eyes were smaller than when she had arrived but not very red. 'Sorry again.'

'That's all right. . . . Good-bye.'

'See you Saturday,' she said as he turned away.

Saturday? Saturday! Dies irae, dies illa solvet saeclum in favilla. And ballocks. Real ballocks. Very serious ballocks indeed.

22 Phallus's End

'Eve, Eve, what is Eve? Well of course when we've looked at the books and got our sums right and done our bigs and wiped our bottoms and at the end of the day, Eve is Eve is Eve is Eve is Eve, and I don't mean the mother of mankind or any such form of words inconsonant with the meaningful and relevant vocabulary of our secular society in these the closing decades of the second millennium, no sir, no siree, ya bedder believe it, right on, daddio, you cotton-picking bastard, get with it, stay tuned as leading Oxford campus hostess and elegant conversationalist Eve Greenstreet, wife of uncontroversial ithyphallic banker Syd Greenstreet, goes on about what she's sorry but she simply can't avoid describing as her endlessly fascinating self, and why don't you piss off?'

Lancewood screamed quietly, as if half to himself. 'No. No. It can't be. It's not in nature.'

'I assure you I've reproduced it with toiling fidelity, the most aridly pedantic literalism conceivable. Except of course in point of duration. You'll have some idea if you imagine what you've just heard lasting about three hundred times as long.'

'I daren't, I'd go mad.'

'I'd had as much as flesh and blood could stand after five minutes,' said Jake. 'My most obvious counter was feigning illness, but that's not as straightforward as it may well sound. Any really serious disorder is ruled out – heart-attack, stroke, apoplexy, all of them most alluring, and in the circumstances extremely plausible, but quite apart from how you deal with the doctor you find you can't face the upset, the ambulance and all that. At the other end of the scale, headaches and so on have been worked to death. So you need a dose of something incapacitating but not dangerous, in the 'flu mode let's say. The trouble with that is you can't just suddenly start quivering like a jelly and saying you've got to go home – well actually in this case I'm pretty sure I'd have got away with it, but I didn't know that then. I thought then I'd need acting ability, again wrongly, and a reasonable build-up, call it an hour at least from the first passing shiver to deciding to pack it in, plus time for getting the bill, finding a taxi and being loyally seen home. And time was the very thing I couldn't spend any at all of, so I went on the booze.

'Now as you know Damon, I don't enjoy getting drunk and I absolutely hate being drunk, not understanding what you're saying and feeling as if you're moving about on the sea-bed but still able to breathe. But I didn't think it would come to that when I started off, you see. I was working on the principle of lowering the old critical faculty, blunting the responses and such to the point where she'd merely be boring the arse off me. But I never got there, I can't have done, I mean I can't remember what happened late on or even latish on and I can only reconstruct bits of it, but I must have got utterly smashed and found I still couldn't stand her and threw a pass purely and simply to shut her up, which I'd as soon have thought of doing before she turned up, throw a pass I mean, as fly in the fucking air, as you shall hear. I don't know why I didn't just go home instead because it must have been quite late by then and I don't know where I did the throwing but I do remember it worked, that's to say it shut her up. And also to say it was accepted, or since short of rape it's always the woman who decides, it was encouraged, never mind she hung out a don't-try-anything sign when I invited her and a rotten-sod-for-taking-advantage one this morning. This morning, Christ. Anyway . . . encouraged. She couldn't have got it all worked out as a conscious strategy could she? If you want cock talk balls kind of style? No of course she couldn't.

'It wasn't just balls though, as I hope I conveyed to you. One's used to that. This is Oxford, let's face it, as she'd say screwing up her nose to show she was being witty. No, it was her thinking she was the thinking man's rattle that made me want to watch her being eaten alive by crocodiles. You know, don't be so dazzled by how terrifically brilliant it all is with all those frightfully clever little cameo parts and absolutely marvellous imitations and accents, don't be carried away by all that so that you don't see that underneath it's *bloody good stuff*, wickedly observant and cruelly accurate and actually very concerned about the state of the language and of our society too. Like Mencken only sexy with it. Oh dear oh dear oh dear. And the insensitivity. I've been given to understand in the last few weeks that I'm not as good as I used to think I was at disguising my feelings, especially when they're feelings of contempt, hatred, weariness and malicious hilarity as they are most of the time these days. Well with Eve, for the first hour or so, until my face got tired, I smiled and nodded and twinkled and tried to laugh, and then, but this was well *after* I'd realised she was going to bat through to the end, then I stopped bothering. Cold. And she didn't notice a thing. Brenda would say of course she'd noticed and that made her nervous so that she couldn't think of any other way of going on. Well I've had my nervous moments but I doubt if I've ever been so frozen with terror that the recourse of shutting my trap has fled my mind. But then Brenda's been. . . .'

Jake paused. After a moment Lancewood got up and put two more logs on the fire, then went out carrying the electric kettle. The room was pleasantly warm and Jake's chair, his every time he came here, more comfortable than any in his own rooms or at Burgess Avenue. Beside it stood a small table bearing a teapot with an embroidered cosy, a Minton cup and saucer and plate, a silver dish with shortbread on it and a glass that had held Malmsey, the only after-dinner wine he really enjoyed. The lights were too low for him to see any of the pictures in detail but he liked them to be there. Outside he could hear rain and wind and nothing else. Physically he was almost himself again, and though it would be different soon enough he felt completely safe, not just secure from harm but in some positive sense he couldn't define. A passage of Horace stole into his mind unbidden, so he booted the bugger out again a bit sharp, and quite right too.

All manner of clocks started striking ten-thirty. Lancewood came back and plugged the kettle in at his side of the fireplace. He was wearing what he called his upper-crust old queen's smoking-jacket in mulberry-coloured velvet.

'One or two questions occur to me,' he said. 'For instance, since you seem to have started hating the lady very much almost as soon as she arrived, why didn't you just tell her you found you had a headache and must leave at once?'

'Oh, Damon. Chivalry. And a long way behind that, memory of the fact that I see her every other day I'm here in the course of duty. To have walked out then and there would have been an insult, whereas my later behaviour in taking advantage of her did no more than damage her self-respect a lot. And I didn't know what my later behaviour was going to be until later, if then.'

'Very well, why did you invite her to dine with you? Had you forgotten all about her? Or I suppose she'd changed out of all recognition, had she?'

'That's more like it, as a question I mean, or questions rather. I invited her because I wanted to confide in her on a matter soon to emerge. As regards her revoltingness, I did try the Marx-Brothers theory briefly, that she had been great fun then and had stayed exactly the same but the lapse of time, it must be fifteen years or more, had made me see her as bloody awful. Change of taste in the world at large, not just in me. It's tempting but I'm afraid it won't do.'

There was a longer pause. Lancewood made tea; it was a China blend you never saw anywhere else but in this room. Even before he had expected, Jake's sense of safety began to slip away from him. He said without much solid intention that he must be going soon.

'Soon or late, you're not going till my curiosity is entirely laid to rest, and if that takes another three hours, so be it. Drink your tea.'

Jake obeyed, which is to say he took a sip; it was delicious. 'Quite amazing, the consistency with which I saw everything about her as what it wasn't, I'm talking about the past. I mistook her egotism for sparkle, her knowingness for judgement, her cheap jeering for healthy disrespect and her . . . vulgarity for plain speaking. Oh, Christ, and something I haven't mentioned up to now, her habit of saying I know I talk too much and then going on talking too much, I thought that was engaging insight and disarming frankness instead of bullshit. She gets things wrong all the time too. Now the reason I never even rose to the level of giving her the benefit of a couple of dozen doubts whenever she did or said anything . . . let's take it in stages. I hardly knew her before I started having a sucessful affair with her, I mean we suited each other physically. But it wasn't that, because I went on seeing her after it was over, on at least one occasion for a whole evening, and I thought I'd forgotten all about it but later on I remembered one thing, or realised one negative thing, I hadn't started wanting her to be dead the moment she opened her mouth – that would have stuck in my mind. And I'm sure, this I can't remember but I'm sure from experience with other ex-girl-friends that I didn't sit there goggling at her tits and thinking about how it used to be and what fun if we tried it again. No, it was just that in those days I was a normal man with a normal interest in women and now I'm not. Yes Damon, I've lost all desire, though funnily enough not all performance, so last night might have been worse. Different, anyway. But since I can't remember anything about it, not a hell of a lot. I'm undergoing "therapy" for my condition, needless to say without the slightest effect.

'You see the really awful part about last night wasn't anything that happened during it. I'll have to go back a bit. Without ever really thinking about it I'd been working on the assumption that the only reason women were tolerated was because the world was run by men, normal men who by definition didn't see them as they really were because they were looking at them through, er, a kind of distorting – '

'Horn-rimmed spectacles.'

'Sod you. Yes. Once I even played with the fantasy that the point of women being in season all the time with only brief interruptions, and even those aren't treated as interruptions among primitive peoples I read somewhere, anyway if they were like dogs or rather bitches with intervals of several months during which they aroused no sexual feelings at all then most of 'em wouldn't make it, they'd get their bloody heads kicked off before they could come on heat. Well that was all very well, quite harmless, the sort of thing a lot of men say on the understanding that they don't really mean it, not really, especially men who are ones for the ladies.

'Now we come to last night, the awful part about it. The reason I could be so wrong about her wasn't so much that I'd been looking at her through horn-rimmed spectacles as that I hadn't been listening to her at all, not a word she ever said, she just didn't interest me. And I could have sworn she did, I could have sworn I'd identified her as what did I say, lively and clever and plain-spoken and so on. But I'd really – only – wanted – one – thing. She told me so this morning and that's when I saw it. I don't even like them much. Women. I despise them intellectually – as the Governing Body now knows. Christ, that reminds me, I must write to the Master.'

'What about?'

'What about? Me blowing my top at the College Meeting, that's what about.'

'Oh, that. You did cause a bit of a stir at the time but these things soon blow over as you know, or rather as you would know if you'd always attended as regularly as I have. Behaviour that would be taken as evidence of madness or brain damage or the utmost malignity outside is just something that helps to make life interesting when we do it. Comes from being in college. Rather like the Army. For instance Wynn-Williams and the Jehovah's Witnesses, were you there or did you ever hear about it? I'll tell you another time. Go on about not liking women.'

'Yes. Well, last night was a sort of illustration of it. I think in a nasty way I quite enjoyed it, at least until I got pissed, watching that female make an exhibition of herself. The thing is, it's not them, it's me. I don't see them as they are any more than I did before. I haven't got those spectacles any more but that doesn't mean my sight's improved. Is it possible to be objective in a case like this? What I feel is imagine me thinking I liked them all those years when I didn't really care for them one bit. Rather sad. Makes you wonder, too. I mean can it be only me? Eve used to screw around a lot at the time I knew her, so there must have been plenty of other blokes who failed to notice she was intolerable company. And blokes who screw girls who screw around a lot are usually blokes who screw around a lot, like me or rather me as I was. More support for the idea that womanisers don't like women. Whereas in fact, in fact they are nice, aren't they Damon? You ought to know, you've never fancied them for an instant and you like them.'

'As you say, but Jake love, you're depressing yourself, it's not as bad as you think, you're still suffering from the various tolls that have been taken of you.'

'I'd better go to bed.'

'Not in your present mood. I understand now why your final contribution this afternoon was so emphatic. A lot of what you said was true but only as far as it went. There's one thing you ought to try to remember. Men have their own ways, just as efficient ways, of being evasive and overbearing and dull and thoroughly unsatisfactory. Perhaps I see some of them a little more clearly than you do. That ought to make me more tolerant when a girl tells me she thinks Hamlet was a woman. I don't say it does but it ought to. What about Brenda? She's the only one who matters.'

'She says I only want one thing too. Of course I don't know how far she. . . .' Jake spread his hands.

'Oh dear. That is rather untoward, I do see.'

'I'm supposed to be working out what I feel about her. I don't dislike her, which is a start of a kind. I like having her about the place. I like chatting to her, but I don't find myself wanting to tell her things – I remember in the old days whenever I read or heard or thought of anything funny or striking or whatever it might be, my first thought was always, I must tell Brenda about that. Not any more. I suppose I ought to tell her just the same – my "therapist" works on the principle that the way of getting to want to do something you don't want to do is to keep doing it. Which seems to me to be a handy route from not . . . pause . . . wanting to do it to not-wanting, wanting not, to do it. But I am paying him to know best. Brenda wants affection, physical affection. She also needs it and ought to have it. My chap is always on at me to go through the motions of it on the principle I've described. I'm a bit scared of being shifted from not-pause-wanting to do that to not-wanting to do it. Do you know what I think I am, Damon? A male chauvinist pig. Until the other day I'd never have dreamt of saying that about anybody, least of all myself. Just goes to show, doesn't it? I think if you don't mind I will bugger off, before I depress myself into a decline. But thank you.'

It was of Kelly, not Eve or Brenda, that Jake was thinking as he trotted through the rain to his rooms. How did she fit in? He didn't think he felt any affection for her, which might have had something to do with what she had said about things like his dick – easy to forgive, not so easy to forget – but he couldn't be sure while his main feeling for her was still pity. She certainly aroused his interest, genuine interest as opposed to the testosterone-fed substitute that had graced his sometime dealings with Eve, but again that interest might well attach to her as a phenomenon rather than as a person. Oh well.

On arrival he shut his outer door in case Mrs Sharp should be on her way into college to hear from his very lips whether he wanted his study curtains washed, and took the plastic phallus out of the drawer where it had lain for the past fifteen days, out of sight all the time and out of mind too except when he had been in London or on his way there. With a paper-knife, a razor-blade and his bare hands he eventually reduced it to fragments too small for it to be made recognisable again by anyone but a three-dimensional-jigsaw-puzzle grandmaster, should such a person exist. As he worked Jake muttered to himself.

'Ah now me poor owld bogger, sure it's athackun your own masculinithy yiz are. Ochone, ochone, yiz do be performun an acth of sexual self-thesthroction, do yiz know. Guilth and shame have been rakun havoc wid yiz so dey have, acushla machree. Jasus, Mary and Joseph, de resolth of inorthinathly sthricth thoileth-thrainun thoo be sure, wid maybe a spoth of sothomy ath your poblic school trown in. And bethath and be-fockun-gorrah, loife's a soighth aisier dis way if yiz ron tings roighth.'

23 Extreme Bourgeois Puritan Conventionality

As well as Kelly's visit to Oxford, that day had seen ball lightning in Glasgow. Later in the month the weather improved, with long spells of sunshine that reminded Jake of one of his summer terms as an undergraduate before the war, he couldn't remember which. At the beginning of June, while Brenda stayed with her Northumberland cousins, he spent a couple of nights with Lancewood and his friend John at their cottage near Dry Sandford, sitting out on the lawn with them till an advanced hour. It didn't last: the rain came back, accompanied by cold and thunder, in nice time to damage Eights Week and plague examinees scurrying to and from the Schools. The last day of term, the last of that academic year, was one of the worst.

Even so, the Oxford end of Jake's life over those weeks had been normal, even satisfactory to the limited degree possible: he hadn't trampled Miss Calvert to death, the little bastard from Teddy Hall had taken to cutting (no doubt it was called boycotting) his lectures and it looked as if Thwaites, the Bradfordian, was going to get his First in Part I, as against which the Cardiff man had been offered the job and had accepted. The London end, beyond question the larger one, had in the meantime not done too well. Jake kept up his visits to Rosenberg who displayed, whether or not he really felt, great interest in the Eve episode; it was possible that his mill had been getting a little hard up for grist. Naturally he tended to concentrate on his patient's fragmentary recollections of the act of sex he had performed, trying to elicit more of them from him.

'Let's go over the whole thing again at a snail's pace,' he would say.

'I honestly don't think I can do it more slowly than last time.'

'Ah, you can try. Now you commenced manual manipulation of her breasts.'

'Yes, I thought pedal manipulation was ruled out one way or another,' Jake ventured to reply on one such occasion. 'For instance etymologically.'

'I'm sorry, I'm afraid I don't quite follow.'

'Never mind. Yes, manual manipulation of her breasts was just what I did commence.'

'And what were your feelings as you did so?' Rosenberg would pursue.

'I've told you. That it was odd, that it was bizarre.'

'You mean you found it disgusting.'

'No, again as I've told you, all I found it and everything else I can remember was odd or bizarre.'

'You suffered feelings of shame.'

'No, and not of guilt either. Not even whatever you called it, personally orientated guilt about my wife. I wasn't thinking of her at the time.'

Another recurrent theme had to do with Jake's fantasies, in the sense not of his private daydreamings but of his commissions of these to paper for Rosenberg's inspection. Each fresh attempt brought the same response, the same as the very first, the one about the fantastically beautiful girl with the unbelievable figure. The holder of that MA (Dip. Psych) shook his small head, drew in his breath and sighed, cleared his throat repeatedly and in general behaved much as Jake would have done if confronted by an essay attributing the origin of Mediterranean civilisations to colonists from outer space. There was the same effect of not knowing where to start.

'I'm a doctor,' was a favourite opening of Rosenberg's. 'I'm *your* doctor, Mr Richardson. I'm not going to be shocked, you know, by anything you think or say or write.'

'No, I believe that.'

'If you do – I beg your pardon, seeing that you do, why don't you come clean? Or rather' – it was well worth watching, the deliberation with which he steeled himself the first time he leaped the yawning semantic chasm in front of him – 'come *dirty*!?'

'Well, that's the dirtiest I could do. You must admit I've made progress, cutting out all the soft and warm stuff and being heavy on the Anglo-Saxon.'

'True, true, but it's all too normal, too straight. I've never worked with anybody who hadn't some slight deviation, often more than one – voyeurism, fetishism, a very wide field there, sado-masochism, even more so. . . .'

'I'm sorry to disappoint you, I must be a very straight man.'

'In some ways indeed you are, to the point of extreme bourgeois puritan conventionality partly resulting from your having attended a single-sex school.'

'Oh come off it, man.' Jake never quite got over his incredulity at this accusation.

Twice at least Rosenberg tried to support his view by referring to the goings-on at the McDougall. 'Several of the photographs that were shown to you there you found offensive. In particular one featuring the female sex organ.'

'Yes, I remember. I said it was ugly and so it was, to me, and I bet a lot of other men would say the same and to find it an ugly sight in a photograph isn't the same as finding the whole idea disgusting which I know is what you're working towards.'

That usually stopped that one, though Jake's eccentric and psychologically sinister dislike of undressing in mixed company was sometimes taken into consideration. Like all Rosenberg's others, this line of inquiry was continuously and abundantly boring but at least, by the relaxed standards of the matter in hand, it had some observable relevance. The same could not be said of an occasion when Rosenberg produced a machine either called something like a GPI or designed to do something called something like GPI. It was somewhat smaller than the nocturnal mensurator (itself long since returned to him and never mentioned since) and was supposedly designed to measure nervous tension. The thing worked by in the first place measuring something else, sweat, perhaps, or changes in skin temperature; Jake, who didn't listen to Rosenberg whenever it seemed legitimate, wasn't listening. Pads connected by wires to the machine were fastened on his thumb and middle finger, a switch clicked and a different sort of click, as from a small loudspeaker, followed. It proved to be the first of a series of such clicks, one every five or six seconds. Rosenberg took him on an imaginary stroll round Orris Park and the clicks stayed the same, sat him in his study and the rate increased slightly, put him in the bedroom with an undraped Brenda and the machine behaved like a Geigar counter in a plutonium shop. They didn't try that again.

Actually that happened on the first Tuesday of the summer vacation. The dating was fixed in Jake's mind because something much more extraordinary happened then too: there was a moment of mild interest, nothing to do with the 'therapy' of course. He had mentioned the end of the Oxford term as he sat down on arrival.

'Ah yes,' said Rosenberg, 'to be sure. That means you'll be having several months at your disposal which you'll be able to devote exclusively to research because of your freedom from teaching responsibilities.'

He spoke with marked reluctance, indeed with sullenness, as if he had been offered too good a price for reciting those couple of dozen words to be able to turn down the job but wasn't going to throw in anything in the way of pretending to care. Jake came back with something like Yes and the psychologist's manner changed completely, became just that, in fact, as he set the ball rolling with a fervid inquiry after his patient's early morning erections.

He must have got an answer but Jake knew nothing of it. His mind had sped back to their very first encounter when Rosenberg had used the same grudging tone in talking of his ancestry, then forward again a week and a bit to their convivial chat in the Lord Nelson. There had been an air of resentment, almost of hatred, about the way he had planked down that couple of miserable facts about his friend (friend? friend?) the editor of *Mezzanine* and how long he might or might not go on editing it – yes, in that way worse for Rosenberg in the pub, because pubs were places where you were supposed to have real convivial chats, not like consulting-rooms or hospitals where you ran the show and need only waste a few seconds on tittle-tattle before getting on with *what really mattered*.

'No, no erotic dreams,' he said to Rosenberg. Another one was what he was saying to himself, another fucking displaced egotist. As the ordinary sort cared only for maintaining or advancing their own position, judging always in terms of what was useful, never of what was interesting, so this sort put a cause or subject in place of self, identified with it to a degree seldom envisaged by those fond of that term and made everything an example of something, some theory, generalisation, set of facts already in their keeping. He had run across plenty of them in his time at Oxford, as he had half-remembered while he ordered his drink in the Lord Nelson: atheistical religionists who talked, not all that much better than Eve had done, about the hidden powers of the mind, philosophasters, global-equality persons – all or any of whom Rosenberg had reminded him of on the same occasion. That was today and yesterday; the day before yesterday had been far less daft, with Marxists of various sorts predominant or thought to be: as an undergraduate he had had pointed out to him a not very old man at Exeter to whom all evils flowed from what he still called Bolshevism.

Some of this occurred to Jake on his way home after the consultation. It was then too that he reconsidered Rosenberg's fitness for his job. He had tentatively decided, that time when the Workshop was assembling, that a psychologist could afford not to know a great deal outside his subject and still do well enough within it. What about a psychologist who didn't care in the least for the world outside it, even resented its existence? There were fields of study in which indifference or antipathy to all other matters could be no handicap, those fields in which the presence of an observer had a negligible effect on what was observed – astronomy, for instance. Jake felt that psychology must be a different case, so much so that he now doubted his earlier view. Any student of the mind would surely be a good deal hampered by lack of all acquaintance with some of its more note-worthy products – art, for instance. But he didn't bother to pursue the thought because whatever conclusion about Rosenberg he might arrive at he was stuck with him.

And that was because of Brenda. It would be unfair to say that she had faith in Rosenberg; to her, he was simply the expert whose instruction must be followed regardless. No, a little more, in that to query any of those instructions was seen as captious at best, as showing less than a burning desire for sexual betterment. Other things were similarly seen, most of all Jake's persistent refusal to accompany Brenda to the Workshop after the first try. Ed had it in for him, he said; there was no knowing what the man might get up to next, given the chance. He also said he was uncertain, unhappy, unconvinced, things like that about the procedures followed, pale versions of his real feeling that if Rosenberg was a bit suspect Ed was a ravening charlatan. (Didn't Rosenberg's readiness to send his patients to work with Ed make Rosenberg worse than a bit suspect? Not quite necessarily: he might find he gained fresh insight that way, might be standing by to intervene should the facilitator require one of the participants to be disembowelled by way of smartening him up. He – Rosenberg – got a mark for not having put any pressure on Jake to resume attendance.)

Another thing Jake didn't tell Brenda was as much as the bare fact of Kelly's call on him in Oxford. His silence was variously motivated. Admitting in effect that she had been right and he wrong about the girl would have gone against the grain, though he minded that sort of thing less than most men. It would have distressed him too to recount the incident in full, and although some people might have consented to be fobbed off with a fifty-word synopsis, Brenda was certainly not one of them. There was also the good rough rule that said that telling one female anything at all about your dealings with another was to be avoided whenever possible. And there was a fourth reason which eluded him at the time. Anyway, keeping quiet was another discouragement from changing his mind and starting to go to the Workshop again: one little extra apology for having invaded him, accidentally or accidentally-on-purpose within Brenda's hearing, and that would be shit. Well, he wasn't exactly palpitating with hunger for Kelly's company but he did want to know how she was getting on, for which his only source was Brenda – Rosenberg had gone all professional-ethical on him when approached. Since he couldn't hurry things up by admitting his interest he had to sit through Brenda's weekly bulletins with the best grace he could muster, and recent experience made him see to it that his best was pretty bloody good.

'Well, we started with scanning pairs and free scanning as before,' she said on the first Saturday evening, 'and then we did parents and children.'

'What's that?'

'First you're your father and then you're your mother and then you're yourself as a child.'

'How do you mean?'

'You act it. You pick somebody of your own sex and talk to them as if you were your father talking to you.'

'Oh yes?' said Jake, leaning forward eagerly. 'What about?'

'Whatever Ed decides. About your father, about sex – you try and remember what he did say. Telling you off. A good deal of that.'

'Really. It must call for quite a bit of acting ability.'

'You'd be surprised how good some of them are. Lionel was marvellous as his mother, he even managed to look like her. Well you know what I mean.'

'Yes of course.' He gave himself a mental pat on the back for having detected intimations of queerdom in Lionel.

'Martha was very interesting when she was her mother – you remember her mother's horrible to her, but Martha wasn't horrible at all, when she was being her mother I mean. You know, reasonable and kind and every-thing. Most odd.'

'Mm. It sounds absolutely – '

'Your friend Kelly was really the star turn.'

'Was she?'

'As herself as a child. Honestly it was quite frightening. The voice particu-larly. If you'd shut your eyes you could have sworn it was a child speaking. She was different from the time before. Much madder. Of course she wasn't putting on a show for you today. She asked after you in the lunch-break.'

'That was nice.' Quite safe, he thought; Brenda wasn't one to save things up, very much the contrary.

'She hasn't been round here since last Saturday has she?'

'Good God no,' he said, sounding shocked. 'Whatever gave you that idea?' He wasn't acting; his shock had come from the immediate perception that only the luck of the draw had made Brenda ask what she had asked instead of whether Kelly had dropped in on him, say, and from the thought of how he might have reacted if the draw had gone against him. Anybody would think I was having an affair with the bloody girl, he said to himself irritably.

'Just the way she asked after you. I expect that was to get at me.'

'Why should she get at you?'

'Because she's after you, or was. Probably moved on to somebody else by now. You're not still falling for that investigative-journalist imperson-ation, are you?'

He frowned in thought. 'I don't know. Anyway, if you're right she sounds a rather pathetic character.'

'Oh yes she is, some of the time.'

'Sorry darling, I'm afraid I don't quite get you.'

'I mean she has a pathetic act to go with her bright act and all her other acts. She's never genuine. That's what's wrong with her.'

He didn't dispute this aloud and the talk moved on eventually reaching Geoffrey and causing Jake momentary but keen regret at not having been there to see for himself. Perhaps Brenda had sensed his interest in Kelly, because in subsequent Saturday debriefings she would tend to mention her late and cursorily or not at all. To take it out of him deliberately in such a way didn't quite fit her character as he had come to know it over the years, but then she seemed as the weeks went by to be changing in other ways too, nothing spectacular or even easy to pin down, in fact the nearer he got to doing that the sillier it sounded. She was becoming more friendly and at the same time less intimate; amiable and talkative, never anywhere near chucking crockery about and yet not, or not so much, or not so often, or perhaps indeed not turning her eyes on his in the full deep glance he had known before. He found something comparable in her behaviour during the non-genital sensate focusing sessions on which, after the almost total failure of two successive genital dittos, Rosenberg had ordered them to fall back.

'Is that nice?' she would ask, stroking his chest. 'Or at least comparatively nice, I know this isn't your kind of thing much but there must be degrees, quite good and not so good. How is it?'

'Oh, quite good.'

'Or would you like it sort of harder, you know, pressing down more?'

'No, that's fine as it is.'

'You're meant to be really relaxed to benefit from it. I'm sure it's beneficial anyway, in general, I mean. Anything that reduces stress must be, don't you think?'

'Well, so people keep saying.'

'I think it's generally accepted. . . . Right, my turn, but let's have a kiss first. . . . Now you do my hip. Let me show you. All the way from here down to here and up again, slowly. Try it. . . . That's it but not quite so lightly. I find it helps at first to shut your eyes and think of something peaceful, like a garden or a lake. You ought to try that.'

This matter-of-factness helped Jake. He still didn't look forward to the focusings but the gloom their prospect had aroused in him was somewhat alleviated. The hard work he put in each time not to seem to be gritting his teeth seemed to have its effect: there were no more complaints of lack of affection. On the two occasions when Brenda went with him to see Rosenberg in Harley Street and was asked what she thought of her marital situation, she answered in summary that it could be better but was coming along not too badly. Even her reproaches for not coming to the Workshop fell away. He began to feel occasional stirrings of hope, though his relief each time Rosenberg didn't order a return to genital sensate focusing was as heartfelt as ever. Funny how it had worked all right with Eve, he thought to himself more than once, or perhaps the difference was simply that then he had been free, responsible to nothing and nobody.

Over the weekend after the end of term the same small thing happened three times: the telephone rang, Brenda went to or across the kitchen to answer it and was hung up on as soon as she spoke. She mentioned burglars; Jake said they'd be wasting their time. He would have forgotten all about this if a not-quite-so-small-thing hadn't happened on the Monday evening while he was watching the nine o'clock news on BBC 1. The telephone rang; cursing mildly he made his way out and answered it.

'Is it possible to speak to Mrs Richardson please?' asked a very hoarse voice with at least two accents in it, one foreign, another perhaps regional, and a couple of speech impediments.

'I'm afraid she's out.' Earlier, Brenda had said she was going to a film about gypsies with Alcestis, the sort of thing she had done two or three times recently, if not a spiffing scheme in itself then a bloody sight better one than bringing Alcestis here.

'Can I get her later?'

'She won't be back till eleven at the earliest. I suggest you – '

Click, Jake would have forgotten all about this too if, ten minutes later, the door-bell hadn't chimed and it hadn't turned out to be Kelly who had caused it to do so.

'Jesus Christ,' he said.

'It's all right, no trouble I promise you, I'm perfectly okay, I can only stay a minute, can I just come into the passage?'

He looked at her. She seemed to have shrunk a good deal since he left her to Ernie, perhaps because of the head-scarf that flattened her hair against her skull and the tightly drawn raincoat, but her manner was much what it had been then. Anyway, what could he do? He stood aside and shut the door after her.

'What do you want? Was it you on the telephone just now?'

'Yes, Brenda hates me. She's probably quite right. Have you told her about me coming to see you in Oxford?'

'Certainly not.'

'Good, I didn't think you would have done. I haven't told anybody, not even my parents. What I wanted to ask you was about this weekend Workshop.'

'What? What weekend Workshop?'

'Didn't Brenda tell you?'

'No. You'd better. . . . You can't just stand there, take your things off and come and sit down.'

'It's okay, honestly.'

'Do as I tell you. Now what's this all about?'

'It's the weekend after next, starting on the Friday evening, the 8th, at least that's when we're supposed to get there so as to be able to start work in good time in the morning. The place is near Salisbury.'

'I see.' He saw more clearly that she had had her hair cut very short like a kind of rufous helmet. It took three or four years off her apparent age.

'Funny Brenda not telling you, Ed and Dr Rosenberg announced it last Saturday week. I. . . .'

'What?'

'I expect it slipped her mind. Why did you stop coming after just the one time?'

'It simply struck me as frightful rubbish and a complete bore.'

'Oh I quite agree, but. . . . What I wanted to ask you, do you think you could possibly come to it, the weekend Workshop I mean?'

So many expressions, most of them impure, tried to get out of Jake's mouth at once that for the moment he said nothing articulate.

'You see I'm absolutely dreading it, I can't tell you how much, but my parents want me to go and they're so sweet to me I really can't not go, and I thought if you were there, just there, somebody I trusted, I wouldn't feel so bad. I wouldn't, you know, do anything, I couldn't with Brenda about all the time, could I?'

'I'm sorry, Kelly, but you must realise it's quite impossible.'

She got up at once from the corner of the settee where she had been sitting for less than a minute. 'Never mind, it doesn't really matter, I'm sure I'll manage all right, it was just a thought, of course it was ridiculous to expect you to, I quite understand.'

'I am sorry,' he said, following her into the passage.

'No no, don't be, forget it, I shouldn't have asked, put you in an embarrassing position, just thinking of myself as usual.'

Being an erstwhile successful womaniser Jake had acted against his better judgement a number of times, but never more directly and more consciously than when he said, as he did now, 'All right, sod it, I'll see if I can fix it up.'

24 Something I Want to Show You

Fixing it up was not straightforward. To approach Brenda – yes, why *hadn't* she mentioned it? – with stuff like thinking of popping up to Dry Sandford again about the 8th or 9th would be to put in an urgent request for trouble. Luckily the next day was Rosenberg-day, though here again care was needed: no Kelly-told-me or Rosenberg might in his innocence or whatever it was drop that one in front of Brenda. After a résumé of his latest self-abusive adventures Jake casually let fall that he was thinking of another try at the Workshop, not on the Saturday to come because he had to be in Oxford then, but on the one after, the 9th. Expressing no surprise at either his ignorance or his change of mind and not the heartiest approval of the latter, perhaps because it damaged his guilt-and-shame thesis, Rosenberg gave some particulars of the proposed weekend and went straight on, or rather straight back since they had been there several times before, to Jake's early sexual feelings and experiences. Of these he had managed to remember a very fair amount he thought he had forgotten without thereby changing his condition in the slightest.

When he brought the weekend up with Brenda she did express surprise, saying she had told him about it on the evening of the day she had herself been told, but now she came to think of it it had been at the end of the evening, most likely after he had taken his Mogadon and so was in a drowsy inattentive state. Her approval was a shade warmer than Rosenberg's but not unqualified: he had always said the Workshop was rubbish so what had happened to change his mind? Well, he had been thinking, and couldn't help being impressed by the fact (it was a fact) that she constantly said she was the better for the experience, and a weekend in the country would be nice. All right, but he wasn't to piss on the proceedings; he promised not to.

No sooner was the the thing fixed up than the tonic effect of the actual fixing-up subsided and his qualms began to mount. It was true that Brenda's reports had included much activity that was daft, pointless, unpalatable and (wait for it) boring but nothing positively unsafe, lewd or illegal; just give that Ed bugger a free hand for forty-eight hours though, in a house as comparatively remote as the one designated seemed to be and for openers, as he would say, you'd be getting off lightly with gladiatorial games. And what might Kelly get up to? He turned his mind away from that, concentrating it on the thought that whatever dire possibilities occurred to him he couldn't fail her, not appear. Once, he was hard at it when he fancied he recognised the extra reason why he hadn't told Brenda about Kelly-in-Oxford: if he had he would never have been able to get away with wanting to join in on the weekend. Funny what you could see coming without knowing it.

As the day approached it began to look less baleful. He had found out by indirections that Geoffrey was to be of the party, so a touch at least of entertainment and satisfaction of malice was guaranteed. Then there was plain curiosity. And then there was the weather, hot and sunny all week long. When Friday arrived with more of the same and the time began to move along to six o'clock Jake felt little tingles of expectation, as he had once done before every out-of-the-way journey with the prospect of someone new and wonderful at the end of it.

Almost dead on the hour a fair-sized yellow car of foreign manufacture drew up as arranged outside 47 Burgess Avenue. It was driven by Ivor, whom Jake wouldn't have recognised after their one meeting a couple of months before. He turned out to be in his thirties, tallish, fairish, serious-looking and doing quite well in a building society. Beside him was Geoffrey. As could be seen when he emerged and came to the front door, he was most peculiarly got up in a sports jacket and flannel trousers, a shirt with an unobtrusive check, a plain woollen tie that matched his socks, and brown brogues; it was almost as if he had *tried* to choose clothes appropriate to a weekend in the country. Mind you, he must be bloody hot in them, there was that to be said. While giving a hand with the Richardsons' luggage, shutting the boot, getting in beside Jake at the back and waiting for Brenda, he explained with a thoroughness such as to defeat all misunderstanding that he had left Alcestis their car, his and her car, to do with as she pleased; this one, this car, the car they were sitting in, belonged to Ivor, was Ivor's car.

Jake remembered very well the senile-dementia treatment he had had meted out to him at the original Workshop and wondered whether Geoffrey intended his last few hundred words as more of the same with more yet to come. If so, he was going to be in trouble quite soon, but before Jake had fixed on just what kind he caught sight of Brenda hurrying up the tiny garden path and forgot all about Geoffrey for the moment.

After so many weeks of conscientious dieting she had lost something like two and a half stone and could no longer be called fat. With the weight she had taken off some apparent years too and would have passed for forty. She was wearing what must be a new dress in pale green silk, some not very serious brown-and-white shoes and an openly frivolous white hat. How fetching, how pleasant, how *nice* she looks, Jake thought to himself; must remember to tell her so at first opportunity.

There was some trouble with the hat when she got in beside Ivor but it passed off easily enough and they were soon on their way across town to get on to the M20. The traffic was thickish, though not so bad as it would have been if most of the people motoring out of London to the West of England countryside and resorts hadn't downed their shit-shovels about noon (Jake decided).

'What a glorious day,' said Brenda in a dreamy voice. 'And how lovely to be driving; just think of fighting one's way on to a train at Paddington in this heat. I mean to be driven. It is kind of you to take us, Ivor dear.'

'Not at all Brenda, I had three empty seats, and this is the only way I can travel. Has that come up, incidentally? My psychiatrist says it's quite common, chaps who can't face any kind of public transport or even a car or even being driven by someone they trust in their own car aren't bothered at all driving their own car. To do with being in control apparently. Isn't that interesting?'

It interested Jake, who remembered now about Ivor's phobias, in more than one way. As soon as they reached the M20 they moved into the fast lane and stayed there. Jake wasn't at all a nervous traveller but after a few miles he did start wondering what substantial fraction of the speed of sound they had reached. The object seemed to be to overtake everything else going in their direction: container trucks, articulated lorries, quite serious-looking private cars appeared in the far distance, swelled hectically in size and in effect hurtled past them like express-trains. Beside him Geoffrey stirred, shifted and made sudden darting movements with his head in pursuit of items that, seen clearly enough for long enough, might prove to arouse his puzzlement or dissatisfaction. At one point the momentary placing of a tall vehicle in an inner lane meant that he clearly missed a sign that Jake had happened to catch.

'Services in so many miles,' he said, pretending to be trying to be helpful. 'I couldn't see how many.'

'What?'

'Services some distance ahead.'

'What distance?'

'Services,' Jake began, then noticed that Geoffrey's frown, in being from the start, deepened slightly at this third utterance of the noun. 'Services are things like food, cups of tea, facilities for – '

'Wouldn't it be better to push on until we're nearer the other end?'

'I'm sure it would, I was just explaining about Services. As well as food and tea they have petrol and probably – '

'Are we low on petrol, Ivor?'

'No, I had a full tank when I picked you up, Geoffrey.'

'There you are, Jake.' Geoffrey gave a hesitant smile. 'Right as rain. Nothing to worry about at all.'

'I wasn't worrying for Christ's sake, I was telling you about Services because of that sign.'

'Sign?'

'Yes, Geoffrey: *sign*. The generic name for flat objects, often rectangular in shape, on which instructions or as in this case information – '

'Do please shut up, Jake,' said Brenda.

Jake held his peace. After about another three minutes' driving they came off the motorway and found to their surprise an authentic old-fashioned family and commercial hotel where it proved possible to dine. All the dishes were firmly in the English tradition: packet soup with added flour, roast chicken so overcooked that each chunk immediately absorbed every drop of saliva in your mouth, though the waterlogged Brussels sprouts helped out a bit there, soggy tinned gooseberry flan and coffee tasting of old coffee-pots. Jake wasn't hungry anyway: foreboding had driven out his earlier feelings of looking forward and there was some tension among the party, no doubt as a result of his surely pretty mild brush with Geoffrey in the car, so he didn't say much. The only one who did was Ivor, whose prowess behind the wheel had made them early and who had filled in the spare time with a few large gin and tonics.

'I don't think these psychiatrist chaps are much good,' he said a couple of times in his agreeable fully modulated voice. 'Or perhaps the phobia lot are particularly lousy. I'm on my third and none of them have made a blind bit of difference. In fact . . . well never mind. Do you know what my latest one tried to tell me the other day? You don't mind me going on about this do you? I don't often get the chance.'

'You go on as long as you like, my dear.'

'Thanks, Brenda. Well – do you know what this bloke tried to tell me?'

'No,' said Geoffrey on brief consideration.

'Well you wouldn't would you Geoffrey? Now you've heard me go on about how I don't like the Tube, the Underground. Right, he took me down there the other week, we went all the way from Warren Street up to Hampstead and I was fine, didn't turn a hair. Next go-off, next day I've got to make the return trip on my own. I went down in the lift and on to the platform and in half a minute I was absolutely terrified. I got myself over it in the end with that deep breathing, but it wasn't funny. So I said all this, and he was *surprised*, because I'd done so well when we went together. And him with a syringe in his pocket with half a gallon of tranquilliser in it, enough to calm down King Kong. And he's *surprised* it makes a difference. That wasn't it though, the really marvellous thing he told me. Now . . . I'm an only child, it was a difficult birth, looks as if my mum and dad decided not to take any chances, I don't blame them. We've been though all that. Anyway, he asked me, when I said I'd been frightened he asked me if there was anything in particular I was frightened of, and I said yes there was, there was nothing on the indicator, no train signalled, and I thought, oh my God it'll never come, I'll be down here for ever. And he said, now this is it, he said, me being afraid of nothing arriving in my Underground was all to do with my mum being afraid of something arriving in her Underground. Isn't that marvellous? Especially nothing being the same as something. I tell you, that cheered me up, it really reassured me, I thought, I may be a bit peculiar but at least I'm not as bloody barmy as to come up with that.'

Jake, who had enjoyed the opening of this speech too, laughed a good deal, more than either Geoffrey or Brenda. Soon afterwards Ivor said they still had to find the house and he'd like to get there in the light, so the bill was called for. To Geoffrey's perplexity but without eliciting anything from him in the way of protest, thanks or contributions, Jake paid it; he considered that to save every spare penny for his retirement, every penny, every time would do its bit towards shortening that retirement. They went off. In less than ten minutes, before the sun was quite down, they had pulled up in the large asphalted front yard of a fair-sized red-brick building that must have dated from about the year 1900. Various creepers ran up its walls and there was an ochre-coloured lichen on part of its tiled roof. It was situated near the top of a slight depression that ran down from the main road to Salisbury. Ivor said interestedly that it looked a bit on the big side, to which Brenda demurred; Jake heard later that the place had once been a nursing-home and was now hired out for conferences and other enterprises of that kind, many of them no doubt perfectly serious and useful. They went inside.

In another ten minutes the four were reassembled in one of a pair of rooms run together by the disposal of folding doors. Both had the look of meagreness attached to being used rather than lived in: large table to discuss business round, dark-green leather armchairs to hold informal discussions in, reproductions of abstract paintings to do what with? Surely not look at; perhaps to be flattered by, flattered into fancying yourself a cultured person. Ed was on hand to greet them, giving Jake a smile not so much of geniality as of amusement; Rosenberg, little legs atwinkle, must still be pedalling gamely down the M20. The others already arrived were Lionel (stealing), Martha (mother), Winnie (shyness) and three men and a woman Jake had never seen before and whose names he didn't bother with for the moment because he would get to know them so very well the following day. After the introductions he stuck to Ivor, whom he had rather taken to and who seemed to need to talk to somebody.

'We're going to be sixteen altogether and that won't fill this house. It really is big.'

'Is that bad?'

'Not as such, but it means parts of it will be empty so that I can't sort of account for them.'

'I think I can see what you mean. But there's bound to be quite a large staff at a joint like this, and offices and so on.'

'That's true, I hadn't thought of that. Thank you, Jake.'

'Don't pills help? Tranquillisers?'

'Yes, but my bloke's made me give them up. Just gloss over the problem, he says. I take his point in a way, but I'm the one that needs them, not him.'

'Is there anything I can do?'

'It would be good if you could tell me you wouldn't mind if I came up to you and started talking rather fast and saying some pretty silly things.'

Jake had just told Ivor he wouldn't mind when a taxi drew up outside the window near which they were standing. It delivered Ruth (despair), Rosenberg, Kelly (you name it), an unnecessarily tall young woman with a head designed for somebody almost as short as Rosenberg, and not Chris (aggression or something), which was nice. When in due course Kelly came into what called itself the conference-room with the other new arrivals she had just the same easy, amicable manner as on first meeting Jake. She greeted everyone in turn, leaving him till last and taking a step or two beyond him so that he had to turn about to face her. Over his shoulder she gave Ivor a superb experienced-hostess look that apologised for removing Jake and at the same time indicated her confidence that the need to do this would be understood.

'Jake, we may only have a second or two so please don't interrupt, all right?'

His mental alarm-bell started up. It was some comfort that the chatter of other voices and the opportune arrival of a trolley with coffee and sandwiches would prevent their being overheard for the moment; not a lot, though. 'All right, but make it quick.'

'I'm in room 33, second floor just next to the landing. There's something I want to show you. It won't take long, five minutes, ten at the very outside, but I think it really must be in private. Will you come to my room, number 33, and look at it for me? Leave it till everyone's bedded down, midnight or later, I won't mind, I've got something to read.'

'You must be. . . . You must think I'm off my head.'

'Listen Jake, did I enjoy you turning me down? Would I enjoy it any more the second time? . . . Well there you are.'

'What do you want to show me?'

'A letter. Well, a kind of letter. I'd like you to read it for me.'

'Brenda's a light sleeper, I'd be almost certain to wake her up.'

'Has your room got a loo attached to it? Mine hasn't.'

'No.'

'Well there you are. Only five minutes. I'll expect you. Hallo Brenda, hallo Geoffrey, isn't this marvellous weather?'

Geoffrey understood without apparent trouble and said it was, but Brenda said in that colourless voice of hers, 'How are you getting on with your plans for exposing Ed? It's been a long time since we discussed them.'

'Oh, that.' Kelly laughed in a relaxed way. 'More or less on ice these days.'

'Really. You were quite keen on them before.'

'Yes, I do rather act on impulse, I'm afraid. I get crazes.'

'I see.'

'But it's not only that. I've pretty well completely changed my mind about Ed. I've come to the conclusion he's rather good. He's helped me.'

Jake would have chuckled if he had dared. The girl might be a bit touched but nobody could have improved on the deftness with which she had taken the initiative away from Brenda by forcing her into agreement. Add to that the way Geoffrey was looking from face to face, not merely unable to deduce anything whatso-bloody-ever from what he had heard but seeming to think that not to be in prior possession of every relevant fact about anything at any time was a novelty, and a shocking one – add this and you had the makings of quite a jolly party as long as you didn't add anything else. After constraining Brenda to extol Ed's qualities an extra couple of times Kelly took herself off, first to the snacks trolley and not long afterwards out of the room, presumably in the direction of bed.

Other people were drifting away too, just as presumably to allow for the early start promised for the morning. Jake's bedtime was at least an hour ahead, preferably more. He was about to go up and fetch his weekend reading (another slice of sizzling suspense by the author of *The Hippogriff Attaché-Case*) when he caught sight of what looked like, and proved indeed to be, a TV set in the further conference-room. To his considerable surprise it was in working order and could be switched on. He was soon settled down to a just-about-endurable film about Paris in 1944; it had in it Kirk Douglas, whom he didn't mind, and Charles Boyer, whom he minded a lot, and there was also some female. Two of the strangers and Martha and Ivor watched with him. Unusually for her, Brenda sat up too, but she was in the other room talking to Geoffrey. Ed and Rosenberg were also to be seen there. It was after midnight when the party dispersed. Before it finally did, Jake told Ivor he was to come and wake him at any time if he wanted company. Their rooms turned out to be on different floors – Jake's on the first, Ivor's on the second – but there wasn't a lot to be done about that.

Upstairs was a little more homely than downstairs but not much. The Richardsons' room had twin beds, plain curtains, a plain rug, papered walls that would have been nicer plain, a dressing-table of military (World War II junior officers' quarters) appearance and a few other things. Jake sat on his bed and told Brenda what Kelly had asked him to do, wishing he had also told her of the Oxford encounter at the time: too late now.

'Whether you go or not is entirely up to you,' said Brenda in a friendly tone, answering his question. 'You remember I told you to feel free; that still holds. But you know what she's like, or rather I don't think you do quite, not as well as I do, seeing her every week. Of course a straight pass is what it looks like but with somebody like that you can never be sure. This five or ten minutes business. . . . If she's got it in for you for any reason, and people like that don't need a proper reason, then she might do anything. Rush about screaming you tried to rape her, anything. But it's up to you, completely.'

In the end, what with one thing and another, he didn't go.

25   Increased Insight

'Jake, Jake, wake up!'

It was Ivor. The light was on. Jake got out of bed very fast saying things like steady and calm down, but Ivor said there was nothing wrong with him, it was Kelly. Brenda sat up in bed. The two men ran out and up the stairs, where it was dark, and into another room with the light on. Kelly was lying in bed on her side with her eyes shut and breathing deeply. Ivor handed Jake a page torn from a pocket diary with a few words written on it in ballpoint in a rather neat script. They were Sorry everybody, but it's better this way. The Ivor handed Jake a small empty bottle made of brown glass. The label said Mogadon – Miss J.V. Gambeson.

'Do you know where Rosenberg's sleeping?' asked Jake.

'No.'

'Go into every room till you find him. I'll call an ambulance.'

He remembered seeing a telephone near the front door and hurried down to it. The emergency-services operator answered in three seconds. Within another twenty or so he had passed his message and was walking back upstairs when he noticed it wasn't completely dark outside. He looked at his watch: thirty-one minutes past four. And still hot, or hot already. In Kelly's room he found Brenda and Rosenberg. Kelly was lying on her back now. Brenda came over and squeezed his hand but didn't speak.

'Ambulance on the way,' he said. 'Any idea of her chances? Doctor?'

Rosenberg shook his head. In pyjamas and with his hair ruffled he looked about nine. 'I don't understand, there's something crazy about the timing. We'll have to wait for Ivor. Oh, her chances, we don't know how many she took or how long ago she took them so medically nobody could say at this stage. If that bottle was full when she started it would have held around eighty of the things, quite enough to do for her.'

'I thought you couldn't die of an overdose of those,' said Brenda.

'I grant you it isn't easy but it can be done, that is if you've been taking other pills as well, which she no doubt was. The trouble is it's very widely believed that there is no fatal overdose. If she believed it . . .'

Jake made an effort. 'I noticed she was one of the first to go to bed. She could have been swallowing them by ten-thirty.'

'If so they'll be well into her by now. She can't have wanted that.'

'How do you mean?'

'Her object was not to die but to punish someone or call attention to herself or both. Unfortunately. . . .'

He stopped speaking as Ed hurried in with Ivor. The note and the bottle were produced. Ed stood still for a moment and looked at the floor. Then at the sound of approaching voices he went active, moved to the threshold and said, 'Hold it there, fellows. Kelly's been taken sick and will have to be moved to the hospital but she's going to be okay. And that's all.'

'Anything we can do?' asked somebody who sounded to Jake like Lionel.

'Yes there is. There's an ambulance coming – you go down to the front door on the double to let the men in. You stay right where you are and don't let anyone past. I don't want a crowd in here. Thanks.' He shut the door and looked round the room, at Brenda in an unluxurious armchair, Jake standing near the head of the bed, Rosenberg sitting on its foot, Ivor by the boarded-up fireplace. 'All right Ivor, let's have it all and in the right order.'

'Jake kindly said I could wake him up any time I felt bad,' said Ivor at a brisk rate, as one who has worked out in advance the best and shortest way to impart a set of facts. 'I woke up suddenly and I was frightened because it was a strange place. I started to go to Jake but his room's on the floor below and I needed somebody at once. So I went into just the nearest room, I didn't know whose it was, and I turned on the light and it was here and she was like that and I saw the note and the bottle. So then I stopped feeling frightened about myself and fetched Jake and he sent me for Frank and I found him almost straight away.'

'So: she had no way whatever of knowing that you even might come bursting in at four a.m.'

'None.'

'What woke you?' asked Rosenberg.

'I don't know, I just woke, found I was awake.'

Ed rubbed his cheeks alternately with one hand after the other. 'It's off pattern, Frank.'

'I agree. What's worrying is that you can kill yourself with those things but hardly anyone – '

'Is that right, I didn't know that.'

'There you are, if you didn't know there's a good chance she didn't either.'

'So she goes for a cut-me-down, a joke, a phoney attempt without knowing what she's using can be deadly.'

'She could have found out about that,' said Jake, hoping even as he spoke to be taken as stating a rather obvious general possibility rather than showing a special knowledge.

'Maybe. We'll know more later. You did well, Ivor. You too, Jake. Now you can all go along to bed. Frank and I'll take care of everything here.'

It struck Jake then that he wanted to stay and see Kelly safely taken off the premises, but he felt he couldn't argue the point so he glanced at her, saw that one of her cheeks was reddened, where Rosenberg might have slapped it to try to arouse her, but nothing else of significance and left with the other two. When asked, Ivor said he would be fine now because it was nearly light. As soon as he had gone Brenda said,

'You're not to blame for that in any way at all.'

'If she dies I'll be responsible. That stuff has had three or four more hours to work on her because of me.'

'You're not responsible. Either she is or God is or nobody is, not you. It's nothing to do with you except in the sense that she did it to get you involved with her and make you feel awful about her, and she picked you because she knows you quite like her or have a bit of time for her and nobody else does.'

'All right, but poor little bitch.'

'You can't afford to think that. Dangerous little lunatic is the only safe thing to think about her. Remember, it's *not your fault*. You couldn't possibly have foreseen what she was going to do, how could anyone?'

They heard the ambulance approaching. Neither spoke while it came up and halted outside the building and, after what seemed a remarkably short time, drove off again. Jake had heard no voices or footfalls in that time and wished he had, feeling that that would have been some sort of guarantee of Kelly's actual departure. By now he and Brenda were tucked up in their beds, or rather lay there in the hot twilight each covered by a single sheet.

'Do you think I did right not to tell them about her asking me to go and see her?'

'I should think so, darling. I suppose it might be a bit awkward if it ever came up, but I can't see why it should. And it doesn't make any difference, does it?'

'Not now.'

'I'm going to rest. I shan't sleep but I must rest or I'll feel terrible in the morning. I mean later on. Try not to worry. As I said, you're not to blame in the least.'

Jake agreed with Brenda about resting and sleeping but got it wrong: he dropped off almost at once and was woken by the heat four hours later. Much the same turned out to have happened to her. On the feeling-terrible front his achievement was well above par, nothing on the scale of the morning after Eve but with similar all-round coverage of the physical, mental, emotional, spiritual, moral. As for worrying he was well into that by the time his eyes were open, so far that he couldn't get round to considering whether he was to blame or not: perhaps he was an innocent instrument but there was no doubt whatever that he was an instrument.

If breakfast was to be had at all he must do no more than dress, comb hair and pee before plunging downstairs. With Brenda at his side, full of complaint about how ghastly she looked, he found something called a dining-room. The sun shone brightly on the non-prestige furniture, plastic tablecloths and haircord carpeting. There was a kind of sideboard with doll's-house packets of cereal, quarter-pints of milk, 'sachets' of sugar and other easier-for-them items that recalled the Comyns buttery. No cooked food was available. You got your coffee out of a machine, and having done that you couldn't get it back in.

The room was set with tables for four, only about half of which were to any degree laid, so Ivor had been right in his estimate of the non-fullness of the house. Here he was now, hurrying over to them.

'Ed and Frank would like to see you in the committee-room as soon as you're ready – same side of the hall as this at the back,' he said and was gone.

Brenda had agreed with Jake that it would be more comfortable to discuss Kelly's case as little as possible, so they picked the table already part-occupied by Ruth and Winnie, an ideal pair for the present purpose at any rate. On his left Jake had a window that gave him a view of a stretch of lawn in need of cutting, a tall thick hedge and then nothing until some low hills with a few trees and clumps of bushes and what looked from here like smooth densely growing grass, and sky of course, in no way remarkable but quite grand on such a bright day. And yet not so grand, he felt, as the same scene would have looked to him five or ten years ago. *Then* it would have been apparelled in ti-tum ti-tum, the glory and the freshness of a dream. Was that what Wordsworth had been on about without knowing it? How old had he been when he wrote the Ode? Thirty-something? But then he aged early in other respects. Get on to Lancewood.

Within five minutes both Jake and Brenda had had enough 'breakfast', he not wanting much, she not allowed much. They soon ferreted out the committee-room, which might well have once been the office of the chief administrator of the nursing-home, though most likely not designed by him: it was low-ceilinged and, even on a morning like this, dark enough to need artificial light. A minor obstacle to the natural sort was afforded by the panel of stained glass that took up the top third of what there was of a window. Although several degrees below the ones at Comyns it was the only thing in the entire place, large or small, inside or out, that might stick in the mind for ten seconds after the eye had passed over it. Human figures were represented but making out who they were, if anybody in particular, wasn't easy, at least to Jake.

Rosenberg and Ed, who was wearing sunglasses of the deepest dye, sat together behind a table with a telephone on it and enough in the way of notebooks and pens to establish them in a business-conducting posture. Ivor was in attendance, also, unexpectedly, Geoffrey. As he took one of the identical straight-backed chairs with dark-green seats, Jake asked if there was any news of Kelly.

'Not yet,' said Rosenberg. 'There won't be for hours.'

'Have her parents been informed?'

This time Ed answered. 'She has no parents. Not in any real sense. Her father died of drink and her step-father, who lives with her mother in Belfast, won't have her in their home after she tried to burn it down the second time.'

'Everybody please understand that's confidential,' said Rosenberg.

'The only person to inform,' Ed went on, 'is her landlady in Hampstead, and that can certainly wait until we know more.'

Jake nodded his head. He looked at the stained-glass panel. It was divided vertically into three scenes: a kneeling girl above whom a heavily robed male figure was raising a sword, the same figure with a lowered sword contemplating a quadruped about the size of a large dog, and the girl from the first scene accompanied by someone of uncertain sex carrying a curved wand and directing her towards a classical portico. He knew the subject but couldn't place it.

'We asked you to stop by,' Ed was saying, 'to let you know we decided on a cover-story for Kelly. Suicide, even a fake one, well, it depresses a lot of people, just the thought of it, and we want the folks to get on with their work without being bothered. Frank and I have staked a lot on this Workshop and we want it to be a success. So we pass it around that Kelly's suffering from an acute allergy that needs hospital attention but isn't dangerous.'

'With a very high fever as the main symptom,' put in Rosenberg.

'She woke up, knew she was sick, found Frank, he got her back to bed to wait for the ambulance. Long as we all tell the same tale if we're asked we'll be okay.' Ed gave a quiet reflective laugh. 'Isn't it great? Allergy. They'll swallow anything. And I go for that, it solves our Kelly problem nice and neat.'

The last phrase made Jake speak more sharply than he had intended. 'I take it you have been in touch with the hospital?'

'Like Frank said, Jake, they won't know anything for a long time.'

'You mean you haven't rung them up.'

'That's what I mean, Jake.'

'Well I suggest you ring them now. They'll know whether she's alive or dead, I imagine.'

'If she was dead we'd know soon enough.'

'Quite possibly. All the same I'd like to be told one way or the other.'

'Anybody else like to be told?' asked Ed, looking round the room.

Brenda didn't speak. Geoffrey had obviously seen through the cunning attempt to betray him into indiscretion, and likewise kept quiet. Ivor said he'd like to be told.

'All right,' Ed Looked through a ring-spine notebook, drew the telephone towards him and began to dial. While he was doing so he said without looking round, 'Ivor, go tell the folks we'll be starting late, like fifteen minutes. We're having . . . administrative problems. That'll hold 'em. . . . Good morning, I'm inquiring after a Miss Gambeson, a Miss Janet

Gambeson who was admitted as a casualty around five o'clock this morning. . . . No, I'm afraid I don't.' He turned towards Jake. 'Her name isn't Kelly. I doubt that it's Janet either. Or Gambeson. Not that it matters a damn what she calls herself. . . . Yes?. . . . Thank you.' He rang off. 'She's still unconscious. Just like we said.'

Ivor had come back in time to hear this. 'Well, that's something.'

After a pause, Ed said pleasantly, 'That's all we need you for, Brenda, but we'd like Jake to stay.' When she looked inquiring, he added, 'There's a little bit of digging we'd like to do about Kelly.'

'I wouldn't mind staying for that too, unless you. . . .'

'No no, fine, you stay if you want, you'll probably be able to help. Now Frank, do you want to carry the ball for a bit?'

'Thank you, Ed.' Rosenberg did want to. He didn't actually grasp the lapels of his unsightly cream-coloured linen jacket, but his tone made up for that. 'Now as some of you may know, when a person of this kind enters a suicidal situation there are two main aims or objectives. One is to arouse attention and concern, the so-called cry for help. The other objective is to carry out an act of revenge on some other person, usually for a sexual or family reason, to make that other person feel guilty, anxious and so on. An invariable accompanying feature is that the subject takes very careful precautions against dying. If that does happen, it's an accident. Something has gone wrong – the person in the next room doesn't smell the gas, the rope round the neck doesn't break.'

Jake had now identified the subject of the window. The curved wand was a bow, its bearer was Artemis, the portico was that of her temple at Tauris, the girl was Iphigenia, daughter of Agamemnon and Clytemnestra, and the beast was the deer supernaturally substituted for her by Artemis to forestall her sacrifice at Aulis. Shockingly rendered, but then. For a moment he felt pleased with himself.

'Now I strongly suspect,' continued Rosenberg, sounding very Irish for some reason, 'that that was what happened in this case, but I don't know what went wrong. If that second person, the one on whom an act of revenge was intended, if he exists, who is he? He might be somebody we don't know of, somebody who was supposed to telephone at midnight, say, but telephones are too unreliable and I just don't believe it. Since this happened here, I strongly suspect that the second person – if he exists – is also here. Here in this room. I've . . . eliminated Lionel.'

'I'm your man,' said Jake at once. 'She asked me to come and see her some time after midnight to be shown what she called a kind of letter. Which it was in a sense. I talked it over with my wife and decided it would be safer not to go.'

There was silence. Ivor looked incredulous, Geoffrey puzzled for once in his life. Brenda glanced at Jake and gave him an approving nod and smile. Ed did the same in his thank-Christ-quite-different manner and said,

'Good, Jake. Excellent. I hope you're not feeling bad about it? We all understand why you didn't go along. None of us would have – I hope. You were absolutely right not to.'

'How can you say that after what's happened? Of *course* I'm feeling bad about it.'

'Jake, you mustn't, you mustn't!' Ed spoke with great and impressive earnestness. 'Can't you see, you idiot, it's what she wants, it's her malice and her awful ... You're falling for it, you're playing it her way by feeling bad. She's *sick* Jake, it's not like you've mistreated some normal human being as we all do all the time and pay the penalty. See it for what it is, a vicious child's game with you cast as loser. Have the flexibility to ... oh, God.'

'She won't die, darling,' said Brenda. 'You can be quite certain of that. I'm sure there are accidents as Dr Rosenberg says, but Kelly isn't going to have one, she's too bright in the way she's bright. You said last night, I mean earlier this morning, you said she'd have found out about the dose. Indeed she would, she'd have found out what was a completely safe dose, and it doesn't matter to her if it's a laughably safe dose and everybody knows it was that *afterwards*. She'll have had her hour and made her point and be on to something else by then.'

'Right, Brenda. Very good.'

For a moment Jake tried to push out of his mind the memory of a weeping face, then stopped trying. He had wondered at the time what Kelly had been 'expressing' at Mr Shyster's; now he knew. Hatred. Of whom or what? Of self. But there could be no such thing: all that could be meant was the hatred felt by one part of the self for another. Perhaps in her that hating part was powerless, able to do no more than look on aghast at the acts the other displayed and to grieve at them. How dismal, if true.

'Er, may I ask a question?' This was Geoffrey. He was frowning. 'There's something I'm afraid I can't quite follow.' (Like the arrow to the Gents, you sodding moron, thought Jake.) 'If, er, if Kelly was revenging herself on Jake, what was she revenging herself for, I mean because of what? Had Jake offended her or something?'

'Yes I had. She tracked me down in my rooms in Oxford and offered herself to me, Christ, bloody well tried to rape me, and I . . . fended her off in a very ungraceful, ungracious way, and she called me every filthy name she could lay her tongue to and said everything she could think of that she thought might hurt me. . . .' He turned to Brenda and said, 'I'm sorry I didn't tell you before, I wish I had. I was going to and then it sort of got too late.'

'I understand perfectly.'

There was an edge to her tone he didn't much care for but he forgot about that when Ed, who had been nodding slowly and sapiently in time with Rosenberg, butted in by saying,

'Then I guess we got the hysterics and tears and self-reproaches bit, right?'

'Right, I mean yes. And then, I suppose it was the pathetic bit.'

More nodding. Geoffrey held up his hand like a schoolboy.

'Er. . . . It must have been a very unpleasant experience for you.'

'Good, I'm glad I managed to get that across.'

'Well then, why did you come here when you must have known you'd be bumping into her?'

'Because she asked me to,' said Jake, raising his voice. 'Because she came round and saw me and did her pathetic *bit*.'

'After what had happened in Oxford?'

'Precisely. That was the order of events.'

'All right, you two,' said Ed. 'We're all finished here. Very good Jake, you seem to have it straightened out now. And thank you for straightening us out, me and Frank. We have everything we need. Case closed. Come on everybody, let's go do some work.'

'Just a minute if you don't mind.' Jake's voice was back to its normal level. 'What exactly do you mean by case closed?'

'That there's nothing more to be said. With your help we have assembled one classic sortie of one type of hopeless neurotic.'

'I can think of one or two more things to be said. Doesn't either of you feel any sense of responsibility for what's happened?'

'We feel concerned, of course, since she's our patient, in very different senses in our two cases.'

'Do you now? But I was talking about responsibility. Anyway, how long has she been your patient in very different senses?'

'Just over a year,' said Rosenberg. He seemed curious to know where this discussion might lead.

'Since March.' Ed seemed to know roughly where and not to mind.

'And has she made one of these suicide attempts or phoney suicide attempts before?'

'Not that I know of,' said Rosenberg.

'Well you know of one now. Doesn't it strike you at all that that means she's got worse while you've been "treating" her? While she's been undergoing your "therapy"?'

Ed squeezed his chin and said rather wearily, 'It might have happened at any time. Any time at all.'

'And you've always been and always will be quite powerless to prevent it or render it to the slightest extent less likely. Which matters a bit, some people might think, because even a phoney suicide attempt is quite a serious matter, not just a fairly interesting example of something, which is all you seem to see in it. As your mate was saying, they do sometimes succeed. Kelly isn't alive yet.'

'No let him finish, Frank. After all, he's our patient too, remember.'

'Only for the next couple of minutes, and that only in case I may say something I'd prefer to be privileged, if that still counts at all. Let's try a spot of adding up. You've done less than nothing for Kelly. How about Ivor? Ivor, have you improved since you started going to Ed?'

'I think I'm about the same, thank you Jake.'

'Nothing for Ivor. What about Chris? Perhaps you cured him and sent him on his way rejoicing. Did you?'

'Jake, I don't deal in cures.' Ed sounded angry but in full command of himself. 'Did I offer you a cure? I aim to release checks on emotion and to improve insight, that's all.'

'Funny how it's got about that both of those must be good. Stop bottling up that emotion that makes you want to hit your wife with a sledge-hammer. Gain insight, you're bound to like what you see. To prefer it to what you couldn't see before. Let me tell you, *Ed*, there's no such thing as a totally phoney suicide attempt. They all want to be at least a little bit dead for a little while. If you were Kelly and found out more about yourself, how would you feel? More likely to knock yourself off or less? And talking of Kelly, there's a small piece of her that can see properly, of course there is or what is it that's gaining insight, but you'll never reach it, not with your methods. Methods, Christ. You just make it up as you go along, which I suppose you call being empirical if you know the word, and there'll always be plenty of applicants, lonely pansies like Lionel who want a nice chat and poor old dears like Ruth who want a good cry and fatheads like Geoffrey who want to show off. What you're up to is hideously boring to anyone without wants or needs of that sort. But then on the other hand it's intellectually beneath contempt – I should have made it clear that the whole of this bit applies equally to your undistinguished colleague. As against all that what you do is dangerous in the extreme. And yet when you come to weigh it up it's funny too, in other words it would be impossible for anyone with a grain of humour in them. All you have, but in abundance, is arrogance and effrontery. Oh, and a certain amount of greed.'

'Have you finished?' asked Ed.

'I think so. Should there be more?'

'You're the best judge of that, Jake. I've let you run on because anybody can see you have this most painful conflict between concern for a martyr-figure and anger at having been made the victim of a – '

'I'm not letting you run on, old boy, I can't have you explaining me, that would be, as you would certainly say, too much. I cease to be your patient as of this moment. And also, in a very different sense of course, Junior's patient too.'

'Mr Richardson,' said Rosenberg, 'may I talk to you in private for just a few minutes?'

'Certainly. Hang on.' Jake moved across to Brenda and tried to signal or will her to leave the room with him, using every means short of verbal directive, but she sat on in her chair next to the doorway and looked at him without curiosity. It occurred to him that in the last couple of minutes he had rather pissed on the proceedings, thereby breaking a promise, and pissed on Geoffrey, shown himself to be at least momentarily against him, too. 'Sorry,' he said to her, feeling hard up for words. 'Things sort of got on top of me. I'd better be off, get a train. Sorry.'

'I understand,' she said as before.

'Well . . . cheerio, love. See you when? Tomorrow night? Okay, fine.'

As he made to kiss her cheek she seemed to relent and kissed him on the mouth with some warmth. He waved in a general fashion at the rest of the room, looking at nobody, and went. After a word to Ed to start without him, Rosenberg followed.

'I suggest we move outside,' said Jake. 'You probably wouldn't want us to be overheard.'

There was a door near by. A gravel path with bald patches took them to a rough lawn that was much larger than the one to be seen from the dining-room. It gave extensive hospitality to buttercups, daisies, dandelions, chickweed, groundsel, charlock, viper's bugloss, plantain, moss and couch. Near its middle stood a large elm tree which might well have been on the point of toppling over from disease but for the moment kept the sun off satisfactorily.

'It's most important – ' began Rosenberg.

'First me, then you,' said Jake. 'I don't want to hurt your feelings unnecessarily or say anything I might regret, so I'll just tell you you're a disgrace to the medical profession, which admittedly is saying something. As practised by you, sexual therapy doesn't exist. There are things that are merely treated as parts of a figment called that, the pathetic bits and pieces of machinery and pornography and genital and non-genital sensate focusing and early sexual experiences and fantasies and Christ knows what that you've tried to make me mistake for a technique, a coherent method. Yes, those fantasies. You were quite right about them, not that it matters in the very least, that stuff I wrote for you wasn't "serious" at all. I told you I have no homosexual feelings, no sadism or anything like that, I'm not a voyeur, anyway not in the usual sense, but I am given to thoughts of subjecting women to certain indignities, I'll say no more than that. Except that I've never put those thoughts into practice and never will now. I knew none of it would have shocked you, but that's not the point: it's private, you see. And I don't think the fact that I was born in 1917 has any bearing. Plenty of my contemporaries wouldn't have minded telling me all about such matters, let alone you. And there must be the same division among youngsters, though I'm sure you apply the same "method" to everybody. People's behaviour changes, "society" changes, but not feelings. And while we're on "society" let me remind you of something you said to me in that terrible pub, something about repressive attitudes making me feel sexually unrelaxed. Repressive? In 1977? I was doing fine when things really were repressive, if they ever were, it's only since they've become, oh, permissive that I've had trouble. In the old days a lot of people, men as well as women, didn't know quite what to expect of sex so they didn't worry when it didn't work too well. Now everybody knows exactly what's required of them and exactly how much they've fallen short down to the last millimetre and second and drop, which is frightfully relaxing for them. No wonder you boys have got enough trade.

'Hence guilt and shame at inadequacy – all quite superficial according to you. Do you still think so? As regards the other lot, your lot, I mean my alleged deep-down guilt and shame about sex itself, what makes you think that what's deep down is more important than what's up top? Anyway, I suppose it is possible they'd been there all the time but totally screened by my libido, which eventually receded and left them in full view. But if that's what they are they're only the foundation of something quite different, as I tried to explain when I was telling you about that woman I had in Oxford.' He paused again. 'What outlandish bits of anatomy, what an extraordinary thing to do, what curious reactions you keep saying to yourself. It's like being a child again, when an older boy's telling you the story and it all seems too unlikely for words. And when you do it, any of it, it's as if it's abnormal, almost monstrous. I know it isn't really, You can't imagine how you ever. . . .'

Jake gave it up. A scream sounded from the house, no doubt uttered by a participant occupied in self-draining or ensconced in the hot seat.

'And you wouldn't have minded being overheard telling me any of this?' Rosenberg had received Jake's strictures with a composure that indicated an extreme of either humility or complacency.

'Good for you, Frank. No, because I won't be seeing any of them again.'

'Except your wife.'

'Yes, but that's rather different. Now you must excuse me.'

'What about my turn to speak?'

'I've cancelled it. Nothing you could say would interest me.'

'Mr Richardson, if we were to go on from where you've just brought us, I'm sure we could make a very – '

'No we couldn't, you'd never reach me, I say, that sounds like one of your words, any more than you could reach Kelly. Not really the same sort of person as I am. I'd think about that if I were you, doctor.'

'I'd be glad to recommend other practitioners with different approaches.'

'Thank you, but for one thing they'd all be too unconventional and unpuritanical for me. Good-bye.' There was a handshake. 'You know, now it comes to it and I realise I shan't be coming to see you any more I can't help feeling, how shall I put it, full of fun.'

Jake's last sight of Rosenberg had his little figure standing under the elm in sad thought for a moment, then violently slapping the back of his neck at the assault of some serviceable insect. It was the only fully human thing he had ever seen him do and it seemed to show up his total nullity as a person. The house was very dark after the glare of outdoors. No sound came from the conference-room. Jake telephoned for a taxi, went upstairs, shaved and packed his bag. He thought of writing a note for Brenda but soon decided against it: if he was to say anything he would have had to say a great deal, and he would be seeing her the next evening.

Shortly after five o'clock that afternoon a nurse told him that Miss Gambeson was now sleeping normally. He said thank you, declined to leave a message, went to the station and was back home for a full Saturday evening's viewing.

26 What, and Miss Television?

Brenda didn't get home till midnight on the Sunday. She explained that there had been a little party ofter the official closure of the Workshop, nothing very wild, just a few bottles of Italian wine. Thanks to Ivor's abilities and the lack of traffic they had made an amazingly quick journey. Yes, all things considered the weekend had been a great success. These and other matters were treated with the affable remoteness he had begun to observe in her recent behaviour. Soon they agreed that it was getting late and retired to their separate rooms as usual.

The next morning Jake awoke rather before his usual time, but feeling more rested than he had for weeks, so instead of turning to and fro in bed on the off-chance that a girl would cross his mind he got up, put on dressing-gown and slippers and went down to the kitchen. While he waited for the kettle to boil he opened the back door. It was going to be another hot day, though with that faint heaviness of or in the air that can betoken the imminent end of a fine spell, especially to someone who has just read in the paper that unsettled weather is forecast. He looked at the garden, advanced a step or two into it. Rain or shine the grass would have to be cut soon, the chrysanthemums staked and all the roses dead-headed, and ideally much else done besides, but in the last four or five years even this tennis-court sized plot had begun to be too much for him, not physically but mentally or morally – he couldn't be fucking bothered. These days what he did do he did largely to prevent it being said that he had let the place go to rack and ruin. Once, Brenda would have given him a hand with the light jobs just as he had done his bit indoors; now, their respective spheres were theirs almost exclusively.

Thinking of things being too much for him stirred the thought that he was going to be sixty the following week. This seemed to him an indefensibly ludicrous proposition; there must be some mistake. If, when he was in his twenties, anybody had advanced to him except as a puerile joke, the notion that one day he would be sixty – not survive to be, just be – he would have told him not to be a bloody fool. Sixty was what all those old people were. It was something he ought to have taken steps to postpone indefinitely, if not evade altogether, while there was still time. Six-oh. LX.

What a silly bugger. Well, at least no one could say he was wiser or more sensible or understood anything better along with it.

He made tea, poured some of it into Brenda's favourite Diamond Jubilee mug, remembered with a morsel of self-satisfaction not to add milk or sugar as formerly and carried the filled vessel to her, once their, bedroom. She sat up as he entered the room, thanked him and asked if he was doing anything special that morning.

'Not really. I thought I might stroll down to the bookshop in Philby Road. The fellow there has got some stuff for me.'

'What stuff?'

'Eh? Some *Greece and Rome* back numbers I've been after. Why?'

'Just wondered. There's something I'd like your advice about before you go, if that's all right.'

'Attend me in my sanctum.'

When he turned the corner at the top of the lowest flight of stairs he saw that Mrs Sharp, having let herself into the house with her own licensed latch-key, was standing in the passage with her back to him, a most sensible position to take up if what you wanted was to enshrine in your memory the look of the inside of the front door. As he went down the flight Jake trod more heavily than was his habit and cleared his throat a couple of times, but to no avail. The female turned, saw him and jumped, the third verb to be understood in a more literal sense than the context would suggest. She managed not to cry out, however. Her response would have been about right for one faced by a spectral Cavalier with his head firmly on his shoulders.

'Morning, Mrs Sharp. Sorry I startled you.' Perhaps a leper's bell fastened irremovably round the neck, he thought. Or were those hand-bells they had?

'Good morning, Mr Richardson. Don't worry, it's just my silly way.'

This said, she moved to her favourite station between the foot of the stairs and the kitchen, again hard to find fault with if you assumed that he had been intending to make for the street attired as he was.

'Excuse me.'

'Can you – '

'Just a – '

'There we are.'

'Thanks.'

There were further evolutions in the kitchen while he assembled his grapefruit and coffee and toast and she collected brooms, buckets and other matériel from this cupboard and that, but he got away in the end, even managing to dive into the bog under less than full scrutiny. He was feeling quite good when, shat, shaved, showered and wearing his green lightweight crease-resistant suit, he went into his study to find Brenda already there looking out of the window.

'Sorry the garden's in such a mess,' he said. 'I'll try and make a start on it tomorrow.'

'Good. Darling I don't actually want your advice, I just wanted to make sure of talking to you.'

He nodded, inwardly squaring up. There was a certain amount of ground to be covered and no mistake, not all of it coverable in any cosy spirit.

'I wish I hadn't got to say this. I'm leaving you.'

'Oh,' he said, and went and sat down behind his desk. He saw that she was trembling slightly.

'I'm going away with Geoffrey.'

'*What?*'

'I know exactly what you're thinking and please don't say any of it or it'll make me hate you, and I don't want to do that.'

'All right.'

'You see . . . he can perform, or he wants to, anyway he does.'

'Thanks very much.'

'Jake, I'm not a fool, not completely, I can understand how hard it must be not to take it that way, and of course it is the way, so. . . . But I'm only stating a fact, no I'm not only doing that but it is a fact. You've lost interest, your sex-drive, but I haven't, and I'm going to be forty-eight in October. I shouldn't think any sort of adventure will ever happen to me again. And it isn't only that. He's interested in me.'

'He's changed tack pretty fast then. At that Workshop I went to he said there were people he liked but they didn't interest him. His very words.'

'You mustn't take things so literally, he was having a gloom. Anyway he pays attention to me and he talks to me.'

'About himself. Sorry.'

'You used to talk to me about yourself and it was fine with me. I used to enjoy it, I didn't mind why you did it, I expect it was mostly because you wanted to impress me, like a clever schoolboy who's still a bit excited by finding out he's clever. In that sort of way you hadn't grown up and you still haven't, which was all right in those days, really rather nice, but it's not so hot when somebody's getting on. Anyway – it wasn't all like that, you talking to me. You thought it would interest me too, sometimes you probably even wanted to know what I thought. There's none of that these days. Do you remember, it must be three or four months ago, you brought a bottle of wine home and Allie was here and she asked for some and you did something in the kitchen, swapped the bottle or – '

'Got you to offer her some actually, and what I did was pour – '

'Don't tell me now, I don't want to know now. In the old days you'd have told me the whole story and we'd have enjoyed it together. But you couldn't be bothered, could you? And just this morning, an hour ago, you said you were going to the bookshop and I asked you on purpose what you were going to pick up there, and you answered as shortly as you could and wondered why I wanted to know. You'd have been sitting on the bed before I had a chance to ask and telling me all about it and what you needed it for, that's what you'd have done *then*. When you still fancied me. In the days when you used to take me out. Before you stopped wanting to talk to me.'

Jake was paying very close attention, but things from outside kept occurring to him, motives, explanations, even why when last seen Geoffrey had been garbed like an adult Caucasian.

'But what decided me was the Kelly business. Going back again, about eight weeks I suppose, that's right, I was talking about the Workshop and I mentioned her, and I've forgotten what was said but there was a moment when if you'd wanted to you could have. . . . I know, I asked you if she'd come round here again and you said no and I knew you weren't lying, you've always been a hopeless liar. I suppose it's because you've always thought the truth was very important, that's one of the things I respect about you. Anyway there was something, I thought afterwards there was something I didn't know, but then I thought there couldn't be, because you'd have told me.'

'Well, it would have been embarrassing, and I didn't want to – '

'I'm sure it would have been a lot of things, but the chief thing it would have been was boring. For you to tell me about it. A mad girl hunts you down in Oxford and tries to go to bed with you and has hysterics and God knows what else happens, and you'd rather watch television than tell me about it. Even though she might come round here in any sort of state at any moment, indeed *did* come round to con you into the weekend, I wonder how she made sure I wasn't going to be here, no don't bother. And even though you *knew* I wouldn't be angry or anything like that if you did tell me. Why should I live with someone who thinks I'm as bloody unrewarding as that?'

Jake didn't say anything.

'When I went on about you to Frank that time and when I gave you that lecture about being affectionate to me and how I'd be able to tell if you were one of those men who only take notice of women when it's to do with sex, that was all . . . theory, Jake. A comparison. An awful warning. I'd met plenty of men like that, what woman hasn't, but I never thought you were going to turn out to be one. In the end. To have always been one, I couldn't believe that of you. I went through bits of thinking you were getting slack and a bit selfish in your old age and needed gingering up, being told if you weren't careful you'd find yourself turning into one of *them*. That's when I wasn't thinking it was all me. Well I've gone off physically but not all that much it seems, and I can't have got so many times more boring in just a couple of years, I worked that out over the weeks, and after I thought I'd warned you as clearly as I could and you went on just as before not talking to me except when you needed an audience and putting up with stroking me and me stroking you twice a week, well, the Kelly business just clinched it. Incredible.'

'Why did you keep on with those pissing sensate sessions?' asked Jake after a moment.

'Well, you know I love massage, I don't really care if it's badly done. And I'm like you, I tend to do what doctors tell me. And I sort of couldn't not go on without a showdown. And I kept thinking it might conceivably start to come right next time.'

'So did I.'

'Did you? Looking back I'd have thought you'd made up your mind none of it was going to be any good from the word go. You expect too much of people.' Brenda looked at him consideringly. 'You've changed, Jake. In other ways too I mean. Kelly again. I can't see you getting involved with a screwed-up little bitch like that in the old days.'

'I wasn't involved with her.'

'Emotionally you were, and still are I imagine. No, you'd have seen through her from the start, because you'd have been observing her that much more closely. You'd have asked yourself what it would be like to get physically involved with her and have said no thanks, not with those complications round the corner. As it was, well, if it had been anyone else I'd have said they were a bit soft. It's odd, in one way you'd have expected a man in your position to see things as they are, especially women. Take away love or sex and the impression ought to be clearer, not distorted by emotions and wishful thinking and so on. But it's the other way round. You used to see as most men see, now you don't. Or it's more like. . . . What's that stuff they put in ships to keep them from going all over the place?'

'What? Oh . . . ballast?'

'That's right. People's sex drives are like ballast, they keep them steady. It sounds wrong, but they do. So as I say, you're worse equipped to deal with Kelly than you would have been before, not better.'

Brenda had long since ceased to tremble. With every sign of ease she sat down in the red-leather chair and went on talking in an interested tone, as if they had been sitting in a restaurant together. Her manner had lost what he now saw as the false amiability of the preceding weeks.

'So much so, in fact,' she said, 'that you virtually take her side against Ed. Now Ed has too good an opinion of himself I quite agree, but he does help people, or lets them help themselves which is just as good. I'm sure there are good reasons for saying he couldn't or he shouldn't or he doesn't really, but he does. For instance Martha now regularly tells her mother where to get off, goes out at night and all that. Anyway. I've got over it now, but I felt rather jealous of Kelly at one stage. Indignant too. You cared more about a destructive delinquent than you had about me for years. Not your fault and not the same sort of thing, I know. But let me give you a parting piece of advice – she's spilt milk, Jake. If she comes here again, chuck her out. Call the police if necessary. Do you think you can do that?'

'I don't know. I haven't thought. When are you off?'

'Probably about the end of the week. Geoffrey thinks he has a temporary place for us in Highgate. Are you going to stay on here?'

'I haven't thought about that either.'

'No of course you haven't. I should if I were you, stay on.'

'It would cost quite a bit to set up a new place.'

'That too. I mean I might come drifting back one day.'

'And put up with being found unrewarding?'

'Oh, I shouldn't be surprised. I like you and I don't care for being on my own as much as you do. And we might get on better with neither of us expecting you to find me rewarding. The thing is, Geoffrey hasn't said anything about divorces and Alcestis has always had a pretty strong grip.'

'On Geoffrey or in general?'

'Both really.'

'I thought her first husband left her.'

'Only physically. Allie gave him the boot.'

'I didn't know that. You must tell me the story before you go.'

'Actually there's not a hell of a lot to it.'

'Pity.' Jake got up from his seat at the desk. 'I'll miss you.'

'Without any malice in the world, darling, it'll be interesting to see how much.' Brenda too rose. 'Frank Rosenberg told me you said you weren't going to go to anybody else for treatment.'

'I probably said that in the lukewarmth of the moment.'

'I hope so. Another piece of advice. Don't let yourself not mind being as you are. Do a lot of thinking about the old days. Will you be in to lunch?'

'I expect so. I mean yes.'

'See you then.'

When she had gone he went on standing by his desk for a time. What hurt him most, and also shamed him, was her not having said she would miss him because she wasn't going to. Then he started remembering a holiday they had had in 1971 in Bodrun, where a gang of Danes had been excavating a fresh part of the ancient Carian city of Halicarnassus that had stood on the site and by so doing had involuntarily made it possible for him and Brenda to semi-diddle the taxman over their expenses, Brenda too because she had been designated his research assistant. The weather had been lovely, the Turks very agreeable and the scrambled eggs with tomatoes one of the best dishes he had ever eaten. They had stayed part of the time in a sort of private house infested with mosquitoes and Germans and, to anybody reared in the West and no doubt others besides, most remarkable for its lavatory. The night sound-track had been remarkable too: goats, chickens, donkeys, cattle and naturally dogs separated from them at times only by the thickness of the outside wall, together with, towards dawn and some yards further away, scooters. But they hadn't really minded any of that. To look back on it now was a bit like looking at a museum postcard of some archaic wall-painting or mosaic: you knew the official version of what the figures were up to and unquestioningly believed it, but found it hard to imagine with any clarity how they had felt about what they had been up to. So perhaps it wasn't really in order for him to be hurt a lot about Brenda not going to miss him.

Eventually Jake decided he might as well go and pick up the back numbers as he had planned. He needed them, the walk would do him good and it would probably be raining tomorrow.

27 Smudger Turns up Trumps

The week passed in a flurry of tedium. There was the money to be settled: all four parties had some, Jake what there was from his academic posts and the odd bob from his books, Brenda a little from her family, Geoffrey a competence from the recklessly spendthrift chutney-merchants, Alcestis something from her terrifying tenure of a post as a social worker and perhaps something too from shares. What held things up was everyone being decent; a touch of rapacity here or stinginess there would have worked wonders. As it was they got no further than deciding that for the moment you hung on to what you had. In the same sort of way the furnishings of 47 Burgess Avenue were to be left as they were down to the last china cat till Brenda had somewhere else to put them, or rather a yet-to-be-agreed proportion of them. She could have the bloody lot as far as Jake was concerned but he couldn't say so.

Several times he considered getting the hell out and making for Oxford, not just for now but for the rest of his time there, letting the house despite Brenda's guarded forecast and doing up his rooms in Comyns and perhaps finding a cottage later. But he always came up against the thought that Oxford wasn't very nice really, not any more, and he had as many or as few friends in both places, and he might not enjoy the garden exactly but he wouldn't like to be without it, and there was the club, and above all he was used to being here, though admittedly not on his own.

There was some minor hitch in Geoffrey's arrangements when it came to it and Brenda didn't leave till the following Monday. The days in between had been normal to a degree that might have been comic: television, desultory work, the club, to the Thomsons' for drinks Sunday midday, the garden, television. Finally he was standing in the bedroom among her packed suitcases.

'That's the lot for now,' she said. 'I'll be back tomorrow for another load if that's all right. I'll ring you first.'

'Yes of course. Er, it's a bit late, but you remember that evening we went to the Bamboo Bothy?'

'How long ago?'

'Well, it must have been the same night you gave me the pep-talk about affection. I was waiting for you downstairs after we'd had a. . . . You came in and I said you looked beautiful.'

'Yes, I remember that all right. What about it?'

'You were touched and so was I. I thought if that could still happen, after all it's only a few weeks ago, then we still have something, and we could sort of build on it and make more of it. Oh I mean have your fling now but perhaps in a month or six weeks. . . .'

'We'll always still have something darling, after all those years but it wouldn't be enough, it wouldn't, you know, come round often enough. It would be very nice when it did, but at the moment I honestly can't see. . . .'

'No, I suppose not, you're right. I thought I ought to mention it, though.'

'Yes, I'm glad you did. It was sweet of you.'

'Good. Well I'll get this stuff down.'

'I can take these two.'

'No, leave the zip one to me. You take that one there.'

There was a horrible interlude in the sitting-room while the driver of the pre-ordered minicab sat in traffic, couldn't find the house, stopped for a hamburger, chatted-up a bird, anyway didn't appear. In the end of course he did appear and proved most surprisingly willing to deal with the luggage. While he did so Brenda walked round the room crying. Jake knew that she was crying because of the room and the house and her life there rather than because of her life with him. That part didn't take very long. When it was over he went out into the front garden with her. The air was cool and the sky covered with cloud but no rain was falling.

'I'm sorry,' he said. 'For it and about it.'

'You are a silly old Oxford don.'

'Off you go now. Good luck. Hey, hold it. I've just thought, we're mad. You have the house, you've put so much into it and made it so nice, you must have it. I'll find a couple of rooms somewhere and you can move back in. Give me a week or two to look round. Thank Christ I thought of it. Insane.'

'What about you and the garden?'

'Well I'll miss it but nothing like the way you'd miss the house. That's decided then. Ring me tomorrow. I'll be here all day.'

Back in the sitting-room he thought about Geoffrey properly for the first time since hearing that Christendom's premier fucking fool had taken his wife off him. Not that there was a great deal to be said about that circumstance, because it was so hard to imagine anything of what it must be like. Geoffrey and Brenda out to dinner at a restaurant, Geoffrey handed the menu, Geoffrey baffled not by the language or by where a Dover sole came from but by the concept of choosing what he wanted to eat from a proffered list of available dishes. Geoffrey and Brenda off on a trip to the land of the mango and the tamarind, Geoffrey with his papers at the airport — incidentally there must be someone at his office who knew which way up to hang a map of the world and had the authority to stop him darting off to the Yukon or Monte Carlo to do his shopping. Jake's mental two-shot of Geoffrey and Brenda regularly cut to a close-up of Geoffrey frowning as some aspect of reality came to his attention. That was just as well; long might it remain so.

One o'clock: nearly time for lunch. What had Brenda – but Brenda had gone. All the same she might well have left something for him in the larder, in fact now he came to think of it she had said as much. He went out to the kitchen and found a saucepan of brown soup (oxtail? chocolate?) on the electric stove. He turned the ring under it on full, thus ensuring it would be warm enough to eat by nightfall. The larder revealed most of a cold leg of lamb and a salad; he carved the meat and made a dressing, then uncorked the remains of the Médoc they had shared the previous evening. All this was very fine but things would assuredly take a turn for the worse in a few days. In pursuance of the principle that those who are always about when they're not wanted are never about on those admittedly very rare occasions when they are wanted, Mrs Sharp, who had been known to collect the odd pound of sausages on her way to work here, was going to be on holiday for the next three weeks; her usual replacement had fallen out at the last minute and Jake didn't know how to find a replacement for the replacement, at least he knew how to summon candidates for the situation but not how to separate the thieves and arsonists from those at the other end of the scale, the merely idle and inefficient. But perhaps he would find a lodging before any of this should start to matter; he had no idea how long it would take.

While he was assembling his lunch things, which included a jar of sweet pickle with the name of Geoffrey's firm on it, on the little round table Jake heard the door-bell chime. His immediate thought was of Kelly, Kelly couched till a moment ago in a hide in a neighbour's garden and now, with Brenda well and truly gone, moving in if not for the kill (and better not be too bloody sure about that) then certainly for the fuck-up. But it wasn't Kelly, it was Alcestis.

'Christ,' he said in simple surprise and dismay. He had thought vaguely that one (on its scale considerable) offset against Brenda's departure would be to see no more of the Mabbotts, by which term he would really have meant Alcestis, because Geoffrey was quite good value for the mean-minded, but of course that was, well, wrong.

She looked at him with her eyes slightly narrowed and her mouth bunched up in an awful Churchillian grimace about finest hours and fighting on the beaches. 'Hallo, Jake,' she said gruffly and with a tremendous amount of quiet courage packed into three syllables. 'Mind if I come in?'

He minded a lot but was still too taken aback not to go along with convention. 'No, no of course not, do come in.'

'Am I interrupting your lunch?'

'I was just going to start, but I haven't actually . . . started.'

In she surged; he noticed she was carrying a supermarket plastic bag. *Christ*, he thought, that's her nightie in there, she's come to start the other half of the wife-swap, and fought down a squeal of panic. Not knowing quite what else to do he followed her out into the kitchen, where a lifetime of experience showed in the way she grasped the state of his soup. With that on the record she sat down at the table next to the place he had laid himself and here eventually he had to join her. Asked if he could get her anything she shook her head slowly, staring out into the garden with eyes that were now slightly wider than normal and looking like some picture of a hundred years before called *The Bereaved*.

'Well, Jake, there's not a great deal to say, is there?'

'Almost nothing.'

'Except perhaps this.' As Alcestis paused, the sound of a jet engine began to be audible. At the exact point where it prevented you hearing anything else she started to speak again. Jake watched fascinated as her expression and movements went from tender to grim and back again, from indignant to forgiving, wistful, desolated, philosophical, wry, brave, as amid the huge uproar she bit her lip, clenched her fist, bowed her head, lifted it, frowned, raised her vestigial eyebrows, sighed, half-smiled. He nodded and shrugged and so on repeatedly and farted once. As the jet started to wane she said, 'Which as far as I'm concerned is an end of the matter.'

'Well, I don't think anyone could put it better than that, Allie.'

'No. Thanks. Well. Now. Right. Go. Here.'

She stood up and successively took out of the supermarket bag and planked down on the table a pork pie, a packet of cereal, half a pound of butter, a tin of tomatoes and half a dozen other unelaborate foods. Finally and more ceremoniously she produced a tear-off pad with a hard back and a pencil attached by a cord.

'Don't know what you've got,' she said, 'don't know what you want. Get a copy of your front-door key made and drop it through my letter-box. Anything you need, just whack it down here and leave it on the table. I've got to fetch my own stuff, no point in two of us at it and I've got a car. Yes, I've been left that. However. Settle at the end of the week or whenever you like. You can be in your study when I deliver, no need for us ever to meet. We can't help each other emotionally but I can help you practically, so why not?'

'Well, Allie, that is most kind of you, I do appreciate it very much.'

'Rubbish, man, nothing to it. So long. No, I can see myself out.'

And in a moment the front door banged. Curious thing, human nature, Jake thought to himself as he started on his cold meat and salad. You get someone like that, by no means the most attractive of women, in fact pretty plain and full of irritating mannerisms, to all appearance entirely self-centred, and then she comes in at the end, so to speak, to show that underneath it all as so often there's more than a spark of decency – and of shrewdness too. Yes, that was certainly a legitimate view. On the other hand it might be tentatively argued that old Smudger was still just as much of a raving monster as she had ever been, or rather substantially more of one with her 'shrewdness' seeing him as a threat to her charter to talk balls all the time and her 'decency' trying to make him feel bad with a coals-of-fire job. He was delighted at this confirmation that she knew he hated her like hell and hoped devoutly that shopping for him would cause her great inconvenience. What about a couple of hundredweight of cement for a birdbath or something in the garden? It had begun to look as if finding somewhere to stay, somewhere really satisfactory and also cheap, would be no easy matter. He poured out the last of the wine and took it in front of the television set.

28   Physical after All

Later that year, in the November, Jake became troubled with excessive shitting. He would have to go seven or eight times a day and between those times his innards were never quiet, popping, chuckling and fizzing their head off and emitting moans of poignant grief that attracted the concern or the interest of his classes and pupils. A preliminary exploration of his bum by Dr Curnow proved inconclusive; he must pay another visit in the third week. So one afternoon he duly made his way through rainy gusts to the bus stop and, preceded on board by two pairs of coffee-coloured children, the first in the charge of a white woman, the second of a black man, was soon being carried towards Harley Street.

Not much had happened to him in the intervening months. He had cancelled his holiday in Sicily in favour of a trip to Crete with Lancewood and his chum. There he had accused the hotel staff corporately of having stolen his money, traveller's cheques and passport a sufficient time before their discovery under his mattress, where it could only be that he had stowed them out of some freak of caution put beyond recapture by retsina and Mogadon. Brenda was settled in the Burgess Avenue house with Geoffrey, Jake in a perfectly bearable couple of rooms in Kentish Town, nearer the centre on the 127 route. He often wondered how much he missed her but never for long at a time. Wynn-Williams fell down dead. Two days before he (Jake) moved he had had a very brief visit from Kelly, first in what Brenda had called her investigative-journalist persona and on being told to go away straight into the apologising self-accusing waif he had had two previous doses of. Then bugger pity, he had said to himself, lest you let a fiend in at your door. But he was always going to feel he had let her down, or rather not always, what crap, just to the end of his days, not nearly as long. He finished his article about Syracuse and sent it in.

The bus passed between the tiled facade of Mornington Crescent station and the roughly triangular paved area with the statue of Cobden near its apex, pitted and grimy and lacking its right hand, Richard Cobden the corn-law reformer and worker for peace and disarmament, too famous for his Christian name and dates to be needed in the inscription. Almost at the foot of the plinth what looked like the above-ground part of a public lavatory, black railings draped with black chicken-wire, bore a notice saying London Electricity Board – Danger Keep Out and gave a limited view of a stairway with ferns growing out of it and its walls. Two bollards painted in rings of black and white were to be seen not far off, their function hard even to guess at. Weeds flourished in the crevices between the paving-stones, a number of which had evidently been ripped out; others, several of them smashed, stood in an irregular pile. Elsewhere there was a heap of waterlogged and collapsed cardboard boxes and some large black plastic sheets spread about by the wind. Each corner of the space was decorated with an arrangement of shallow concrete hexagons filled with earth in which grew speckled evergreen bushes and limp conifer saplings about the height of a man, those at the extreme ends crushed by traffic and the greenery run into the soil along with aftershave cartons, sweet-wrappers, dog-food labels and soft-drink tins. Turning south, the bus stopped at its stop across the road from Greater London House, through the windows of which fluorescent lighting glared or flickered all day. It stood on ground filched from an earlier generation of dwellers in the Crescent who had woken one morning to see and hear their garden being eradicated.

Fifteen minutes later Jake was walking down Harley Street, buffeted by damp squalls as he went. He noticed a man and a woman in Western dress before he got to Curnow's place and was admitted. Thanks perhaps to the default of a bashaw or begum the receptionist showed him in straight away.

'Sit down, would you please?' The doctor made it sound as if this procedure would quite likely be painful and was certainly unusual but would turn out to serve his patient's interests better than any alternative soon come by. 'And how have things been?'

'Oh, not too bad. A slight improvement on the whole.'

'You've kept to your diet?'

'Pretty well. I've laid off the fruit and the spices but I have backslid a couple of times with the wine.'

'You must cut it out altogether. You've passed no blood or mucus or anything of that character or nature?'

'No, nothing of that category or description.'

'Any pain? Good. Now if you'll just take down your trousers and pants and lie on the couch.'

Curnow pushed a light up Jake's bum and had a look round there while Jake made hooting noises to relieve his fairly marked discomfort. When Curnow came down again it felt as if he had brought far, far more than his light with him but this proved not to be the case. Soon Jake was back in his chair and very glad of it too.

'Well, there are some unformed stools up there but nothing abnormal. Keep on with the Lomotil and the diet and it should clear up. But remember: no wine,' said Curnow doggedly, adding with extreme reluctance, 'for the time being. If you must drink stick to spirits.' He paused, following up a memory perhaps set off by a glimpse of Jake's genitals a few minutes before. 'Ah – your libido. I sent you to Dr Rosenberg, didn't I? What was the result?'

'Nothing whatever. No, that's not quite true. My . . . libido declined further during the "therapy" and has gone on doing so since.'

'I gather from that that you have ceased the therapy. Why?'

'Things like it being offensive and nonsensical.'

'I could recommend you elsewhere. There are others in the field.'

'If any of them could help me I shouldn't need to go to them.'

The doctor said impressively, 'Let me suggest an altogether different approach. When I measured the level of your testosterone in the spring, it was average.'

'You mean that hormone test you did?'

'Yes. It's been established more recently that what is significant is not the crude testosterone level but the level of that part of it that isn't bound to plasma protein. It would be perfectly simple to establish what yours is. If it's below average it can be supplemented artificially.'

'You mean it may be physical after all? And cured just by taking something?'

'Yes. As I said, we'll have to run tests.'

Jake did a quick run-through of women in his mind, not of the ones he had known or dealt with in the past few months or years so much as all of them: their concern with the surface of things, with objects and appearances, with their surroundings and how they looked and sounded in them, with seeming to be better and to be right while getting everything wrong, their automatic assumption of the role of injured party in any clash of wills, their certainty that a view is the more credible and useful for the fact that they hold it, their use of misunderstanding and misrepresentation as weapons of debate, their selective sensitivity to tones of voice, their unawareness of the difference in themselves between sincerity and insincerity, their interest in importance (together with noticeable inability to discriminate in that sphere), their fondness for general conversation and directionless discussion, their pre-emption of the major share of feeling, their exaggerated estimate of their own plausibility, their never listening and lots of other things like that, all according to him.

So it was quite easy. 'No thanks,' he said.

STANLEY AND
THE WOMEN

Contents

1 Onset

It had been one of Susan's most successful evenings. After weeks of hot sun in late June and July, the weather had turned cool and some of the people, especially the women, must have been quite glad of the candles round the dinner table. The room, which she had recently had redecorated, looked bright and cheerful. There was a comfortable, friendly atmosphere with everybody contributing something to the conversation. The first course, cold avocado soup with a sprinkling of red pepper on top, had been made by Mrs Shillibeer, the daily woman, under Susan's supervision, and it went down extremely well. So did the cold cooked salmon with cucumber, fresh mayonnaise and a sauce made out of chopped olives also by Mrs Shillibeer. They drank a rather good white Burgundy with that, four bottles between the eight persons there, and a small glass each of a sweet Rhône wine with the raspberries and cream. By the time Susan took them upstairs for coffee they were in excellent form.

The sitting room on the first floor had a low ceiling and a rather awkward shape, but she had done her best to turn it into an attractive place with carefully chosen lamps and bright rugs and cushions. The pictures were all personal in some way too, done by artists known to her or the gifts of friends. A long row of gramophone records, mostly orchestral, instrumental and chamber works, stood in a specially built wooden case, part of which housed the rather old-fashioned hi-fi. But naturally it was books that predominated – no science, no history, a bit of biography and some essays alongside a lot of plays, poetry, novels and short stories. Her own two books of collected pieces were among the essays somewhere, not in any particular place.

Quite a few of the books had come her way as review copies in the literary department of the *Sunday Chronicle*. Others she sold off in regular batches, an established perk that went some way towards making up her salary as assistant literary editor of the paper. Not far, though, especially considering how much of the literary editor's work she had to do besides her own. He was there that evening, old Robbie Leishman Jamieson, in fact she had very much set it up as his evening, with an American novelist also present and a new writer of science fiction or something of the kind, and their wives. Old Robbie was the centre of attraction on the pale-grey velvet settee with a shot of his favourite malt whisky in a cut-glass tumbler and Susan encouraging him to tell all his best Evelyn Waugh stories, especially the one about Noel Coward and the Papal Nuncio, which had to be explained to the American novelist's wife.

People used to say about Susan at this stage of her life that things were going not too badly for her after some rather rough times earlier on. Back at the beginning there had been a husband nobody seemed to know a great deal about, an unsuccessful painter or book-illustrator she married to spite her family, according to her, and started divorcing as soon as she found the family had been right about him all the time. Her main attachment after that had been to a considerably more successful left-wing playwright she lived with for six years but could not marry because he already had a wife, and as well as being left-wing was a Roman Catholic, not one of the sort that went in for divorce. That part lasted till the end of '78, when the fellow's wife developed a serious illness and he went back to her. On 12 February 1980 Susan began her second and present marriage and later that year moved into the substantial Victorian red-brick house up near the pond in Hampstead, once the property of a minor poet and antiquarian of those days.

She had passed her thirty-eighth birthday a fortnight before the party for Robbie Jamieson. At first glance she could have been quite that, a rather tall woman who walked and stood a bit off centre with her hands on her elbows very often, frowning, blinking rather above the normal rate and always pushing her upper lip down over her teeth and pressing the lower lip against it in a doubtful kind of way. In one of her grey cardigans or unsensational dark summer dresses she could have been mistaken for a librarian or even a secretary in a local-authority office, but only for a second and before she realized someone else was there. Close to and in conversation she showed up as younger, better shaped for a start and also much more definite in her appearance, with large clear brown eyes and a very distinctly outlined mouth, and glossy black hair that had a little grey in it but no more than was enough to show how black and how genuinely black the rest was. She looked clever, nervous, humorous, something like devoted or loyal when she gave a person her full attention, and gullible, and beautiful. It was true she lacked the withdrawn expression to be seen in most women considered beautiful, but there ought to have been a word for her combination of features, which was among other things completely distinctive, meaning less good versions of it somehow never seemed to show up, and the obvious word always had a lot to be said for it, quite enough in this case. Anyway, that was the conclusion I came to every time I thought about the matter. In fact I told her she had been looking beautiful that evening, when the guests had gone and I was helping her take the coffee things and the glasses out to the kitchen.

'That's good,' she said, kissing me. 'Even in my present state, you mean.'

'I don't know what you're talking about,' I said.

'What? Even attired in one of my old school nighties and without so much as having passed a comb through my hair.'

'I didn't say a word. Did I say anything at all?'

'You didn't have to, old boy. When I appeared as hostess you radiated courteous disapproval. Fairly courteous disapproval. For three seconds or so.'

'I very much doubt whether I radiated anything. You guessed I'd be feeling it, which isn't the same at all.'

'Well, you were, weren't you, so it's not so different. Not that I'm complaining, I promise you.'

I said, 'I don't think it's egotistical or funny or like a Jew or like a gangster of me to fancy the idea of my wife getting herself up in a bit of style. Which would indeed include a much more expensive dress than the one you're wearing. Nicer, too. Also something in the way of earrings or – '

'Of course it isn't funny, darling, it's sweet of you, but you know how hopeless I am, I'd still only pour soup over it. Here.' She pulled part of her skirt into the light. 'Actually this is probably mayonnaise. *Bugger.*'

I managed not to press the point. In spite of what she had said just now Susan always kept her hair neatly trimmed and shaped, but with everything else I could think of her careless attitude to her appearance did seem pretty firm. It connected up somehow with her ideas about art and her position as a writer, an obviously important part of her life she had never wanted me to inquire into. I thought in one way it was rather a shame, not getting the most out of a complexion and colouring as good as hers, but I have always been a great believer in letting people decide things like that for themselves, and there was not much I could have done about this one in any case. So when she asked me in various ways if I thought the evening had been a success I not only said the right things but said them enthusiastically. I went on record as being quite sure the meal had been remarkably popular, old Robbie had had the time of his life, the Americans had gone down well enough with the others and had also been suitably entertained, and more in the same strain, not that she was in much real doubt in her own mind, of course. By this time we had finished in the kitchen and were back in the sitting room.

'Shall we have just one more last quick drink?' I said.

'Why not?' said Susan, screwing up her face.

I poured her a small brandy and myself a smallish Scotch and water. As I did so I realized I had put down a couple already that night.

'Good old Stanley,' she said in a very slightly dreamy way. 'Without whom none of it would have been possible.'

'What do you mean? You organized the whole thing.'

'That's exactly what I do mean.'

'It's true I was responsible for the wines, and there I feel I can claim some credit. The Beaumes-de-Venise in particular. Never been known to fail. Actually I think even old Robbie approved, don't you?'

'Darling, what I'm trying to say is, you let me have the entire evening exactly the way I wanted it even though it wasn't really your sort of evening. Just like you let me have my life the way I want it, as far as you can. Even though, well, parts of it aren't quite your sort of life, I suppose.'

We looked at each other and she smiled and half-shut her eyes in the way she sometimes did.

'You don't hear me complain,' I said. 'Shall I come and sit over there?'

'Let's go up.'

The words were not even out of her mouth when the buzzer from the street door went, a short burst but long enough.

'*Shit*,' said Susan with an annoyance I shared.

When I took the phone arrangement off the wall there was nobody at the other end, though not quite silence, more like a very loud seashell. I said Hallo several times and there was still nothing.

'Probably a drunk going home from a pub,' Susan said.

'Not this late I shouldn't think. Nobody left anything, did they? I'd better go and see.'

The outside door was at the far end of a short glassed-in passage over a dip in the ground. I opened it and looked around and saw nothing at all even when I stepped out, only street lighting and a few parked cars, in fact I was just about on the point of going back in when I heard somebody say something, a mumbled couple of words in a man's voice. I said Hallo again, still without getting any answer. Then after more silence the same person spoke again, tentatively.

'Dad?'

'Steve!'

There was no one else it could have been, though even now I had not really recognized the voice. I already knew that something was wrong, before I could think of any possible reasons. At the same time I felt the slight muzziness slip away from my head. I walked up the street a few yards and found my son alongside the next-door garage, or just stepping out from that corner. Nineteen he was that year, a tall lad, taller than me, also fairer, and of course less bald. He seemed to be wearing his usual assemblage of dark jacket and trousers and light-coloured open-necked shirt. I thought he was avoiding my eye, but it was hard to tell in the patchy light. Usually we hugged each other on greeting but not this time.

'Well, fancy seeing – '

'Okay if I come in for a bit?'

'Of course it's okay. It's great to see you, Steve-oh. What can I offer you? Drink? Bed? Food? Anything within reason.'

I turned away towards the house but he stayed where he was. 'Got some people in, have you?'

'No. We did have, but they've gone. There's just Susan and me. We were – '

'Have you got those colour photographs I took that year in Spain?'

'Hey, you're supposed to be in Spain now, aren't you, you and, er, you and Mandy? Why aren't you there? Didn't you go, or what?'

'Oh, yeah. See, I wanted to get my head together.'

'What?' That last bit bothered me for a moment, until I put it down as another of the vague phrases he and his mates picked up out of nowhere, rode to death for a few weeks or months and suddenly forgot. 'But did you go? When did you get back?'

'Just now.'

'You mean today.'

'Just now. Victoria. I walked.'

'Not all the way here from Victoria, surely to God? It must be about . . .'

About six miles, I reckoned later, a couple of them noticeably uphill. Steve had no estimate or anything else to offer. He stood there on the pavement like somebody at the start of a long wait, not facing me quite head-on. His manner was not so much cold or off-hand as completely devoid of the friendly concentration on whoever he was talking to that he had always shown as long as I could remember. Suddenly I felt an absolute fool, a wash-out as a parent, nosey, pernickety, dull, only wanting to ask tiresome questions about taxis and buses, phoning, luggage and things like that. My head was full of some tougher questions about my son's state of mind, but they were going to have to keep likewise.

'Shall we go inside?' I said it very casually, as though the last thing on earth I wanted was to put pressure on anyone – I had no idea why.

'All right.'

We met Susan in the hall. 'I was just . . . Oh hallo Steve, it was you then, how super, darling,' she said. 'We thought you were meant to be away.' She seemed to notice nothing out of the ordinary, I was glad to see, not even when she went to hug him and he held back for a moment at first. She went on, 'Dad and I were just having a last drink upstairs. You did get to Spain in the end, did you? Where was it, not that bloody place all the Brits go, what's it called, not Torremolinos? Well, that's a comfort, anyway. They tell me it's all frightfully cheap over there now.'

More of that kind of thing got us to our seats upstairs and Steve answered up, not in his old way but enough like it to make me begin to tell myself he was only tired, or had been feeling embarrassed about something he would let out to us as soon as he felt relaxed enough, not that he had ever been particularly easy either to tire or to embarrass. Then Susan turned to him in a way that could have meant nothing to anybody but that she was going to move nearer home, and I saw him shut himself in.

She said, 'Tell me, Steve, is Mandy still reading *The French Lieutenant's*

Woman? I remember you saying she was never without it. Quite a read for anybody, of course.' She sounded and looked like a very expensive nurse, being very good with him, so good you would hardly have noticed. I suppose there was quite a lot for her to be good with him about, his accent, for instance, which was considerably worse than mine. I was very much aware of it when after a long uncomfortable silence he started to speak.

'Mandy and I don't have an amazing amount to say to each other, know what I mean? I mean we do talk all right, but we don't seem to communicate. So I thought, well, we're not getting anywhere, it doesn't really mean anything, it didn't really happen, so I thought I'd better try and get my head together, you know, try and get things sorted out, so I could decide what I was going to do. I mean you've got to do it for yourself, like sort out what you . . .'

He took some time over saying this because he put more silences in. There was a sort of comic contrast between the importance Susan and I had been attaching to his account of himself before it came and what he had actually said, but I thought that as regards things like originality and clearness and compared with almost anything else from one of his generation his statement was not too bad. What had made it hard to listen to or sit through was nothing in the words themselves, not even in the way he delivered them, which was lackadaisical enough but no more so than would have been natural for somebody rather bored at having to explain himself or merely ready for bed after a long walk. No, he just left out completely all the small movements of face and body and inarticulate sounds that you get from people talking, all the familiar signs of an interest in being understood. I would never have thought that a negative change could be so noticeable, and certainly not that having noticed it I was going to take something like half a minute making up my mind exactly what it was. I did notice that he frowned once as he was speaking, but very briefly and not at anything in particular that I could see. Otherwise he was completely without expression, even when he said what he did about getting his head together and I had been so sure he would remember he had said it before, outside in the street, and would let me have some signal that he knew I was thinking it was funny or awful of him to say it again. That was the worst part.

Susan said, quite rightly, 'Do I gather you're not seeing Mandy at the moment?'

'Well, you know, not much going for it.'

'Is she staying behind in Spain for a bit?'

'Decide what I'm going to do.'

There was another silence. I was very relieved when he got up, sprang to his feet in fact with no sign at all of being tired any more, but then in another second he had gone back to his lifeless, wrapped-up style. He muttered something about a drink of water.

'Of course,' I said, looking across to where we kept the tray with the bottles of Malvern and Perrier, but it had gone downstairs with the rest of the stuff. 'Sorry, there doesn't – '

'It's okay, I'll get it.'

'What's the matter with him?' asked Susan when he had gone out.

'He's exhausted. He walked all the way from Victoria, or so he said.'

As though we had both been dying for the chance we had moved instantly into what sounded like accusation on one side and excuse on the other. We kept it up while Susan went on about why no bus or taxi – I came back with queues at the station, why no phone-call – all his generation were like that, and why no luggage – well, nothing much to say there. Neither of us turned anywhere near fervent but it was odd just the same, especially since she had taken a lot of trouble over Steve and they seemed to like each other. Perhaps not so odd on second thoughts, merely a result of being a stepmother and a father and not one hundred per cent cool. I stepped out of the pattern when she mentioned his passport.

'No,' I said. 'I can't believe he's got it on him. Nor any cash either.'

'Well, you could . . .' She stopped. 'So he can't have come from Spain. Where has he been?'

'I don't know. I think I'll go and get a beer.'

'I don't blame you,' she said, meaning for wanting to keep an eye on Steve.

When I got to the foot of the stairs it was like being in a Channel steamer with the drumming and shuddering of the water-system in the walls and all about. In the kitchen the sound of the water itself as it hit the sink was more noticeable. There were pools of it, not very large or deep ones, on the floor and on the various work-surfaces near by. As I came in Steve was adding to them with what was bouncing off the glass in his hand. This he seemed keen to rinse as thoroughly as possible. Feeling ridiculously self-conscious I went past him not too quickly to the refrigerator and took out and opened a can of Carlsberg lager. He knew I was there, of course, but he took no notice of me, or perhaps he did, because he turned off the tap and turned it on again just long enough to fill the glass, which he drained and refilled the same way, all at top speed as though he had taken a bet, and without any signs of pleasure or of anything else. Obviously I had no way of knowing how many glasses he had drunk before I arrived.

By the time he was starting the fourth round of the process I had got a glass for myself, poured my beer and thrown the can away, so that from then on I was hanging about. I tried to force myself to stroll out of the room. Perhaps I ought to say something. I was sure I remembered reading somewhere that children could actually welcome discipline.

'Come and have a spot of Scotch,' I said, and tried to infiltrate lightness into the way I said it. 'All that water can't be the best – '

He looked at me for the first time. It was a glare that lasted less than a second. 'Jesus fucking Christ!' he shouted, so loudly that I jumped. After a weird moment of hesitation he hurled the half-full glass on to the floor and rushed out. Finally I heard the faint slam of the door of his old bedroom at the top of the house.

Susan found me brushing the pieces of glass into the dustpan. I tried to make what had happened sound more ordinary than it had been, but without getting anywhere much. She listened carefully and said in a reasonable tone that no one in fact wanted or needed so much water. I agreed with her.

'He's not normally given to throwing glasses on the floor, is he?' she asked. 'No, that's just it.' He had always been a quiet, easy-going sort of fellow, rather apt to walk out of situations when he felt cross or frustrated, but less so lately than as a boy, and never inclined to violence in any form.

'He doesn't seem to be . . . Something's upset him.'

'Something certainly has,' said Susan, nodding her head several times. She clearly thought there was more in the phrase than I had reckoned with. 'I bet you I know where that young man has just come from, and it's a long way from Spain. Unless of course *she* happens to have been there, which would explain a good deal, I suggest.'

The person referred to was my former wife and Steve's mother, Nowell by name, now married to somebody called Hutchinson. She had left me for him in 1974 and since then, or rather since the end of the legal hassle, we had not met more than a couple of times. Steve hardly ever mentioned her and I had stopped asking him about her. 'Oh, I don't know,' I said. 'I don't think he sees her much these days.'

'What about the time he appeared out of the blue after that cricket match and didn't speak the whole evening? And it turned out she was stoned in the Shepherd's Bush flat the entire time he was there. You remember.'

If other things had been different I would have enjoyed as usual her tone of voice for talking about Nowell, not a bit hostile, better than objective, sort of *interested*, putting the expression in like someone reading aloud in the family circle. 'Yes, but that was years ago.' I wondered if she would still be able to go on like that having met Nowell even for five minutes.

'And the school outing.' Susan glanced at me and went on in her usual way, though quieter. 'Tell me what you think is wrong.'

'I don't know what I think is wrong. He could have had a row with Mandy. They haven't been going together very long, but . . .'

'Three months? I expect that's quite a long time in their world, don't you?'

'Yeah.'

Having turned off lights and locked windows we got to our bedroom on the second floor. Steve's room was up a curving flight of stairs at the far end of this floor, and for a moment I tried to remember if the bed in it would be made up before telling myself that there were plenty of blankets within reach and that anyway he was not five years old any longer. I shut our door behind us. Susan came over and put her arms round me.

After a couple of minutes she said, 'You're upset too, aren't you? In a different way.'

'I suppose I am. I didn't think I was.'

'Have one of my sleepers. Quick and no hangover.'

The next morning things had settled back into proportion. The main event of last night had of course been the dashing and enjoyable dinner party. Steve would probably have slept off whatever had been bothering him and might be talked into staying on for a couple of days. He had always got up late and it came as no surprise that he was still out of sight when I cleared off my Blue Danube coffee and boiled egg in the kitchen and checked my stuff before leaving for the office. Susan appeared in a white terry robe just as I was on my way to the door. She had never been a great early riser either and had her hair hanging down loose round her face. There were faint brownish blotches on the fine skin near her eyes.

'I'm off this morning,' she said.

'I thought as much.'

'You haven't forgotten mummy's coming to lunch?'

'I had. Or else you forgot to tell me.'

'Perhaps I did. Anyway, can you come? Please? I know it's a nuisance but she does like to see you.'

Susan did it just right, appealing to me without putting the pressure on, making her mother out to be fond of her own way but in an amount I could probably put up with or not far off. In fact I was a long way from clear whether the old girl did like to see me in quite the usual sense of the words, but I was as ready as I ever was to see her any time, that is any time bar a Friday lunchtime, my preferred procedure being to take a sandwich at work midday and then beat the weekend rush-hour. Susan knew that perfectly well, and I was just going to remind her of it when I realized she had not tried to use my perhaps difficult son as an extra reason why I ought to be around. I thought that was excellent.

'All right then,' I said, 'I may be a bit late but if I am I'm still slated to attend.'

'Oh Stanley, you are gorgeous.'

She came round the table and began kissing me in a very friendly way. In a moment I tried to put my hand in under the terry robe, but she prevented me.

'Later,' she said. 'I'm not awake yet.'

Susan knew I worried about being on time at work. The weather that morning was damp and blowy and I got a sufficient sample of it just walking the few yards to my garage door. Inside and soon afterwards outside was the Apfelsine FK 3. I could really have managed my surface travel perfectly well with taxis and the occasional hire, but I could hardly have justified keeping the Apfelsine if I had done that, and I was set on keeping it until something replaced it in its class. It was what used to be called a status symbol. I always thought it was much easier to understand than most symbols. I parked it at the other end in my personal space in the office park without turning a hair.

It happened by chance to be motorcars that I discussed in the way of business a couple of hours later. This was in a wine bar just off Fleet Street called La Botella that when I first went to it had been a sort of local for men from the nearby newspaper offices and law places, but for some years now had attracted drinkers mostly of no particular description. Spirits were sold there as well as wine.

As well as operating a stuffy rule about men wearing ties, the management at La Botella was hard on women, forcing them to sit down in the long narrow room at the side of the premises and then making it next to impossible for them to order drinks once they had done that. Lone women who were new to the place or had screwed their plans were always being stood or advanced drinks in the side room by decent chaps. When the man I was talking to there that morning had been called to the telephone, much to his disgust, and half a minute later Lindsey Lucas pitched up in search of a seat and a gin and tonic, I could hardly have turned her down even if we had been total strangers.

I had known her much longer than I had known Susan, though the two were exact contemporaries and old friends without ever having been close. In fact I had an affair with Lindsey after my first wife left me and had given her one or two a bit casually a couple of extra times between then and taking up with Susan. In those days a husband of Lindsey's had come and gone, perhaps still did. She was reddish-fair and well formed, medium-sized, with a good skin, very well-chosen glasses and a banked-down manner like a newscaster's. With this went a hard flat Northern Ireland accent which I liked as a noise without feeling it suited her especially well. For the past three years she had had a column on the women's page of one of the down-market dailies.

'You saw your ex was on the box the other night,' she said with very little delay. To someone else she might have sounded accusing but I could tell it was only those tight vowels.

'Yes I did see, I mean I saw she was going to be but I didn't see the play. Was it good? Was she good? Did you see it?'

'I did, the first half. One of those drama-documentaries about life in our hospitals today. She was the maverick matron who didn't really think they ought to be torturing the patients to death just yet. But get that – matron. Oh, it was called senior nursing officer or some such jargon but she was a matron. Fiery and vital and everything but a matron. Looking not too bad it must be said. What is she now, forty-four?'

'Just over. She's the same as me.'

'Looking quite good. A wee bit miscast in the role, maybe.'

Lindsey took a quick look at me from behind her glasses to see if I had fully appreciated this touch, then another, slower one. She knew well enough that chatting to an ex-husband about the wife who ran away from him was not altogether the straightforward business you might think it would be, even when there was no nonsense whatever about any lingering fondness, as in this case. He might thoroughly enjoy hearing of her misfortunes and love being reminded how terrible she was to have around, but the very next bit might throw doubt on his good sense or taste in ever having got involved with her in the first place. So Lindsey took her time.

'It wasn't a very big part,' she said, 'but I *think* I'm right in saying it was her first for . . . quite a while. And before it I can't remember anything since she was whoever it was in that version of *The Letter*, you know, the woman who shoots her boyfriend and then says he was trying to rape her when really he was trying to ditch her. We, uh, we thought she was just right for that, but it didn't go down very well, I believe. In fact that career of hers in television, which I remember you telling me she was so set on . . .'

So set on, I muttered under my breath and through my teeth, that you could almost say she left me to have a better crack at it – 'Yes, that's right.'

'I may have missed some things, but it doesn't seem to have come to very much. What about that husband of hers? – what's he called, Hutchinson is it?'

'Bert Hutchinson. What about him? Horrible bleeder. Wears suede shirts. And drinks like a fish, I hear.'

'Oh? Well, she should be used to that, Stanley. Perhaps she likes her husbands to put it away. Not that I blame them.'

'No rudeness, please. He drinks like a fish, I just drink, right? Basic distinction. Anyway, he never turned out to produce or direct anything at all as far as I know. There was meant to be going to be a pricy series about Mr Gladstone, with Nowell as I imagine it would be Mrs Gladstone, but then it fell a victim to some axe or quota or whatever.'

'Oh my God,' said Lindsey, undoubtedly thinking of Nowell as Mrs Gladstone, though I had no real idea of why that should be so bad. 'I don't suppose you see much of her, do you?'

'No point. It was bad enough being married to her.'

'Have you seen their child?'

'No. I'd forgotten it existed until now.'

'You should. I can't imagine why Nowell ever agreed to have it. It's a girl. Naturally.'

'I don't know why you say that. Get invited there, do you?'

'Oh, somebody took me along. Are you doing anything for lunch? I don't think this fellow of mine's coming.'

'I wish I wasn't, but I am. In fact it's starting to get tight already.'

'Come on, it's only – '

'I know, but I've got to get home.'

'To Hampstead? Do you go home to lunch every day now?'

'No, not every day,' I said, wishing I was queer and need never explain anything to anybody. 'Today, though. My mother-in-law's coming to lunch.'

I was scowling at Lindsey so fiercely that she just grunted and took a good swallow of her drink, but she was not the sort to leave off when she wanted to go on. I caught sight of my bloke on his way back from the phone, and she saw at once that some interruption was a few seconds away. With an extra dose of the accent, or so I thought, she said, 'You certainly do marry some extraordinary people, Stanley,' obviously reckoning on any real comeback being ruled out. But the bloke, instead of keeping on his way towards us, veered aside in the direction of a pee, so there was no rush after all for the moment.

'Now I realize you haven't got much time for her,' I said, 'Susan that is, but I have. You don't think I know what I'm getting, do you? Well, I think I do, by and large. I like most of it, and the bits I don't like so well I can put up with quite easily, because there's nothing that says I've got to agree with her idea of what she's doing. So she'll pretend she's helping someone or being nice to them, and she really is too, but she's also showing off her genius and drawing attention to herself, which is what a lot of people do, and I'll go along with it. And that works out perfectly well, because she's not a thought-reader, you see. As I say, it's only a small part of the time. We've been married two and a half years now, and going together nearly four, so I reckon so far I'm probably going to be all right.'

'I hope so,' said Lindsey with a smile that looked okay, but making it sound as though she was rather hoping against hope. 'No, I'm not so much down on the old thing as perhaps you imagine. But according to me she's slightly mad, you know.'

I was far from sure how that sounded. 'What does that mean?' I said.

'Well . . . she can't really believe that anything or anybody exists unless they concern her personally.'

'My God, all I can say is it's a good job we haven't got you in charge of committals to the nut-hatch or we'd all be in there.'

'Yeah, we all do most things but some of us do some of them more than others do. Of course I haven't seen her for years. She's probably grown up by now.'

'What's that bleeder *doing* in there?' I asked her, looking at my watch. 'Ah, how's . . . how's Barry?' I was pleased with myself for having come up with her husband's name just when required, but what I tried to get across to her was more that naturally in an ideal world there would most likely not be people called Barry. It seemed from her reply that this particular one was still around, at any rate not yet dead or required to keep his distance by court order. My bloke returned at last, closely followed by Lindsey's apologizing for his lateness. I settled things with mine in about five seconds, got her latest phone number off her, and left. By now I was medium late, so I grabbed a passing taxi.

*

My mother-in-law's lime-green Saab, with a fresh scrape on the rear door, was parked across the road from the pottery shop. In the quite recent past I had watched her have two minor accidents in it at walking pace, one with a stationary furniture van, the other with a simple brick wall, both in excellent conditions of visibility and road surface. At higher speeds she obviously took more care, or else was under some sort of special protection. I could let Susan see nearly all of what I felt about her mother's driving.

In the hall of my house Mrs Shillibeer was rubbing the stain off the floorboards in an area by the fireplace. At the first sound of this name I had imagined a chain-smoking old witch in a flowered overall and one of those turban affairs I had seen on the women who came to clean my parents' house in South London. In other words I had not expected a tall fat girl in her twenties whose usual get-up was a tee-shirt, jeans and pink brocade slippers. Under one of these at the moment there was a pad of wire wool with which she was doing her stain-removal in an upright position. In theory the person at work could have been someone different because her face was hidden by the paperback book she was reading called *The Myth of the Vaginal Orgasm*. Then when she heard the street door latch behind me she lowered the book far enough to see over the top of it.

'Hallo,' she said in a loud affected voice. 'Lady Daly,' she went on in the same voice and paused for quite a long time, 'hazz . . . arrived-uh.' She was given to making announcements of this sort. I could never tell whether she was being cheeky to me or so to speak joining up with me against whoever the announcement was about.

Lady Daly was naturally my mother-in-law. Her husband, fallen down dead before I ever came along, had been a Conservative MP for a safe Hertfordshire seat, given a knighthood for never having done anything. When I opened the sitting-room door she tried to shove back into its place on the shelves the book she had taken out and turn round and face me innocently at the same time, like Ingrid Bergman interrupted in a bit of amateur spying. They were not my books anyway.

'Morning, Stanley,' she got in quickly.

'Morning, lady. How are you today? Can I get you something? What about a spot of sherry?'

'Oh no. No. No thank you.' She gave me a peck on the cheek, as near as someone without an actual beak could. 'But you have . . . have one.'

'I don't see why not,' I said, and started to make myself a small Scotch on the rocks. There were rocks on hand in the plastic pineapple instead of to be fetched from the kitchen because Susan had got Mrs Shillibeer to interrupt her other duties to put them there. Where was Susan? One of the troubles with getting on all right with people like your mother-in-law, or looking as if you did, or trying to, was that people like your wife took to leaving you alone with them to have a nice chat.

My mother-in-law managed to stop watching my operations at the drinks tray. 'Filthy traffic,' she said as one committed road-user to another.

'Wicked. Of course there's the weekend coming up.'

She turned on me indignantly. 'But it's barely Friday afternoon.'

'I know, but you know how it is.'

'I wonder some of them bother to go in to work at all. Well, a great many don't, as we see. They're *unemployed*.'

'Yes, I know.' I raised my glass. 'Cheers, lady.'

Mum was what I had called my first mother-in-law but this one had other ideas. I thought they were on the wrong lines. Lady Daly had to be a dodgy thing to be called in the first place and the nickname or whatever it was reminded you of that dodginess. Also I very much doubted whether she had ever done what I once had out of curiosity and looked up the word in *The Concise Oxford Dictionary*. Apparently to use it in the vocative and the singular, which was what I had just been up to, could only be either poetical or vulgar, nothing in between. I thought that was very interesting.

'I gather you have *Steve* staying with you,' she said after a pause, quite chuffed at getting over all the various difficulties raised by bringing out this name.

So nothing really awful had happened in between. 'Yes, he dropped in to stay for a couple of days. So it seems. Just turned up on the doorstep. As they do at that age.'

'Such a nice boy. Still working at his writing, is he?'

'Yes, I think so, yes. Plugging away.' It would hardly have been fair to say that Steve had ever plugged away at anything. What kept him going usually was pound-note jobs with gardeners and handymen and dribs and drabs from me.

'Tell me, Stanley, it's dreadfully stupid of me, but I seem never to have taken in just what it is that he writes. Is it verse or prose? Essays? Plays, perhaps?'

'No, it's not plays.'

'How would you describe it?'

'Well . . . '

I tried to remember anything at all about the few badly typed pages that, in response to many requests and with a touching mixture of defiance and shyness, Steve had planked down next to me on the couch one Sunday afternoon the previous winter. But it was the same now as then, really. I had not been able to come up with a single word, not just of appreciation, but even referring to one thing or another about the material. But surely I had managed to tell whether it was in verse or prose? Hopeless.

'Of course, he hasn't shown me a great deal of it.' I looked across and met the old girl's eye and wished she could find a way of coming a little less far to meet me – sometimes you would give anything for a spot of boredom. 'I don't know about you but I'm a complete wash-out when I come up against any of this modern stuff.'

'Oh, I do absolutely agree. But what would you have – '

Susan came in then. 'Sorry,' she said in a half-whisper. I was relieved to see her, as I often was, and it was easy enough to see that her mother felt something similar, say like after spending an unpredictable length of time with a small half-tamed wild animal. When Susan kissed me she gave the top part of my arm the special little squeeze that meant she was thanking me or apologizing or hoping to cheer me up. I imagined she was doing a minor bit of all three that time. She took the dry sherry I poured for her and went and stood with her mother near the china-cupboard. Seen as a pair like this they could look more alike than I cared for, and today was one of the days, with them both wearing darkish skirts and lighter-coloured tops. Lady D would have been in her middle or late sixties but she had kept her figure, and one way or another her hair was almost as dark as Susan's. But then again her eyes were much lighter and she looked less clever, more nervous and not humorous at all.

I drank some of my Scotch and said, 'Any sign of the young master?'

'Oh,' said Susan, 'he – '

She stopped suddenly because the door was thrown open, also suddenly, so that it banged into one of her embroidered stools, though not very hard. Even so, the effect was quite noticeable, especially when nobody came in or could be seen from inside the room. The three of us stood still and said nothing, not in the least like people wondering what the hell was going on. Then Steve strolled round the corner, very casual, I thought, preoccupied but normal enough, scruffy enough too, having probably spent the night in his clothes.

'Hallo, dad,' he said quietly. 'Hallo Susan. Hallo . . . lady.'

'Good morning, Steve,' said my mother-in-law rather like a fellow playing in Shakespeare.

'Er . . . ' he said, and stopped. I could hear him breathing deeply through his mouth. 'Can I borrow a book?'

'Help yourself, my dear,' said Susan, spreading a hand. 'Fiction there . . . poetry there . . . politics, psychology, what you will . . . Art and so on down there.'

Steve, who had not followed this closely, turned his head towards the bookshelves. The other three of us moved into the window-bow so as not to seem to be watching him looking. We talked about something like the Labour Party or what we might do for Christmas. After a minute or two he moved away from the books and apparently started examining a painting on the end wall. It was mostly blue, but some parts of it were white. As far as I knew he had never taken any particular interest in pictures and this one had hung there all through his dozens of visits to the house. He went on examining it. Susan had no idea – if she had been playing the adverb game 'normally' would have been the one she was doing. Her mother handled it differently, putting all her effort into not running for her life. I sympathized with her at the same time as wondering what exactly it was we three had to be so on edge about. Before I had solved it there was a tearing sound and I saw that Steve was in fact tearing the cover off a book. I shouted out to him. Having got rid of the cover he tried to tear the pages across but they were too tough and he put the remains of the book down on a cushion on the back of a chair. By the time I went over there he had gone. The book was *Herzog*, by Saul Bellow.

'I'm sorry, love,' I said to Susan. 'I don't know what he thinks he's doing. He must be off his head. I'll get you another.'

'It's all right, darling,' she said, 'I'd finished with it, it was just hanging about on the shelves. Lunch in ten minutes,' she called after me on my way to the door, sounding as normal as anybody could have managed.

With my mind on the water-drinking event I checked the kitchen, then briefly the upstairs in general before catching up with my son in the small bathroom, or rather lavatory with washbasin, next to his bedroom. As before, there was plenty of water about – on the mirror behind the basin, into which he was staring, on his face and hair and clothes and on the floor. He had evidently not touched the clean towel on the metal rack beside him.

'What's the matter with you?' I said, trying to sound angry instead of worried. 'What do you mean by tearing up a book like that?'

He just stood there with his hands by his sides and said nothing.

'These things cost money, you know.'

'I'll pay for it,' he said wearily.

'Like hell you will.' Now I was really angry. He was always offering to pay for other people's things he had used up or broken or lost, going on every time as though it was very sweet of him to be so patient with all these small-minded idiots, and then somehow not having the cash on him until I forked out. 'Anyhow it's a waste, and it might have been a special copy, and it might not be able to be replaced, and what did you want to go and do it for in the first place? Are you crazy or something?'

By way of reply he turned on the cold tap and started to slosh handfuls of water on to his face in a tremendous, ridiculous hurry, throwing more of it down his shirt and trousers and round his feet. He did this in complete silence.

I waited till I had stopped feeling angry and said, 'Have you been to see your mother?' I tried to make it sound interesting, as though his mother had been a film.

At once he dramatically turned off the water and snatched up the towel, and started drying himself, but you could soon tell he had nothing to say this time either.

'If something's upsetting you I wish you'd tell me about it,' I said. 'Or if I've done anything you don't like. I know it sounds dull but I want to help you.'

It sounded dull all right. Perhaps that was what Steve was trying to get across by the way he finished drying his face and neck, peered into the mirror, turning his head to and fro to catch the light, and then started drying his face and neck again. Or perhaps he had really not heard. I tried to think how to go on. At no particular point he said suddenly and in a trembling voice, but just the same like someone continuing a conversation,

'I was hot, that's all. Haven't you ever been hot? What's so peculiar about trying to get cool? All got to be the same, have we? All like you. Anybody who isn't is mad, according to you. Why don't you come out and say it?' He was still looking in the mirror, though not catching my eye in it. 'You want to get bloody Dr Wainwright over and certify me, don't you? Go on, admit it.'

He turned round and stood in front of me, stood about, in fact, not showing the least interest in what I might say back to him. But I began telling him he was wrong and of course I had never even thought of getting him certified, and I would have gone on to appeal to him to forget the whole thing and come and have some lunch, only he pushed past me not all that rudely and went off to his room, still holding the towel. The door slammed.

Susan was waiting for me just inside our bedroom. I shut the door behind us and we hugged each other, with her giving a little half-joky shiver. I told her about the water and the accusation and she listened attentively, arms crossed and lips pressing together. When I had finished she said, 'I waited till he was in the bath and I sneaked into his room and looked in his coat and the chest of drawers and places, everywhere. No passport, no traveller's-cheque stuff, no ticket stubs, nothing. So . . . ' She jerked her shoulders.

'So he hadn't come from Spain, or not straight from there. No knowing where he was or how long he's been, well, whatever he is now.'

'Before he had his bath he didn't appear at all so I went up to see how he was getting on, and he was just lying in bed, not asleep, just lying there. Then about half an hour ago I was nearly blasted off my chair in the study by Mahler on the record-player. Not just loud, you know, but absurdly loud. Grotesquely loud. And then of course when I asked him to turn it down he turned it off.' She shook her head a few times.

'Yeah,' I said. 'It must be his sex life. At least it's all I can think of.'

'Oh, I brilliantly rang her flat, having brilliantly but I forget why put its number in my book, but somebody I thought sounded Swedish said no, Miss Blackburn was not there.'

'Didn't they say anything else?' Asking that question was rather dishonest of me, because actually I only wanted to hear some more of what Susan must have thought was a Swedish accent. It reminded me strongly of the Italian accent she had put on the previous evening to tell a story about Toscanini.

'No, in fact I never made out whether Mandy wasn't there just then or on a permanent basis.'

'Oh. Well, I think all we can do is leave him to himself until he snaps out of it. Sorry about that book, by the way. I couldn't get him to say why he'd done it.'

'Never mind. But actually I would rather like another copy if possible.'

'No problem, I'll send one of the girls out for it this afternoon. You go on down now and I'll give it a couple of minutes.'

When I went into the kitchen Lady D swung round on me with an expression that showed clear as a bell that she expected a full report on the case of the buggered-up book. I had used most of that couple of minutes to pour and swallow a stiff Scotch. I wished now I had brought another one with me, that or a brass knuckleduster. Hoping her idea might go away if I said nothing, I took my place at the table opposite Susan, who rolled her eyes slightly.

Fat chance. 'And what did *Steve* have to say about destroying that book?' asked her mother, getting a totally different effect this time from leaning on poor old Steve's name.

'Well, he made it pretty clear that something had just come over him, he couldn't say what. But he was obviously very embarrassed about the whole thing and wished it hadn't happened.' True in parts, I thought.

Lady D gave a kind of one-syllable laugh that in the standard way left it open whether she was coming clean about not believing a word or thought she was keeping it to herself. Mrs Shillibeer helped things along by standing at the cooker doing a marvellous imitation of somebody not listening to what somebody else was saying because of being so completely wrapped up in heating and stirring a saucepan of soup. Susan said,

'Stanley thinks he's had an upset in his love life and I must say I'm inclined to agree.'

'And that licenses him to *rend* apart other people's books?'

I frowned. 'Oh, I wouldn't say that. No, I . . . wouldn't say that. In fact I can't agree at all. Explains it, perhaps.'

'Let's just hope he'll sort of unwind,' said Susan.

'After shedding the gigantic burden of responsibility he habitually carries about on his poor shoulders,' said Lady D with tremendous faces and head-movements as she spoke. Previous to that she had sent me the latest of a series of looks which the chances were she thought I never saw or possibly failed to understand, burning looks, looks that showed she was wondering what sort of bloke it could be that had a son who did diabolical things like tearing covers off books. I stopped trying to think what to say when I noticed that Mrs Shillibeer had pointed her face at me, opened her mouth and started blinking non-stop to show she had a message for me.

'Oh, Mr Duke,' she said, or rather called.

Instead of screaming I said, 'Yes, Mrs Shillibeer?'

'Oh, Mr Duke, would you like me to take Steve up something on a tray?' Her voice climbed the better part of an octave on the last word.

I looked at Susan. 'I don't think so, thanks. Best to leave him. He'll come down and get himself something if he feels like it.'

'Of that there is no room whatsoever for doubt,' said the old girl.

'Oh, I couldn't agree more, lady,' I said.

Mrs Shillibeer doled out the soup and the three of us had lunch. While we were having it I thought to myself that someone else, someone apart from Steve, was behaving unusually, and that was my mother-in-law. It had been clear to me for some time that she reckoned Susan had not taken much of a step up in the world by becoming one of the Dukes, but up to just now she, Lady D, had managed to keep that sort of feeling more or less to herself. But then of course there had not been anything much in the way of reason or excuse or provocation before.

'Are you going in this afternoon?' I asked Susan at one stage, meaning to work.

'I wasn't, why?'

'Well, good, I've got to and I just thought there ought to be someone here.'

'But that'll leave Susan alone in the house,' said her mother in amazement. She had a chain on the ends of her glasses and round her neck so that in between times they sat on her chest and when she was wearing them, like now, the chain hung down in a loop behind and waggled about in a quaint way every time she moved her head, and she had never thought of that.

'Except for Steve, yes,' I said.

'It's all right, mummy,' said Susan.

We never found out what her mother thought of the idea in so many words because just then there was the noise of an assault platoon coming down the stairs and a few seconds later the crash of the street door.

'Would that be Steve?' asked Lady D, doing another variation by putting on no emphasis at all.

'I think it must be,' I said.

'Perhaps when he comes back he'll be in a more gracious mood.'

Soon afterwards I went out and picked up a taxi on its way back from dropping somebody at one of the Jewboys' houses in the Bishop's Avenue.

The phone on my desk rang and a man's voice grunted once or twice and said, 'Is that, er, is . . . is, er . . . '

If whoever it was had really forgotten my name he would have had to do it very recently, since asking the switchboard for me. Another day I might have played him along. 'Stanley Duke here,' I said.

'Ah. Duke . . . you're a shit. A *shit*. Ha. Don't ring off, don't ring off, somebody here who wants a word with you, you . . . '

The words died away in mutterings. Those few seconds had been enough to remind me first of a big fat body, a round dark-red face, a scrubby beard and glasses, and then of a name, Bert Hutchinson, and immediately after that I guessed some of what had happened and felt scared. I was glad I was alone in the office just then.

'Stanley,' said a faint, suffering voice.

'Yes, Nowell. What's the – '

'Stanley, it's Nowell. Could you possibly come round? I can't deal with him at all. I don't know what's the matter with him, I think he must be mad.'

'What's he been – '

'Stanley, you've simply *got* to come round, I can't stand it, it's absolutely terrifying. He's been saying the most horrible things to me.'

'Oh,' I said. That in itself was no atrocity from my point of view. 'What's he doing at the moment?'

'He's upstairs,' my ex-wife admitted.'But he's in the most awful state. You must come, Stanley. You don't know what it's like, honestly.'

There was a vague kind of bawling in the background during the last part of this, which I thought was probably Bert suggesting some other remarks she could make. I asked her what she expected me to do and generally made difficulties, but I knew I had to go. For one thing, there was nothing to stop me. I checked that they were still where they had been, not in Shepherd's Bush any more but nearer the centre and perhaps classier in Maida Vale. Then I hung up and to show my independence or something rang the High Commission of one of the South-East Asian countries and failed to raise the Commercial Attaché, which was nothing out of the way. Finally I got moving – in the Apfelsine, naturally.

The traffic was a bit hard and I used up some endurance just getting out of the car park. At the lights at the bottom of Fetter Lane I was behind an enormous tourist bus from Frankfurt. The guide spotted me and pointed me out to his passengers as a typical Fleet Street editor. They all seemed to be about sixteen. I tried to give them their money's worth by looking energetic and ruthless, also thoroughly up-to-date in my approach. Or perhaps it was just the car. Talking of which, as I pulled away and again by the Law Courts the clutch was definitely on the heavy side, still, after everything I had done to it. I would have to get somebody in who knew a bit about the subject. Not my field, clutches. When it came to gearboxes, now, I reckoned I could hold my own, even with the paper's motoring correspondent, not that that was saying much. In fact, a good half of my published works, articles as well as letters, had to do with gearboxes one way and another, trade press only of course. So far, at least. But if . . .

No, I must not let myself get out of thinking about what was on the way up. First, though, I was going to go back to that short phone conversation with Nowell. Had she really not named Steve, not laid it on the line that that was who she was talking about? Very likely. It was the sort of thing distracted females did in films – it just went to show how distracted they were. It was also the sort of thing some females did in real life distracted or not, and that went to show, really show, how wrapped up in themselves they were. In a small way. They knew who they were talking about and that was it. Not that they knew who they were talking about and you could bleeding well catch up as best you might – no, just they knew who they were talking about. Another time I might have pretended I thought she was talking about Prince Charles, but not today.

I had never felt I had had too much to do with either marrying Nowell or not being married to her. After going round with her for about six months I had suddenly noticed that I was already well on with a trip that ended in marriage and had no places to get off. Not that I had wanted to. Then after thirteen years and at no particular point that I could see she had gone and set up with this Bert Hutchinson. Between then and now I had done a great deal of thinking about him and how he compared with me, but it had not taken me all that long to decide that about the one difference between us there could be no argument about had to do with him being showbiz and me not being. In talking to people like Lindsey Lucas I would admittedly say that Nowell had gone off with Bert to be got better parts in television by him, but the fact that it had not happened told against that idea – she was too shrewd to be so wrong about what somebody could do for her. No, it was just that Bert fitted in with her by presumably liking to spend as much time as possible with showbiz people and I never had. I could stand spending quite a lot of time with them and looking after myself the rest of the time, only from Nowell's point of view that was unsatisfactory in at least two ways. No prizes for seeing a connection here with her not having been able to run the whole of her and my life whereas perhaps Bert let her run the whole of theirs and even liked it, but that you obviously could argue about.

I had got to that point, and also to the Marylebone flyover, when it suddenly came to me that it was not trouble with or about Mandy or any other girl that was the cause of Steve's behaviour. He had come in for that sort of trouble in the past and it had affected him differently, not in any kind of violent way, more prepared to hang on and keep quiet and tend to make the best of it. That went for how he had handled other kinds of upset. Whatever had happened to him was completely new.

The house was in Hamilton Terrace, stone and dark brick, hard to get into under a quarter of a million. In the garage at the side I noticed one of the first Jaguars, plate impressively DUW 1, well kept but not ridiculous. I pressed a button and heard a chime with a cracked note in it. The door was opened by a girl of seven or eight with straggling dark curly hair and a white dress down to the ground, like a kid in an old photograph. She also had a very boring face with no Nowell in it that I could make out.

'I've come to see your mother,' I said.

'Who are you?' Her voice reminded me of Mrs Shillibeer's.

'Well, I used to be married to her. She's – '

'Do you do commercials?'

'No.'

Shoving past her was the thing, but she was holding the door only a little way open and standing in the gap, and I felt I could hardly trample her underfoot just yet. While I wondered about this I heard a lavatory-plug being pulled and an inner door opened, followed by a sharp thud like someone's knee or head hitting the door, and after a moment the top half of Bert Hutchinson came in sight. I had forgotten – I had only seen him about once before – that he was one of the school that parted their hair just above the ear and trained it over the bald crown, a policy I thought myself was misguided, but only on the whole. Without noticing he pushed a colourful picture on the wall askew with his shoulder.

'What the bloody hell are you doing here?' he asked me hoarsely and at the second attempt, and went on before I could answer, 'Go on, get . . . get out of it, you . . . '

'I talked to Nowell on the phone and she asked me to come round to give her a hand with Steve.'

'That's right, she did,' he said, just as hoarsely. He could see straight away that this made a difference but was far from clear how much. Anyhow, he stayed where he was and so did the small girl, who had to be his daughter and did look rather like him in a frightening way.

'Is he still here?' I said to keep the conversation going.

'Who? Oh . . . yeah . . . fuck . . . ' He looked me over, hesitated, then decided to stretch a point and pulled the door wide open. 'You . . . '

'Is that your Jaguar I see there?'

Nothing definite came of that. The hall was stacked with great bulging brown-paper parcels tied up with hairy string. Some of them had been partly torn open to show what looked like blankets and bolsters. It was rather dark and smelt of old flowers or the water they had been in. Not poverty-stricken, though.

I found Nowell in a lounge where there would have been plenty of room for a couple of dozen commercial travellers to hang about for the bar to open. All the pictures, including a large one let into the wall at the far end, were by the same artist or squad and showed one or more sailing-ships having a bad time. Nowell was sitting on a circular couch in the middle being talked to by a white-haired chap in a jacket put together out of suede, fisherman's wool, rawhide and probably canvas. When she saw me she held up her hand with the palm outwards so as to get me to fight down my impatience till she had finished her listening. You could have told a hundred yards off that she was listening, hard enough, in fact, to make any normal person dry up completely in a few seconds. There was no sign of Steve, like pools of blood or blazing furniture.

It must have been a good three years since I had laid eyes on Nowell, either in the flesh or on the screen. She had not visibly aged, though her thick-and-thin look seemed to have become more noticeable. I had often tried to analyse it in the old days, but could still get no further than being nearly sure it consisted physically of a slight permanent rounding of the eyes and raising of the eyebrows plus the top teeth being a bit sticky-out in the English mode. In those old days it, the look, had been one of her great attractions as far as I was concerned, along with things like her breasts. I had not known then that the thick and thin in question was not what she would be at my side through but what she was prepared to battle through to get her own way. On the other hand there was nothing deceptive about her breasts, not then anyhow. Not much about them could be made out today through the top part of her faded dungarees. They and the polka-dotted handkerchief on her head gave the idea that she might be just going to get down to stripping the paint off a door or even hanging out the washing, whereas in fact she would have been easily as likely to be going up in a balloon. There was all that to be said and more, but sitting in the same room with her I found it impossible to be simply glad I was not married to her any more and not to flinch a bit at the thought. Stopping being married to someone is an incredibly violent thing to happen to you, not easy to take in completely, ever.

Funny old Nowell. Nowell? It was amazing, but in all those years I had never realized that of course that was wrong. Nowell was to do with Christmas – there was a carol about the first one. Noel was her name but she or her mother had just not been able to spell it. There were cases like Jaclyn and Margaux and Siouxie where no no one seriously imagined that was right, but this was different. Nowell was like Jayne and Dianna and Anette where somebody had been plain bleeding ignorant.

I sat on and the bloke in the fancy jacket talked on. What he was saying must have been extremely important, because so far he had not had time to notice I had turned up. After a minute Bert came in carrying a glass with a blue-tinged liquid in it, perhaps drawn off from the insides of some appliance. I saw now that his glasses were similarly tinted. He looked over at me round their sides more than through them.

'Listen,' he said, 'have a . . . er . . . Do you want a drink?'

As a matter of fact I did, but I was not going to have one with him. 'No thank you,' I said.

He thought that could not be right and spoke more loudly. 'I said do you want a *drink*.' When I refused again he slumped down on a padded corner-seat some distance off. The little girl, who had followed him into the room, clambered up beside him in a complicated, drawn-out style and started leaning against him and rolling about all over him the way some of them do at that age with men in the family, not sexually quite because they leave your privates alone, but sexually all the same because you would have to take it like that from anyone else. In the meantime the kid watched me from under her eyebrows as though I had to be half out of my mind with jealousy.

After a bit of this I started to feel restless. I went over to Bert and said, 'Where exactly is Steve, do you know?'

He lifted his arm up slowly to point at the ceiling. Nobody tried to stop me when I went out of the room. I reckoned to find Steve laid out in one of the bedrooms and walked up to the top floor, stopping on the way for a pee. The wc had a fluffy crimson mat round its base and another on its lid in case you wanted a comfortable sit-down. The place led off a bathroom with pine panels round the bath and one of Nowell's classy loofahs, looped at the ends to help you do your back, on a bright brass hook behind the door.

Steve was in a bedroom that had large windows, no curtains, bare lemon-yellow walls and the late-afteroon sunshine streaming straight in, so it was never hard to see what was going on in the next few minutes. I thought of Susan's description when I saw he was not only not asleep but not even in the sort of attitude sleeping people get into. Apart from the unmade bed he was lying on I noticed two rather neat piles of sheet-music and a newish bar-billiards table. That set me wondering, a third of a ton of slate and mahogany lifted all this way, and how, and why, but I soon dismissed it from my mind when I took another look at Steve.

'What about getting on home?' I said. 'There's nothing for us here.'

He muttered something I failed to catch, just a few words, rather fast.

'Sorry, what did you say?'

'No, I was just . . . ' His voice petered out in a sort of quiet gabble.

I tried again. 'Let's be off. We could take in a beer at the Pheasant.'

'Possessing all the relevant information to the most incredible degree,' he said quickly.

'What?' I said, though I had heard well enough.

No reply. After a pause he suddenly swung his legs round and sat on the edge of the bed so as to face the main window. Then he raised one hand in what might have been a waving movement. Obviously there was nothing out there, but I went and looked to make sure and that was what there was, just a lot of roofs and down below not a soul in sight, a cat sitting on a wall and that was it. When I turned back to Steve I thought his face was not quite the same as what I was used to, not in any way I could have described but enough so that if I had seen him unexpectedly in the street I might not have recognized him for a second. Yes, it was something about the way his features related to each other. There was so much I wanted to ask him, no deep stuff, no more than what he had actually been doing before he turned up the previous night and what he had in mind to do, but there seemed to be no way to start. Another pause.

'Let's get going, shall we?' I said, trying not to sound too jolly. 'I've got the car outside.'

'Do you believe in past lives?' he asked me, in a rush as before.

'Eh? I'm sorry, son, I just don't understand what you mean.'

'You know, people living before and then being born again. Do you believe in it?'

'Oh, reincarnation. No, I don't think so. I haven't really . . . How do you mean, anyway?'

'People that lived a long time ago — right? — being born again now, in the twentieth century.'

'But they . . . ' I stopped short — there was no sense in starting on what was wrong with that. 'Say I do believe in it, what about it?'

Steve was staring out of or towards the window. The line of his mouth lengthened slowly in a thin, tight, horizontal grin, and he began to giggle through his closed lips in a half-suppressed kind of way, not a habit of his. Nothing much seemed to be happening to the rest of his face, except perhaps his eyes widened a bit. After a few moments he stopped, but started again almost straight away, this time putting his hand over his mouth. Even though it was not a specially disagreeable sound in itself I had soon had all I needed. I went brisk and businesslike, looked at my watch and turned to the door.

'I must remember to get petrol,' I said. 'Would you keep a look out for a place on the way? I had a full tank on Tuesday, you know. It's all the low-gear work in town.'

He nodded and got to his feet, but then he said, 'Are they still there, those people downstairs?'

'What? Well, they were when I came up. Why?'

'What were they saying?'

'I don't know. Nothing of any consequence, I imagine. Mum was listening to that white-haired — '

'What were they smirking and carrying on about?'

'They weren't carrying on about anything that I could see. They were just — '

'Why are you pretending?' He sounded no more than irritated.

'Steve, I honestly — '

'Don't try and tell me you don't know what I mean.'

I failed to come up with any answer to that one. For the first time I wondered what the horrible things had been that Nowell had told me over the phone he had said to her. She tended to have horrible things said to her more often than most people, though most people would probably not have counted a few of them. One lot had consisted of some stuff about his garden that a neighbour had said to her when he could have been saying how brilliant she had been as the publican's wife in the film spin-off of that TV series. I remembered feeling quite indignant with him at the time.

Whatever Steve might have been saying earlier he seemed peaceable enough now, and when he and I went back to the lounge place we might have been any old visiting father and son looking in to say goodbye. Nowell and the white-haired fellow were not there, Bert and the child were, sprawled in front of the television set, or rather he was sprawled while she wriggled about next to him or on him. A cartoon was showing with the sound turned down so far that you got nothing more than the occasional faint clatter or scream. After a minute Nowell reappeared, having seen her chum off as I had sensed.

'That was Chris Rabinowitz,' she explained when we were still only half-way out of a pretty brief clinch of greeting. The name meant nothing to me, but the grovel in her voice made me think he must be on the production side rather than just another actor.

Steve seemed to take no notice and just said, rather flatly, 'We're off now, mum.'

'Oh, are you, darling?'

There was a big hug then, with her very decently forgiving him for the horrible things. I looked at the television. The cartoon was the sort where as little as possible moved or changed from one frame to the next so as not to overwork the artists. Something went wrong with the hug but I missed what it was.

'Cheers, Bert,' said Steve, and started to move away.

'You *must* come again soon,' said Nowell to Steve and me, as though the present once-a-week arrangement was nowhere near good enough.

Immediately – though I soon saw there was no connection – Steve turned back to her and said in the same flat way, 'Is he a Jew, that pal of yours?'

'Who, Chris? I don't know, darling. I suppose he is. Why, what of it?'

'Do you get many of them coming round here?'

'What, many Jews? Some, probably. But what on earth are you driving at?'

'They're moving in everywhere to their destined positions.'

'Oh, come on, Steve, don't be bleeding ridiculous,' I said. 'That's not your style at all.' It certainly was not, in fact he would sometimes call me a Nazi for making the kind of mildly anti-semitic remarks that came naturally to someone like me born where and when I was. 'Or is it the way your pals are talking these days?'

'You don't understand. This isn't that old-fashioned shit about Yids in the fucking golf club. None of you know what's going on. They're not ready, see, not even through the whole country yet, never mind some of the other places. But the map is there, and it projects, you know, if you can just get on to it. You want to get your head together.' He seemed to think that this was an important secret and well worth knowing for its own sake too. 'Take warning. When the pattern's complete, the prediction of the ages will emerge. Surely you must have seen something, one of you. Doesn't the colour of the sky look different after dark?'

This made Nowell quite cross. She tried a couple of times to interrupt and finally got in a burst. 'For goodness' sake shut up, darling. I can't bear that sort of poppycock.' That might well have been true – the sort of poppycock she could bear or better, like astrology and ESP and ghosts, was well worked over and properly laid out. 'You've been reading one of these frightful mad paperbacks about cosmonauts or flying saucers or something.'

'No,' said Steve in an agitated way, shaking his head violently. 'No.'

'Of course you have. Or you've been sniffing glue or taking horrible speed. I've got enough troubles of my own without listening to your nonsense hour after hour.' So Chris Rabinowitz had not come up with the offer or prospect he had been supposed to. Without looking at me Nowell went on, 'Get him out of here, Stanley, please, and leave me in peace. I've had about all I can take.'

Before I could say anything he shouted, 'You poor fools! You're in terrible danger!' He looked wildly round the room as though he needed a place to take cover.

I tried to get him to look at me. 'What danger, Steve? What from?'

'You have to trust me, dad.'

'How do you mean?'

'You've got to put your whole trust in me, completely. Swear you'll trust me whatever happens.'

'Of course I trust you, lad, we all do, but what do you mean, whatever happens? What's going to happen? Who – '

'No, swear – you have to swear. Mum, you swear first – come and stand over here by me.'

'Don't be ridiculous, Steve,' said Nowell, but she said it without any conviction at all. And incidentally she looked like the way she had looked one time years before, I remembered, when she had wanted a holiday in Morocco and I had said Majorca was far enough.

Steve was shouting again. 'Will you listen! It's going to happen any minute now!'

I said, 'What is? For Christ's sake, what's supposed to happen?'

'I can't explain, you have to trust me.'

Silence fell, but from the way Steve looked it was not going to last long. He was trembling in a jerky way and wincing as though he was cold, and his expression and even the set of his shoulders showed total bewilderment, though the word was not strong enough for a feeling that in this case was obviously as painful as extreme fear. At that point I knew what I had known on his first appearance the previous night, or rather I was forced to admit it to myself. On the other hand I was stumped for what to do. It seemed Nowell was not. She put her arm round his shoulders and talked to him with a loving sort of indignation, taking his part against the world.

'You've had about enough, you poor little thing, haven't you? It really is too bad. You've been under the most terrible pressure. I'm not surprised you're upset. Anybody would be. It must have been absolutely awful,' she said, and more in the same strain.

In a minute or so she had him sitting on the couch and not trembling in the same way. I knew and cared nothing about why she was doing it or what she was saying to herself about it. Bert had no way of understanding what was happening but that bothered him not in the least. His offspring was more up with things, staring while resting her cheek on her shoulder like a kid watching a couple of sweet little baa-lambs. I went over and asked for a phone.

He decided not to trust himself to speak, which I thought showed sound judgement. Kicking over on the carpet his fortunately empty glass he made a last-straw face and noise and pointed at the ceiling as earlier, then flew into a temper and shook his head a lot and pointed at the floor. I found what I was looking for in the next room, which set me wondering rather where Bert thought he was for the moment.

'May I speak to Dr Wainwright? It's Stanley Duke.'

'I'm sorry, Mr Duke, I'm afraid – one moment.'

After a short pause Cliff Wainwright's mellow voice suddenly spoke. He came from one station up the Clapham Junction line from me but he had done a thorough job on his accent, only letting out an unreconstructed SW16 vowel about every other visit. 'You're in luck, Stan,' he said. 'I was literally going out of the door. What can I do for you?'

'It's about my son, young Steve. I'm afraid he's very sick. I'm afraid he's mad.'

'Really? I shouldn't have thought that was on the cards. What's he been up to?'

I did some explaining.

'Oh, yes, well, m'm, slightly hopped up is about what it sounds like to me. Unless he's having fun, of course. No. Ever done anything like it before? You sure? Ah. And I assume he's not pissed. I'd better have a look at him, hadn't I? At home, are you?'

I did some more explaining.

'Fine, no problem, with any luck I should be along in about fifteen minutes. Don't worry, my old Stan. If he turns violent just hit him with an iron bar.'

The phone was a prewar one, or a replica. I went on sitting in front of it after I had hung the receiver back on its hook. The room had probably got itself called the study, or even the den, with a roll-top desk like in the films, a word-processor, a row of theatrical directories and an incredible number of photographs of Nowell – in what looked like Shakespeare, in something to do with Dracula, talking to Princess Margaret, talking to Sean Connery, as a tart, as a nun, on a TV quiz-show, on a TV chat-show. The ones I recognized had an out-of-date look. Bert was in two or three of them but there were none of her with Steve at any age.

Words like mania and schizophrenia and paranoia ran through my mind. I tried to remember what I had heard and read about madness and the treatment of it over the years but it was all a mess. I just had the same settled impression as ever that the fellows in the trade had a very poor idea of what they were up to. Now I came to think of it I did recall looking at a classy paperback where a psychiatrist had said that the only actual help they could give you when you went off your head was to keep you comfortable and safe and stop you doing things like killing yourself until you got better of your own accord if you were lucky or for the rest of your life if you were not. Cheers. But he had been making out a case, exaggerating, paying off scores or trying to write a bestseller. Of course he had. The business was bound to look pretty ropy from outside, all wild theories and rich people going to the shrink every week for twenty years and mental hospitals with no roofs, and never mind the successes, the new drugs and therapies, the thousands of patients quietly though perhaps slowly improving. That was certain to be going on. Things were just the same with medical science, you only heard about the scandals and the mistakes and not about the marvellous cures. Well no, it was not the same exactly but there were similarities. And that psychiatrist's book had been published quite a long time ago.

I decided to ring home while I was about it just to say what was going on, but there was no reply – Susan must have slipped out for something. Till then I had not realized how much I had wanted to hear the sound of her voice. Immediately after that Steve shouted something next door and there was a violent noise that was really two noises at once, a crash and a kind of giant pop, and then more shouting and some shrieking. I guessed what had happened and I was roughly right. When I dashed in I saw a lot of glass on the rug in front of the television set and a large hole in its insides surrounded by odds and ends of electronics, also the remains of a puff of smoke. A big grey stone ashtray was lying among the glass. Steve still looked bewildered but not in such a detached way, more as though he was worried at not understanding what the excitement was about. All the other three were yelling, Nowell at him, Bert more or less in general and the small girl at everybody, and that was the worst of the three. I shouted in her direction, not too loudly but I probably looked a bit alarming. Anyhow, she shut up and so did the other two, only a moment though, in Nowell's case at least.

'Get him out of here,' she ordered me in ringing tones.

I tried to ignore her and tell Steve he was all right. It was not very constructive, I dare say, but it was all I could think of.

'Get him out of here,' said Nowell, bravely sticking to her guns. 'He's raving mad, the boy's raving mad.'

I said, 'Never mind about that. Now just quieten down, will you? Come on, cool it. The doc's on his way.'

At this stage Bert tried to shove himself in. 'You heard, you . . . Out, ha, bastard.'

'Look, old chap,' I said, 'I don't want to find I've got to put a bit of weight on you, do I? And I'm very nearly doing it already, you know,' which was really not much at all but it soothed our Bert's feelings in no time.

Nowell had taken a few steps nearer the smashed set and quite likely it looked worse from there. She certainly seemed more furious on her way back.

'It's ruined.' She was starting to shout again. 'Completely ruined!'

'That's right,' I said, and did what I should have done straight away and pulled the plug out of the wall.

'I'm not putting up with that kind of behaviour in my house. If he's not out of here in one minute flat I'll call the police and ask them to remove him. I won't have it, do you hear me?'

All of a sudden I remembered exactly what it had been like being married to her, a large piece of it anyway – her saying something quite short and uncomplicated that gave me a couple of hundred things to say back, all of them urgent and necessary and with a bearing and all completely hopeless, all pointless. I remembered too how it had felt to start saying them regardless, rather dashing and plucky, like knocking back the drink that you know will put you over the top. The present set were at least as urgent and the rest of it as any, mostly to do with Steve and her being his mother, but with a few here and there about the police and how they might react to the idea of evicting a son from a parental home, plus how serious was she about that, etc. This time I refrained from starting, not actually out of concern for Steve but because I could see clearly what I would only have got as far as dimly suspecting in the old days, that she wanted me to start. And that was because she could be sure of dominating a scene with me whereas she could not with Steve as he was or might be at the moment. After all these years. But that never made any odds.

Some of this I worked out later. I answered her quite quickly. 'Cliff Wainwright'll be here any minute. I'll take Steve then.'

'You take him now. You can wait outside. It's not raining.' She was certainly putting on a wonderful demonstration of somebody having to stand up for what they thought was right.

'Sorry about the telly,' said Steve briskly. 'Only thing to do.' There was nothing brisk about his looks. He was breathing unsteadily and his mouth was trembling.

The cracked chime sounded from the front of the house. 'That one's yours, Bert,' I told him. 'Soon as you like.' With almost no interval he picked up a visual okay from Nowell and went off, followed by little girlie looking over her shoulder and pouting till she was through the door. I put my hand on Steve's arm but he shook it off and turned his face away. 'Nowell, do see what you can do,' I said. 'You were so marvellous with him before.'

I watched her hesitate. Meanwhile I wondered whether perhaps she was taking her current line because Steve had scared her, before deciding that all that scared her was the prospect of everybody not looking at her for five seconds. That was just as she plumped for being distracted rather than marvellous and began blinking a lot and making small sudden movements. By the time Cliff appeared, looking more ridiculously handsome and like a Harley Street doctor than ever, she was well into it, also starting to talk about thank God he was here and so forth. But it cut no ice with him – of course he was used to all that, and not only from her. In some way that was too smooth for me to catch he had her on one side in a flash and after a nod to me was strolling over towards Steve and giving him the kind of casual but wide-awake look-over I knew from visits to his consulting room. Steve backed off a pace or two.

'This doesn't concern you in any way, Dr Wainwright,' he said. 'You're not wanted here.'

'Oh, I don't know,' said Cliff, and glanced at the shattered television. 'Was that you?'

I fancied Steve looked uncertain. 'Yeah.'

'Really.'

After nearly a minute Steve said, 'Like I said, I had to,' firmly this time.

'Had to? Bad as that?'

'Yes, I . . . There's something been done to it.'

'What sort of thing?'

'Something been done to it. Fixed. You're going to say it's crazy, but I know it was recording us. It's happened before, see.'

'What, you mean as it might be on a video-tape.' Cliff went over and peered for a moment into the guts of the ruined set. When he came back he tried to walk Steve to a seat but Steve declined to go along. 'I doubt it, you know. In fact it's impossible. A VTR's quite a bulky affair, you couldn't possible fit one into a box that size.'

'Sophisticated development. Just a microchip.'

'Oh, one of *those*,' said Cliff, sounding very tired indeed. 'Too small to see. I know.' He looked up because Bert had come back into the room, unbelievably carrying what looked like a glass of water. I caught on when Cliff took the glass, produced a pill from nowhere in particular and held the two out towards Steve. 'Here.'

'Look, doc. I don't need any pill. Thanks.'

'Maybe not. Up to you. It's a tranquillizer and I gather you're a bit tensed up by this and that. No lasting effect. It won't – '

'What's your name, *doctor*? Your real name.' Steve sounded unfriendly all right but in other ways he seemed just adrift, half out of touch with what was going on. I was pretty sure he had not connected me with Cliff's arrival, which would have made it seem quite like the result of some conspiracy.

'Oh, get out of it, lad,' said Cliff. 'My name's never been anything but Wainwright. Now you just – '

'Not Isaac, is it? Or Moses?'

Cliff gave me a quick glance which I read as him wanting me to see what I could do. Anyway I said, 'Go on, Steve, knock it back and we can get off home.'

'You keep your nose out of this,' he said without looking at me.

'Its only effect will be to make you feel better,' said Cliff, going on rather awkwardly holding out the pill and the glass.

'Stuff it.'

So everything was in position for Nowell to move towards him slowly, hesitantly, with her arms hanging down at her sides in a way they never did, and stand in front of her son just looking at him, not saying anything, her eyebrows raised a tiny bit more than usual and her eyelids possibly lower and a very slight smile of hope and trust on her lips, which you could just see were apart at the middle but together at the corners. All things considered she was lucky I had somehow not remembered to bring my flame-thrower with me, I thought to myself, then forgot it when he suddenly took the pill off Cliff and washed it down with a gulp of water.

'Well done,' said Cliff to them both. 'We should start getting the benefit of that pretty soon. There is just one more thing, Steve, and then you can relax. Who's behind this business? You know, monkeying with the . . . The Jews, is it?'

'I'm not saying.'

'Right, fair enough, you go and rest for a bit.'

Nowell, with her arm in a protective position round Steve, took him off to the couch where she had been sitting with Chris Rabinowitz an unbelievably short time previously.

Cliff said to me, 'Well, you don't need me to tell you he's disturbed. But there are several possible reasons for it. In my experience the likeliest is a shot of something like LSD. He ever gone in for that?'

'Not as far as I know. Nor even smoked pot. I don't think he'd have felt he had to tell me he hadn't if he had. No, I just don't think this lot use it.'

'Well, whatever's the matter there's plenty can be done. But in the meantime you and Susan had better stand by for a large dose of boredom and inconvenience, I'm afraid.'

'I reckon we can face that.'

'Ah, you don't really know yet what you're . . . '

He stopped speaking at the approach of Bert, who said quite distinctly, 'Can I get you a drink? Gin? Scotch?'

Cliff asked if he could have a gin and tonic. I hesitated and then said I would like one too. When Bert had gone I said, 'That bugger was pissed five minutes ago.'

'Oh, he still is, he's just making a special effort for me. It's amazing what people will do for doctors, you know. Even today. Barring nobs, of course.'

'Have you met him before?'

'No, but you get to tell straight away. I don't wish him any harm but it would be fun visiting him when he's ill. That sort of hair-do looks great when they've been tossing and turning for a bit and it comes adrift and you get a bald noddle with flowing locks down to the shoulder on one side only. Old Nowell's a wonder, isn't she? Christ, it must be getting on for ten years since I saw her and really she hardly looks a day older. But then egotists always do wear well. Like queers. Interesting, that. Cheer up, Stan boy, you've done all right so far. He'll be okay for tonight, I'll pop in in the morning to see how he's getting on and I'll try and bring a trick-cyclist of some sort along to run the rule over him.'

'Thank you, Cliff, you're being very good about this.'

'Only fairly good at the moment. I had some time to fill in.'

No puzzle there. As long as I had known him Cliff had been a tremendous hammer of the ladies, quite a reckless one too – he had found himself within shouting distance of getting struck off a couple of times. That made him not all that much different from any other doctor I had ever heard of. It occurred to me like once or twice before that a day spent mucking about with ugly and decrepit and sick bodies might make you particularly keen on collecting a young and pretty one after work. I decided against taking the point up with Cliff there and then because Bert was bringing our drinks over. When he had done that he stayed with us, but apparently not so as to say anything, not at first. But then, when Cliff had told the one about the fellow who was afraid to go to bed with girls because his mother had told him there were teeth down there, and I was trying to think of one to tell back, he, Bert suddenly spoke.

'Do you mind if I ask you something?'

Drinking his drink as I was I felt there was not a lot I could say to that, so I said No.

'Er . . . do you keep a bottle of vodka in the bed at home?'

'No,' I said again, though it took a bit more out of me the second time round. 'Why?'

'I don't know really. No offence. I used to keep a half of Scotch in mine sometimes.'

'Sorry to be so dense, old chap, but I'm afraid I'll have to get you to explain the joke.'

'I think we might as well be getting along if you're ready, Stan,' said Cliff.

When Nowell realized we were off she slowly got to her feet and slowly helped Steve to his. He looked not so much tamed as washed out, emptied, or perhaps like a mental defective. She walked him to the door as though they were going into church, then turned and gazed at the two men who in their wisdom were about to take from her bosom the son she had not quite been trying her hardest to persuade to stay when she had the chance. After that she made a slight effort to prevent herself from hurling her arms round him but soon gave up the unequal struggle. It just so happened that her face was pointing towards Cliff and me at that stage, which meant I could easily spot the tears that were trickling out of her nearly closed eyes, and I thought he probably could too, but then he looked not greatly impressed.

Over her shoulder I saw Bert go back to being drunk – his neck seemed to turn to jelly. Of course, he had stopped making his special effort for Cliff.

*

'I've got hold of a fellow,' said Cliff when he rang the next morning. 'Name of Nash, Alfred Nash. You might just conceivably have come across it. Well, anyway, he was something of a celebrity in his younger days. Not so much been heard of him since then, in fact he hasn't got a regular job any more and was quite chuffed to be asked to do something. Everybody seems to think he's a very good man – I wouldn't know exactly. I've run into him I suppose half a dozen times in the way of business.'

'An analyst, is he?' I asked.

'Of course he's not a sodding analyst,' said Cliff, quite cross until he remembered it was no use expecting me to know how bad that was or would be. 'No, he's a doctor and a psychiatrist, not a quack in other words. I'd say he was a bit . . . Well, you'll be able to see for yourself very soon because I'm off to pick him up in a few minutes.'

'Are you sure you'll be all right, Stanley?' asked Susan shortly afterwards. She was wearing a round woollen hat that gave her a trustful, childish look. 'Say the word and I'll hang on till they get here.'

'No no, Sue, you go on in.' Saturday was of course press day at the *Chronicle* and they were all undoubtedly expected to turn up, even though according to her half the reviews and stuff had been sitting in the office since Tuesday.

'It would be quite ludicrous for me to try to tell you not to worry about this,' she said. 'But there is one part to do with it where you can feel absolutely safe and secure, and that's anything involving me in any way. I'll do whatever I can and whatever you want me to. I may not always know what that is and whenever you see I don't you're to tell me straight away without thinking. What I mean is, it doesn't matter if it seems a lot to ask, or even too trivial to ask – you tell me and I'll do it. Now have you got that, darling?'

'Yeah. Thank you, love,' I said, wishing I could find it natural to call her darling at times like the present, up-and-about times. 'And thank you for what you've done already. See you this evening.'

She squeezed my hand – hers was in a woollen glove to go with the hat. I noticed the faint little dark hairs at the corners of her mouth. The previous evening after we had seen Steve safely tucked up, she had spent the best part of two hours pulling me out of a state where I was quite certain I could face nothing more personal and outgoing than watching television and getting drunk – out of that and into allowing myself to be made a great fuss of and finally into bed. I had called her darling then all right.

The street door slammed and immediately there was total silence in the house. When looked in on an hour before, Steve had been asleep or, almost as good, pretending he was. He was going to appear as soon as he felt like it, which would be soon enough to suit me. I felt very reluctant to be in his company – oh, I felt plenty of other things too, and disapproved of that one, but there seemed to be nothing I could do about it and for the moment it was neither here nor there. All the same I had some time to fill in, not much, but some. I could go over the closely argued letter I proposed to send to the editor of the journal of the Classic Car Club on a subject – exhausts – rather outside my usual area. I might work it up into an article – after all, Susan was not the only writer in the family. But when I dug it out and looked at it I found that even to take in what I had been saying was beyond me. So I settled for drinking a weak Scotch and water instead.

I had just decided I would not have another till they arrived when they arrived and put the idea out of my head for the moment. Nash turned out to be about sixty or a couple of years more, tall, pale, moustached, with a better head of hair than mine and a posher accent than the Queen's. He was wearing what he probably called some well-worn tweeds and what was a rather dirty old polo-neck sweater in anyone's language. Cliff took all of two seconds introducing us, I told Nash it was good of him to come over, he told me he was sorry to hear of Steve's troubles, and we were off. My life was getting low on small-talk. For the time being at least there seemed to be no prospect of a drink – I felt shy of suggesting it and Cliff had given me nothing in the way of a lead. Well, it was still early.

I did some filling-in. Nash listened and wrote things down in a notebook, or rather on a new 25p memo-pad with lined leaves. He asked about Steve's early circumstances and history and wrote down some of what I said about that too. Then he wanted to know if there had been any recent emotional upsets.

I hesitated. 'He broke up with a girl – it could have been the day before yesterday or a bit longer ago. But . . . it's not his style to go off the deep end about things like that, and anyway it never struck me as being a particularly serious affair.'

'But it was an affair? Forgive me, but on the rare occasions when I peep into the world of the young I find it about as recognizable as, as medieval Patagonia.'

'He keeps things pretty quiet but from the look of his girl, if she wasn't sleeping with him she was going against a quite firmly established habit.'

Nash glanced up sharply from his pad, as if what I had said interested him in some way he had not expected. 'I see,' he said, paused and went briskly on. 'Ever been mad yourself? Or gone to a psychiatrist or seen a doctor about your nerves? M'm, didn't think you had really. What about your family, brothers and sisters, aunts and uncles, grandparents, any mad people there.'

'Well, there's my mother's sister. She never stops talking.'

'What about?'

'Oh, what she's been doing, where she's been, in insane detail. You can't – '

'No no, merely in foolish and fatiguing detail. Perfectly normal behaviour in a what, an elderly female.'

'But she – '

'Is that the worst you can do, Mr Duke? No uncles who didn't know what was going on, or cousins who sat in a chair all day without speaking or moving? No one they used to say was always rather a funny chap, always a bit . . . you know. Ordinary people are usually good judges of that, or they were until some lunatic went round telling them it was really the sane ones who were mad. Yes, funny, a bit odd, a bit peculiar, you never quite knew where you were with him, never really knew what he was thinking, you got on well enough together but you wouldn't have been surprised if one day out of the blue he'd said that he'd always hated you. Shocked and hurt, all that, but not *surprised*. Nobody like that at all. Oh well. What about your wife, I mean of course your ex-wife, the boy's mother, Mrs . . . Hutchinson. What about her?'

'Well . . . ' I looked over at Cliff, who made an encouraging face, dilating his eyes. 'Well, I think she is a bit mad.'

This wild understatement had Cliff blowing out his cheeks. 'Why do you say that?' asked Nash. 'In what way? Mad in what way?'

'She can't seem to . . . You mentioned something just now about somebody who can't make out what's going on. I don't think she can do that, not what's *really* going on. I mean she knows your name and what day it is, but she sees it all differently. Nothing's what it is, it's always something else. Her sense of other people's not good. They can be sweet to her, and they can be foul to her, and that's about as much scope as they've got. If they can't be fitted in as one or the other they don't exist, no not quite, they're like Mr Heath or David Bowie, no more than facts. Of course with her personality and everything she just goes on like that through her life. Even if everybody got together and dug their toes in and told her it wasn't like that it still wouldn't do any good. No use telling her to stow it or cheese it or come off it because she really believes it. That would just be everybody being foul to her at once. I'm sorry, Dr Nash, I've said enough.'

'Indeed you have. But the first part was good. M'm. Would you say, would you assent to the proposition that all women are mad?'

Cliff did about ten tremendous nods involving the whole top half of his body with lips pressed tight together and eyes goggling. I said, 'Yes. No, not all. There are exceptions, naturally.'

It was such a gift for Nash to say Naturally back that I had no idea how he avoided it, but he did, just pushed his mouth forward and went on staring at me in what seemed to be his way, not offensively, seeing either quite a lot or not much of anything, it was hard to tell.

'Yes,' he said after some of this. 'We won't pursue the point. I'll be having a word with Mrs Hutchinson. Well. I must say this is a most convenient arrangement, acquiring copious information before so much as clapping eyes on the patient. On other occasions I've found it to be markedly different, you know. Now, Mr Duke, I suggest you go and ask your son to come and have a talk with me. Yes, I'm a doctor if he wants to know, and yes, I'm a psychiatrist. Of course I am.'

I put this proposition to Steve in various not too different forms as he lay in bed in what I thought had to be a mightily uncomfortable position looking towards the ceiling, though his eyes were probably not reaching that far. The room smelt rather, but not as badly as it might have done if he had been really grown-up. I opened a window. I also noticed a couple of new shirts still in their plastic covers and some sets of underclothes out of the chest of drawers – Susan's doing. She had understood straight away that he had nothing to wear but what he stood up in.

After about ten minutes and nothing special about what I had just said or how I had said it Steve got quite actively out of bed. He was wearing grubby underpants and a sort of vest. With the same willing manner he put on his old shirt, his intensely crumpled trousers and a pair of multi-coloured rubber shoes fit for an Olympic track event. I still didn't believe it until I had gone downstairs and into the sitting room with him, introduced him to Nash and seen Nash stare at him in the way I had noticed, and hung on for a moment before Nash politely waved me out of the room.

Cliff had come out with me. On our way down to the kitchen he nodded to me again, not so dramatically as before but at least as expressively. I got us a gin and tonic each and we sat down at the table. The chairs there were supposed to be particularly good in some way, but to me they were straightforward all-wood jobs with slatted or splatted backs.

'We're doing well so far, obviously,' said Cliff. 'Him being so amenable. You should see some of them. But it's not just handy for everyone else, it's a good sign. I can't believe he's really ill. He'll have been sniffing glue or chewing this, that and the other – you see. Anyway, what did you think of him? Freddie Nash.'

I said, 'Well, he's hardly my cup of tea, is he? That voice. And isn't it rather a performance?'

'Oh *Stan*, of course it's a performance, among other things. Doctors are colossal actors, you know that well enough. Worse than actual actors, because they've got more power.'

'What were you going to say about him over the phone earlier? You said you thought he was a bit something but you didn't say what. A bit what?'

'Oh, a bit . . . Well, a bit rigid. Inflexible, kind of style. If that sounds as if he thinks he knows everything then I've got it wrong. Just, when he does know something then that's it. And I've heard one or two of the younger people say there are areas he hasn't kept up with. You'd expect that at his age. But they all agree he's very good.'

'Has he got a wife?'

'Yes, lots. Four at least. He may still be on the fourth, or he may not, or he may be on the fifth by now, I don't know, but it's one of those. Why?'

'Well, I naturally wondered, when he came out with that about all women being mad. Does he believe it himself, would you say?'

'Oh, I see. Christ, after all those wives he can't help but, poor old bugger. Only in a manner of speaking, you understand, in the sense you and I believe it – no, sorry, of course *you* don't think they're all mad, do you? Just most of them.'

Cliff laid great stress on it being me who made the exceptions, as an indicator or a reminder that he made none, especially not his own present wife, one of the few women I had met who could give Nowell a hard game. I remembered an evening not long after we first started to get chummy, which had not been all that long before Nowell had sheered off. Last thing that night, while she and I were getting ready for bed, she had launched into a long monologue which I had thought at first was an amazingly, almost frighteningly clear-headed analysis of her own character and conduct, put in the third person so as to be extra clinical and objective, and it had taken a sudden reference to Cliff being spineless to reveal to me that she had been on about Sandra Wainwright all the time. There was very little from my first marriage that had stayed so clear in my mind as those few minutes.

Cliff had gone quiet, probably thinking about Sandra. I said, 'Yes, I didn't actually imagine it was Dr Nash's professional opinion that all females over the age of eighteen were suffering from recognized mental disorders. But then it's not only an expression, not *just* a manner of speaking. There's more to it than simply them being a pest. A lot of them. That's what I was trying to say just now. The ones like that have got a distorted picture of reality. Not as distorted as thinking they're Napoleon, but distorted. More distorted than a bloke who thinks the earth is flat, because you can have a decent discussion of football with him. Their thing covers everything.'

'What? That's right. Absolutely.' He looked at his watch, finished his drink and stood up, so perhaps he had not been thinking about Sandra after all. 'You'll be okay now,' he said. 'He'll take a bit of time yet. When he's through he'll tell you the score so far.'

'What about his lunch?'

'He'll tell you that too. Don't worry yourself on that account. Fellows like that don't wait to be asked anything.'

'Does he drink?'

'No. You know, wine. He won't mind you having a couple, but he might mind you falling down in front of him. Use your judgement.'

Cliff added that he felt sure things would turn out all right and that I was to ring him later, I thanked him and he left. I would have kept him if I had had an excuse. Today I might have welcomed even Mrs Shillibeer's company, but she said her husband made her stay with him all the time at weekends.

There was some of her not-bad soup on the stove, enough for two at a pinch, and in the larder a board of cold meats, a jar of gherkins and some prepared celery and spring onions, and normally just my fancy – not today. I imagined I had anything up to an hour to get through before the next stage was reached. The only thing I could think of to use up some of the time was making myself another gin and tonic, and that used up less than a minute. On a normal Saturday at past twelve-thirty I'd have been somewhere else, at the golf club, at the squash club, at friends', always with people. So how was unaccompanied Duke to fill in? Read? Read what?

Suddenly Mandy came into my head, Mandy's flat with perhaps a Swede in it, perhaps still in it but perhaps by now Mandy as well or instead. The next part was slower. Susan had mentioned the surname. Blackburn. Here was a chance of establishing that there was nothing gruesome or otherwise interesting in Steve's recent past, and I suppose I also had some dim idea of getting a spot of help, though I could hardly have started to think what sort.

Finding the house phone-book certainly used up some time. When it turned out to be missing from its slot alongside the cook-books I searched the kitchen as usual before running it down in Susan's study. No helpful crossed lines or wrong numbers turned up, though. Quite soon a young girl's voice said Hallo with a great deal of alertness and amiability packed into two syllables, English too, very much not the reported Swede, and when I mentioned Mandy I was told she was speaking.

'It's Stanley Duke here, Mandy, Steve's father. I'm afraid he hasn't been too well. How was he when you saw him last?' That should fetch anything worth fetching, I thought, and very likely much else.

The silence at the other end was so complete that I wondered if I had been cut off. After a moment I said, 'Mandy?' and she said simultaneously, 'Who is that speaking, please?'

'Stanley Duke. I'm – '

'Sorry?'

'Stanley . . . Duke. Father of Stephen . . . Duke. *Steve*. You know.' Good God, I wanted to bawl, you were going round with him for four months at least, probably more like six, and it can only be three or four weeks since, etc.

'Who did you want to speak to?'

'To you, Mandy. You are Mandy Blackburn, aren't you? Well then, you remember Steve, surely.' More silence. 'Tall, rather thin, fair, with a slightly crinkled nose,' I struggled on, feeling a perfect idiot, but not knowing how else to go about it. 'Leans forward when he walks . . . Likes Mahler . . . Always cleaning his fingernails.'

'Oh . . . uh . . . ooh . . . ' The girl made long remembering noises. Then she said briskly, 'I'm all booked up today and tomorrow and next week.'

'I'm sure you are. I just wanted to tell you that Steve's been a bit poorly these last couple of days, and I was wondering – '

When the dialling tone sounded in my ear I was fooled a second time, and imagined for a moment that something technical had happened. For another moment or more I was filled with rage and amazement, almost with disbelief as it struck me that Mandy had not sounded at all fed up with her own thickness, let alone apologetic – not a bit of it, she was too busy being tickled pink by her powers of recall. To hear her, anybody would have thought she had managed to come up with the name of the pet rabbit belonging to the boy next door but two when she was little.

Thinking of childhood fitted in well. Then, places you had been to and people you had seen shot out of mind with incredible speed, not necessarily into oblivion but somewhere more remote than the ordinary past, like another life. Steve really had seemed to Mandy very far away. But she still needed a good hiding.

That set me remembering him myself. I turned out not to be much good at it. Innumerable things were in my memory as having happened, but not as full events with visual bits I could play back in my imagination. For instance, I was very clear that when Steve was fourteen I had gone to see him take part in his school's swimming sports, or rather in the finals of them, that he had been in the diving competition and that he had come second in his age-group, but I could not pick up a mental glimpse of the swimming-baths where this had taken place, let alone of Steve in them. When I tried to picture him in his pram, sitting on Nowell's lap, as the boy of eleven he had been when she left me, all I got was a version of present-day him scaled down as required. The few little flashes I had were no more than that, not so much as a face, just a smile, a look. I still had a few photographs, but Nowell had taken most of them with her when she went.

I had just not been able to do any of the *Daily Telegraph* crossword when I heard Nash calling my name from upstairs. His tone of voice made it clear that while there was no crisis on at the moment no delay was needed. My mother-in-law would have handled it in rather the same style.

'Gone for a bath,' Nash explained when I found him alone in the sitting room. 'Most opportune. Some interesting books here. They yours?'

I said, 'No.'

'What, none of them?'

'No. Is he mad?'

'I think so.'

'Oh my God.'

'But most likely not in any settled or irreducible way and very possibly not even for more than a short time. Mad – oh, without any doubt a depressing and frightening word,' said Nash, staring at me, 'but advisedly or not you were right to use it. There's no sphere in which it's more important to call things by their right names.'

'How sure are you, doctor? That he's mad?'

'In one sense I'm not sure at all. There's always the chance, on the face of it quite a fair chance these days with a person of that age, that some drug or other chemical influence has been at work, but you ruled that out earlier, and your son was quite clear on the point, and . . . '

'But my son's mad. He might say anything.'

'He's also frightened. If he had taken anything harmful I think he would say so when asked, and anyhow . . . There are remoter possibilities too. But in another sense I'm perfectly sure. I was sure within five minutes of setting eyes on him. Less.

'One of the troubles with psychiatrists in England is that because of the system here they often don't see a madman for months on end. In my youth I worked in the admissions department of a large mental hospital in Sydney and I saw madmen from morning till night. Fresh ones, if you follow me. And there's no teacher like simple quantity of experience. You yourself, now. Young Wainwright . . . ' Nash lingered over this characterization, though without making any point with it that I could see. 'Er . . . tells me you know a great deal about cars. When there's something wrong there, aren't you . . . sure . . . what it is before you establish the fact?'

'Yes, but – '

'Of course there are differences. But go back to the time you describe, when your son appeared late at night. Isn't it possible that you were sure then that he was mad,' – for once, just on that last word, Nash's voice softened – 'or nearly sure, or you might have been sure if you hadn't told yourself you knew nothing about the subject, or you would have been sure if it had been anyone less close to you? Mr Duke? Nearly sure or just about quite sure? Yes? Straight away?'

I hesitated, remembering what Cliff had said about Nash being rigid and the rest, but it made no difference. When Nash answered my first question just now, I knew at last that I had indeed been sure straight away, and that only huge powers of self-deception had kept the memory buried till that moment, through all his wild talk and behaviour – even over the phone to Cliff I had still not meant the word seriously, not altogether. Anyway, I nodded my head at Nash. 'Quite sure,' I said.

He nodded back with his eyebrows raised, then said with heavy emphasis, 'My judgement would be that he's suffering from acute schizophrenia.'

'Oh,' I said.

'Another frightening word. Two, in fact. The acuteness distinguishes not the gravity or intensity of the illness but a stage in its development, an early stage. Schizophrenia itself has of course nothing to do with split minds or multiple personalities or colourful stuff of that sort, which comes in well enough for the films obviously, and in life I can see there must be great advantages in pretending there's somebody else in your head who does all the shoplifting and child-molesting that you wouldn't dream of doing yourself. M'm. Nowadays I'm told chic persons use the adjective schizophrenic to mean something like inconsistent. But then. As to what it is, what schizophrenia is, discussion can be deferred. More important at the moment, it responds to treatment, and I'd like him in hospital for that.'

The last bit came quite fast and I had not considered the idea at all. 'Is that necessary?' I asked at about the third try.

'Desirable. Highly desirable.' Nash looked down at his hands, which were big and rather battered, not upper-class at all at first sight. 'It's only fair to let you know why and how. Briefly, then – your boy hasn't offered any violence to persons so far, but he's plainly shall we say unpredictable and *needs* treatment that'll work fairly quickly. Which in practice means full doses of tranquillizing drugs,' he said with his voice going slightly sing-song, 'which will probably have side-effects which may be alarming and even a little bit risky if not professionally supervised and which may lead the patient to shirk taking his pills, which again can be dangerous. For instance he might – '

Here I interrupted him. I had been trying to follow what he said while fighting off memories of visiting my mother in hospital three years previously. The place itself had not been too bad and she had thought she was coming out in a few weeks – so had everybody else until the last couple of days. What had stuck in my mind were things like the sight and sound of those other sick people everywhere and my mother's feelings of being cut off and not in any control of the situation, and she had been completely clear about what was going on. Steve had been confused and scared in his mother's sitting room, and where he looked like being sent would be worse in some serious ways than where my mother had been, I thought, and I said to Nash,

'Can't he just stay here and go to the hospital as an out-patient? My wife and I could give him his pills and see he took them.'

'Do you really think so? Can't you hear him telling you he's not a child, stop treating him like an idiot, don't stand over him like that, don't you trust him? What you actually have to do to see he takes his pills, to monitor compliance as I'm afraid it's called, is a rather undignified and intrusive business, you know. Much better left to nurses. He'd agree.'

'Surely it can't do him any good to be surrounded by . . . '

'All those loonies. Yes. I can only say it won't do him any harm. No doubt that sounds rather a breezy remark. The fact is that mental illness isn't communicable.'

'But he'll be frightened.'

'He'll be under medication. Tranquillized. As I said. There's really no need to worry about that.'

'What happens then, doctor? Does he get some sort of therapy, or does he just go on being tranquillized? I'm only asking.'

'He gets chemotherapy, which is drugs. As for what you probably mean, psychotherapy, which is corrective training – not recommended in this case. But let me explain about the drugs. They're quite distinct from palliative tranquillizers like Valium and Librium that you may have come across and which are almost useless in treating schizophrenia. Over the last thirty years these, these others have helped a great many patients to recover quickly and well. I realize you may have gained the impression from me or in some other way that all that can be done is keep the patient quiet until he either recovers or doesn't. No, much more than that.' Perhaps he misread or read correctly something in my expression, because he went on to say, 'Or possibly you have ideas of your own on the point.'

'How on earth would I have ideas of my own on that kind of point? All I'm doing is trying to take this in. It's rather a lot in one go and I'll probably get some bits wrong the first time round. If that, doing that, sounds like me having ideas of my own it's not meant to,' I said. Christ, I also said, but not out loud.

Nash smiled for the first time, showing a couple of rows of old-ivory teeth and looking like an unreliable dog. 'I really beg your pardon, Mr Duke, but these days everybody seems to think he knows something about the subject, about psychiatry that is, usually after reading a newspaper article to the effect that all the work so far done has been mistaken. A little crushing, you may think. I mean *all* the work? Imagine an astronomer hearing the same. I agree not a close parallel. A jurist. To revert to your son. There's at least one other good reason why I want him in hospital – he needs various medical and neurological tests which would be much better done with him there.'

'Can't he have them done as an out-patient?'

'Yes. Theoretically. But finding the right building, and the right part of the right building, and waiting for the clerk to come back if she isn't there when you arrive, and don't be too upset if it turns out the machine isn't working that day, and fix up another appointment and turn up on time for that, but don't be too sure, don't be too sanguine about its working then either, and don't walk out in a huff if they're rude, and don't lose the form I gave you because they won't do it without, and remember always to leave yourself plenty of . . . well . . . '

'I could take him myself.'

'Mr Duke, I must stress to you that it would be very much simpler and more straightforward, and quicker which is important, if these tests were done in the normal way, with everything organized by the hospital.'

'Yes, I can see,' I said. What I said to myself this time was what it was I could see, or a good half of it – that the ones it would be simpler for in the first place were the doctors, the hospital staff, Nash himself, all of them, the other lot as against Steve's and my lot.

Nash too seemed to have seen something. He said, quietly for him, 'People in your position usually find it hard to face the prospect of their child disappearing for an indefinite period into the shadowy world of mental hospitals, which they don't understand in the way they feel they understand places you go to with something wrong with your inside and have it cut out. They find the notion of madness easier to accept than that of mental illness, which can't be an illness really, can it? Doctors and nurses for that? Something that just comes over you? Then a lot of them feel they'd be abdicating the proper . . . Ah, here we are.'

Steve had put on one of the shirts Susan had got for him, in fact part of the cardboard stiffening it had been packaged with was showing under the collar. I noticed his trousers were very shiny as well as shapeless. His whole appearance and manner seemed ordinary, not worth bothering about, so completely free of strain that just for a moment I thought I was going to tell Nash we were not going to need him after all. Then I caught Steve's eye and he recognized me instantly, which does sound like what he should have done in a way, and it was not that he mistook me for someone else he knew or thought he knew, at least that never occurred to me then. He looked at me in a contented, relieved, friendly way that held not an atom of what gets built up and taken for granted between a parent and a child who get on all right together, different from anything else. After that he gave Nash a polite glance and dropped suddenly on to the velvet settee, soon wriggling into one of his awkward positions.

'Good bath?' Nash asked loudly, rather like somebody talking to a foreigner in a sketch. 'Splendid. M'm, now just, if you would . . . ' He made what were probably encouraging movements with his hand. 'Er . . . just . . . '

Without any more prompting Steve said, 'I told you I couldn't blame her.'

'Yes, you did, but let's go into it again. Why not? Why couldn't you blame her?'

'Well, she couldn't have done any different.'

'Why not? Why couldn't she have done any different?'

'She couldn't for my sake. She had to freeze me out.'

Nash shook his head and drew in his breath. 'I don't see that,' he said firmly.

'She didn't want to know me,' said Steve, with a lot of patience and a look in my direction. 'Did she?'

He really seemed to be appealing to me. 'Not when I spoke to her,' I said.

'You what? You . . . spoke to Fawzia?' That was what the name sounded like.

'I thought you meant Mandy,' I said, blushing like a schoolkid.

'Mandy? That slag?' He sounded quite good-natured, but was a bit bothered or suspicious when he said, 'What was she on about then?'

'I rang her, just to see if she could – '

Holding his hands up now, shushing me, Nash said, 'This freezing you out as you call it, what was the point of all that, it makes no sense to me at all.'

'Well, you know, she was protecting me, wasn't she?'

'I'm terribly sorry, but do you mean she was protecting you by freezing you out? I should have thought . . . '

Steve nodded in a tolerant way, prepared to admit that parts of his story did need some explanation. 'This girl Fawzia, right? She and I had a big thing going, not out in the open, but I knew, just from the little things she said, wouldn't mean a thing to anybody else, and even just the way she looked at me sometimes, it was all there, I just knew. Then she became involved in certain undercover activities, which made her extremely unpopular in certain quarters.'

'When was this?'

'Year ago.'

This seemed to disappoint Nash. He smoothed his moustache and waited.

'So then they get after me, because I know too much. So she starts ignoring me, see, to try and throw them off and to warn me. I know too much not only about her but their systems. Also their organization, which is extremely high-powered, extremely ruthless, and extremely . . . undercover.' Then, coming to the climax of a horrendously embarrassing and pathetic take-off of a hundred would-be brilliant films, he said, 'The gentlemen involved . . . call themselves . . . the chosen.'

Poor old Steve of course belonged to one of the generations which had never been taught anything about anything, and he obviously thought his reference to the chosen was about as advanced and wrapped-up as words could get, well out of sight of a poor bugger as cut off as his dad, let alone any associated other-worlders like Nash. The next moment I remembered him once or twice just about a year before bringing along to the house somebody who could have been a fellow-student of his during his brief stint at the polytechnic, a remarkably unaccommodating female with a short upper lip and a sallow skin and a name very like Fawzia.

With that established, a lot of things became as clear as they were probably ever going to. Jews, or people who might have been Jews or counted as Jews or Israelis, were after him because he had once known – not, I was sure, ever very well – a girl who was quite likely one kind of Arab or another and on that ground could, at the sacrifice of all the common sense and humour in the world, have had them after her too, or something of the sort.

The realization shoved me into a state of combined gloom and boredom. Had Steve really put himself through the whole business of going mad just so as to be able to believe that? At the same time its moderation was a relief – it was only untrue, silly, ridiculously improbable, not mad in itself. There undoubtedly were such things as Arab intelligence agents, even if a female one was a pretty dodgy concept, and presumably Israeli counter-intelligence went around trying to do them a bit of no good. It was another relief that however confused he might actually be he seemed not to feel confused for the time being, nor in the least frightened.

He had been looking at me with cheerful mild contempt, an expression I had never seen on his face before. I tried to remember where he had finished speaking. 'You don't believe any of that, do you?' he asked.

'You've been going a bit fast for me,' I said.

He nodded as before. 'Okay,' he said, and got energetically to his feet. 'We can take a look outside now. Yeah, come on.'

Nash and I followed him to the window, which gave a good view of the street. Hunched up in the slight drizzle a man I immediately recognized was walking along it at that very moment, a man who worked at one of the banks in the High Street and whom I had seen a few times in the Pheasant and who looked like half the other men you would expect to see in places like that. Otherwise there was nothing moving in sight at all.

'There you are,' said Steve.

After a moment I said, 'How do you mean?' because he seemed to think I knew. I wished Nash would join in.

'Joshua,' said Steve.

'What?'

'Oh come on – *Joshua*.' For the first time he showed some impatience. 'He's only just . . . You saw him with your own eyes.'

'I saw a man. What . . . which Joshua are you talking about?'

'More than one, is there? That one's the one that took out Jericho with ultra-sound and saw off the Canaanites.'

He mispronounced this name and I took a second to disentangle it. 'How do you know about Joshua?' I asked. It was nowhere near the most urgent question I had for him, but even now I could not imagine anything that would drive him to the Old Testament.

'There are methods of obtaining the relevant information,' he said, dropping back into his master-spy act for a moment, but soon coming up lively and self-confident. 'Anyway, you saw him, didn't you, what, twenty yards away? Less than a minute ago?'

'You're telling me that that was Joshua out of the Bible out there in the street just now, are you?'

Evidently I was almost there but not quite. 'Well, in a kind of way. You know, that was him born again. They're all that in the key section.'

I had no excuse now for complaining that Steve's new view of the world was short of imagination or scope. When I looked at Nash, hoping for a sign that that sort of thing was to be expected, would soon pass, perhaps even had a nice touch of technical interest to it, there was nothing but a long, serious stare. Before I could speak to him Steve cut in.

'You still don't believe me, do you?'

'I don't see what made you think that was what he was. I don't see how you could tell. I mean you must admit he looked like just an ordinary bloke.'

'What do you expect him to look like, a geezer in white with a long white beard? It's nothing to do with what he looks like, it's who he is.'

'Yeah, but what is it about him that tips you the wink who he is? You can't have – '

'Look, I just know, got it? I know.'

'But . . . ' I had seen at the start it was no use arguing but I only stopped now because I could think of nothing to say.

'I'm sorry, it's not the type of thing you can explain.'

He turned to Nash to appeal for support on the point that there were types of things like that. I said to Nash, 'I think what you suggested, I think we'd better do that.' Nash nodded silently. He still looked grim.

'No, I'm not going there,' said Steve as soon as he understood the proposal. He showed no anger or fear but he would not have it. 'I wouldn't be safe in a place like that,' he kept saying. Nash explained that if necessary he could have him put inside willy-nilly. Steve told him he was bluffing, and after a bit I stopped being clear what I thought. I said a lot of things I immediately forgot. A couple of times I felt so hungry I thought I was going to die, then the next moment not at all. Time passed as though it was never going to do anything else. I was sinking into a drowse of apathy and despair when something reminded me of something and I plunged downstairs to the phone. I forgot what I said there too, just like a drunk person, but no matter. 'Your mother wants to speak to you,' I said to Steve when I got back.

He went straight away. I explained to Nash, who merely grunted. He obviously thought it was no time for a chat, turning over his notes with a great rustle of pages and hissing through his teeth, and I tried to hold off but soon I was saying firmly, 'He's very sick, isn't he?'

'Well, we're not quite clear, are we, on exactly when, er matters took their present course,' he said a bit at a time, 'but his illness does seem to have progressed as fast as any I've known, of its type. From your account, and Wainwright's, a remarkable rate of development. And to be so specific, comparatively specific, at this early stage, about his delusion that is – most unusual, if not . . .' His voice died away, and it did seem just briefly that for once in his life he was not sure, or had let it be seen he was not. Then he charged on, 'But very sick in any sense of unusual resistance to being made better, no. At least there's no sign of that at the moment. We're only at the beginning, you know.'

'What causes it, doctor, this sort of illness?'

Nash shook his head, either not knowing or knowing but not saying. 'What . . . triggers it off is often some sort of shock to the emotions. Which means I think that it's always that but sometimes the psychiatrist can't find it or is uncertain about it. In this case the Fawzia episode looks rather a long time ago and the Mandy episode looks rather slight, but one never knows. It isn't all-important to find the shock.'

'He seems less frightened than he was.'

'These things come and go. Large changes of mood from no visible cause are characteristic.'

I thought of that when Steve reappeared, so soon I thought at first my luck had run out and Nowell had failed or not tried to do what she had promised. But I soon saw that was wrong. He had stopped being animated and he looked different, physically exhausted, like somebody who had been up all night. I was sure Nash noticed it too.

'All right, I'll go there.' Steve said that without much expression, but he sounded quite convincingly fed up when he went on to say, 'So I changed my mind. Does it matter why?' The question was for me personally, though I had not been conscious of even asking myself anything on those lines. 'You're getting rid of me, aren't you? That's what you want. Father.'

Those last few words of Steve's turned out to be very easy to remember. They stayed around while I watched him silently – except for eating noises – get through a couple of bowls of soup and some ham and some bread in the kitchen, and incidentally while Nash sat on in the sitting room and wrote a lot of stuff for the hospital and ate Brie and cream crackers and drank a glass of red wine, just what he had ordered actually, though without specifying the rather pricey Burgundy that, feeling a bit of a coward, I had opened for him. There was a distraction when a young man dressed like a dustman, or so I thought, came to the front door and turned out to be the municipal psychiatric social worker summoned earlier by Nash to take Steve off. He, the social worker, wasted no time, but made two phone calls, handed me a piece of card that had an address and phone number written on it with amazing legibility, made it clear in the same movement that I would not be needed on the expedition and started a move to the door.

'Cheers, dad,' said Steve, not at all hostile now and so a lot more effectively reproachful than he could ever have been on purpose.

'Cheers, son.' Hugs were out, so I said a few things about him being well looked after and me coming to see him soon, and more deep stuff like that.

When the two had gone, Nash said, 'He should indeed be well looked after at St Kevin's,' surprising me slightly – I had put him down as a man who saved his attention for the job. 'There really is a saint called that, you know. Irishman, of course. How he got his name on a hospital near Blackheath I can't imagine. Anyway, it's a cheerful sort of place, not one of your Victorian dungeons. Amusing lot, the Victorians, but when it came to institutional interiors they just gave up. I know somebody there called Dr Abercrombie who's a very good man. I couldn't get hold of him just now, but, er, he's a very good man.'

After that Nash made a whole operation of taking a last look at his notes and bundling them up and into his pocket. He seemed to me to be trying and failing to come up with a hopeful but true remark that also meant something.

'Bit of luck, getting hold of that chap this time of the week,' I said.

Nash thought not, on the whole. 'Saturday afternoon's time and a half. Monday morning's when you won't find them. All day Monday, in fact.'

'Oh yeah,' I said. I could not have accounted for it, but this information depressed me. 'Could you have put him in, put my son in if he'd gone on refusing to budge?'

'Oh yes. Yes. But it's not easy with a patient who isn't grossly mad, mad on inspection so to speak, there he goes waving a great knife, that kind of behaviour. Not at all easy. All these vile rights of the individual, you know – it's becoming more and more difficult to get anything done. M'm.'

He gave me his card, engraved to the nines needless to say, with an address in Eaton Square as well as one in New Harley Street. 'Mr Duke,' he went on, staring at me, 'I do want to impress upon you that I'm most inordinately interested in my subject. So much so that even after all these years I still catch myself wondering how supposedly intelligent people can absorb themselves in these various secondary pursuits. Mathematics. Literature, even. This means in practice that I'm prepared, I'm very willing to talk about your son's case with you at any remotely reasonable time by telephone, in person by arrangement. Such a discussion couldn't fail to touch on points of significance, do you see. Just try to bear that in mind, would you?'

As soon as I was alone I started thinking about what Steve had said when he agreed to go into hospital, or rather just remembering, because I failed to get any actual thinking done on the subject. I stood about in the sitting room, then in the kitchen, where I tried to think about food instead and got nowhere there either. Obviously it was time I settled down to what I always did when I wanted to relax, to unwind, to take my mind off things, to potter through a couple of hours without having to think. Only I was short of anything like that, it seemed, except small stuff like a beer and a read of the paper. How had I managed before and after Nowell left me? It had been different then, I was not very clear how – something to do with being away a lot, changing jobs, having the builders in, and other rubbish I had forgotten after eight years.

On past form on a Saturday Susan would not be back for a fair while, but sometimes she was early, and when she was going to be she usually rang to say, but not always. I was feeling powerfully like ringing her, but was uneasy about making her feel she ought to be home when she could still not leave work. All the same I had moved to within reach of the phone when it rang and made me jump.

'Stanley? Is that you, Stanley?'

It was like something out of a dream, not what that usually means, something marvellous, too good to be true, dreamy in fact, but something very hard to take, not at all vague, most precise, hard to take in too because the thing is wrong in a special way, like black and white at the same time. Anyway, for a moment I really thought Susan was talking to me with Nowell's voice. Then I realized that of course it must all just be Nowell.

'Yes, Nowell, as a matter of fact I was – '

'It's Nowell here, darling. Did it work?'

'What? Oh yes. Like a charm. Thanks very – '

'You might have taken the trouble to let me know.'

'I was going to, honestly, but I haven't had a chance – he's only this absolute second gone out of the door. We couldn't get hold of the chap.' Already without the least sense of strain I had slipped back into Nowell's world, a place where, among other features, the truth or untruth of a statement rated rather low when you came to decide whether to state it or not. Not that you actually bothered to go into that side of it.

'What? What chap?'

'Oh, the . . . the chap at the hospital,' I answered more or less at random. 'Still, it's all done now, thank God. I don't know what line you took but you were pretty good, obviously.'

'Well . . . ' she said, and in a way I wished I could have been there to see her saying it, 'you know. Look, Stanley, tell me, where have they taken him, how is he, what are they going to do to him? It's all happened so quickly.'

'I don't know any more about it than I did when I spoke to you an hour ago, except they've taken him to – '

'Darling, we must have a proper discussion, it's too absurd. After all, we are both responsible for the poor little thing.'

'Yes of course, but for the moment there's really not a lot to discuss. He's gone into hospital – that's done, as I say. If you want to talk about his, well, his illness then Dr Nash is the fellow for that. He'll be getting in touch with you anyway. He's the one with all the – '

'That's not what I mean. We ought to *discuss* it. You and I. Surely you can see it's an extremely serious matter, and it's a thing we know more about than anybody else, I'm not talking about doctors, and if you want my opinion it's our *duty*, and surely it's a reasonable thing for me to ask in my position.'

'Oh absolutely, but wouldn't it still be sensible to wait till you have seen Nash and heard what he thinks are sort of the most important points?'

In Nowell's book a discussion was not a matter of views being put forward and argued over, let alone a method of working out what it was best to do about some problem. At the same time it was a cut above your straight chinwag, anyway morally. A discussion had such a serious subject that you could go on as long as you liked about any bit of it you fancied, because you were only trying to get at the truth, not showing off or holding the floor or any of those. The chosen bit could be as far-fetched as you liked too, because these days nobody could be sure what might or might not throw light on this or that. The seriousness also made it all right to be things you were usually supposed not to be in conversation, starting with rude and embarrassing.

For these and other reasons I felt I could really do without a discussion with Nowell about Steve. What I had just said was nothing more than an attempt to hold her off – I had felt like going quite a way further but, as she had reminded me with her last few words, she had been the one who had talked Steve round when my lot could not, twice in twenty-four hours too, and there was plenty of time to go yet.

Until she got to that last phrase about her position, her voice and the looks and movements I could so easily imagine going with it had been chummy, almost cosy, with a definite hint of only-yesterday going on – not her usual style with me. She went back to it when she said, 'After all, this isn't some sort of scientific experiment, darling. It's to do with our son. My son. I don't mind admitting I'm awfully ignorant about all sorts of things, but I do know a lot about him.'

'You certainly do,' I said admiringly, also thoughtfully. 'You can read him like a book. Always could. What was that place in Brittany you took him to a couple ot times?'

'What? When was this?'

Her tone had completely changed in that second, but I was too slow to take it in. 'Oh, years ago, he can't have been more than eight or – '

'What did he say to you?'

'Well, he'd obviously loved having you to himself. I was tied up here with all the – '

'Perhaps you hadn't noticed, Stanley, but the poor boy was in the most frightful state. Confused . . . terrified . . . '

'Eh?' For the moment I was baffled. 'Look, Nowell, I don't mean just now, I'm talking about then, when you and he came back to Maida Vale and I asked him if he'd had a nice holiday and he was full of the way you'd – '

'For Christ's sake, any *reasonable* man would have been *pleased* to be helped out of a problem he couldn't cope with himself. I must say I had thought I was doing you a good turn.'

'You were, and I'm very grateful – I didn't – '

'I can see you may be upset but you've no need to take it out on me. There's no point in trying to deal with you in your present mood. Thank you for your information. Good afternoon to you.'

Most of the things old Nowell said and did were funny really. The difficulty had always been in laughing at them, especially when they were coming your way. The dignified-restraint component in her final offering illustrated the point well. At this distance I was unsure how I had taken that type of thing when we were first married – as rather dignified and restrained, probably, though also hasty, perhaps, or confused. I had gone straight from something like that to what I felt now, a desire to chop her off at the ankles, without so much as an embarrassed smirk in the middle.

At the moment any sort of smirk could only have been at my own expense, with first place going to my brilliant attempt to lead her away from the topic of the dreaded discussion. I had forgotten until too late that she was sensitive about Steve's younger days, when she had boarded him out with friends more than she should have, got in unsuitable girls to look after him, and so on. I had only been fool enough to bring these things up once, just before she left me or perhaps just after, but I always might again, she never knew. And then of course when I was baffled near the end of our conversation I knew I had started speaking quicker than before, and a bit louder, and with a certain amount of force or emphasis, and from her point of view I might easily have gone on to set about being foul to her any second, and she could hardly have been expected to take a chance on that. For Nowell, if one patch was dodgy the whole area was dodgy, even if the other fellow seemed to be sticking to the far end of the field. This little way of hers often tended to limit conversation to the here and now.

But when she had gone there I was on my own again. I turned on the radio, a Danish job called a StereoBoy, something I rather wished I had noticed before I bought it, and went not very searchingly over the bands. Most of the stations were evidently playing the same yobbos' war-chant, but even the others were somehow impossible, too far on with what they were doing to be caught up with. I had just started on a second run-through when I heard Susan's key in the door.

I went round the corner into the hall and there she was, coming down the passage with her briefcase and stubby umbrella and shaking out her woollen hat. Her eyes looked extra large.

'Oh, I am glad to see you, love,' I said. 'I don't think I've ever been so glad to see anybody.'

We stood with our arms round each other. 'There's nothing awful, is there?' she asked.

'No. Well. They've taken him off to hospital. And he's mad, the doc says.'

'Tell me all about it.'

We went into the kitchen, where a woman with a North-country accent was talking seriously about senile dementia. Susan turned her off, or rather, not knowing how to do that, shifted off the frequency, which was good enough for me just then.

I said, 'You're back early, then. Do you mind if I have a drink?'

'Of course not. You sit down. I tried to ring, but the switchboard had blown up or something. Whisky and water?'

'Yeah, lovely.'

When I came to the bit about Nowell and her getting Steve to agree to be taken off, I kept a careful eye on Susan. I took no decision to – I just found I had started t6. In nearly four years, longer if you went back to our first meeting, I had never known her say or do anything that showed how she felt about Nowell. I realized this was a pretty big statement to make on any woman's feelings about any other woman, not just her husband's ex-wife, if by anything you meant *anything*. She had obviously found some third way of getting across to me her total hatred, contempt and horror. Her words to me on the subject that Friday night, reminding me that Steve had seemed upset once or twice after visiting his mother, had come over with about the punch of a traffic report. This time round it was the same story – nothing that could show on the tapes, audio or visual, and great waves of umbrage. Fair enough. Still, I thought there was no point in piling it on by going into Nowell's phone-call to me, which had really not added anything, so I ended up with Steve going off in that docile way.

When she could see there was no more to come, Susan said, 'Good. What a relief,' and got up and started to put the kettle on. She had not once interrupted me or even shifted about much.

'Yes, it is,' I said. 'It seems a bit sudden, though, that's all. Doesn't it?'

'Shoving him in on sight, so to speak. Very sudden. But by what standards? If he'd had a ruptured appendix or whatever it is, not sudden in the least.'

'It can't be as urgent as a physical thing.'

'Maybe not – I wouldn't know. I'm just saying, what you mind isn't Steve going into hospital suddenly, without warning – you mind Nash suddenly deciding he should go in. The way you see it, he should have thought about it longer, a serious step like that, gone away and come back again. That's because you don't know any more than I do about psychological things, mental things. They seem like just a branch of ordinary things, don't they? Literature's rather the same, to a lot of people. Anyway, I see no reason why Nash should be less right today than he would be on Monday. I can't remember whether I've ever told you, but I had a barmy cousin once, so I've been through part of this before. Would you like some tea?'

'No thanks,' I said. 'No, yes, I will. Thanks.'

'What have you had to eat?'

'Not a lot.'

Susan washed out the teapot at the sink and carefully dried the inside, a thing of hers. Then she said, 'Those points Nash made about the drugs and the tests and so on, it's much easier to do them in hospital, you agreed with all that, I thought.'

'Yeah. Yes. Didn't you?'

'Oh yes. And that Joshua business put the lid on it, you said yourself. So I don't quite see . . . ' Standing behind me, she put her hand gently on my shoulder and went on in a gentle voice, 'What's really bothering you, darling?'

I put my hand over hers. 'Well, it was what he said when he told Nash and me he was prepared to go in – I ought to be pleased because I was getting rid of him and that was the only thing I cared about, according to him.'

'Is that all? I don't suppose he meant it very seriously, do you? And even if he – '

'It's not that so much, I'd just hate to think he was right and I wasn't actually interested in what'd be best for him, only in getting him off my back.'

'Without you realizing it. Give it a rest, Stanley, you're much too self-aware for any of that kind of crap. Also much too bright not to be able to see that what's best for somebody can quite easily be what's best and most convenient for somebody else as well, you for instance. But too bloody sentimental and silly to take it in, to believe yourself. And what's wrong with getting him off your back in the state he's in at the moment? And there's my back to be considered too, you know.' There had been no gentleness in her voice for a bit, but I could hear some of it when she said, 'And too silly to ring me up.'

She leant down and kissed me. With me sitting at the table as I was we were only able to hug each other in a rather badly-organized way, but it seemed not to matter much. There was plenty I wanted to say to her, all good, all nice things, only I could not sort them out or get them to sound right in my head, so I made pleased, friendly noises and stroked her neck. In a minute she straightened up and went to make the tea.

Later I rang the hospital number the fellow had given me, and after what I thought was an uncommonly short space of time an Asian voice said Yes, Mr Duke had been admitted that afternoon. But I could find out nothing else whatever, not even whether somebody might tell Mr Duke that his father had called.

2 Progress

When I rang the hospital the next day the response was much as before. Another Asian voice, or quite likely the same one, said Mr Duke was comfortable but, it turned out, was not to be visited – not must on no account be or taking everything into account had better not be, just was not to be. After a repeat on the Monday morning I decided unenthusiastically to try and get hold of one of the doctors, but to put it off until after eleven, when there would be no excuse for such people not being on duty.

People like advertising managers of daily newspapers needed to get off the mark a bit earlier. I arrived in my office to find my deputy and our joint secretary already in position, which was right. Everything they told and showed me was very dull except the news, passed on a strip of flimsy that Thurifer Chemicals were cancelling their half-page.

'That leaves them five light,' said my deputy, a capable but non-drinking Welshman called Morgan Wyndham who liked being what he called realistic. 'Five out of eight.'

'I know,' I said. 'He can't do that.'

'He won't be there yet,' Morgan told me when I started to dial the agency.

I ignored him. After the last digit there was a click or two and then a colossal silence, as though I had been put through to the house of the dead. Another try ended the same way.

Morgan looked over from his own phone. 'Was he there?'

'Probably not, but I didn't get that far.' Next time I did a switch in the hope of flushing out the bugs, and got the ringing tone in fine style.

'Penangan High Commission, good morning,' said a girl's voice.

'Is the Commercial Attaché there, please?' I knew that sounded none too clever, but the thing was that like all his pals, apparently, the chap had three names, just one syllable each and, to look at on his official card, perfectly pronounceable as small chunks of near-English. But when I had tried them over the phone a few weeks before, this girl or her colleague, though as English as your hat, had not known what I meant, or so she had said and gone on saying. Eventually she had produced three amazing noises that according to her I must have meant, and I must have, because the right chap at once came on the line. And thereupon became the Commercial bleeding Attaché for ever in my book.

'Just a moment, sir,' the operator was saying politely. I thought she sounded marvellous. 'Er . . . did you want to speak to Mr One Three Five or Mr Two Four Six?'

Of course that was not what she said, but it was no further from it than half the other ways I could have put it. Her question put me in a bit of a quandary. 'What's the difference?' I asked eventually.

'Well . . . Mr One's the old Attaché, and Mr Two came last week.'

'Oh, yeah. Right, give me Mr One, if you would.' This sounded like, or rather probably was, the right chap, and also incidentally a chap destined to go jetting back to Penang at any moment, but there was not a lot I could do with that thought except bear it in mind.

I gave my name and that of the paper, and after a moment a high-pitched voice that made you think of sweet and sour pork said, 'Hallo, yes?'

'It's Stanley Duke, Mr Attaché,' I said for good measure. 'You remember we discussed a possible special report in my paper. I wonder if you'd had a chance to think about it.'

'Ah – Mr Joke. Oh *yes*.' He sounded pretty well overcome with joy. 'Now everything is being arranged. I'm communicating with my government and they're being very interested. Extremely interested. Particularly the Minister of Trade will be coming to Europe next month and will be spending three days in London. He's being very intelligent and very well educated and has visited Australia. Now I think with your good assistance he'll be understanding the commercial advantages of my proposal.'

Mr One tended to speak of his fellow-countrymen as worthy but limited, needing a Western nudge of some sort to fall in with his proposals, of which the latest known to me was the buying of space in the paper to tell its readers, or a couple of dozen of them, about his country's achievements. Actually that particular proposal had come from me in the first place, but I found I could face having the credit hogged.

'You and I,' he tinkled on, 'will be making some arrangements beforehand. We mustn't trouble the Minister with details. Please come to lunch here. I think you like our food.'

'Oh, delicious.' I liked their ginseng stuff too, though delicious was probably not the word for it. 'I'll look forward to that. Well, I mustn't keep you, Mr Attaché.' Then a thought struck me. 'By the way, I gather you have an assistant these days.'

It had not been a good thought. 'Assistant?' said Mr One in a voice like a blast off the Eiger. 'What assistant?'

'I don't know, the switchboard seemed to think – '

'Oh no. No no. I'm not having an assistant, Mr Joke.'

'Sorry, I just – '

'He's being an observer, you understand. We're calling him an observer, you see. Please telephone my secretary shortly to arrange lunch. And please give my regards to your charming wife.'

No light on the replacement question, then, but the stuff about the advertising space was good news as far as it went. Lunch with Mr One, assuming he managed not to vaporize first, would be no huge treat, still, worth it for the experience and for telling Susan afterwards. She had got a mention just now because she had given a small party for the Penangan Cultural Attaché, and he had invited us to a do at his High Commission, and among those present had been Mr One, in on whom I had homed as soon as I had heard what he was, and then Penangans were the sort of people who took a lot of trouble over things like wives.

I glanced up and saw a short bearded man watching me from the doorway, or what might have been the doorway if the walls of my office had come up high enough to contain a door instead of only reaching about as far as the top of this fellow's head. That was as far as the walls of nearly everyone's office had come up since the inside of the whole building was remodelled at some stage in the Seventies. Perhaps he had not been actually watching me, only looking at me, but I felt a bit watched that day.

When I reckoned I had noticed him he said, 'Got a minute?'

'Sure,' I said, standing up behind my desk. You always had a minimum of that much for the Editor, whoever he might be. This one's name was Harry Coote and he had not been in the job long, anyway not as long as I had been in mine, which was what counted, and what made me feel a little uneasy too from time to time. Harry struck me as one of those men who very much preferred their own ideas to other people's on all sorts of issues, including ones like who should and especially who should not be advertising manager of the paper they edited. Of course nobody took a blind bit of notice of what editors thought about that unless the paper was putting on readers, but then rather to my surprise the paper was putting on readers, and doing it at a time when its rivals were giving all their readers cars to try and coax them to go on being their readers a bit longer. And I liked my job – I thought I was good at it slightly more than I liked it, but still.

On my way out I dropped the Thurifer note in front of Morgan. I followed Harry along to his office, which had walls that went all the way to the ceiling, also enough hardware to launch a smallish satellite, also a long tank for tropical fish with no fish in it, no other creatures either, no greenery, no water even, just sand, stones and empty shells, and a light still going that probably no one knew how to put out. In its active days the tank had tipped you off that a great man worked here, along the lines of a flint-glass sherry decanter or an antelope-hoof snuffbox further back.

'How are things?' asked Harry. That just meant he was not yet ready to come to the point, if any.

'Fine,' I said, pretending to hesitate before turning down one of the dusty, gnarled cheroots he showed me. 'You remember that business about the Penangan report we talked about.' I ran through part of my phone conversation. When the subject had been mentioned before Harry had shown guarded approval. To print four or any number of pages of guff about a distant and irrelevant hell-hole would do nothing, or nothing good, for circulation but it would raise the tone, lift the paper a millimetre up market. More than once I had noticed him saying he thought it was time to improve the paper's image, give it a touch of quality, etc. Perhaps he really hated to have it putting on readers. Anyway, it might be interesting to see his reaction to the nearer approach of the Penangan report.

It was interesting, but not encouraging. 'Yes, well, that's what you get,' he said firmly and vaguely. He wanted to register doubt or disapproval without knowing how. 'Of course, it's nothing to do with *me*.' There he was telling the strict truth, only it lacked conviction.

'Well, we'll see how it goes.' Not easy to quarrel with that either.

'You're, er, you're going to meet this Minister of Trade bloke, are you?'

'I thought I would, yeah. When he comes over.'

'If he does.'

'That's right, if he does.'

Harry's mouth buckled behind the beard with the exertion of dragging air through his cheroot. You could tell they were a cruel smoke just from the look of them. For some reason I thought of what he had been known to do, perhaps invariably did do, when he had you up to dinner at his bachelor joint in Tufnell Park – give you an admittedly not too bad Chinese takeaway meal and make you eat it with chopsticks, real ones though, mind you, bought or stolen on some all-expenses trip to Peking. I had never been asked along myself, but had had the facts on the first-hand authority of the Features Editor, who had heard from somebody else, somebody not even in Fleet Street, that at one of these blow-outs Harry had given them tea to wash it down with, pointing out that actually with any national food you were supposed to drink the national drink, the wine of the country, which in this case any fool could see was not wine. There had been times when I found the tea story a bit hard to believe, but at the sight of Harry now, looking quite upset at the way his cheroot would not draw to suit him, I could manage it all right.

After a short silence he said, 'I've been thinking about you, Stanley.'

I could think of one or two rude answers to that but no polite ones, so I just looked expectant.

'You really, you really *enjoy* doing what you do, do you?'

'Yes,' I said, sounding terrifically certain and relaxed at the same time.

'And you think you ought to be doing it, do you?'

'Without any question whatever. How do you mean?'

'Well, you know, I was just wondering whether you felt you had the proper scope for your talents in the present job.'

'What? What talents?'

He gave a slight laugh. 'Get stuffed, Stanley,' he said, or rather must have meant to say, but what he in fact said was something far nearer 'Gat steffed, Stunley.' That was because he came from up North, so much so that if he ever got tired of editing he could have walked into a job as a chat-show host on any of the TV channels. 'I know more about you than you give me credit for,' he was going on. 'I'm not such a fool as I look, you know.' It seemed a good idea to let that one go too. 'For instance, er . . . Oh yes. Tell me, do you ever see anything of old Nowell these days?'

I had always thought that one of the most appealing things about Harry was his complete openness, if you could use the word to cover being incapable of successful deceit. So I knew straight away and for sure that he had heard not a word about my recent contacts with Nowell – whom many years previously and for a very short time he was supposed to have been in the same digs as – and was just being pushy and nosy in his usual way. 'No,' I said. 'Practically nothing. Why?'

'Oh . . . I always thought it was a pity you two couldn't manage to make a go of it.'

Always? Until he joined the paper, Harry would not have known of my existence much. 'Well, there we are.' I looked at my watch.

'I see Whatsisname, Bert, in the Ladbroke Arms occasionally.'

'Oh, yeah.'

'I suppose you haven't got much time for him.'

'Not a lot, no. Well . . . '

'Oh, he's not so bad when you get to know him.'

I glared suddenly at the fish-tank as though I had noticed something starting to come to life there. Another short pause followed, long enough all the same for it to dawn on even our Harry that the time had not yet come to fill me in on all those good points of Bert's that I had been missing up to now. A knock sounded at the door and the Political Editor put his bald head round it. Harry told him to come on in, sounding quite relieved. 'Well, if you don't mind, Stan,' he said, smiling, 'I seem to have this conference.'

'No, I don't mind, Harry. I really don't mind a bit.'

'Right, see you. Oh, and, er,' he turned his smile off, 'I hope everything's going fine at home.'

He conveyed to me that I was not to not manage to make a go of my second marriage if I knew what was good for me, using so much wattage that something of the sort got across to the Political Editor, a man I knew only from his photograph in the paper, who looked at him and then at me and had started to look back at him about the time I left them together. Outside I just missed butting under the chin, luckily on the whole, a seven-foot female in a knee-length cardigan also bound for the conference. Harry was quite capable, I thought to myself, of believing that what he had been up to back there was showing sympathetic interest in me, kindly concern about someone who was not his responsibility in any strict way but about whom he nevertheless felt a certain this, that and the other. At least he would have said he had been doing that if challenged, gone on saying it to the death too if necessary. But what had he really been up to?

No answer. I had no clear idea why, but I went straight on to do a bit of wondering, for the tenth time, about Harry's sex life. He appeared to have none at all – his name had never been remotely linked with any man's, woman's or child's, though he was seen around with plenty of people. He never went near the subject in conversation – so for instance when his long-ago alleged chumminess with Nowell arose, as it did from time to time, I was at least spared any hint that they might have had it away together, which comparatively few men in that situation would or could have kept themselves from suggesting. He gave nothing away in his clothes or mannerisms or speech. And so on. The consensus was that the bed he kept his distance from had a little boy in it. Of course, it still could have been a big boy, even though Harry must have been getting into his middle fifties by now. After all, you never knew, did you? Not with them.

I forgot about Harry straight away when I got back to my office. No secretary. Morgan made a nothing-to-do-with-me face and at the same time I saw there was a woman standing by my desk. Her back was half turned and for a moment I thought it was Nowell. Then I realized I had been misled just by the hair, which had the right rough texture and shortish cut, though it was rather too dark, and by the vaguely foundry-style rig-out in slate-coloured denim, and it was true that Nowell had been fresh in my mind. I soon saw that this woman was hardly like her at all really, younger, longer in the leg, thinner, with a thin face and a nervous or restless manner. For the second time in a few days I guessed something was wrong without being able to say what.

'Mr Duke?' She had a deep, harsh voice with one or other regional accent.

'Yes. What do you want?'

'There's no need to be unfriendly, surely.'

'So you say.' I felt somehow I had had enough laughs for one morning. 'Now, please tell me who you are and what you want.'

Morgan had been following this, and called, 'She said she had an appointment, Stan. There was nothing in your book, but I couldn't, er . . . ' He left it there. He was a very capable deputy advertising manager.

'Okay,' I said, and nodded to the woman to go on.

She ducked her head and said with souped-up humility, 'My name is Trish Collings, and I'm a friend of your son's, and I was – '

'What's up? Is he all right?'

She stared at me. 'Well . . . that's rather what I've come to ask you, Mr Duke. I thought you might have some news of him.'

'Oh,' I said. Morgan's phone rang and he answered it. 'Now,' I went on, 'how did you make your way here, to this room?'

'Does that matter?'

'Certainly. You're not supposed to be allowed up without personal permission. Standard procedure.'

'That's what I figured, so I got straight in the lift and asked around. It didn't take me long. Anyway, how is Steve?'

'How long have you known him?'

Up to this point she had seemed not to be giving me her full attention. She had kept glancing at, or towards, the photographs and other cuttings that were pinned to the cork runner on the wall by the desk, most of them scattered with handwritten comments. They would have been very largely unintelligible or at best uninteresting to anyone outside a narrow local circle, and even I could have spared a few of them. Now she tore herself away from all that and faced me more squarely. 'I don't see that matters much either,' she said, and I put her down as probably West of England.

'What are you doing here? Why didn't you ring me up?'

'Look, Mr Duke, all I want to know is how Steve is. That's not classified information, is it?'

'Of course not. He's . . . all right. A bit under the weather but nothing serious,' I said without thinking. 'Why? What have you heard about him?'

'Oh, is there something to hear?'

Across the room Morgan put his phone back. I went over to him and said, 'Look, Taff, could you lose yourself for a few minutes?' I was hazy about why I wanted him to do that – I had no theories to speak of about Trish Collings, if that was her name, except that she was not what she said she was, but even so embarrassment of some sort could safely be predicted. If in due course she came at me with a razor I could call for help from the dozens of people within hearing, run away, etc. Still no secretary, a temporary who was going the right way about making herself even more so than had been agreed in the first place.

Morgan had done quite a good job for him on hiding his astonishment at my request. 'Sure,' he said. 'Er . . . sure.' By the way his eyes flickered I could tell he was starting to wonder too.

'Have you tried him?'

He cottoned on to that instantly – no trouble with anything like that. 'Not reachable, but somewhere in the building, so we're getting warm. I left a message.'

'Great. Well . . . '

The sudden quiet reminded him that he had undertaken to leave. 'Er . . . see you later,' he said, and went out at a near-run.

I started on the female again. 'Now. Who *are* you?'

'Mr Duke, why all this fuss about a simple inquiry after somebody's welfare? What's the matter?'

She spoke, as she had done from the start, in a reasonable tone, in fact with slightly overdone reasonableness. By now we had had quite enough time to finish looking each other over. The female was not all that much younger than Nowell after all, with good features except for that thin mouth, which had something wrong about its shape or perhaps the way she moved it in speaking. I thought there had been sexy bits in her expression part of the time, to show she might be interested in me and inquire whether I might be interested in her, but it was hard to be sure of that because she moved her mouth about even when she was keeping quiet, and also kept shifting her eyes to and fro. Her face was never still. That meant I had no chance of telling whether she was attractive either. What she was mostly looking at was a not very large man with a rather small moustache, probably with a suspicious, hostile look as well and certainly with the nearest he could manage to a deep-frozen eunuch's one.

'State and authenticate your identity in the next ten seconds,' I said, quite enjoying this part, 'or I'll call Security and have you buzzed out.'

'What are you so afraid of?'

'Plenty of things, thanks, and one of them's that you might be off your head whoever you are.'

'Ah,' she said as though she had won a bet with herself.

'Ah? Two seconds.' I moved towards the phone. 'Sorry about the script.'

'All right, you can call off the panic, I've got what I wanted,' she said, still a good deal more mildly than the way I had gone on from the start. 'My name is Trish Collings, and I'm helping to look after Steve at St Kevin's.'

'He is all right, is he?'

'No cause for alarm.'

'Nurse, are you? Or doctor or what?'

'I am a doctor, yes. So – '

'I thought a Dr Abercrombie was supposed to be in charge of his case.'

'Dr Abercrombie suffered a small heart attack a few days ago. He'll be off work for at least a month.'

'So are you in charge of Steve?'

'I don't like that phrase, it has the wrong implications, but yes, I am a senior psychiatrist.'

'Really. What identification have you?'

'Oh, for Christ's sake.' She unzipped what looked like a man's black imitation-leather sponge bag and turned through it.

'I'd just like to be on the safe side if it's all the same to you,' I said, I had meant to sound indignant and rather grand, but it came out apologetic. As I spoke I realized I felt it too, and could not quite see why, except there we were and Dr Collings was a woman.

After a moment she passed me a letter addressed to the person she claimed to be, even down to the Trish. It was from the librarian of the British Psychiatric Association, which somehow worsened things slightly for my side. By this time I was fighting hard not to say I was sorry, also wondering whether my uneasy feelings at the sight of her were all accounted for now.

'You didn't give me much of a chance, did you?' I said as I handed her back the letter. 'What am I supposed to think when a strange female barges in . . . '

I had lost her – something in or about the letter had caught her attention. She peered short-sightedly at it while I remembered that the book it referred to had been called *The Parenthood of Madness* and started feeling uneasy again. Then, taking her time, she folded up the single sheet and pushed it back into her sponge bag. 'Sorry?' she said.

'Nothing, I was just – '

'I know, I shouldn't have done it really, but it sometimes helps to catch people off their guard.'

'I see, yeah. Has it helped this time?'

At this piece of repartee she shook her head in a way I thought was more preoccupied than negative – I noticed that whichever it was none of her hair moved. At the same time she gave a smile of a sort, turned down at the corners, not very wonderful to look at, really, but with something awkward or shy about it that I could not object to. She sent me one or two of her short glances but said nothing.

I said, 'How's Steve?'

'Ah,' she said again, but went on straight away, 'He's all right, he's fine, he's just got some problems which we're beginning to get a sense of, we need to know more about him, his early history, all that, I hope you'll be able to help us in those areas.' Where had I heard that sing-song before? 'Which means I'm going to have to ask you to give me some of your time.' Time – toime – West of England it was, the very thing for Long John Silver, of course, but extraordinarily ageing for any young or youngish woman, almost as bad as a southern Irish brogue. 'I thought the atmosphere here would be more relaxed than in hospital.'

'Did you really? Far from ideal, I should have thought.'

As I spoke a phone rang from what sounded inches away, closely followed by another, and a small young man and a bigger older man went by some yards apart with pieces of paper in their hands, shouting back and forth. Further off a voice yelled, calling, swearing, yawning.

Dr Collings seemed to take my point. 'Or would there be somewhere you'd feel more relaxed?'

'There would, quite a few places.' Places like one of the little rooms at the top of the Bar and Press Club would be private all right but for that very reason not relaxing, not for me, not with this female. 'Er, but I doubt if you'd think they were suitable.'

She frowned. 'Oh? What sort of places are they?' It was obviously nothing to do with the frown itself, but I suddenly realized that her breasts were a size or two bigger than the rest of her. Usually, in fact I dare say every time up to now, seeing a thing like that had me paying the woman concerned much more attention automatically, which in this case meant straight away and without thinking. But the breasts of Dr Collings had no such effect, merely adding up to one more out-of-place piece of her. Still, they were breasts.

'What?' I answered.

'Where are you thinking of?'

'I thought we might go to a pub,' I found I had said. 'If that's all right.'

'Sure, why wouldn't it be?'

'They're usually pretty quiet for a while yet.'

'Fine, fine.'

'There's quite a nice one, well, anyway, just the other side of Fleet Street called the Crown and Sceptre. Not a hundred yards away. Almost opposite.'

'All right. Let's go.'

'Well . . . I was wondering if you'd mind going on and I'll join you in a few minutes. There's just a few things I'd like to get squared away here first, if it's all right with you.'

'Can't they wait?'

'Well yes, in a sense of course they can, but, er, unless you've got a particular urgent bit for me I'd very much like to, er . . . After all, you did – '

'Mr Duke,' she said in her controlled way, 'which is more important to you, your son or these matters you seem to be so interested in? Whatever they are.'

One day quite soon a woman was going to say something very much like that to me, something hardly at all more noteworthy than that, and I would collapse and die without recovering consciousness. I put out a hand, not too fast, and gripped the edge of the desk. 'My son, of course,' I said, 'when it comes to it. If it has come to it you'd better tell me now, hadn't you?'

I thought that was quite good, but before it was half over I lost her again. She walked out of the office at average speed without looking at me. I could think of nothing to do but assume I would find her in the designated pub in due course. Morgan reappeared so immediately that he must have been hanging about in sight of the doorway.

After a quick glance over his shoulder he said, 'Who was that?'

It was undoubtedly a fair question, but for some reason I found it an impossible one to answer in any satisfactory way. 'She's . . . a friend of my son's.'

He waited till he was sure there was no more to come before saying 'Oh yes' in a voice that dripped with disbelief and suspicion. The Welsh accent came in handy for that. There did seem to be rather a lot of accents around that morning, but then I hardly ever came across anybody without one, apart from me, of course.

'Yes,' I said, and gave him a dozen or more boring things to do and make other people do. When I had finished I rang the Thurifer agency again and got the fellow I was after. His story was that not he but someone at Thurifer had gone off his head and I was to stop worrying. So I stopped worrying and rang Cliff Wainwright, who answered at once and in person and sounding quite angry. He calmed down somewhat when he discovered who it was, but went back to being fed up when I asked him about Trish Collings.

'A bit off, you know, this, Stanley, quite frankly. Surely you realize it's most improper for me to go sounding off about all and bloody sundry. *And* I don't possess a card-index system on the whole of the medical profession and areas adjacent as you appear to think. However, by some freak of chance it does so happen I've heard of the bag. Well above average was what was said. Thoroughly in touch, very good with the patients. That can be dodgy, of course. Well, what patients like isn't necessarily good for them. They're keen on not being cut open. For instance. Anyway, there she is.'

'Do you have any other children?' asked Collings.

'No,' I said. 'Surely Steve must have told you that, if you've talked to him at all, as you say you have.'

'Not even by your second wife?'

'No, not even by her. Why?'

'Why not?'

'Eh? Oh, er . . . Nowell said she couldn't face going through all that again.'

'That's not what she said to me. Yes, I spent nearly an hour with her before coming along to see you. She was very helpful.'

'Really? In my experience nothing's what Nowell says to anybody, whether it's you or me or the postman. I mean whatever she said's got nothing to do with what happened. Ever.'

'How long is it since she left you?'

'Eight years. Nearly nine. I'm not bitter, it's just I know her. At least I am, bitter, to some extent, I can't ever see myself not being, but it's much more I know her, that I say things like that about her. It's true anyway. She can't . . . You'll see what I mean when you've seen a bit more of her. Well, you might, I suppose.'

'In fact she did face going through it again.'

'That's right. She wouldn't have not done it just because she'd told me she couldn't or wouldn't. If you remind her that she's said something it doesn't suit her down to the ground at that moment to have said, she says she didn't say it, even if you're fool enough to produce a boatload of other people who heard her say it. Simplifies life no end. She makes the past up as she goes along. You know, like communists. Why are we talking about this, anyway?'

'You still haven't told me why there are no children of your second marriage.'

'No, I haven't, have I? I can't think what it can have to do with anything, but you're the doctor. So. Susan was nearly thirty-six when she married me and that's oldish to start having children, I should have thought. She hadn't had any by her previous husband, and presumably she wanted to go on not having any – well, that was what I presumed. She said she reckoned she wasn't cut out for motherhood, which I took as a sign that she probably wasn't.'

'Was that all she ever said on the matter?'

'Just about. I didn't try to get any more out of her. It sounded quite reasonable to me. After all, it's not as if she was the Queen.'

'Did you try to get her to change her mind?'

'Certainly not.'

'Why didn't you?'

'Well, I had no particular, special desire for any more kids. Lots of men would have felt the same, perhaps most of them. No child of Susan's and mine could have been any kind of company for Steve. And I didn't think it was my place to talk her into a thing like that. The woman should decide, and Susan was absolutely definite about it.'

'Is that your usual line, would you say, leaving the basic decisions to your female partner?'

'No, I said in a thing like that, that concerns her more than me.'

'You mean you think the role of the mother is much more important in the raising of children than that of the father.'

'Well, not ultimately, perhaps. I was thinking of pregnancy and confinement and the rest of it. Obviously a young child's going to make more difference to the mother's life than the father's.'

'Confinement. That takes me back. Anyway, what about an older child? Does the mother continue as much more important there?'

'I don't know about much more. It depends. But more, more important. I mean that's the view the courts take, after all, when there's a split-up. It's the wife who usually – '

'I suppose it was your first wife who took the decision to become pregnant?'

'I can't say what happened. She said it was an accident. I was still believing a lot of what she said in those days but of course that was ridiculous. It wasn't my decision anyway, which I take it is the point.'

'Would you ever have taken that decision if it had been left entirely to you?'

'I can't say about that either. Quite likely not. I don't think all that many men actively want children, not when they're twenty-five. Look – '

'What was your reaction to the news?'

'Well, I was pleased in a way. The timing was off, though, financially and that. There's always a case for not having a baby in the next twelve months when you're that sort of age.'

'So really you'd have preferred the pregnancy not to have occurred when it did.'

'Yeah. Yes, I think I would. Do you mind telling me what all this is leading up to?'

'I think we're almost there actually, Stanley. We're close to establishing that you had a negative attitude towards parenthood and resented the difficulties it occasioned.'

'Are we hell! That was just at the start, before I'd had a chance to adjust to the idea. By the time Steve arrived I was as thrilled and excited as, I was going to say Nowell but there again – '

'It's quite common in young primogenitors of high activity – first-time fathers. And it often persists even in association with definite positive behaviour. That can produce some pretty bizarre results.'

Trish Collings started to laugh while she was saying the last part of this and went on after she had finished, her shoulders shaking and her slightly spaced-out teeth glistening. The scale of it went beyond what you normally expected from someone just struck by a witty thought, in a civilized country anyway. When it was over she got up from her bit of bench and without another word walked past me in the direction of the lavatories at the rear of the pub. I was hoping that on her return she would get her questions over and with luck explain the point of them, no insistence there, and then let me ask her about Steve. Well, I said to myself, if one of the first things she wanted to know was how I had felt when I heard he had been conceived, there was probably not so very much wrong with him.

The pub was as quiet as I had said in the sense that there were not yet many people in it, though of course it was noisy as well – I had forgotten about that, as I still often did after all these years, not as noisy as it could be, nor noisy absolutely all the time, but noisy. A fat ginger-haired fellow in – among other things – a whitish tee-shirt and a burgundy plastic anorak, which between them made him look amazingly undressed and dirty and dangerous as well as horrible, was playing the fruit-machine, in this case a new improved model that broadcast at top volume an extract from a harmonium sonata every time anything happened and part of the sound-track of a Battle of Britain movie in between. In case you were deaf and trying to think, it flashed different combinations of coloured lights on and off like billy-ho. Apart from that there was not much to see by, just a couple of table-lamps with tasteful imitation-parchment shades on the bar and some feeble sun from the street, cut down further by the criss-crossed strips of painted lead glued on the windows.

What with the semi-darkness and being preoccupied I failed to spot Lindsey Lucas until she was almost within arm's reach, and the gritty Ulster tones made me jump. Her hair-do and clothes had their usual neat, slightly dated look.

'When are you going to start managing some advertising? Whenever I run into you you're boozing your head off in a well-known Fleet Street watering hole. My turn – what can I get you?' As she spoke she was taking in the half-full glass of gin and tonic opposite where the Collings woman had been sitting.

I tried to think and found it hard going. The trouble was that although I knew quite well that it would be a good idea to get rid of her and at once, I was so cheered by the sight of her that the words took their time about coming. It was not my day. Before I had done much more than stand up and open my mouth Lindsey's expression changed in a way that showed that Collings was on the point of joining us, and I was still turning my head when she actually appeared. Even now it was not too late to send Lindsey packing with talk of deal, rate, space, block and so on, but instead of that I found myself introducing them, or rather saying their names one after the other and pointing at each one in turn at the same time, perhaps in case either of them started wondering which was which. While my vocal cords went on being selectively paralysed my eyes were more than up to snuff. They showed me Lindsey quietly transmitting a claim to part-ownership of me, but when I looked to see how the other female was reacting I found her sending the same message back in a different style, more obvious, jerky, where Lindsey was smooth, but there. Or so I thought.

That finished me off, for the next half-minute at least. I went on standing about while Lindsey again offered a drink, to Collings as well this time, took an order from her for a single gin and ice and asked me whether I wanted water or soda.

'What?' I said, having heard perfectly well. 'Er . . . soda. Water.'

'Are you pursuing that girl?' Collings asked me when we were alone. Her manner was morally accusing, not at all sexual now.

'Of course not. No. What if I were?'

'But you want her to join in our conversation.'

'No. Why should I? Absolutely the opposite.'

'In that case, why didn't you tell her we were talking privately?'

'I don't know really. I suppose I couldn't face explaining that you were a psychiatrist dealing with my son's case.'

'Oh, *case*. Why couldn't you? It's nothing to be ashamed of. You wouldn't mind telling her your son had broken his leg, would you?'

'No, I just . . . '

'I'd have expected you to be well educated enough not to take that view.'

'It's not a view. I couldn't face going into it with her. Surely you can see that. And now would you mind just telling me what you were getting at with your questions about my attitude to Steve before he was born?'

'Isn't it obvious? You resented him as an intruder. You made him feel he wasn't wanted. Not calculated to foster a sense of security.'

'But that's not true,' I said, trying and failing to catch her eye. 'It just isn't true. I can remember, I didn't resent him when he was born. I wanted him by the time he was born. I couldn't have made him feel he wasn't wanted because I wanted him. Honestly.'

'I don't mean you consciously behaved to him in an unloving way.'

'Oh I see. I thought I was thinking one thing when really I was thinking the opposite. I know.'

Her lips came apart with a little smacking noise. 'Have you ever asked him about this?'

'No. Have you?'

'I didn't have to. He told me. There was plenty of it. "Dad was always trying to freeze me out. Dad never really accepted me. Dad had as little to do with me as he could." That kind of thing. Of course you often get – '

'What's the address of your hospital? Out Blackheath way, isn't it?'

'I'm sorry, Stanley, I can't let you see him at the moment. Not just yet. It wouldn't be at all a good idea.'

'How do you stop me?'

'Only by telling you that. But it's enough, isn't it?'

'Yes. Sod it.'

'As I said, this is quite common. And you often find an element of exaggeration, centralizing what are objectively relatively minor grievances.'

'Ah, cheers.'

'I have to get through some more work with you on this session, so can we cut the social get-together short?'

'She won't stay long.'

It was not till then that I realized that Lindsey's eyes were at least as good as mine. She was obviously going to think I was not just with Collings but so to speak going round with her. But Lindsey must not think that – I could simply not bear her to think that. I knew very little about why I felt so strongly on the point, except that the reason had to do with Collings rather than Lindsey. At that moment she was turning carefully away from the bar clasping three glasses in her hands. I should have followed her over there earlier and fed her some plausible de-sexing tale, but it was too late for that, and even at this late stage I could have bounded across the room to give her a hand and dole out a compressed edition, but I thought of that too late as well. Normally I would at least have jumped up to help her put the drinks on the table, but today I forgot.

'Something wrong, Stanley?' asked Lindsey.

I pulled myself together. 'No. I remembered something I should have done. But I can't do it now.'

At this she led off reliably by explaining how she came to have a quarter of an hour to spare, then switched to friendly interest and good manners – no curiosity showing – to ask Collings if she worked in Fleet Street too. This is it, I thought.

'I do and I don't,' said Collings, smiling suddenly. 'I'm in the Accounts Department of the *Sunday Chronicle*.'

'Oh really? Of course, eh, that's where Susan works, the *Chronicle*.'

'Yes, the people on the editorial side, we don't see much of them in Accounts as a rule.'

'No, I suppose not.'

It struck me later that to have Ulster and Dorset or wherever it was coming back at each other in this style was like something out of a very carefully cast radio play. Not at the time, though. At the time I was pretty well too terrified to think at all. I sat there staring at Lindsey, willing her to look my way so that I could twitch my face to signal at least that something was up but, as always in these situations, I might as well have gone to see my aunt.

'In fact I don't know her at all really,' Collings was saying. 'Just by sight. I expect you know her though, don't you? Being a journalist yourself and everything.'

'As it happens I've known her longer than that. Nearly twenty years, in fact. Why?' Lindsey gave the last word quite a shove.

'Oh, I'm just interested. You'll be able to tell me – is it Lindsey? – I imagine she is a very intelligent woman?'

'Christ, you don't have to know someone for twenty years to reach a conclusion on that. Yes, she is very intelligent, exceptionally intelligent, as anybody who's ever talked to her for five minutes is well aware. Including her husband.'

Collings gave one of her hearty laughs and laid her hand heavily on my shoulder. Somehow I managed not to fling it off or bite it. 'Oh, he says the same, but you know what men are, he could be biased, couldn't he? But Lindsey, you mustn't mind me going on like this, I'm curious, but I've heard people in the office who do know Susan say they've found her a bit, well, not stand-offish exactly, but very very reserved. What would your comment be on that? Stanley won't mind me saying what I've said.'

That did make Lindsey look at me, but there was no need for signals now. She had gone rather red, which suited her looks no end. Glaring through her glasses, she said, 'Stanley may or may not mind what you've said, but I can assure you that I do. And my comment would be, Fuck off, whoever you are. What's the matter with you? Why don't you listen? I told you she was an old friend of mine. What do you think I am? Be in touch, Stanley. Go carefully.'

She gave me a quick kiss and a squeeze of the hand that reminded me of Susan, and hurried away without another glance. Collings, who had kept up quite a good detached sort of air while Lindsey had been telling her her fortune, twisted her mouth at me as though it had been Lindsey who had behaved oddly or badly. I sat down and for a moment just gazed.

'What the bleeding hell were you playing at?'

'I'm sorry if I've upset you.'

'Me being upset's not the point. What did you think you were doing? I mean that literally. What did you actually think you were doing? For God's sake.'

'Gathering information,' she said in her patiently reasonable voice.

'Yeah, and a great roaring success you made of it, I'll give you that. You extracted the precious secret that Susan's intelligent and you're where you started on whether she's reserved or not. Terrific. All that at the price of a few lies and a spot of trouble-making.'

'There was information there right enough if you knew what to look for.'

'Oh I get it, you could tell what she meant when she thought she was meaning the opposite or not meaning anything at all. You're a marvel, you are.'

'I have upset you. Please try to – '

'Well I would be upset, wouldn't I?' I stopped for a moment and then went on more gently. 'Look. You're not just a woman I happen to have taken to the pub, you're the doctor who's looking after my son or however you want to put it, and he seems to be very sick. So what do I think when I see you behaving in such a daft and irresponsible and *pointless* way? What am I supposed to think?'

For the first time she met my eyes steadily for something over a couple of seconds. Her own were narrowed while at the same time her eyebrows were lifted. At least that was what it looked like, though admittedly when I tried it later in front of the mirror I got nowhere with making my own face do both those things at once. She also seemed to have drawn in her nostrils. I could not have said what that expression expressed but it was nothing encouraging, that was for sure. I thought for a moment she was going to cry and got ready to start apologizing for everything I could think of, but the moment passed and her face went back to its constant movement. When she began to speak it was in a flat voice without much inflection.

'Now listen to me, Stanley. First of all you'll have to take it from me that my experiment just now wasn't pointless. As regards the rest of it, you'll have to agree that no actual harm was done. That little Irish girl went off quite charged up with having stood on her dignity, and nobody said anything to hurt your feelings that I heard. But the important thing is for you to reshape your image of psychiatry and psychiatrists, which you've got from people like Alfred Nash. Oh, a brilliant man undoubtedly, made a fine contribution, only trouble is he's still stuck in Sydney in the 1950s, and the world's moved on since then. Everything's got much more flexible, there aren't the old rigid categories any more. The way Nash sees the human race, there are mad people and sane people . . . '

'Dr Collings,' I said, 'if I could just – '

'Do call me Trish. The medical title is so compartmenting.'

'M'm, but if you don't mind I think I'll stick to Dr Collings, but you can go on calling me Stanley if you want. Anyway. We've talked about me and my first wife and my present wife and Lindsey Lucas and me again and now Dr Nash. Could we talk about Steve? I dare say you haven't finished examining him or whatever you want to call it yet, but you must have some thoughts about him. I wish you'd give me an idea of what they are, if that's all right.'

'Sure.' She gave me a smile I had to hold on to myself not to look away from. 'Let's have another drink, though. My round. The same again?'

She was good in pubs, I thought to myself, promptly naming her preference when I asked her earlier and correctly taking that single off Lindsey to put in her half-drunk gin and tonic. It seemed not to go with the rest of her. Whatever that was like. I groaned quietly. Just when I could have done with a spot of mind-battering the fruit-machine was vacant and silent but for an amplified hum and the general noise-level seemed to be down. There was nothing to stop me from worrying about whether I really had tried to freeze Steve out when he was small. What was it about the idea that was familiar? – not the accusation itself but the type. Familiar from long ago, not the more recent past. Of course! Nowell. It had been a favourite trick of hers to denounce you for doing something or being something that had simply never crossed your mind, so that when it came to answering the charge you had nothing to show, no register of dates and places that showed you doing or being conspicuously the opposite, just a load of denials and undocumented general stuff, no alibi, in fact. But then people without alibis were often guilty.

I had got that far when Collings came back with the drinks. She plunged into business straight off, talking in a much less jittery, uncomfortable way than before.

'Nash's diagnosis of Steve was schizophrenia,' she said, lighting a Silk Cut. 'I just can't accept anything as prefabricated as that. What's at stake here is far from simple. On the information available so far, I think we're dealing with a problem in living, something involving not just him but also the people close to him, especially his parents. You've got to remember first that all kids of that generation have got a lot to cope with, a lot to try and make sense of – unemployment, of course, but also the nuclear holocaust, racial tension, urban pollution, alienation, you name it. They're very vulnerable and they feel powerless, it's a big, dangerous world over which they have no control. Someone like that senses that he's at risk. Then there comes a crisis in his emotional life, like breaking up with his girlfriend, and he's defenceless. So, what does he do? He creates a defence. He doesn't have anywhere to hide, so he makes a place to hide, a place we call madness, or mental illness, or delusions, or hallucinations.'

She paused for a swig, also probably for effect. I felt drunk or something, but asked her, 'Do you mean he's just putting on all that stuff about Joshua and the other fellows in the Bible?'

'Not consciously. He believes every word of it, for the time being.'

'But that's . . . I'm afraid I still don't quite see what he's defending himself against or hiding from.'

'Well, there are various ways of putting it. Escaping from reality, or his own inner feelings, or inner needs might be more accurate. He's trying to keep other people at a distance emotionally, so he puts up a wall, a wall consisting of what the likes of Nash call delusions. In cases like this that's often due to an appalling fear of being hurt. Now at this stage one can't be sure, but I rather think that with Steve it's more that he's afraid of hurting other people. He's a very nice boy, that I do know.' Here she sounded quite defiant, as if she thought I was obviously not going to let her get away with that, and putting me strongly in mind of my mother-in-law. 'Our job is to persuade him to lower his defences. He won't do that unless we can help him to get in touch with his own feelings, including especially his own anger.'

'Get in touch with his own anger,' I said. 'I see. What sort of chance would you say there is of that?'

'It's too early to say. You're anxious about this, I know, Stanley, but believe me it's most important not to jump to conclusions. This is very tricky and difficult ground. We're dealing with a scared, confused, insecure boy who has to be helped to find out who he really is.'

A frightful feeling that had been growing on me ever since we came into the pub suddenly got much worse, so bad I could no longer pretend it was not there or was really something else. It was roughly that Collings's general style and level of thinking would have done perfectly well for a psychiatrist in an American TV movie but might have looked a bit thin in a Sunday magazine article. And this could simply not be anything like a correct description. I was drunk, stupid too at the best of times, unable to take in ideas of any difficulty. But I had been perfectly sober when I arrived, and Steve talking about Joshua because he was afraid of hurting other people was not a difficult idea. It was not an idea at all.

I told myself it had to be, had to make sense somehow, somewhere. The resemblance to TV must be a mistake, an illusion based on my ignorance, which had made me miss all sorts of subtle points and misunderstand phrases and expressions that were nearly or even exactly the same as bits of drivel but actually conveyed a precise scientific meaning to those in the know, and getting in touch with your own anger and finding out who you really were, etc., were technical terms referring to definite, observable processes. Or Collings's approach was so new that they had not yet worked out a what, a terminology for it. Or she was hopeless at talking about what she did but shit-hot in action. Or something else that made it all right, because something must. Whatever she might say and however she might behave, the bint was a *doctor*.

Anyway, there was no alternative to going on trying to listen. I went on doing that for forty minutes or so, the stage at which we shunted from presumable technical talk to further inquiries into my early relations with Steve. That part went quite well as far as I was concerned, because I had had time to do some remembering and get my confidence back. I could see now that for some reason, like to fit a theory, Collings was trying to make out that father and son had got on badly or in a distant sort of way. I told her different and thought she seemed to notice. At the end we fixed that I should come and see her at the hospital in a couple of days, Nowell too perhaps.

Back in the office I went straight to something the improvers had unaccountably overlooked, a boxed-in part where you could make phone-calls in private. It was the Sundays' day off and I got Susan at home. Just having her at the other end listening put a lot of things right. She agreed to keep a careful look-out for twitching females with cider-apple accents.

I hesitated a moment over the next, but quite soon had Nash on the line reassuring me it was all right to call. I passed the news about Dr Abercrombie.

'Oh,' he said quietly. 'A small one, you say.'

'That's what I was told. By somebody calling herself Dr Trish Collings, who seems to have taken over from him. She's taken over my son, anyway.'

'*Oh.*' Quite a different noise, and followed by silence.

'Do I gather you know her?'

'I know of her.' A great sigh sounded in my ear. 'You do realize, Mr Duke, that medical etiquette is unmistakable and strict on the point that no practicter may say anything derogatory about another, or more accurately anything at all beyond the barest facts. So I won't. Say anything at all. For now.'

'I see.'

'She'll probably ask you a lot of questions about yourself. Oh really. M'm. Well, it can't do any harm to answer them. I suppose she didn't say anything about those tests I asked to have done on your boy. No. Of course everything takes time these days. Er, now I come to think of it there's another fellow in that hospital I have some acquaintance with, at least there was two or three years ago. More like five. Fellow name of Stone. He's . . . different from the . . . from Dr Collings. I'll get after him and tell you what I find out. Cheer up, Mr Duke. The boy's quite safe in there.'

My third call broke the run of abnormal luck. Lindsey was out, not back yet. Where from? Sorry. I looked at my watch and thought. From what I knew of her she would look into her office if she could before going to lunch. As I rushed off to look into mine I wondered why it had suddenly got so urgent to see Lindsey in the flesh, too urgent for any rubbish like message-leaving. Oh yes, she must not be allowed to go on thinking or suspecting that Collings and I were having an affair a moment longer than necessary, and stopping her had to be done face to face.

I had wondered whether Morgan Wyndham would be inquisitive or tremendously casual or just determined to delay me, but he was not even there. Only a major disaster could get me now, and before one could arrive I ran out. Rather than wait for the lift I charged down the stairs, along the street, across and along again, and almost banged into Lindsey coming out of the swing doors of her paper.

'*Ah*,' I said, feeling a great surge of relief. 'Are you lunching somewhere?'

'Yes, but I've got a minute. Right.'

She meant she agreed to a quick swallow in the pub next along but two, the one she and her mates always went to. Like all newspaper pubs it was nothing like the nicest in walking distance, not even the nicest a minute away, just the nearest. Inside, the noise from the people almost drowned the music. There was nowhere to sit, and there seemed to be nowhere to stand either, except in the hearth each side of an unlit gas fire. I bought drinks and carried them over, trying to keep them unspilled by moving three-quarters backwards through the customers, who were huddled along the bar three or four deep and shoulder to shoulder like a crowd waiting to watch a procession go by. The row seemed to have got worse since we came in, but it was too late to go anywhere else and the Crown and Sceptre would probably have been as bad by this time.

'How did you know how to find me?' shouted Lindsey, having sensibly held back till we reached this stage. Then she shouted something else I missed.

'Genius.' I found that at least I could put my glass down on the mantel-piece. 'I had to tell you – '

'Who was that madwoman you had with you just now? What the hell was the matter with her that she went on like that? Do you know your tastes are getting quite extraordinary.'

'That's actually what I came to tell you about, love. Listen, will you believe me if I swear something is true?'

'I might. Try me and see.'

'She and I are not, repeat not, having an affair.'

'Not . . . I've got it. Oh, you're not? She went on as if you were.'

And a sight less subtle on the subject than you were, darling, I thought. I said, or rather bawled, 'That was just her, I've no idea what she was playing at. But surely you saw me going on as if I wasn't?'

'Well, you would, wouldn't you, in the circs?'

'Maybe. But it's not so, I promise you. It's *not so*.'

'Stanley, have you come all this way just to tell me that?'

'Yeah. Don't ask me why, eh?'

'Oh, come on. Between old friends. What makes you feel so strongly?'

'I just couldn't stand the idea. Of you making that mistake. She revolts me.' I had said the last part without thinking, and it was close, but still not quite right. 'You believe me, don't you?'

'I might if you tell me who she is. She obviously isn't anything to do with the *Chronicle*. I think I get full marks there for keeping my Irish temper in check and not retorting to the insult to my intelligence. And you'll have to tell me too what you were doing with her, and it had better be good.'

'Some check. You went for her like a bleeding pickpocket. Quite right, though, mind you. But what if she'd been on the point of buying an acre of space off me?'

'No serious concern would let a cow like that buy pussy. Fess up now, Stanley – who is she?'

'Who'd you think she is?' I said to hold off the inevitable.

'Christ, I took her for something you'd picked up when you were pissed and were desperately trying to ditch. You greeted me like a hundred-pound note. And then she buggered it up for you.'

'I never get as pissed as that. I wouldn't touch her with yours, if you know what I mean.' Again, true as far as it went. 'And I don't pick up anything when I'm pissed these days.'

'Tamed. Poor old Stan. Now . . . deliver.'

'She's the psychiatrist who's looking after my son Steve who's had a psychological breakdown.' On the way here I had reconciled myself to telling her that, though perhaps not to yelling it at her as I had had to do, but there it was.

'What?' She screwed her face. 'Sorry.'

'My son's in a mental home,' I roared, 'and she's the doctor.'

After a second of shock she laid her hand on my left shoulder and her head on my right. I put my arm around her waist and took her free hand. There was a short pause. When she moved back she looked at me in a kind way I had never seen before, miming the message that nothing much to the point could be said here and now. I nodded.

'Would you like to tell me about it? Some other time?'

I nodded again. 'I'll give you a ring. Thanks.'

Not long after that Lindsey took herself off to her lunch. I got hold of a Carlsberg Special Brew and tried for a cheese sandwich, but they only had Brie and French bread, so I took that. I ate it jammed in a corner with the plate under my chin taking alternate bites of Brie and bread because there was nowhere to put the plate down and spread the one on the other. Then I went back to the office and kipped for a spell in the library. Nobody ever disturbed you there.

I tried to get Lindsey next morning at her office, but she was out. So I tried to leave a message, but nobody knew how to find the person I could leave it with. I had another go in the afternoon, no more successful, and after that sort of gave up. In any case there was less incentive now, after the long cheering chat I had had with Susan the previous evening. On the Collings wordage she took the line that the jargon of any trade was likely to strike outsiders as crude and rubbishy.

'I'd try to forget it if I were you, darling,' she said. 'And the other thing of course is that some of the best people in their line are bloody hopeless when they try to explain it.'

'Yes,' I said, 'I thought of that.'

'You certainly get that with writers. There are all sorts of examples. Oh . . . Yes, Nabokov. You know, *Lolita*. Talks balls by the yard about what he does and yet he's an absolutely super novelist. Wait and see, that's the ticket.'

But when I got on to what I reckoned had been Collings's general approach, as opposed to just her style, Susan was less encouraging.

'What kind of theory?' she asked.

'Well, something like mental trouble being caused or anyway helped on by experiences in childhood, where obviously what the parents did or didn't do is important. I was reading an article by some American the other week that said something like that.'

'Some American will say anything, won't he, if you give him time. So Steve had a breakdown because you took no notice or the wrong kind of notice of him when he was little. Nasty as well as crap. Did she act hostile, this creature? Why aren't you drinking?'

'I thought I'd had enough for a bit.'

'Yes, I noticed you were rather pissed when you came in. You can afford to be a little more pissed than that after the day you've had. Where were we? Oh yes – hostile?'

'More clinical,' I said en route to the drinks tray. 'I don't want to say she was hostile when what I mean is I didn't like what she was telling me. No, but there were definite hostile bits.'

'You said she was sort of sexy but getting it wrong. Did – sorry, you must be fed up with answering questions, but did she . . . issue anything in the way of an invitation to you? It wouldn't surprise me, with such an attractive man.' She beamed at me.

I beamed back. 'Yeah, I thought so.'

'And I presume the lady received a dusty answer. You know when you were talking on the telephone I thought it sounded as if she was taking it out of you for something. I bet that's it. I bet that's it.'

'You seriously . . . you mean because she flies a little kite and I don't want to know, she decides to even up by trying to prove I neglected my son. My God.'

'Oh, I'm sure she didn't decide to do anything. None of it would have been conscious. She'd have said she was doing a perfectly ordinary piece of objective analysis. You know what women are like. You ought to by now.'

'Now I come to think of it she did remind me of Nowell. More than once. But I mean, my God.'

Then Susan said it was only a guess and went off to run up dinner. On further inspection I threw out her guess – doctors were trained not to behave like that. I held firm even though I had in my possession one solid piece of evidence in its favour that was hidden from Susan. It showed great powers of something-or-other to have got there unassisted by knowing about Lindsey's little demonstration that she had a stake in me, which

Collings could not have found at all funny. And I had probably made things worse by if not actually dribbling with lust then at least by making some sign that feelings were mutual. But that assumed that Collings was capable of . . . Sod it.

Actually I had shut up about Lindsey altogether, both today and last Friday. This keeping-dark was required anyway by the regular blanket ban on mentioning as much as the name of one female to another unless it was absolutely necessary. More than that, though, I had told Susan about the affair I had had with Lindsey pretty well straight away, in one of those fits of blurting that come over some men when they fall in love. In the telling I had made it as plain as a dozen pikestaffs that the whole thing had been over before I had ever met her. Never mind – my confession, which was what my harmless bit of reminiscing had turned into almost from the word go, ended up a disaster, needing a pair of Regency candlesticks and dinner at the Connaught. I had forgotten, or perhaps in those days had yet to learn, the rule about comparability, avoidance of. You can let on that you once slept with the Richard who sweeps the floors and sells the french letters at the barber's or with a royal, and mostly get away with it, but not when it was someone they were at Oxford at the same time as, even if the two have barely set eyes on each other since. Except perhaps to announce her death I could never again mention Lindsey to Susan.

Over kedgeree and Spanish plonk in the kitchen I mentioned Nash and his reaction to the news of Collings. When I had finished my mention Susan said, 'Old Robbie telephoned today about something and I told him I'd run into a shrink called Nash, because the name had rung a faint bell in my head, and Robbie knew it straight away. Apparently apart from being very eminent in his field he made a terrific splash in the Fifties with a book for the general reader about madness in literature. It seems Cyril Connolly raved about it, but of course he often . . . Anyway, Robbie said he thought he could get hold of a copy for me. Well, it's a fascinating subject.'

I could never have explained, even to myself, why it was that my general estimate of Nash, highish almost from the start and inclined to lift under the influence of today's events, took a small but sharp dive at this disclosure. Of course I kept my mouth shut about that. Later Susan played the hi-fi, Bach and then I thought Nielsen. Later still she did a marvellous job of impressing on me that I was not to blame myself for whatever it was that had happened to Steve. She had hardly started before I became too drunk to remember afterwards any of the individual bits, but the general effect lasted me well into the next day and even took some of the punch out of my hangover. Nothing actually happened that day – two men and a woman told me at different times that Thurifer Chemicals were staying with their half-page after all, and Trish Collings phoned me at work to make an appointment at her hospital at 9 the following morning. Nowell had prom- ised to be there too, said Collings. Fat bleeding chance, I thought to myself, as regards your 9 a.m. anyway. And why 9 a.m., come to that? To show who was boss, said Susan, and I tried not to agree, because I had decided it was better all round to give Collings the benefit of any doubt. Well, almost any.

An alarm phone-call woke me at 7. My first action after ringing off was to grab the usual large jug of water beside the bed and take a hearty gulp. This turned out too late to contain some live creature which had no doubt fallen or flown there, not long before, probably, because to judge by the results inside me there was still quite a bit of flight left in it. I stumbled out of the dark bedroom and hung over the wc for a minute or two, thinking very hard about not being sick and impressing on myself a fact learnt in childhood, that there was enough acid in my stomach to burn a hole in a carpet.

After some long, unaffected groans, a go with the toothbrush and a hot shower with shampoo I felt very tired. Nothing occurred between then and the time I left the house that would surprise anyone who has ever got up in the morning in London or a similar place. When I took Susan up a cup of tea she again offered to come on the trip with me and I again thanked her and said there was no need.

It was raining busily away when I started on my disagreeable journey. I took the Apfelsine through the middle – straight down the hill, along past the office, across Blackfriars Bridge, to the Elephant and into the Old Kent Road. Very likely other routes would have been cleverer, but that morning the thought of even trying to be clever seemed dreadful, not to be borne. At first the traffic was so light that I looked like getting there in about ten minutes, but then an almost stationary Belgian container-lorry, stuck trying to back into a side-turning and so gigantic it must have been built for laughs, put my mind at rest. South of the river I was on home ground, or not far off. By the time I got to New Cross I had come to within five miles of where I had been born and brought up.

For all I knew, this part and that part had been different then, built at different times with different ideas, anyhow not interchangeable. That was no longer so, if it ever had been, unless perhaps you happened to have an eye for churches. Not that I cared, of course – I had left South London for good as soon as I had the chance. And yet in a sense what I saw from the Apfelsine was the same as ever, was cramped, thrown up on the cheap and never finished off, needing a lick of paint, half empty and everywhere soiled, in fact very like my old part as noticed when travelling to and from an uncle's funeral a few weeks back. Half the parts south of the river were never proper places at all, just collections of assorted buildings filling up gaps and named after railway stations and bus garages. Most people I knew seemed to come from a place – Cliff Wainwright and I got out of an area. This might have spared us various problems.

On Shooters Hill I picked up a sign for St Kevin's and was directed across some strikingly unrepulsive parkland through a couple of open gates in a low red-brick wall surmounted by railings. Following further signs I found myself winding through what added up to another park, though this one was in full fig with lawns, flowerbeds, shaped hedges and ordered groups of shrubs, all looking cheerful enough even if fairly well saturated just now. But most of the view consisted of houses, again in red brick, probably of the Thirties, and enough in size and number to shelter a great many people, in fact a small New Town of loonies and their attendants. That sounded like the sort of novel by a dead foreigner that got reviewed in the *Sunday Chronicle*, not with Susan doing the review, of course.

The car park was right at the end, at the back of a one-storey building with a husky-looking creeper trained along it. Having duly parked I walked round to its front, not hurrying because I was early and the rain had stopped for the moment. I turned the corner to find that an ambulance had drawn up outside the entrance and the two crewmen were helping down an old fellow who was going on like a madman in a Bela Lugosi movie. Shock-headed, wild-eyed, wrapped in a grey blanket, he was spreading his hands jerkily about in front of him as he shuffled forward, not actually screaming but crying out in a high wordless voice. The men told him he was fine and doing great. I was trying to look like a piece of the wall and had no idea how he saw me, but he did, and swung and swayed round.

'Hoo-oo!' he howled, pointing a shaky finger. 'Urhh!'

The man quickly soothed him and the younger one steered him through the glass door. The older one came over to me. He had a very long neck and small ears and was blinking and frowning.

'Nothing for it, just got to stare, have we?' he said hoarsely. 'Reflex action, is it? See a nut and goggle like a kid?' He gazed past me and let his lower jaw hang to help to show me what he meant.

'I'm sorry, I wasn't thinking, I was waiting to go in here myself.'

'I mean he's not a bloody freak, you know. He's a poor old man who's a little bit confused and a little bit frightened, and he don't need very ignorant people gawping at him, right?'

'Yeah,' I said. 'My son's in here somewhere.'

'Oh, well I expect you'll learn then, won't you?' He looked me up and down once or twice before letting me off whatever he still had up his sleeve for me, and hurried off into the building, stopping abruptly on the way to light a cigarette.

Something prevented me from following him for the moment. I stood muttering excuses and looking vaguely about, soon catching sight of someone in a white coat who peered out of the entrance of the house opposite, probably a woman, but the white brimmed hat like a cricket-hat made it hard to be sure. Two pairs of eyes met for I suppose two seconds, then the figure threw up both hands and waved them and started towards me, crossing the threshold on widely separated legs. That sent me indoors all right. There was a desk and a girl there, and the ceiling struck me as unusually low.

'I'm looking for Rorschach House,' I said.

She scratched her neck and said without looking up, 'This is it.'

'No really?' I had been fully expecting to be sent on a hike back to the front gate.

'It's over the door,' she said, sighing. 'Was there somebody you wanted to see?'

We went into that and I started walking down a narrow, dimly lit corridor with doors along the sides made from extremely cheap wood and the floor loosely spread with white cotton lengths like the ones decorators put down. I saw nobody and heard no sound before I knocked on a door of similar quality at the end of a section of passage. Like the others it had a number on it but no name.

On request I went inside, and nearly went straight out again on failing to recognize the female sitting behind the metal table with her back to the window. Then I saw that the dark-rimmed tinted glasses, swept-back hair-do and old-style office get-up belonged to Trish Collings – so too with a vengeance did the thin funny-shaped mouth, where I should have looked first. She held out her hand, which I shook, and asked me to sit down, which I did, on one of the kinds of chair you never see in a private house.

There was not much in the room, and nothing personal or unnecessary, no photographs, newspapers, flowers, books except what looked like text-books and reference works, none of the usual desk-clutter. Except of course there was no desk either, just the bare table with a couple of files, a couple of wire trays, a couple of loose papers, a telephone, a canteen saucer for an ashtray and a white plastic institutional wastepaper-basket. Not so much as a typewriter – but a small voice-recorder on a shelf. Strip-lighting gave an effect much more like daylight than any electric light ever did, and at the same time not like daylight at all.

Collings allowed me plenty of time to take this in by finishing, or so far just going on with, the letter or note she had been writing when I came in, my second reminder of the world of the cinema since parking the car. When the wall-clock, one of the sharp sort with no face or hands, just figures, showed 09 11 she looked up at and said, 'Mrs Hutchinson is late.'

'I know, it's incredible,' I said incredulously, 'I can't think what can have happened to her.'

'Usually on time, is she? I suppose with her – '

'No, I'm sorry, no, she isn't usually on time. She's always late, you see. It's because she's a . . . Er, I don't think we'd better wait for her. Tell me, how's Steve?'

'He's all right, he's quiet, no cause for alarm.'

'Can I see him?'

She hesitated. 'Later. For now you might answer a few basic questions.'

The basic questions started with one about the date of my birth, but its precise hour was not required, which ruled out the casting of my horoscope. They went on with ones about things like whether I had had a serious illness, all from what looked like some sort of form. Necessary for her theory? Possibly. Or then again she could have been softening me up for a sudden really rotten one slipped in after one about my grandparents. If so she had still not got to it when at 09 22 there was a knock at the door and Nowell came in.

She was smiling with demure triumph at having made it on time – well, 22 minutes late was on time unless you were going to start being foul to her. At 10 22 she would have gone on in just the same way, plus being ready, if anyone started being foul to her, to state wonderingly that she was sorry but she had been asked for 10 00. She had on a very upstanding kind of suit in some khaki material, and with her short hair reminded me of the ATS girls I had seen during the war. Collings got up and Nowell went across and I could have sworn they were going to kiss, but without going that far they made it clear enough that they got on famously together. Then they both turned and looked at me. I knew that look, I would have known it even if I had never seen it before – it was the look of two women getting together to sort a man out. And on the way here I had said to myself well anyway, it would be fun to see those two wills battling against each other. My trouble was that I kept mixing women up with men.

Nowell came conscientiously over and kissed me on the cheek. Then she went and sat down on a chair just like mine but ended up rather nearer Collings than me, underlining the two-to-one effect. Intentionally? Not a useful word when talking about Nowell.

'Well,' said Collings in chairpersonal style, 'let's get on, shall we? What I'm trying to do is put together an informal biography-in-depth of Steve so far. I've managed to get quite a lot from him – oh yes, it's not that difficult if you know what to look for – but I've hardly started on you and Stanley, Nowell. Let's go right back to the time he was born.'

She could have meant me but she really meant Steve. The first twenty minutes or so went suspiciously well – at least no physical blows were exchanged. Collings took quite a few notes, which reminded me that I had not seen her take any on the Monday. Nowell went on being conscientious, but in a different style. From the events of Steve's life up to puberty, such as they were, the talk shifted to parental relations. In general, had he got on reasonably well with his mother? On the whole yes, Nowell thought. Did I have any comment on that? No, that seemed fair enough to me. What about how he and I had got on?

'There again,' I said, all systems on full alert by now, 'I think reasonably well.'

'You confirm that, Nowell, do you?'

'I . . . think . . . ' said Nowell, dripping with objectivity, '*I* think . . . that that's putting it . . . rather too low. Stanley and Steve seemed to *me* to get on . . . considerably better than the average father and young son. In fact

I'd go further than that. In *my* view the two of you had a . . . quite remarkably close relationship. Considering how little you saw of each other.'

I stared at her with a sort of grin. 'What? We saw a hell of a lot each other. Don't you remember how every evening I – '

'It's perfectly understandable, darling,' she said, and gave Collings an I-told-you-so smile. 'Nobody's blaming you. As I say, it was a great success – you got on marvellously well whenever you did actually set eyes on each other. I often remarked on it at the time.'

'This is ridiculous. It wasn't like that at all. For instance, what about those weekends when I – '

'We have here the standard behaviour-pattern in the situation.' Leaning over her work-table and blinking her eyes pretty fiercely, Collings marked the important words by tapping on it with the butt of her black ballpoint. 'Again, it's the norm for young primogenitors with strong external drives, not necessarily producing negative effects.'

Something that might have been the strip-lighting was making a high-pitched humming noise. There was no view through the window, just a flat brownish surface which filled the space and was probably the outside of more of the building, and nothing on the walls, not even a calendar, not even a list or a timetable. All this and the grey paint on those walls made the room seem a long way from anywhere much, like a satellite tracking station in the Mojave Desert, say. I looked over at the two females and saw that, quite naturally really, they were looking at me, Nowell with a hesitant smile and her own, wider-eyed style of blinking, Collings with her usual mish-mash of expressions and what might not have been expressions at all. Much sooner than I had expected, the three of us had reached the point I had foreseen ever since this meeting was proposed, foreseen it intermittently and vaguely and yet with certainty.

Starting with the set of my shoulders, I did my best to look and sound like the very picture of meekness, goodwill, sincerity, tolerance, respect and disposition to admit mistakes, and lumbered off on what had to be done.

'Now I take it the reason we're all here is that we want to do the best we possibly can for Steve.'

'Of course we do, darling,' said Nowell reassuringly, showing that she really was on her best behaviour, because I instantly saw that opening had been far from brilliant after all – I might easily have been getting ready to tick her off for being there for some other motive.

'For the moment I'm afraid I frankly don't understand just where our, er, inquiries are leading, but maybe I will later, and anyway I'm sure there's a reason and a purpose to them.' In the meantime I was pushing my hands down between my thighs and crossing both sets of fingers.

'You bet there is,' said Collings with a couple of peals of laughter.

I struggled on, addressing myself to her because I had to. 'Obviously, if – er, for the best results we've got to get as near the facts of what happened as possible, it's some years ago now and people forget things, of course they do. But, for Steve's benefit, that's all, Nowell is mistaken when she says I saw rather little of him during his childhood. I could give you the names of friends who would describe to you the situation as it was in fact. Neighbours, parents of school friends. Why, before he could walk I – '

While I was speaking, Nowell had been looking from me to Collings and back and giving little quiet puffing and grunting laughs. Now she said, 'Oh Stanley, you are being rather a bore, darling. You do go on, don't you? And there's no need to, you know. Okay, now it's come up you feel bad about having neglected Steve a bit. Forget it! Nobody blames you. It's normal, as Trish told you. It's all over. Past history, old boy. Now could we possibly all manage to be sensible and get on with the job, yes?'

Having been brought up not to interrupt I kept quiet, against my inclination, until the end of that. When I started, my voice sounded like something off very early radio, or disc, or cylinder. 'In this context I have nothing to feel bad about. It was you, not I, who neglected Steve. One instance. The evening I – '

'Stanley, please.' Collings had got to her feet, and I had to admit, very unwillingly again, that the old rough tones had some authority in them. 'Can I prevail on you not to conduct your private quarrels in this office?'

I said slowly and quietly, and as I guessed afterwards sounding this time incredibly sinister, 'That's not what I was up to, Dr Collings, whatever it may have sounded like to you. I was trying to get the facts straight, not very cleverly it seems, but surely ... Now presumably you hold some theory or whatever you prefer to call it about the state people like Steve get into being something to do with the way their parents treated them when they were small. Fair enough. But a theory can only give the right answer in a particular case if the facts of that case are properly established. It will give the wrong answer or no answer at all if the information supplied is incorrect for any reason. So in the case of Steve, if the received information says that I – '

'Oh for Christ's sake,' cried Nowell after a leave-this-to-me look at Collings that went on for less than a second, 'Steve isn't a *case*, he's your son! He's a human being, not a bloody motor car! You and your information supplied and theories and answers, I don't know how you can ... ' Etc.

There had never been any hope at all for my side, from how far back you bleeding trembled to think, but in peace no less than in war hopeless efforts must be made. This one had been such a blow-over for the opposition that Nowell had had no need to send in the second wave by asking me why I was being so foul to her, nor Collings to hit me with science. Even so I continued to resist sporadically as the story swept, or rather slouched, on. For instance what kind of school experience had Steve had?

How did Collings mean? Had he been a success at school? No, he had not – he had left with a single 'O' level, in biology.

'Were you disappointed with that result?'

'Well I wasn't, Trish dear, I tell you frankly,' said Nowell. 'But then I don't happen to think exams are important. I think what matters is what a person's like. I know Stanley doesn't agree with me.'

'No,' I said, still quietly. 'I think both are important. Sorry, of course that's not agreeing with you. No, exams get you jobs, that's the point.'

'I must say I haven't noticed them getting youngsters much in the way of jobs in the last couple of years,' said Nowell in a concerned, caring voice.

Collings cut in before I could answer that, which was probably just as well. 'So you were disappointed with the result, Stanley. Did you let Steve see your disappointment?'

'You bet I let him see it. It was his second try. I wanted him to have another go, but they – '

'And had you put pressure on him beforehand to do well? Not only for that exam but for earlier ones too?'

'Yes I had. Of course I had. Short of tortures and death-threats, I'd better say. Plus rewards for success. If any.'

'It used to worry the poor little thing to death,' said Nowell.

'And when Steve didn't do well, you made it clear you were disappointed in him, you thought he'd let you down.'

'I was disappointed with the result. I don't think I gave him a bad time, I didn't say anything, but I didn't go round pretending I hadn't noticed either. Perhaps I was a bit disappointed, in him, but you get that. There were other ways he was so much more than I'd ever expected.'

'But surely you must have realized he wasn't academically orientated?'

'I could see he wasn't Einstein, but I still wanted him to do his best. Like English 'O' level. He sometimes talked of being a writer. You'd think he'd have had the interest.'

'Stanley's very keen on writing,' said Nowell seriously. 'His second wife's a writer, you know. She doesn't write a lot but she does write. And he sometimes writes himself, articles for the magazines about cars.'

To my surprise Collings seemed interested in this information and made quite a lengthy note. When she had finished doing that she pushed back her chair, which matched the table and had only one leg, and lit a cigarette. 'Of course with changing social conditions the elitist role of education is passing too.'

'Oh, yeah,' I said.

'Nowadays there's much more emphasis on the social function, training the kids to relate to each other and preparing them to take their places in the adult world.'

'At my school we got that thrown in, just by being there. We didn't attend classes in it.'

'No, and we can see the results, can't we?'

I thought about it. 'Can we?' She probably meant sexism and censorship and things like that.

'Don't you think it's at all important to help kids learn to express themselves and develop their identities?'

'Of course I do. I mean no, not really, and anyway I don't see how you teach that, and that's not what you go to school for. Any more than you join the police force to learn about community relations or whatever. You may pick up some of that on the side but the business of the police is to see to it that people obey the law.'

Nowell had been watching me in a furtive kind of way that somehow made it no more difficult for me or anybody else present to see that that was what she was doing. Other bits of her expression showed how she was slightly thunderstruck to see that her ex-husband was even more stupid or brutal or out of date than she remembered, or perhaps had been able to take in before. She took no interest in politics, but she had been to too many parties in Islington and Camden Town not to know that the idea of the police seeing to it that people obeyed the law, or doing anything really, was a very bad one. So she produced a hissing inwards whistle and gazed wide-eyed at Collings, who managed to convey that she too was shaken by my last remark before saying, 'Don't you find it rather revealing that you see fit to equate the educational process with the British police of the 1980s?'

'I don't myself. I can't see how I would, but I dare say you do. Except I didn't equate them, if the word means what I think it does. I was merely making a comparison on one point, not . . . '

I nattered on a little longer, but I had lost them again. Nowell did one of her controlled yawns, looked at her watch, bounced a hand over her hair-do. Collings pulled her chair back in to the table and put her cigarette part-way out in the saucer, getting it across that the enjoyable frivolous intermission was over and the serious work about to recommence. I wished Susan were there. She would have seen to it somehow that the story Collings went off with was a few kilometres nearer the truth. If that mattered.

So to Steve and sex. He emerged even to Collings as hopelessly normal, standard, average. She rather surprised me by apparently finding nothing macabre in his slight but visible shyness with girls, not so much as a castration complex. Anyway, she gamely wrote bits down. Nowell came up with a few more of her own-brand facts, but all they did was fill out the picture of Steve spending his early years with his mother in constant attendance and his father at the office, out getting drunk and never remembering his birthday.

At no particular juncture that I could spot, Collings said that that was enough for today, put the top on her pen and gathered up her papers. Nowell glanced over at me. For once in our lives, it seemed to me we were both thinking the same thing, that some kind of round-up so far or tentative communiqué would be welcome. I knew enough about Collings to be reasonably certain that it would never occur to her to wonder whether Nowell and I might perhaps be thinking along those lines, so I spoke up.

Sure enough, Collings was evidently thrown into some confusion by the idea, but she made a quick recovery. 'Well,' she said, 'on the understanding that we're still at a preliminary stage and this is only speculation . . . ' For the first time she was addressing Nowell and me more or less equally. 'What Steve needs,' she said slowly, sounding quite thoughtful, 'is to be accepted as he is, and not as other people might wish him to be. That's something that goes very deep in everybody, the need to be oneself. It takes precedence over almost all other drives. So . . . when it's frustrated, the effect can be devastating. Steve is suffering from years of being treated and responded to, reacted to, as if he were someone else, someone quite different, someone created by other people. What we're seeing now is his protest against that kind of treatment.'

By the end of that lot she had gone all the way back to talking entirely in my direction. 'Don't tell me,' I said, 'it's me, I'm the other people you're talking about, I'm the one who's to blame for the state he's in.'

'Please don't think that, Stanley,' said Collings, and Nowell put her head on one side and half-closed her eyes in a way that showed that she was against me thinking that as well.

'Why not, if it's true?'

'Thinking in terms of blame won't do any good. It won't help you to help Steve, which is what this is all about, after all.'

'I ought to have seen it coming, oughtn't I? All the time I was sending him to a private school and getting a tutor in and bothering him about his homework I was actually setting him up for . . . '

'You did it all for the best, darling,' said Nowell.

'Oh, super.'

'I can tell you very seriously and professionally, and without any qualification that you're not to blame,' said Collings. 'Instrumental, perhaps. That's rather a different thing.' After a moment's hesitation she went on, 'I must say it would be a pity if you let concern with your own moral position get in the way of more important things,' and Nowell looked at the floor because she was afraid she took the same view.

'I'm with you there,' I said, and meant it. The trouble was that just then I could see no way of putting the idea of blame out of my mind whatever anybody told me. Without thinking I said, 'Not everyone whose father puts pressure on him to pass exams ends up with schizophrenia.'

'Of course there are other factors. Oh and by the way, I thought I'd already made it clear that Dr Nash's diagnosis is quite mistaken, I'm sorry to say. If we must use these reductive terms, what Steve's suffering from is something we call a schizophreniform disorder, which may sound similar to you but I assure you is quite different.'

'Oh.'

Nowell did a little forward semi-circle with her head and said in a semi-whisper, 'Do you think I could possibly see him for a moment? Please?'

'Yes,' said Collings shortly. 'He's in Ebbinghaus House, which you'll see on your left as you make for the main entrance.'

'Aren't you coming, Dr Collings?' I asked.

'No, it's a rule of mine.' Again she hesitated. 'You may find some of his behaviour a bit unexpected. You know, unusual.'

'Un . . . usual?' repeated Nowell over a great surge of music on the inaudible soundtrack. 'And what exactly is that supposed to mean?'

For the first time a tiny rift could be seen in the idyllic relationship between those two. Collings said with her laid-on patience, 'Certain physical reactions that are often observed in cases of this kind but people in your position are unlikely to have come across. That's all.'

'What sort of physical reactions?' asked Nowell, taking a pace to one side to head Collings off if she tried to run out of the room.

'Eye movements, changes of expression and so on. Nothing gross.'

Nowell seemed satisfied with that. Collings indicated that she had gathered enough information to keep her happy for the time being. In the middle of doing so she threw me out completely by giving me a really powerful sexy look, one that almost qualified as a leer. At least that was what I took it to be, though given her skimpy control over her face it might almost equally well have stood for impersonal sympathy or moral disapproval. Not that that mattered much either.

A minute later Nowell and I emerged from Rorschach House, whose name was indeed over its door, into watery sunshine. I was again struck by how neat the whole scene was, too neat perhaps, obsessively so, the kind of loonies' garden this lot preferred to head-high grasses, holes dug in the ground and constant bonfires. Inmates strolled on the shaven lawns or walked up and down the weedless gravel paths. Well, I assumed they were inmates, but in these days of any old dress they could easily have been a convention's worth of forensic psychiatrists out for a breath of fresh air after a lecture. Somebody who looked straightforward was approaching, a tall thin woman with a froth of white hair, a tic, a frown and a mouth that moved vigorously, also, as I saw when she was nearer, a copy of the *Journal of Behavioural Psychology* under her arm, which I felt must have meant something, though I was not clear what. I was hungry and I was nearly sure I could have done with a drink, even at whatever time it was, not yet eleven.

'What an extraordinary woman,' said Nowell as we walked, referring I assumed to Collings. 'What did you think of her? Did you fancy her at all?'

'Good God no, and even if I did I wouldn't dream of laying a finger on a dodgy little bag like that.'

'You must be getting old, Stanley. You used not to be so particular. As regards dodginess, that is.'

There was a good deal I could have said on this subject, especially to Nowell, but I gave a peaceable grunt instead.

'I thought it was a bit thick, the way she went on about you being to blame for what's happened to poor little Steve. I hope you didn't take that too seriously.'

'Actually she went on rather a lot about me not being what you'd call *to blame*, didn't she?'

'Oh yes, but that was only what she said afterwards, you could tell she was really trying to blame you. I think that's really mean, it's bad enough to have your son have a breakdown without being told that it's your fault on top of it. Bloody disgusting.'

I moved my eyes to take in her face. Its thick-and-thin look was very much on view at the moment, plus a touch of generous indignation. There had been a time – I could remember it distinctly – when I would have at once asked her why, if that was her view of the matter, she had told Collings those lies about my having neglected Steve in his childhood, and would have been amazed when, instead of answering the question, she asked me why I had suddenly started being foul to her, what was the matter with me and the rest of the list. That certainly made me feel old.

'Well, whatever you may think of her,' she said, 'the bag fancies you.'

'Surely not.'

'Oh yes, darling, I'm never wrong about that kind of thing. So no wonder she gave you a bad time – hell hath no fury, no? Now I'm sorry, Stanley, but I'm afraid I've suddenly realized that after that grilling in that frightful room the thought of picking my way through a bunch of madmen to see Steve doing unusual physical reactions is just too much for me. I'm not like you, tough as old boots, I simply can't face it. Is that awful of me? I'd be afraid of upsetting him. I wonder, could you angelically give him my love and tell him I'll be over to see him in a day or two? And let me know how he is, yes?'

I said I would, and found myself going on to say, 'I should think probably one visitor at a time is as much as he can cope with at the moment.'

Nowell gave me a radiant smile, full of affection and gratitude, and kissed me warmly on the cheek. 'You are a nice man, Stanley,' she said, holding me at arm's length a moment and gazing at me. Then she was off with a spring in her step. I had been sweet to her when I could just as well – rather more easily, in fact – have been foul to her.

I remembered Cliff Wainwright saying once that women were like the Russians – if you did exactly what they wanted all the time you were being realistic and constructive and promoting the cause of peace, and if you ever stood up to them you were resorting to cold-war tactics and pursuing imperialistic designs and interfering in their internal affairs. And by the way of course peace was more peaceful, but if you went on promoting its cause long enough you ended up Finlandized at best. Calling this to mind now somehow helped me to see that Nowell's line on Steve's childhood came out of no sort of hostility, just self-protection, forestalment of the possible and well-founded charge that it was she who had done most of the neglecting. I had forgotten that her whole character was based on a gigantic sense of insecurity, not that remembering that had ever done me the slightest good.

Ebbinghaus House was more of a house than the other place, with two storeys and proper windows. Inside too it was laid out after a different mode. I went into a small ante-room with a linoed floor and a porter's cubby-hole behind a partition drawn far enough aside for me to see that there was nobody behind it. However, there was somebody in front of it, a young black man standing with his hands clasped together, I thought at first over his privates but actually, as a not very searching second glance showed me, just above them, for the time being at any rate. He was rolling his eyes, though not towards me, and opening and shutting his lips about every second. I decided quite quickly against asking him for directions. The partition and a board on an easel were covered with notices, but they all referred to places like bathrooms or the library or to amusements like chess and boxing. Boxing? Here?

I had just given the notices up when a middle-aged woman in some sort of overall and with a pleasant, capable look about her came bustling towards me out of a passage at the rear. I only got as far as drawing in breath to speak to her, because she shook her head at me and in a flash lay down on her back on the lino with her arms crossed over her chest, like a crusader on a tomb. So I stepped over her and left her and the black fellow to it.

The corridor here had a carpet running down it, one of a pattern my mother would have really liked, and a lot of rooms opening off it. Most of them in fact had their doors open to show quite nicely and brightly decorated insides, rather in the style of a mid-market boarding house in somewhere like Worthing or Hastings. Usually there were people sitting on the beds and chairs or standing, some chatting, some reading, some drinking from paper cups, but all the ones I noticed looked as though they were just filling in time and the rooms were parts of one large waiting room — half of them glanced up and away again as I passed. None seemed in any way mad. After going round a couple of right angles and through a kind of arcade of dispensers of soft drinks, hot drinks, peanuts and bubblegum I came to a doorway beyond which a female sat at a desk with papers and telephones on it.

She leaned over slightly in my direction. 'Can I help you?' she asked, meaning what the hell was I doing there and making me wonder whether she had nipped down here from behind the Rorschach House desk.

'My son is a patient here,' I said, and gave his name.

'Wanted to visit him, did you?'

'If possible. Dr Collings said I could.'

The girl, in her middle twenties with pale hair and a great many moles on her face, consulted a list at her side. 'Stephen Duke, was it?'

'That's it.'

'He's in one of the rooms upstairs.' This too seemed to mean something more or other than what it said.

'How do I get there?'

'By the stairs.' Before I was actually forced to ask another question she went on, 'Along on your left.'

I thanked her and she silently went back to whatever she had been doing before. The conversation had made me feel old again, also this time out of touch, high and dry, a survivor from a bygone era.

The stairs were indeed along on my left, a single steep flight ending at a closed door. Here a worryingly incompetent hand-lettered notice asked me to ring and wait. When I rang I heard a pair of feet running away from just inside the door to some remoter part. After about a minute, in other words a longish time, the door opened a few inches and stayed there while a high-pitched voice spoke in a very foreign language, angrily I thought. In the end the door opened properly and a male Asian stood there, Indian or Pakistani, small, middle-aged and without any expression at all. I explained my errand and whether or not he understood he let me in. I just had time to notice that this floor looked quite different from the one below, more like what I had seen of Rorschach House, when he showed me into a small room containing four beds. Three of them were empty and made up and the fourth had Steve in it.

Steve was apparently asleep. He was rather pale in a sort of transparent way. When I said his name his head made a sudden twisting movement and his eyes opened, though if he recognized me he gave no sign. He began to sit up while his head and neck went on jerking sharply backwards and to one side in a way that must have been most uncomfortable, if not painful. His eyes focused on me again for a few seconds, but then they rolled up and sideways in the same direction as his head, which soon followed, along with the shoulder on that side. I said his name again, louder, and he said something back, or perhaps just made a noise, a distressed noise. When he had been taken by another, more marked spasm I went back into the passage I hurried back into the passage and called for a doctor.

The Asian put his head out of the next room but one to Steve's. 'Yes?' he said, not sharply, not kindly or in a concerned way either.

'Would you come here, please? Something's wrong.'

He frowned and put his head back in for a moment before emerging and moving towards me carrying a millboard with papers clipped to it and followed by a Caucasian girl of about thirty in a uniform with something that looked like an officer's badges on the shoulders. When the three of us got to Steve his tongue was sticking out quite a long way. The Asian nodded his head as if satisfied.

'What's the matter with him?' I asked.

'He is suffering from schizophreniform disorder.'

'Yes, but does that cover these . . . whatever they're called . . . colossal twitches? Are they all part of the disorder?'

'They're normal.'

'*Normal?*'

'Normal for the patient at this stage.'

'Well, what's he doing in bed? Is that another part of the disorder?'

'He's in bed because he prefers. He spends a very great deal of his time there.'

'But he's much worse now than he was when he came in. He reacted to his name but I doubt if he knew me.'

'In some respects he may indeed be worse.' The Asian spoke with a touch of impatience. 'That too is not uncommon.'

'But what does he . . . Does he go on like this all the time? How does he get to sleep?'

'No no, it's intermittent. It may be brought on by some sudden change in environment, some unexpected thing. Some unwelcome thing.' He was staring at me.

'Like his father coming to see him?'

The fellow did a sort of shrug with his face and looked away.

'Oh my God,' I said.

'Now I'm going to try something.' The Asian took a pace towards Steve. 'Stop that! Stop what you're doing!'

Obediently Steve relaxed almost in the act of twitching and his tongue crept back between his teeth. He caught my eye briefly, then drifted away.

The Asian sniffed daintily. 'It's nothing so terrible. Mainly a matter of attention-seeking, you see.'

At my side, the nurse or more likely sister made a small sound or movement that might have meant she disagreed. She was dark and serious, not pretty but wholesome-looking. Also sympathetic in manner.

'Attention-seeking?' I said.

'Yes, er, my colleague Dr Collings and I agree between ourselves that that is the main thing that the patient is doing, namely seeking attention, though not necessarily in any planned, purposive way. As you yourself saw, the behaviour there is under his control. He can pull himself out of it if he so desires. To my mind, to *my* mind, that rules out the possible alternative explanation, that what we are witnessing is catatonic phenomenon. When he feels a little more relaxed and confident, when he realizes he's in good hands, then we shall see a very great change for the better. Oh yes.'

It struck me that this Asian, quite apart from being an Asian, looked tremendously unmedical, much more like a bloke in charge of loading stuff on to a ship or train, not necessarily in this country, what with his khaki-style shirt worn outside his matching trousers, the row of pens in his top pocket and of course the millboard. Steve, sunk back on his pillows, seemed completely apathetic, more than half asleep. From the sister I got the message that she was going on disagreeing with the doctor.

I said without thinking much, 'It's not his way, trying to make people notice him. He's always been one to keep himself to himself.'

There was a colossal click from somewhere, a roaring whisper and then a loud boxed-in voice that said, 'Dr Gandhi to B.1, please. Dr Gandhi, B.1. Thank you.' Then a silence that was a bit like being slapped lightly across the face.

I reckoned it was just what you might have expected when the doctor in front of me obviously took his message to refer to him and without hesitation, or anything else, left the room. The sister at once turned to me in a friendly confidential way.

'There's no need to be actually alarmed, Mr Duke.' Her voice sounded like nothing in particular, which was a relief. 'I couldn't have said this in front of Dr Gandhi, and perhaps I shouldn't be saying it to you now, but I've seen patients with those symptoms before, and attention-seeking may come into it, I don't know, but what they mostly are are side-effects of drugs. You see, he's had big doses of this powerful tranquillizer which have certainly tranquillized him all right, but they've also given him those involuntary movements you saw.'

'But don't the others, Dr Collings and Dr Gandhi, surely they know about anything like side-effects, don't they? Or are they using some new treatment or something?'

'No, it isn't that, they know about them. They just haven't recognized them in this case. I mentioned them to Dr Gandhi, you know, said that was what I thought they were, and he said Oh no, and went on about attention-seeking, well, you heard. The thing is, Dr Collings thinks it's that, and Dr Gandhi, he always tends to agree with her. It's not easy for him. She rather . . . I can't say any more but perhaps I don't need to.'

I thanked her and said, 'I've just come from Dr Collings, and she mentioned these reactions, but she didn't seem to think they were all that important.'

The sister looked back at me without replying. She had very clearly defined black eyebrows.

'But those twitches can be no fun at all,' I said.

She nodded. 'And they'd start to clear up in minutes if the drug was changed, not the treatment, just the drug.'

'There's a Dr Stone here, isn't there? Couldn't he . . . '

'He's tried before,' she said at once, 'in the past, I mean. There's a limit to what anyone can ever do. Just, doctors have their patients.'

'I suppose so. But surely if – '

Between being ordered to stop by Dr Gandhi and a moment ago, about when I mentioned his twitches, Steve had hardly moved. Now, having slowly sat half up, he made a clumsy turning movement so that his legs dangled over the edge of the bed, and the twitches began again. They seemed worse this time, more violent, perhaps because in his unstable position they threw him about more. The sister put her arm round his shoulders and told him to stop in a firm and strict but not unkind voice. I said he was all right and similar things, rather like the two ambulance men with the old loony outside Rorschach House about fourteen hours previously. It had no effect, but just when his eyes looked ready to roll up and back in that unpleasant way the tension left him in a couple of seconds, the twitching stopped and he let himself be eased back into a more restful position under the clothes. He had always been a docile sort of chap and still was, even now he was mad.

Soon afterwards the sister went away, having assured me that these attacks would do no lasting harm and that his medication was bound to be changed soon. I wanted to stay and talk to him, but that was obviously not a good idea if I had set him off on a round of spasms just by turning up – perhaps it had been the sound of my voice that had done it again a minute before – so I left. When I inquired, Dr Collings was not in her office. Would I like a call to be put out for her? No thank you, I said, and went back to the Apfelsine and drove to work.

I thought it best to keep out of Steve's way, for the time being anyhow. Phone-calls told me he was satisfactory, nothing more. After turning it over in my mind for twenty-four hours or so I rang Nash. He listened to only a small part of my story before suggesting I might go to see him at noon the following Tuesday. When I asked if I could bring my wife he said I could if I thought it would help, making the helping sound a fairly remote possibility. It would have taken a good deal more than that to get me to leave her behind, not that I expected anything remotely like a replay of the morning at St Kevin's, but you never knew.

Down Rosslyn Hill we rolled when the time came in a brisk downpour. With her ideas about Nash as a literary figure Susan had dressed in a bit of her best in a check suit and black-and-white shirt, but I had allowed for that and knew that she was perfectly serious about whatever might turn up. At the lights at England's Lane I said, 'Have I ever told you about Don Barley?'

'I don't think so. Who's he?'

'Oddly enough, I was just coming to that. Don Barley and his mother lived next door but two to us in SW16 during the war. There wasn't a Mr Barley, I've forgotten why. I suppose things might have turned out different if there had been. I can't really remember what he looked like either, Don. I was only about five at the time and he was seventeen. Anyway, one day

Don got a poisoned foot from cutting it on a tin or something. His mother
fetched the doctor along. He did the necessary and said he'd be back Friday.
He must have rubbed it in somehow that there was absolutely no need for
him to see Don before the Friday, Mrs Barley being a bit of a fusspot.
Well, Friday comes and the doc turns up, and he takes one look at Don
and rushes out for an ambulance, and gets him into hospital right away.
And he died there at nine o'clock that night – they hadn't got penicillin in
those days, you see. His mother had noticed he was poorly, but the doctor
had told her nothing needed doing till the Friday, and doctors (a) knew
what they were talking about and (b) you did what they said regardless.

'I can't really say I remember that happening, any of it. I doubt if I was
as much as five. But I remember very clearly my mother telling the story,
time and again and always in a very horrified way. It was a rotten thing
to happen all right, but she went on about it sort of more than that. It
wasn't that we knew the Barleys all that well. My mum certainly didn't
blame Mrs Barley or anything like that – she always said how awful it
must be to have to live with it for the rest of your life. What it was, I
think, I didn't see it at the time, actually I didn't see it in full until I started
telling you about it just now, what it was, she realized that if it had been
her and one of us she'd have done the same, or she easily might have done.
My dad would have had more sense, probably, but only probably, and
there again he could have been off on his travels. I'm pretty sure his
Midland trip used to take the inside of a week. Just right, in fact.

'So if you should think I spent rather a long time making up my mind
to get hold of Nash this last time, I don't say you do or you have or you
ever will, but if you ever do, or anything else like that, just remember I'm
a boy from SW16 whose parents were so much in awe of the doctor that
they might have let him die of blood-poisoning rather than do what the
doctor didn't order. I suppose I might have reacted against it, but I don't
think you do with that sort of thing. Anyway I haven't.'

Susan put her hand gently over mine on the wheel. 'How dreadful.' She
was nearly crying. 'Poor Mrs Barley. And I understand about your mother
too. But as far as I'm concerned you can forget the rest of it, the last part
of what you said. Remember I'm not like the others, Nowell and Trish
Collings and the rest of them. I don't think things like that about you.'
Now she was cheering up. 'With me you don't need excuses. I say, how
terrifically Jewish that sounds, doesn't it?'

'*By* me would be even better,' I said, squeezing her hand. 'There must
be an accident or a demonstration or something. They're not moving at all
up there.'

But in the end we were being let into 100 New Harley Street at only
two minutes past the hour. It was a big old place with eight doctors in it,
if as I assumed they were all doctors. Nash's part was at the back, looking
out on to a garden with a lot of trees in it now being rained on steadily.
The room reminded me of a men's club in St James's, the sort where they

keep out the under-seventies. Nash himself was got up in full professional gear, including a tie that was obviously the tie of something or other, no doubt for Susan's benefit, and the same could be said of his manner – bland, almost hearty. Not quite so obviously, but nearly, he found her a good deal better-looking than he had expected to, which I thought was a bit cheeky of him. Susan must have taken that in, though busy at the same time on the furniture, curtains, etc.

On Nash's suggestion I began again at the beginning of the main Rorschach House episode. He seemed to be paying close attention, not interrupting, now and then holding his breath for a moment and letting it out in a kind of voiceless groan, either as a comment on what I was telling him or because it was a thing he did while he was listening. Susan never took her eyes off me.

When I had reached the schizophreniform-disorder passage near the end of Part 1, Nash came to life and said, 'Thank you, Mr Duke, I think perhaps I've heard all I require to know of that conversation. But you mentioned an earlier encounter with, with Dr Collings in – am I quite mistaken or was it in a *pub*?' He shook his head slightly once at what things were coming to. 'Can you describe that occasion to me? Not in full, please, just the general drift, or anything that impressed you particularly.'

I tried to oblige. After a minute or two of highlights Nash gave a faint whimper with his mouth shut, like someone taking a nap and dreaming.

'Would you mind,' he said, 'could I ask you to repeat that, Mr Duke? Your son is trying to – what was it?'

'To find out who he is.'

'That of course is an approximation, your paraphrase of a partial recollection of what she said.'

'Word for word, I promise you. Only half a dozen of them, after all.'

'I find that very difficult to believe.'

'It stuck in my mind the moment she said it.'

'Which doesn't mean I can't believe it, I just find the effort rather extreme. Just as – if you told me that a foreigner, say a Frenchman, had said to you, with serious intent as far as you could make out, er, "You English, you are so cold," or a writer, a novelist, a practising one, had solemnly assured you that his object was to strip away the smooth surface of things and show the harsh reality underneath, well, I would quite likely be sceptical, would I not, properly too. Then I might well reflect that somebody, some real person, was bound to pronounce those words sooner or later and it was just a question of waiting long enough and being in the right place at the right time. I'm sure you take the point.'

With a touch more than simple even-handedness, Nash delivered the item about the novelist to Susan. He would naturally have heard from Cliff Wainwright what she did and was, but even so there was more than a touch more than up-your-street to the way he handled it. She chuckled very prettily and did one of those little sweeps of the eyes showing polite sexual approval. All of which was perfectly fine with me.

'There are a couple of further comments I might make at this stage,' he went on. 'Schizophreniform disorder. The Collings woman gave you to understand that it was a condition substantially different from schizophrenia itself. This is not the case. The difference is no more than legal. She clearly, even she clearly agreed with my diagnosis but couldn't face letting you see that. I could have wished to be spared the insult of her confirmation, in fact the danger-flag, the, the, the *tocsin* of it. M'm.

'Now as to the matter of your son's, er, need to be himself, not what . . . other . . . people . . . want . . . him to be, this as the cause of his illness. That's rather surprising in a way. Not fashionable any longer. Nowadays it's more the sort of stuff peddled by quacks and gurus and social workers rather than psychiatrists. But it has the advantage of leading directly to attaching blame for the patient's condition to his parents or parent. Now any decent parent, almost any parent whatever, is going to be upset, harrowed, thoroughly daunted by that accusation and will show it, will very likely protest, make an issue of it, claim good intentions and so on, which leaves the way open to the supplementary accusation that he's allowing his own self-esteem to take precedence over his child's welfare. Checkmate. Or rather, one more to their side.'

I said, 'I didn't think I'd mentioned that part.'

'No, I don't recall your having done so.'

'So how did you . . . '

Nash went into an elaborate dumb-show, sucking in his breath, dilating his eyes, shaking his head slowly from side to side and turning his hands palm upwards on his lap. Then he caught sight of Susan and went back to normal in a twinkling. 'Oh, I've come across that sort of,' – here he faltered slightly – 'person before.'

'But why would anybody play a game like that?' asked Susan indignantly.

'I don't know, Mrs Duke,' he said, having done the first half-second of the dumb-show over again. 'I've no idea. Why anybody should behave in that fashion.'

'There you are,' she said to me, meaning she had been broadly right about Collings.

After waiting politely for a moment or two, Nash said, 'Following your . . . interview with Dr Collings you say you were allowed to visit your son. Tell me about that if you would.'

I told him, a selective version only because I found I had got a bit tired of telling people things. He listened as before, nodding every so often in an as-I-thought way. Susan was as before too.

'This other doctor you saw,' he said firmly. 'Dr Gandhi? Was he, er, did he, er, an Asiatic I take it?'

'Yes.'

Nash sat on for a long time behind his desk without saying anything.

He might have been trying to make up his mind to say something he had on the tip of his tongue, or just as likely wondering what was on television that evening. If it was the first he never got there but woke up suddenly and said, 'I can't tell you that your son didn't resent your arrival at the place where he was, I can only tell you that his distressing behaviour wasn't caused by anything of that sort. As Dr . . . *Gandhi* must have known.'

'What?' I said, totally baffled. 'Why did he say it was, then?'

'Why? You'd been making a nuisance of yourself, hadn't you, asking questions and generally using up time he could have spent reading his sex manual. A brilliant method of getting you out of the way.'

'But a doctor doing a thing like that, even a – '

Nash interrupted me by sighing theatrically. 'I've noticed, Mr Duke, I've noticed before that you have an exaggerated respect for doctors. Before it's too late you must learn that doctors are no better at doctoring or about things to do with doctoring than . . . m'm, motor-mechanics are at what they do.'

'Oh no. You don't know what you're saying.'

'The point is clear. Now. One would have to see him to swear to it but I'm sure, h'm, that your son's discomfort was the result of large doses of one of a group of tranquillizing drugs. Not nice to see, no, but . . . no actual harm, the sister was right there, and of course he won't remember any of it when it's over. Anyway, don't worry, I'll get it changed. Yes, I'll just tell Dr Collings. After I've had a look at the boy, naturally.'

'But then she's bound to know I've been on to you, and I thought you weren't supposed to . . .'

'There's nothing to prevent me visiting my patient in hospital, and I also intend to follow up the matter of the tests I asked for, none of which have been carried out, perhaps needless to say, or at least I haven't been told of the results. And then you see I can suggest things to the doctor in charge of his case. And as regards medical etiquette, allow me to tell you, Mr Duke, I'm too old and rich and powerful and fed-up to be unduly swayed by that. You can go straight from here to the Collings woman and tell her I have told you I consider her to be a disgrace to her profession, which incidentally would be saying something, and I won't *turn a hair*. Not that you would of course.' He had got up as he spoke and stood now over his desk with his knuckles resting on its top, as though he expected to have his photograph taken. 'Would you care for a glass of sherry? Mrs Duke?'

'Well, yes, thank you very much, Dr Nash,' said Susan, sounding slightly astonished as well as pleased.

'Mr Duke?'

What Mr Duke would have cared for at this stage was a small tumbler of absolute alcohol, but he had the sense to see that it would not be available and said Yes to the sherry instead. This came out of a cut-glass decanter that came out of an expensive rosewood cabinet with an inlaid top. Some digestive biscuits came too, in a silver-bound barrel, but there

Nash must have been joking. Now the room seemed like a don's study in one of the snootier colleges at Oxford or Cambridge. There were certainly plenty of books. Most of them were across the room from me and the light was none too marvellous, but from the look of their jackets a lot of them were not on psychiatry. I saw Susan giving them a good going-over during the sherry production.

By the time we got to my turn what had been a consultation or something like that had started to turn into something else. Before it could finish doing so I said, 'If my son gets taken off the drug he's on, what sort of happens after that?'

'Of course. Oh, he goes on to another tranquillizing drug that doesn't have the effects you saw but works in the same general way, acting on the so-called neuro-transmitter system in the brain and in a great many cases, as I told you, bringing about positive improvement, it's not known how or why. But it does frequently happen.'

I tried to take this in. 'So Dr Collings is aiming in the right direction, so to speak, but so far she's missed the bull's-eye.'

Nash nodded, swallowing sherry. 'Broadly, yes. There's not a great deal of choice in the matter. Electro-convulsive treatment – not much help to us, except with patients so far gone in withdrawal that they're in danger of dying of hunger and thirst because they can't be bothered to eat or drink anything. Neurosurgery – obsolete. Psychotherapy, which is talking to the patient and getting him to talk – appallingly difficult, with the risk of encouraging him to elaborate and naturalize his fantasies. Troublesome, too. Group therapy – useless in my view, likely to be popular with Collings, no matter, harmless as well as useless. Anyway, drugs are easiest and most effective. There we are.'

'But she has all these terrible ideas,' I said.

'Has she? I mean I too think they're terrible, perhaps even more . . . passionately than you do, Mr Duke, but I wonder to what degree she can be said to have them, to hold them. They're to her taste all right, obviously, but then she must hold some ideas or views, or must seem to, to, to do so. It would be virtually impossible for a woman, an individual of that type to say to you, "Your son has schizophrenia, just as that old man said and as any qualified observer could have seen. I'm giving him a lot of drugs to try to make him better. And that's that." Wouldn't it? Be . . . So she told you your son was trying to find out who he is and a great deal more in the same strain.' He spread his hands in the air.

Susan gave me a cheerful look that said she and I had never thought of that. I wondered.

'There's also the point,' said Nash, 'that, assuming she takes a similar line when talking to your son, going on about his efforts to surmount the difficulties imposed on him by other people, all that, she'll be likely to acquire his confidence, which will tend to reduce his anxiety. However unfortunately in other respects, she is, well, on his side. A supportive approach, as the trade odiously calls it.'

Susan was showing more signs of relief. 'I see that, yes.'

I saw it too, and tried to feel relief, but mostly what I felt was a slight sense of being conned. I realized I had hoped, and almost expected, that after listening to my tale with mounting horror Nash would grab the phone or even go tearing out of the building as the first step towards getting Steve out of Collings's clutches and under the care of Dr Stone or some other angel of mercy. All right, not on, but I found it hard to swallow the idea of Collings as a well-meaning blunderer with a duff line in conjuror's patter. At the same time I was reflecting that here I was after twelve years' marriage to Nowell still assuming that unless people were actually lying they meant what they said.

'Is that all?' I asked Nash.

He gave me a sharp look. 'Nearly all of this section, Mr Duke. For the moment I've only one more question for you. Which of the following, if any, would you apply to your son's disposition? Cut off, dreamy, diffident, unintimate, unsociable, solitary, moody, touchy, uncommunicative?'

'Diffident,' I said. 'And a tendency to be dreamy.'

'None of the others?'

'No.'

'Not uncommunicative?'

'No.'

When appealed to, Susan agreed that that was fair. There was no sign that this registered with Nash, but he did come round again with the sherry, which she turned down and I accepted. When he had finished with that he half-sat, half-leant on the side of his desk. I thought he looked clever, grim and crafty, also upper-crust.

'The trouble with discussing schizophrenia,' he began – he was obviously just beginning, 'is that almost nothing is known about it after seventy years of study by some very intelligent men, and a great pack of blithering idiots too, of course. Some of what is known isn't very helpful, for instance you're more likely to develop it if you were born early in the year. North of the equator, that is. The helpful parts are elementary and mostly negative. Schizophrenia is an illness, one in which the brain becomes disordered. The cause has not yet been established, though there's quite a long list of things that don't cause it, like cell senility as I suppose they have to call it, and food allergy and any sort of virus, and anything to do with society. For a time it was thought to be tied up with unhappy families, until someone noticed that there were lots of unhappy families in which nobody had schizophrenia. Heredity comes into it, though it's not known where or how.

'As I told you, Mr Duke, the subject fascinates me, but not as anything but itself. It leads nowhere. All schizophrenia patients are mad, and none are sane. Their behaviour is incomprehensible. It tells us nothing about what they do in the rest of their lives, gives no insight into the human condition and has no lesson for sane people except how sane they are. There's nothing profound about it. Schizophrenics aren't clever or wise or witty – they may make some very odd remarks but that's because they're mad, and there's nothing to be got out of what they say. When they laugh at things the rest of us don't think are funny, like the death of a parent, they're not being penetrating and on other occasions they're not wryly amused at the simplicity and stupidity of the psychiatrist, however well justified that might be in many cases. They're laughing because they're mad, too mad to be able to tell what's funny any more. The rewards for being sane may not be very many but knowing what's funny is one of them. And that's an end of the matter.

'I consider you should know of these matters. Think of your son's illness like a physical illness of the dullest and most obvious kind, after which he may be restored to you undiminished, healed, healthy, or he may be more or less impaired, and the process may be a long one. Meanwhile I'll see to what has to be seen to.'

'Thank you, doctor,' I said, and stood up. At the same moment he looked at his watch and then at Susan.

'I was thinking, if you're not doing anything special for lunch,' he said, looking at me now, 'you might let me take you round the corner to my local, my local restaurant. It isn't awfully good but at least it's pretentious, with the added merit that at this sort of time of day you can just walk in. And from here you can walk to it as well. Two minutes away. It's stopped raining.'

Not for me, in line for a couple of stiff quick ones and a sandwich in Fleet Street followed by a slog in the office. I drew in my breath to explain some of this, caught Susan's eye and said, 'That's very kind of you, we'd love to.'

Nash was delighted. He went and helped her on with her mack as though nobody else knew how to handle a thing like that. She played up to him about the proper amount.

'I see you're an Anthony Burgess fan, Dr Nash.'

'Yes. I find him a very interesting writer.'

That was it. Susan said, 'I didn't notice a copy of *Don Juan and the Lunatics*.'

'Oh, that,' said Nash, pretending not at all strenuously to have nearly forgotten what I took to be the great work on madness in literature, its title now successfully researched. 'Out of print for many years.'

'I'm ashamed to say I've never read it. In fact I don't think I've ever set eyes on it. I suppose there isn't a copy I could borrow?'

'I may have a spare somewhere, I'll have a look. But, er, you mustn't expect too much, you know. I'm afraid you'd find some of the literary judgements ill considered. Where they're not painfully obvious.'

'Oh, I doubt it.' She seemed to think he was a tremendous old tease to say that, then immediately went serious. 'But after what you said just now about mad people being incomprehensible and madness not telling us anything about the human condition, which I thought was absolutely fascinating, well, I just wonder what's left, what you found to say in your book.'

'Internally, in itself, madness is an artistic desert. Nothing of any general interest can be said about it. Like sex. But the effects it has on the world outside it can be very interesting indeed. It has no other valid literary use. But that's by the way. My subject was just how well or, mostly, how badly writers have described madness. As a gardener or a cook might with their speciality. A medical doctor.'

'Mostly badly?' asked Susan in a companionable way.

'Yes. A fellow wants to put some madness into his novel because it's strange and frightening and quite popular. But if he bothers to go into the reality he finds it's largely unsuitable, an unsuitable topic for his purposes. So he gets hold of a pamphlet by some charlatan or crank propounding a suitably colourful fantasy and makes a character kill his wife because he's got an Oedipus complex, or find he's strangled a prostitute while under the impression he was a Victorian sex murderer. Which may be great fun but makes it hard to take the thing seriously. I mean you wouldn't have much confidence in Graham Greene if he tried to tell you Haiti was in the Mediterranean. Good morning.'

The last bit was said to a waiter, because here we were in the restaurant, which at this first sight looked quite modest to me, but then probably Nash was better at detecting pretentiousness than I was. I rather handed it to him for making no bones about enjoying the way the head waiter and the manager practically carried him to his seat at the best table in the place. He had put my mind at rest here and there, and I reckoned I bought his general approach, but I would have had a little more time for him if he had gone pounding off to see after a patient of his in some distress instead of going out to an elaborate lunch and flirting mildly with the patient's stepmother. Still, that part was very likely just me being mildly jealous. And I could see a large whisky coming straight at me.

'Hasn't anybody got it right?' asked Susan when we had ordered. 'Describing madness.'

'Shakespeare got it right. Lear, of course. Cerebral atherosclerosis, a senile organic disease of the brain. Quite common in old age. Periods of mania followed by amnesia. Rational episodes marked by great fear of what he might have done while manic and great dread of the onset or renewed onset of mania. That way madness lies – let me shun that – no more of that. Perhaps even more striking – Ophelia. A particular form of acute schizophrenia, very thoroughly set up – young girl of a timid, meek disposition, no mother, no sister, the brother she depends on not available, lover apparently gone mad, mad enough anyway to kill her father. Entirely characteristic that a girl with her sort of upbringing should go round spouting little giggling harmless obscenities when mad. In fact it's such a good description that this . . . subdivision of schizophrenia is known as the Ophelia Syndrome even to those many psychiatrists who have never seen or read the play. He was content just to describe it, you see. No theories or interpretations. Oh, she says and does plenty of things that mean a great deal to the other characters and to the audience, but she doesn't know what she's saying or doing or who anyone is, because she's mad.'

Our starters came then and I thought we might have heard the last of the topic, but not a bleeding bit of it. I had no great objection to Shakespeare as an author – it was just that I thought he was rather far back as something to talk about over lunch. Also I reckoned I had learnt enough about schizophrenia for one day. Anyhow, in less than a minute and without waiting to be asked Nash was off again.

'The play's full of interesting remarks about madness, among other things, yes. Polonius. A rather underrated fellow in my opinion. To define true madness, what is it but to be nothing else but mad? Not bad. Not bad at all. Not a complete definition, but an essential part, excluding north-north-west madness. Later in the same scene, you remember, he has a chat with Hamlet, the fishmonger conversation, and is made a fool of – the very model of a dialogue between stupid questioner and clever madman as seen by that, er, that, er, that unusual person R. D. Laing – you know, *The Divided Self* and all that.

'But actually Hamlet's only *pretending* to be mad, isn't he? No problem scoring off the other chap if that's what you're up to. Polonius gets half-way to the point. How pregnant sometimes his replies are, he says, a happiness that often madness hits on, which reason and sanity could not so prosperously be delivered of – a remarkably twentieth-century view. If he'd paused to think he might have found it just a bit suspect. But Hamlet in general very cleverly behaves in a way that lay people who've never seen a madman expect a madman to behave. Ophelia doesn't go mad till Act IV.'

The two of them went on having the time of their lives, working their way through Gothic novels and then Dickens, who either left mad people out altogether or was no good at them, though evidently terrific on neurosis. There was something about King Charles's head.

'Penangan High Commission, good afternoon.'

'Good afternoon,' I said, and went on to say who I was. 'May I speak to the Commercial Attaché?'

After a moment I heard the dying-away of a phone bell and after a longer moment a hollow voice that said, 'Yes, hallo, yes?'

I said who I was again, but there followed only a rumble that might or might not have been human, followed by more silence. 'Hallo?'

The man – I assumed it was a man – at the other end breathed out heavily a couple of times. 'What . . . do you want?' I could not help being impressed by the quantity of both fear and menace he managed to pack into those four simple words, with a bit of despair added on.

A certain amount of despair came over me as I sweated away at explaining what I wanted, talking about report, supplement, feature, advertisement, publicity in the hope of grazing the target with one of them. Eventually I just ran out.

Another rumble. Then, 'When were you speaking of this before?' I gave the exact date and had hardly got it out when he came back, 'No no, finish, all done, cancelled, cancelled.'

'Does that mean your Minister of Trade has – '

Dialling tone. I rang the High Commission switchboard again and established quite easily that, as I suspected, I had been talking not to my pal Mr One but to his rival or replacement, Mr Two. Mr One had presumably returned to Penang, then. Not yet, said someone on an extension, he was in consultation with Mr Two but was not available.

Cheers most awfully, I thought. Win some, lose some. Well, lose some, certainly. Not that it really mattered, but it would be nice to have something go right for a change. I hoped slightly that it had been panic rather than fury that had made Mr Two bang down the receiver on me.

It was quite late and I was quite tired. I had had another early morning over at St Kevin's, where Steve had turned out to be in more comfortable shape, true to Nash's report the previous day that he fancied he had put the hospital on the right track. Good, but all the same I had found him, Steve, no more responsive than last Thursday, not really. He lay on rather than in his bed and now and then sat up on the edge of it while I talked, but that was all. Already, not nine hours later, I had a pretty poor hold on what I had taken quite a long time telling him, rambling recollections of holidays, places where we had lived or stayed, bits of school, that type of thing interspersed with even less reliable stuff about how nice the hospital seemed and the great strides made in medical science since the war. At just three moments altogether I thought he looked at me properly and perhaps recognized me, but they were only moments. In the room when I arrived, and still there when I left, there had been a small prematurely white-haired man in his forties looking out of the window and making the sort of little grunting, moaning, wincing noises that might have come from a chap watching something like a fist fight in which a friend of his was rather getting the worst of it.

I had made no move to see Trish Collings during my visit, in fact on my way back to the car park I hurried past Rorschach House with my head down. Not much digging inside it was needed to show me that I was afraid that, if I had happened to run into her, she would tick me off for having complained about her to Nash, or for perhaps having done that, which of course was just as bad. Old Don Barley up to his tricks again.

After staring at the wall of my office for some few minutes I left the

building. Almost everyone not directly implicated in bringing the paper out
had done the same. Quite a few of them would have made their way, as
usual at this time, to the Crown and Sceptre. Apart from my own staff I
had never known more than a few of them, even by sight, and none was
visible now. I carried a large Scotch over to a stool so placed that I either
had to face the wall or turn completely round each time I put down or
picked up my drink. I solved that one by holding it on my lap.

The racket was colossal, not just a lot of people talking loud and fast
but with a kind of ferocity to it I had often doubted if you could find
outside Fleet Street. I would stick it while I downed this and another and
then go home and take a bottle in front of the telly. Susan was out, spending
the evening with her mother, though when she debriefed me earlier over
the phone she had said she would not be back late. Still, on the whole
things were well placed for Lindsey to make one of her unscheduled appearances. You could say too well placed. She had been on my mind quite a
bit over the past days – I had been very touched by her kindly concern
when I told her about Steve. Not only that, though. Anyway, it was not
she who pitched up at the bar just when I was thinking of leaving but
Harry Coote, my short, bearded editor. He looked at me for a moment in
the way he had, without smiling or raising his hand or anything, as though
he had found out from somewhere that it was quite funny not to smile or
anything at times when other people usually did. Then he came over.

'Got time for one?'

'Sure,' I said. 'Large Scotch and water. No ice.' It would normally have
been a gross breach of pub protocol to specify the quantity, but that
protocol included the clear provision that it was all right to do so when
there was a reasonable doubt whether a large one would come as a matter
of course. And in this case there was reasonable doubt. But one way or
another it was indeed a double that Harry rather grandly delivered to me
before taking up a standing position next to my stool. He was short enough
for his head not to be so very much further off the ground than mine.

'How are things?' he asked, quite audibly because the uproar seemed to
have fallen off a bit.

'Fine.' I could very easily have told him about Mr Two, true, but I kept
quiet.

'I suppose you haven't seen anything of old Nowell recently?'

This was routine, Harry playing himself in with me, or it always had
been in the past. If it turned out to be different this time, if he started being
wise or quietly sympathetic or anything else about Steve, I was off. I said,
'Yes, as a matter of fact I ran into her just last week. Had a nice chat with
her.'

'Did you, now? Oh.' No, he had heard nothing. 'Tell me, how was she?
How was she looking?'

'Great. She's unchanged, you know. Absolutely amazing.'

'Oh dear,' said Harry, shaking his head, his eyes gone glassy with wonder.

'Makes you think, doesn't it? She's all woman is Nowell, if you know what I mean.'

'I think so,' I said. I said to myself that if I hung on long enough he would tell me he had always thought it was a shame Nowell and I had not managed to make a go of things, but as it was he told me almost straight away and almost in those exact words.

After that he made a great business of lighting one of those rugged cheroots of his, peering at me every few seconds and generally behaving as though he had in mind some tremendously important project or request or revelation which he considered the time was not quite ripe for. This could still have been routine, though by no means a bit you took no note of. He asked after Susan in an intent sort of way, and seemed relieved at the news that she was very well, but I doubted whether hearing so was his whole objective. There was another of the same when he asked for and got my views on the Government's financial policies. After he had given me his I went and bought him a drink, a predictable vodka and tonic. It occurred to me that having a round of Harry's to return was indeed a rare experience.

At my return he intensified his weighty look, then switched off and said casually, 'Going to the Boxes'?'

'Eh? What sort of boxes?'

'Julian and Paula Box.' He seemed astonished when I shook my head in ignorance. 'I could have sworn I'd seen you there. They're on a barge. On the river.'

'Oh, yeah.'

'Why don't you come along? Drinks party. Completely informal. They're a very free and easy couple. Paula doesn't give a toss.' The noise had got up again and I missed the next bit, so he had another shot. 'I thought we could, er, I thought we could have a chat on the way, like.'

After weighing things up I said, 'All right. Where are we off to?'

'Got the car, have you? Oh it's,' he hesitated, 'it's out by Chelsea.'

'Chelsea? Not artists, these mates of yours, are they, or writers?'

'No, no,' he said reassuringly, 'they'll all be in accountancy and insurance and suchlike. No trouble. You'll enjoy yourself, Stanley. You see.'

Outside it was blowing half a gale but hardly raining at all, and there was lots of daylight left. All went well for a time, just one hold-up on the way down to the Embankment and no trouble after that. We slid along the river at a rate that left to itself would have got us to Chelsea in about five minutes, so I held back to give Harry a chance to finish talking about the World Cup and start recruiting me into MI6 or whatever it was he had in store for me. He was cutting it pretty fine, I decided, when we reached the corner of Tite Street and he had still not done with the referee problem.

'Where to now?'

'Well, I'm afraid I'm not much of a navigator, Stanley. Comes of not running a car, you know. The best plan is for you to make for Putney Bridge and we'll think about it there.'

You bleeder, I thought wearily. So much for Harry's famous lack of subtlety. Not that subtlety of a very high order had been needed to con Muggins into saving him the taxi fare to Walton-on-Thames or Reading or Oxford or wherever this perishing barge was going to turn out to be and back, not forgetting the time and difficulty that finding transport at the far end would have cost him in the ordinary way, all for the price of a large Scotch and a slice of somebody else's hospitality. But no getting away from it, I had wanted to come on my own account. It was years since I had gone to a party with any intention of picking up a girl, and a Harry-generation get-together was unlikely to feature many or any girls, just females, and I was someone's husband, but you simply never knew.

We came to Putney Bridge and thought about it, or Harry thought about it, and then we crossed over and went along the A205 until it became the A305, and not much later he made me stop while he thought about it again. After another couple of goes of this and only one wrong turning we reached a yard where a number of other cars were parked and drove in there.

The rain had finally packed up, the wind had risen a little if anything, the sun was shining low down through a hole in a great mass of black cloud and producing the rather unpleasant effect usual at such times. When we started walking there was no sign of the river, but it came into view at the first bend down a long alley. None of the buildings here had probably been touched since the beginning of the century, by human hands at least, though they had certainly got a great deal dirtier, slimier, damper, more battered and no doubt smellier in the meantime. Huge piles of rubbish smeared with oil, tar and soot, from postcard-sized pieces of creased paper to what could have been ship's boilers, went back about as far. I was expecting a trudge through half a mile of mud at least, but when we made it to the waterside there was gravel and then a paved strip, and a long college-type structure on the far bank really looked pretty good after all with the sun on it.

Four barges were moored in line in front of us, moving about quite a bit, it seemed to me, also faster than I would have expected, never mind preferred. Ours was evidently the second along. Harry moved ahead of me across a rope-and-board gangway, which turned out to be all right but not the sort of thing to make sure of not missing. I reached the deck successfully and found two lots of noise going on, a remarkably loud and varied mixture of creakings and groanings from parts of the structure and, further off, the gabble of a party into its second half-hour, loud enough for anybody but without the Fleet Street snarl. Following Harry I ducked through an opening, crossed a narrow platform and, still not too comfortably, went down a short steepish flight of stairs into what, but for the lack of windows, looked very much like the sitting room of a rather well-off house in North London. Clearly the Boxes were living here on purpose, so to speak, and had had the sense to rip out or plaster over every possible trace of what had been there before.

When produced by Harry, the Boxes turned out to be a bit of a mixed bag. He seemed perfectly sound, the kind of fellow who, one minute flat after the last guest had gone, would be in an armchair in front of the large TV set in the far corner, in fact by the look of him I thought he could have done with being there now. She let you know she was the one behind the party, as if you had been in any doubt, and behind a lot else as well, like them being on the barge in the first place. I was given a full and satisfactory explanation of that part and what it entailed.

'I suppose it's not often as rough as this?' I asked after a time. The movement had not eased at all since I came on board, indeed just as I spoke an old boy near by staggered and clutched at the woman next to him, burning his hand on her cigarette, but then he was drinking.

'No no no no,' said Mrs Box, frowning and shaking her head, 'it's only the turn of the tide. Either that or the wind blowing against the tide. Happens quite regularly.'

'Oh, well that's all right then.'

At that she screamed, or rather at that point she made the female sound meaning someone more interesting had appeared, and was away past me without a word or a look. I wondered whether this was her not giving a toss. I also wondered whether the general clearance as regards artistry and writing that Harry had given could be applied to her. She had the look of wondering whether to agree with some of the things you said, and not listening at all to others, that I had noticed in some of Susan's mates.

While I was wondering I took two glasses of Scotch and water off the white-coated waiter and made a drink out of them that was somewhere near what I would have poured myself at home. It lasted me while I made a thorough circuit of the scene that did me no good beyond what I got out of taking a pee in the very nice little toilet I found near what could have been the blunt end. The snag was not exactly that all the women were females, more that they all seemed to be wives or daughters, bar an aunt or so. And establishing the absence of anything pursuable or worth pursuing meant the party was a write-off, did it? Of course not, I could try and get a conversation going. Yes, about cars, golf, advertising, whisky or the price of onions. Oh, and women. Good God. Sometimes I wondered how Susan put up with me.

That last section saw me halfway into another jar. It would be easier if I found someone I knew, even Harry. Had he gone? No, there he was talking to a tall fat man who had his back to me but looked somehow familiar. When I got round to his front I found it was Bert Hutchinson. Yes, Harry and he shared a pub.

'Hallo, Stanley,' he said, and added 'Christ' when the floor dipped slightly more than usual and sent him lurching to one side. Again, the drink could have been helping, but he looked comparatively sober, more so than when

I had last seen him, at least. 'You know, people can only take so much of this. If it goes on they'll be throwing up all over the bloody shop. Well, how have you been?'

'Not too bad.' I was going to move on as soon as I decently could, very soon, in fact. 'I haven't seen Nowell anywhere.'

'She's not here.' He spoke flatly.

'Stanley kindly drove me down,' said Harry.

Bert stared at me through his bluish glasses. 'What have you got?'

'Apfelsine. FK 3.'

'Oh, you have, have you? They're very quick, I'm told. What we used to call a quick motor. Dear oh dear.'

'Hey,' I said, remembering, 'haven't you got one of the first Jaguars? I saw it outside your place that time.'

'Yes. I have it, I own it, I possess it, and I derive from that fact such satisfaction as I am able. And that is all there is to be said.'

'How do you mean?'

'How do I mean? How – I beg your pardon, Harry. This is very boring for you. As a non-driver. Lucky man. Who doesn't know what he's missing. Unlike those who once upon a time . . . I'm sorry, I mustn't go on.'

'No really, Bert,' said Harry, who I thought looked a little bit tousled. 'Do carry on. It'll interest Stanley.'

Bert made a great growling noise and then stayed quiet for so long, looking towards his feet, that I started thinking he had forgotten all about whatever he had been going to say. With his head tipped forward like that he gave me a first-rate opportunity to inspect his scalp and the condition of the strip of hair he wore stuck down across it. I reckoned it, the strip, had become both narrower and less dense or luxuriant as the growth area above his left ear declined, but I would have had trouble remembering when I had last seen it close to. Finally he spoke.

'I suppose in a way I shouldn't complain,' he said wisely and like someone completely above the struggle. 'My generation received a wonderful gift – well, earlier generations had had it too, but in a less fully developed form. And the name of the gift was – motoring. For a few brief years after the second war and before the advent of the motorway and all the, all the *vile* things it brought with it,' he went on, in some danger now of losing his calm, 'it was possible to take an evolved automobile on to the roads of Great Britain and . . . drive, by what way and in what way, er, you could do as you liked. No longer so. No longer so. I *have* my Jaguar, I *own* my Jagular, fuck, Jaguar, but I don't drive it. No sir. Not a chance. It's all over. Thing of the past. Ancient history. Now Stanley, you tell me, am I, has the, is that complete balls? Or what? You be the judge.'

'No, no, Bert, you're absolutely right,' I said. Well, I did think he had a point of a sort. 'All too sadly true.' Admittedly I could have done without the king-in-exile approach. 'Never again.' But it would have been unkind and perhaps dangerous to disagree with him. 'Absolutely right.'

He sent me a look that was not so much kingly as saintly, as though after that affirmation of mine he could face the lions with a quiet heart. Then his glance shifted and he nodded his head emphatically. 'I knew it. There goes one now. Told you, didn't I?'

I turned round in time to see an elderly man who looked like a retired ambassador, hand over mouth, making for the corridor that led to the toilet at an unsteady run that included a glancing collision or two with other guests. This caused comment.

'It could be just the drink,' said Harry, who for the last couple of minutes had been looking from Bert to me and back again in amazement at all this emotion he had had no suspicion of. He looked as if he thought he had missed something important in life.

Bert shook his head just as emphatically. 'Oh no. A fellow that age, he wouldn't be taken suddenly like that, the way a youngster might. No, that was motion sickness and no mistake. Look,' he said in some excitement as a similar chap, white-faced and staring-eyed, stumbled over to the foot of the stairs, 'there's another one. No doubt about it. Not that I'm feeling any too clever myself, let it be said. Ah, bloody good.'

This was addressed to the waiter who had just approached, or more likely was just a reflex reaction to the tray of drinks he was carrying. There were quite a few glasses of Scotch on it, but even so I would not have dared to repeat my tactics under these conditions if Bert had not poured one into another on the tray itself. I did the same. Harry took a white wine rather slowly.

'How did you get here?' I asked Bert.

'Taxi.' He pointed his head at my drink. 'Aren't you afraid of being picked up?'

'They'll get me in the end, I expect. But probably not in the middle of the evening, like eight o'clock, which is when I intend to be on my way. If that's all right with you, Harry.'

'Super,' said Harry unenthusiastically. He had put his wine down untasted and there was sweat on his forehead and under his eyes. 'Think I'll . . . have a pee.'

'You do that,' said Bert, and went on almost before it was safe, 'Right, let's bugger off.'

'I can't leave him, Bert. I brought him here.'

'You bet you did. But what of it? It may be a bit off the beaten track here but it isn't the middle of the bloody Sahara exactly. Three minutes' walk and he can get a taxi. Do the little bastard good. To put his hand in his own pocket for a change.'

'I thought you and he were supposed to be drinking mates.'

'*Christ*,' said Bert, but because the floor had misbehaved again. 'It's getting worse, it's like the Bay of bloody Biscay. I'm not going to be able to stand it much longer. What did you say?'

'He told me he sometimes saw you in some pub in Notting Hill.'

'Unfortunately he does. I grin and bear it. I'm not going to let a little sod like that drive me out of my pub, am I?'

'You were talking to him when I came over.'

'He was talking to me. He thinks he's a buddy of mine. And I don't seem to know anyone else here, except you.'

'Who invited you?'

'I can't remember. It wasn't Harry. Look, what the bloody hell is this, a bloody inquisition? You're like a bloody chick, you are. Actually it is quite interesting. I found I had this very neatly drawn map and all the details written out, you see, so of course I assumed it was them, the Boxes or whatever they're called, and I'd forgotten who they were. Then when I got here I not only didn't recognize them, but they didn't recognize me. Took some getting round, that. The missis turned quite stroppy. I had to tell her I was in TV to quieten her down. A right one, she is. Well, is that enough for you?'

'Quite enough, thanks,' I said. 'I'm going up top. I've got to get some air or I'll die.'

'I'll join you. I'll just get a freshener first.'

Closely following an elderly woman with an enormous backside under some ribbed grey material, I climbed to the deck. It was not quite dark, with hundreds of lights showing on both banks and a few more round me and on the other barges. Out here on the water it seemed very quiet, or it might have done but for the long hallooing retches that came from somebody up at the far end. Half a dozen other figures leant or slumped at various points. I found a secluded spot and had soon taken in all the air I could handle. Having done so I felt just slightly worse. The back of my neck prickled and my mouth kept filling with saliva. There were only three things I could do – leave, lie down or be sick. The first was the one to go for, but I would have to try at least to find Harry first.

Outside the opening that led to the stairway I came across a man of about fifty kicking the corded step below it and biffing at the sides with the heels of his hands. He had obviously given the business some thought. 'I think it's going to rain again,' I said as I approached.

He looked round and nodded cheerfully while going on bashing away and incidentally blocking my path. 'I shouldn't wonder if you weren't right, lad,' he said in an unreconstructed Northern accent. He had a broad pink face and sandy eyebrows and wore a towelling jacket with military pockets and drill trousers. 'Just working off my feelings, like,' he went on, then evidently made up his mind that I deserved some further explanation, because he stopped what he was doing and turned towards me, panting slightly. He was rather drunker than I had thought at first.

'The wife's been being a little bit provoking,' he said in a half-whisper, smiling and screwing up his nose. 'You know, feminine. Now whenever that happens I don't say a word, I come straight outside wherever I may be and I do what I just been doing for two minutes, and then I go back in full of the joy of spring. When I got married I told myself I could be happy or I could be right, and I've been happy now for twenty-two years. Ee, sorry, lad, here I go gassing away and holding you up.' He stood aside, looking at his watch. 'Another . . . forty seconds should see it through.'

I had been away no more than ten minutes, probably less, but the scene down below had changed quite a lot in the time. I thought to begin with that everybody was being sick, then I saw that only quite a small number were or had been, but they were naturally getting all the attention. One fellow had – I turned my eyes away. A woman was – no. Even now there was no general move towards the stairs. The bleeding idiots had stood their ground hoping the whole thing would pass off until it was too late to move a step. If I had been Julian Box I would have been very angry with them, but if he was he was getting no chance to show it, because his wife was giving him a going-over for not stopping them or not holding the boat steady or something like that.

Harry was nowhere to be seen, not in the main room anyway. Literally gritting my teeth and trying to think of rose-gardens I tried the revolting areas round the toilets and shouted his name through the door of each one with no result. In the first bedroom a man was lying with his grizzled head hanging over the edge. The second bedroom was empty – no, there was a pair of legs sticking out from the far side of the bed. They were Harry's. He had helpfully squeezed his head in under to be sick there. Somehow I got him moving. I tried not to look at his beard. When we were nearly at the stairs Bert came up.

'Can you give me a lift, Stan?'

'All right. Lend a hand here.'

There was a hold-up at the gangway, and when he got ashore Harry failed to perk up at once in the usual way of seasick people on landing. He stayed propped up against the Apfelsine while Bert and I moved aside for a pee. The three of us climbed aboard. Bert insisted on going in the back, which called for a semi-climb over the tipped passenger seat, no doddle for a bloke his size even cold sober, Harry got in beside me unaided though unsteady, and we were off.

Bert swore now and then. Harry said once or twice he was feeling better. I kept quiet until I spotted a vacant taxi halted at a traffic-light on our left.

'Get him,' I said to Harry, pulling up and pointing. 'Bert wants a taxi. Quick about it.'

He only just made it but he made it, and came back almost simpering. 'Okay.'

I said, 'I'm afraid it's not okay here, Harry. He's passed out, I can't shift him. Not a hope. Look, *you* take that taxi, go on. I'll see to him, don't worry.'

'But you can easily – '

'No, it's all right, I'll deal with him. Off you go now, I'll manage.'

There was nothing he could do, especially when I put the window up. The wheels started to turn.

'He's taking it,' said Bert's voice behind me. 'Not much choice, really. Five quid up his shirt from here. That was brilliant, Stan. Real touch of class.'

'It was your idea.'

'I'm talking about the execution. Fantastic. Bloody noble, you were. Anything for a pal.' When he was settled in the passenger seat he gestured towards the instrument panel and said, 'Don't let's do this now. Motors another time, right? Hey, I bet you thought that bugger was seasick, didn't you? Well, he may have been but he'd drunk too much too.'

'Do what? In that minute? We weren't there more than – '

'That's the point. When you go hurling it down it only takes half what it does spread out. When I started talking to him, not so long before you turned up, he was working his way through a bloody trayload of gin and tonics. Just started on the last one as you came along. *And* the rate he was going there'd been other trays before. It was free, you see. Like what, red rag to a bull? One of those. In the boozer we tell him when it's his shout. It's a joke, except we don't think so, and he doesn't think so. How do you stand him?'

'I haven't got to stand him,' I said. 'Good editor, though. Gets the readers.'

'Oh shit,' said Bert in disgust, then shut up for a bit, then suddenly said, 'Five past eight. Fixed up for dinner, are you?'

'No.'

'There's a place I go to sometimes in Soho. Little Italian joint. That sound all right to you?'

'Fine. But aren't you rather pissed, Bert?'

'Not by my standards, old son. Anyway, they know me there.'

They certainly seemed to from the reception they gave him, which reminded me of Nash's at his place, only this one was of course a class or two down the social scale. What was similar was the way Bert basked in it. Pissed or not, he soon saw me noticing.

'Friendly bunch, eh? I come here quite a lot, actually. In fact I'm quite famous here. I'm not famous in any famous places but I am here.' He drained his wineglass and filled it again. 'Because of the people I'm usually with. I do a lot of TV commercials. More interesting work than you might think. Reasonably well paid, too.'

'So I gather,' I said. This explained several things, including the general impression he gave of prosperity and non-failure. I realized I had known almost nothing about him except that he got drunk and had a first Jaguar.

'You might even have seen the odd one. Er, Prosit lager?'

'What, those two fellows in the helicopter? Marvellous. You did that?'

He looked modestly into his minestrone, which he was coping with rather better than I had expected. 'That's me, yeah. That's one of mine. I do all those. So I'm quite famous in that line, you see, in the business, but you don't get known to the general public there. I don't mind that myself, as I say the money's good, but . . . And then . . . If . . . ' He put his spoon down. 'Stanley, I've got to talk about her. Say I can. Say it's all right. Please.'

'I've seen it coming for hours, mate. Go ahead and enjoy yourself.'

'Because you're the only man on earth who'll understand.'

'I wouldn't be too sure of that, but I see what you mean. Anyway.'

'Yeah anyway, but where had I got to?'

'Wait a minute. Oh yes, you don't mind not being famous everywhere, but presumably she does.'

'Yeah, she does. She wouldn't like me being famous everywhere either, but she'd get something out of that, or she thinks she would, or you can't prove she wouldn't, any more than you can prove anything else about her. She reckons if I was a famous director of feature films she'd meet a lot of other famous directors and get parts in their films and that would be some compensation for being married to the likes of fucking me. I said once directors would be much more likely to give her parts if they hadn't met her.'

'You said that? Out loud? To her?'

'I told her. I was cross with her about something. I didn't get the chance of telling her anything else for a couple of weeks after that, but she turned up. It was partly she likes to spend a lot, you see. Christ, you know. She got it wrong about the career, didn't she, but the cash held up all right.'

'You mean she married you to get parts in films?'

'That's right. Like she married you because you were earning a lot for your age. Sorry, Stan. Sounds crude, doesn't it? I suppose it would if I meant she'd planned it and really knew what she was doing. But it's only men who plan things like that. You could fill her with what's that truth drug stuff, that's right, scopolamine, you could dose her up to the gills with fucking scopolamine and she'd still deny it. Another thing she knows without knowing she knows is that she's a not very good actress who isn't very beautiful and she'll be forty-six by the end of the year, so where's she going to go? She's much too neurotic to set up on her own. No, I'm stuck with her. By Christ, you're a long time alive, Stanley.'

'Why don't you get out yourself?'

'You must be joking. Get out? I couldn't face it, not again, not now. I did it before, perhaps nobody told you but I had to get unmarried too, and it bloody near killed me then. And soon enough I'm going to be fifty-three. But there's a snag attached to what you might call the zero option, which now I come to think of it is a bloody marvellous name.' He laughed, then sighed. 'What? Snag, there's a snag. And I don't mind telling you what it is. It's not much fun . . . living with somebody . . . you don't like much.'

Over a rather good scaloppina of veal and interrupting himself with swigs of Valpolicella Bert told me some of his grounds for not liking his wife much. All of it, or nearly all of it, was familiar territory. Not that that made it any less interesting – on the contrary, it was wonderful to recognize variably sized almost-forgotten offences against common sense, good manners, fair play, truth, all those, with just the names and circumstances changed.

One short section was new. Bert described, believably enough, the way she hated you to be there, within range, in the room when she did some footling manual task like safety-pinning something to something else or tearing a stamp off a sheet and sticking it on an envelope. You were watching her, she said, waiting for her to be slow or clumsy or to get it wrong. Needless to say you were doing nothing of the kind, you had not got as far as taking in what she was up to, but as always you might have been watching and waiting, you could have been, there was no way of proving you were not. It gave me a ridiculous pang to think that I had never noticed her doing that, not as one more tiny absurd awful thing about her but just as a thing about her. I had thought I knew her better than anybody else ever could.

When Bert called for coffee, grappa and cigars it became clear to me, in so far as anything now could, that he was one of that number who could go on when most others had fallen by the wayside, in other words got drunk but had the power of drinking more, perhaps much more, without collapsing, at least for the moment. Also without losing hold of the conversation. He had repeated or partly repeated a couple of his stories, but he was still better than some people I knew cold sober. At the time I had reckoned that his funeral address on motoring could only have come from somebody well on with his last half-hour before blacking out. Not so, evidently. When the grappa arrived he went halfway back to that style for a moment, holding up his glass and staring at it like an actor.

'The great refuge,' he said as though he had just thought of it himself. 'The great comfort. And the great protection.'

'I'll drink to that.'

He scowled at me. 'It's a protection in a way that probably hasn't occurred to you, sonny, as well as the obvious. Now. She thinks I'm pissed all the time, right? You probably think the same, why shouldn't you? But I'm not. Obviously. A piss-artist couldn't do my job. Of course I am *sometimes* pissed, like now, like tonight, partly though not wholly in consequence of a little discussion of a carved walnut armchair, probably early Georgian. Hence also my presence on that fucking barge. But mainly, usually, normally not.'

'You were pretty far gone that afternoon I came to your place, remember?'

'Oh, bloody good,' he said, laughing. 'I take that as a real tribute. By the way I'm sorry I bad-mouthed you over the phone and so on. My line on you with her is that you're a shit, you see. There's no such thing as a safe line on anything with her, as you may have noticed, but I just thought that would be the least unsafe.'

'You mean you weren't pissed at all that time?'

'What? Oh, no no. Couple of beers at lunchtime. I was hamming it up.'

'You hammed it up like mad when I arrived and she wasn't even in sight.'

'Ah, but that's the rule. The rule is, I've got to have a rule, I'm always pissed there, if not for real then I act it. Too confusing otherwise, too bloody risky too. I work from an office just across the road from here. That's good because she thinks I'm getting arseholes drunk round the clubs. I don't know where she thinks all the money comes from. But that's not interesting, is it? Not so long as it keeps coming.'

'What's the point?'

'Of acting pissed? I'll tell you,' he said in a much quieter voice. 'When you're young, you're ready to fuck anything on two legs. That's almost enough on its own. But as time goes by, you get choosy. You know, if they chat to you about Harold Pinter while you're on the job or they throw their food about and swear at the waiters or you find out they used to work for the Gestapo or the KGB or one of those, well, you notice, it puts you off a bit. And by the time you're fifty, Stan, you're even more demanding. You expect them to be a bit pleasant occasionally, *right*? To listen now and then, *m'm*? To be good company, *eh*? A lot of unreasonable things like that.'

He had not said the last bit very quietly, and he had started to slur his words too. When he went on he kept the volume down but he still talked in a mumbling kind of way. 'If you don't like 'em, you don't want to fuck 'em. And who could like her after they got to know her, after they'd seen her in action? The milkman worships her, but he's new and he hasn't not brought the bloody cream yet. The accountant, well, he's not new, I suppose, just an idiot. She's a . . . she's a fucky *nuck* case, that's what she is. Ought to be put away. For her own protection.'

'Well then, there we are. If you don't want to fuck your wife you have the option of telling her it's because she's such a horrible bloody creature, which actually I wouldn't dare to do, I'd be too afraid of a knife in my guts. Seriously. She could justify anything she did. Unendurable provocation. How do we know it was unendurable? Use your eyes, she couldn't endure it, could she?'

I watched him while he struggled to get his mind round his next, clinching point, ready to help out if needed, but he made it on his own. '*Or*,' he said triumphantly, '*Or* you can be pissed all the time so the matter doesn't arise, ha ha ha. By well-established convention. And for real too, I should imagine. Variation by Hutchinson – be pissed some of the time and act pissed the rest of the time. I must be pretty bloody good at the latter by now because she's never noticed the difference. As far as I can remember, that is.'

'Things must have been all right at the beginning,' I said. 'When you first went round with her.'

'Till we'd been married a couple of years. By which time she'd finally got the message that I didn't really like parties full of TV and film people. She couldn't believe it at first.'

'Was that when you stopped wearing suede shirts?'

'Eh? Sorry, Stanley, I don't get you.'

'Never mind.'

'I heard about your boy. I'd offer to help but ... but no.' He gave another sigh, one that went into a huge single hiccup. 'If you're going to drive me home, Stan, and my honest guess is you've more or less got to, you'd better do it before I pass out.'

I tried to, but he was too quick for me. Much too heavy, too. It was a judgement on me for the Harry stunt, on Bert as well perhaps. I hauled at his arm for a time, then gave up and went and rang the front-door bell, which clunked as before. Nowell answered it quite soon, wearing a dress which looked to me as though it was made out of a well-known brand of dietary biscuit. I realized I was very drunk myself, nowhere near fit to be in charge of a motor vehicle on any grounds bar necessity.

'Stanley!' she said, all welcoming smiles. 'How nice to see you. Come and have a drink. Bert's gone to a – '

'I've got him in the car,' I said.

Before I could think of a winning way to describe the problem she turned round and went back across the hall. She had started to catch on as soon as I spoke, without showing a wink of surprise or even curiosity about how her husband came to be out with a fellow he always said was a shit. After half a minute or so she reappeared carrying a fat bunch of cushions under one arm and a roll of some thickish material under the other. She seemed definitely shorter than before, and when she passed me on the step I saw she was wearing bedroom slippers, little green affairs with turned-up toes. Her manner had a sort of professional steadiness about it. I followed her into the street with my brain not working too well. The wind was still blowing pointlessly away.

'Where are you?'

'Along here.'

I was parked a dozen yards off, near side to the pavement. She opened the door as wide as it would go, looked at Bert for about a second, took his glasses off his nose and handed them to me, laid out the cushions on the nearest bit of ground, which was damp but not watery, unrolled the roll of stuff, a length of carpet as I now saw, and placed it next to the cushions. Having done that she got in at the other side and, bracing her shoulder against the doorpost, shoved at Bert with her slippered feet until he fell off the seat and out of the car. Then she rolled him on to the bit of carpet and started dragging him along the pavement towards his front gate, a job made easier for her by the suitcase-handle let into the front edge of the strip. I locked the Apfelsine and collected up the cushions, one of which she took off me in the hall and put under his head before turning him on his side. She held out her hand to me for his glasses, which she stowed on a nearby oak chest beside pieces of outdoor clothing like gloves and a child's mack. The last thing was a blanket from the top shelf of the coat-cupboard thrown over him. The whole operation had taken two minutes at the outside.

'You must love him very much,' I said.

'Fuck off, darling.' Nowell stared at me. 'Do you know, I don't think you'd better have that drink after all.' She looked down at Bert and then at me again. 'They say however many times you get married it's always to basically the same person, don't they? Watch out, Stan.'

I drove home in exactly the style of a very very good driver who had had two small glasses of wine with his dinner and was taking no chances but of course not dawdling. And I was lucky. Well, it was still not half-past ten. Quite a few points needed chewing over, though not before the morning. One, probably not the most important, was whether Bert always or even sometimes got himself given the cushion-and-carpet treatment when he was only acting pissed. Another came from what Nowell had said. Had she only been talking about drink?

3   Relapse

Steve was worse when I saw him next. He talked, but not to me or to anybody else who was there. I could not make out half of what he said and the rest made no sense. His mouth was very dry, with the drugs presumably, and there was a crud or something of what looked like half-dried-up saliva sticking to his teeth. He obviously had no idea of where he was or what was going on, and the way he moved his eyes, which had dilated pupils, made me think he was seeing things that were not there. Still, he seemed calm.

On the next couple of visits his hallucinations, if that was what they had been, seemed to have blown over, but nothing or very little was getting through to him. That was what I thought, anyway, and Susan agreed the day she went with me. So it came as quite a surprise when Trish Collings rang up that evening and said she was transferring him to the St Kevin's day clinic, which meant he would be spending his nights at home, and would I please come and fetch him at 5.30 tomorrow. His condition had significantly improved, she said.

I held down any desire to cheer, no longer knowing what I thought of Collings. 'Since this morning?' I asked.

'The improvement has become obvious since this morning, but it's been taking shape for some time now.' As before, she sounded extra west-of-Winchester over the phone, bursting with cricket and cream teas. 'Anyway, you'll be able to judge for yourself very soon.'

When I got to her terrible office she started explaining about how it was up to me to arrange for Steve to be brought to and fro. I interrupted her.

'Aren't we going to wait for Mrs Hutchinson?'

'I didn't ask her to attend. This is between you and me, Stanley.'

'Oh, so when it comes to getting something done I'm not such a disaster.'

'Will you please try to contain your aggression towards your ex-wife at least while you're here.'

She spoke quite stroppily. I apologized, and she went on to caution me against assuming that Steve was now completely and permanently cured, and put it on record that she was not a magician. After that she talked about what a bad thing it would be if I or anybody else, but particularly

I, showed any resentment towards him for any upset or inconvenience he might unintentionally cause. She also warned me against thinking that quite run-of-the-mill possible bits of behaviour on his part, like smashing crockery or staring into space for a couple of hours at a time, were really abnormal violence or withdrawal respectively. If anyone, me for instance, got it across to him that that view was being taken, then he would become more alienated.

'May I ask a question, doctor?'

This set her off on one of her merriest guffaws. When she was able to she said, 'My, we are being formal today.'

'Well, I thought so. Anyway, just, if he's done so well in hospital, and there are likely to be these difficulties at home, wouldn't the logical thing be to keep him here?'

Her mouth slid sideways. 'That's a bad question if it means you're thinking of the disruption likely to be caused in your routine and your wife's.'

'Of course I'm *thinking* of it,' I said, glad that as I felt just then I was indoors and sitting down. 'That's natural. But in another sense I'm also *thinking* of my son. Parents often do think of their children in ways like that.'

'I'll accept that,' she said, doing so with suspicious willingness. 'Perhaps you have been taking a balanced view of the situation. Yes, in some circumstances continuing hospitalization would be the answer, but here we have to consider the long term. What we're all trying to do, you'll agree, is get Steve to be able to stand on his own two feet, and the first step towards doing that is to allow him out of the artificial hospital environment and into the community, as far as possible at the moment, when he's ready to spend his evenings and nights with family, and I think he is ready for that.'

'I see. Can we look forward to a steady improvement?'

'Hopefully yes. But in these situations there's always the possibility of relapse. That's why I stressed the importance of responsible handling.'

'I see,' I said again. 'One more thing if I may. I've got a wife at home and I'm no unarmed-combat expert myself. How likely is he to get violent?'

'Now here again that sort of thing can't be ruled out, but any purposeful violence is much more to be associated with psychopathiform disorders. Steve may well appear threatening and alarming without engaging in any violent behaviour at all.'

'Well, that's something, I suppose.'

She told me a bit more about what to expect, none of it markedly confidence-building, and at the end of it said in a voice that was quite gentle by her standards, 'I expect you're looking forward to having him home.'

My God, I thought to myself, if anybody ever looked off their bleeding rocker then this was it, never mind what Nash and his lot might say. She was sitting hunched up at her table clutching a fag in her right hand, opening and closing her left hand, smiling unsteadily at me with the left side of her mouth and blinking her left eye. Her head jerked a couple of times. The nearest thing would have been out of an award-winning Mexican movie made in black and white on purpose and called *Las* something. If she bothered at all she probably read my expression as embarrassed paternal feeling. At any rate she got up after a minute, nodded at me and went noisily out of the room. When she came back she had Steve with her.

'Hallo, dad,' he said, and shook my hand. He was looking me in the eye and smiling. 'How are you?'

'Hallo, son, I'm fine.'

'Is everything all right?'

'Oh yes, absolutely.'

I was very nearly sure that I would sooner have had him as I had last seen him than as he was now. He, his normal self, would never have shaken hands with me like that without a private signal that of course the whole thing was a joke, an act, an imitation, anyway not what it seemed to any idiots who might have been watching. And he had met me eye to eye right enough, but if he had not just called me Dad I would have said without recognizing me, certainly without the least touch of the humorous warmth I had always had from him on meeting and whenever we were at all specially aware of each other for a second. Again I wondered whether I would have instantly recognized him out of context, and fancied the proportions of his face had altered in some small but unmissable way.

'Isn't it nice to seen him looking so well, Stanley?' said Collings.

'Yes, it certainly is. Well, Trish, if there's nothing more for the moment we may as well be getting along.'

'No no, you're free to go,' she said, and choked back another peal of merriment, unless I imagined it. 'I'll just walk you to the entrance.'

It seemed a long hike to the hall of Rorschach House. The lengths of material underfoot, which on my last visit I had thought must be for something temporary, were still there, only more crumpled and stained than before. I was dying to be rid of Collings and at the same time dreading being alone with Steve. Her farewell when it came was fully up to standard for embarrassment, with a terrible roguish bit about it being au revoir not goodbye for him and her.

The car park was in weak sunshine. 'Well, how did they treat you back there?' I asked, and when I got no answer, 'All right, were they?'

'Yeah.'

'What was the food like? Okay, was it?'

'Yeah.'

He had spoken so lifelessly that I was filled with a sudden panicky suspicion – he had indeed not recognized me, he still had not the slightest idea of what was happening, he had simply had it drummed into him to address as dad the man who turned up and to go wherever he was taken.

No, that could not be, that was daft, he was simply nervous, confused, frightened, shy of committing himself or saying more than he had to. He would talk all right when he had settled down and felt safe.

There was not much sign of that for the first couple of days. On arrival he said Hallo to Susan quite nicely and shook hands with her, a bizarre sight if I ever saw one, but after that he only spoke without being spoken to when he wanted the coffee jar, an extra blanket, a light for his cigarette, the time of day. He ate little, read nothing, watched television, took long showers, left the television on, left the shower on, left the lights on. I could find nothing abnormal about any of this, nothing unusual, and yet it was different. The most different part came first thing in the morning – so far from having trouble getting him up I found him fully dressed sitting looking shell-shocked on the edge of his bed or on the broad sill of the big window on the landing. But he certainly seemed calm.

About the third evening early on he said to me quite normally, 'Just popping out to get some Marlboros.' Susan was there too.

It was the first unnecessary thing he had said for a long time. Partly because in a very unimportant way I was fed up with having to give him lights every ten minutes and partly to provoke some sort of reaction I said, not at all crossly, 'You might as well buy yourself a few boxes of matches while you're about it.'

I got my reaction all right, also notice that he had some sort of grasp of the state of affairs. He glared at me with astonishing hostility, showed his teeth in a way I had never seen before and said in a sort of choked-up or choked-off voice, 'Don't you fucking dare talk to me like that, you bastard. Who the bloody hell do you think you are, giving me your fucking orders?'

Knowing at once there was no point in it I still said, 'I wasn't giving any orders, I was merely making a suggestion.'

'Like fuck you were. You were trying to make me into part of your bloody little police state, weren't you? You're just a pissy little dictator. You don't care about anybody but yourself and other people can go and jump in the fucking lake.'

'That's not true.' Susan sounded pretty cross herself. 'Your father sweats his guts out for you. Look at the way he – '

He turned on her so savagely that I got to my feet. 'You keep out of this, you fucking bitch,' he said with shocking sincerity. 'You've done enough, pushing my mother out and now you won't let me go near her, you bloody. . . '

'She's not there,' I shouted. 'I can't get hold of her. She's not around.' I had phoned three or four times on my own account and only got an answer once, from a foreign voice that said helpfully that Mrs Hutchinson had gone to London. Not that Steve had so much as mentioned her until this moment since the evening I first fetched him. But it was no use going into any of that.

With a growl of hatred and disgust he took a step towards me and jerked his fist in the air, but then shoved past me and hurried out. Susan and I stood without moving until the front door slammed, on which we clung to each other.

'That's not his way,' I said, trying to remember something of Collings's about helping him to get in touch with his own anger. Was that what I had done?

'No, well he's not himself. He's all in a muddle, poor little thing. He probably feels bloody awful from all these drugs and things and when you're like that you lash out at whoever's nearest. Come on, darling, let's have a drink.'

After ten minutes or so we heard the door slam again and after another moment a burst of working-class music from the television. When I went in last thing I found a semi-circle of used matches round Steve's chair, one of which had burnt the carpet slightly. It seemed not much to be bucked up by.

The next day Susan's mother came to lunch. So did Alethea, Susan's elder sister by half a dozen years. Alethea had been married to a doctor, a chest man at a London teaching hospital who had run off with one of the cleaning women there. I still thought that was a pretty peculiar thing to have done, though not as peculiar as before I met Alethea. She had gone white early, wore her hair in a short bob and, with her tallish, stooped figure, looked a bit like a country parson in an old number of *Punch*, dressed differently, though. When I turned up, rather late on purpose, she greeted me quite heartily and made a great thing of insisting on a full double kiss in the continental mode.

'Stanley dear, how marvellous to see you, it's been absolutely ages.'

'Lovely to see you, Alethea,' I said, only just managing not to burst out laughing in her face. Although we had met a good dozen times over the years I had never learnt to be altogether ready for the way she talked, which sounded to me like a fellow trying to get you to hate and despise the upper classes by ridiculously overdoing their accent. My mother-in-law looked quite startled at the way I came rushing over to embrace her. Susan was out of the room.

'And how are things going in Fleet Street?' asked Alethea. 'Have you had any good scoops lately?'

'I'm not on that side of it,' I said, 'but nobody gets much in the way of scoops these days because – '

'They're pulling down the whole of that lovely William IV terrace just round the corner from where I am,' Alethea told me. 'You remember, on the north side of the square?'

Her mother answered, not that I had any objection. 'Oh darling, they can't,' she said, with a quick glance my way to check that I was not grinning with satisfaction at this news. '*Not* the one where Sickert lived?'

'I'm afraid they can, darling. I've a number of friends locally, as you know, and I hear on the best authority that it's all coming *down* and a block of flats and a supermarket are going *up*. Damn-all chance of stopping it.'

'People like that will do *anything*,' said my mother-in-law.

'Terrible,' I said. 'Terrible.'

'Of course you're all right round here, aren't you, Stanley?' said my sister-in-law. 'All these rich socialists with their Georgian mansions, nobody's going to lay a finger on *them*, oh dear no, don't make me laugh.'

Good advice, that last bit, I thought, successfully remembering what it was like. 'Yes, they have been quite reasonable, actually,' I said. 'There's a place in Flask Walk called – '

'They're stopping the season-ticket arrangement for those concerts of the Friends of the Baroque,' said Alethea to the old girl and me more or less jointly. 'Something I don't really understand about the laws about charities. Apparently there is or was some loophole that some little bureaucrat has cleverly managed to close.'

'A magnificent achievement. Obviously a man destined for the highest office.'

Lady D had let me off that one, but I went and poured myself a Scotch anyway. While I was doing it Susan came in and we had a quick exchange – all well, no news, lunch in ten minutes. I took the sherry round. We had an item on the duty on wine and another on the Royal Shakespeare Company. Then there was something about the Saab wanting its boot repaired and I pricked up my ears, but before we could be told about the latest slow-motion bump good old Alethea cut in. She made sure there were only the four of us in the room and said into a minimal pause,

'I rather gather . . . poor Steve . . . has been a little . . . under the weather lately.'

'He's better than he was,' said Susan. 'As I told you, they let him – '

'Is it . . . some sort of breakdown?'

'Evidently they don't use that word,' I said, 'but yes, that's what it seems to boil down to.'

'Poor you, how frightfully worrying for you both.'

'Has he been behaving violently again?' asked Lady D.

Alethea twisted round on her. 'Behaving violently? How do you mean, darling? What sort of thing?' Now was the time I could have done with hearing about the terrace or the tickets, but it was obviously too late for anything like that.

'Well, when I was here three weeks ago he flew into a rage about nothing in particular that I could see, grabbed a book of Susan's off the shelves and tore it to pieces, and then rushed out of this house and round to his mother's, where he proceeded to smash the television set to fragments.'

I said, 'A very distinguished psychiatrist – '

'But that's nothing very terrible or extraordinary,' said Alethea, really disappointed.

'I quite agree, darling, exactly my own view of the thing,' said Lady D, causing me to blink slightly. 'But then of course these days everything has to be . . . Stanley,' she went on, and lifted her head up in a confidential way, so as to let the world know we were all on the same side, 'is that boy really to be regarded as ill, would you say?'

'Well, he's not physically ill, lady,' I said. 'As regards mental illness I have to leave it to the – '

'Mental illness?' said Alethea. 'What sort of thing?'

'I don't think Stanley wants to go into any of that,' said Susan.

'Just in the family, darling.'

'*No*, darling.'

'What does Steve do with himself here?' My mother-in-law swung her glass out of the path of the sherry bottle. 'How does he get through the day?'

'He gets through the day at the hospital. As regards the evenings here he just sits in front of the television. No trouble to anybody.'

'And no good to himself, it appears. I suppose he'd die rather than go for a walk. Does he never help Susan in the house?'

'Well, there's nothing really for him to do, darling,' said Susan. 'I have two people coming in and I'm not going to put him on to papering the best bedroom just for the hell of it.'

'So he never so much as washes up a teacup,' said the old girl, sending her elder daughter a glance of wonderfully covered-up horror and getting back one of the same sort.

'There's a machine for that, as you know.' Susan was beginning to fidget.

'Which requires to be loaded, I believe.'

'Darling, Steve's in a very strange state, he's not just another idle teenager with a fit of the mopes. He needs to feel sympathized with and that nobody's trying to get at him.'

'And it would be *getting at* him to induce him to perform some portion of his share of household tasks. I see.'

'Surely there are simply dozens of things he could do in the garden,' said Alethea.

'*Please*, both of you,' said Susan, getting up. By now she was quite agitated. 'We're going through a very nasty time in this house at the moment and we don't need lecturing on how to run it. Really we don't. So could we please drop the subject.'

'I'm sorry,' said Lady D in one of the plenty of ways of saying that without doing any apologizing. 'I was only thinking of Steve and what a shame it would be if he were actually encouraged in his. . . .' She took a long time over that one. 'Slackness,' she said eventually. 'But of course I quite realize that it's much too late to talk along such lines,' she said with her voice beginning to die away, 'and that these rather unhappy strains in his character probably go back to his early training and the unfortunate influence of his mother,' she said with the last word coming through strongly enough and a glance at me that left no real doubt in my mind that the mother she was thinking of was rather bald and had a little moustache and drove an Apfelsine.

'Shall we go down to lunch?' said Susan. When the other two had finally cleared off she said to me, 'I don't know what happened, darling, honestly. That's about as bad as I've known her. Alethea being there comes into it somehow, I've noticed it before. But . . . part of it was to do with concern about Steve, I would like you to believe that.'

Yeah, I said to myself. And some more of it was to do with making out that what was wrong with Steve was nothing more than a severe case of being lower class. Not all of it, no.

When I got back from the hospital with Steve the following evening I could see Susan had news for me. I waited till he had settled in front of the TV with his usual coffee and slice of bread and honey, then followed her up to our bedroom. What she had was something to show me rather than tell me, a square-cornered length of metal or heavy plastic about four inches by an inch by half an inch with a roughened surface. It looked like the handle of something, which was what it actually turned out to be when I pressed a stud at one end and a stout pointed blade shot out of the other.

'In his chest of drawers,' said Susan. 'Not even covered up. It wasn't there yesterday. I look every morning.'

'Quite right. But when did he get it? Unless he was keeping it somewhere else before. And even then . . . Must have been at the other end, out near the hospital. I just drop him there, you see, I don't bodyguard him all the way to the ward. It's quite a walk to the shops. Not impossible, though, I suppose. Anyway here it is, eh?'

'Must have cost a bit if he got it new.'

'I gave him fifty the other day. I can't have him coming to me every time he wants a packet of fags, can I?'

'What are we going to do?'

'I don't know.' I clicked the knife back into its hilt. 'I honestly don't know. Well, we can confront him with it.'

'No need for that, we can just ask him what it's for. Can't we?'

'That's confronting him with it. Or we can throw it away. That's confronting him with it as soon as he finds it isn't there instead of now.'

'Well, what about confronting him with it?'

'Yes,' I said trying to think whether concealed possession of a flick knife would count as normal or abnormal in Collings's book. 'We can predict his reaction from what happened the other day. Rage, curses, accusations of spying, and so on.'

'Which can be faced.'

'Oh, sure. But . . . It's a pity about the spying. I support you on it, I mean if you'd asked me whether you should look through his things I'd have said go ahead. But if you look at it it is very much the sort of response that . . . Well, that Dr Collings said would alienate him.'

'So you're in favour of putting it back.'

'I can't see what's to be gained from not. We know it's there now, and he doesn't know we know. And it's not as if it's the only knife in the house. Those non-stainless French kitchen jobs of yours, you could tackle a bleeding elephant with one of them. I suppose we could lock them up. You're not really with me over this, are you, Sue?'

'I just think if you said very casually and calmly that I'd happened to come across it when I was – '

'Then he'd fly into a rage and accuse us both of spying. Don't forget he's Nowell's son too. Can you imagine how she'd behave if you casually and calmly told her you'd happened to come across something in her handbag? Of course, she is a . . . er, we all know what she is. I'll check this with Collings in the morning.'

Collings said putting the knife back was right – Stephen had probably only got hold of it in the first place so as to feel secure. In case I went for him with a hammer, I said to myself but not to her. Further reports would be welcome. His action on being encouraged to take a shower, which was to take a shower so thorough that he used up all the hot water and made me late for work, had its annoying side but hardly seemed worth reporting.

At the start of the second week he took to going to his room earlier than before, at ten o'clock, nine o'clock, straight after arriving home. That time, feeling a perfect idiot, I sneaked up about eight to spy out the land. The light was on in the room. One or two slight sounds told me nothing except that he was not in bed. Reading? Conceivably but not much more. Looking at dirty pictures? Quite possibly. Staring into space? Quite likely. I left it and Susan and I forgot about him for the whole evening, until we heard him coming down for his late-night snack and our conversation, which had been bounding along before, soon petered out.

Five days after the knife incident Susan again had something waiting for me when I got home. In the bedroom she handed me some sheets of cheap lined paper covered with Steve's familiar and terrible handwriting. 'It was on the little round table in his room,' she said. I thought she looked tired, rather pale anyway. 'He must have meant us to find it there.'

'What is it, a letter?'

'You'd better read it.'

I sat on the edge of the bed and she settled herself next to and partly behind me in one of those kneeling or squatting female positions with her arm on my shoulder. Although terrible enough, full of unnecessary loops, leaning, falling over and straightening itself up again, the writing could mostly be read, and the spelling mistakes were plentiful, but the intended words could mostly be rescued. Put right as far as it could be put right, Steve's message went like this:

BE IT KNOWN TO ALL THE PEOPLES OF PLANET EARTH —

Light years ago in the secret heart of the galaxy an Element created itself. For centuries it had no name, then ancient Atlantean physicists discovered it with scanners and named it POTENTIUM. But when Atlantis perished neath the waves the secret of POTENTIUM perished also.

More centuries flew by on the wings of time, until Lemurian mystics got to know about it in dreams and visions sent by MITHRAS, but when they went and told their king he was displeased and had them slain. So alas the secret was lost once more.

Then as NOSTRADAMUS had predicted the Alchemists brought POTENTIUM back into existence, but no man knew what it would do.

Then one day the great AVERROES was experimenting on some POTENTIUM by bombarding it with Photon Particles and this mutated it into an isotope that could live in the human brain.   REJOICE!

HENCEFORTH MAN WAS ARMED AGAINST EVIL.

    POTENTIUM IS THE SOURCE OF THE SPIRIT THAT FIGHTS FOR GOOD.

> The element that had no name,
> Through the centuries it came,
> Through all the smoke and flame,
> POTENTIUM God's gift to man,
> By his great plan,
> The war against evil began,   EVIL
> Against those who live for greed,   LIVE
> To smash their vile creed,   VILE
> And make them all bleed,   LEVI
> POTENTIUM gives the power,
> To strike at the right hour,
> And all the evil devour.

Atomic Number 108
        Symbol Pt
            Atomic Weight 303
                    Valency Number 99
                            Rainbow Metal

    THIS IS A DEMOCRATIC DOCUMENT OF GREAT IMPORTANCE
CREATED FOR THE PRESERVATION OF PEACE
                      AND THE DESTRUCTION OF THE
                      WICKED

    HAIL POTENTIUM THE POWER OF THE LORD

Underneath the text there was a drawing of a person with a beard stretching out an arm towards some buildings that seemed to be falling down among small figures probably intended to be human beings. It, the drawing, was done in ballpoint and I thought showed very little talent.

I had just had time to take this in when Susan gave a sort of shrieking gasp right in my ear and I looked up rather quickly to see Steve standing by the door, which I could have sworn had been shut, and glaring at us. He might have been there for a couple of minutes. When he saw us see him he came towards us in a determined way. I jumped up.

'What are you doing with that?' he said, or rather snarled.

'Reading it. That's what you meant us to do, isn't it?'

'Fucking snooping!'

'You left it lying about,' I said, and tried and failed to get the energy together to go on about people having to go into his room to make the bed, etc.

The next moment, probably just by chance, his manner changed. All menace left it. He looked alert and preoccupied at the same time, like somebody trying to remember something or to hear a distant sound. He soon gave this up and focused on me with his mouth hanging open. Slowly he closed it and pressed the lips together until his expression was one of smothered amusement, also shyness and a modest kind of pride, reminding me of how he had looked at me the first time I saw him walk. Then he broke out into laughter, completely amused and amiable, no awful side to it at all in itself. The trouble was I could see nothing much that was funny in what was actually happening or what was there in front of us. I tried to make out he was laughing at me and Susan for being serious or stupid or worried or frightened, or at himself for being angry just now, or anything like that, but it was no good. Nash had talked about schizophrenics being too mad to know what was funny. I stood there longing for a drink till Steve jerked his head back and scampered out of the room.

Susan had come up and taken my hand and now she put her arms round me and squeezed. 'Stanley, I'm scared,' she whispered.

'Not much of a treat, was it?'

'No, I mean I'm still scared. All that . . . *mad* stuff about Atlantis and alchemists and smashing the evil ones, it's like . . . I don't know.'

'Bleeding ridiculous.'

'Darling, it's not just ridiculous. That boy, he's very seriously disturbed.'

'We knew that,' I said. 'I'll discuss the matter when I've got a glass in my hand and not before.' When I had, and we were in the sitting room with the door firmly shut, I said, 'Sue, love, listen to me, now. This thing is just an old piece of sci-fi, that's all it is. Tripe, in fact. I thought it had gone out. Plus the sort of stuff you get through the post from the green-ink brigade – you know, the pyramids one minute and lasers the next. The thing's not worth taking seriously, really.'

'He believes it,' said Susan. 'He thinks it's true.'

'Oh, come on. Believes it? It's like a kid scribbling. Doodling.'

'There's violence there. To smash their vile creed and make them all bleed. I suppose that's more doodling.'

'I'd say maybe he was trying to get a rhyme, but then I wouldn't know about a thing like that.'

'The destruction of the wicked doesn't sound very funny to me.'

'Well, he wasn't going to threaten to let their dog out and knock over their pint in the pub, was he?'

This was the moment where she should have looked up at me and smiled and said she was sorry to have gone on like that, and I would have said of course I saw why and more in the same strain while saying to myself, in this case, that although Steve's document might not be worth getting steamed up about it was a long way from reassuring in itself. But instead of that she went on sitting there on the grey velvet settee in one of her grey cardigans and dark skirts, pressing her lips together, her head down in a way that showed off the blackness and glossiness of her hair. I felt I was a long way from knowing what she was thinking, not that I would have gone round claiming I regularly did know.

Partly to break the tension I said, 'I'd better give Nowell a ring.'

Susan looked up then and no mistake. 'Why? What for?'

'I'd like to tell her about this just now and, well, the general situation. I should have got hold of her earlier.'

'What for? What can she do?'

'Nothing, love. I don't want her to do anything, I just want her to be informed. She probably doesn't even know he's here.'

'I dare say she doesn't,' said Susan sharply. 'She never takes the slightest interest in him.'

'Look, I'm not calling her in as a consultant, all I'm after is putting her in the picture so if he does act up, like walking in there out of the blue as he's quite liable to do, she can't complain she was kept in the dark. Okay?'

'Yes.' Susan sighed and blinked apologetically. 'You know, it's hard going on being reasonable all the time when you're feeling a bit shaken up.'

'Oh, absolutely. Listen, Sue, I'm sorry all this is happening, and it's sort of none of your doing.'

'It's none of yours, either. Forget it, darling.'

'No, you know what I mean. I don't really feel I can leave him alone in the house much for the moment, but you can go out. You must go out on your own a bit more.'

'I don't like going out without you.'

'Then we must have a few more people in.'

'Don't worry, there's always plenty to do here. And you're here, aren't you?'

'It's not much of a life for you.'

'Yes it is. We'll make sure he doesn't get into the bedroom again, darling.'

When I tried the Hutchinson number it answered immediately. I remembered feeling very slightly baffled when there was no answer before – what if I had been somebody who might have had work for Nowell? But no point in going into that now because it was Bert at the other end.

'Stan here. Hold on a minute. How did you get away with it the other day, going out on a blind with your favourite shit?'

'No problem,' said Bert with his mouth close to the phone. 'I told her she had to be joking at first, then I couldn't remember anything about it, could I? Well, it wasn't all no problem, because it still didn't look good. But she was over the moon that morning because Chris Rabinowitz wanted to talk to her about an idea he'd had. She can be quite agreeable when everybody's doing what she wants at once. Remember? Anyway. Was I all right that time? When I look back, it starts getting a bit vague over the veal.'

'You were fine. Not that I was in much of a state to judge.'

'Not offensive? . . . Good. Hang on, I'll get her. Ah, you . . . shit,' he said, his voice getting louder and further away at the same time, fuzzier too. 'You bloody man. Ha . . . darling,' he continued with a quite impressive off-mike acoustic. '*Darling*, it's that, er. . . .'

Nowell came on the line full of simple wonder and pleasure at hearing the sound of my voice, but changed it to sincere puzzlement when I seemed to think she might want to be told what Steve had recently been up to, where he was, etc. When I actually started to tell her she switched again and stopped listening. How she got that across on a non-visual circuit without saying anything or making any other kind of noise I had very little idea, but the fact made me realize I must have seriously underestimated her acting ability in the past. Then something I said about the flick-knife business evidently broke through, and she came over all motherly – to me, not Steve.

'I'm very glad you've told me about this, Stanley. You did quite right. *Of course* it's an upsetting, disturbing thing, suddenly coming across *a knife* hidden away like that.'

'Actually it wasn't – '

'Anybody who wasn't upset, even a bit *frightened*, in those circumstances would have to be rather stupid. Fair enough. But darling, you mustn't mind me saying this but it's really not very sensible to go *on* being frightened because of it.'

'I'm not – '

'Because a lot of young boys go in for that sort of thing, you know, having a knife and so on, it makes them feel big. They've no intention in the world of *using* it. And as for *Steve*, I'm quite staggered you think he might take a cut at you, or Susan. I mean surely.'

'I don't – '

'He's such a *gentle* creature, always has been. I don't believe he'd be actually violent to anybody, however frantic or worked up he got. It's just not in him.'

That was more or less how I felt myself, but hearing her say it almost made me want to change round. 'M'm,' I said.

'But I want you to be quite certain of one thing, Stanley,' she said, and her voice started to tremble slightly with thick-and-thinness, so that I could visualize every last millimetre of her expression. 'If ever you need me, if there should ever be anything I can do, you only have to say the word and I'll be there, depend on it.'

'It's good to know that.'

Speaking at three times the speed and steady as a rock, she said, 'You must understand quite plainly that he's not coming here, Stanley. I won't have it, I've got to think of Joanne,' their daughter, presumably. 'It wouldn't be fair on her. Surely you can see that. I'm sorry but I really have no alternative. Goodbye.'

I got it almost straight away. Although I was pretty convinced that my last remark had sounded quite all right, devoid of any hint of malice or sarcasm, I could always have got it wrong, and in any case from Nowell's point of view I might easily have been having malicious or sarcastic thoughts, and I might even have been getting ready to be foul to her about not going near her son while he was having a not very good time. Well, this was the sort of thing that helped me to go on not making any mistakes about my first wife, like spending a few seconds every couple of months wishing she had not run off with Bert.

The next morning I told Collings about the potentium stuff and she told me it was normal. That evening Steve started whispering to himself as he sat watching television, or rather with the set turned on. From the way he kept pausing and looking attentive I reckoned he was having a conversation with a voice inside his head. While a journalist on the screen talked about and tried to illustrate the decline of bits of Liverpool Steve listened to this other voice, disagreed with what it said, disagreed quite strongly but consented to listen further, made a couple of reluctant admissions and finally caved in. For five minutes nothing more happened, but then he started disagreeing again and I went upstairs for a stiff Scotch.

The morning after that I drove him over to St Kevin's as usual. At first he kept quiet, also as usual, but about half-way there he said or muttered, 'Leave me alone,' not for my benefit. For the rest of the journey he said the same thing or variants of it every couple of minutes, plus excuses like there was nothing he could do about it. If he had been on the end of a phone trying to get rid of a bore he would have sounded completely normal. At last we arrived.

'See you tonight, son,' I said when he was getting out. Twice before when I said it or something similar he had given me a terrific bawling-out for treating him like a child and so on, but I found it was impossible to let him just go off in silence.

Today was different. He bent down to get a proper look at me and said, 'Goodbye, dad,' shut the door and moved off.

I watched him cross the car park, head slightly forward as always, and pass out of sight. Should I have gone with him to the ward and to hell with his objections? Should I now find Collings or that Gandhi bloke and tell them about the whispering? Well, presumably they knew already or soon would, unless he put it on specially for me, which I doubted. And it was probably normal anyway.

The thought of him saying goodbye like that came back to me several times in the next few hours, especially when I got back to the office after a rather long lunch break and Morgan Wyndham handed me a slip of paper and told me to ring that number urgently – the St Kevin's number with Collings's extension. He then took himself off as though the thing was his own idea, one which another time would have earned him a lot of marks.

I got Collings in ten seconds flat. 'Hallo, Stanley,' she said like a real old pal. 'What have you done with that boy of yours?'

'No jokes if you don't mind. What's up?'

'Well, that's what I was wondering. Where is he?'

'You mean he didn't – I brought him in as usual.'

'Well, we haven't seen him here. Any idea where he might have gone?'

I tried to think. 'His mother's. He went there before once. I told you.'

'No reply. Or from your home number. Of course he might be there all the same and not answering. Anywhere else? . . . Right, I'll let you know if anything turns up.'

'Hey, hold it, hang on a minute.'

'Yes?'

I had been desperate to prevent her ringing off, but now I could find very little to say. 'Er . . . he will turn up all right, will he? How long . . . ?'

'If he's still loose tonight we'll set things moving in the morning. Don't worry, Stanley, they very seldom come to much harm.'

'He's been talking to himself.'

'Yes, he has aural hallucinations. Very common with disorders of this kind. Usual, in fact.'

At least she had not said normal. 'He wasn't doing it or having them before yesterday as far as I know. I thought he was supposed to be getting better.'

'He is. You should have seen him on his first couple of days here.' This would have been a good moment for one of her horse-laughs, but it failed to show. 'Anyway, I warned you not to expect his progress to be smooth.'

'You said he might have a relapse. Is that what this is?'

'I simply can't say at this stage, Stanley, I'm afraid. It depends what he's doing. If he's just sitting in a park somewhere, which he probably is, then there's not much to worry about.'

Except for him being rather wet and cold in the kind of drizzle I could see through my window. After Collings I rang home. Still no reply, which meant nothing. Before I did anything else I had to see a punter about a quarter-page. I saw him, though without result, and got home just on 5.30. When I let myself in the phone was ringing. I took it in the kitchen.

'Mr Stanley Duke?' a man's voice asked pleasantly.

'That's me.'

'Oh, it's the Metropolitan Police here, sir, Superintendent Fairchild speaking. I've got a young fellow with me who says he's your son. Name of Stephen. Is that correct?'

'Yes. Is he in trouble?'

'Well, I'm very much afraid he is, sir, yes. He's in our custody at the moment at the Jabali Embassy, where I'm speaking from now. I have to ask you to come down for a short interview.'

'Jabali? That's Arabs, isn't it?'

'Yes, sir.' He gave me an address near Regent's Park. 'Just down the road from you, really. You'll be making your own way, will you, sir?'

'Yes – can you give me some idea of what's happened?'

There was a short silence. When the Superintendent spoke again it was in a slightly different voice, one that made him sound bored stiff with what he was saying. 'I have to tell you there are diplomatic aspects to the matter which preclude it being discussed over the telephone.'

'Oh. Is my son all right?'

'Oh yes, sir,' said Superintendent Fairchild quickly and unreassuringly.

I had a quick drink. Of course I did. Not being a blithering idiot I never even considered taking the Apfelsine and phoned for a minicab, a quicker bet than a black cab hereabouts and in the rain. But I was idiot enough not to remember the flick-knife till the driver had rung the doorbell. No knife, at least nowhere I looked in my top-speed search. All the way down the hill I told myself that Fairchild would have taken a different tone over a stabbing, and got nowhere.

The embassy turned out to be one of a row of between-wars houses of upper-bank-manager status, rather small for St Kevin's but in a similar style. In a back corner of the hall a uniformed constable was standing outside a closed door. He let me into a sort of waiting room newly decorated and furnished in an extremely down-market Western way. There was Steve, presumably Fairchild, also in uniform, and an Arab in a three-hundred-quid suit.

Steve's appearance was a shock, but at the same time a relief after what I had been imagining. He had the makings of a black eye, a bashed nose and a cut lip and had probably been crying, perhaps still was in a small way. 'Hallo, dad,' he said, not at all cheerfully.

The Superintendent seemed about my age, tall when he stood up, with red-grey hair and a clean-shaven gloomy face, rather a good-looking chap.

After introducing himself he nodded at the Arab and said, 'This is Mr Fuad.'

'Major Fuad.' The man spoke in a stroppy way. Arab or no Arab, seen close to he looked incredibly Jewish to me, but who was I to judge?

'All right – Major Fuad. Er, Major Fuad would like to advise you of certain circumstances relating to the present matter, Mr Duke.' Without actually waving his arms about, the Superintendent signalled to me that this was something that would have to be gone along with.

'I see,' I said, and sat down on the indicated hard chair and waited respectfully.

In quite good English, but speaking at a pitch of disrespect no Englishman would have dared to use in front of another, even to a foreigner, Major Fuad said, 'You must realize that under international law this embassy is deemed to be part of the sovereign territory of the Republic of Jabal and that intrusions upon it will be treated in the same spirit as intrusions upon the republic itself,' and more in the same strain. He had a small moustache which made me wonder about my own. He also reminded me of somebody, but not because of the moustache. Superintendent Fairchild watched him with an expression on the far side of contempt or distaste, more like continuous quiet amazement. I kept nodding my head at what Fuad was telling me, or rather while he told me. Finally he said, 'I call upon you to see to it that your son understands these considerations in future, because it seems that those of us here have been unable to do so. Will you undertake to carry that into effect?'

'Yes, Major Fuad, I'll do my best.'

'You would be well advised to. Tell your son he may not get off so lightly a second time.'

'I will. Now may I ask what's happened?'

'Superintendent?' Fuad handed the ball over but went on to listen closely to the next part.

'Well, sir, it seems in brief that this young man called here earlier this afternoon and asked to speak to someone in Intelligence. He was taken in to see, er, Major Fuad's assistant and told him he had information about the activities of Israeli secret agents in this country, in London. When questioned about the source of his information he began to talk wildly, became violent and had to be restrained by the official and one of the guards here. At this point the duty PC was called in and he fetched me along.' Fairchild's manner sharpened. 'That's not quite all, I'm afraid, Mr Duke. Your son had this in his possession.'

The flick-knife right enough. I looked at it and kept my mouth shut.

'Did you know your son was in the habit of taking this kind of weapon round with him?'

'No,' I said, thanking God for the form of the question.

'I see, sir. Now you do know, it might be sensible to discourage him from carrying one in future. For one thing, as you're no doubt aware, such weapons are illegal. They may not be offered for sale, bought, possessed, borne on the person, anything. You and he have Major Fuad to thank for asking us to overlook the offence. Perhaps you'd like to dispose of this.' He handed the thing to me and stood up. 'I have some further questions which I'll put to you in another place. Thank you, Major Fuad. We're all grateful to you for your restraint in not taking the matter further. And now we won't keep you.'

I did my best, not a very good best, to imitate a man being grateful, got in return a glare of hostility with nothing imitation about it, and left the room with the others.

Outside in the hall, the Superintendent said to Steve, 'Are you all right, sonny? Do you want a doctor?'

'No, I'm all right.'

'You sure, now? You didn't get any nasty kicks? What do you say, Mr Duke? Do you think your son should see a doctor?'

'I reckon we can leave it for the moment.'

'Okay, fine. There aren't any further questions actually, sir, but there is a little more to be said, later, when we've run you home. I'll just have a word with the PC a minute.'

I squeezed Steve's arm and muttered that he had had a rough time and he nodded and looked at the floor with his mouth open. It occurred to me to wonder what he had told those Arabs. About Joshua and the rest of them milling around Hampstead? No wonder they had asked him to name his informants. What was he thinking now? About which embassy to try next, possibly, or something as far out as the rim of the galaxy, where Jews in phylacteries and Star of David teeshirts sat in intersystem ships tuning their hyperspatial receptors to his brain currents. The cleverest thing I could think of to say to him was not to worry and we would look after him.

When we got to the house Superintendent Fairchild sent his driver to the pub and made a phone-call in the kitchen. Susan was terrified at the sight of the police uniform, but I soon calmed her down and told her what had happened. I called the hospital and spoke to Dr Gandhi. Should I bring Steve in for the night? Unnecessary since he appeared calm – but bring him all the way in the morning. Agreed. Steve side-stepped me when I went to comfort him, asked for and was given aspirins and slouched off to his room without another word.

'I owe you an apology for that ragtime carry-on down the road,' said Fairchild when the three of us settled in the sitting room with our drinks. 'But there was no help for it. Now I expect you'd like to know what really happened down there, wouldn't you? Right.'

He was facing me directly. 'All okay up till the point where your lad starts giving them funny answers to their questions. So he's a joker or a nutter or an unbelievably useless would-be infiltrator, but anyway he's not what he says he is. So they set about working him over out of habit, till one of them remembers they're not supposed to do that, even if this is the

Jabali . . . Embassy. Then they call in the PC and say it was the boy that went for them in the first place, and there we are. How do I know? There wasn't a mark on either of the two I saw, Captain Abdullah or whatever he calls himself and some goon. And that knife, it was closed-up in his pocket when the PC searched him. They hadn't even done *that*, would you believe it. You'd have thought at least . . . I don't know.' The Superintendent shook his head and sighed in professional vexation. 'Oh no, I know those fellows of old.

'Because – I'm not an ordinary copper, I belong to a special corps that does all the security on the embassies and what-not. Now, you see, Mr Duke, my standing orders say that whenever possible I must promote cordial relations between their side and our side. Cordial relations. What that means in this instance, there's that Fuad knowing full well his side have made a bit of rubbish, an error, and the thing these blokes can't stand is losing face, right? So we all pretend he's the one with the grievance, and we have you down to be given a going-over on behalf of your son, because he's too young and helpless to be worth a going-over, you know, to get any real satisfaction out of it. And you heard me being grateful to him, Fuad that is, for not pressing charges when he knew I knew what I knew. So now he's won that one we'll have cordial relations for a bit. Meaning instead of him being unbearable on purpose he'll give us a dose of being unbearable not on purpose.

'Oh, it's a funny old job sometimes. You'd hardly credit it – I have to get into this clobber every time I put my nose inside the door, else they go on about not showing proper respect. Nothing wrong with Fuad going round in his fancy suits, of course. It's all right when they do it, you see.'

'But he can't think he's really won,' I said.

'Not a bit of it, Mr Duke, not a bit of it. As I say, he knows full well. But he *seems* to have won, everybody goes on as if he has, and that's all that worries him. These fellows, they're like,' he glanced at Susan and away, 'like children, really, aren't they? Just big talk,' he wound up vaguely.

Susan was sitting with her legs under her on the grey settee. Now she straightened her back and said quite fiercely, 'I don't see why that pair of bastards should be allowed to just get clean away with roughing up poor Steve.'

The Superintendent reacted unfavourably to the swear-word, though I could not have said what he physically did. But he politely turned in his seat towards Susan, giving her his full attention for almost the first time since they had met. 'Oh, they won't, Mrs Duke, far from it,' he said decisively. 'Our friend Fuad will see to that. I must say I'd quite like to know what he's got lined up for them, just out of curiosity. No, I understand your concern for your son, but I can – '

'Stepson.'

'I'm sorry, I just assumed. Oh yes, those two'll be taken care of all right. Thank you, just a drop if I may, I really must be going.'

Saying something about putting the meat in, Susan took herself off – we were having a couple of neighbours in that evening. Fairchild conscientiously looked round the room, nodding to himself once or twice.

'Are you a writer, Mr Duke?'

'Not really, Superintendent. My wife is. I'm in advertising myself.'

'M'm.' His face seemed to go slightly gloomier. Then, making it as clear as daylight before he spoke what was coming up, he said, 'Your boy, I take it he is, er . . .'

'Yes, he's disturbed. He goes to a day clinic at a psychiatric hospital. They say he's improving.'

'I thought it was that pretty well straight away. At first I thought glue-sniffing or one of those, but then I thought no no. You get to recognize it. You know, if those fellows down the road were any good, they'd have got on to it and just turfed him out before he could start making a nuisance of himself. They'll never learn, I'm afraid.' He paused and hung out another sign. 'That knife of his, now. You'd seen it before, hadn't you?'

'Yes, but I didn't know he was taking it around with him. I or rather my wife had just come across it in his drawer.'

'And you left it there? What a silly way to behave, even for someone who didn't know that weapons of that sort are illegal. I mean as I say, I'm quite satisfied in my own mind that this afternoon that knife never left his pocket, but nobody with any gumption would bet on a thing like that in advance, surely to God.'

'I see that now, but the hospital people were on at me not to let him feel – '

'Misprize common sense at your peril is my motto. Well, it's not my place to go on about this, especially when I'm drinking your excellent whisky. Which I must now very reluctantly tear myself away from.' He got to his feet, drained his glass and gave me a look. 'Bury that nail-file good and deep, eh?'

I followed him to the front door. He put on his uniform cap, making himself look quite grimly official, and seemed to be thinking something out. Finally he said,

'You know, Mr Duke, from a personal point of view, speaking just for myself you understand, the Major Fuads of this world have got one thing to be said not *for* them at all, just *about* them. They do seem to have got the women problem sorted out nice and neat. Whether you like it or not. Well, here I go. Thank you for your hospitality. Say good night to Mrs Duke for me if you would. And good night to you, sir.'

He hesitated for a moment, then turned away. While I strolled back upstairs to get my drink that last mention of Major Fuad got it across to me who he had reminded me of. I winced and groaned to myself and felt bad, all in vain – it was Nowell, no question, not just the tune being more important than the words and the no nonsense about forbearance towards a helpless victim, but also the sort of substitutional effect, saying A and meaning X, or rather talking about A but *really* talking about X, and not caring who knew it — especially that. At the same time I realized I had started to wonder whether I ought to ring her and tell her about the dust-up at the embassy. Not now, that was for sure — perhaps in the morning, from the office.

'What a horrible bugger, that policeman,' said Susan when I joined her in the kitchen.

'Is he, was he? What was wrong with him?'

'Oh, the ghastly bloody complacent way he could see through everyone and *know* exactly what happened out of his vast experience.'

She was being pretty definite about it, but I held on a bit longer. 'Well, with a bloke like that, I should imagine experience would be quite a reliable guide.'

'And the way he sneered at me for being your second wife. Fucking cheek. Who the hell cares what *he* thinks?'

I had been looking fairly closely at the Superintendent at that stage in the conversation, and I had seen nothing but a passing embarrassment. Still, it was probably not an interesting enough point to be worth a mention, so I made a semi-agreeing noise instead.

'Incidentally,' she said with a look that failed miserably to convince me that what she was going to say would be incidental, 'it wasn't such a good idea to let him have his knife back, was it?'

'No, it wasn't. Your friend the Superintendent said the same sort of thing. I just didn't think of him going and doing a thing like that. Good job he didn't actually *do* anything.'

'According to that cop.'

'Well, yes.'

She came over and put her cheek against mine. 'Bit frightening, isn't it?'

'Yeah. And awful. Let's have another drink.'

The next morning Steve was nowhere to be found. His bed had been slept in, in fact I had seen him sleeping in it when I looked in last thing. He had evidently made himself a cup of coffee. We reckoned or hoped he had gone out to buy cigarettes, though five to eight seemed a bit early for that, and there was rain about and he had not taken the mack I had lent him, but none of that counted for much. If buying cigarettes was all he was up to he would be back by 8.20 at the latest. 8.20 came and went. I could think of nothing to do but get on with shaving and dressing.

Half a dozen decent-sized trees stood in a line in the bit of garden at the side of the house, elms that had somehow escaped disease. As I shaved, the mirror in front of me reflected a view through the window of the upper parts of two of these elms. I was working my way round my moustache when I caught a movement in one of the two. As soon as I went over and looked I saw Steve standing on a branch next to the trunk about thirty feet from the ground. He was holding on to and also leaning on another branch in a position that was probably quite comfortable for the moment. I tapped on the window and after an eerie interval he turned his head and caught my eye. The light was poor but good enough to show me that he was very pale. I collected Susan and we rushed out and round.

It was not actually raining all that hard just then, but there was a lot more to come in the sky and a gusty wind was blowing. In just his shirt and jacket and trousers Steve was going to be wet through before very long and thoroughly chilled, unless he already was after however long he had been up there. Some rooks or crows were flying about near the tree-tops and cawing a good deal, perhaps because of him. He watched us approaching as though it was barely worth his while. When I asked him what he was doing he took no notice, in fact he looked away and seemed to stare into the next garden or the one further, where there might have been something interesting going on for all I knew. His hair clung to his head with the wet.

I decided it would be impossible to climb the tree to a height where I could hope to get through by talking to him face to face, and pointless to go up to any lower level. So I stayed where I was and said all the things you would say in the situation, or as many as I could think of, and no doubt some more than once. Susan went in and fetched the mack he had left behind, and then I did do a climb and managed to loop the thing over the branch he was standing on. He ignored it. A little after that he pulled himself forward and I thought for a moment he was coming down, but he was going up, up to the next tier, so to speak. I stepped back for a better view, remembering rather late in the day that he had been given to this sport as a young boy and had once, on holiday in Wales, climbed some horrible height like seventy feet to get to a bird's nest, not to take the eggs, just look at them. Now I saw him find a fork and another bit that between them made a kind of seat where he had no need to hang on to anything.

'He could be up there all day,' I said. 'What are we going to do?'

'I don't think there's anything we can do.' Susan had pushed her hair up and under a red mackintosh hat with a fairish brim. It made her look French or Italian, anyway not English and absolutely not like her mother. 'I can't imagine what would make him come down while he still wants to stay there.'

'We can't just leave him there to get wetter and wetter.'

'It looks as if we'll have to, darling. We're not helping him by standing about here getting wet ourselves. I'm not being callous about it but he'll come down in his own good time. When he's had enough.'

'Oh sure, but when's that going to be? He's mad, love. He's probably got voices telling him to stay there for forty days and forty nights.'

'Maybe, maybe not. Didn't one of those doctors say something about attention-seeking? Anyway, it's their job to sort it out.'

'But surely to God . . .'

'I think we ought to try leaving him to himself. Taking no notice.'

'Hey, dad!' called Steve, so unexpectedly that I jumped. 'I couldn't do anything else. I didn't want to come up here but I had to, where I can't be looked into. I kept giving things away in the house, even when I was asleep.' He was shivering and making hissing noises between the words. His voice came out odd but distinct in the damp air. 'I didn't mean to but I just couldn't help it. I haven't got to be awake to be tapped because the storage circuits are always active, but there's got to be conduction too and that means metal or stone at ground level. I can always be looked into if there's that and I don't even know when it's happening. The street's nearly as bad even with the location tuning. But up here I've got all this insulation with vegetable matter and the gap's too wide to jump at normal power. I just hope they don't realize what's keeping them out. With stepped-up power I wouldn't even be safe up here.'

His cheeks were shiny with rain and probably tears as well and his mouth was turned down at the corners. I could not imagine a better example of a person full of fear and misery. I called to him, 'Please come down, son, I beg you. Just for your dad. Please.'

He shook his head and turned away, his face crumpling.

'I'm going to ring Nowell,' I said to Susan.

She stared at me for a couple of seconds and then said in what I thought was a cheerful voice, 'I hope you're joking, Stanley.'

'No I am not joking. I told you about the way she calmed him down when he got violent at her place that time, and talked him into going into hospital over the phone. Well, let's see if she can work the trick again.'

'Surely you know how I feel about her.' No, there was nothing cheerful here.

'I fancy I've a pretty fair idea, though you've never actually said. I understand all that, and in the ordinary way of course I wouldn't dream of letting her get within a mile of you, but this isn't an ordinary situation. Your feelings are very important to me, make no mistake, love, but just at the moment Steve's feelings are more important. And his state. Now you must be able to understand that.'

'Yes, I understand,' she said, and turned round and went back into the house.

For a moment I felt a pang of a kind of fear I had not even thought about for nearly ten years. Then it was gone. I called to Steve that I would be back and left him there.

I got through to Nowell straight away. When I did I realized I had been half or a quarter hoping she would be unreachable. As soon as she understood what was required of her she started thick-and-thinning away like nobody's business and after doing enough of it to last me, or herself, said she would come at once.

'Great. Don't – ' I said, and stopped.

'Don't what, darling?'

'I was going to say don't break your neck, then I remembered you don't drive.'

She sounded a bit puzzled when she signed off, as well she might. I had been going to ask her not to queen it too hard over Susan, but then it had flashed on me that it was very much the wrong time for being foul to her.

Exactly as I put the phone down the doorbell rang, as if she had found a way of literally coming at once. But of course it was Mrs Shillibeer's early morning. She was wearing a pale blue plastic mack with a hood and resembled an enormous child.

'Hallo,' she said in her geriatric-minder voice. 'Horrible weather.' She mouthed the words so that if I was too deaf to hear them I stood a fair chance of lip-reading them.

'Oh, yes, it is,' I said with a slight quaver.

'Mrs Duke upstairs?' she went on, actually pointing.

'I shouldn't be at all surprised.'

I could hear very little sting in the last one, but it was the best I could do at that moment, and probably just as well. I went out and told Steve his mother would be here soon and saw him nod. Then I went to the bathroom and finished shaving, and then to the bedroom to finish dressing. Susan was there. The whine of the vacuum-cleaner came from somewhere under our feet.

'Has she arrived yet?'

'No,' I said. 'I'll come and tell you when she has.'

'I don't want to set eyes on her.'

'Oh, fair enough. I shan't be bringing her up here.'

'How long will she be around, do you think?'

'Not long, I'd say. If nothing happens in the first few minutes then that's it, probably. Anyway, she won't want to hang about.'

'I've got things to do in here, clearing out drawers and so on, so I shan't be wasting my time.'

It was sporting of her to throw that in. All the same I would have settled for a smile or two. Not that she was cold or I had done any better myself. The two of us had been relaxed but not intimate, like people who had worked in the same office for years without ever having met outside it.

I was in the kitchen trying to eat a yoghurt when Mrs Shillibeer barged into the room. Her forehead looked amazingly huge compared with her chin.

'There's a man in one of the trees out there,' she gabbled, no geriatrics now.

'Yes,' I said, 'I know.' My mind was a total blank. I had not stopped thinking about Steve or him being in the tree for more than five seconds at a time, but somehow it had never occurred to me that this female was going to have to have something said to her on the subject.

'What's he doing? Who is he?'

'He's my son.' This slipped out a second before I got to ideas about branch-lopping, man from the Council and so on.

'The one who's staying here? The one you ... What's he doing up a tree?'

'I suppose he just felt like it,' I found I was saying. Perhaps I really had gone senile.

'*Felt* like it?' she asked indignantly. 'In this weather? What's the matter with him? On drugs, is he?'

Here was my out, but I was too thick to recognize it. 'Nothing like that,' I said with conviction, realizing as I said it that this was not even true in any literal way.

'What is it then? People don't go sitting in the middle of a tree in the pouring rain like that, not if they're ... normal. What is the matter with him?'

I coughed. 'He's ... upset. Confused. Unhappy.' Nobody hearing the words could have believed they were honestly spoken.

'That hospital's not just for anxiety and depression,' she said, suddenly gone all calm and wide-eyed. Susan and I had worked out that that was the best story to cover any unforeseen puzzling or perhaps alarming bit that might have emerged. But it was no use this morning. Mrs Shillibeer had guessed the truth, near enough anyway. 'He's barmy. I'm not having that.'

She started to fling out of the room but then froze and, while I watched in fascination, retraced her steps to where I sat at the table, moving with ridiculous caution like somebody imitating a burglar. First looking over each shoulder in turn she bent forward in my direction and gave me a slow wink.

'I'll tell you this much,' she said in a throaty undertone about as far as possible from her usual mode. 'It's a relief, that's what it is. I've been dying to get away from this job almost since I first started here, that's almost two years now, not that long after you moved in. The money's good quite frankly and my husband would never have let me walk out of here just because I didn't fancy coming. But now I've got a reason, see. He knows I've got this thing about loonies. So I'm off the hook at last. Whoopee.'

'Why don't you like working here? Not because of me, I hope?'

'Ooh no, not you, Stanley, you're a darling, you are. No, it's that stuck-up cat you married. What did you want to go and do that for, a nice guy like you? Have you ever noticed the way she talks to me?' Actually I had, but I kept quiet. 'No reason why you should. Oh Mrs Shillibeer, would you very kindly, very sweetly chop up these shallots, not too fine, you know the way I like them, and tell me when you've done them.' It was — of course — an unkind imitation but not quite an unrecognizable one. 'Never once talks to me like a human being. It's not much to ask. And that mother. And that sister. You want to watch the mother. That's the way Susan'll end up. Well, she's most of the way there already, I reckon.'

Mrs Shillibeer seemed again ready to be off. I said, 'Are you going up there now to tell her some of that?'

'Christ no, what do you take me for? I'm much too scared of her. I'd sooner cross my husband. And that's saying something. Good luck, Stanley love. I'm afraid you're going to need it. Oh, and I hope your son gets better soon. They can do a lot these days, you know.'

She went out in the same sort of style as she had come in, getting into trim for the action. Instantly the doorbell rang. It was Nowell. Who else?

'Darling Stanley.' A warm hug came my way, one full notch below sexiness but no more and accompanied by the usual good smell. 'Am I going to be asked in?'

'Of course. I . . .'

'Is he all right? Will he be all right for the next two minutes?'

'Yes.' I took her into the kitchen, which was all she seemed to want. Much against my expectation she showed no interest in her surroundings. 'Would you like some coffee?'

'No thanks,' she said, not sitting down. 'Stanley, I want to say this. I know you think I've behaved pretty badly over Steve and his troubles, not doing my fair share and all that. Of course you think so. And in a way you're right. The thing is, I've got troubles of my own. Or rather Joanne has. You've seen her, so perhaps you've some idea of how difficult she can be. Difficult, that's hardly the word. It's a full-time job just keeping an eye on her. Not long ago I had to take her to Portugal for a week because she wanted some sunshine. It may be all my fault in the first place but there's no point in arguing about that now. As you can imagine, I don't get any help from Bert.' The mention of this name had a knowing look packaged up with it. 'There it is. She's got me and Steve's got you. Simple as that. I'll lend you a hand when I can but mostly I can't. There we are.'

Again, it was not the moment to query any of this or boggle at the idea of a human being who could make Nowell have to do things, so I was sweet to her instead. Before I had quite finished somebody came tearing down the stairs and went out by the front door. Nowell ignored this completely. I told her to hang on a moment and went up to the bedroom.

Susan was sitting on the bed with about five hundred waist-belts on the counterpane. I was a bit flummoxed on how to open the conversation but she led off straight away.

'Mrs Shillibeer has gone. Walked out.'

The way she spoke these half-dozen words sounded incredibly and horrendously like what I had heard in the kitchen five minutes before. I was reminded in a more disagreeable way than usual that snobbily or not I was quite tickled by being married to someone who talked like that. 'Yes,' I said, 'I heard her.'

'She said you told her Steve was mad and mad people frighten her. She had a mad brother. What the bloody hell possessed you to tell her?'

'I didn't mean to. It just sort of . . . She guessed. I wasn't ready for her.'

'You knew she was here, you let her in. A clever man like you.'

'I'm sorry, I got flustered. We can discuss it later. Nowell has arrived.'

'I can't understand why you didn't call the hospital. They must have people who are used to dealing with this sort of thing.'

'Perhaps I should have, I don't know. I will if this doesn't work. Anyway, she's here now.'

'Well . . . good luck,' said Susan with a smile that came and went.

Whether by good luck or not, it worked. Nowell took her previous line about what a rough time he must have been having and in less than five minutes Steve was down, soaked to the skin, pale, shivering, wretched, but on terra firma. Nowell hugged him, but he seemed unresponsive and had nothing to say for himself. Having called off his performance, though, he was keen enough to get back indoors, and without fuss set about obeying instructions to go up and take off his wet things.

I walked Nowell to the door. Her behaviour had impressed me rather. As well as hiding all curiosity about the house and its contents she had not once mentioned Susan's name or raised the subject without actually referring to it, something she was very good at, and at no stage had shown any triumph or complacency at getting Steve to quit his perch, just pleasure and relief. True, she had more or less blamed me personally for his wetness, coldness and lack of topcoat, but I could think of quite a few people who would have taken that tack.

At the threshold I said, 'Thank you for coming so quickly. That was a damn good show just now.'

'Think nothing of it. Just a knack I have.' Then she gave me a look that signalled the advent of something in bold. 'You're a good chap, Stanley,' she said very earnestly. 'No wonder Steve's devoted to you.'

'Oh.'

Here it came. 'I miss you, you know. Do you believe me?'

'Why not? I miss you. Every day.'

The warmth in my voice took her by surprise, and me too a bit. For an insane moment I could see her seriously wondering why I had said that, how much I meant it, what it might indicate for the future – then it passed, and the Eternal Woman once more looked out of Nowell's eyes. She threw her head back, kissed me lightly on the cheek and tripped away to a waiting taxicab whose driver was doggedly picking his nose.

I was glad I had said what I had. I had indeed meant it, though it was not a complete statement of the case, perhaps not even accurate as far as it went. But if you could miss somebody, feel somebody's absence, without ever wanting to be with them again, then yes, I missed Nowell every day. More to the point, I had been sweet to her in spades, which was not going to come in unhandy when Steve climbed on to the roof of Buckingham Palace or hijacked a jet.

I got him into a hot bath now and went to the bedroom and said, 'All over. She talked him down and she's gone.'

'I know.' Susan had moved on to long thin strips of different-coloured material the purpose of which was very difficult to guess. 'At least I gathered he was down. Is he all right?'

'Well, he's better where he is than where he was. I don't know what more you could say.'

She was still on her limited-friendliness tone, the nearest thing to a female freeze-out I had ever had from her. But when the time came to take Steve off we held on to each other for a fair time, with her seeming not to want to let go as if I were off to the States or somewhere. At the end she gave me a smile, a real one this time. So that was all right.

When I had escorted Steve to Dr Gandhi's manor I went in search of Collings and found her in her room. She was looking really rough that morning, with her hair got up to remind you of carefully prepared paper. I told her about Steve and the tree and she said it was part of the pattern.

'Look, it may be part of your pattern, Dr Collings,' I said as quietly as I could, 'but it's not part of mine or my wife's. We're not used to handling this kind of thing.'

'I understand that.'

'Terrific, but could you do something about it? We're getting near the end of our resources.'

'Of course it's a period of great tension and distress for you both. It would be far from unusual in this situation for your marriage to suffer severe strain,' she said, ready with more technical data if they were needed.

'I dare say it would. I wasn't actually thinking of that side of it. What I was driving at, my wife and I don't know how to deal with someone like Steve. We've managed so far but any moment he might do something we couldn't cope with. Would you please take him back in as a full-time patient where there are trained people to look after him. In his interests.'

'It's in his interests to stay as he is, believe me, Stanley. Do you want him to be a hospital case for the rest of his life?' She went on to describe a few of what she called hospital cases in some detail, and if she wanted my honest agreement that the general run of them would have been as well or better off dead she could have had it for the asking. There was more than a touch of overkill here and I wondered where we were due next. At the end of her cases she said, 'I hope you'll agree it's worth a lot of sacrifice to make any of that less likely to happen to Steve.'

'Oh, absolutely,' I said, letting myself off a question about how much sacrifice and how much less likely, and another one about how likely in the first place.

'He must be helped to live in the world, to make a successful transition to family and community.' On she went about that while I grew more and more uneasy. As she spoke she looked more steadily at me than ever before. This part was so boring that when the punch came I almost missed it. 'These current difficulties are all part of the process of adjustment to the withdrawal of chemotherapy. A progressive – '

'Chemotherapy? That's drugs, isn't it? You mean you've taken him off drugs?'

'Drugs are a crutch, an artificial support. He's got to learn to do without them if he's ever going to live any sort of normal life.'

'But he's *mad*. You should have seen him when he was up that tree. Not just the loony stuff he was saying but the way he looked and everything. He wasn't in a difficulty or adjusting, he was raving bonkers, poor fellow. He was in a *state*. Anyone could have seen.'

'It's very difficult and painful for him and that's why he needs all the understanding and encouragement you can give him.'

'Please take him back. For a bit. He's not ready.'

'You must let me be the judge of that.'

After a bit more along the same lines I came away, trying not to feel scared about what might be in store. Just after starting back I remembered the flick-knife, still in my pocket. I had not exactly forgotten it but so far kept finding I was short of a good place to dump it. Now I soon had one – the river off Blackfriars Bridge. When it was gone I felt a glow of relief, which was not very logical but well worth having on a day like today.

That afternoon, while I was on my way back from an advertising agency somewhere off Oxford Street, an accident up ahead kept me sitting in a traffic block for forty minutes. On my desk in the office I found a note from Morgan telling me to ring home – urgent.

'How long ago was this?' I asked, dialling.

'Oh, getting on for an hour. It was your wife.' He hesitated, then said, 'She sounded a bit upset.'

After half a dozen rings a man's voice spoke at the far end.

'This is Stanley Duke,' I told him.

'Stan, it's Cliff. I'm afraid there's been a bit of a dust-up here, old son. All under control now, but you'd better get along as soon as you can. I'll stay till you come.'

'Anybody hurt?'

'Nothing that can't be taken care of.'

When I got home by taxi and let myself in I found a trail of blood, drops of it the size of a 10p piece, running into the kitchen. 'Up here, Stanley,' said Cliff's voice.

Susan was in her usual chair in the sitting-room. She was pale and had a fair-sized bandage on her left forearm. There was more blood on the carpet and furniture, not a great amount but quite enough. I hurried over and we hugged each other. She said she was all right. I asked what had happened. Cliff answered. 'Steve came at her with a knife,' he said.

'Oh, God. Where is he? Where is he now?'

'In his room. With a shot in him that'll make him not want to go anywhere for quite a while.'

'How bad is the arm?'

'Well, it's nasty, but it's not, it's not bad. In the fleshy part, no major blood-vessel punctured, I've put three stitches in, under a local anaesthetic of course.' He spoke in a dead sort of way, almost as though these details bored him. 'There'll be a certain amount of pain when it wears off and for a couple of days afterwards. I'll leave some pills for that. And I'll look in tomorrow.'

When he had said that I quite expected him to leave, but he stayed where he was, standing by the empty fireplace. I had pulled a stool up to Susan's chair. 'Tell me what happened, love,' I said. 'If you can bear to.'

'Oh, I can bear to. I think the worst part was the fright at the beginning,' she said, a little quietly for her but well under control. 'You did take him to the hospital, darling, did you?'

'Yeah. Right to the ward.'

'I didn't even know he was in the house. The door just burst open and he came rushing in with this knife shouting that I was a bloody bitch who'd driven his mother and father apart and wouldn't let him see his mother. Like that bit of hostility last week, you remember, only this time he meant business, and I just had time to get to my feet before he . . . struck at me.' She started to lift her left arm to show how, but winced and used the other one instead. 'I tried to catch his wrist but I didn't manage it properly, and he cut me.' I squeezed her hand. 'And I thought I was done for, but then he stopped, I don't really know why, perhaps it was the sight of blood, anyway he dropped the knife and gave the most awful sort of groan or moan, an absolutely harrowing noise, and then he simply ran off and I heard his bedroom door slam, and it was over.'

She had not actually started to cry but she was not far off it. I thought she was being pretty good. 'Thank God for that, anyway,' I said. 'What knife was it?'

'There,' she said, and there it was on one of the low tables almost in front of me, though I saw it now for the first time – a kitchen knife from downstairs with, as I knew, a sharp point and edge, now with dried or drying blood on it, some of which had leaked on to the sheet of newspaper underneath. 'Well . . . I went down to the kitchen and tried to get you, and couldn't, and then I got Cliff, and he sweetly said he'd come straight away, and I sort of hung about near the front door, ready to run, until he arrived, and there we are.'

'I know it's a bit early but I'm going to have a drink,' I said after a moment. When I looked at Susan she shook her head. 'Cliff?'

'No thanks, I've got to get back.' But he still made no move.

'So then you turned up,' I said from the drinks tray.

'Yes, I turned up,' said Cliff. As soon as he started to speak I knew that he was not at all bored, just choosing his words carefully, and also that there was something that had not been mentioned, something to do with him – actually I had known it almost since coming into the room. 'I put in the local,' he went on, 'and that was going to take a few minutes to work, so I went up to have a look at Steve. There he was, lying on his bed, not asleep, but quite relaxed I thought, you could almost say torpid, but after what Susan had told me I was taking no. chances. I gave him Valium intravenously, which is pretty quick-acting. He didn't object.'

'Didn't he say anything at all,' I asked, 'why he'd done it or anything?'

'Oh, he said something. I asked him why, why he'd attacked his step-mother, and he said he didn't know what I was talking about. He'd let himself in and come straight up, thinking he was alone in the place, he said.' Cliff snapped the catches of his bag. I fancied his hands were shaking. 'He said he hadn't done it.'

A horrible pause followed. What felt like a hundred thoughts went through my head in two or three seconds, bits of remarks about Steve from Nash, from Collings, from Nowell, cloudy memories of Steve himself when younger, sharper ones of Susan the other day, this morning, and behind it all something I could neither face nor define. At last, very late, I said, 'Amnesia, presumably.'

'Does rather suggest that, doesn't it? Yes, it's quite common in these cases.' He sighed, scratching his head elaborately and sending a thin shower of dandruff on to the shoulders of his incredibly dark green suit. 'Well, that's it. I shouldn't say much about this to anyone, but then I don't suppose either of you will want to. Except of course to the people at the hospital, Stan, when you take Steve in in the morning. It's quite likely they'll want him back in full-time, I suppose. Yeah, and better let them know where he is now.'

'What did you say, you suppose they might want him back in full-time?' Susan asked. 'But surely, I mean after a thing like this they must, mustn't they? Or has he got to murder somebody first?'

'If you're talking about legal committal, I can assure you it wouldn't be at all easy. Not really worth a shot, in fact.'

Cliff had still not sounded his normal self and Susan had spoken so faintly I could hardly hear her, almost without expression too, a new voice for her as far as I was concerned. Shock, that would be. Fatigue. I felt dazed, like with a very bad hangover, wanting to start using my mind on what had been said and what seemed to have happened but unable to get there.

Now Cliff handed over pills and gave instructions about them and other things and I tried to listen. When he started to leave I went with him.

He kept well ahead of me all the way down the stairs and nearly to the front door. 'Nasty,' he said as I opened it. 'Look, er, it might be as well if Susan went and stayed somewhere for a couple of days while we sort things out with the hospital and so on. Just to be on the safe side. No need to worry tonight but she ought to be out of the way tomorrow. So long, Stan. I'll be in touch.'

I rang the hospital, but could find nobody who gave any sign of having heard of Steve, so without a lot of hope of success I left a message at the switchboard. In the teeth of a whacking reluctance I went back up to the sitting room, though once there I landed up at the drinks tray without any trouble at all. Susan was sitting in the same position, her injured arm on the arm of the chair.

'What did Cliff say to you?' she asked in the same tone as before.

'He said tomorrow you ought to get out for a bit. Stay with someone.'

'Did he really.'

'Can I get you anything, love? What about a nice cup of tea? Tomato sandwich with the skins off? Do you good to eat something.'

She looked at me with her eyes half-closed and her mouth drooping and said in another voice I had not heard before, low and level, 'You little bastard. Swine. Filth.'

I was so surprised I knocked a bottle of tonic water over with my elbow, and yet I had been fully expecting it. 'What have I done?' I said.

'You think I gave myself that cut, don't you? Three stitches there are in there. I'd like you to see it.'

'But I don't, I don't think you gave yourself it.' I had no idea what I thought.

'I was watching you when Cliff told you Steve had said he didn't know anything about it and you stood there weighing it up. Weighing it up.'

'I wasn't, there were just some things I couldn't help – '

'You believe what somebody says your deranged, deluded, fucking raving maniac of a son said instead of what your wife tells you happened. You see what that makes me, don't you?'

'I don't believe – '

'Or rather what it reveals about what you think of me. You think I'm so neurotic, so self-centred, so . . . unprincipled that I'd expose that boy, that poor madman to being locked up and Christ knows what and I'd put you through it and suffer all that pain myself just to . . . just for what? Attention? Is that what I was after?' She spoke in the same level tone.

At least I had the sense to see that this was a question with no good answers.

'And you think I'd do that. As well as tell a lie on that scale. That seems to me about the worst insult one person can give another. And I'm not having it.' She stood up. 'I'm off. And I'm not waiting till the morning as your friend suggests, I'm leaving straight away. Catch me hanging on here with someone who thinks I'm like that.'

I stood up too. 'You're not fit to travel, you need rest,' I said, and got out of her way as she moved towards the door.

'I'll risk it.' At the door she stopped and turned round. 'If anybody wants me they can get me at my mother's. Though you'll be wasting your time if you try me there yourself. I suppose you think that's funny. Yer, ass right, the wife's gorn orf to er muvver's,' she said in a very poor imitation of perhaps a Hackney or Bow accent as much as anything. 'Just up your street, you lower-class turd. I don't know how I've put up with you for so long, with your gross table-manners and your boozing and your bloody little car and your frightful *mates* and your whole ghastly south-of-the-river man's world. You've no breeding and so you've no respect for women. They're there to cook your breakfast and be fucked and that's it. So of course nothing they say's worth taking seriously, and when one of them says something quite important and serious and a man says something different then you believe him even though he's out of his mind. Oh, I wish to Christ I'd found out about you sooner.'

I watched her saying this, looking as brainy and nervous as ever but not humorous any more and nowhere near vulnerable. Her eyes were wide open now, though blinking pretty fast, and I had seen them more or less like that a thousand times, but if she had ever before had her lower lip pushed forward as it was at the moment then I had missed it. She had taken a few steps back into the room from the doorway and stood there with a brown striped cardigan thrown over her shoulders and her right hand clasping her left elbow just above the top edge of the bandage. This set my mind running on whether she had had her arm in the sleeve or not when . . . but I pulled guiltily back from that. I was still dazed and could think of nothing to say. Well, I said 'Cheers, love' at the end.

'*Love*,' she said through her teeth, and made for the door again.

'Are you coming back?'

'I shan't be able to take everything with me in one go if that's what you mean, so yes to that extent.'

She said this from outside the room. There was no one I wanted to see and nothing I wanted to do. Except have another drink, of course. By the time I had seen to that I was into my second minute of having no wife.

Had she really stabbed herself? What a perfectly ridiculous sodding question. Who ever heard of the assistant literary editor of the *Sunday Chronicle* stabbing herself a bit and saying her barmy stepson had done it to pay her husband out for thinking the barmy stepson was more important than she was? But perhaps she had. And of course perhaps she had done it to make the stepson seem barmier than he was, more violent, so violent he would have to be shut up and her life could go back to normal. But that would have been calculation in pursuit of comfort – too squalid to suit a woman like Susan, a woman who might incidentally let an innocent party in for damage while following her ends but would never make that damage her aim. If she had done it, she had done it for ego, as in her own scenario, not for peace and quiet. Wow, I thought to myself – I had come quite far quite fast too. Could she have done it? Surely not the woman who had put so much into cheering me up when I needed it, who had only the other day seen off her own mother and sister on my behalf. But perhaps she had. Could Nowell have done it? Perhaps. Probably. Yes. But what of that?

At least one fact needed establishing. When Cliff said Steve had said he knew nothing about any attack, had I really — what had she said? — had I weighed up the chances? Not a lot — it had been far more a matter of telling myself in a completely slow, thick way that that was funny, what Steve said had happened was different from what Susan said had happened. And when I tried to do some weighing a moment ago I had not even been able to start. Never mind, at the time in question had I looked as if that was what I was doing? That depended not only on how I had behaved but on who had been watching. But what was absolutely bleeding certain and inescapable was that I could have been weighing up the chances, which was the same as I could easily have been, which meant I might even have been going to be foul to her. Good God. Surely not.

I was going through this for about the fifteenth time when the doorbell rang. Having got half-way across the room I remembered hearing the phone give its little end-of-call chink a few minutes earlier and reasoned that a minicab stood below, so I went back to my chair, not before I had topped up my drink. Almost at once I heard Susan coming down the stairs and in a moment she appeared in the doorway. She was carrying the large red suitcase she always took on holiday and was wearing her round woollen hat and gloves. I got to my feet so as not to show unwilling, but she just stayed where she was and looked very seriously at me. If I had had a bit more time I might have gone over to her and confessed to or admitted anything she liked — as it was I too stayed put. There was no knowing, then or later, what was going on inside her, from profound sorrow to wondering whether it would be all right to touch me for the cab fare. Anyway, the bell rang again and without saying anything or changing her expression she went out, and soon enough the street door slammed.

Later on I went and looked at Steve, but he was obviously out for the count, so I came down again and had another drink or so. About 4 a.m. I woke up in my chair and went and drank a couple of litres of water and got into bed.

4   Prognosis

First thing the next morning I took a cab down to Fleet Street and drove
the Apfelsine slowly and dangerously back to Hampstead. I wished I had
a headache or anything else like that, out where I could see it so to speak,
instead of how I felt. Steve was still half-full of the sedative Cliff had given
him and I had a hard time getting him to get up. When he finally came
downstairs he ate nothing, not that he had done much different on previous
mornings as far as I could remember, but now I was in charge of breakfast
I noticed more. I managed a glass of apple juice and most of half a bowl
of posh continental cereal with nuts and raisins that had been cunningly
turned the same dusty white as the cereal itself. On an ordinary day I
would have said that of course I preferred this sort of thing to any old eggs
and bacon or sausage or kipper in the world, but now, again, I remembered
that neither of my wives had been the sort to fancy cooking their husband's
breakfast, never mind what the second one had had to say on the point
the previous evening. I drank a lot of Lapsang Suchong, which I really did
quite like and which helped the other stuff to stay down.

When the time came I told Steve so and went and had a pee and collected
my gear. He had not appeared, so I went back to the kitchen and found
him in exactly the same position as I had left him in, sitting near rather
than at the table with his shoulders hunched, hands clasped and head
down. I wanted to fetch him a thump that would lay him full length on
the floor, in the first place for not doing what he was told, but also for
being a bleeding pest, being dull, being off his head, being around the place
all the time without a word to say for himself or even a glance to spare,
and taking over my life and mucking it up. But instead of thumping him
I shouted his name. He looked up very quickly and just for a second I saw
him as he always had been before that first evening he came to the house,
but then almost at once his face changed in ways I had no hope of making
out and went back to being something different, more different than it had
been, I thought, with a funny sort of twist to the corner of the lower lip.
I told him we were off, quietly now, and he got up straight away.

As always it was a relief being in the car because people often said
nothing to each other in cars, and anyway there was the driving to be

done. After a few minutes, though, I started asking Steve what he had been up to the previous day and he answered after a fashion. He had walked out. He had got on a bus. He had arrived home. What time? No idea. He had gone to his room. Susan had been in the sitting room, had she? No idea. What had she said to him? From here on the answers stopped coming. It looked as if I was never going to know any more about that afternoon.

I had one last shot. 'There must be something you remember,' I said. 'Never mind how trivial.'

He seemed to reflect for half a minute or so, then nodded slowly. 'Actually there is something.'

'Let's have it then.'

'You're not going to like it,' he mumbled.

'Don't worry, I'll manage.'

'Promise not to be angry.'

'Of course. I promise.'

'Well,' he said, staring in front of him, 'I remember being born.' I just managed not to drive into the side of a bus. 'What?' I said. 'I remember being born. Everybody's done their best to make me forget by telling a different story. Mum says she brought me into the world and you say you're my father and I don't really blame either of you – you probably believe it yourselves by this time. And everybody else believes it and no wonder. But I've had the message so often on television and in ads and the street names and the names on shops and even the labels on bottles of sauce and things, so many times I can remember it, actually being born. Well, I say born, attaining consciousness would be better, more precise. It was like a great light being switched on.

'Yeah, I was put together by these alchemists using the philosopher's stone.' He was smiling cheerfully now. 'Kept in a vault in Barcelona till needed, then triggered off by radio beam. And here I am, ready to begin my task.' At that he looked guilty and nervous, as though he felt he had let slip something important. 'Er, I want to thank you for all your kindness, Mr Duke. Oh, and I think we should go on calling each other father and son in public. For security reasons. You understand.'

I pulled in to the side of the road and stopped behind a van delivering a lot of eggs. I spent five minutes or so trying to get myself to think that it was all just part of his madness, nothing to do with rejecting me or his mother, while thinking under zero pressure that whatever happened or was said in the future I would always feel I had had some hand, somehow, in bringing about his condition. Nobody could prove the contrary. Perhaps nobody could prove anything of importance. Having reached this conclusion I drove on, since I was going to have to some time.

When Steve and I eventually reached Gandhi's pad Gandhi was not in it. But Collings was, which would save me a walk. Also in attendance were the sister I had seen on my first visit and since, name of Wheatley, the white-haired moaning loony I had also seen before, not actually moaning at the moment, and another with no teeth who was new to me.

Almost straight away I said to Collings, 'It looks as if he stabbed my wife. Took a knife to her. Nothing too serious.'

She followed it up in a flash. 'Looks as if?' she repeated. 'Did he or didn't he?'

'He did,' I said without thinking at all. To believe anything else was ridiculous again. 'I just wasn't there when it happened. But he did it.'

'Are you sure?'

'Of course I'm sure.' This time it was more that I spoke before I could think. 'There she is with a gash in her arm. What are you talking about?'

She was hardly listening, looking into Steve's face, looking at his eyes, feeling his pulse. 'This boy has been sedated,' she said.

'You bet he has. That was Dr Wainwright's doing, our GP, when he came to stitch up my wife. I should have thought it was common sense.'

More no-listening. She sat on the corner of Steve's bed next to him with her hand on his shoulder, still looking at him closely, asking him now a string of quite friendly questions about what he wanted to do and where he wanted to be, soon agreeing that he should stay as he was for the moment and then get into bed if he felt like it. I was just starting to think that she might be some good when she turned towards me and said, 'What have you been doing to your son?'

I stopped breathing. The sister sent me a glance of sympathy with a touch of despair. The white-haired loony did nothing but the toothless one, either catching the feel of things or driven by a sudden extra bit of delusion, backed into a corner and crouched there with his arms held out in front of him like a wrestler's. When the sister went over and spoke gently to him he dropped his arms to his sides and started blinking and shaking his head very fast.

After a while I gave up watching this and said to Collings, 'Can we go somewhere and have a talk?'

'Here will do, for anything you have to say to me, Stanley.' Her tone, somewhere in the anger-resentment bracket, did an unusually good matching job with her expression. At the same time during what followed she kept switching them both off and paying attention to Steve, now and then muttering to him too quietly for me to hear.

'Well,' I said, 'what do you mean, what have I done to him?'

'It's obvious enough I should have thought. He goes through an acute phase, he starts responding to treatment, he's gradually pulling out and coming to terms with himself and getting in touch with his emotions, doing so well that I put him back with family, which in practice means you, and he promptly turns round and retreats behind his defences again.'

'Oh, that's what happened, is it? I thought you took him off his drugs and he promptly tried to join the Arab secret service, climbed a tree to insulate himself from blokes who were reading his mind with radio waves and went for his stepmother with a knife.'

While I was saying this she sent Sister Wheatley out of the room to fetch or do something or other and then took a bit of notice of me. 'If he did. It's just the sort of tale somebody might dream up if they wanted to get him taken off their hands and back into hospital.'

'You think I,' I said, and stopped, taking good care not to move my head suddenly in case it fell off. 'But if he didn't. . .' I stopped again.

This I thought she missed altogether for what it was worth. 'He's obviously suffered a major relapse and requires rehospitalization. All those weeks of work gone for nothing,' she said, glaring indignantly at me.

'You're a scream, you are, Collings, and no mistake.' I realized I must have sounded fairly angry. 'You decided Steve was ready to spend some of his time at home. Wrong. You decided he was ready to come off drugs. Wrong again. Two whacking errors of judgement that might have got somebody killed. And you put it all down to me. Incidentally till a moment ago you must have thought I was a quite fit person to be in charge of him, mustn't you? Another floater.'

'What's the matter with you? Been having trouble with Nowell again?'

'Oh for Christ's sake,' I said, and the white-haired loony gasped and winced and the one with no teeth raised his arms as before. 'You can't stay ten years old for ever,' – the best I could do at short notice.

'Don't you talk like that to me, my lad.' She stared at me with her eyes half-shut and her eyebrows lifted in the mysterious expression I had seen in the Crown and Sceptre that time, only now there was no mystery any more. Sheer rage was there but also menace, a stated purpose to level the score. 'One more crack out of you and I'll discharge him and then you'll fucking know all about it. Is that clear?'

All my own anger died away. I just felt a dull horror that a doctor, a woman, anybody could turn a madman loose to avenge a passing slight. No, I felt incredulity too – surely not, no one would, she was merely furious for the moment. But this brought no comfort.

The Sister came back into the room having fetched a file or part of one, presumably Steve's part. Collings started checking through it. I said goodbye to Steve in the hope that he might at least raise his head, but he gave no sign of having heard, so I went.

While I was making my way through the boarding-house part of the ground floor I heard my name called. As more than half expected it was Sister Wheatley. I turned back.

'I just wanted to say, Mr Duke, I'll keep an eye on Steve for you. Can I have your telephone number?' She wrote it efficiently down on a small pad from her top pocket. 'If anything, well, untoward happens I'll let you know. It won't because she can't afford it to, not anything awful, but I thought perhaps you might like to have something you felt you could rely on. She's all right really, just a bit funny sometimes.'

'That's very kind of you, Sister. Thank you,' I said, and, and thought to myself you got good and bad in every crowd. You know, like Germans.

Outside there was a lot of sunshine, more than usual for the time of year, as bright as early evening in summer. Immediately everyone and everything I had been thinking about up to that moment fell away and I was stuck with just myself and having no wife. It stayed with me throughout the drive to the office, the ride in the lift and the short walk to the private phone, and barely started to shift when Lindsey Lucas answered her extension, though it moved a bit further off when she agreed to meet me in the Crown and Sceptre after work. When that was over I spent a minute or so paying close attention to the wall, which had a great many unspecified people's numbers ball-pointed and otherwise written on it. Then I rang Nash's New Harley Street place and after an interval got some other male who told me to ring him, Nash, at home that evening. I said I would, fine, but the bloke hung about.

'Is it, er, very urgent?'

'I couldn't say *very*, no. But I would rather like to see him as soon as convenient.'

'Oh. Have you rung him before at that number? Recently?'

'No, never. Why?'

'I should, I should leave it till after seven if I were you. To make sure of getting him, you know.'

'Oh, I see,' I said. I wondered if I had struck Nash's grandfather, or at least somebody of that age-group. Then I thought whoever it was had sounded rather as though he would have liked to warn me about something but had not known how. Then I put the question aside. In my own office I sat for a time trying to work up the energy to tackle the whole immense matter of Stentor PA Systems' half-page. I had not got even as far as being able to start to think when my phone rang and I clutched at it.

'Stanley Duke? Good morning, Penangan High Commission calling. I have the Commercial Attaché for you.'

After a pause and a click a voice I knew said, 'Am I having Mr Joke?'

'Yes, speaking. Good morning, Mr One, I mean Mr Attaché. What can I do for you?'

'Mr Joke, I'm wanting to make some arrangements with you for four pages special report in your newspaper. It must be soon because our Minister of Trade will come to London next month for three days. Please telephone my secretary shortly to arrange lunch.'

'Is this definite, Mr Attaché? The last time we discussed the project it was still at the planning or provisional stage.' I remembered that it was only simple sentences that might throw Mr One – anything at all complicated he sailed through.

'Oh yes, definite. My government has completed its explorations.'

'That's fine – highly satisfactory. Tell me, sir, shall I be working with you direct or with that observer I spoke to recently?' Pretty crafty, I thought.

'Observer? What observer?'

'At the High Commission. That was what you – that was his official designation.'

'Observer,' said Mr One, lingering over the syllables. Eventually, '*Haw*,' he howled at some length, carried away by wonder at his own feat of memory. Like Mandy. 'He has been subducted.'

So now I knew. The lunch itself would be eatable and drinkable and there would be the fun of telling . . . Oh well, I had had a minute off.

When I had put the phone back Morgan was there. 'Stanley, you know that new girl, the one with the cage?'

'With the what? Is that the same as the one with the rope?'

'That's right. Going on like the hammers of hell she's been, about sexual harassment.'

'Really? Lucky to get any you'd think, with that comb. The limping porter again, I suppose.'

'No, it's the bloody tea-lady. Asks her if she had a good you-know-what last night and says she bets her boyfriend's got a nice big how's-your-father. In a nasty way, she says, the girl.'

I groaned. 'M'm, it's sexual in a sense, of course it is, and I can see how it might be harassing for her, but it doesn't quite add up to what the phrase is supposed to mean, does it? Not that there's the slightest point in telling her so, I realize that. When were you talking to her?'

'Now, just while you were on the phone.'

'Oh, yeah, that was the King of Penang wanting four pages. Firm.'

'Great. Come and have a word with her, would you, Stanley? She's in a hell of a tizzy.'

I looked round for an escape route and there was Harry Coote brilliantly standing in the doorway. I had not set eyes on him since what he quite likely thought of as the night of the taxi. 'Got a minute?' he said.

Well, I would have had a minute and more for Yasser Arafat at that stage rather than a word with a female in a hell of a tizzy, in fact one in almost any foreseeable condition. I told Morgan I would have the word later and he covered up his disappointment like a man, meaning none of it showed.

Since my last visit somebody had replaced Harry's fish-tank with a piece of sculpture in a dark blue veined material. The subject was probably a horse, or perhaps a cow, but it was impossible to be sure because the artist had died half-way through the job, or perhaps got fed up and left it. There was a new potted plant too with hairy leaves.

Harry sat down at his desk, which was completely bare but for a glass ashtray the size of a dustbin-lid, and took out his cheroots. I noticed that the packet design had a depressing Third-World look to it. 'Any news?' he asked.

'Well, the Penangans are taking those four pages.'

'Really.' He showed at least as much enthusiasm at hearing this as Morgan had done. 'How long have you been in the job now?'

'About eighteen months longer than you've been in yours. That's . . .'

'Ever thought of making a change?'

'Not seriously. Seeing as you ask.'

'That young fellow, now, what's he called, your number two, nice young fellow, Morgan something, Morgan, Morgan, Morgan *Wyndham*, Wyndham, tell me, Stan, in your view, is he, would he be, er, assuming he was interested of course, but do you think he'd be capable of running the show there for a time?'

'Well there again I haven't done much in the way of thinking, Harry, to be quite honest. Off the top of my head I reckon that's about what he'd be, capable. He doesn't get ideas much. Why?'

'Well, as I've told you before I have my doubts whether advertising manager has ever been the ideal outlet for your particular kind of expertise.'

'Have you now?' I asked him when it seemed he had had his last word on the subject. To my mind the conversation needed to get much funnier fast. 'You wouldn't be trying to tell me something, Harry, would you?'

'Yes,' he said quite briskly. 'Yes, I would, I am. Unofficially, I'm telling you unofficially that as from the end of the month your services in your present post will no longer be required.'

'Oh, yeah,' I said, wondering if the house in Hampstead was burning down as I sat there, and then saw he was looking at me with an awful sort of World War II film admiral's smile.

'But your services as motoring correspondent of this newspaper are very much in demand, my dear Stanley. Unofficially, the Board have been dissatisfied with the present arrangement for some time. Then, well, I just happened to run into your ex's husband, old Bert Hutchinson, I think I told you I see him in the Ladbroke Arms from time to time, and he said, well, he said he'd had a long talk with you recently and he said he'd never come across anybody who knows as much about cars as you do.' Did he? What had I said? When? 'And *cares* about them, he made a big point of that. And that's . . . essential,' said Harry with a lot of sincerity. 'And I know you've always wanted to be a writer.' How could he know that? What could possibly have made me tell him? Where? 'So . . . I went away, and I had a small think, and I dropped a word, and you'll be hearing . . . soon. I hope you're pleased, Stan.'

'Oh yes.' I was, or I would be one day. 'Thank you very much,' I went on, trying to sound as though I believed he had done it all himself.

'Forget it, lad. I just passed on a thought, that's all. Yes, nice to do that little thing on my way out. I'm er, I'm changing jobs myself. Going to edit a new English-language newspaper in South Africa. Quite a, you know, what would you say, a challenge.'

'You bet.'

'I thought it was time to make a shift. I thought if I don't do it now I'm never going to.'

'That's the spirit.'

As soon as I had spoken a horrible silence started. I could hardly spring up and be gone so soon after hearing these two fair-sized bits of news, at least I felt I hardly could, but at the same time I could think of nothing to say. Neither could Harry, it seemed, or rather, much worse than that, I saw he could think of something all right, but was far from sure whether he could or should or wanted to say it. The moment had come for him to ask me to marry him. His mouth opened. I slid my right foot round till it was alongside the front leg of my chair, heel lifted ready to give me a good take-off on my dash for the door.

'I'm going to tell you something I've never told anybody else,' he began. He had his hands clasped in front of him on the desk. 'You'll have noticed I not only have no wife, I also have no lady friend of any sort and as far as you know never have had. That's right. Some people of course have worked out that that must mean I'm, you know, queer.' He considerately went straight on at this point to save me having to start pretending I had never been one of those people. 'Well, I suppose I might be, deep down. All I can say to that is, it would have to be bloody deep down, Jack. No, as regards the *direction* of my sexual urges, you might call it boringly normal. But when we come to their *intensity*, then it's a different picture.'

He ground out his cheroot in slow motion while we both in different ways thought about the picture. 'Sub,' he said abruptly. 'Definitely sub. About once a month to six weeks. Speeds up a bit in the winter, I've noticed, funnily enough. Anyway, no problem, I get on the blower, by the time I'm along there she's ready and waiting, back indoors within the hour. Never let them come to me. Last time that happened she wanted to *stay the night* and I had a devil of a job shifting her. I've been going to the same one for over ten years now. No point in chopping and changing. They're all built the same.'

While he told me this much Harry had mostly looked away from me but had kept flicking his eyes to my face. Now, with the hard part presumably done, he relaxed a bit, lit another cheroot and gave me more of a proper glance, and when he went on he took his time.

'I don't suppose it's ever occurred to you, Stanley, to work out what it costs you to be married, even with the wife working. Well, it wouldn't, I dare say, your type of bloke. It occurred to me, though, very early in the game. You obviously get considerably more out of it, out of marriage, that is, than I would in all sorts of ways. But for someone like me it's simply not on.'

He spoke in an impressive, statesmanlike way, thumping the desk with his fist. 'As a commercial transaction it's just *not on*. Your money,' he said, managing to make it sound really grand, up there on a level with your country and your old mother, 'draining away twenty-four hours a day, seven days a week on goods and services that are . . . *non-requisite* and . . . *non-pleasurable*. Like Christmas all the year round. In 1969 men in Great Britain lost control on average of sixty-two per cent of their disposable income on getting married, according to my calculations. And it won't have gone down since, will it? Not with all this liberation. That's a laugh, that is.' He laughed. 'Liberation from what, pray? But we'd better not start on that. Just remember that wives in developed countries are in effect many times more highly paid for their contribution than any other group, certainly any other unskilled workers. And all this is assuming an average sex life. Whereas in my case . . .'

'What about companionship?' I asked, feeling somebody should.

He seemed puzzled. 'Having another person round the house, you mean?'

'Well, a bit more than that. To talk to, share things with kind of style.'

'M'm. I should imagine that would go along with a normal sex drive. Obviously does, in fact. I'm not trying to lay down a general law. The arrangement suits most people. I mean most men. Needless to say it suits most women. Well . . .'

He looked at his watch and we both stood up. But he had not quite finished. 'In a way, you know, I don't really mind if here and there I get suspected of being a faggot. It's nothing so dreadful these days. Certainly far less objectionable to me than giving someone else my money to spend for the rest of my life. But the result is, of being suspected of it is it's harder to make friends, men friends that is of course. For instance I'd have liked to get to know you better, Stan, but it wasn't to be. And then when a man on his own has passed his first youth there's a lot he doesn't get invited to. Eh, the world's made for the marrieds. It's taken a mortal time for all that to sink in in my case. I intend to do something about it when I get to Cape Town. I can't do anything about being on my own, at least I won't, but I can have had a wife in England now rather long dead. Something never discussed. See you before I go.'

All the way back to my office I succeeded in not collapsing with woe at the thought of the friendship that never was. Once or twice during Harry's recital I had wondered whether his sexual policy might be based on a deep, perhaps unconscious hatred or horror of women, but I concluded now that it was nothing more than hatred and horror of exposing his wallet to the light. In the eyes of most men this was surely a more powerful disincentive to chumming up with him than any inklings of faggotism. He had incidentally not explained what he had against the common practice of other non-marriers, picking girls up at parties and putting them down on the morrow – cheaper, you might have thought, than a Harry-type solution. Ah, but only in theory. You never knew what you might be letting yourself in for in the way of providing a hot bath or a cooked breakfast, lending cab fare with nothing in writing about getting it back, etc. Still, I had to thank him for neither saying what a shame he had always thought it was that Nowell and I had failed to make a go of things nor asking meaningly if things were all right at home. But then perhaps he had never felt much personal commitment to either concern.

Lindsey was looking very trim when she turned up in the pub just after six, even healthier than usual and sort of better defined, as though I were seeing her closer to. Her high-collared metal-buttoned jacket and tan boots gave an outdoorsy effect. From the start she paid close attention to everything I said and quite soon she was paying it to my story of what had happened up to and including Susan's exit. She, Lindsey, made some faces and a few noises at high or low points but she came out with none of those dispensable prompts I had known females to hand out so as to stay in shot while someone else tried to talk. I carried on for about ten minutes instead of the couple of weeks I could easily have filled. When it was over she went to the bar for more drinks, getting them just in time before the place filled up in a wink like a lift on the underground.

'Well I never did,' she said. 'Do you think she actually went and stabbed herself like that?'

'No, I . . . No. A clever, educated woman like Susan, with a responsible job, always in such marvellous control of herself? Surely not. After all I've been living with her for four years now. The thing's too messy, too hasty. Rubbishy. Silly. No. Though I suppose I must have – '

'She'd have been doing it on the spur of the moment right enough. And when somebody like that loses control they lose it good and proper. Oh, she's capable of it, believe me.'

'So you say.'

'So would others say if you ever got a chance to ask them. Listen, in those four years have you ever met any of her friends from before?'

'Well, there's her boss, old Robbie Whatname Jamieson, and his wife, and a fellow called . . . No, not a lot, not really.'

'She does that, she cuts off completely and moves on. Do you know, she's never been near any of the people we used to know at Somerville in the Sixties? What you've got to grasp, Stanley, what you've got to take in is she's mad. Off her educated head. It was educated in an interesting way, which I don't imagine you know about either.'

The fruit-machine started up. Apparently without meaning it or even noticing, someone gave me a boof in the small of the back that nearly sent me off my stool. Someone else came with his pint and stood so close that his bent elbow hid Lindsey's face. She shifted and looked at me through her glasses, which were very clean and had crimson frames that day.

'Would you like to come home, Stan?'

'Oh, I'd love to.'

When we had been at home, in her stately garden flat off Fulham Road, for some little time, she said, 'You're not really Jewish at all, are you darling?'

'No. My grandfather came from East Anglia. Well, I suppose he could have come from Tel Aviv before that but he didn't. I know I look it a bit.'

'All right, but what about this then?'

'Lindsey, where have you been? Oh, of course, I was forgetting. Just let me tell you that over *here* that's been done to practically everybody from way back. Even lower-class turds. It's supposed to help you to pee or something.'

'Look, I know it's a dodgy topic, but you are lower-class, aren't you darling? Just between ourselves, naturally.'

'I was before I came up in the world, true, but lower-middle-class, not working-class. Very important distinction. My old dad got really wild if you said he was working-class. Worse than calling him a Jew.'

'You do go on about it a bit, don't you?'

'I'd drop it like a shot if people would let me. And you asked. And which bit of the mick working class do you come from, Lucas?'

'That's much worse than calling your father a Jew. Micks are Catholics, bog Irish, and I'm right bang in the middle of the middle class – I'll have you know my father's a big wheel in the Manpower Services Commission, and everybody there talks with this hick accent except the real nobs who've been to school in England. *And* the family home's in Lisburn, which is the Godalming of the Six Counties. A very nice place, Northern Ireland. Lovely and quiet. Oh, if you're a bloody fool and know just where to go you can get your head blown off all right, but it's quiet everywhere else. No race problem. Peaceful.'

She stopped speaking on the last word. I thought of suggesting that it was rather quaint to say a place had no race problem when it was all Irish there, but then thought not. In a minute or two I was deep into one of the nicest silences I could remember for a long time. It was not quite total – not much traffic came down this way, but I heard a couple of taxis, muffled though by the old thick windows and the heavy curtains, scattered footsteps passed, and now and then I caught Lindsey's breathing, so slow I thought she must be asleep. The things in the rest of my life were still there, only for the time being there was nothing they could do. Very little light came into the room, just enough to make out the dark patch that was her head and the white of her shoulder. Eventually I sighed and shifted. She was awake after all and got me wrong, though not seriously.

'Do you want a drink?' she asked without moving.

'Not yet, thank you. Darling.'

Later on I did have a drink, a Scotch and water actually, and called the number I had been given for Nash. It answered so quickly that someone must have either happened to be dusting the telephone at the time or been sitting waiting for it to ring.

'Yes?' A harsh, uninformative voice.

'May I speak to Dr Nash, please?'

'Who are you?' A woman, not very young, posh, like Alethea as much as anyone.

'Duke's the name. I was hoping to – '

'Who are you?' Drunk.

'My son is one of Dr Nash's – '

'Get off this line and stay off it.' Like a send-up of a ham actor being threatening. Also mad. 'He's not coming . . . *got it*? He's staying right here, okay? And that is straight from the horse's mouth, brother. You can tell your *floosies* that Dr Nash regrets he will be unable to attend the . . . ffffunction.'

I went on standing there by the oriental-style earthenware umbrella jar in Lindsey's hall listening to this and feeling a certain amount of a charlie, none the less quite incapable of coming up with something to say. Then after another word or two from the drunken upper-crust madwoman there was a sudden complete silence at the far end, the sort you get when somebody puts his hand over the mouthpiece. Then Nash came on.

'Hallo, Alfred Nash here, who is calling?'

His composure was so ironclad that for more than an instant I thought I must have dreamt up the contents of the last half-minute. Of course, being that much older he must be more used to them, though perhaps . . . I just beat him to asking again by telling him who I was, then went on to fill him in about Steve, who I said had attacked his stepmother. 'I wish you'd go and see him there, doctor,' I said finally. 'I'm worried about him. The woman is a dangerous psychopath, sorry, I mean, you know, a hysterical neurotic.'

Only a touch more sharply he said, 'What, what woman is that?'

'Er, Dr – '

'Yes yes, Dr Collings, m'm. M'm. As it happens I can visit your son tomorrow morning.'

'I was going over then myself. Shall I meet you there?'

'Would you forgive me a moment?' More dead silence, for a bit longer this time. When he emerged again there was a sort of echo of a yell in the background. 'No, I think I should advise you to stay away, Mr Duke,' he said consideringly. 'I'll see you at New Harley Street at twelve, if that's all right.'

'I'll be there. This is very kind of you.'

'Well. The alternative was a workshop on social psychiatry.'

He hung up with headlong speed, so much so that he chopped off half the last syllable. I helped myself to another drink and took a refill in to Lindsey, who was sitting up in bed, though not very far. She looked about two without her glasses.

'Cheers,' she said. 'Every success.'

'Thanks. With what?'

'Your new job. Car critic.'

'Oh that.' I had honestly not thought of it above once since telling her on the way here. 'I hope I take over in time for the Motor Show. Of course I was going anyway but only as a bloke, as it were.'

She could just about have managed without this information, I reckoned, and the same was true of one or two of the things I went on to tell her, but I was set on keeping control of the conversation because of a superstitious feeling that it would be a good-luck sign if Susan stayed unmentioned till we were out of the flat and, as arranged earlier, in the quite good Greek restaurant a couple of streets away. As it turned out I won bonus points for a further hold-off up to when we had ordered. Then I could stand it no longer.

'You were saying something about the way she was educated. Susan.'

'None other. Yes, she didn't go to school, or only for a term, then her parents had to take her away and get her tutored at home. She was terribly homesick and was subjected to the most frightful bullying.' Lindsey did a better job on Susan's accent than I would have expected, but she was still not as good as Mrs Shillibeer. 'You hadn't heard that, I take it.'

'No. How did you hear about it? Isn't that funny, she never said anything to me about that part of her life and I never thought to ask her.'

'She told me is how I heard about it. Well, by the time you came along it must have dawned on her that those facts are a pretty unprepossessing lot.'

'What are you talking about? She couldn't help them.'

'Only if you take them at their face value. You think of what happens at school, at any school. There are two things everyone gets plenty of, enough and to spare, especially at first – opposition and competition. Susan hates those. She won't have them. Who does she think she is or he think he is, that was her watchword at Oxford. When the answer would be like the Principal of the college or the Professor of English Language and Literature, you know, bloody understrappers of that kidney, with no right to make Susan Daly do what she didn't want to do or prevent her from doing what she wanted to do. And then, she was bright as hell and that tutor must have been damn good, but when the final exams came along she had a breakdown. Couldn't sit. Well, you can never know with a thing like that, but my feeling was at the time, she might not have got a First, you see, and Kate Oliver who we were both friendly with was going to get one, and did. She wasn't speaking to Kate anyway by then because Kate had told a lot of lies about her to her boyfriend and taken him off her. Maybe. How it looked to me was he met Kate through her and fancied Kate better. I wouldn't have said thank you for him myself. He was reading engineering.'

'Oh, yeah. Er, did you ever met her first husband? Book illustrator, wasn't he?'

'Mainly. I never met him but I heard a bit about him. Illustrating books was what he liked doing best, well you know what I mean. What he liked doing next best was looking at books that had illustrations by other people and reading books about them. He liked doing anything like that much better than going to parties that had writers and artists and people like that at them.'

'Well, I must say I can see his . . . Good God.'

'What's up?'

'Nothing, I've just remembered something somebody told me about Nowell. Any more on this fellow?'

'Apparently, I've forgotten who I had this from but he didn't go about the business of illustrating books in an intelligent way. He wanted to do good illustrations in serious books, proper books. Not trendy illustrations in trendy books that made a lot of money.'

'I don't believe it,' I said, not telling nothing but the truth.

'Suit yourself, Stanley, it's only what I heard.'

With disastrous timing the waiter brought the humous and the taramasalata and the rest of it at this point, failing miserably to encroach on an intimate moment or kill a punch line. I put my hand out to my glass and then left it. Easy on the ouzo tonight, and not just that either.

Lindsey caught my movement. 'You're not drinking. Not by your standards.'

'No, sod it. Daren't. Getting into practice. Motoring correspondent loses licence? It's going to change my bleeding life. Turn driving into just another thing I do, like playing squash or writing letters to the motoring press. Don't know how I'll adjust to it.'

After a pause she said quietly, 'Do you want to talk about your son?'

'No,' I said. 'No, I don't want to talk about him.'

'Worse than Susan, isn't it?'

I nodded.

'I know, I nearly lost my younger one six years ago. Hit and run. She was . . . Sorry.'

'Go back to those bleeding schooldays of Susan's,' I said. 'And what were they exactly, those unprepossessing facts?'

'She had to be taken away from school – had to be? – because, one, she was homesick. Translation – she very much wanted to be back in a place where she could do what she wanted to do all the time. Two, the bullying. Translation – some of the other little girls got rather cheesed off with the way she kept trying to do what she wanted to do all the time, including queening it over the rest of them, and showed her a bit of opposition. I used to wonder how much. Telling her to pipe down, I dare say. Perhaps getting together and jeering at her and even pulling her hair. Fiendish things like that.

'Her parents came up to Oxford once, at least I saw them once. The old lady was very straightforward about looking at me as if I was talking Swahili whenever I opened my mouth, which wasn't often after the first minute as you might imagine. And looking at the others for help too. You know, for Christ's sake don't leave me alone with this savage.'

'Yes, actually I do know.'

'But the old gentleman was the one. Would you believe it, you probably wouldn't believe it but he said to me when she'd gone off for a pee or something, he said, honest he said, "What do you think of my little gel? Rather splendid, isn't she?" That's what he said. I told you you wouldn't believe it.'

'Nor I do. Else he was trying to be funny.'

'He was not trying to be funny, Stanley. He was, how shall I put it, he was the archetype of the ridiculously indulgent father who worships the ground his little gel walks on and, you know, fancies her quite a bit. Oh yes. Seriously. I don't mean of course anything happened, nowhere near, but it was there, there was something there. Obviously it's all years ago now.'

'Look, love, this is fascinating, and I believe every word of it, but you started off by saying you thought she was quite capable of er, putting on a show like the one with the knife, and that's what I really want to hear about. Is there any more to come? I mean what you've told me so far . . .'

'What about it?' asked Lindsey when I failed to go on.

'I was going to say just, the whole thing sounds no worse than the dossier of any other deranged bleeding completely wrapped up in herself female, and then I remembered I always thought she was better than that. I thought she was, you know, reasonable and listened to what you said to her and you could disagree with her.'

'You could until it started to matter. You gave her a soft ride from what you've told me in the past, and then quite suddenly she finds she's coming second. And the lady simply is not cut out for coming second.

'Now Stanley dear, I hope you believe I'd never have breathed a word of this if things had been going on as before. But now they're all over the shop . . . I wasn't going to tell you, sweetheart, but there was this time a friend of Kate's gave a party in her digs, nothing grand, I was there, just drinks before hall, and old Susan thought she ought to have been invited, well maybe. Anyway, after about an hour she walked in carrying a bottle of champagne and looking, well, I'd read about people's faces looking like masks, but hers really did. Everybody said Hallo, rather awkward like, and she didn't say anything, but she hurled the bottle of champagne clean through the window of this sitting room place which was on the first floor, and the thing burst like a bloody bomb in the street, lucky it didn't hit anyone, and then she just went wild and smashed every glass and everything she could get her hands on until she was, you have to say overpowered, it took about four rugger-players to hold her down. Then she started crying and apologizing, and that went on a long time. Oh, there was no doubt about who'd come first that evening, not in popularity, no, but in attention-grabbing she was well in front.

'Afterwards she said she didn't know what had got into her. I thought about it a fair amount. That bottle of champagne now, a fucking expensive missile if that's all you'd ever wanted it for. A half-brick would have done just as well. I reckoned what she'd done, she'd bought the champagne and was going to come and hand it over as a gift to the hostess, a gift with a kind of a string to it because it would put paid to any crap about not being invited. A performance that would have made a bit of a stir for a short while, nothing like what she did do. She changed her mind at the last minute, perhaps as late as when she came into the room and saw all the buggers laughing and chattering and boozing happily away without her. Acting on the spur of the moment. Like I bet she did with that knife last night.' Lindsey had turned quite grim, staring at me through the big lenses. 'As for being mad, you should have seen her face that time. She was unrecognizable, well I recognized her but I wouldn't have if, what, if I'd passed her in the street. Off her head. Temporarily. Or temporarily letting it show.'

From being well on the way to something like certainty that Susan had been telling the truth about the knife I was now back to not knowing what I believed or felt about any of that. Or anything else I could turn my mind to. Trying to think was like picking through a rubbish-dump looking for nothing in particular. Eventually I said, 'If this hadn't come up I might never have found out about her,' only because I had been able to see how to get to the end of the sentence.

'Something else would have, it was bound to. People like that, it's as if they have to make something like that happen sooner or later. Their natures need it. Like a drunk wanting a fight. They're more bothered about getting one than where it comes from.'

'Why did she marry me?'

For once Lindsey was stumped for a quick answer, or more likely turned down the one she first thought of. 'Well,' she said, 'you're successful, but in a different line so you wouldn't be competing with her, you gave her a lot of rope and what the fuck can I say, Stanley dear, you're a nice enough fellow and quite an attractive fellow and I should imagine she was as fond of you as she could be of anybody. Still is, I dare say, or could be again.'

With the last few words the waiter brought the moussaka and the stifadou and the rest of the rubbish, which was not much but the worst he could manage in the circumstances. Susan was shut out of the conversation after that but she hung about in my head, not the look of her but the feel of her presence, the kind of thing I got when I came into the house and knew she was there even though there was nothing to see or hear. Oh well, it would be all right when we were back in the flat, I thought to myself, and Lindsey seemed to have the same idea, turning down sweet and coffee and looking at her watch. But then when we were back drinking the coffee she had made she put me right on more than one point. Actually the way she measured me with her eye told me most of it before she opened her mouth.

'I'm sorry, Stanley, but – '

'Barry due back, is he?' I had seen signs of male occupation, though long rather than short term, suits but no shirts, boots, slippers and plimsolls but only one pair of shoes. 'Or somebody?'

'No, nobody. Just, I have these interviews fixed in Glasgow tomorrow and I'm getting the sleeper up there tonight, and I have to put my gear together first. So if you – '

'Fly up in the morning,' I said, knowing it was hopeless. 'I'll drive you to the airport.'

'No, sweetheart, I can't, I'd like to but everything's arranged.'

'But as long as I . . . No of course, I see.'

She refused my offer of a lift to the station in half an hour from now, as it would have been. Whether to put her gear together or not she clearly wanted some time to herself before she took off. Quite understandable. On the way to the front door I realized I had got as far as not being sure what names to give our second child if it was a girl. Ha ha, very funny.

'Sorry, darling,' she said. 'This was all fixed up a couple of weeks ago and you only rang this morning.'

'I know. It's all right. See you when you get back.'

'I don't like thinking of you going back to that empty house.'

'I'm not mad about it myself.'

At the Paki supermarket in Hampstead I bought a jar of crunchy peanut butter, a pot of savoury spread, a large jar of pickled onions, a jar of sweet pickle, a small sliced white loaf, a packet of Cheddar, a packet of Brazil nut kernels, a box of liqueur chocolates and a box of chocolate truffles. The other things I needed, butter and whisky, were in stock at home. I unpacked the stuff on the kitchen table, drank some whisky and thought about laundrettes, Chinese takeaways and kindred matters for some minutes. Then I rang Cliff, late as it was, and told him the score. By now I had got it down to about five sentences.

He seemed more shaken than I had expected him to be. After a silence he said, 'So you're on your own there.'

'Yes.'

'Has she gone for good, do you think?'

'I don't know.'

'Well, we can't discuss it now,' he said rather peevishly, and there was another short pause. Then, 'Come to dinner tomorrow, I mean supper. Just the three of us.' When I had accepted he said, 'So I'll see you in the Admiral Byron about seven, where it'll just be the two of us. Stan, I'm sorry.'

Nash said, 'I think we can be reasonably confident that he'll now be more or less suitably looked after and will be given suitable treatment, at any rate for a time. The effect of that assault . . . which you described to me. . .' he went into his spaced-out mode, 'one effect . . . has been to put the fear of God into Dr Collings. Even she rather balks at the idea of an unmedicated and . . . presumptively violent patient of hers on the loose. You can discount her threat of discharging your boy. Sheer anger. She spoke out of sheer anger at her . . . apparent professional failure. As you surmised.'

'I'm still not happy about leaving my son in her charge,' I said.

'Nobody could be *happy* at the thought of someone in that position with the ideas that she professes to hold. But while in the intervals of talking modish twaddle, or even démodé twaddle, she administers reasonably appropriate chemotherapy . . . The boy would find much the same thing in most other places. A different line in twaddle, perhaps.'

'I see. Dr Nash, I should tell you that there is a possibility that my wife's wound was self-inflicted.'

He looked as though I had told him that somebody was dead, lowering his eyes, sighing deeply and sitting in silence for a time. Eventually he said, 'With the aim of bringing about the result I've just described to you? To get shot of the lad, was that the idea?'

'Could be. But I think more likely for my benefit, to draw attention away from him and on to herself.'

He had started doing little rapid nods before I was halfway through. 'If you come to any conclusion on the matter, however tentative, I hope you'll let me know. Talk to Dr Wainwright about it.'

'I will. When she thought I doubted her story she walked out. Left me.' It came out without much in the way of intention.

This news he took more or less in his stride, as something almost to be expected, but he said seriously enough, 'You have my profound sympathy in all senses of the word.'

'Doctor, if we assume my son did attack my wife,' – now there was a ridiculous phrase if ever there was one – 'does that make his prospects of recovery a lot worse? I'm afraid that's not very well put.'

'I follow you perfectly. No. In effect, in itself no. In the sense that very violent cases may recover and harmless peaceable ones become and remain isolated. But as I said I would welcome information on the point.'

I waited for a bit in the hope that he would offer me sherry for something to say, but he held his peace. I said hesitantly, 'Could we go back to Dr Collings for a moment? When we talked about her before, I thought you were saying, of course it was difficult in front of my wife, but I thought you were saying that she was getting at me, sorry, that Dr Collings was getting at me out of sheer malice, and I *thought* you meant that she was simply trying to . . .'

'Fuck you up because you were a man,' said Nash, disconcerting me to some extent. 'Yes, Mr Duke, that was what I meant. As you say, I was a little inhibited by your wife's presence.'

'But surely, Dr Nash, that's not enough of a motive on its own to make somebody, you know, in a professional matter like that, with these very important things at stake . . .'

'Not enough of a motive?' His voice had gone high. 'Fucking up a man? Not enough of a motive? What are you talking about? Good God, you've had wives, haven't you? And not impossibly had some acquaintance with other women as well? You can't be new to feeling the edge of the most powerful weapon in their armoury. You must have suffered before from the effect of their having noticed, at least the brighter ones among them having noticed, that men are different, men quite often wonder whether they're doing the right thing and worry about it, men have been known to blame themselves for behaving badly, men not only feel they've made mistakes but on occasion will actually admit having done so, and say they're sorry, and ask to be forgiven, and promise not to do it again, and mean it. Think of that! Mean it. All beyond female comprehension. Which incidentally is why they're not novelists and must never be priests. Not enough of a motive? They don't have motives as you and I understand them. They have the means and the opportunity, that is enough.'

At the start of this he had stared at me in what looked like stark fear, wondering whether I might not be an android or have been taken over by an alien entity. After that he calmed down, though not completely by any means, and now went back most of the way to the stark-fear mode when he said, 'For God's sake tell me you know what I'm talking about.'

'Oh, of course I do. But the way I see it, they have motives of a sort. It's the sort that's frightening. I think Collings let Steve out of hospital and took him off drugs to punish me for ticking her off for – '

'Oh, there'll have been some trigger, no doubt,' he said, making a side-ways neck-chop motion. 'In sufferers from rabies a touch on the arm or showing a bright light is sufficient to provoke a violent suffocative paroxysm. No doubt you did annoy or displease the woman in some way. What of it?'

'Well, I think that makes her unfit to be in charge of – '

'Forget it, my dear fellow. If things went that far, can you imagine yourself telling a tribunal that in your opinion a certain qualified doctor and psychiatrist is unfit to be in charge of a certain case because in your opinion she has been swayed by personal motives? A tribunal that included at least one woman? Take your time.'

'I don't need any. No.'

'So be it. Let's leave Dr Collings, Mr Duke. I'll, I'll see to her, or keep her in order. My turn to go back. On our first meeting, at your house, do you remember my asking you if you thought all women were mad?'

'Very clearly,' I said. 'And I told you I thought a lot of them were. Well, what's happened in the meantime hasn't exactly forced me to change my mind.'

'I find that very natural. Would you say, would you go as far as to say that the real mad people are not the ones in mental hospitals, like your son, but . . . women, certain women?'

'It's tempting. Or rather – '

'It is tempting. Half of it, anyway.' Yes, he was calm, and yet not relaxed, holding himself down or in, mentally biding his time to leap out at you. 'It seems you hold to your view on certain selected women. M'm. That's young Wainwright's view, of course, or on the way to it. He thinks they're all mad, or says he does. Of course one must bear in mind that in the ordinary way a general practitioner has very little contact with insane people. Neurotic people, on the other hand . . .'

'For God's sake, Dr Nash, does somebody have to be frothing at the mouth or going for you with an axe or chattering about reincarnated Old Testament prophets before you'll pass them as mad? Can't they be mad part-time, a bit mad? Like you can have a grumbling appendix without actually . . .'

Nash was not listening. His chest slowly filled with air. This was going to be the big one. 'Would . . . that . . . they . . . *were* . . . mmmmad,' he grated out in five loud sliced-off screeches, displaying his off-white teeth and looking far from sane himself. 'If only . . . they *were* . . . off their *heads*. Then we could treat-'em, lock-'em-up, bung-'em-in-a-straitjacket, cut-'em-off-from-society. But they're not. They're not.'

He sprang up, came round his desk and advanced on me. I wondered briefly if he took me for a transvestite, a male impersonator, but he was only on the first leg of a series of pacings to and fro. 'Mad people,' he went on in a tone not much less strung-up than before, 'can't run their lives, they're incapable of dealing with reality. How many women are like that? Mad people are hopelessly muddled with their thoughts, their feelings, their behaviour, their talk at variance with one another and all over the place. Does that sound like a description of a woman? Mad people are confused, adrift, troubled, even frightened. What woman is? – really is, I mean.

'No,' he said, starting another crescendo. 'No. They're not mad. They're all too monstrously, sickeningly, *terrifyingly* sane. That's the *whole trouble*. That's the whole trouble,' he repeated in his normal voice, blinking and moving his head about like a fellow coming round after a blackout. 'Well, Mr Duke, I hope your marital difficulties sort themselves out. Because after all one has to *be* married. That's where they've . . . Now I know you're a busy man and I too have things to do. We will be in touch.'

At the door he said, 'Your boy has a good chance.'

I was as busy as I could manage to be for the rest of the day. I kept trying to throw off the thought of Steve, then when trying to think about Susan instead kept breaking down. I switched to trying to work out why I had the feeling that he would never be back. Perhaps it came from something

Nash had said that morning. But he had said very little on the matter and nothing new. Perhaps there had been something in his manner, something more unhopeful than his words. Perhaps, more likely, it went back to the previous morning and the tiny glimpse I had had of Steve as he used to be, an instant and complete reminder of the person I had already started to forget. No doubt what could happen once for a second could in theory happen again for longer, and I did my best to believe it without getting very far. In the end I had no real idea at all why that Steve seemed gone for good and the one I saw every day, the miserable, quaking, humourless nitwit who was also my son, looked like being a fixture. As for him, it would be better if he were dead, provided that could be arranged without him having to die.

Some of this went through my head while I sat drinking Scotch and waiting for Cliff. As I had found on previous visits with him, the Admiral Byron was frequented by Scottish labourers, probably building workers, given to shouting unreassuringly to one another. However, it seemed he had never seen an actual fight in here, perhaps because of something one of the Scotsmen had gone out of his way to explain to us, that anybody who looked like starting one was given a right good hiding and thrown out. The staff changed frequently and only the landlord ever knew what the place served or where it was kept, apart from the stuff on tap. Nobody would have called it cosy – it was vast, hangar-like, the result of the knocking-into-one of several smaller bars or even, to judge by the differences of structure and style from one end to the other, a couple of separate pubs. But it had no juke-box or fruit-machine and at the moment, before the Scotsmen, it was quiet.

Cliff came bustling in a little later than he had said, complaining as usual, quite cheerfully as usual, this time mostly about the one-way traffic system and the hospital staffs' trade union with a bit about a urologist thrown in. Then quite soon he looked at me and nodded his head several times and sighed.

'There's a splendid fellow called Sydney Smith,' he said. 'I don't mean, you know, that fucking old fool.'

'What fucking old fool?'

He gave a growl of disgust. 'Of course, I keep forgetting you haven't looked at a book since you left school and precious few before. There was a posturing old ponce of a clergyman in Jane Austen's time, oh Christ, never mind, anyway he was called Sydney Smith and a lot of people, people like, well I was going to say Susan, er, think he was a bloody scream. But as I say I don't mean him. Jesus. *Anyway*, my Sydney Smith wrote the standard work on forensic medicine, which I suppose I'm going to have to –'

'No, I can do that,' I said. 'Legal medicine. Medicine as regards the law.'

'Man's a genius. Well, in this work there is naturally a chapter on self-inflicted wounds.'

'Oh.'

'Yes, oh. How a genuine wound inflicted on a person trying to protect himself or herself against an assailant with a knife is usually on or in the hand, sometimes the wrist, the inside of the wrist. That's point one. The characteristics of a self-inflicted wound are, made in a safe part of the body unless of course we're talking about throat-cutting et cetera, so not for example the inside of the wrist where there are dodgy things like veins but for example the forearm, the top or outside of the forearm.' He made gestures in case I had never bothered to find out what a forearm was. 'Where Susan, er, was wounded.

'Next thing, the cut will not penetrate what we medical johnnies call the true skin, that's your corium, a quarter of an inch or so deep in places like that. As with Susan's wound. Then, the cut follows the curvature of the body if that part is curved, like the forearm. You can see how that wouldn't happen with a real stab. I'd have liked to take a better look but it's a pound to a pinch of shit that Susan's wound did that. And the last thing but perhaps the most telling, I've never quite understood why, but they all seem to have a dry run or two first, little tentative nicks alongside the main wound, even the cut-throat brigade – I've seen it. Anyway, there were a couple of those on Susan's arm. And there we are. I'd take my chance with a jury on it.

'Bloody silly of her, wouldn't you say, apart from anything else? You'd think an intelligent girl like that would realize it was on the cards there'd be some sort of give-away. She must have got the idea one moment and done it the next, on impulse. Mad as a hatter, like the lot of them. Must have seemed like a heaven-sent opportunity when poor old Steve came wandering in. What a marvellous bloody irony, eh, that it took that to get Collings and her gang to start looking after him properly at Kev's. I talked to some Paki there.'

'Yeah. Nash went over.'

When Cliff saw I had nothing more to offer about Nash he said, 'Disasters are just crappy things that happen, you know, Stan. It's a waste of time to try to explain them or make sense of them.'

'Which one are you talking about?'

'Steve, of course. I'm afraid I don't regard the other one, her walking out that is, as all that much of a disaster.' When I made no reply to that he said, 'Another irony, if we're collecting the buggers, is that she attains her object and successfully got Steve out of her hair and now she's not around to enjoy it. What?'

'Oh, I don't think that was her object. I think she was scene-stealing.' It was clear that he understood me immediately. 'At least that was what I thought at the time. I'm not so sure that I'm so sure now. It's hard to feel it makes much difference. I'll tell Nash about her arm and the rest of it.'

'I'll tell him, I want a word with him anyway. Let's have it again now.

She walked out on you because she thought you thought she'd stabbed herself and said Steve did it, right?'

'Next time, take more care. She walked out *after saying* she knew I thought that. After saying a great deal more besides. She was . . . mad with rage that I'd seen through or I might have seen through an extremely dodgy operation she may already have been regretting – as unwise, naturally, not bad form or anything silly like that. If seen through, eh? it would show her up as some kind of monster. At the same time she was calculating that anything short of mad rage would be as bad as a half-hearted denial – but there of course she was going by what her own reaction would have been and didn't realize that a wholehearted denial would have cut much more ice with me, or you or any other man. But then again she was mad with rage. I must have annoyed her quite a bit in the past and she'd bottled it up and it all came out at once. She was frightened too – you showed you suspected her. What was that for, by the way?'

'For just that, to frighten her, frighten her off. I didn't know what she might have got up to next. I meant to signal to her but not to you, but I was so bloody cross myself that I muffed it, clearly. Terrible how they drag us down to their level, isn't it? Crikey, you do know her well, Stan. Pity you didn't before, but then you never do, one doesn't I mean. Did you work all that out in just those couple of minutes just now?'

'No, I was on it all the time I was going round telling myself that of course the whole thing was perfectly genuine. Men's minds are funny things too, you know. Oh, the rest of it was, the walking-out was an escalation of the bawling-out. Plus it would have been a wee bit awkward for her to stay in the same house after some of the things she'd said.'

'She'll come walking back in again, won't she?' said Cliff a moment or two later.

'No. Live with a man who thinks or knows she did a thing like that?'

'She'll pretend you don't think or know it. So will you. It never happened. Easy as winking.'

'Some of what she said . . .'

'That's your problem. She was upset, wasn't she, after being attacked with a knife? Who wouldn't be?'

'She won't be back.'

I went and got more drinks. The place was filling up, though mostly down the far end in the part that looked like an old-fashioned railway waiting room. When I gave my order the little slut with her hair green and half an inch long all over cut me off by saying 'Sorry?' almost as soon as I opened my mouth. When I was a kid you hung on a bit if you missed the first few words and hoped to pick up the drift later. Anyway, I had more luck with my second go and at least she knew where the Famous Grouse was.

Cliff was looking thoughtful. 'According to some bloke on the telly the other night,' he said, 'twenty-five per cent of violent crime in England and

Wales is husbands assaulting wives. Amazing figure that, don't you think? You'd expect it to be more like eighty per cent. Just goes to show what an easy-going lot English husbands are, only one in four of them bashing his wife. No, it doesn't mean that, does it? But it's funny about wife-battering. Nobody ever even asks what the wife had been doing or saying. She's never anything but an ordinary God-fearing woman who happens to have a battering husband. Same as race prejudice. Here are a lot of fellows who belong to a race minding their own business and being as good as gold and not letting butter melt in their mouths, and bugger me if a gang of prejudiced chaps don't rush up and start discriminating against them. Frightfully unfair.'

'The root of all the trouble,' I said, 'is we want to fuck them, the pretty ones, women I mean. Just try and imagine it happening to you, everyone wanting to fuck you wherever you go. And of course being ready to pay for you if your father's stopped doing that. You'd have to be pretty tough to stand up to it, wouldn't you? In fact women only want one thing, for men to want to fuck them. If they do, it means they can fuck them up. Am I drunk? What I was trying to say, if you want to fuck a woman she can fuck you up. And if you don't want to she fucks you up anyway for not wanting to.'

'I read somewhere about a Hollywood film star,' said Cliff. 'I forget which one, years ago anyway, she was getting on a bit, used to go to a lot of parties, it might have been Madeleine Carroll, one night she went to one and nobody made a pass at her, so she went home and took an overdose. That was coming out into the open a bit, I agree.'

'Actually they used to feel they needed something in the way of provocation,' I said, 'but now they seem to feel they can get on with the job of fucking you up any time they feel like it. That's what Women's Lib is for.'

'It's getting worse,' said Cliff, 'now they're competing on equal terms in so many places and find they still finish behind men. They can't even produce a few decent fucking *jugglers*. Like the race thing again.'

'They say people go on getting married to the same person time after time,' I said. 'Well men certainly do. There isn't another other sex.'

'It's no use saying anything to a woman,' said Cliff ultimately, and drained his glass.

I waited, but there was no follow-up. 'When what?'

'What?'

'It's no use saying anything to a woman when what? Or unless what?'

'When nothing. Ever.'

We had a couple more drinks and were quite merry by the time we got to the Wainwrights' house in Holland Park, and were quite unmerry again two minutes later. Sandra was cross about something. I could not have said what was different from usual in her manner or tone or expression or anywhere else, not really, not in detail, and yet I could tell. I could have told at a hundred metres. Of course I could. Any man could. Any man was meant to. I had sometimes wondered if they thought we thought they were really trying to keep their feelings to themselves at times like these, but if you knew *that* you could destroy the world.

I got half a minute of it to myself at the start because Cliff had broken off for a pee in the hall cloakroom. Sandra embraced me with all the warmth of a recent rape victim.

'Cliff tells me Susan's walked out on you,' she said. 'That must be upsetting for you.'

'Yes it is rather.' I wondered how she would talk and look if she were telling me instead that Susan was to be congratulated and whatever upset I got from this or anything else would do me a power of good.

'I suppose it's six of one and half a dozen of the other,' she said, meaning such was the impudent travesty I was preparing to palm off on the public. 'It usually seems to be.'

'Probably.'

'I expect you want a drink.' To go with the fourteen I clearly had inside me.

'Well . . .'

Cliff came in. While Sandra asked him if the pub had been fun and he told her it had been, thanks, I watched him notice, wonder what he had done, think of something, think surely not for Christ's sake, and resign himself. He widened his eyes at me but said nothing. I said nothing. In fact all three of us said nothing, pretty near literally, until Sandra went out to the kitchen. When he was sure she was clear he opened his mouth to start, but the phone rang first.

He went across the room and answered it. 'Yes,' he said, and held the handset out to me with a completely blank and completely informative face.

'Oh Stanley, thank God you're there,' said Susan's voice, strained but calm. 'I was going to give up if you weren't. Can you ever forgive me?'

'What for?' I said.

'Well, those terrible things I said to you.'

'Oh, those.'

While she hurried on about having been so desperately frightened and upset and one thing and another I turned towards Cliff, who did the brief lift of the chin South London people use to mean Told you so or Here we go again or Wouldn't you bleeding know. People elsewhere too, I dare say. Perhaps all over the world.

THE OLD DEVILS

Contents

1   Malcolm, Charlie, Peter and Others

1

'If you want my opinion,' said Gwen Cellan-Davies, 'the old boy's a terrifically distinguished citizen of Wales. Or at any rate what passes for one these days.'

Her husband was cutting the crusts off a slice of toast. 'Well, I should say that's generally accepted.'

'And Reg Burroughs is another after his thirty years of pen-pushing in first City Hall and later County Hall, for which he was duly honoured.'

'That's altogether too dismissive a view. By any reckoning Alun has done some good things. Come on now, fair play.'

'Good things for himself certainly: *Brydan's Wales* and that selection, whatever it's called. Both still selling nicely after all these years. Without Brydan and the Brydan industry, Alun would be nothing. Including especially his own work – those poems are all sub-Brydan.'

'Following that trail isn't such a bad – '

'Goes down a treat with the Americans and the English, you bet. But . . .' Gwen put her head on one side and gave the little frowning smile she used when she was putting something to someone, often a possible negative view of a third party; 'wouldn't you have to agree that he follows Brydan at, er, an altogether lower level of imagination and craftsmanship?'

'I agree that compared with Brydan at his best, he doesn't – '

'You know what I mean.'

In this case Malcolm Cellan-Davies did indeed know. He got up and refilled the teapot, then his cup, adding a touch of skimmed milk and one of the new sweeteners that were supposed to leave no aftertaste. Back in his seat at the breakfast-table he placed between his left molars a small prepared triangle of toast and diabetic honey and began crunching it gently but firmly. He had not bitten anything with his front teeth since losing a top middle crown on a slice of liver-sausage six years earlier, and the right-hand side of his mouth was a no-go area, what with a hole in the lower lot where stuff was always apt to stick and a funny piece of gum that seemed to have got detached from something and waved disconcertingly about whenever it saw the chance. As his jaws operated, his eyes slid off to the *Western Mail* and a report of the Neath-Llanelli game.

After lighting a cigarette Gwen went on in the same quirky style as before, 'I don't remember you as a great believer in the integrity of Alun Weaver as an embodiment of the Welsh consciousness?'

'Well, I suppose in some ways, all the television and so on, he is a bit of a charlatan, yes, maybe.'

'Maybe! Christ Almighty. Of course he's a charlatan and good luck to him. Who cares? He's good fun and he's unstuffy. We could do with a dozen like him in these parts to strike the fear of God into them. We need a few fakes to put a dent in all that bloody authenticity.'

'Not everybody's going to be glad to have him around,' said Malcolm, giving another section of toast the standard treatment.

'Well, that's splendid news. Who are you thinking of?'

'Peter for one. Funnily enough the subject came up yesterday. He was very bitter, I was quite surprised. Very bitter.'

Malcolm spoke not in any regretful way but as if he understood the bitterness, even perhaps felt a touch of it on his own part. Gwen looked at him assessingly through the light-brownish lenses of her square-topped glasses. Then she made a series of small noises and movements of the kind that meant it was time to be up and away. But she sat on and, perhaps idly, reached out to the letter that had started their conversation and fingered it as it lay in front of her.

'It'll be, er, fun seeing Rhiannon again,' she said.

'M'm.'

'Been a long time, hasn't it? What, ten years?'

'At least that. More like fifteen.'

'She never came down with Alun on any of his trips after whenever it was. Just that once, or twice was it?'

'She used to come down to see her mother at Broughton, and then the old girl died about that long ago, so she probably . . .'

'I dare say you'd remember. I just thought it was funny she never really kept up with her college friends or anyone else as far as I know.'

Malcolm said nothing to that. He swayed from side to side in his chair as a way of suggesting that life held many such small puzzles.

'Well, she'll have plenty of time from now on, or rather from next month. I hope she doesn't find it too slow for her in these parts after London.'

'A lot of the people she knew will still be here.'

'That's the whole trouble,' said Gwen, laughing slightly. She looked at her husband for a moment, smiling and lowering her eyelids, and went on, 'It must have come as a bit of a shock, the idea of, er, Rhiannon coming and settling down here after everything.'

'Call it a surprise. I haven't thought of her since God knows when. It's a long time ago.'

'Plenty of that, isn't there, nowadays? Well, this won't do. All right if I take first crack at the bathroom?'

'You go ahead,' he said, as he said every morning.

He waited till he heard a creak or so from the floor above, then gave a deep sigh with a sniff in the middle. When you thought about it, Gwen had given him an easy ride over Rhiannon, not forgetting naturally that it had been no more than Instalment 1 (a). A bit of luck he had been down first and had had a couple of minutes to recover from some of the shock – rightly so called – of seeing that handwriting on the envelope, unchanged and unmistakable after thirty-five years. Gwen had left the letter on the table. With a brief glance towards the ceiling he picked it up and re-read it, or parts of it. 'Much love to you both' seemed not a hell of a lot to brag about in the way of a reference to himself, but there being no other he would have to make the best of it. Perhaps she had simply forgotten. After all, plenty had happened to her in between.

Finishing his tea, he lit his first and only cigarette of the day. He had never greatly enjoyed smoking, and it was well over the five years since he had followed his doctor's advice and given it up, all but this solitary one after breakfast which could do no measurable harm and which, so he believed, helped to get his insides going. Again as always he filled in time by clearing the table; it was good for him to be on the move. His bran flakes and Gwen's chunky marmalade enriched with whisky went into the wall-cupboard, the stones of his unsweetened stewed plums and the shells of her two boiled eggs into the black bag inside the bin. He thought briefly of eggs, the soft explosion as spoon penetrated yolk, the way its flavour spread over your mouth in a second. His last egg, certainly his last boiled egg, went back at least as far as his last full smoking day. By common knowledge the things tended to be binding, not very of course, perhaps only a shade, but still enough to steer clear of. Finally the crocks went into the dishwasher and at the touch of a button a red light came on, flickering rather, and a savage humming immediately filled the kitchen.

It was not a very grand or efficient dishwasher and not at all a nice kitchen. At Werneth Avenue, more precisely at the house there that the Cellan-Davieses had lived in until 1978, the kitchen had been quite splendid, with a long oak table you could get fourteen round with no trouble at all and a fine Welsh dresser hung with colourful mugs and jugs. Here there was nothing that could not have been found in a million cramped little places up and down the country, lino tiles, plastic tops, metal sink and, instead of the massive Rayburn that had warmed the whole ground floor at Werneth Avenue, an oval-shaped two-bar electric fire hanging on the wall. Most mornings at about this time Malcolm wondered if he had not cut down a bit too far by moving out here, but no point in fretting about that now, or later either.

There came a faint stirring in his entrails. He picked up the *Western Mail* and without hurrying – quite important as a matter of fact – made his way to the slant-ceilinged lavatory or cloakroom under the stairs. The old sequence duly extended itself: not trying at all because that was the healthy, natural way, trying a certain amount because that could have no real adverse effect, trying like a lunatic because why? – because that was all there was to do. Success was finally attained, though of a limited degree. No blood to speak of, to be conscientiously classified as between slight and very slight. This was the signal for him to sit to attention and snap a salute.

In the bedroom Gwen was at her dressing-table putting the foundation on her face. Malcolm came round the door in his silent, looming way and caught sight of her in the glass. Something about the angle or the light made him look at her more closely than usual. She had always been a soft, rounded, fluffy sort of creature, not ineffectual but yielding in her appearance and movements. That had not changed; at sixty-one – his age too – her cheeks and jaws held their shape and the skin under her eyes was remarkably supple. But now those deep-set eyes of hers had an expression he thought he had not noticed before, intent, almost hard, and her mouth likewise was firmly set as she smoothed the sides of her nose. Probably just the concentration – in a second she saw him and relaxed, a comfortable young-elderly woman with gently-tinted light-brown hair and wearing a blue-and-white check trouser-suit you might have expected on someone slightly more juvenile, but not at all ridiculous on her.

To get her voice as much as anything he said, 'More social life? No letting up?'

'Just coffee at Sophie's,' she said in her tone of innocent animation.

'Just coffee, eh? There's a change now. You know it's extraordinary, I've just realised I haven't seen Sophie for almost a year. One just doesn't. Well. You'll be taking the car, will you?'

'If that's okay. You going along to the Bible?'

'I thought I might sort of look in.' He went along to the Bible every day of his life. 'Don't worry, I'll get the bus.'

A pause followed. Gwen spread blusher – called rouge once upon a time – over her cheekbones. After a moment she dropped her hands into her lap and just sat. Then she speeded up. 'Well, and how are you this morning, good boy?'

'Perfectly all right, thank you.' Malcolm spoke more abruptly than he meant. He had prepared himself for a return to the topic of Rhiannon and the query about his bodily functions, though usual and expressed much as usual, caught him off balance. 'Quite all right,' he added on a milder note.

'Nothing . . .'

'No. Absolutely not.'

As he had known she would, she shook her head slowly. 'Why you just can't deal with it, an intelligent man like you. The stuff that's on the market nowdays.'

'I don't hold with laxatives. Never have. As you very well know.'

'Laxatives. Christ, I'm not talking about senna pods, California Syrup of Figs. Carefully-prepared formulae, tried and tested. It's not gunpowder drops any more.'

'Anything like that, it interferes with the body's equilibrium. Distorts the existing picture. With chemicals.'

'I thought that was what you were after, Malcolm, honestly, distorting what you've got. And what about all those plums you go in for? Aren't they meant to distort you?'

'They're natural. Obviously.'

'How do you think they work? Just chemicals in another form.'

'Natural chemicals. Chemicals naturally occurring.'

'How do you think your guts distinguish betweeen a bit of chemical in a plum and a bit of the same chemical in a pill or a capsule?'

'I don't know, love,' said Malcolm rather helplessly. He thought it was a bit thick for a man not to be able to win an argument about his own insides, even one with his wife. 'But then I haven't got to know.'

'Don't take my word for it – fix up to see Dewi. Yes yes, you don't hold with doctors either, and why do I have to go on at you. Because you're foolish, that's why, you won't help yourself. Unteachable. You know sometimes I'd almost take you for a bloody Welshman?'

'There's nothing to see Dewi about. There's nothing wrong with me. No sign, no sign of anything.'

'Just ask him for a prescription, that's all. Two minutes.'

Malcolm shook his head and there was more silence. In a moment he said, 'Can I go now?'

They embraced lightly and carefully while Gwen made another set of little sounds. This lot meant that although she still thought her husband was silly about himself she would let it go for the time being. There was affection there as well, if not of an over-respectful order.

As often before, Malcolm could see strength in the case against ever having mentioned his defecations in the first place. He had never intended more than an occasional appeal for reassurance and so on. As an apparently irremovable part of the daily agenda the subject had its drawbacks, while remaining streets ahead of his shortcomings as a man, a husband, an understander of women, a provider and other popular items dimly remembered from the past.

In the bathroom across the landing he cleaned his teeth, first the twenty or so surviving in his head in one form or another and then the seven on his upper-jaw partial. This was such a tight fit that putting it back was always a tense moment; bending his knees and moving them in and out seemed to help. What with the five crowns in front, of varying manufacture and recency, the ensemble was a bit of a colour atlas, but at least no one was going to mistake it for snappers top and bottom. They would have to come some day – which meant not now, bless it. The thought of having a tooth extracted, loose as nearly all of his had become, bothered him in a way he thought he had outgrown many years before.

The face surrounding these teeth was in fair trim, considering. In shape it was rather long, especially between the end of the nose and the point of the chin, but the features themselves were good and he was aware without vanity that, with his height and erect bearing and his thatch of what had become reddish-grey hair, people usually found him presentable enough. At the same time he had noticed that now and then a stranger, usually a man, would glance at him in a way that always puzzled him rather, not quite hostile but with something unfavourable about it, something cold.

He had seen a good deal of that sort of glance at school, where he had been bullied more than his fair share for a boy not undersized, foreign or feeble, and he remembered asking Fatty Watkins, one of his leading persecutors, why this was so. Without thinking about it, Fatty had told him that he looked the type, whatever that might have meant. Twice in later life, once down Street's End on a Saturday night and then again on a train coming back from an international at Cardiff Arms Park, just minding his own business both times, he had been picked out of a group of mates and set upon without preamble by an unknown ruffian. Perhaps without intending it he sometimes took on an expression people misinterpreted as snooty or something.

Whatever the ins and outs of his face he was going to have to shave it. He hated the whole caboodle – teeth, shave, bath, hair, clothes – so much that he often felt he was approaching the point of jacking it all in completely and going round in just pyjamas and dressing-gown all day. But for Gwen he would probably have got there long ago. She kept on at him to play himself through with the portable wireless and he still tried it occasionally, but he cared for chatter about as much as he cared for modern music, and that was about all there seemed to be apart from Radio Cymru, which was obviously just the thing if you were set on improving your Welsh. The trouble was they talked so fast.

Welsh came up again and in a more substantial form when, having heard Gwen drive away, he settled in his study to put in a bit of time there before going along to the Bible. This, the study, was on the first floor, a small, smudgy room where water-pipes clanked. Its dominant feature was a walnut bookcase that had not looked oversized at Werneth Avenue but had needed the window taking out to be installed here. One shelf was all poetry: a fair selection of the English classics, some rather battered, a few Welsh texts, all in excellent condition, and a couple of dozen volumes of English verse by twentieth-century Welshmen. One of these, not painfully slim, had on it Malcolm's name and the imprint of a small press in what was now Upper Glamorgan. On taking early retirement from the Royal Cambrian he had intended to set about a successor, completing poems left half-done for years and years, writing others that had only been in his head or nowhere at all. He ought to have had the sense to know that intentions alone were no good in a case like this. Not a line had turned up in all that time. But some day one might, and meanwhile he must practise, exercise, try to get his hand back in. Hence the Welsh.

Among the books on his table there was a publication of the Early Welsh

Text Society – to give its English designation: the poems and poetical fragments of Llywelyn Bach ab yr Ynad Coch (*fl.* 1310), open at his funeral-song for Cadwaladr, quite a substantial affair, three hundred lines odd. Malcolm's translation of the first two sections was there too, a lightly-corrected manuscript, also a pamphlet containing the only other translation he knew of, done and published by a Carmarthen schoolmaster in the Twenties but in the style of fifty years earlier. Never mind – whatever it lacked as a piece of poetry it came in bloody handy as a crib.

Moving at half speed, Malcolm opened the pamphlet now at the beginning. His glance shifted to and fro between the Welsh original of this passage and the two English versions, picking out words and phrases in either language that he felt he had never seen before: the tomb of the regal chieftain . . . red stallions . . . ye warriors of Gwynedd . . . I the singer, the minstrel . . . heaps of Saxon slain . . . chaplet . . . hart . . . buckler . . . mead . . .

Malcolm jerked upright at the table. A great God-given flood of boredom and hatred went coursing through him. That, that stuff, fiddling about with stuff like that was not living, was not life, was nothing at all. Not after today's news. No indeed, poems were not made out of intentions. But perhaps they could come from hope.

He made to tear up his manuscript, but held his hand at the thought of the hours that had gone into it, and the other thought that he would go back to it another day and transform it, make something wonderful of it. For now, he could not sit still. Yet if he left the house now he would be much too early, or rather a good deal, a certain amount too early. Well, he could get off the bus at Beaufoy and walk the rest of the way. On more of the same reasoning he went and gave his shoes a thorough polish; not much point hereabouts, agreed, but virtuous.

When he finally went out it was overcast with a bit of black, damp already, mild though, with a gentle breeze clearing the mist, typical Welsh weather. If you can see Cil Point it means rain later; if not, rain now. As he started down the hill he could see it, just, a dark-grey snout between the ranks of black slate roofs shining with moisture. Soon the bay began to open out below him, the sweep round to the west where coal had once been mined on the shore and inland along the coastal plain, and steel and tin-plate were still worked and oil refined, for the moment anyway, and behind all this, indistinct through the murk, the squarish mass of Mynydd Tywyll, second-highest peak in South Wales.

It was mid-morning in the week, and yet the pavements were crowded with people darting in and out of shops or just strolling along like holiday-makers – here, in February? Children and dogs ran from side to side almost underfoot. Crossing the road was no joke with all the cars and the motor-cycles nipping about. There was a queue at the 24 stop but, even so, nothing showed for a long time. Staff shortages, they said, recruitment down since the automatic-payment system had meant good-bye to days of plenty, when the conductor fiddled half the fare-money on the out-of-town part of the route and handed over half of it, or nearly, to the driver when they got to the garage. To save going round the end of the queue, youngsters on their way to the opposite corner kept breaking through it, always as if by pre-arrangement just in front of Malcolm.

The bus came. While he was climbing the litter-strewn steps his left ball gave a sharp twinge, on and off like a light-switch, then again after he had sat down. Nothing. Just one of the aches and pains that come and go. No significance. He would not always have taken such a summary line, in fact at one stage cancer of them, or one of them, had been among his leading special dreads, distinguished as it was by its very personal site and alleged virulence. There had even been the time when, after a day and most of a night of just about unremitting twinges on both sides, he had spent the dawn hours compiling in his head a draft list of books to take into hospital: mainly English poetry with one or two descriptive works about Wales, in English naturally. The following morning, by one of the most rapid and complete recoveries in medical history, the affection had vanished. So far so good, no further. But then he had read in the *Guardian* that recent advances had put the survival rate for testicular tumours up to or above ninety per cent, and for the rest of that day he had felt twenty, thirty years younger, and something of that had never been quite lost.

Reflecting on this and related matters took him past his stop and almost into Dinedor itself. With an air of transparent innocence that luckily escaped remark he got off by Paolo's Trattoria. Just round the corner was the Bible, more fully the Bible and Crown, the only pub of that name in the whole of Wales. According to local antiquarians the reference was to a Cavalier toast, though research had failed to come up with a date earlier than 1920, some time after it had become safe to proclaim loyalty to the King's party in any or all of his dominions, even this one.

On the way in Malcolm's spirits lifted, as they always did at the prospect of an hour or more spent not thinking about being ill and things to do with being ill. It was still early, but not enough to notice.

2

'But uglier still is the hump that we get from not having enough to do. You know who said that?'

'No.'

'Kipling. Joseph Rudyard Kipling. He was usually right, you know. Had a way of being right. No use sitting about, he said, or frowsting by the fire with a book. Wonderful word, frowst, isn't it? Wonder what it comes from. Well anyway, the thing is, get out in the fresh air and take a bit of exercise. A brisk walk, two miles minimum, three preferable. No need for

any of your sleeping pills after that. I haven't taken a sleeping pill since . . .
Guess when I last took a sleeping pill.'

'No idea.'

'1949. That's when I last took a sleeping pill. 1949. Morning, Malcolm.
Another early bird.'

'Morning, Garth. Morning, Charlie. Now what can I get you?'

The two had nearly-full glasses and declined, but the offer was standard
arrivals' etiquette. Malcolm went and got himself a half of Troeth bitter at
the hatch in the corridor, the nearest place. During his absence, Garth
Pumphrey let Charlie Norris know more about the benefits of exercise and
the dispensability of sleeping pills. Charlie followed Garth's talk with only
half his attention, if that, but he found it comforting. He knew that nothing
Garth said would surprise him, and as he felt at the moment, which was
very much how he felt every morning of his life at this hour, even a pleasant
surprise, whatever that might be, would have been better postponed. He
flinched a little when Malcolm reappeared more abruptly than he had
bargained for.

'Ah, here we are,' said Garth cordially, holding out an arm by way of
showing Malcolm to the chair at his side. 'There. I've been treating young
Charlie to a highly authoritative lecture on the subject of health, physical
and mental. My number one rule is never sit over a meal. Breakfast least
of all.'

It was amazing, thought Malcolm to himself, how invariably and
completely he forgot Garth when looking forward to or otherwise weighing
up a visit to the Bible. Forgetting things like that was probably one of
Nature's ways of seeing to it that life carried on. Like the maternal instinct.

'Of course, you know Angharad says I'm turning into a real old health
bore – a notorious pitfall of age, she says.' In the ensuing silence Garth
took a good pull at his drink, which looked like a rather heavy vin rosé
but was really gin and Angostura. Then he shaped up to Malcolm in a
businesslike way. 'You were quite a performer in days gone by, Malcolm,
weren't you? Sorry, with the old racquet. Oh, I was saying earlier, I
remember the way you used to bash that ball. Give it a devil of a pasting,
you would. That serve of yours. Famous. Deservedly so.'

'Many years ago now, Garth.'

'Not so many as the world goes in our time. November 1971, that's
when the old place finally closed its doors.' Garth referred to the Dinedor
Squash Racquets Club, of which all three had been members since youth.
'The end of an era. You know you and I had a game in the last week very
nearly. I took a proper clobbering as usual. You were really seeing them
that evening. Then we had a drink after with poor Roger Andrews. Do
you remember?'

'Yes,' said Malcolm, though he had forgotten that part, and Charlie
nodded to show that he was still in the conversation.

'He seemed so full of life that time. And then what could it have been, six weeks after we started coming in here, eight at the outside, off he goes. Like that. Sitting just where you are now, Charlie.'

Malcolm remembered that part all right. So did Charlie. Roger Andrews had been nothing out of the way, a building contractor of no more than average corruption, not even much of a good fellow, but his fatal collapse in the so-called saloon lounge of the Bible had had a durable effect, confirming the tendency of a group of ex-members of the defunct squash club to drop in regularly midday and in the early evening. Over the years the room had become a kind of relic or descendant of that club, its walls hung with inherited photographs of forgotten champions, teams, presentations, dinners, its tables bearing a couple of ugly old ashtrays that had escaped being sold or stolen when the effects of the DSRC were disposed of. The habitués had even acquired something of a prescriptive right to keep out intruders. The landlord of the Bible made no objection, in fact it suited him well enough to have up to a dozen or so comparatively well-behaved drinkers perpetually occupying the least convenient and agreeable corner of his premises. From time to time the old boys complained among themselves about the discomfort, but there they were, the dump was almost next door to the Club building, which was what had drawn them there in the first place, and in winter the genial host actually let them have the benefit of a small electric fire at no extra charge.

After a moment of reverie or premeditation Garth Pumphrey again turned his face on Malcolm, a dark serious lined face with a hint of subdued passion, an actor's face some might have called it. 'What exercise do you take these days, Malcolm?' he asked.

'Just about zero, I'm afraid.'

'Just about zero? A fellow of your physique. A natural athlete like you. Dear, dear.'

'Ex-natural athlete. I'm not going to start going on cross-country runs at my age.'

'I should hope not indeed, it's altogether too late for that.' Garth whistled breathily to himself and moved his hand crabwise along the table in front of him. Then he said, 'Do you find you fancy your food all right? I hope you don't mind me asking, we're all old friends here.'

Charlie thought a distinction could be drawn between Garth's boasting about his own insides if he had to and his involvement with others', but he was not the man to put it into words. His second large Scotch and dry ginger was beginning to get to him and already he could turn his head without thinking it over first. Soon it might cease to be one of those days that made you sorry to be alive.

'No, that's all right, Garth,' Malcolm was saying gamely. 'No, my trouble's all the other way. Keeping myself down to size.'

'Good, good.' Garth's small figure was huddled up in the cracked rexine chair, turned away from Charlie. He smiled and nodded. 'And, er . . .' His eyebrows were raised.

In a flash Malcolm knew or as good as knew that the next second Garth was going to ask him about his bowel movements. He felt he would do, must do, anything at all to prevent that, and mentioned what he had not even considered mentioning, not there, not yet, not until he had hugged it to himself as long as he could. 'Alun and Rhiannon are moving down here in a couple of months,' he said quickly. 'Coming back to Wales to live.'

That did the trick. It took quite some time for Garth's incredulity to be mollified, likewise his craving for information. When that was done he explained that, what with being stuck out at Capel Mererid and so on, he had not known the couple in early years, but had met Alun many times on trips to these parts and anyway, he finished strongly, 'the bloke is a national figure, let's face it.'

'You face it,' said Charlie, who had reasons of his own to feel less than overjoyed at Malcolm's news. 'I realise he's on television quite a lot, though we don't usually get it in Wales, and when anyone wants a colourful kind of stage-Taffy view on this and that then of course they go to him. With a bit of eloquent sob-stuff thrown in at Christmas or when it's dogs or the poor. He's the up-market media Welshman. Fine. I can take him in that role, just about. But as for Alun Weaver the writer, especially the poet . . . I'm sorry.'

'Well, I'm no literary critic,' announced Garth. 'I'm just going by the general acclaim. I'm told they think highly of him in America. But we've got a writer here now.'

'Oh, no,' said Malcolm, embarrassed. 'Not in that sense. Well, what can I say? It's true that a lot of his work falls under Brydan's shadow, but I see nothing very shameful in that. And there's more than that in it. I'm not saying he didn't get quite a bit from Brydan, but they were also both drawing on a common stock to rather different effect. Something like that.'

Charlie said with a bland look, 'Everything you say may well be true – it cuts no ice with me. Brydan, Alun, you can stick the lot. Take it away. Forget it.'

'Oh, Charlie,' Garth pleaded. 'Not Brydan. Not *Tales from the Undergrowth*. Known and loved all over the world as it is.'

'That in particular. Write about your own people by all means, don't be soft on them, turn them into figures of fun if you must, but don't patronise them, don't sell them short and above all don't lay them out on display like quaint objects in a souvenir shop.'

'I didn't realise you felt that strongly,' said Malcolm after a silence.

'I don't, I don't feel strongly at all. Not my field. But I do think if a chap decides to make a living out of being Welsh he'd better do it in a show on the telly. Which I think Alun realises part of the time.'

'Oh dear.' Malcolm too seemed quite cast down. 'And you see that in the poetry, in Brydan's poetry too, do you?'

'Yes I do. What's that stuff about, er, the man in the mask and the man in the iron street. All he'd done was juggle two phrases about and had the

Americans going on about childlike Welsh vision. Stark too it was, boyo. It's not serious enough, that kind of thing.'

Malcolm set about considering the justice of parts of this in his conscientious way. Soon Garth, who had been looking anxiously from face to face, made a permission-to-speak noise. Charlie nodded encouragingly at him.

'I was just going to say, what about, what about her? I have met her, of course I have, but I think only the once and long ago.'

'Well, what about her?' said Charlie. 'Just a very pleasant – '

'Rhiannon Rhys, as she was when I first met her,' said Malcolm fluently, raising himself in his seat like a panellist answering a question from the audience, 'was one of the most stunning-looking girls I've ever seen in my life. Tall, fair, graceful, beautiful complexion, grey eyes with just a hint of blue. An English rose, really. And a lovely nature – modest, unassuming. She made no attempt to be the centre of attraction, but she was, in any company. No, I haven't seen her for a long time either, and she may look a bit different now, but there are some things that don't change, not in thirty years. I'm glad she's coming back to Wales.'

Malcolm believed that he had on the whole said this in a conversational, down-to-earth way. Garth paid close attention. Charlie drained his glass for the second time, sucking fiercely to get the last couple of drops.

'Well, er,' said Garth, 'that sounds absolutely marvellous. Thank you, Malcolm. I'll look forward to renewing my acquaintance with, with Mrs Weaver.'

Before he had finished Charlie was urging Malcolm to have a real drink, assuring him that what he had before him was piss and getting up from the table. This was not as straightforward a procedure as might be thought, in view of the table itself and his chair and their respective legs, and his own bulk and state. On the way out of the room he gave a muffled cry of shock when the side of his heel bumped against the door-frame. By standing quite still for a moment and concentrating, however, he successfully avoided the hazard in the passage floor where for some years most of a tile had been missing. His shoulder grazed but did not dislodge a framed photograph on the wall showing a row of men in hats standing outside a thatched cottage in Ireland or some such place.

As he waited at the hatch for Doris to finish giving change for a couple of twenty-pound notes in the bar, Charlie thought about Malcolm's speech just now. Almost every phrase in it had been all right in itself, would have been, at least, if said in a different voice or eked out with a few oaths or perhaps seen written. It was the way the silly sod had looked and sounded so pleased with himself for having had no false shame about coming out with it – that was what had called for a frantic personal exit headfirst through the closed window or, more prosaically, overturning the table in his lap. And that clear holy-man's gaze . . .

Doris ambled along and Charlie ordered a large pink gin, mentioning Garth's name, and three large Scotches and water. Down went one of the

Scotches in its entirety while Doris was ringing up and right away the old feather duster twirled at the back of his throat and he was coughing his heart to bits, right there at maximum first go, roaring, bellowing like an imitation, in a crouch with his fists shoved into his guts, tears pouring down his face. A silence fell widely round him. When he tried to look he thought he saw somebody, several people, hobbledehoys, leaning over the bar to peer. Doris gave him a glass of water and he sipped and breathed, then drank. With a great exhalation he straightened up and mopped his eyes, feeling now quite proud of himself, as if his well-known toughness and grit had got him through another testing external assault.

He had not yet touched the tray of drinks when the door banged at the end of the passage and a large lumpish figure creaked towards him through the gloom, recognisable after a moment as Peter Thomas, runner-up in the open tournament of the DSRC a couple of times in the 1940s but more of a golf man. Neither one nor the other these days, of course.

'Hallo, Peter. Early for you.'

'No, not really. Yes, I'll have a gin and slimline tonic.'

If Charlie Norris had ever been thought of as big and fat and red-faced, and some such description was hard to avoid, a revision of terminology might have been called for at the sight of his friend. Charlie's backside pushed the tail of his tweed jacket into two divergent halves, true, and his paunch forced the waistband of his trousers half-way down to his crotch, but Peter could have given him a couple of stone and still been the heftier, not so obviously from front or back where the cut of his suit tended to camouflage him, but to be seen in anything like profile as even thicker through than wide. And Charlie's cheeks and forehead were no more than ruddy compared with Peter's rich colouring. Their faces in general were different: Charlie's round and pug-nosed, with the look of a battered schoolboy, Peter's fine-featured, almost distinguished between the bulges and pouches. At the moment Charlie was smiling, Peter not.

'Well, how are you today?' asked Charlie. A duff question on second thoughts.

'How do you think? But as you see I can get out of the house. Who's in there?'

'Just Garth and Malcolm.'

Peter nodded and sighed, accepting it. His massive, bottom-heavy head turned sharply at a burst of laughter and jocular shouting from inside the bar. The voices sounded youthful. Frowning, he limped to the hatch and stuck his head round.

'According to Malcolm,' began Charlie, but stopped when the other turned back, speaking as he moved.

'I thought we were supposed to be in the middle of a depression. Have you looked in there? Three-quarters full, at this hour.' It was all coming out as if freshly minted. 'Most of them in their twenties or younger. Unemployed school-leavers, no doubt. Who'd be anything else these days if he had the chance, eh? What happens if we ever have a boom? They'll be falling down drunk from morning till night, presumably. Like the eighteenth century. You know, Hogarth.'

Charlie wanted to grin when Doris put the slimline on the tray next to the (large) gin. Talk about a drop in the ocean. Like an elephant going short of a banana, he thought. He also thought Peter looked distinctly fatter since he had last seen him, though admittedly this was doubtful after no more than a couple of days. Nor did he appear well. He had been breathing hard when he arrived and seemed to be sweating, though it was far from hot outdoors or in. High blood-pressure. Not good.

Still talking, he preceded Charlie down the passage. 'You should see the old bags coming out of the supermarkets with the goodies piled up on their trolleys like Christmas.' His hip thumped considerably into a table against the wall, agitating the leaves of the flowerless pot-plant that sprawled there. 'And I don't mean in the middle of town, I'm talking about wretched holes like Greenhill or Emanuel.' He opened the door of the lounge. 'And the point is you can't tell anybody. Nobody wants to know.'

Peter Thomas had to hold the door open because an ancient shoddiness of workmanship would have made it swing shut in a few seconds, and Charlie was much occupied with the tray after a pair of speedy over-corrections had nearly sent the stuff piling over opposite edges. At last they were in and settled and Garth had finished welcoming Peter.

A glance at Peter showed there was no more to come from that direction for the moment. Half to provoke him, Charlie said, 'Anybody happened to go by St Paul's recently? They're having fun there.'

Malcolm said, 'Are we talking about St Paul's Cathedral in London?'

'No, no, the church off the Strand here. Old what-was-he-called, old Joe Craddock's church.'

'Used to wear a green tweed cap with his dog-collar.'

'That's the fellow. Well, he should see it now. So should you, it seems. Sex cinema is what it is now. You couldn't invent that, could you? You wouldn't dare. Nobody would.'

'Come on, Charlie,' said Garth right on cue, 'you don't mean to sit there and – '

'I bloody do, mate. Adult movies on Screens 1 and 2. In the nave and chancel respectively, I presume. "Come Play with Me" and another witticism.'

'I dare say they exerted themselves to deconsecrate the building,' said Peter.

You fat old hypocritical Welsh cunt, thought Charlie. 'It would have appealed to Joe, anyway,' he said, and added for Garth's benefit, 'Used to fuck anything that moved, old Joe did. Bloody marvel, he was. Pulled in an enormous congregation too. Very tough on drink. Of course, I'm talking now about twenty years ago.'

'I didn't know that,' said Malcolm, trying not to sound shocked. 'I mean about his activities.'

'No, well . . .' Again Charlie kept to himself what he thought. Still grinning, he met Peter's eye, only for a second, but quite long enough to be sure that Peter was trying not to join in an admiring, part-horrified laugh in reminiscence, something he would certainly have done up until more recently than twenty years ago. 'Amazingly lucky with the horses as well, Joe was. He said he used to count on five to six hundred a year, which in those days was all right. You never ran into anyone who reckoned that was fair.'

Another silence followed. Silences were a great feature of these Bible sessions. Peter sat on with his hands spread on his bulky thighs, sniffing and groaning quietly, perhaps trying to think of something that summed up what he felt about the fate of St Paul's, if so failing. Finally Garth said in his eager, quacking voice, 'Malcolm was telling us, Alun and Rhiannon Weaver are coming back down here to live. They – '

Peter swung himself round almost fiercely on Charlie. 'Had you heard this? Well, you didn't mention it to me just now.'

'You didn't give me much of a chance.'

'Down here to live, you say.'

'Apparently. Yes,' said Charlie, signalling with his face to Malcolm to come in, and after no great delay Malcolm started explaining that the Weavers had rented a house in Pedwarsaint to look round from and things like that while Peter stared at him or in his direction through his thick glasses and Garth listened as if every fact were new to him.

Malcolm did not disclose that, while Peter had been a young lecturer at the local university and Rhiannon in her second year as a student, they had had an affair, and she had got pregnant and had had an abortion performed on her at his expense by a doctor in Harriston, a man incidentally struck off the medical register soon afterwards for another of the same and now long dead. This had been a remarkable train of events in the South Wales of 1947–8; more remarkably still, Peter had not been thrown out of his job at the university, in fact nothing official was ever said on the matter. What counted, after all, not only in South Wales, was not what you knew but who could prove you knew it. Quite soon, however, Peter had given up a promising career in academic chemical engineering for a different sort in the real thing not far away, a few miles along the coast to the west in Port Holder. Rhiannon had promptly vanished to London, where after an obscure interval she had got a job as a receptionist at the BBC, where in turn a year or two later she had met Alun Weaver.

That was, of course, not all that had happened. Just about when Rhiannon had become pregnant, Peter had shifted his attentions to another female, someone outside the university, and after another few months had turned out to be engaged, presumably to this other. His fiancée was a certain Muriel Smorthwaite, the daughter of one of the managers at the tin-plate mill he now worked at. In those days Peter had been considered rather lucky, given his record, to be engaged to anyone at all west of Offa's Dyke, for although the Smorthwaites were from Yorkshire originally, not local, some conscientious neighbour must surely have passed the word. But the two had got married, living in Port Holder for a judicious couple of years before settling in Cwmgwyrdd just on the far side of town.

Charlie had been a student in the same year as Rhiannon, though older than she through war service, and acquainted with her and her mates. He had heard as much about all this as most people not directly involved but had learnt no more since. He had not tried to find out and not been told; he had forgotten about the whole business until that morning. He wondered how well informed the other two here were: Malcolm well enough, as was shown in his every movement and inflection as he spoke, Garth probably not at all.

Malcolm finished his short recital. Evidently Peter, with Garth looking at him in expectation of something or other, could think of nothing to say. His glistening bald head moved from side to side in an agitated fashion.

Charlie gave him an easy one. 'Of course, you were never a great fan of Alun's, were you? As man or writer that I remember.'

Peter turned on him again, but appreciatively this time. 'Bloody Welshman,' he said with relish, doubtless referring to Alun.

'Oh, come on now, Peter,' said Garth, laughing steadily, being very good about not being indignant, 'we're all Welshmen here. Including you as far as I know.'

'More's the pity,' said Peter, draining his glass with a flourish.

On this the door burst open with a suddenness and violence that might well have killed Charlie half an hour earlier, its edge striking the back of his chair, though not hard. Into the sudden hush stepped a man and a woman, both young, both having on knee-boots and other wearables of synthetic material, both carrying crash-helmets. It was at once evident that the tumultuous door-opening had been the result of thoughtlessness rather than any kind of hostility. Unaware both of the hush and of the four looks that went with it, from Peter's glare to Malcolm's mild curiosity, the couple strolled across the room and started looking at some of the DSRC mementos on the wall there and along the mantelpiece above the boarded-up fireplace. When they spoke their accents were not local, perhaps from Liverpool.

'Ladder as at 31st December 1949,' read out the young man and took a pull of what was probably lager. 'What kind of ladder would that be?' He spoke in simple puzzlement.

'Must be all the landlord's stuff,' said the girl. In her hand was an opaque greenish concoction with pieces of ice and fruit floating in it.

'Annual dinner . . .'

The girl studied the slightly mildewed photograph. 'Nowhere here is that.'

'Chairman . . . committee . . . You know, like some sort of club?'

'Served us all right, didn't they?'

The pair had begun to turn shyly towards the group of old men when Garth, having recognised without any sense of novelty that Peter and Charlie were too fat to be expected to make a move and Malcolm too windy, got up and shut the door as loudly as he could, which was not very loudly because it had already come close to shutting itself.

'Er, excuse me,' began the youth.

Garth stared at him without speaking.

'Er, is this some kind of club?'

'Not exactly a club, no,' said Garth, moving his head about and screwing up his face in a confidential way. 'It's more, well, we had been hoping to hold this private committee meeting in just a few minutes. Personal matters, you'll appreciate, er . . .'

'Oh . . . well . . . sorry . . .'

After an exchange of glances and no delay the two invaders set about leaving. The girl, who was rather tall and walked with a firm tread, looked briefly over at the seated three as she passed.

'And *shut* the *door*,' said Peter with elaborate movements of his mouth.

When the door had shut, almost soundlessly, Garth puffed out his breath, Charlie said, 'Well done, Garth, you're a great man,' and Peter gave a short roar like a lion keeping in voice.

Malcolm made no sound. He thought the girl's eye had caught his for an instant, not of course out of anything but habit or even politeness, and yet it set him thinking. How many years was it since he had noticed a girl? And what exactly had he seen in this one? – she was not all that attractive. She was young, yes indeed, not that he could have said what age, but not so much young either as fresh, new, scarcely out of the wrapping-paper with no time for anything to have got at her and started using her up. It was hard to believe that there had been a time when he had lived his whole life among people like that with occasional unimpressive distractions from an aunt or a teacher or a ticket-collector.

'That, that *breed* haven't necessarily been badly brought up, they're gross and boorish by nature.' It seemed that Peter thought the affray of a moment before had been far too lightly passed over.

'On the contrary,' said Malcolm, quite sharply for him. 'They blundered in rather crassly because they knew no better, but as soon as they grasped the situation their decent instincts took over and they were perfectly civil.'

'I'll go and invite them back in if you like,' said Charlie.

'It's my shout,' said Garth.

'No, mine,' said Peter.

But before he had got properly started on rising to his feet the door opened again, nearly as wide as before but smoothly and silently. There followed a frozen pause which a stranger might have found unsettling. Then a man came into the room and shut the door ceremoniously behind him, a man of the same sort of age as the company, a tall broad man, not fat, wearing an unusually thick natural-coloured cardigan with scuffed leather buttons. This was Tarquin Jones, known as Tarc, landlord of the Bible as long as any of the others could remember. On first sight of him standing behind the beer-pulls in the main bar, perhaps as far back as 1950, Malcolm had thought that he must have suffered a bereavement earlier that morning and had on the instant decided that he, Malcolm, was in some way responsible. But he had stood his ground and quite soon discovered that Tarc always had that expression on, at least in public. Now, grasping the backs of Charlie's and Peter's chairs, he leaned over the table and looked them all in the eye one after the other.

'So you managed to dispose of the intolerable intrusion,' he said in a grave tone, at once diffusing a cloud of the ambiguity that hung about so much of what he said.

'They went like lambs,' said Charlie. 'No trouble at all.'

Tarc nodded impatiently, already done with the matter. 'Last night,' he went on, lowering his voice, 'they were out there for an hour after I'd shut my house, revving up their bikes and the rock blaring out on their radios and yelling their heads off. They – '

'How extraordinary,' said Malcolm – 'as Charlie said they couldn't have been more tractable a moment ago. No hint of any . . .'

His voice died away as Tarc looked round the circle again, this time with stoical weariness. 'I was thinking in fact,' he began, suddenly affecting a sunny forbearance, 'of a different group of young people altogether. Not the two who went in and out of here just now. No. Others. Who are given to behaving in the way I have tried to describe. As I was saying,' he went on, then said nothing for ten seconds or so before resuming in his original manner, 'They're not from round here, you know, most of 'em. Come batting down the M4 from Cardiff or Bristol like fiends out of hell any time of the day or night, all with a chick behind there. I tell you, the other Sunday I was coming back from seeing my daughter in Penarth and a crowd of 'em caught up with me and started carving me up as I understand it's called, overtaking me and fanning out in front and then staying level three or four abreast and looking at me, staring at me for, I don't know, it seemed like minutes at a time and going at seventy. Seventy. And talking about me, shouting out to each other about me and pointing at me. I don't mind admitting to you,' he lowered his voice further, 'I was scared, honest I was. Scared.'

When he paused, none of his audience showed any sign of responding, then or at any future time. 'Because this isn't just high spirits or youthful exuberance – we're used to that. No no, what we're faced with is an orchestrated onslaught on our whole culture and way of life. And this concerns you gentlemen particularly. In your position it behoves you to take note and consider what is to be done. If the likes of you won't give a lead I don't know what is to become of us.'

'If you ask me,' said Malcolm, 'what could be at work there is an actual enmity towards the very structure of society.'

This observation seemed to take all the fight out of Tarc. He said in a bleating tone and with a slight quaver, 'I'm very glad to find you hold that view, Mr Cellan-Davies, because it's rather the one I was trying to put forward myself.' Then as he gathered up the empty glasses his manner began to rally a little and grew almost friendly for a moment. 'Er, warm enough in here, are you? Miserable old day out. Now remember all of you, you've only to say the word and I'll bring in the fire.' No one said it, so he withdrew, pausing at the door for his closing line. 'I do beg you to consider seriously the points I've put to you.'

'Dear, dear, there's a character,' said Garth, very much the sort of thing he always said after one of Tarc's visitations.

'I seemed to quieten him down all right,' said Malcolm modestly.

'Yes, you did, didn't you?' said Peter.

'He goes too far sometimes, old Tarc,' said Charlie. 'We know we have to take it and so does he, so he really shouldn't talk about orchestrated onslaughts and behoving, especially behoving. No, that was naughty.'

'I'm sorry, I don't understand what you mean,' said Malcolm.

'Well, teasing us. Defying us to tell him to come off it.'

'Are you saying it's all an act? I know he exaggerates and all that, but . . .'

Peter answered. 'Tarc doesn't know how much of an act it is himself, not any more. He's got so he couldn't tell you whether he means what he says or not. Far from the only one in these parts to have reached that condition.'

'Anyway,' said Garth, 'you and he do seem to see very much eye to eye on the modern world and the youth of today and the rest of it.'

Fortunately, before Peter could answer that one old Owen Thomas (no relation) turned up with a guest of his, a retired chartered accountant from Brecon, and soon after them came old Arnold Spurling and then old Tudor Whittingham, who had beaten the British Empire amateur champion 9–3, 14–12, 9–7 at Wembley in 1953. Arnold had just won a few quid in one of the newspaper bingo competitions and insisted on drinks all round. Charlie started feeling quite good, and even Peter seemed able to put up with the presence of old Arnold and the others.

Owen Thomas went off to the bar for ham rolls and came back with all there was in the eats line, a plate of egg-and-cheese quiches prepared by Tarc's granddaughter, who was doing a course in culinary studies at the university. For different reasons Peter, Charlie and Malcolm turned them down. The three decided to leave after the next drink, or rather Peter, whose car was outside, decided that and the other two went along. They had that next drink, and then another quick one which Malcolm declined, and then they left. Garth lived within walking distance, so of course he was going to walk, perhaps as soon as he had finished explaining to Owen Thomas's guest about the importance of not brooding.

3

Peter's car was a Morris Marina of an archaic buff-orange colour relieved here and there by small archipelagoes of rust. With nothing said, Charlie got in beside Peter and Malcolm got in the back. This was not easy for Malcolm with his long legs, because Peter had to keep his seat pushed back as far as possible in order to get his stomach behind the wheel. The other half of the back seat was taken up with wooden trays spilling earth and small stones and piled with potatoes, leeks, parsnips and perhaps turnips freshly out of the ground, or at any rate untouched since. Empty tissue cartons, very dirty cloths that had wiped the windows, dog-eared technical pamphlets, graphs and thick bundles of duplicated sheets with a forlornly superannuated look, publishers' circulars, an empty tube of children's sweets, a biscuit wrapper and several books and leaflets about dieting lay elsewhere. When Peter set the car in motion a small capless bottle that might once have held slimline tonic came trundling out from under his seat.

Malcolm peeled one of the diet leaflets off the floor at his side and looked through it. He wanted to be covered in some sense against the possibility that the subject of Rhiannon might come up again. Also diets interested him. His own eating and drinking practice was a conflation of several, often irreconcilable with each other. Thus the two halves of beer a day he reckoned he needed to help to keep him regular meant a cutback in calories elsewhere with the risk of a deficit in vital fibre. More generally, you never knew what one programme or another might come up with in the way of a new hankering-reducer or safe volume-limiter. And there was not such a hell of a lot to read anywhere these days.

Soon enough Malcolm was pretty sure that what he had picked up was no good except to get him through the five minutes now in progress. After forbidding all alcohol except a small glass of dry white wine every year or so, it ran through a remarkably full and imaginative list of everything anybody had ever enjoyed eating and forbade the lot, though surely with some risk of infraction. Anyway, your own eyes were enough to tell you that if old Peter, now listening to something Charlie was telling him about the price of a house in Beaufoy, had ever observed these constraints he had forgotten them again after a couple of hours. Then why did he bother to read or at least buy diet literature? To feel virtuous by laying out nothing more than money. To make promises to himself like a man looking at travel brochures of exotic places. No, more a man reading about polar explorers living off snow, moss and boot-leather. About Red Indian tortures.

Malcolm became quite dreamy. As in his boyhood he had deliberately used thoughts of school, of homework to obscure the prospect of a treat or a birthday before wallowing in delighted expectation, so now he let Peter's overweight problem be obliterated by memories of Rhiannon. The only trouble was that they were not as sharp in his mind as *Lettres de mon Moulin* and the South Africans playing at Gloucester. His clergyman uncle had taken him.

'Soft as lights, that fellow,' said Peter when Malcolm had been dropped at his front gate. 'Perfectly pleasant, I agree, but dead soft.'

'Something like that, yes,' said Charlie.

'I bet he fills in the month and year on all his cheque counterfoils.'

'Yeah, and writes out the number of pence in words.'

'And sends in box-tops to save three-fifty on a hand-crafted presentation decanter.'

'Oh really I think that's going a bit far. But I bet he watches documentaries on the telly.'

'In Welsh.' Peter spoke with genuine rancour.

'And I swear he swings his arms when he walks.'

'Do you know they have wrestling in Welsh now on that new channel? Same as in English oddly enough except the bugger counts *un – dau – tri* etcetera. Then the idiots can go round saying the viewing figures for Welsh-language programmes have gone up. To four thousand and eleven.'

'The commentary would have to be in Welsh too.'

'Doubtless, doubtless. Did you gather that young Malcolm had, let's say, an attachment to Rhiannon in the long-ago?'

'Something like that,' said Charlie again. 'He wasn't at all specific.'

'I thought he sounded a bit as though he had been attached. But I rather wonder when.'

'He gave a great lyrical spiel about her just before you came. Non-specific, as I said. That doesn't sound very nice, does it?'

'M'm. Non-specificity could cut either way. Meaning he never laid a finger on her but would like us to think he did. Or meaning he did but for some reason doesn't want us to think he did so he goes on as if he didn't. You've got to remember he's a Welshman too.'

'Christ, Peter, nobody would take you for one after that analysis. Anyway I don't think Malcolm's that sort of Welshman.'

'Oh, is there another sort? Actually you know I had a . . .'

Peter's voice cut off so abruptly that it was hard to be sure he had said what he seemed to have said. He sat in a round-shouldered yet strained posture, arms out to their fullest extent to reach the wheel, legs and feet stretched too and still only just finding the pedals. After a moment Charlie got a quick half-glance from him where a steady look would have been more characteristic, and also feasible with the car drawing up at the Salt

House lights. A growl of effort escaped him as he reached even further forward, squashing his paunch severely, and set the wipers going in the fine rain.

'Hard to be sure, of course, that any given bloke hasn't done a touch of finger-laying in a specific case,' said Charlie reflectively. 'Even young Malcolm. I wouldn't put it past – '

'You see, I was having an affair with her myself. You must have heard that, Charlie.'

'Yes.'

'And a bit more besides I shouldn't wonder. I didn't come out of it looking particularly well, I know. I didn't behave particularly well, either.'

After a pause, Charlie said, 'I suppose we all – '

'Not as badly perhaps as some people probably imagine but still not well. Not at all well. So one way and another it was something of a bolt from the bloody blue just now, hearing about her turning up again. Obviously I'll do my best to keep out of her way.'

'Not very obviously after all these years, surely.'

'No, no, there's an awful lot of stuff . . . I'll tell you later. For the moment I'd just ask you to, you know, stand by. And there's more to it than steering clear of her. I mean there's him, you see.'

'Yes, there is him.'

'It's not the time now to go into that either. But I expect you can imagine how I feel. Part of it, at least.'

'I can. And I'm quite sure you can imagine quite a bit of how I feel,' said Charlie, making it clear with tone and look that he in his turn was making mentionable what had been known but unmentioned.

'Indeed.' Something not utterly unlike warmth entered Peter's manner. 'Does, er, does Sophie ever mention it or anything? I mean there was never very much in it, was there?'

'Not as far as I know, and Alun wasn't exactly the only one, but then you only need one Alun if I make myself plain. And it was supposed to be all over before I came along, or rather what there was of it was, but there again . . . Well, there was an afternoon while he was down here on one of his trips five or six years ago when the shop rang up for Sophie and she couldn't be found, and then I heard quite by chance that no one knew where he was at the time either. Probably nothing, I agree. And anyway there was nothing *else*, which is the main point. Because it's not *it* that matters so much, it's the bloody side-effects. Great man for side-effects, Alun. Of which a traumatically embarrassing poem would be a very mild example.'

'I see that. By Christ I see it. The time he broke down at that service for Brydan – at St Illtyd's?'

'Yeah, and the way he broke down. "*Gwae och*, I am unworthy to pronounce his praise" and the rest of it.'

'Welcome flash of realism,' said Peter.

'Oh, do you think so? According to me nobody could have been more suitable.'

'Well, yes, all right. When are they coming down, did you say?'

'Not yet. Couple of months. Could you drop me at the Glendower?'

'Sure. What shall I tell Sophie?' Peter's destination was the Norrises', where he would pick up his wife after the coffee-party.

'Just you've dropped me at the Glendower. It won't come as much of a shock.'

When they arrived Charlie asked Peter in for one, but Peter said he thought he had better push on, so Charlie went by himself into the Glendower, in full the Owen Glendower (no Owain Glyndŵr crap thank you very much) Tavern and Grill. Being part-owner of this, Charlie was by himself only for a very short time, in fact he found a couple of fellows he knew from County Hall in the bar, which thoughtfully offered seventeen different kinds of Scotch whisky, and in just a few minutes he was at the top of his form.

4

Two empty 1½-litre bottles of Soave Superiore (DOC) stood on the glass-topped table next to a silver tray bearing ten or eleven used coffee-cups, some of them half full of finished-with coffee. The air in Sophie Norris's spacious drawing-room was misty with cigarette-smoke and loud with several conversations. True to Welsh punctuality, most of the ladies there had arrived at or slightly before the off at eleven and so not missed any part of what was going. The coffee and attendant biscuits, having conferred a kind of legitimacy on the session, had been made short work of, swallowed down by some like bread and butter before cake, scamped or skipped completely by others, and the real business was uncorked and poured after about twenty minutes. Obviously it was drunk at different speeds thereafter, though you could have guessed that a couple of those in the room had been at the Soave, or perhaps the Frascati, earlier and elsewhere. After all, it was only wine.

Sophie herself was not one of the couple. Standing by the french window that gave a view of garden, golf links and, remotely, sea, she looked confident and comfortable, very much like the wife of a prosperous caterer recently semi-retired or more, and hardly at all like someone who in her time had been one of the surest things between Bridgend and Carmarthen town – quite a distinction. In tweed skirt and angora sweater her figure was still impressive, though her breasts no longer jutted out of her trunk like a pair of smallish thighs as they had once famously done. At the moment she and Gwen Cellan-Davies were talking about that day's star topic.

'Quite a good-looking man, I suppose you'd have to admit,' said Gwen fair-mindedly. 'Or he was, anyway.'

'Oh, not too bad if you like that rather flashy type.' Sophie spoke in the unreconstructed rather shrill tones of Harriston, well suited for expressionless utterances. 'Of course she's lovely.'

'Mind you, he's a terrible old sham.'

'Sorry?'

'At school with Brydan my eye. Oh, they were both at the Grammar right enough, but three years between them. He can't have known him. Well if he did, it means Brydan was taking an interest in boys three years younger, and I've heard a lot of things about him but that never. You ask Muriel. She'll tell you Peter's the same age as Alun exactly, they were in the same form, and he doesn't remember Brydan at all from then.'

'Yeah, well . . .'

'And evidently according to Peter that "Alun" business is a lark. "Alan" it always was at school, Peter said, in the English way. That was before he went in for being a Welshman professionally.'

Not many general topics appealed to Sophie, and the question of Wales or being Welsh stood high in her uninterests. 'Oh yes,' she said, quite dully enough to have checked anyone less tenacious than Gwen.

'When he came back after the war he'd been out in the great world and discovered the advantages of Welshness.'

'For Christ's sake tell me what they are, Gwen, and I can pass them on to my old man,' said Muriel Thomas in her breezy, booming voice as she moved closer. She held a freshly-opened bottle of Soave, just a litre one this time, from which she refilled Gwen's glass. 'He seems to think it's about on a par with the brand of Cain.'

'I really meant just to appeal to the Saxons, Muriel, you know, the way Brydan used to go on. But actually we were talking about Alun.'

'Oh God, were you? I'm afraid here's one Saxon who's managed to resist the appeal of both Brydan and Alun. I'll say no more because I am, after all, a guest in your country.'

'You're one of us, darling,' said Sophie.

This was certainly true in the sense that, for all her often-proclaimed Englishness, Muriel conformed closely to a prevalent Welsh physical type with her dark hair and eyes and slender build, a fact often remarked on, at least in Wales. If it occurred to her now she gave no sign. Holding back whatever had been on the tip of her tongue, she said, 'My purpose in grabbing you chaps was not to discuss the great Alun but to recruit a rescue expedition for poor Angharad's benefit. La belle Dorothy hath her in thrall.'

After a minute the trio began rather carefully to cross the room. The level of atmospheric pollution seemed if anything to have gone up slightly. Drinking rates among the company might have varied but there was a pretty uniform deep commitment to cigarettes, with the smoke from those actually being smoked well backed up by the three or four stubs left in ashtrays but not put out. Empty or forgotten packets and various bits of wrapping littered the rugs.

On the rug in front of the lighted gas-fire, a large and elegant appliance with fully simulated coals, sat Dorothy Morgan, who had been on Sophie's doorstep at ten to eleven. At her side stood a half-full 40 oz. flask of California Pinot Chardonnay and a brimming blue-glass ashtray with the distinction of having two cigarette-ends burning away in it at the same time. She was indeed talking strenuously though not loudly to Angharad Pumphrey, who often had to lean down from her leather armchair to catch the words.

Angharad was not deaf, or no worse than most of them; she was not drunk, not even drinking. What singled her out from those around her was her looks, which were those of a real old lady, though she was not the oldest in years. Part of it came from her clothes — no bright trouser-suits for her — and part her untouched or unretouched hair and the like, but there seemed nothing to be done about her collapsed mouth or the knobbly protrusions of jawbone on either side of her chin or the criss-crossed flabbiness round her eyes. There had been talk of a disfiguring illness at some time before she arrived in these parts from Capel Mererid and presumably after she married Garth, but nobody really knew or would tell.

Dorothy Morgan was saying, 'But it's not just that, their whole outlook is different, their whole view of life.' Her neat short haircut and unadorned black-framed spectacles gave her a misleading air of intellectual strictness. 'You can tell from the structure of their language. Do you know Russian at all? Well, it's full of conjugations and inflections. For instance . . .'

Meanwhile the arrivals were moving into position in businesslike style, Muriel on the arm of the chair, Gwen on a quilted needlework-box and Sophie squatting on the rug. As they did so they all said hello to Angharad and asked how she was and told her they were glad to see her and she said something to all of them back.

During the last part of this Dorothy rose to her knees and, in a slightly louder voice than before, said, 'I was telling Angharad about Russian and how extraordinarily more complicated a language it is than Welsh, and of course English, which means . . .' She spoke with an unvarying slight smile and her gaze fixed on some neutral point. ' . . . not necessarily more sophisticated than we are, at least not all the time . . .' It was not known when she slept, because nobody had ever been there to see her departing for bed or, when staying in the same house, come down to breakfast and failed to find her already at the table with a cigarette and most likely a glass of wine. ' . . . very primitive because they drop the verb "to be" whenever they can. Like Red Indians.' She was said to have been found once telling the man who was laying the carpets about eohippus.

Dorothy's heavy-duty mode took an appreciable time to come round from, so that when she paused for a second or two, as she did after the

Red Indians, nobody had anything to say at first, until Sophie just scraped in on the last of the amber by asking to hear about the trip to Leningrad. Not again, surely? Yes, again, insisted Sophie, and very soon she was having the case for going by Aeroflot put to her with undiminished conviction.

Under this covering fire Muriel, Gwen and Angharad were able to withdraw in good order. Standard Dorothy procedure said that when she got into that sort of stride and someone had to sacrifice herself for the sake of the others, then whoever happened to be hostess stepped forward. The punishment seemed to even out pretty well except that on neutral ground, like Dorothy's own establishment, Sophie got landed oftener than her turn. The others would agree rather sheepishly among themselves that she somehow sounded as if she minded it less.

There was no trace at the drinks table of the almost-full litre of Soave Muriel had left on it some minutes earlier. An untouched magnum of Orvieto, however, stood within reach and she set efficiently about opening that, cigarette in mouth, eyes screwed up.

'We haven't seen you here for a long time, Angharad,' said Gwen.

'No, you haven't, and I wouldn't be here today if I hadn't happened to have to take a clock in for repair at that place in Hatchery Road.' Angharad's voice was not old, so much not so that public-utilities men and other strangers still occasionally tried to flirt with her over the telephone. 'I bumped into Siân Smith when she was more or less on her way here.'

'Of course, it is quite a step from where you are.'

'Yes, and it's not much fun when I get here, either, if this is anything like a fair sample.'

'Sorry about old Dorothy. We're sort of used to her, you know. We could see you were stuck.'

'I hope I never have the chance of getting used to her. What makes that woman think I want to hear her paltry little observations on Russia or Russian or Russians? Or anything else on God's earth?'

No awareness, let alone appreciation, of having been unstuck showed itself in Angharad. On the contrary, her resentment of Dorothy's conduct seemed to grow when no one looked like offering to excuse it. Closely and with apparent curiosity she had watched Muriel expose and pull the cork of the Orvieto; now, all but incredulously, she followed every detail of its pouring, her own nearly-empty glass held austerely to one side. People tended to forget about Angharad in the same sort of spirit as they forgot about her husband, whom, by the way, no living person had ever seen in her company, any more than anyone had ever seen the inside of their house. They wondered about the Pumphreys' domestic and marital life quite as much at these coffee-parties as at the Bible.

'Well, that's just how she is,' said Gwen, defending Dorothy rather late in the day and without much fervour. 'She's always been like it but she's got worse lately. Like everybody else.'

'I mean it's not as if I were a great friend of hers,' said Angharad, accusingly now. 'I hardly know her. Hardly even spoken to her before.'

'You were there, that's enough,' said Muriel.

'What sort of a husband does a woman like that have?'

Muriel lit another cigarette and said, 'Very nice chap, old Percy Morgan. She doesn't do it to him. Not when we're about, anyway. They get on together like a house on fire.'

'He's a builder,' added Gwen.

'A *builder*.'

'Well, he builds things like town halls,' said Muriel.

After studying Muriel's next inhalation of smoke, Angharad returned to her point. 'But she wouldn't let me get a word in, not a single word. Not even to tell her how riveting she was being.'

'You always get one person like that at this sort of jollification,' said Gwen.

Angharad raised her bushy eyebrows. 'Oh, so that's what it is. Quite frankly, if it stopped short at one person like that I wouldn't mind so much,' she said, graciously looking over Gwen's shoulder as she spoke. 'I don't mind telling you it'll be quite a time before I come this way again. This sort of jollification, as you call it, quite defeats me. I'd better make my farewells. Where's . . . where's Sophie?'

The other two watched Angharad take brief, undemonstrative leave of her hostess and, without a glance at Dorothy or anybody else, limp heavily from the room.

'That's what I call mellowing with age,' said Muriel, topping up the glasses. 'Oh, I'm thrilled that she didn't mind telling us what she told us.'

'I thought only beautiful people could behave like that. Poor old thing, though. She's probably in pain.'

'I hope so. It didn't do us any good, sticking up for Dorothy.'

Gwen screwed up her face. 'Not a lot of that, though, was there, actually?'

'Now you mention it, no, there wasn't. It's not much of a defence of a burglar to say he's always been a burglar.'

'Perhaps we should have agreed with her about how terrible Dorothy is.'

'Then she'd have had it in for us for knowing her. There's no pleasing some people, as you've probably noticed yourself.'

A general stir began. Glasses were drained, but not always left empty because there seemed to be a feeling that no opened wine should be allowed to remain undrunk, perhaps out of some old Cymric superstition. Things might have gone differently, or just further in the same direction, if Sophie had broached the 3-litre box of Selected Balkan Riesling on top of the drinks cabinet, whose contents of gin, whisky and other strong liquor were of course perfectly safe from any or all of the party. Two, three women went to say good-bye to Sophie, who was so relieved at being able to speak again that she refused to let them go, at any rate until after she had answered the door-bell. Siân Smith fell down on her way out but soon got up again and made it into the hall. When Sophie reappeared she had Peter Thomas with her. The sight of him standing alone on the doorstep had been enough to let her know that he had dropped Charlie at the Glendower. Without consulting him, still less offering him a glass of wine, she crossed to the drinks cabinet.

Peter looked rather shaken. After a moment's hesitation he advanced into the room with a real reluctance that he tried, late on and not very convincingly, to hide in a comic pretence of reluctance. He and Muriel waved to each other and it was the same or similar with him and Gwen, him and Dorothy, him and a couple of others. Flapping his hand at the smoke-filled air, he said in a bantering tone,

'So this is what all you busy housewives get up to while your men-folk are slacking and boozing their heads off in the pub.'

It was not very good, though surely better than nothing, and he had done his best to sound pleasant, and he had sounded quite pleasant, at any rate for him, but nobody seemed to hear much and nobody came over, not even Dorothy, until Sophie brought him a gin and tonic, offering to fetch ice which he forbade. He and she chatted about something, very likely more than one thing, for however long it was before Muriel collected him and took him off. If his shaken look had departed it was in place again by this time.

Of all the guests only Dorothy remained. She would not move before another piece of standard procedure fetched Percy over from Pedwarsaint to shift her, probably, though not certainly, by the power of words. There was no standard procedure for that.

5

'Good party at the good old Bible, I trust,' said Muriel. 'Who was there?'

Peter told her.

'You wonder why on earth you go, especially when you've got there and find it's exactly like it always is, and then you realise that's why you went. I suppose once upon a time we did things for a change. Malcolm full of the news about the Weavers, was he?'

'Well yes, he was rather.'

'What was your reaction?'

'It came as no surprise. Alun's always threatened to return to his Welsh roots, as perhaps you remember.'

'Perhaps I do, but that doesn't mean I want to remember.'

'Nor me. How was the do at Sophie's?'

'Much as usual, as I was saying. Quite enjoyable, that is, and many thanks.' With no perceptible pause and almost no change of tone, Muriel went on, 'Certainly not the assemblage of fools, bores and madwomen you made it crystal-clear you took it for, losing no time in doing so let it be said. You emptied that drawing-room in sixty seconds flat. Congratulations. Super. Your best yet.'

Peter, behind the wheel as they drove towards Cwmgwyrdd, thought as many times before of a film he had seen about half a century earlier. In it, a sadistic sergeant broke the spirit of a soldier in a military prison by beating him up at systematically random intervals, from more than a day down to a quarter of an hour, so that the victim never knew when the next attack was coming, never felt safe. Life with Muriel, it seemed to Peter, had over the last seven or eight years turned into a decreasingly bearable version of that. There were times, it was true, and this was one of them, when you could be morally certain a drubbing was on the way, not from anything she said or did but because you had spotted something disagreeable to her, either in itself or in its associations, drifting to the surface over the past few minutes or so; that was enough for her. For some strange reason, though, this kind of early warning did little to soften the eventual impact. He actually felt the sweat break out now on his forehead.

'Could I ask you to hold it for a bit, until we're home? If you don't I might drive into something. I'm not threatening to, I just might.'

'You might well, I agree with you, any time, with your belly forcing you back into that dangerously distant and also incidentally ludicrous posture.' Muriel's style made it sound as if she had spent weeks thinking of nothing else. 'I don't think you can have appreciated quite how unattractive an object you are. I'm not *just* talking about physically though I certainly *am* talking about physically for a start. You emanate hopelessness and resentment and boredom and death. No wonder everybody shrank away from you.'

Again familiarly, this had an uncomfortable quasi-sense about it. If Peter had really wanted peace at this point, however limited, he might have done well to leave it there or to beg for mercy. Instead he found himself showing what defiance he could. 'I just happened to come in at the end. They'd started leaving before I arrived.'

'You sent them on their way unrejoicing. Which incidentally you're in process of doing to me. I'm not sure how much longer I can stand you.'

'The past is past. Nothing but a waste of time wishing it had been different.'

'Who's said anything about the past?'

'You have. Of course you have. Your great theme, isn't it?'

That one failed to go off. Muriel just talked on at a slightly enhanced rate about what supposed friends of his had said to her about him and harmless things like that. He concentrated as fixedly as he could on driving. If he could have been reasonably sure of killing them both outright he would have been inclined to swerve into the path of an oncoming bus or builder's lorry, but as it was he took them safely past the War Memorial, through Irish Town, across the River Iwerne and into what had once been the mining village of Cwmgwyrdd, now a semi-smart outer suburb. Every so often he tried to make himself believe something he knew to be true, that Muriel would not go on like this for ever and that after a few minutes she would go back to being rather mechanically affable until next time, but he stayed unbelieving.

They were home, getting out of the car in the built-on garage of their quite decent Thirties villa on the pricier seaward side. When Peter had locked up, Muriel gave him a glance of studied neutrality, the signal for some kind of change of direction. He was glad he had followed his instinct and left the vegetables (out of old Vaughan Mowbray's patch that morning) unmentioned in the car. To flaunt them now might have led to requests to come out and say what he had against the way he was normally fed, and further.

On the front doorstep she said to him, 'You know, I don't think that news about the Weavers is good news for anyone.'

After all these years they really understood each other very well. Her saying that in an ordinary tone meant that hostilities were suspended and more, that that subject was now free, cleared for bringing up at any later stage without penalty. Further yet, as might not have been instantly clear to anyone but him, it constituted an apology, or the nearest she was ever going to get to one.

These thoughts occupied him while he went and got a couple of cold fish-fingers out of the refrigerator for his lunch, so that he failed to consider whether he agreed with the content of what she had said or not. Muriel pulled on her wellies and tramped off into the garden. She never ate lunch.

2   Rhiannon, Alun

1

A train, a particular train, the 15.15 out of Paddington on an afternoon some weeks after Peter Thomas had decided to leave the potatoes and leeks in his car, emerged from the Severn Tunnel into Wales. The area had once been called Monmouthshire but because of a decision taken in London was now called Gwent, after an ancient Welsh kingdom or whatever it was that might have formerly existed there or thereabouts. Anyway, it was Wales all right, as Rhiannon Weaver reckoned she could have told by the look of it through the carriage window. There was no obvious giveaway, like road-signs in two languages or closed-down factories, but something was there, an extra greenness in the grass, a softness in the light, something that was very like England and yet not England at all, more a matter of feeling than seeing but not just feeling, something run-down and sad but simpler and freer than England all the same. Ten minutes to Newport, another hour in the train after that and ten or fifteen minutes more by road.

This journey was the Weavers' final move and tonight would be their first night on Welsh soil as residents, though they were booked to stay with Gwen and Malcolm Cellan-Davies that first night. Rhiannon had rather expected to make the trip by car, and so among other things to be saved a fair amount of packing, but had soon realised that, for somebody wanting to be noticed arriving, trains had the great virtue that they turned up at a fixed place at a fixed time. In one way it would have been better to fly down, but scheduled flights only went as far as Rhoose, which was wrong anyway because of being the Cardiff airport.

She turned her head away from the window to find Alun in the next seat giving one of his special beams with the eyes half closed and mouth slightly lifted. It meant more or less that in spite of everything, which was saying something, he was devoted to her and that she knew, in spite of everything again, that there was no one like him. She would have had to agree with Gwen that he was quite a good-looking man, but more than quite — remarkably, at least considering the life he led. The skin had held up well, no more than pink, as if after a day watching cricket; the famous mane of hair, once and for a great many years a deep bronze, was now snow-white, at any rate much whiter than the streaky, lifeless grey it would have been if left to itself. Most of his friends were pretty sure that he improved on nature in this department as in others; not many of them would have guessed that Rhiannon put the whitener on for him while they giggled and had drinks.

Suddenly Alun jerked himself upright and started waving vigorously to the buffet-car steward who had come into sight at the far doorway. The man was smiling and nodding and coming for them at top speed, but Alun still waved. In the rear another, younger and subordinate, buffet-car steward approached less swiftly.

'Sorry for the delay, Mr Weaver.' The first steward looked and sounded really cut up as he unloaded a miniature of Whyte & McKay, a can of Idris ginger beer and trimmings. 'Always a crowd before Newport,' he added. Then his manner changed momentarily to conditional consternation. 'You did say no ice, didn't you, Mr Weaver? Now you have got everything you want, have you? Mrs Weaver? Are you sure? Nothing to eat?' He looked swiftly over their shoulders and back again and went on, mouthing the words to show that they were not for all ears, 'Toasted sandwich, bacon or Danish Blue and ploughman's pickle? Are you quite sure now?'

Alun said he was, and reeled off a string of heartfelt appreciative expressions while he paid and moderately tipped.

Maintaining it had been a pleasure, Emrys said, 'Now here's a young man who as good as went down on his bended knees to me to be given the chance of meeting you. May I introduce Darren Davies. This is Mr Alun Weaver, OBE.'

The lesser steward was brought forward. He looked rather uneasy and not at all the type to go out of his way to meet an elderly Welshman famous for something unintelligible, but he managed a smile.

Alun sprang up and stuck out his hand. 'Actually, it's CBE. How do you do, Darren. What part of Wales do you come from?'

'Llangefni. Anglesea.'

'Yes, Darren's a North Walian,' said Emrys in the unshocked tone he might have used to announce that the lad was a soccer-player or a Roman Catholic.

'Anglesea's beautiful. I was up there two years ago. Aberffraw. Now Emrys I mustn't keep you any longer from your duties, it wouldn't be fair on other people.'

'Very well, Mr Weaver. But before I go I want to say just this. Everybody is delighted to learn that you and Mrs Weaver have determined to come and live among us here in South Wales. Proud too. Honoured.'

When Alun had said he was grateful and very touched and had shooed Emrys and Darren away and beaten down some of the stares from nearby passengers, not all of them reverential, nor all comprehending, he turned to Rhiannon and raised his eyebrows in a rueful, resigned way. 'You've got to do it,' he said as he had said many times before.

'Of course you have,' she said likewise.

'He'll be telling them in the pub tonight how he had that boring old fart Alun Weaver on his train.' He had said something like that before too but less often.

'Nonsense, he was thrilled, you could see.'

'Anyway a bloody sight more thrilled than he'd have been if I'd asked him to actually produce a bacon bloody sandwich.'

At Cambridge Street station it looked for nearly a minute as though there was not going to be anything that Alun had got to do, but then there appeared a squat man in a white raincoat with what Rhiannon considered was a very small piece of machinery in his hand.

'Alun Weaver?'

'Yes indeed – BBC?'

'Jack Mathias. No, Glamrad,' said the fellow hoarsely, referring to the local commercial radio station.

'Oh. Oh, very well.' Alun peered vainly about for a moment longer, then switched himself on. 'Good to see you, Mr Mathias, and thank you for coming. I hope you haven't had to wait too long. Now what can I do for you?'

Mathias seemed to be suggesting that he and Alun should conduct their business on a public bench on the station platform. They were under cover but drizzle came gusting in from the open and there was a good deal of noise of people and trains.

'Can't we go somewhere warmer?' asked Alun. 'And quieter?' He tilted his head in an unnatural way to keep the wind from blowing his hair out of position.

'Sorry, we need the noise for the actuality.' Mathias was efficiently setting up his recorder on the bench beside him. 'The ambience. One, two, three, four, testing, testing.'

'Are you going to need my wife for any of this?'

'No,' said Mathias. The question evidently puzzled him.

'All right.' Dissatisfaction with the proceedings showed in Alun's face, but also acceptance. He said to Rhiannon, 'Go and have a cup of tea, love. No need for you to stand about here.'

She felt the same, but thought she would stay and just see or rather hear the start. Soon, so soon as to constitute a vague put-down, Mathias was ready. He had not yet looked either of them in the eye.

'Alun Weaver, Cambridge Street station, take one,' he said to nothing in particular. 'Tell me, what does it feel like to return to live in Wales after all these years away?'

'Many things grave and gay and multi-coloured but one above all: I'm coming home. That short rich resounding word means one simple single thing to a Welshman such as I, born and bred in this land of river and hill. And that thing, that miraculous thing is – Wales. Fifty years of exile couldn't fray that stout bond. Heart is where the home is, and the heart of a Welshman . . .'

The warm, lively voice was soon lost when Rhiannon started to walk towards the barrier carrying the overnight case that Emrys had fought so hard for Darren to be allowed to carry. She held herself very straight and still answered physically to most of Malcolm's description, though her grey eyes had never held the touch of blue he had said he saw in them.

On her two recent trips to these parts she had travelled by car and she had not seen the station for over ten years. So far, except for the signs, it looked more or less unchanged, and of course the outlook was just the same, the view of an expanse of hillside with those unmistakable terraces of small houses, some running along from left to right, some up and down, among patchy grassland with stretches and bits of cliff of bare rock, few trees and no bright colours anywhere. She had always thought it was incredibly typical, South Wales at one go, though not the kind of thing you put on a picture postcard, and looking at it now under thin rain she felt she had remembered it exactly as it was.

What they called the station concourse, the hall, was more or less unrecognisable: coffee-shop, travel bureau, passport-photograph booth and electronic-looking screen of arrivals and departures. Let into the wall below this she noticed a commemorative plaque, perhaps the one Alun had been so fed up at not being asked to unveil the previous year. After a nose round she went into the coffee-shop, where everything that was not colouring-book red, blue or yellow was black. There was a very poor selection of things to eat and drink and only one girl serving, who seemed to be waiting for something or somebody that was not Rhiannon and who, like that interviewer, never looked at you. When she had given up hope of whatever it was she wordlessly produced and handed over a cup of tea.

The tables and chairs each stood on a single immovable stump to prevent them being picked up and thrown about. In Rhiannon's experience Welshmen had never gone in for that type of behaviour, but probably that had changed too. The tea turned out to be as nasty as that served in the old torn-down refreshment room, but in a different way; hot, though. As she sipped it she wondered what Alun had been seriously expecting, what a radio man was a let-down from. The mayor, the MP, the chairman of the Welsh Arts Council, a crowd of fans with autograph-books? Well? A TV team? He did a lot of TV and knew much more about it than she did, but . . .

Rhiannon had never settled in her own mind at any stage how important or well-known Alun thought he was, or even really was except very roughly, but at times like this it crossed her mind that he might be making too much of that part of himself. That might go with being his kind of writer. And that was a bit of a puzzle too, how he was always saying he wanted to be regarded as a writer first of all and then always going on television and being interviewed.

He came in sight now, striding towards the glass door, stopping all at once as somebody recognised him, shaking hands, grinning, nodding enthusiastically and writing something – not in an autograph-book but never mind. That was a bit of luck. But when he reached her he had his discontented expression on, with frown and nose-twitches.

'That chap was a prick,' he said, staring at her. 'A *prick*. Do you know what he asked me? Whether I found my books still sold reasonably well. Can you beat it? And when I said Yes as crappily as I could – what else could I do? Well, then he said he meant in England as well as in Wales. I mean Christ, you'd think they'd have told him.' He stared at her a moment longer before letting his shoulders collapse and laughing through his nose, and she joined in. 'Let's get out of this place. Sorry, finish your tea. Are you sure?'

They went outside and stood where a sign used to say Taxi and now said Taxi/*Tacsi* for the benefit of Welsh people who had never seen a letter X before. It was starting to get dark and the lights were coming on, reflected in the wet pavements. Some of what she saw was no different or not much, but other things that she remembered well enough, from the old Mountjoy Arms hotel with the green-and-tan frieze of classical figures to that mock-rustic shop where you could get very good doughnuts, had vanished so thoroughly that it was impossible to say whereabouts they had stood. But the town was still the place where some of the special parts of her life had come and gone.

When thirty seconds had passed with still no taxi Alun started making tutting noises. 'I do think Malcolm might have met us,' he said. 'Lazy bugger.'

'I was there when you told him not to because the train might be late. Which it was, wasn't it?'

'Oh, were you and did I? Perhaps that's why he's not here. Let's say partly, anyway.'

After another minute, which was quite as long as any such minute with Alun about, a taxi arrived, in fact a London-model taxi, rare in this part of the world. Something about this displeased him. As they moved off he settled himself insistently on the jump-seat behind the driver and tried to talk to him through the open glass panel with a lot of shouting and calls for repetition. It was possible to guess that he had been expecting an ordinary saloon with a passenger-seat up front. Eventually he abandoned the struggle and came and sat beside Rhiannon.

'You can't have a proper conversation under those conditions,' he said.

'Of course you can't. What did you want one for?'

'Well, you know, I always like talking to drivers and people when I'm here. Very Welsh thing. It's a completely different relationship to what you get in England. Difficult to explain.'

'You needn't to me. I am Welsh too as it happens. Boyo.'

'Piss off,' he said, squeezing her hand.

2

Rhiannon and Gwen settled down in the kitchen after Alun and Malcolm had gone along to the Bible for a couple of beers before supper. The two women had been close friends at the university, members of a trio whose third party was Dorothy Morgan. Gwen had put a strong case for leaving Dorothy out of the evening's doings altogether, but Rhiannon had overruled her, mostly on the grounds that after all it was her inaugural, so to speak. Accordingly a false time of arrival had been circulated and the coast was reckoned to be clear for a good hour yet.

In Rhiannon's as well as Malcolm's eyes it was not an attractive kitchen, long and narrow with barely room for six people to sit down. At the moment you would have had trouble finding a vacant flat surface big enough to make a pot of tea on, the sink was full of pans not left to soak, just dumped there, and two or three of Malcolm's shirts hung from a cup-hook on the dresser. It took her back to Gwen's room in Brook Hall, the women's hostel – spick and span every Monday morning and in a fright-ening piggy mess by tea-time, all sandals, jam and lecture-notes, with plenty of sand underfoot in the summer term. There was always something that needed doing first, she used to say. Rather different now, you might have thought, but then it never worked like that.

With a small start Rhiannon noticed that the bottle of white wine on the table in front of her was not the same as the one they had started on quite a short time earlier. This had a green instead of a blue-and-white label and was also about half empty already. The excitement of getting here and of a sudden feeling, dim and out of nowhere but still real, that things had not stopped happening to her after all, that there were unknown possibilities lined up, had carried her away. Had she drunk two glasses? Three? Well, more than was sensible in the time. It would not do to start following in Dorothy's footsteps, if they were at all as Gwen had described a little while back and was now going on about again.

'Absolute hell. Sophie had to tell her there was no more wine and Charlie put on an act of trying to persuade her to have whisky. Of course if she had . . .'

If anyone was following in Dorothy's footsteps, thought Rhiannon to herself, it might be Gwen. A bottle's-worth of wine had gone down that throat since the start of the session and there was no one around to say how much had before that. The mini-story about Dorothy and the whisky had been touched on already that evening. It seemed quite a distance from the shandy-sipping Gwen of Brook Hall days. But the rest of her was unchanged: a little bit nosy, a little bit catty, but sensible, shrewd, down-to-earth, now as then the one to see through the shams and the wishful thinking. She was absolutely as before when, mixing hesitancy with cheek, she said,

'Haven't really had a chance to ask you this before, old thing, but, er, how do you feel about coming back to live round here?'

Rhiannon would have liked to hear Alun answering that. 'I've always thought I would in the end,' she said tamely. 'Nearly all the Welsh people I've talked to in London say the same thing.' And anyway here I bloody am, she felt like adding.

'But they don't actually come, most of them, do they? Too settled where they are, I dare say. Mind you, I always thought you and Alun were pretty firmly fixed there in Highgate. Especially you yourself, Rhi. You really cut yourself off from down here, didn't you, in the last few years anyway. Not like Alun. He's kept up with, oh, a lot of people here and there.'

'No, well I'm sorry, but you know, you keep leaving it and then all of a sudden you find it's too late, anyway without a lot of explanation.'

'Of course, and then your mother dying, you haven't got her to come down for. You'll soon pick up the threads again.'

There was a silence that was pretty clearly an interval before more of the same from Gwen's side. Rhiannon let it go on; she never minded silences. On this occasion she partly filled in with the thought that one of the reasons for not accompanying Alun on his Welsh trips, the one that had always seemed to come to mind first, was to give him a free hand in keeping up with certain people, people like that doctor's wife by Beaufoy and the woman with the extraordinary hairdo who had been second-in-command at the mental home. He had been a model husband for days, weeks afterwards when he got back. But Rhiannon was not going to tell Gwen any of that, nor that she hoped Alun would set about finding some people to keep up with out at Capel Mererid or further, once he was settled down here.

Gwen looked at her in an understanding, caring sort of way. 'But you did, *you* did really want to come? I mean you weren't talked into it however nicely?'

'No,' said Rhiannon, trying not to sound too flat or final.

'No qualms? I know you've got some painful memories of the old days.' Gwen had turned quite sad now, as though some of it had happened to her as well. 'Aren't you afraid at all of stirring them up?'

However much wine might or might not have gone down it seemed kind of early to get on to such matters, but they had been bound to arise some time. 'A bit. But it's all a long time ago, what went on then. That's if it's the thing with Peter you're talking about. Do you know, I never think of it.'

'Oh really. You can't forget it though, can you?'

'No, but you can stop feeling bad about it, I mean I have. No point.'

'No point, no, but women have an awful way of feeling things there's no point in them feeling.'

'I know what you mean all right. I suppose I've just been lucky.' Again, Rhiannon wanted to say something like there were times when one person could get away with murder as far as another person was concerned, and even after the times had changed completely, for good, that part stayed the same, but she had never told anybody that. She said, wanting to know though not necessarily from Gwen, 'How is Peter? Do you see him much?'

'Not a lot, no. Malcolm runs into him at the pub occasionally. He's fine as far as I can gather, for his age you know. Run to fat rather. And, well, I get the impression he's not very pleased with life.'

'I suppose he's retired now.'

'According to Malcolm he hasn't a good word to say for anyone or anything.'

'He's not the only one. Muriel's around, I suppose?'

At this name the two caught each other's eye and as if by pre-arrangement made remarkably similar frowning, blinking, whistling faces. On instinct they drew closer together in their chairs.

'Oh yes,' said Gwen. 'Yes, she's around. There's a strange one as they say.'

'Well, I hardly know her. I can't really say I know her.'

'I can never tell what she's thinking. There she is going on as nice as pie and I've no idea what's in her head at all. I realise I've no idea what's going through her mind.'

'She gives you that look, sort of measuring, summing you up. Actually I haven't seen her for God knows how long.'

'She may love us all but somehow I doubt it.'

'It's not exactly cold, is it, because in a way she's very friendly. It doesn't go with her voice.'

'I wonder how those two get on. They're funny together. Like two people at work who've got to hit it off while they're there but you can bet they never go near each other outside. Like in front of the servants.'

'What?' Rhiannon wondered if she was falling asleep. 'Does Malcolm hear anything, I mean from his mates?'

'Don't know. Sometimes I catch an awful look on Peter's face when he doesn't think anybody's watching. Afflicted. Stricken.'

'Oh, I know that stricken look from the old days. I used to tell him he was only . . .'

When no more followed, Gwen said, 'Christ, she doesn't half put it away, young Muriel. Not regularly, not every day, just occasionally, but then – wow! It doesn't show on her but whenever I happen to catch sight of her glass it's either full or empty. Not that she's anything special, mind. There's Dorothy . . .' Gwen paused, perhaps trying to remember whether she had told Rhiannon the one about the whisky. If so, the effort was successful, because she went on, ' . . . and Charlie of course . . .'

'I haven't seen Charlie for –'

'No use expecting much sense out of him after about six o'clock at night.

He's got this restaurant in Broad Street now. Co-owner of it with his brother. I don't know whether you remember Victor. Not my type at all. Absolutely not my cup of tea. He's . . . you know.'

'What, you mean . . .'

'You know,' said Gwen, nodding slowly. 'Well, we're not supposed to mind them these days but I can't help it. I came to them late, sort of. For a long time I didn't know there was any such thing. And there wasn't really then, not in Wales. When I first heard about them they were in places like Paris and London. You know, Oscar Wilde. You can say a lot against the chapel but it least it kept them down. And I reckon everybody being poor helped. They couldn't dress up or anything.'

Rhiannon remembered Gwen talking in that style in her room in Brook Hall, about chaps among other things, saying what she probably really thought but being jokey too so as to stay in the clear about something. According to Dorothy, who had always been a great one for psychology, it showed a basic insecurity. Whatever it showed it was quite fun to listen to but it did tend to slow down the conversation, as now in fact. Gwen seemed to have dried up though she showed no sign of being insecure about that. 'This queer brother of Charlie's,' said Rhiannon.

'*Victor*, yes. He runs the restaurant with his, with a friend of his. Nothing for Charlie to do but chat to the customers and knock back the Scotch and tell himself he's working. Not conducive to health. Eventually he nods off at the table or in the bar and Victor sends him home in a taxi.'

'Not much of a life for Sophie.'

'Oh, I don't think she minds too much. She has got this shop – just a sort of boutique,' said Gwen in response to Rhiannon's quick look and hurried disappointingly on. 'The thing is, Charlie's got nothing else to do and he can afford it. It's quite a problem for retired people, I do see. All of a sudden the evening starts starting after breakfast. All those hours with nothing to stay sober for. Or nothing to naturally stay sober during, if you see what I . . . We used to laugh at Malcolm's dad, the way he used to mark up the wireless programmes in the *Radio Times* in different-coloured pencils. Never caught him listening to any of them but it was an hour taken care of. Drink didn't agree with him, poor old Taffy. Some of us have got a lot to be thankful for.'

Watching Gwen refill her glass and also send a minor stream down its outside, Rhiannon wondered what, if anything, she told herself she was doing. Did she just not know what she was really doing? As any wife of Alun's would have had to be, Rhiannon was almost as used to people getting drunk as she was to them having a drink, but she had learnt too that there was a stage beyond that. It was a little discouraging to find, a couple of hours after arriving to live among them, that everybody round the place seemed to be getting there regularly if they were not funny in some way. Or (Muriel) had a touch of both.

Gwen was turning serious and inquisitive all over again. She said, 'How did you actually react to the idea of settling down in these parts?' This had not got to be another bit of maundering; it was a trick of Gwen's to keep coming back to a point until her curiosity was either satisfied or else knocked firmly on the head – a very minor improvement on the maundering option if you asked Rhiannon.

'Thrilled,' she said rather loudly.

'You don't mind my asking? I suppose the two of you discussed it pretty thoroughly before you took the decision.'

'Not really, no. Over in a moment.'

'Oh yes. Which of you in fact got the idea first?'

'We found we'd both been thinking about it for some time.'

'But who was the first to mention it? Was it you? Just interested.'

'No, it was Alun. He came out with it one morning at breakfast.'

'And you fell in with it straight away.'

'Yes. I seemed to have my mind already made up. I don't really know why.'

'Oh. I expect you had a lot of friends in Highgate.'

Rhiannon nodded from the waist upwards. 'Yes, I was quite firmly fixed there. Look, old thing, if you're trying to get me to say Alun was the one who wanted to come and he managed to browbeat me into it then you're wasting your time. He was keener than I was to start with but I was keen enough. Not that that would have made any difference in the end to whether we came or not.'

'Have you always done what he wanted?'

'Yes, of course I have, in anything like that. He earns the money.'

'You let that man walk all over you, Rhi. I told you he would.'

'Did you? Well, this is one time he hasn't.'

At this Gwen seemed to give up. She scrumpled bits of cigarette-wrapping and stowed them in vacant parts of her ashtray and carefully blew some ash off the table-top. With a quirky smile she said, 'How is Alun?'

That sounded really nice for about half a second, like an easy exam question: anything you feel like saying on the subject will do. Rhiannon half wanted to answer with a run-down on Alun's medical check-up last month, featuring the part where the doctor had told him, rather coldly, apparently, that his liver as well as his heart and lungs was in excellent condition. But she felt she had to be a little more forthcoming than that. She saw that Gwen had switched to a smile with raised eyebrows. What a lot of expressions she knew.

'He's just the same as ever,' said Rhiannon. 'Always jolly and lively except when I don't want him to be. That's the chief thing about him as far as I'm concerned.'

This went down less than well. Gwen got up quickly and toddled to the litter-bin behind Rhiannon. There, having let the empty bottle rustle and thump down inside, she was to be heard knocking out the ashtray on the edge of the bin. Silence followed while she presumably regrouped. When she spoke it was clear from the acoustics that her back was turned. Rhiannon shifted uneasily on her chair.

'You know, Malcolm was absolutely knocked sideways when your letter came. We'd heard talk but nothing definite. Knocked him completely sideways.'

'Not with horror, I hope.'

'Of course not with horror. With delight. With joy.' A loud smacking pop indicated what Gwen had been up to while out of sight. 'But something else as well, Rhi, you know that.'

Gwen came into view again with the new bottle and the emptied but still dirty ashtray and rather flung herself down in her seat at the table.

'You were his first love,' she said matter-of-factly.

'That's nice to hear. He's one of the sweetest men I've ever met.' Rhiannon meant what she said, and could not understand why she so much disliked speaking the words.

'He never talks about it,' said Gwen, looking at her watch. 'Never says what happened.'

'Gwen, really, there's nothing to talk about. *Nothing* happened.'

Rhiannon felt what was almost admiration for her friend and at the same time wanted to hit her a certain amount for the way she accepted the message without any nonsense about believing it or even somehow not believing it. She finished nodding her head and sat for a time fiddling with her glass, which she had refilled, and moving her eyebrows about, as much as to say that here came the punch. At the instant she drew in her breath to deliver it the door-bell rang, a peremptory, office-type sound. When a moment later Rhiannon heard Dorothy's voice she sniggered to herself.

Then Dorothy came in, embraced Rhiannon at length, apologised for being early, asked to hear all her news and listened, or at least stayed quiet and watching, while she told some of it. This startling behaviour intrigued Rhiannon and obviously disconcerted Gwen, who twice at least seemed on the point of breaking in to protest that the whole thing was a put-up job, meant to bring her into disrepute, most unsporting and certain to wear itself out soon. On the last point at any rate she would have scored, for Dorothy sent her first glass of wine down in a little over ten minutes and her second in a little under, and not before Alun, Malcolm and Percy got back from the Bible, but well before the end of the evening, she started telling them all, and then telling just Gwen, about a tribe in probably New Guinea she had been reading about who built houses in trees that they never occupied and had perhaps at some distant era intended for the spirits of their ancestors to live in, but perhaps not, and other things like that. When the time came, however, she went off quite meekly, taking less than a quarter of an hour to move from just inside the front door to just far enough outside it. More than once in that time she had invited Gwen and Rhiannon to coffee at her house the following morning.

'Is she like that all the time now, did you gather?' asked Alun as he and Rhiannon were undressing in the little guest bedroom. 'Malcolm said something.'

'Quite a lot of it, evidently. but I think some of it tonight was the excitement of seeing us.'

'Seeing you, more like. She's never had much time for me.' He stood on one leg and shook the other with tremendous force to rid it of that part of his trousers. 'I can't think why not.'

Rhiannon got into bed and started on the considerable routine necessary to shape her pillow correctly. 'She was sober when she arrived.'

'Yeah, well when you're knocking it back like that all day every day you get a sort of float, or do I mean balance. You only need a bit of topping-up and you're off, gone. A plateau.'

'Poor little thing.'

'Poor little thing be buggered,' said Alun musically, also getting into bed. He turned the light out, lay down and put his arms round Rhiannon as he did every night, or rather every night he was there, with her. 'We're the poor little things having to take it. And poor old Percy's the poorest littlest thing of the lot.'

'I think he can handle her. No, I meant it means she must have some idea of what she's like. She stayed sober all day because she wanted to be in a good state to meet me, her old friend. Means she must know she normally gets into bad states. Mustn't she?'

'She may or may not know but she obviously doesn't bloody care or she wouldn't get into them.'

'I don't suppose she can help it much, it's a bit late for that.'

'If she can help it once she can help it again.' Alun worked his way through an intensive spell of sniffing, throat-clearing and grunting. When he had finished he said, 'Old Gwen hadn't been exactly short-changing herself either, had she?'

'No. Far from it. She didn't use to do that. She's a bit different all round, I thought.'

'Well, speaking from the old lofty pinnacle, I imagine decades of piss-artistry can't help leaving their mark on the character. Christ Almighty, what sort of lot have we got ourselves into? Well, should be fun. Of a kind, at least. One thing about you, sweetheart, you're never going to be any trouble that way. Or any other way. It's a marvellous thing. To know that.'

After a minute or two he pulled his arms back and turned away over on to his side of the bed. That was not what he did every night.

3

A few days later Cambria Television made arrangements to record an interview with Alun at the Weavers' rented house in Pedwarsaint, the suburbanised former fishing village in or near which they hoped to settle down. From the vanished quay the smacks had gone out in numbers for the oysters in the bend stretching over to Courcey Island on the east side, and sold their product from Bristol to Barnstaple until overfishing and industrial pollution wiped out the beds before the Great War. A marina stood there now, completed only the previous year, the resort of owners of medium-grade casinos or smallish chains of coin-op laundrettes from Birmingham and points north who came in at the weekends down the M5–M4 or, increasingly, by air taxi to the strip at Swanset on Courcey. And of course, where not so long ago it had been hake and chips, bottled cockles, pork pies and pints of Troeth bitter, these days it was cannelloni, paella, stifado, cans of Foster's, bottles of Rioja and – of course – large Courvoisiers and long panatellas, just like everywhere else.

Barring perhaps the oyster details for their elegiac potential, none of this would have been worth a second thought to Alun, certainly not today. He was charged up by the television presence, more by the simple expectation of appearing in front of its cameras than by having pulled off any sort of coup in securing a spot, even the lead spot, on *The Week in Wales*. Necessary, though. Perhaps on reconsideration not insignificant after all. He had done England, got out of it what there was for him to get out of it; he could never have hoped to be omnipresent there. In Wales he could, or was going to have a bloody good try.

The house belonged to a remarkably opulent official in a local housing department, at present holidaying with his wife in the Caribbean, a man whose future acquaintance could not, given reasonable luck, be a bad thing. Nor could being filmed in his sumptuous drawing-room, as far as the *hoi polloi* went, at least. Any lefty sticklers who might find a bit too much silver, glass and teak on display there would be placated, when the future-plans question came, by talk of a swift removal to a modest place of one's own and a single half-amused glance about. At this stage he had not yet fully worked out minor finesses like that, but he was a great believer in thinking as far as possible round any subject beforehand.

Now he set out to ingratiate himself with the crew, but circumspectly, not in the style which had been good enough for Emrys on the train. He sensed that a little went a long way with this sort of youngster, especially a little of anything that could be described, however unjustly, as Welsh flannel, Taff bullshit, etc. Having done what he could in this out-of-the-way mode he turned his attention to the interviewer, a fair young man in a wine-coloured jacket who had nothing discoverably Welsh about him and who let it be known, with enviable speed and clarity, that this morning's task was no more than the sort of thing he was prepared to go through with while waiting briefly for a proper job a long way away. In other circumstances Alun would have sorted him out in five seconds flat, but as it was he concentrated on pretending not to have noticed and on not trying to make the young shit like him – that had to come naturally or not at all.

The interview went well enough. Alun soon saw the fellow had no particular approach, was in the manner of such fellows merely concerned to establish his superiority to the overall run of the play. So the angle to go for had to be knowing a lot, seeing a lot, caring a lot but only in unpredictable ways, or ways that could be passed off as unpredictable. It was not an occasion for pulling out the stops, but near the end, after magnanimously letting pass a touch of ignorance about the Attlee governments' policies for industry in South Wales, Alun took the chance of getting into his stride rather.

'It's all too easy for an exile come home to stay where he lands up, to cultivate his garden and never look over the hedge, to become something of a vegetable himself. That won't do for me, I'm afraid. I'll be going out, out in search of Wales, looking at things, looking at people. A small private voyage of discovery. I'm sure I'll find plenty of changes, for the worse, for the better, but there are some places where change can never reach . . .'

He went on to list, rather fancifully, perhaps, a few of that kind. In the normal way he forgot everything he had said in a broadcast as soon as it was finished, and good riddance – remembering might interfere with spontaneity next time. But now for once some of it stuck. Cultivating his garden he could dismiss right off, as anyone might who was as keen as he on what you could get up to indoors. In search of Wales, on the other hand, sounded distinctly good, might become *In Search of Wales* one day; it was a pity that old Brynford had done those programmes so recently. Meanwhile, the pursuit of a nebulous project of this sort would be just the thing for getting him out of untimely invitations and the like, and also covering any sudden disappearances he might feel impelled to make.

When Rhiannon came into the drawing-room after the TV lot had gone, she found him full of enthusiasm for his new scheme, full of ideas too: trips to Courcey Island, to Carmarthen, to Merthyr Dafydd, to Brecon; visits to metal works at Port Holder and Caerhays; rounds of the pubs in Harriston, in Cwmgwyrdd, in Bargeman's Row; a pilgrimage and a piss-up in Birdarthur, where Brydan had settled after his last trip to America. As he talked, she moved here and there round the room in an unsettling way.

'What are you doing?' he broke off to ask.

'Nothing. I'm listening. I was just making sure everything's all right.'

'What? How do you mean all right?'

'Just nothing's been broken or anything like that.'

'Don't fuss,' he said, but not sharply. 'You tip-toe round this place as if you're afraid to chip a bloody saucer. These blokes are very professional, you couldn't tell they'd been here if you didn't know.'

'All right, but I am afraid to chip a bloody saucer, and so should you be. People get attached to their things. Anyway, how did it go?'

'Uh? *Oh.*' He tossed his head, indicating that the presumably-meant interview was nothing, no trouble, of no significance, already forgotten but satisfactory. 'I was thinking, I thought I might look in at the Glendower for lunch, you know, toe in the water kind of thing. See if it's any good. Why don't you . . .'

'There's this cleaner turning up, and then Rosemary's train gets in at 2.40,' said Rhiannon, naming their younger, unmarried daughter. Rosemary was taking a long weekend off from St John's College, Oxford, where she was reading law, to come and help her mother look at houses round about. 'Be a bit of a rush.'

'Oh God, four to one again. Still, it's only for a couple of days, I agree.'

'Come on, let's hear it.'

'I told you before and don't pretend you don't know perfectly bloody well in the first place. Any man in the company of two women is outnumbered four to one however amiable they may be. By definition.'

'So when it's just you and me I outnumber you two to one, is that right?'

'Affirmative. And it's not twice two when there are two of you. I mean if we had Frances on the party it would be nine to one. What they call a square law.'

'You will have your little joke, won't you, *was*? And I'll go along and glad to as long as we all know it's a joke. You outnumbered. That'll be the day.'

'Oh now now girl, easy by there, *cariad*,' he said, taking it off wicked of course but getting something out of it at the same time, or fancying so. 'No ruffled feathers now.' He put his arms round her.

'Relax, boyo,' she said.

The family car was Japanese and why not? – Alun would tacitly claim a special Welsh exemption from any lingering sense of duty to drive an 'English' model. It had been brought down from London earlier that week by a minor character from his publishers, minimal in fact and male too, thus rating no more than a gulped-down whisky before being packed off to the station. Today Alun took it into town and parked it in a building contractor's yard just behind Broad Street. A long-nosed man in a yellow helmet came out of a shed as if to order him away, but Alun's face with the distinctive quiff was well enough known to be familiar even when not actually recognised, and a clap on the shoulder and a bellowed but unintelligible greeting did the rest.

The state of play in the grill at the Glendower, half full or more on a weekday lunchtime earlyish, suggested that the concern was doing well enough. It was a big part of Alun's stock-in-trade to seem to know things like what sort of people were sitting at the tables, but he would have tried not to be challenged on this lot. Part of it was that nobody dressed properly any more. Another part was that it was no longer just the young who were too young to be distinguished between. He cast his eye round the room. Tradesmen, he said firmly to himself. Housewives. When he had hung about for a minute or two without anyone coming near him or even looking up, he made for the door, noticing on the way that an attempt, pretty pathetic but not on that account less offensive to respectable sentiment, had been made to give the place a Nineties or Edwardian look with plush, iron, brass, wall-mirrors and long white aprons on the waiters. An ancient map of South Wales (*c.* 1980) hung between the windows.

Upstairs in what was called the cocktail bar there was more of the same: sepia photographs of archaic worthies on the mauve-papered walls and a barman in a striped waistcoat with brass buttons, and not only that. In fact he looked like the sort of girl who might be cast as Toby Belch in a women's-college production of *Twelfth Night*. An older man on the other side of the counter was talking seriously to him, a man with very neat wavy grey hair, a slim figure and uncommonly white whites to his eyes, and in other ways showing himself to be no exception to a rule of Alun's that men over fifty who took care of themselves were not to be trusted. This one was readily placeable as Victor Norris and he turned and so introduced himself with impressive speed, going on with more of the same to order Alun a drink. Then he did a buttering-up job on Alun that was a good deal more efficient than might have been expected in a restaurant in a provincial town, even a Welsh one. When it seemed to be over Alun said,

'Expecting Charlie in, are you?'

Victor scratched the side of his neck, bending his hand back to do so further than some men might, and glanced at the grandfather clock that clunked near by. 'If he's coming he should be here any minute.'

'He told me he usually turns up midday.'

'Yes, he feels at home here. Which is nice for everyone.'

'I should have thought he felt at home in most places with a licence.'

'M'm.' Victor smiled with closed lips. 'Of course he is very outgoing. But behind that, oh dear, there's a very different kind of person. You wouldn't – you haven't seen that.'

'What haven't I seen?' asked Alun, who had found himself beginning to come round fast after the soft-soap session. 'I have known him for quite a few years, actually.'

'Oh, indeed you have, he often speaks of you. But that poor man my brother is vulnerable to all sorts of pressures and more than a lot of people he needs a settled, undisturbed kind of existence. I dare say you think that sounds silly but it's true.'

'Really.'

'Yes really.' At this point Victor took a silent message from somebody in the doorway, doubtless the friend one heard about, and in a flash his manner changed from faint menace all the way back to full warmth. 'No rest for the wicked. Super to have met you – Alun. Oh you are lunching? Do you like scallops?'

When Alun had said truthfully that he did, Victor held his hand out palm foremost, interdicting further speech, and strode rather mannishly away. Back at the bar Alun got another drink but had his money refused, and his respect for Victor went up another notch. Time was getting on, however. He looked round as he had downstairs: more tradesmen and housewives, a fairly unself-conscious sample. Just as he was starting to contemplate listlessly a solo lunch with perhaps bits of Victor thrown in, Charlie appeared. He was followed by someone who at first looked to Alun like an incredibly offensive but all too believable caricature of Peter Thomas aged about eighty-five and weighing half a ton. At a second glance he saw that it was Peter Thomas.

All three men seemed to turn rigid for an instant, then came back to life and motion. Alun raised his glass high, Charlie waved, Peter nodded. They converged. Alun shook Peter's hand not too hard, smiling not too broadly, trying to get it right. The difficulty was, he recognised, that he had grown so used to transmitting amiability, benevolence and all those for unreal that this confrontation rather stretched him. His will was of the best: he had a rooted and sincere aversion to any trouble not of his own making.

'Don't let's think how long it's been,' he said to Peter, genuinely enough. 'Now drinks.' While these were coming he went on, nodding at Peter's paunch, 'I don't know how you do it. I suppose it's just a matter of eating and drinking anything you like.'

'Yes, but it's the slimline tonic that turns the scale. Actually I have managed to reduce the rate of increase of the rate of increase.'

'Nice-looking place, this,' said Alun to Charlie, his glance panning to and fro. 'They won't let me pay here, I notice.'

'Oh, you've seen Victor.'

'*Yes*,' said Alun, enthusiastically this time. 'Impressive fellow, I thought. He knows his job all right. Very professional.'

Charlie seemed rather doubtful of that one, but then raised his glass. 'Here's to us all. Welcome to Wales, you poor bastard.'

The three looked one another seriously in the eye and drank with a flourish. Alun began to relax. He went on relaxing over the next drink, when they got on to politics and had a lovely time seeing who could say the most outrageous thing about the national Labour Party, the local Labour Party, the Labour-controlled county council, the trade unions, the education system, the penal system, the Health Service, the BBC, black people and youth. (Not homosexuals today.) They varied this with eulogies of President Reagan, Enoch Powell, the South African government, the Israeli hawks and whatever his name was who ran Singapore. They were very much still at it when they went down to lunch, or rather when Charlie, explaining that he was trying to keep himself down to just one meal in the evening, went and sat with the other two and prepared to drink while they had lunch. He had brought a fresh drink with him from the bar so as to ensure an even flow.

They had hardly settled in their seats before one of the long-aproned waiters went round unfolding napkins and spreading them across their destined laps. They were unexceptionably large and laundered and of linen, but they were also pale pink. Alun ostentatiously held his arms up well clear during the spreading. When it was over he put on an eager, didactic expression and said,

'This is called a napkin. Its purpose is to protect your clothing from the substantial gobbets of food that your table manners will cause to fall from your mouth or from some point on the way to your mouth, and to provide something other than your hand or sleeve with which to wipe your mouth. Explaining this to one of your understanding would take a long time and even then might not avail, so fucking well sit still and shut up.'

'Oh Christ,' said Peter immediately, his eyes on the menu. They had each been given one in the bar but none of them had looked at it. 'A bloody Welsh lunch and dinner. Well, roll on.' Looking round for someone to accuse he caught sight of Charlie. 'What's the idea?' he asked, apparently in sincere puzzlement.

'You have to do it in a way,' said Charlie. 'People are getting to expect it. We only do it on Fridays anyway, Fridays and St David's Day. And it isn't compulsory even then. Which is decent of us because it's pretty nasty, unless you happen to have a taste for chicken in honey.'

'You mean you actually get people eating that?' asked Alun.

'Not much, no. That's not really the point. Seeing it on the menu is what they like. Same with the signposts.'

'But you don't give an English translation here,' said Peter.

'Well, you see, that would rather spoil things for them. They like to feel they understand it, or could if they paid it a bit of attention. And they probably do understand some of it, like *pys* is peas and *tatws* is taters.'

'Christ,' said Peter again, with weary disgust this time.

'We're not going to war over this, I hope. It's all fairly harmless, isn't it?'

'No it isn't. There you're wrong. It's one part, a small part but still a part, of an immense Chinese wall of bullshit that's, I mean Offa's Dyke that's . . .'

'Threatening to engulf us,' supplied Charlie. 'I know. But I'm afraid I don't think putting a couple of dozen Welsh words on a menu lets the side down very far. Find a pass that's really worth holding and I'll join you there.'

'There never is one. That's the trouble.'

'We need more drinks,' said Alun. 'And I'd advise you to switch, Peter. I don't think that slimline tonic agrees with you.'

'Can I recommend the soup?' asked Charlie. 'I hope you've noticed it's called soup, not *cawl*. I might even have some myself. Potato and leek today, he does it quite well. Unless Peter thinks the leek is there for impure reasons.'

'All right, Charlie,' said Peter.

Just as they had ordered, Victor approached the table, using a much less emphatic gait than when making his exit from the bar. 'Do forgive me, but one of your fans, Alun, requests the honour of a brief word.'

'What kind of fan?'

'Well, I don't know what you'd call her, but if it was left to me I'd say she was a young person. There, over in the corner, just turning round now.'

From what Alun could see without his glasses, which was all he was going to see of her, the fan looked perhaps rather good as well as young. 'All right, but you will see she knows I'm having a little private lunch-party.'

'I'll make sure she understands that, Alun – leave it to me.'

'You more or less have to do it,' said Alun after a moment. He felt a little embarrassed.

'Don't worry,' said Charlie.

'I mean you can always get out of it if you don't mind looking like a shit but I'm afraid I'm a bit too cowardly to do that unless I have to.'

'We understand.'

Seen closer to, the fan looked quite seriously good and late twenties. Alun found himself signalling to Victor, who with what could have been piss-taking alacrity sent a waiter scurrying forward with a fourth chair. The fan shook hands nicely with them all and accepted a glass of wine.

'And what can I do for you?' There was no point, Alun considered, in trying to hide his satisfaction at this turn of events.

'I'd like you to talk to my group.'

'Tell me about your group.'

It turned out to be a literary circle, thirty strong on a good night, though naturally there would be more for someone like him, twenty minutes' drive, and not worth asking about a fee. Yes, a reading would do if he preferred it.

'I'll consider it,' said Alun. 'Perhaps you'd like to drop me a line incorporating all that, care of the local BBC. Very kind of you to ask.'

'Nice to have met you.' Her voice was good too.

Charlie watched her go. 'Is that the lot?' he demanded.

'The lot? I might talk to her group if I'm feeling gracious. What are you getting at?'

'What? A bit off I call that quite frankly.'

'I don't know what you mean.'

'I mean, is that the worst you could do? You didn't even ask her for her bloody phone-number.' Charlie shook his head.

'Oh, I read you now. What I should have done was grab at her bosom. Of course.'

'Well that's how you're supposed to behave, isn't it?'

'You do me too much honour, Charlie. Age comes to us all.'

The fresh drinks arrived, whisky and gin to make up for the relative thinness of the wine. Soon afterwards the scallops arrived, and they were all right, eatable enough anyway for Alun to praise them extravagantly when Victor came to inquire. At this stage too Alun carried his point that he must be allowed to pay for the meal or would feel inhibited in his choice, and Victor gave in very gracefully and accepted a glass of the second bottle of Chablis *grand Cru*. For obvious reasons Alun made rather a thing of not knowing about wine, but any fool could have seen that this one looked and sounded good. At a suitable moment he revealed that he had done television that morning, hence, he said, his desire to get clean away afterwards and have a couple of drinks with a pal or two. He added that that was how he always felt after a do like that, even a little local one.

'You must have done a lot of it in London,' said Charlie.

'Yes I did, and why not? Some of the people up there, you know, bloody intellectuals, Hampstead types, they look down their noses at you if you go on the box more than once in a blue moon. Cheapening yourself. Well I'm not. I don't consider I'm cheapening myself by appearing on television. What else am I fit for? I'm just an old ham after all, so why shouldn't I perform where a few people can see me?'

'Oh, come along now, Alun, really,' said Charlie at once, and Peter said, 'No, you're not being fair to yourself.'

'You're very kind, both of you, but I've no illusions after all these years. Quite a successful ham, mind, but a ham none the less. An old fraud.' Here he paused for a space, as if wondering whether this time he had indeed been to some extent unfair to himself, then went buoyantly on, 'Anyway, forget it. Bugger it. Now who's for cheese? And it must follow as the night the day, a glass of port.'

Charlie said yes to that instantly, and it only took Peter a moment or two to do so. Alun asked for the cheeseboard, two large vintage ports and a glass of the house red, explaining that port had been playing him up a bit recently, and went off to the lavatory with more explanations about being an old man and envying you youngsters.

'We chimed in all right, did we?' asked Charlie. 'About the terrible injustice he was doing himself.'

'We did the best we could. Does he think we think he means that about him being a ham and a fraud? Him seeing himself in that light, that is.'

'I don't know. I doubt it. I shouldn't be surprised if he reckons that just saying that, whatever we make of it, is going to help his credibility in the future. Sort of, a fraud who's come out is more believable that a closet fraud.'

'Maybe. Anyway, he's buying us an excellent lunch. Well, buying me one.'

'There's always that. And it may go against the grain to admit it, but one's spirits do tend to lift a degree or so at the sight of him.'

'I know what you mean. Even I know.'

Alun came hurrying back as the drinks were being handed round by a wine-waiter who came out of the same sort of drawer as the barman and was got up in a fancy jacket with clusters of grapes depicted on the lapels. The cheese was there. Charlie took a small piece of Cheddar.

'What is the vintage port?' asked Alun.

'Port is a fortified wine from Portugal,' said the waiter, having perhaps misheard slightly, 'and vintage port is made from – '

'I didn't ask for a bloody lecture on vinification, you horrible little man.' Alun laughed a certain amount as he spoke. 'Tell me the shipper and the year and then go back to your hole and pull the lid over it.'

The lad seemed more or less unabashed at this. 'Graham 1975, sir,' he said in his Ruritanian accent, and withdrew.

'It's no use just relying on respect to get good service in a restaurant,' Alun explained, still grinning. 'There has to be fear too.'

'Perhaps it slipped your mind that I'm part-owner here,' said Charlie.

'Not at all, that's why I piped up. I could see it would have been difficult for you to say anything.'

'Excuse me a moment.' Charlie got up with deliberation and made off after the wine-waiter.

Alun watched him cross the room in an all-but-straight line, then turned purposefully to Peter and looked him in the eye. 'Gives me a chance to tell you this. What happened many years ago is over and done with as far as I'm concerned. For what that may be worth. I have no unfriendly feelings towards you at all. You'll want to hear about Rhiannon's feelings from her, and forgive me if I intrude, but as far as I know they're the same. I'll never say anything more on the matter.'

'That's generous of you, Alun.' Peter had dropped his gaze. 'Thank you.'

'One moderately interesting thing did emerge from that rubbishy TV chat this morning. It occurred to me while I was yammering away that it might be fun to take a few trips round the place.'

Here Charlie came back and sat down, again in commendable style. 'Keeping staff is a hell of a problem these days,' he said. His manner was conciliatory.

'I bet it is,' said Alun warmly, and went on in the same breath, 'I was just telling Peter I was thinking of going on a jaunt or two in the next few weeks, nothing fancy, a sort of scenic pub-crawl really. With, you know, some eventual literary creation held distantly in mind. Even a poem or two if the bloody old Muse can still walk.'

Charlie and Peter looked at each other. 'It's an idea,' admitted Charlie.

'Bit miserable, running about here and there on your own. Perhaps you two would like to come along sometimes if you're at a loose end. We might get hold of old Malcolm. Make a party of it.'

In those few seconds the expressions of the other two had solidified, Charlie's into cheerful mistrust, Peter's into surly mistrust. The mistrust was natural enough, but out of place on this occasion. Alun liked company, he liked an audience and he liked almost any kind of excursion and that was it. For the moment at least. When he protested some of this his hearers soon started to cave in, not so much out of belief as because each calculated that any attempt at hanky-panky could be better resisted nearer the point of unveiling, and after all it had been a pretty lavish lunch. And what else had they got in their diaries?

Charlie was the first to yield. Peter held out a little longer, declaring that he would have to see, maintaining that he was supposed to be taking things easy, but he was talked out of that in no time when it was explained to him that getting out and about a bit was just what he needed. All the camaraderie that had rather faded away over the wine-waiter was restored. Animatedly they suggested places to visit, discussed them, reminisced about them. Alun ordered two more large vintage ports and another glass of the house red, which he sipped at and seemed to lose interest in. After a few minutes he called for the bill, paid, tipped largely, and departed on his way – to take the car in and have its starter fixed, he said.

4

But when Alun reached his car and set about driving off, the engine fired in a couple of seconds, nor did he go near any garage or repair-shop before parking the machine at the side of the road in a smart residential area. There followed a brisk walk of a hundred yards to a short driveway, at whose entrance he abruptly checked his stride. Standing quite motionless he gazed before him with a faraway look that a passer-by, especially a Welsh passer-by, might have taken for one of moral if not spiritual insight, such that he might instantly renounce whatever course of action he had laid down for himself. After a moment, something like a harsh bark broke from the lower half of his trunk, followed by a fluctuating whinny and a thud that sounded barely organic, let alone human. Silence, but for faint birdsong. Then, like a figure in a restarted film, he stepped keenly off again and was soon ringing the bell in a substantial brick porch.

Sophie Norris came to the door in a biscuit-coloured woollen dress and looking very fit. As soon as she had taken in the sight of Alun her routine half-smile vanished. 'You've got a bloody nerve you have, Alun Weaver,' she said in the old penetrating tones. 'I've a good mind to slam this in your face, cheeky bugger.'

'Ah, but you're not going to, are you, love? And why should you anyway? Just dropped in for a cup of tea. Nothing wrong in that, is there?'

Sighing breathily and clicking her tongue, she gave way. 'Ten minutes, mind. Ten minutes max. I've got to go down the shop. Think yourself bloody lucky I hadn't left already.'

'Sure. Charlie not about then?'

There Alun overplayed his hand a little. 'What do you take me for, Weaver, a fucking moron?' she said more indignantly than before, her eyes distended. 'Do you think I don't know you'd never dream of showing your nose here unless you were absolutely certain he wasn't around? You sod.'

'Come on, only joking. Yes, as a matter of fact I've just come from the Glendower. Peter was there too. The three of us had a spot of lunch. Quite good it was. All right if I sit down?'

She conceded this with an ill grace. 'Why didn't you say something the other night at the Morgans'? Or you could have just picked up the – '

'I didn't get the chance. No, no, that's not true. I probably could have. I didn't happen to think of it then.'

'And when did you happen to think of it, may I ask?'

'Well . . . this morning. Can't remember what time. One moment nothing could have been further from my mind and the next I was full of it.'

'And you reckon you can just turn up like this, out of the bloody blue?'

'You could always chuck me out. I'd go quietly. You know that.'

'Still the same old Alun, eh?'

'Pretty much, yeah.' He paused. 'Go for a drive, shall we?'

This apparently innocent invitation held overtones for them that resounded from thirty years or more back, when their drives had taken them to a convenient spot behind the mental home, in better weather to the woods on the far side of the golf links and occasionally to the Prince Madoc out at Capel Mererid, in whose snug they had more than once behaved in a fashion that had never quite ceased to perturb Alun in retrospect, even today.

'No need,' said Sophie in reply. Her manner was still faintly tinged with resentment. 'There won't be anyone along.'

'What makes you so sure?'

'I'm sure.'

'Yes, but what makes you so sure?'

'I'll tell you later.'

'No, tell me now.'

'All right,' she said. 'When Victor puts him in a taxi he always gives me a ring to let me know. Because once when he stayed very late he pitched up passed out on the stool thing in the passport-photo booth at Cambridge Street station. And it just so happened that old Tudor Whittingham was on his way back from London and spotted him and fetched him home in a taxi, another taxi. He couldn't even remember being put into the first taxi.'

Alun pondered. 'But Victor giving you a ring won't stop him pitching up passed out at the station or anywhere else, will it?'

'No, but it sort of hands over the responsibility, see. I can understand it.'

'Oh, and I can. What does Victor think? About how that arrangement might, er, have a bearing on your own plans for, er, whatever it might be.'

'I don't know. I don't know what any of them think.'

'Who does? Has it come in handy before?'

'If I ever tell you that it's bloody going to be later.'

'Has that arrangement with Victor come in handy before?' he asked later.

'Do you consider you have the slightest right to expect me to answer that?'

'Absolutely not and absolutely none. Presuming on an old friendship.'

'You are a bugger. Well, sort of, just from time to time. Not ridiculous. Not like when . . .'

'No, of course not. How much does he know?'

'Same as ever, the whole score and nothing at all.'

'I'd say you and he have a pretty good life together on the whole.'

'I don't know about together exactly, but yes, we do really. Most afternoons while he's in town I'm down the shop.'

'Yes, the serviceable shop. I remember well. What do you actually do there?'

'I look at a pattern-book occasionally, and friends come in, and I drink a lot of coffee. I do about as much as he does at the Glendower. All quite relaxed. He knew all about me when he married me, of course. Well, quite a lot about me.'

'You two haven't been married all that terrifically long, have you?'

'No, not what you'd call terrifically long, only twenty-two years.'

'Good God, is it that much?' said Alun absently. 'Well now, you've never had children, have you? I suppose that's . . .'

'Just as well and no one could have put it clearer, and quite right too. You've forgotten, you've only just remembered I've always never had children. I don't know, some men would have done their homework before they barged in for a quick snuggle, or at least a bit of bloody revision.' She was dodgy again for a moment. 'How's your life then?'

'Fine. Never changes.'

'Oh? In that case I suppose you'll be looking up a few old friends round the neighbourhood. Like a couple of dozen. Always been like that with you, hasn't it?

'The Don Juan syndrome. Rather a high-flown name, I've always thought. You know what they say? Comes from a desire to degrade and humiliate women. Well, there may be something in it, but if there is you'd have expected me to be particularly hot on women who'd be better off all round for a spot of degradation and humiliation, go round the place bloody well begging for it, like Muriel and fishface Eirwen Spurling. And I tell you frankly they leave me cold.'

Sophie had not listened attentively to this. 'Beats me,' she said, 'why a bloke married to someone like that has to go messing around with all and sundry.'

'You mentioned homework, well homework or no homework I remember you saying that to me slightly more than twenty-two years ago, and I'll tell you again now what I told you then: like buggery it beats you, you understand it through and through. You know you're right – *has* to go messing around. No choice involved – necessity. Easier, wiser, kinder . . . to accept it. But to hell with the years. Forget 'em. No problem where you're concerned. Believe it or not, I can't really remember how you used to look. Whenever I try I keep seeing you as you are now. You're just not different enough. Isn't that amazing, isn't that . . . splendid, isn't . . . that . . . marvellous . . .'

Much too late to spoil it the telephone-bell rang on the landing.

'That might be Victor now,' said Sophie.

Left to himself, Alun glanced briefly and incuriously round the capacious bedroom. Large and small, the things in it looked as if getting through money had been a principle of selection, starting with moulded wallpaper apparently encrusted with gems. His mind was traversed by banal, inescapable thoughts about the passing of time. Quite a lot of time had indeed passed, but so far to surprisingly small effect. What he had said to Sophie just now about her appearance and so on was of course untrue, though it would have been much untruer, one had to admit, of most other people he had known that long. But in a general way, applied to experience, it had a bearing. All sorts of stuff, for instance what had been taking place a little earlier, seemed much as before, or at any rate not different enough to start making a song and dance about. This state of affairs might well not last for ever, but for the moment, certainly, the less it changed the more it was the same thing, and the most noticeable characteristic of the past, as seen by him, at least, was that there was so much more of it now than formerly, with bits that were longer ago than had once seemed possible. Alun went for a pee.

When he came back to the bedroom Sophie had returned and was dressing.

'How long have we got?'

'Fifteen minutes minimum,' she said without looking up.

'I've done it in two and a half in my time, and with cuff-links and shoelaces.'

'Not so much talk.'

Tying his tie, Alun saw in the dressing-table mirror what he had not properly seen direct and earlier, that across from the double bed where they had lain there stood a made-up single bed. 'Who sleeps there?' he asked.

'He does. It's where he usually is.'

'Usually is? You mean sometimes he comes and – '

'No, no, it's where he lands up. I kick out in the mornings, see, and he goes over there when it gets too much.'

'What a jolly sensible set-up.'

Something about its description puzzled Alun, but he had never been one to be afflicted with disinterested curiosity and he had long forgotten the matter when, with six minutes to spare, he and Sophie came to say good-bye in the hall. (Six minutes, eh? Not such a marvellous arrangement.)

'Lovely to see you,' she cried as if he had indeed just dropped in for a cup of tea, then changed register and said 'You are a bugger' again, but resignedly this time.

Rejecting a first thought or so he said, 'You're lovely. I'll be along again soon. But I'll ring first.'

A shitty irony hovered when the car refused to start at once, but then it did. He turned it round, something to get done on arrival in future, and slid off down the hill. Clear. Six minutes, eh? Like the old days. Sophie soon slipped from his mind, but as always at this stage he felt utterly free, not triumphant, just never freer, never so free as now. Softly, shaping the notes, he broke into a pleasing light tenor:

'Was it young Denise who spread disease through all the men in the room?

Oh no, it wasn't young Denise, it was Mrs Rosenbloom . . .'

He took the road above Beaufoy which brought the sea into sight at a distance and, across the bay, the umber and dark-green stretch of Courcey, with vague industrial shapes half misted over in the background. For the moment the sun was out, strong enough to turn the water into something a bit more rewarding than grey-brown. Flat-fronted terraced houses reached by steep flights of steps gave place to semi-detached brick villas put up between the wars, a cluster of 1950s two-storey pre-fabs and then, further along and from further back, the spaced-out stone-built residences of the coal-owners and ironmasters of prosperous times.

Hereabouts Alun eased up on the accelerator and caused his face to take on expressions of boredom, dissatisfaction, even disappointment, getting it ready for a going-over by his daughter Rosemary. There was a definite element of the creepy about the way that girl could get the wrong idea about her father's less significant activities and interests. Up to something was what he could reckon on being charged with having been, not a moment ago either, if at encounters like this he showed any more positive feeling than a fairly plucky resignation. The girl was even worse in this respect than her elder sister, now safely married, or rather safely out of the way most of the time on that account. He could not have explained why these challenges of theirs made him so uncomfortable.

In the drawing-room mother and daughter had staked out a little feminine enclave on the fireside rug and a low coffee-table beside it with coffee-cups, biscuit-tin, box of chocolates, box of tissues, handbags, manicure kit, wastepaper basket, local map and dozens of estate-agents' brochures and lists. If he could get through the first minute in one piece, Alun knew he was probably going to be all right. He crossed in safety the twenty feet of minefield from the doorway and embraced his daughter. As always it was a warm embrace.

'Good lunch?' asked Rhiannon when he had kissed her.

'Not really. Quite bearable. We'll go there some time.'

'You saw Charlie? Like some coffee?'

'No thanks. Yes, he was there. And Peter.'

'Oh, was he really?' said Rhiannon, with pleasure and interest in her voice. 'How was he looking?'

'Not very well I thought. He's put on a lot of weight. But he's, you know, recognisable.'

'Oh. Well, he never was much of a bean-pole, was he?'

Rosemary, a darker and more robust-looking version of Rhiannon, had stood waiting for this part to end. She had been told years previously that before meeting her father in the long-ago her mother had had some sort of attachment to a university lecturer called Peter Thomas. What more she might have heard or guessed was unknown and she showed no reaction now. Indicating one of the brochures, she said,

'There's a house in Kinver Hill with attractive Swedish-type sun-room and unusual walled garden Mum and I are looking at at five. You're just in time to run us along there.'

'So I am indeed. Tell me, how would you have managed if it hadn't been for me turning up?'

'Minicab, same as she's been managing all week while you've been driving yourself to the pub and wherever else has taken your fancy. Come on, how many houses have you actually seen?'

'Christ love, I don't know. Not many. As few as possible. Three was it? Not my kind of thing. There's nothing you can say that'll drive me off the position that that kind of thing's a women's kind of thing.' Alun was busy hiding his relief at not after all being asked to account for himself, despite the unpleasant tilt in his daughter's last speech.

'You mean we've got to do it so we might as well like it. Well, here's one you're not getting out of, boy *bach*. Two, in fact. That's right, the place in Mary Tweed Lane'll be viewable at six, wasn't it, Mum?' Rosemary turned through the leaflets. 'Extensive hall with recessed fireplace and carved Victorian overmantel. Mum tells me you've got some scheme lined up for visiting places of scenic and historical interest in the surrounding vicinity.' She put on a quacking local accent for the last dozen words, efficiently enough though she had never lived in Wales. 'We'll go into the places another time, but of course part of the deal is while you're in Bargeman's Row exploring folkways and getting drunk you can't be in Pedwarsaint and Holland looking over houses. Well, for the next couple of days, Dad, resign yourself to a lot of looking over houses. You're not going to get away with leaving it all to Mum while I'm here. Right? Are you with me?'

Alun nodded without speaking. They always took it out of you for doing anything on your own, without them, however innocent, like glancing at a newspaper. Now he came to think of it, he had seen quite early the avoidance of house-viewing as an extra benefit of going in search of Wales. And by the way four to one was way off – four and a half it was, with Rhiannon, now furtively winking and peering at him, the half and Rosemary the four.

Well, roughly. Far from the least ill-feeling the style of her harangue had shown affection of a sort, but the sort that mitigated the sense of her words not at all. She came and linked arms with him when at last they moved off, kissed him on the cheek and gave him a smile that exactly blended fondness and disapproval. It was the best he could reasonably have hoped for.

3 Charlie

1

When Charlie Norris noticed that the smallest man in the submarine rail-way-carriage had a face made out of carpeting he decided it was time to be off. By throwing himself about and sucking in air fast and deep he got away and back to his bed in the dark. Intensely thirsty as usual he at once reached for one of the several glasses of water lined up on the low table beside him, but before he found it his hand was grabbed and worried by some creature with very long narrow jaws. It made croaking, creaking noises. He cried out, or thought he did, and pulled his body away like a swimmer surfacing, and then he was really back.

He could hear Sophie breathing quietly in the bed across the way and started to throw the covers of his own bed back before going on to scramble in beside her and nestle up to her. Then he worked out that he had done that twice in the last ten days or so and a third time now would be too much. She always woke up at his arrival however careful he was, whether he nestled up or not, and though she always said later that she dropped off again in a couple of minutes he doubted it. And after all, he had not found himself at the edge of one of those huge, brilliantly lit stretches of grassland with ruined pillars and water flowing uphill and changing its course as it went, nor had to deal with small things, small unrecognisable animals or machines behaving like animals. So for the moment he stayed there leaning on his elbow.

It was not really dark. He could even see part of Sophie's outline in the light of the hooded lamp next to him. Other gleams came from the passage doorway and its reflection in the tall mirror by the window. An early car receded towards the town. He was quite safe, also no less thirsty in the real world than in the unreal and standing in need of a pee. Not till he was back tucked up after supplying these wants did he look at his watch: five ten. Not too bad. He felt as if about two-thirds of his head had recently been sliced off and his heart seemed to be beating somewhere inside his stomach, but otherwise he was fine, successfully monitoring his breathing over about the next hour until he fell into a kind of doze, not a very nice kind, admittedly.

It was light when he came out of that and he was not at all fine, nowhere near. As usual at this time, his morning self cursed his overnight self for having purposely left the Scotch in the drinks cabinet downstairs. Without that sort of help it was quite out of the question that he should ever get up. A mug of tea and a plastic flask containing more tea stood on the bedside table. He would in no sense be committing himself to getting up if it so turned out that he drank some. With this clear all round he got on his elbow and drank some, drank indeed the whole mug's worth in one because it was half cold, and dropped flat again. Before very long the liquid had carved out a new and more direct route to his bladder. He rolled over and fixed his eye on the stout timber that framed the quilted bed-head, counted a hundred, then, with a convulsive overarm bowling movement, got a hand to it, gripped it, counted another hundred and hauled with all his strength, thus pulling himself half upright.

In this position, still clutching the frame, he paused again, said 'With many a weary sigh, and many a groan, up a high hill he heaves a huge round stone,' and plunged a foot to the floor. Of course it was understood that if he ever got to the bathroom he would dive straight back into bed the moment he got back in range. Having got back he went and laid his hands flat on the dressing-table either side of Sophie's chased-silver hand-mirror and looked out of the window, looking but not seeing. With a conviction undimmed by having survived countless previous run-offs he felt that everything he had was lost and everyone he knew was gone. Only because there was nothing else to do he stood there assembling the energy to move, to start dressing, rather in the spirit of a skier poised above a hazardous run. Ready? Right . . . Go. Up. Round. Off.

'I'm just popping over to Rhiannon's,' Sophie told him in the kitchen. 'They think they've found a house but she wants me and Gwen to go over it with her. One of the ones backing on to Holland woods. You know, where the Aubreys used to live. Er, Dilys'll be along at eleven and Mr Bridgeman's here, round the front he is now, so you'll be all right.' She referred to the daily woman and the ex-docker who tended the garden and cleaned an occasional window and suchlike. 'I'll be here from about half-four on. Hope your do is fun. Expect you when I see you, love,' she ended on a formulaic note, kissed the top of his head and went.

After ten minutes Charlie had made it all the way from the breakfast-room table to the refrigerator in the kitchen. Here he stood and drank a great deal of apple-juice and crunched a half-burnt, holed piece of toast Sophie had rejected; making his own toast – bread-bin, toaster, all that – was unthinkable. Along with it he swallowed a couple of spoonfuls of marmalade straight from the pot. The sight of a coffee-bag out in the open near an unused mug was not quite enough to make up his mind for him, but finding the electric kettle half full turned the scale. He saw the thing through and even got some sugar in, stirring with the marmalade-spoon. When a speck of saliva caught at the back of his throat he managed to lay the mug down before the father and mother of a coughing-fit sent him spinning about the room and landing up face to face with Mr Bridgeman, round the back now, eighteen inches away on the other side of the window-pane. Then the telephone rang as it always did at about that time of the morning.

'Charles, it's Victor. How are you today?'

'About the same as usual.'

'Oh, I'm sorry to hear it.' Sometimes Victor said that and sometimes he said he was glad it was no worse. 'Listen, Charlie, I'm fed up with Griffiths & Griffiths. Fed up to *by here*, my dear,' he said, turning a local vulgarism to his own purposes. 'Half of what they sent up yesterday was unusable. As you remember we talked of experimenting with Lower Glamorgan Products. May I proceed with that?'

'Go ahead.' Charlie had long since stopped wondering why his brother bothered to pursue the fiction of their joint responsibility for the affairs of the Glendower. The boredom of it was therapeutic, though.

'Good, thank you. The other thing is I've taken against the house white. Horrid little ninny of a wine. As regards a replacement I have one or two ideas to try on you. Will you be in later?'

'Actually I'm not quite sure today. There's the ceremony at St Dogmael's with a piss-up at the Prince of Wales after.'

'Don't remind me, I wouldn't have missed it for anything, the ceremony that is, chance to see Mr Posturing Ponce going all out. The trouble is young Chris. The poor boy's picked up some sort of bug and I've sent him to bed, no one to leave in charge. But listen Charlie, you round up three or four notables at that get-together if you can and bring them along here for lunch on the house. Only if you can. Ring before if possible. The coq au vin is going to be a positive dream. All right?'

'I'll have to study the ground but I'll try.'

'Oh good lad. You sound a little more cheerful now. Take care of yourself, Charles.'

The mug of coffee had not got any hotter but Charlie drank it anyway in the interests of rehydration. By and by he also drank a weakish whisky-and-water, having held off till then because he made a point of avoiding early drinking whenever he could. At eleven o'clock a minicab arrived to take him into town. While, yawning his head off, he climbed aboard he told himself, as he always did at this juncture, that he really must sell his old Renault, which sat in the garage unused for years except by Sophie when her own car was laid up. He would set about it tomorrow.

The journey took him past many places, but none of more interest than Lower Glamorgan County Hall, half a dozen times the size of the old Glamorgan County Hall in Cardiff, indeed a miniature new town in itself. Its inmates were said to enjoy the use of uncounted cocktail bars, tastefully-lit dining-rooms, discos, jacuzzis, hairdressing salons, massage parlours and intensive-care units while not actually defrauding the populace, all this situated conveniently close to Jenkyn's Farm, otherwise the gaol. Notable too, and further in, were the docks where once Mr Bridgeman had earned a very respectable wage and enriched himself in other ways as well. Now, where once ships by the dozen had lain, bringing timber, ores, pig-iron, fetching coal, coke, spelter, there was just the harbour dredger, looking as if it had not yet been out that year, and a single dirty little freighter flying the blue, white and red of Yugoslavia.

Sophie's image as he had seen her an hour before, brisk and neat in her tightly-belted light-blue mack, stayed in Charlie's mind. You only had to look at her to be assured that men with faces made out of carpeting played no part in her life; it took longer to establish that she made every allowance she could for anybody involved with such men. In those twenty-two years of marriage he had not perhaps got to know her very well, but almost his strongest feeling for her, stronger than envy, was respect, even admiration. Provided things were left to her there would never be any trouble, not even over Alun. If Charlie had not felt certain, as early as the moment of sitting down to lunch at the Glendower, where Alun proposed to go afterwards, the clean sheets on Sophie's bed midweek would have told him the score. But let it be. As always, he and Sophie had not exchanged so much as a glance about it. Let it be. Something like half-way through the twenty-two years he had in any case given up a large part of the right to a say in that area of Sophie's life.

St Dogmael's came up on the landward side, another of the town's deconsecrated churches. This one had been converted not into a porno-graphic cinema but, less inoffensively some might have thought, into an arts centre. The structure had been extensively restored in 1895, though parts of the clerestory were traceable to a fourteenth-century rebuilding by Henry de Courcy. These facts and many more were to be found in a pamphlet sold at the extensive bookstall and information office in the west porch. To one side of the porch entrance there had stood, longer than anyone could remember, a short, dingy stone pillar supporting a life-sized figure too badly battered and weathered to be recognisable even as a man, but always vaguely supposed to have portrayed the saint. Today the whole thing was covered with a great red cloth and seventy or eighty people, some hung with civic and other paraphernalia, were standing close by and producing a loud jabber of talk diversified with the sportive female shrieks prevalent in the locality.

Charlie had cut it fine. He stopped his car several yards short, paid the driver, a Chinese with an alarming Greenhill accent, and stole up to the edge of the crowd. A rather fat man of about fifty, with short white hair, a long doughy face and wide eyes, turned towards him.

'Good morning, sir,' he said loudly in a North American accent.

'Good morning,' said Charlie, and felt like running there and then. He had taken a turn for the better in the last half-hour, but it was nothing that could not be undone by any sudden bit of strain, such as this chap looked more than competent to provide.

'May I introduce myself? I am Llywelyn Caswallon Pugh.'

And at that accursed name the whole assembly fell silent. At least that was how it appeared to Charlie for a dazed moment, like something out of the Mabinogion. Then he realised that the hushing agent must have been one or another of the central group of notables and others that, he now saw, included Alun. Throughout what followed, photographers were to be seen and heard near this group and a man wielding what must have been a sort of portable television camera was there too.

A series of semi-intelligible pronouncements began by way of a microphone and one or two loudspeakers. As it proceeded the man Pugh, who now struck Charlie as distinctly deranged, kept sending him purposeful glances, promising him more to come, more to be communicated than just what he was called. Across the way, near the shape under the cloth, a smartly-dressed youth who had to be the mayor introduced the, or perhaps merely a, minister of state at the Welsh Office. This man, who seemed scarcely older, spoke some formula and jerked at the end of an ornamental rope or cord that Charlie had not noticed before. With wonderful smoothness the red cloth parted and fell to reveal, standing on a plinth of what looked like olive-green marble, a shape in glossy yellow metal that was about the height of a human being without looking much more like one than the beaten-up chunk of stone that had stood there before.

There was a silence that probably came less from horror than sheer bafflement, then a sudden rush of applause. The presumed sculptor, a little fellow covered in hair like an artist in a cartoon, appeared and was the centre of attention for a few seconds. Another youngster, who said he represented the Welsh Arts Council, started talking about money. It came on to rain, though not enough to bother a Welsh crowd. On a second glance, the object on the plinth did look a certain amount like a man, but the style ruled out anything in the way of portraiture, and Charlie felt he was probably not the only one to wonder whether some handy abstraction – the spirit of Wales, say – had pushed out the advertised subject. Those close enough, however, could see Brydan's name on the plate along with just his dates, 1913–1960.

Alun's turn came. He played it low-key, avoiding a display of emotion so long after the event, sticking to facts, facts like Brydan being the greatest Welsh poet that had ever lived and also the greatest poet in the English language to have lived in the present century, together with minor but no less certain facts like his utter dedication to his art, though leaving out other ones like his utter dedication to Jack Daniel's Tennessee whiskey and *Astounding Science Fiction*. Llywelyn Caswallon Pugh evidently thought he could afford to do without some of this. He stepped up the frequency of his glances at Charlie and slowly edged closer. He had a considerable power of instilling dread, in Charlie at least. When he spoke it was a little less loud than before.

'Excuse me, sir, but would that gentleman there be Mr Alun Weaver, CBE?'

'It would,' answered Charlie, panting slightly. 'That's him.'

'And would you yourself happen to be personally acquainted with him?'

'I would. I mean yes, I know him.'

'Might you be good enough to introduce me after this ceremony?'

He must be doing it on purpose, thought Charlie, and to no possible benign end. This really was the time to run, or at least walk briskly away – quicker, cleaner, kinder – but he was not up to breaking through the thin but solid cordon of bodies that now stood between him and freedom. So he babbled some form of assent and tried to shut himself off from Pugh and everyone else for as long as possible, dreamily looking back on those distant mornings of mere headache and nausea.

Alun was beginning to take a winding-up tone. As he spoke he moved his gaze slowly from one extremity of his audience to the other so that no one should feel left out. 'Too much has sometimes been made,' he said, 'of the undeniable fact that Brydan knew no Welsh, was altogether ignorant of the language. This was a matter of the purest chance, a matter of fashion only. Parents in the South Wales of the era before World War I saw fit to bring up their children to speak nothing but English. But nobody who knows his work and who knows Wales and the Welsh language can be in any doubt that that land and that language live in that work. He had no literal, word-for-word understanding, but at a deep, instinctive, primal level he understood. He felt and he sensed something beyond words . . .'

When Alun had finished, someone else pronounced a few phrases of thanks or thanksgiving or anyway termination. All present relaxed and looked about, but at first none moved. Charlie was trapped physically and by obligation of a sort, but also by his own curiosity: he was going to be around when this transatlantic Welshman came up against Alun or . . . Well no, not perish, but know the reason why. This resolve flagged rather when Pugh turned towards him again and drew in air to say more to him. He had been mad not to drop in at the Glendower on the way to a horror like this. Would he never learn?

'May I know your name, sir?'

Charlie gave it and found himself throwing in his occupation like a fool.

'I am an official of the Cymric Companionship of the USA,' said Pugh.

At this point something terrible happened to Charlie's brain. Pugh went on speaking in just the same way as before, with no change of pace or inflection, but Charlie could no longer distinguish any words, only noises. His eyes swam a little. He stepped backwards and trod heavily on someone's foot. Then he picked out a noise he recognised and nearly fell over the other way with relief. It had not been fair to expect an old soak whose Welsh vocabulary started and stopped with *yr* and *bach* and *myn* to recognise the rubbish when it came at him unheralded in an American accent. 'M'm,' he said with feeling. 'M'm.'

Pugh's wide stare widened further in a way that made Charlie wonder what he had assented to, but that was soon over and more English came. 'A key objective of the Companionship is the forging and maintenance of ties with the mother country.'

A capful of rain blew refreshingly into Charlie's face and a seagull passed close enough overhead to make him flinch. 'Sounds a first rate idea.'

'Uh-huh. In pursuance of which my purpose today is to solicit Mr Weaver to guest-visit with my home chapter of the Companionship at Bethgelert, Pennsylvania for a designated period. Consequentially my desire to make his acquaintance.'

Charlie appreciated this attempt at courteous explanation. He felt he understood the sense of it too; things were coming a little easier now. While he looked round for Alun he found he could imagine with ridiculous ease – he had perhaps even heard – him saying that all he needed was a free invitation over there, never mind to how God-forsaken a part, anything to give him a base, and he would be off and away. Well, the bloody old Welsh chancer's chance had come at last. But hey, those Stateside Taffs must hold an alarmingly high opinion of the said Welsh chancer. How could they have acquired it?

Alun, closely attended by three or four functionaries, had just begun to move in the direction of a line of official-looking cars, and in no time there was Charlie with Pugh at his side barring the way and doing the introducing.

'Mr Pugh has something to do with the . . .'

'Cymric Companionship of the USA. I'm honoured to meet you, sir. I wrote you care of your – '

'How nice to meet you, Mr Pugh. Where exactly are you from?'

'Bethlegert, Pennsylvania, which is situated – '

'Dear, dear, there are Welshmen all over the world, aren't there? Saxons, give up hope of finding a pie under the sun that we harmless folk don't contrive to slide our sly fingers into. Carry my warmest cousinly greetings to the Celts of Bethlegert, Mr Pugh. Now . . .'

'Mr Pugh wants to invite you there,' called Charlie hurriedly.

The fluid, seamless way Alun converted his unthinking glance towards the waiting car into an urgent request for assistance, for somebody to accommodate his Mr Pugh, was something Charlie was quite sure he would never forget. Good too was Alun's look of measured eagerness to hear anything the fellow might say. Just ahead of them, somebody dissatisfied with some of the arrangements barred their way of departure for the moment.

'Bethlegert is situated in that part of the state containing a large Welsh element. In fact William Penn desired that the Commonwealth as a whole be designated New Wales, but the English government interdicted the proposition.'

Pugh laid special stress on the last few words, but if he had succeeded in whipping up separatist feeling in his hearers they gave no sign, though Alun's air of expectation perhaps waned slightly. But he seemed to cheer up again when Pugh started on his next offering.

'We in Bethlegert have been privileged to welcome many distinguished Welsh persons. We were honoured with a visit from Brydan in 1954. The occasion is memorialised by a plaque inscribed in Welsh and English in Neuadd Taliesin, our meeting-house. There also hangs there a portrait of Brydan in oil paints executed by Mrs Bronwen Richards Weintraub, a member of our council.'

'When were you thinking of – ' began Alun, but Pugh raised a hand, just an inch or two from the wrist, and continued as before.

'Mrs Weintraub relied chiefly on photographs, but visitors who knew Brydan in life pronounced it an excellent likeness.'

There was something final and definitive in the delivery and reception of that remark. Up front, the missing man or car had been found or despaired of and movement was resumed. Alun said thoughtfully,

'Tell me, Mr Pugh, where would I stay in Bethlegert?'

'Why, with me, Mr Weaver. A bachelor establishment, but comfortable enough I assure you. I'll enjoy showing you our neighbourhood.'

'I look forward to it.' Alun stood now by the rear door of his destined car. 'I think the spring of 1995 would be about right for my visit.'

'You must be – '

'No, better say the autumn. The fall. I am very busy just at the moment. Nice to have met you. Good day to you. Charlie, in round the other side.'

At the moment before he ducked his head under the car roof Charlie caught a last glimpse of Pugh, looking not totally unlike an inflated rubber figure out of whose base the stopper had been drawn an instant earlier. Charlie might have felt some pity if he had not been lost in admiration for Alun.

'Bloody marvellous bit of timing,' he told him when they were settled in the back seats.

'Yeah, nice bonus, but on a note like that I could have outfaced the bugger indefinitely. And by the way I reckon bugger is right, don't you? I'd whiffed it even before we got to the bachelor establishment, just in that second.'

'Probably, but I was a bit too overwhelmed with the rest of him to notice much.'

The car had still not moved. Alun squinted forward through his window.

'There he goes, poor dab. I should have recommended him to that Gents by the fire station. Most likely not in business any more, though, like everything else.'

Out of pure devilment Charlie said, 'I suppose he did get the message all right, do you think?'

'What? How do you mean?'

'Well you were frightfully polite to him, you know. Took him very seriously.'

'Perhaps there was a touch of that.'

'I mean you don't want him coming through on the phone asking if he can discuss it with you. Find a way round your objections.'

'No, I don't, do I? My God.'

By now the car had started to crawl along beside the pavement. Again Alun peered through his window, then took a quick glance at the traffic ahead. He started to roll down the window with his left hand and arranged his right with the thumb and first two fingers extended and the other two clenched.

'That's English, what you've got there,' said Charlie quickly. 'Middle finger only for Americans.'

'Christ, you're right, thanks. Well . . . here we go.' Alun stuck his head and hand out of the opening and Charlie heard him bawl, 'Make it two thousand. The year two thousand. And fuck off.'

The car accelerated nimbly. By a blessed chance Charlie got another last sight of Pugh out of the back window, much reduced now from the comparative equanimity he had shown a minute before. What tale of this would he tell in Bethlegert?

'They do say fuck off in America, don't they?' asked Alun anxiously.

'I'm sure they understand it.'

'And it doesn't mean how's your father or anything?'

'Not that I know of, no.'

'I thought I'd better clinch it, you see. Sort of make assurance double sure.'

'Yes, I can't see him bothering you again.'

Alun laughed quietly for a short time, shaking his head in indulgent self-reproach. The driver, who had the collar of a tartan sports shirt turned down over that of his blue serge suit, spoke up.

'Trying to cadge a lift, was he, that bloke back there?'

'Roughly.'

'Funny-looking sort of bloke. He reminded me – '

'Yes, well we can forget about him now and concentrate on getting to the Prince of Wales as fast as we reasonably can.' Evidently Alun had no wish just then to pursue the special Welsh relationship with drivers of taxis as mentioned to Rhiannon. He lowered his voice and went on, 'Hey – timing really was important for that. A clear getaway afterwards. I got badly caught in Kilburn once telling a Bulgarian short-story writer, actually he *was* trying to cadge a lift, anyway telling him to fuck off for two or three minutes while the chap driving the open car I was sitting in turned round in the cul-de-sac I hadn't noticed we were at the end of. Amazing how quickly the bloom fades on fuck off, you know. Say it a couple of times running and you've got out of it nearly all of what you're going to get.'

'And there's not a lot you can go on to later,' said Charlie.

'Well exactly.'

'What really got you down about Pugh, made you dump him? One thing more than another. I mean apart from his interest in rugby. Of course he was unstoppably American, I do see.'

'He can't help that, love him. No, I could have taken that. Well, taken it more cheerfully than him being even more savagely Welsh. I've heard about those buggers in Pennsylvania. You know what they are, do you? Bloody Quakers. You're doing well if they let you smoke there. And you know what they get up to? Speaking Welsh. Talking Welsh to each other on purpose.'

'Yes, he talked some to me.'

'Well, there you are then,' said Alun, glaring indignantly at Charlie. 'How can you deal with a bastard like that?'

'I wonder you didn't give him the thumbs-down as soon as you heard where he was from, at that rate.'

'Oh, I couldn't have done that. That would have looked rude. And anyway at that stage I couldn't be sure he wasn't going to, I don't know, say fuck or something and show he was a human being. I think a drink's what I'd like now.'

They went through the hall of the Prince of Wales, which by some reactionary whim had ordinary carpets on the floor and pictures of recognisable scenes on the walls, up in the photograph-infested lift and into the glittering meanness of what was no doubt called a banqueting-room with slender, softly gleaming pillars. But, fair play, it had a bar in it, plus a table serving wine only, which kept a few unserious drinkers out of the road. One advantage of Charlie's trade, now only to be called that in a manner of speaking but for many years an accurate description, was that he tended to know waitresses. Off this one he got, well ahead of his turn, a whisky and water that would have struck some other men as a nice lunchtime session's worth, and quite surprised himself by finding how much he had needed it. Clutching its successor, he made his way straight towards Alun, who had pleaded for moral support in alien territory. The Cellan-Davieses were also close by, in fact Malcolm was in the middle of asking Alun a question.

'Called what again? Llywelyn what Pugh?'

'I'm not clear, Charlie heard it.'

'It sounded like Caswallon.'

'Oh, Caswallon,' said Malcolm, with a tremendous hissing scrape on the double L. 'Better known as Cassivellaunus.'

'Now you're talking,' said Gwen, nodding busily.

'A British chieftain who fought the Romans in – '

'Look, baby, baby, cool it, okay?' said Alun. 'We've had enough history for one morning. William Penn and Cassivellaunus – next, the Patagonians, many of whom, my friends, are bilingual in Welsh and Spanish.'

'I think it's a pity you ditched Mr Pugh,' said Gwen. 'He and Malcolm sound as if they were made for each other. Can't you get him back?'

To Charlie's ear there was a bit extra there, but when he looked up it was to see someone of consequence joining the group. Nobody was to ask who he was and he knew all he needed to about who they were. In appearance, including hair-style and clothes, he was like a good average town councillor, from Yorkshire rather than South Wales, in a black-and-white film of twenty-five years before. Two lesser persons were with him.

'Well now,' he said in the kind of husky alto often put down to massive gin-drinking, 'what's the state of feeling about our new piece of sculpture?'

'Oh Christ,' said Alun as if before he could stop himself. 'Er . . . actually we haven't discussed it, have we? It's not what I'd call my field. Gwen, you're good on art.'

'That's sweet of you, Alun. Well, it hasn't got any holes in it. You can say that much for it.'

A short guessing-game followed and ended with the disclosure that the start-to-finish, all-in cost of having the sculpture there was £98,000.

'Makes you think, doesn't it?' said Alun. 'You could get a couple of torpedoes for that.'

'Oh, surely they're much more expensive,' said Malcolm. 'I was reading – '

'To hell with it – half a bloody torpedo, then. A quarter, I don't care.'

'It's the principle of the thing,' said Gwen.

'If you don't mind,' croaked the questioner, 'could we forget about torpedoes for the moment and get back to the sculpture? You, Mr . . . ,' he turned to Charlie, 'you haven't said anything yet.'

'No, well . . . I thought it wasn't at all figurative,' said Charlie rather complacently.

'Is that all? Has nobody anything more, er, more, er, more constructive to put forward?'

Nobody had.

'So nobody here shares my feeling that the Brydan monument is an exciting breakthrough for all of us in this town?'

Like everyone else, Charlie at once ruled out the possibility of any sort of irony being intended. There was general silence, with eyes on the floor, until Gwen said in a voice not intended to carry far,

'If you're going to call that, or anything like that, exciting, what do you call the late-night horror movie? When it's slightly above average?' She frowned and smiled as never before.

Alun nodded weightily. 'Very good point,' he said.

'My colleagues and I had hoped for a little bit of encouragement. Here we are going all out, fighting to bring the best in modern art to the people, to whom after all it belongs and not to any fancy élite, and people like you, educated people, don't want to know. You don't, do you? You're happier with your cosy, musty Victoriana. Safe I suppose it makes you feel.

Anything challenging you give a wide berth to. Well, I take leave to doubt whether your reaction is typical. Good day to you.'

The man of position jerked his head at his aides to signal a move in a way that recalled a boss in a different kind of film, returning from a few paces off long enough to add, 'You're entitled to your opinions, it goes without saying, but they're clearly based on ignorance, whereas the artist in question was selected and instructed by a panel of experts. Kindly take due note of that.'

When he was clear, Alun said with great emphasis, his voice shaking slightly, 'It's all right when little turds and turdettes, especially the latter, go on about exciting breakthroughs in advertisements and arts pages, well of course it isn't *all right* but we're used to it, we've got our defences against it. And it was all right when buggers like that were fighting to stop *Desire under the Elms* being put on at the Royal and going all out to get Joyce and Lawrence *and T. S. Eliot* off the shelves of the public library. You're too young to remember a bloody old fool and by the bye frightful shit called Bevan Hopkin who called the police in at a Renoir exhibition at the Trevor Knudsen – in 1953, not 1903. That's how he was supposed to behave. Imagine him in favour of anything challenging. Imagine him *knowing the word*. When Labour councillors in South Wales start blathering about taking modern art to the people everyone's in deep trouble. Come back, Bevan Hopkin, all, repeat all, is forgiven. Well, *Iesu Crist* and no mistake.'

'*Grist*,' said Gwen. '*Iesu Grist*. With the soft mutation.'

'Oh, bugger it. I'm going to give up. Had enough. Oh God here's another lot,' said Alun, turning to Charlie. 'We'd better be off soon.'

'I'm off now but I'll be back.'

Charlie just made it round the flank of the mayoral contingent and, picking up a fresh glass on the way, dodged into the lavatory. Here he waited for the two already present to leave, filled the glass at a basin, locked himself in a compartment and let go the ultimate coughing-fit that had been hanging about him for the last hour. Somebody else came in and used the urinal during it, groaning a lot as if in sympathy. He drank more water and took some deep breaths, feeling much weaker but clearer in the head, like a man in a book by John Buchan after an attack of fever. On departure he noticed that, as he put it later, the place reeked like an Alexandria knocking-shop.

He walked up the corridor, on carpet very luxurious to the eye but somehow disagreeable underfoot, until he reached a row of telephones separated from the outside only by small roofs shaped like Romanesque arches.

Victor answered his ring and sounded pleased. 'How are you, Charles? How reads the latest bulletin?'

'One of the more magical days. Look, er, I'm afraid I shan't be able to manage the lunch idea. There's a pub-crawl thing in Harriston I said I'd go on I'd completely forgotten. Sorry.'

'Charlie, I'm afraid I've no idea what you're talking about. A lunch . . . ?'

'You asked me to try to get some selected shits together and bring them – '

'Oh, that. Never mind, it was just a thought. Another time. How was Posturing Ponce?'

'Quite good, actually. Well, he was terrible at the unveiling thing, but came back stoutly later. There was a collector's-item Welsh-American queer there he brushed off in fine style.'

'Brushed him off? You mean he – '

'No, no. He invited Alun to go and stay with him in his bachelor quarters in Pennsylvania or Philadelphia or wherever it is.'

'I suppose there's no chance of him going? Because that really would be a turn-up for the book.' For a moment Victor's voice went falsetto with laughter. 'PP in Pennsylvania with one of that lot.' That lot stayed in the third person in dealings between the brothers. 'Too much to ask. Well – enjoy your pub-crawl. You'll be in later, will you?'

'Probably, but for once I'm not too sure when.'

'Any time you like, Charles.'

When he got back to it the party seemed to have dwindled a good deal, or perhaps had merely spread out to the edges. At any rate the mayoral squad was on the point of leaving; the chap who had liked the sculpture was nowhere to be seen. An old man with a pink-and-white complexion – pink round the nose and eyes, white elsewhere – stood by the wall opening and shutting his jaws at a great rate. Large oval dishes of uncommonly horrible finger-snacks, a vivid green or orange in colour, lay here and there almost untouched, and quite right too, thought Charlie, also quite understandable now that everybody was either too fat or living off chaff and whey.

The drink, on the other hand, had been very popular, so much so that at the moment there was no Scotch available and no one to serve it anyway. Charlie placed himself at the corner of the bar where he could grab the waitress on her return. Two others with empty glasses had taken up the same station, a fellow in his sixties with a small face that seemed the smaller for the elaborately strutted and cantilevered pair of spectacles on it, and a younger, dark-complexioned man of melancholy, thoughtful appearance, not unlike Garth, a common Welsh type not often noted for either quality. Both looked up at Charlie's arrival and nodded to him in a subdued but friendly way, seeming to know him, and quite likely they did know him, had at least seen him more than once in the way of business, at a function of this sort, in a club, in a bar. Round here you had a pretty good idea of who everybody was, which helped on some kinds of contact without doing anything for others.

Accordingly the two pursued their conversation while going out of their way not to exclude Charlie from it. 'You'll find the same everywhere,' the older man was saying, 'not just in our chosen field. Did you see about that ambassador bloke who brought home too much wine?'

'No I didn't see that, I must have missed it,' said the dark man, glancing at Charlie, and Charlie nodded to show he had missed it too.

'Well, you couldn't have a more perfect illustration of the point under discussion. When you retired, you see, from your last ambassadorial post you got a duty-free allowance, known as your cellar, a certain amount of wine you were allowed to bring back to England as a privilege. The exact number of bottles was never fixed: it was left to your discretion, and everyone was happy. Until one fine day Sir This-and-that turns up with ten, twenty times what was reasonable. And that was it. As from the next day, no more allowance. No more cellar.'

'Ruined it for everyone. What appalling selfishness.'

'Indeed. I hope I needn't ram home the moral. In other areas the custom has grown up over the years of people in certain positions being deemed to be entitled to certain privileges. Of – and this is the point – a modest and limited order. And everyone is happy, until . . . '

'Until somebody goes beyond what is reasonable.'

'Exactly. Human greed,' said the older man, staring into vacancy through his spectacles. 'Human greed. Well,' he went on with humorous impatience, 'where's this bloody Scotch we've heard so much about?'

'What's the use of sitting in the dispensary when there's nothing for a sore throat?'

'A bit thick, I call it,' said Charlie.

'Ah – wait a minute. Remedy in sight. About time too. Grateful for small mercies. The relief of Mafeking. I knew you loved me, darling.' The three of them said all this and much more, until the glasses were refilled and the water, soda and ice had gone round. Everyone was very relaxed.

'Thankfully,' said the older man – 'thankfully the picture is not uniformly bleak. I'm thinking of one bright spot in particular. Aneirin Pignatelli.' This set the dark man nodding with his eyes closed. 'You know who I'm talking about, of course?'

'Well, naturally,' said Charlie, himself nodding. He was nearly sure he had heard the name somewhere.

'And I take it most people are sufficiently aware of what happened to him.'

Charlie went on nodding.

'He showed himself to be a man of the highest integrity. When he came out' – the pause here was not really necessary – 'he couldn't get into his front room for the flowers.'

At this stage Charlie did show puzzlement, slightly, briefly, unintentionally. In an instant the last speaker turned his small face aside. 'From all the people he hadn't brought down with him,' said the other with a hint of vexation.

Charlie hastened to say 'Yes yes' and make a silly-of-me gesture, but it was too late. The spell of something like intimacy was shattered. The interloper took himself off, though not before he had topped up his glass, with a couple of cold stares to speed him on his way.

Looking vaguely about, Charlie saw Alun and Gwen at the far end of the main room. As he came up behind Gwen he heard Alun say in his quick style,

'I try to get out of lecturing whenever I can these days. Would a reading do instead?'

'Oh, er, I should think so,' said Gwen, turning. 'I'll let you know.'

'But don't worry, I'll be there. Charlie, time to be away, old boy.'

'Why aren't you going to the mayor's lunch?' asked Charlie. 'There must be one, surely.'

'Oh, there's a lunch, but I've got a date with my mates, haven't I? Where's Malcolm got to? And even if I hadn't I couldn't face another mayoral do. Had enough officialdom for one day.'

'You've got to remember he's an artist,' said Gwen.

'And, doubtless more plausibly in the eyes of some, the lunch won't be reported, the ceremony will. I'll see you up at the Picton, Charlie – I've got to dash off somewhere first. One of those things that won't keep.'

2

To Charlie waiting at the exit, it seemed to take about as long for Malcolm to get his car out of the multi-storey over the road from Tesco as it would to get the country out of the Common Market. But, having little real alternative, he turned up in the end and drove the two of them through the outskirts on a good old rainy Welsh afternoon. They passed the ruins of the castle and not long afterwards the ruins of the copper-smeltery. Here and there were conical knolls covered with grass and even supporting bushes or young trees, the overgrown spoilheaps of long-vanished collieries. The road led upwards beside the waters of the Iwerne and the walls of the valley began to rise, with bigger hills fuzzily in view further off. Then, just as some sort of countryside seemed about to come into sight, human habitations reappeared, shops, offices, pubs too, all quite as grimy as when the air was thick with coal-dust.

'Here we are,' said Malcolm, steering round a corner. 'Or are we? I can't see any – '

'What's the trouble?' asked Charlie, ducking and peering.

'It just says Streets where the Picton sign used to be. Streets? What are they talking about?'

'Let's have a look.'

Malcolm parked outside a lilac-painted boutique on a site Charlie was nearly sure had once been occupied by a Marxist bookshop, only that would have been a bit too good to be true. Everywhere else was apparently selling either electronic equipment or large steakwiches and jacket potatoes with cheese-and-onion topping. A man's voice crying the *Evening Post* might have been from another world.

As they walked the needful not-very-many yards, huddled up against the thin rain, Malcolm spoke to Charlie, who for the second time in less than two hours had the experience of being addressed with one-hundred-per-cent unintelligibility by someone who had been making perfect sense a moment before.

'I'm sorry, Malcolm, I must be going round the bend, I couldn't follow a single word of that. Could you try again?'

'My fault,' said Malcolm, blushing a good deal. 'It was supposed to be your friend Cassivellaunus Pugh asking about General Picton. I mean I didn't hear him but I assume he had an American accent. I'm afraid I can't have done it very well.'

'Pembrokeshire man, wasn't he, Picton?' asked Charlie kindly.

'Yes, well part of Dyfed as it is now.'

'Fuck the lot of them,' said Charlie in a considered way.

'Who? Fuck who?'

'The London bastards who changed all the Welsh counties about. Even my kind of Welshman resents that. And then gave them all these crappy ancient names.'

'It was done in the interests of efficiency.' Malcolm was nothing if not fair-minded.

'That's where you're wrong. It was done in in the interests of my bum.'

They plunged from the rain into the dark, echoing tunnel or underpassage that led to a side entrance, sometimes in the past scattered with boozers' muck, immaculate now and with its old cobblestones torn up and replaced by concrete. Indoors the continuing gloom was relieved by what looked like, and indeed proved on closer inspection to be, old-fashioned lamp-posts. More light, treated so as rather to resemble daylight, came from or through the glass ceiling. The walls were got up as shop-fronts, brick-pillared gateways, a park with railings, plastic shrubs and a white planking pavilion. The vast shape of Peter Thomas could be made out towards the back, sitting on a green-and-white-striped canvas chair near a stone-and-wrought-iron well-head. As the arrivals closed in on him the stuff they walked on changed from tiles to gravel.

'The affluent society,' said Peter. 'In the bad old days only very rich people could hope to enjoy surroundings like these. Now they're within the reach of all.'

Charlie went to the polygonal bar in the middle of the concourse and called for service.

'Be there now,' called a voice from out of sight, so not everything had changed.

When drinks had been dealt out Malcolm said, looking about him, 'Well, they've certainly transformed this place.'

'You can't even see where anything was,' said Charlie. 'Can you remember where the bar in the back room was? Where the door into it was?'

'I suppose everywhere's like it now except for a few backwaters like the Bible,' said Malcolm. His expression grew serious and withdrawn. 'It reminds me very strongly of somewhere I went a little while ago. Now where the hell was it?'

Peter had started to breathe heavily. 'Everywhere is not like it. I came up on the bus in a leisurely fashion and stopped on the way at the old Pendle Inn – remember? It's all metal now, would you believe it? Walls, floor, tables, chairs, bar, the whole thing. Bare metal. Matt, not shiny. Including the fast-food device. Naked metal. Except for a dozen or so television screens for the rock videos. I freely grant you may think the differences between that and this can't be considered substantial.'

This was a long speech for Peter, but Malcolm answered up readily enough. 'I expect it appeals to the young people. Same as here.' It was true that as far as could be made out through the murk most of the others present were under thirty or so. Some were under ten and ran about crashing into pieces of furniture.

An expression of ineffable loathing swept over Peter's face but he offered no remark.

'It's not meant to appeal to anyone,' said Charlie. 'That's not the idea. It comes to the brewer's turn to give his pubs a face-lift, and of course he hates forking out a couple of million quid on that, but he can just about face it if he grits his teeth and needn't ever think about it again. So he picks a noted designer and tells him to get on with it. A noted designer gets noted through having photographs of things he's designed published in Swedish magazines and stays noted through winning prizes from international committees sitting in Brasilia. And that's that. The poor old . . .'

His voice faded out as Peter, who had been looking from him to Malcolm and back again with increasing speed, was evidently driven into speech. 'Where's Alun?' he demanded. 'I thought he was supposed to be coming with you.'

'He was,' said Charlie. 'He is. Coming, I mean. Later, though.'

As he spoke a telephone-bell sounded and a youngster with a fearsome slouch moved from behind the bar towards what was apparently a fully-furnished old-style red GPO telephone-box standing on its concrete base near the centre of the area.

Peter said with some rancour, 'But it seems he was present, even active, at the ceremony to honour Brydan, which I gather from Malcolm unluckily went through without the gross humiliation of all parties.'

'Yes to all that, but something suddenly came up.'

'What sort of thing?'

'I don't know.'

The way Charlie said this made Peter glance at him sharply, then at Malcolm warily. But all three sat there in silence under an orange-and-white beach umbrella while they rather helplessly watched the crouching youth advance on them.

'One of you Mr Cellan-Davies?' he asked, pronouncing the first element of the name in a way no Welshman would have done.

Charlie hoped with some earnestness that Malcolm would not issue a correction, but it was all right: he responded after no more than his standard interval for uptake.

'Your friend says he's on his way.' A rearward jerk of the head went with this, to allay any doubts about its source.

For no reason that Charlie could define, the information failed to cheer them up, producing instead a condition almost of gloom, certainly one in which no further talk seemed possible for the foreseeable future. It was good old Malcolm who rose to the occasion with details of the event at St Dogmael's, as seen by him, and some account of Pugh for Peter's benefit while Charlie came comfortably near nodding off in his cabana chair.

Alun turned up really quite soon, striding vitally towards them over the tiles and gravel, grimacing apologies and deprecations of the décor, fetching fresh drinks. Though full of assorted prattle he had no information to offer about the preceding hour or so of his life. Charlie, now roused again to somewhere near full consciousness, found that the slowing-down of his intake and the general relaxation of recent minutes had combined to advance considerably his feeling that he might be drunk. He waited for Alun to finish going on about how today might or might not have been the first time for God knew how long since the four of them had been boozing together, and then said to him,

'I thought what you said at that do this morning was quite good.'

'Oh, well one just has to – '

'Except for that stuff about although Brydan couldn't actually understand Welsh he could nevertheless *understand* it.'

'For Christ's sake that's only what they – '

'I want to get this over to you while I remember and before I have too many drinks. When somebody tells you in Welsh that the cat sat on the mat you won't be able to make out what he's saying unless you know the Welsh for cat and sat and mat. Well, he can draw you a picture. Otherwise it's just gibberish.'

'Well, strictly no doubt – '

'The point is it's unnecessary. They'll be just as pleased to hear how Brydan wrote English with the fire and the passion and the spirit of this, that and the bloody other only possible to a true or real or whatever-you-please Welshman, which if it means anything is debatable to say the least, but whatever it is it's only bullshit, not *nonsense*. Stick to bullshit and we're all in the clear.'

'How many of the people there could appreciate the distinction?'

'I don't know, but I can, and so can you.'

Alun sighed. 'You're right, Charlie. I didn't think. I was careless.'

'Look to it in future, good boy.'

'Hey, Alun.' Malcolm was leaning across and grinning rather. He went on in seriously incompetent but this time intelligible American, 'Would you say, Mr Weaver, that this here is a typical or characteristic Welsh pub?'

There came a noise that began rather like a fart of heroic proportions but soon proved to be made by the exhaustive ripping of the canvas seat of Peter's chair under his buttocks. Luckily he was too fat to fall the whole way through to the ground, remaining clasped round the hips by the metal frame of the chair, his drink intact in his hand. Before he or anyone else could move, a piece of rock music, with the compulsory slap on the third beat of every bar, started up all around them at enormous volume, giving the effect of an omission handsomely redressed.

'Out!' bawled Alun. 'Down drinks and out.'

Having downed his own drink he went over and held the torn chair in position while by fits and starts Peter heaved himself upright and was free. They hurried out after the other two. Nobody looked up at any of them.

'That was a near one,' said Charlie as they assembled at the mouth of the tunnel. The rain had of course grown heavier.

'Well.' Alun was glancing to and fro. 'Lunch. There we are, the very thing. Bengal Tiger Indian Bistro and Takeaway. Well, nearly the very thing. Hang on a minute, lads. Case the joint.'

He dashed across the road in full athletic style, marring the effect hardly at all by holding a newspaper over his head. The three left in the tunnel turned morosely to one another.

'Got to watch him, you know.'

'What's he lined up for us?'

'I'm not quite clear. There was something said about a trip to Courcey.'

'Bit late for that, isn't it? Most of the way back and out again.'

'Not half-past one yet.'

'Do I look all right?' This was Malcolm.

'Yes, you look fine,' said the other two. 'Why, don't you feel all right?'

'Yes, I feel fine. I just wondered if I look all right. Looked all right.'

'No, you look fine.'

'Christ, here he is already.'

Making washout signals as he came, Alun hurried back and joined them in the tunnel. 'Bloody awful. You can't even get − I'll hold it for now. We'd better be moving. I don't think we'll find anywhere bearable round here, so let's head for Courcey right away. There's all sorts of tourist spots there now. Where's your car, Malcolm?'

'Haven't you got yours?'

'Came by minicab. More fun if we all go together.'

It was certainly more crowded than it might have been, but really quite pleasant in the warm damp and the half dark. Charlie was comfortable enough in the back, with Peter's bulk next to his seeing to it that, although Malcolm's car was not particularly small, staying unbudged on corners was no problem. As number one, Alun had naturally secured the front passenger seat, and he was soon twisted most of the way round in it to push on with conversation.

'Nightmare place back there, you know. Like a seaside boarding house hung with fairy lights and log-cabin music playing. Completely empty, of course, in fact no sign anybody had been there ever. A nice-enough female appeared and what could I have, well, I could have a cooked dinner, that's beef dinner or lamb dinner with cheese after, or I could have chicken salad, but you gets the Indian chutney-stand with that if you wants it, and pickled onions. And cheese after.'

'As served in Chittagong,' said Charlie.

'Couldn't I have a curry? No, sorry, it's only English till the evening. The Indian, he don't come on till six. She didn't like telling me, poor little thing. I rather cantankerously pointed out that it said Indian-Continental cuisine outside, which she agreed was the case. And then . . . *then* . . . I asked her who owned the joint, and oh, she looked bloody uncomfortable. And what do you think? Arabs owns it.'

There was a united cry of rage and disgust, given extra punch by the effect of the bump in the road that shook the car at that moment.

'I mean my God,' said Alun, glaring seriously. 'Arabs owning airlines, Arabs owning half London you can sort of . . . But Arabs owning the Bengal Tiger Bistro in a clapped-out industrial village on the edge of a mouldering, rotting former manufacturing centre and coal port in a God-forsaken province, it makes you, well I don't know what it does, it makes you sweat. Or something.'

'It's not only the province's fault,' said Malcolm. 'Perhaps not even chiefly.'

'Nobody said it was, boy, nobody said it was.'

Silence fell in the car. Malcolm drove it perhaps a trifle faster than his habit but safely enough, and they ran into little traffic. For some minutes Charlie dozed. When he woke up it was to hear Alun singing to himself in the front.

'Was it little Nell whose nasty smell diffused general gloom?
Oh no, it wasn't little Nell . . .'

Anyone in a position to compare Alun's style of rendering these phrases with his effort on leaving Sophie's might well have noticed a falling off, a downturn in force and conviction. Charlie hardly took them in. It seemed to be shaping into one of his good days. The rain had stopped, or just as likely they had moved out of it as they approached sea level, and there was watery sunlight. Courcey came up on a signpost. Everything was peaceful and safe.

Before people stopped bothering about such things at all, Courcey Island was widely considered to have received its name from the Norman family of de Courcy who had been lords of nearby Locharne. Various authorities had seen that name as actually a corruption of Corsey, from Welsh *cors*, 'bog, fen' and Old English *ey*, 'island', or possibly from an eponym *Kori* with *ey*, or again had derived it from English *causeway* or *causey* or from the Welsh borrowing of the latter, *cawsai* or *cawsi*. In the manner of authorities anywhere they had never reached agreement, though it remained true that a substantial causeway, last rebuilt in the 1880s, carried traffic the thousand yards or so between mainland and island on a fine broad road. It had only been about half as broad until 1965, in which year Courcey's three goods-and-passenger railway stations had been closed and the single track taken up.

Parts of this had once been known to Charlie, and more than those were no doubt still fresh in Malcolm's mind. How he would have enjoyed imparting them to such as Pugh, and how lucky it was for everybody else that it was not happening. What might it not have done to Peter, fast asleep as he was and from time to time giving what sounded like a grunt of brutish consternation.

Once on the island and through Holmwood, the famous grove of ancient oaks once quite mistakenly thought to have druidic associations, Malcolm took the road to the left. East Courcey was always said to be the Welsh half of the island and its place-names suggested as much, including one or two anglicised ones like Treville, where they were making for. The western side had been English or largely English since Henry II planted settlers there in the 1160s. The former port of Birdarthur and nearly all the beaches of the island, overflowing with visitors in summer, lay on that coast. Along this one there ran for the most part a series of dark-coloured cliffs falling to narrow banks of pebbles or straight into the sea. In places they rose to a couple of hundred feet, their highest point being not far off the highest on Courcey. Hereabouts Malcolm stopped the car by agreement, and the occupants set about hauling themselves into the open, for a breath of air, they said, as well as a pee.

Charlie's first breath or sniff of air brought some redolence or other – salt, heather, pine-bark – that was gone before he could give it a name. He peed conscientiously into a grassy drain at the roadside. It was very quiet, or so he had just started to think when a small scarlet aeroplane picked out with yellow came buzzing over his shoulder in the direction of the Swanset strip. He fought his way up a short damp tussocky slope to the inconsiderable summit, which was marked by a fake Celtic cross of some antiquity, flecked with lichen, and a more recent tablet in a purplish material.

Although he had known right away the spot to make for he had no recollection of having stood here before. He had certainly forgotten how the land dropped gently off on almost every side, giving a view of the mainland through a clump of Scotch firs and in the opposite direction an unsteady blur, if that, where Devon and Cornwall must be, but hiding most of the island itself. There was just one clear outlook down a small twisting valley on to the top of a straggle of bushes and low trees, a band of grey rock and a sunlit stretch of turf so dense and green it made him think of the cloth on a snooker table. He found the whole thing a most agreeable sight. At one time he had thought that there must have been more in such sights than he could merely see, perhaps not in them at all, behind them or beyond them but somehow connected with them, and plenty of poems had seemed to tell him the same story. But although he had stayed on the alert for quite a long while to catch a glimpse of what could not be seen, nothing answering remotely to any of his guesses or inklings had ever looked like turning up. Still, if he happened to stroll about in the country or to come across one of the poems he often found the experience appealing, even today. He started back down the slope.

'Come on, for Christ's sake,' called Alun rather irritably. 'We haven't got all night.'

'Indeed we haven't,' said Charlie, the last back to the car, though not possibly by much. As advertised, the breath of air had cleared his head. 'Look, I was in some sort of torpor or stupor when I let you bring us down this way. You won't find anything in Treville — it's all packed up round there.'

'The pubs'll still be going.'

'And with luck they'll be as nice as the one we've just come from.'

'Let's get going anyhow. No, they won't be trendy there, it's not that sort of place.'

'What are you talking about?' said Charlie as they moved off. 'Everywhere's trendy now unless it's actually starving.'

'I know what he's getting at,' said Peter. 'He means they're more authentic. More Welsh, God help us.'

'More suitable for his television series. Shit, I believe you're right.'

'Where do you want me to go?' asked Malcolm.

'About half a mile along there's our last chance to turn off over to the west side. That must be a better bet, surely.'

'What do you expect to find open there at this time of year?' Alun sounded pained and resentful, as if at ingratitude.

'I don't know, you're the researcher,' said Charlie.

'Hey, I tell you what we could do,' said Alun in an immediately livelier tone that would have revived Charlie's suspicions had they had time to abate, 'we could drop in on old Billy Moger just a bit further on. He'd know all that.'

'I haven't seen him for years. Vanished from sight when he moved out, pretty well. Are you sure he's still living there?'

'Well, he was last week when I rang.'

'Was he now?' Some female connected with Moger drifted up in Charlie's memory, not wife, or if wife then second wife, more likely long-standing lady-friend, but anyway also to do with Alun in the long-ago. 'That's good to hear.'

'I was going through my old address-book.'

'I understand.' Laura something, that was the name.

'Shall I take this right turn or not?' asked Malcolm.

Charlie was fully expecting to be swept into the outskirts of Treville, but after no more than a few hundred yards the car pulled up in front of a bungalow built almost at the roadside. It would hardly have been anyone of Billy Moger's era who had required or accepted an original structure on the lines of a cottage in a whimsical book for children, but perhaps he or someone in between had ripped out the old-time twisty windows and goblin's front door and filled the apertures with steel and pine, and in the same spirit had put sensible housing-estate chimneys there instead of whatever funny-hat arrangements had cheered up the roof before.

'Nasty place he's got here,' said Charlie when Alun had gone to ring the bell.

'Who is this Moger?' asked Peter.

'For years he had that sports shop in Cambridge Street next to the off-licence. Jolly handy, that. Nice little chap. Played a bit for Glamorgan before the war. You remember him.'

'After, too,' said Malcolm. 'Left-arm over the wicket. Used to bring them back from the off.'

'Right, we're summoned,' said Charlie. 'That didn't take long.'

His squint at the garden at the side of the bungalow showed him a walled space landscaped like the small-mammal enclosure at some opulent zoo, including the dry bed of an artificial watercourse. But there were no animals in it and little in the way of vegetation either. On the threshold he was met by a strong but not obnoxious perfume, woody and spicy rather than sweet. He and the others got an outstandingly warm welcome from Laura, fully recognisable to him on sight, a small thin woman in a close-fitting black velvet suit, with piled blonde hair and a more than average allowance of jewellery round neck and wrists. Alun really performed the introductions.

Like a lot of people in Wales, though not only in Wales, Charlie had had a much more extensive education in horrible rooms and houses than in attractive or even so-so ones. So he was not much good on detail when, girded for the worst after what he had seen outside, he came across nothing of the interior loathsome to his practised eye, though others perhaps would have drawn the line at the well-stocked bar that filled one end of the living-room. He did notice flowers all over the place, numerous, varied, fresh, bloody marvellous in fact and, as another department of expertise told him, quite expensive in total, like other visible features. Yes, memory added now that at one period Billy had done very well, even too well for squeamish tastes, out of supplying sports equipment to local schools and other educational institutions, including the gaol. Well, that was how he had got his start.

Where was Billy? Laura rejoined them to say that he would be out in a minute. Charlie had missed her departure, having concentrated on the bar, where at her request Alun had started to deal out drinks. Separate from the others, Peter stood and glanced round with what seemed to Charlie an expectantly censorious air, on the watch for vulgarity, affectation, shoddiness, lingering over a suspect water-colour, moving disappointedly on. Malcolm evidently approved of what he saw, or what he had taken in, was enjoying the party. He still looked fine, though his normal gravity of demeanour had begun to show signs of coming apart, like the descended knot of his tie.

Alun set out to describe the supposed purpose of their call, but as soon as he mentioned eating in Treville or any such place Laura would hear no more.

Her eyes flashed fire as in the nick of time she put a stop to this dangerous, degenerate project. 'Quite out of the question,' she affirmed in her startling deep husky voice. 'I never heard such nonsense in my life. Thank God you mentioned it to me, that's all I can say.'

'We were only thinking of a snack,' said Malcolm.

'*Snack*,' said Laura, thereby banishing the topic. 'So let's be practical. Now – bearing time and trouble in mind the answer's obvious. Sandwiches for four is nothing to me, right?' Right, said Charlie to himself, and another fragment of recall checked in: Laura Makins, cold-lunch counter at the Three Feathers in Kinver Hill. 'No problem, gentlemen. Round again, Alun, and I'll see to it.'

'We can't let you do that,' said Malcolm, looking about for support.

'Don't you tell me what you can and can't let me do, young man.' For the first time she allowed humour to soften her pronouncements. 'I don't often get the chance to show off my talents. For making sandwiches, that is,' she explained, mischievously waving her beringed forefinger. 'Ah, here we are, darling – come along then.'

A small white-haired old man moved slowly but steadily over to the group, smiling and looking from face to face. He wore a burgundy-coloured silk dressing-gown with small white dots and a similarly-patterned scarf high on one side of the neck, where it covered most of a reddened swelling. Alun and Laura between them told him who everybody was, and he shook hands and spoke in a thin voice. She handed him the weak whisky-and-water she had started preparing at first sight of him. He raised the glass and again glanced round the circle.

'I'm not off it, you see,' he said.

'Well, you've got this one here to keep you up to the mark, Billy,' said Alun. 'I bet she keeps it coming at you.'

'No, I'm not off it.'

'What do you think of the England bowling prospects this season?' asked Malcolm. 'Not much real quality there, is there?'

Billy chuckled and winked and nodded. 'Made an honest woman of her, I have.'

'About time too,' said Laura.

'I thought it was about time.'

She settled him now in a low leather chair with wooden arms and a Thai-silk back-cover in squares of red, green and buff. Close by was a small circular table on which stood a box of tissues, a box of mints, a silver pencil and a bowl of daffodils with their stalks cut short. The others moved round.

Laura said clearly but not loudly, 'Alun's only just come back to live down here. He was telling me he's seen a lot of changes.'

Alun described some of the changes, with accompaniment from Charlie and Malcolm. Pauses were inserted for possible contributions from Billy but he confined himself to a monosyllable or two, though as far as anyone there could judge he followed the drift of what was said. After a few minutes Laura shifted them all out to the kitchen, placing Billy at the far end of the long scrubbed table and Alun and Malcolm on either side of him. Alun was put on to opening and pouring wine. With speed and skill Laura prepared sandwiches – cheese and onion, tongue and pickle – for all except Billy, who very cheerfully ate baked beans and a couple of digestive biscuits and drank another weak whisky. The sandwiches were quite tasty and moist enough to arouse Charlie's professional respect and even to induce him to eat most of two of them. Soon they were all gone. Laura offered coffee and then at once disallowed it.

'You won't have time if you're to have a drink in Treville.'

'To hell with that,' said Alun. 'We'd all love some coffee – wouldn't we, boys?'

'Not now, darling. Some of us get a bit tired.'

'Oh. Right.'

They said good-bye to Billy there in the kitchen. When it came to Charlie's turn it struck him that at no time had he seen in him the Billy Moger he used to know. Laura went out to the car with them.

'Bless you for coming, all of you,' she said. 'Hope it wasn't too much of a shock.'

'Oh for Christ's sake,' said Alun.

'No really, it was sweet of you. He'll be cheered up for days now. He'll go over it a hundred times. Well, I'll go over it with him. You could, er . . . if you see any of his old mates you could tell them it's not too bad – you know. I think some of them stay away because they're afraid it's worse than it is. Good luck in Treville. I must say I don't fancy your chances anywhere there.'

By common consent they kept quiet well beyond the point where even the most preternatural powers of hearing, or the most sophisticated technology, could possibly have carried their words to Laura.

Charlie opened. 'So it's established that you didn't know what we were in for,' he said.

'I hope so.' Alun again turned to face rearwards, though less jauntily than before. 'Surely you could tell that straight away. Even I couldn't have carried off pretending I didn't if I did. No, she just said drop in when you're passing, we'd love to see you.'

'And what did you say?'

'I said we might make a trip this way today and if we did we might pop in for a drink. I didn't expect her to be expecting us.'

'I wondered about that,' said Malcolm. 'She could have had all that stuff just by her – tongue, cheese, onion. Not that it wasn't delicious and very good of her to do it.'

'Everything bar the bread,' said Charlie. 'Two large loaves. She got that in on the off-chance. Not negligible, I agree. And it's quite possible she primps herself up like that every day.'

'Poor little bugger,' said Peter.

'Yes, no harm in sparing a thought for him.'

'Indeed, but I was thinking of his wife. How many times she must have told herself of course nobody would come. How disappointed she'd have been if nobody had. For half an hour out of twenty-four times God knows what. All right, she smartened the place up a bit for our benefit. In the remote contingency that we came, that is. Not daring to tell him why. But no mere smartening-up could have done that, what we saw. That's years of work, every day.'

'Are you feeling all right, Peter?' asked Charlie.

'Shut up, Charlie,' said Alun.

'Sorry. Well, there seems to be plenty to be said about her. Not a lot about old Billy.'

Nobody was ready to contest this view there and then.

'One consolation, though,' Charlie went on. 'We haven't got Garth with us to say what is appropriate to such an occasion.'

He got quite a good laugh out of that. Other thoughts he kept to himself, for instance that Laura had known her Alun in not saying anything to him on the telephone about her husband's condition. And likewise, if Alun had plotted everything and known everything in advance he could not have contrived a better position for himself: not only full conversance with the situation there but a huge fund of goodwill and a positive duty to return to the scene. Carte bloody blanche at zero cost. Billy must be dead keen for you to have an afternoon off once in a way, love. Oh well, there it was.

A few pieces of traffic turned up as they in fact reached the outskirts of Treville. As the car ducked down the last little hill before the village, the motto FREE WALES was briefly to be seen daubed on a brick wall in faded and dingy whitewash. An ironic cheer went up.

'Now would that be – ' began Malcolm in his frightening American accent before Alun shushed him.

'Belt up, you stupid bugger. What's the matter with you? You hardly set eyes on that clown and everything you see reminds you of him. Forget him.'

'Remember what happened the last time you invoked him,' said Charlie.

'Dismiss Cadwallader *Twll-Din* Pugh from your mind.'

'Hey, I've thought of the thing to say to him about that slogan there. Show me a Welsh nationalist and I'll show you a cunt.'

'He wouldn't say thank you for showing him a cunt,' said Alun reasonably.

'That's my point, you bloody fool.'

'Oh Christ, it's the drink. Fuddling my mental processes.'

'It's certainly fuddling mine,' said Malcolm, wrenching at the wheel. 'Sorry.'

'And mine, thank God,' said Peter.

Despite everything said just now and earlier, expectation mounted as the time of arrival drew near. They passed traces of the railway station and of some of the eleven worked-out pits in the area, reached the shore and turned along it. Here until quite lately cockles and the edible seaweed laverbread had been harvested. In the village itself rusty galvanised-iron roofs and shop-fronts that needed painting were noticeable. The first pub they went into had in it a half-size snooker-table, a TV set showing a children's programme with the sound turned down and only two people, the barmaid and her boyfriend, who while talking to her fed himself continously from a dispenser apparently called a Peanut Colonel. There was a move to withdraw at once, but Charlie remarked that there was no guarantee of getting a drink elsewhere. Nobody was sure about local licensing hours.

Twenty years before, Charlie had passed a whole day from rising to retiring without a drink. Rising in fact had very nearly not taken place at all: he had believed absolutely, would have told anyone who asked, that death was on him. In that frame of mind he had nevertheless found himself playing a hard game in the crowd that afternoon at Wales v. France in Cardiff. In the evening Sophie and he, then recently married, had been giving a party – too late to cancel. Orange-juice in hand, he had watched fascinated as one by one, with unbelievable speed and totality, his contemporaries had crumpled into drunkenness, their faces and voices disintegrating between one sip and the next. From rather nearer the fray he saw it happen to Malcolm now as they emptied their drinks by the coruscating fruit-machine, saw his eyes swell in time with some event inside him. He took a sudden half-pace forward.

Charlie stayed at Malcolm's right hand for the two-minute walk to the other waterside pub Alun had spotted earlier. The tide was out and a strong, not wholly pleasant smell came blowing off the saltings ahead of them, though there was nothing obvious for anybody to have done about that, nor about the rain that had come back into the air. As far as they could see there were only three or four parked cars about, unusually for any inhabited place in the kingdom. Someone, a middle-aged man, let himself in at a front door and disappeared, the only sign of life, apart from brand-new litter underfoot, at a time when the inhabitants might have been expected to be in full circulation. It seemed as quiet as it had been back there on the hill.

'What do they do here?' Malcolm asked quite distinctly as they crossed a side-road up which nothing moved, not even paper blown by the wind. 'Nowadays, I mean.'

'I don't know. Make lemonade or deodorant I dare say.'

'Some of them must commute to town.'

'No idea.'

'Mind you the unemployment figures for the area are as high as anywhere else in GB, along with Merseyside and parts of north-eastern England.'

'M'm.'

'Well, it's a terrible thing, Charlie, you know. A really . . . monstrous thing. I mean, imagine yourself stuck in a place like this with no prospects, no future, nothing going on. You can see for yourself. No . . . no prospects.'

'Ah.'

'I'd like to know, just out of curiosity, whether Maggie Thatcher's ever been out here, Charlie.'

'I shouldn't think so for a moment, not if she's got any sense. Certainly not since she closed down the first colliery in 1910, I think it was.'

More of this sort of thing soon brought them to the door or doors of the Ship Inn, which by appearance might easily as well have admitted them to a public lecture-theatre or bit of local government. But inside it was not at all like any of that, a typical old-style country pub with electric organ, round tables of pitted copper, triple-decker sandwiches and tremendously badly designed and written local announcements. And also a great many people. This was where they all were.

The considerable noise they were making lessened slightly at the entrance of the four visitors and some of those in view turned and had a look at them. This seemed natural enough at the sight of a group of obvious strangers in unconventional clothes like jackets and ties and including one or two – Peter, perhaps Charlie – worth a second glance anywhere. The hum of normality was about restored by the time they had moved to the further and less crowded end of the room and Charlie had waddled to the counter.

'Nothing for me,' said Malcolm when he was asked.

'Have a soft drink.'

'No I think I'll just go and sit down. You know.'

He sank into an armchair with tangerine loose covers that might have come out of a local auntie's front room, the generic source of most of the furnishings up this end, not least the parchment lampshades. In a moment he seemed to fall asleep. The other three nodded at each other, needing no words.

'That's nice,' said Alun. 'No question about him not driving now.'

'He's not the sort to try and insist,' said Charlie.

'No, but it's good to keep it civilised.'

Having unrestively waited rather longer than strict equity would have entailed, Charlie had his order taken by one of the fellows behind the bar, the one whose locks hung to his shoulders from either side of a bald pate. After unhurriedly assembling the required drinks he in due course uncourteously served them.

'Now we're all right for a bit,' said Charlie. 'More water? Well, how was Gwen?'

'Oh, Christ,' said Alun, and then, almost as differently as possible, 'Oh, Christ.' He stared malevolently at Charlie. 'You bugger.'

'Calm down, old bloke, it's all in the family, won't go any further. Not from me or Peter, that is. One of the reasons I've brought it up while I'm still stone cold sober is to warn you very seriously against letting the slightest suspicion enter Malcolm's head for a moment. He's – '

'Good Lord, what do you take me for?'

The grin lurking in this might not have irritated Charlie if it had not made him want to start grinning himself. 'Don't try and go devil-may-care on me. Listen: no sly quips or digs in the ribs or narrow shaves or delicious hints he couldn't possibly pick up and supposing he did what of it really, eh? He's not as, shall I say resilient as some of those we know.'

Alun betrayed little or none of the embarrassment he might have been expected to feel at this. 'No, of course, don't worry. It was her idea, not mine in the first place. She grabbed me in the Prince of Wales. As I was hoping you hadn't seen but knew you had.'

'But you went along with it. Yes, I saw. Anyway, how was it?'

With this Charlie glanced at Peter in the hope of spreading out the curiosity, making it a little more a matter of public concern, but he was looking here and there in his unfocused way, no bloody use at all.

'Oh, Christ,' said Alun, 'it was a . . . I just scraped home if you know what I mean. She was great fun in the old days but she's, well, she's gone off rather. Is that enough for you?'

'Just right, thanks. What sort of a state was she in when you left?'

'Bit on the subdued side.'

'M'm. I expect she'll liven up when she sees Malcolm, poor old bastard. You know, Alun, it might be a good thing all round if you took in the idea that we've rumbled you. We see through you, chum.'

'If you're talking about Laura . . .'

'No, I am not talking about Laura. The diaconate has given you a clean bill of moral health there. More than you deserve. I mean in general. Can't you sort of concentrate your attentions? Narrow them down a bit?'

'It's all this bloody temptation, you see. Growing in amplitude year by year. The percentage of women between my age-group and puberty, both ends inclusive, is unlikely to rise significantly higher.'

'The lower end doesn't seem to bother you unduly. You saw off that fan in the Glendower without any trouble. Any that I could see. And she was quite a – well, time was when I'd have been a horrible nuisance to her myself.'

'The lower end is largely hypothetical. Rather like the invisible cone that in theory extends upwards from the apex of your ordinary real God-fearing cone. The other way round in this case. More practically the young ones lack the essential security-conferring streak of gratitude to be found in the old ones. No problem resisting that temptation.'

Charlie gazed startled at his empty glass. 'Christ, what's gone wrong with this? Er, from the way you talked about it I didn't think Gwen sounded particularly grateful. I dare say you'll keep your mouth shut, but there's her too. Eh?'

'Yeah, I know.'

Vague Peter might be at times, preoccupied even, but shy on his shout never. He took Charlie's place at the counter and produced a pentagonal slice of plastic in which five one-pound coins were embedded: a children's toy, he would say, for children's money. Something between the used glasses and muscular dystrophy collecting box caught his eye and he bent to see better, fumbling for his spectacles. A moment later he gave a kind of snarling bellow, loud enough anyway to cause a nearby head or two to twist in his direction.

'Wouldn't you bloody know,' he said not much less loudly. 'ASH *yng* sodding *Nghymru. Diolch am* . . . What kind of madhouse . . .'

'Never mind, no one understands it,' said Charlie soothingly.

'Not content with trying to stop me smoking they have the bloody cheek to do it in buggering *Welsh*. It's enough to make you . . .'

He flung out a hand, probably just in contemptuous dismissal, but his fingertips brushed the folded card and sent it fluttering to the floor. Before he could have started to face bending down to ground level the man with the divided hairdo intervened.

'Would you kindly pick that up, please.' He spoke not in any Welsh way but in the thick, unvarying tones of generic middle-north England.

Peter grew flustered, sweat gathering on his upper lip, but still he made no move and it was Alun, as one doubtless used to finding himself the only male in the company capable of bending, who put the notice back on the bar.

'If you want to smoke you'll have to go down the other end.'

'I don't want to bloody smoke,' said Peter, 'that's not the point. I just . . .'

'And lay off the language if you don't mind.' The barman gave them an assessing stare one after the other. 'Welshmen,' he muttered finally and turned away.

On later inquiry it emerged that Malcolm had not in fact been roused up by the mild disturbance and come to see about it, but it looked very much like it at the time. His return to action certainly aroused more notice than his withdrawal had. When he reappeared he could not have been said to look fine any more, not too bad though, and his speech was all right too, at least as regards its utterance. But ten minutes' nap could have done nothing very reconstructive for him, and Charlie at once diagnosed a false dawn, being experienced in dawns of that kind if of no other.

Yet Malcolm started off quite well – he was excited, admittedly, but for the moment in a contained way. 'I've remembered what I was trying to remember, it's all come back to me. That awful place in Harriston we were in, with the railings and the lamp-posts. I knew it reminded me of somewhere but I couldn't think where. Well, it was a pub in Chester we went to when we were staying with our son last year. Very similar. Same sort of idea.'

This was obviously no more than a minor shock to the others.

'Don't you see, I'm saying the place in Harriston was just the same as an *English* pub. That's what they're doing everywhere. Everywhere new here is the same as new things in England, whether it's the university or the restaurants or the supermarkets or what you buy there. What about this place we're in? Is there anything in here to tell you you're in Wales? At last they've found a way of destroying our country, not by poverty but by prosperity. I don't mind so much the decline and the decay, we've faced that before and we've always come through. No, what I abominate is the nauseous fruits of affluence. It's not the rubble I deplore, it's the vile crop that has sprung from it. It spells the end of . . .'

When he paused, less perhaps for breath than to concentrate on not falling over, Charlie said, 'Come and sit down and have a glass of dandelion-and-burdock.'

'I may be drunk but what I'm saying is very important.'

'There's no point in getting worked up about it,' said Peter.

'Oh there isn't, isn't there? It'll be all right with you, when everything's gone and we're left with a language that nobody speaks and Brydan and a few choirs, and Wales is a place on the map and nothing else? That'll be okay, will it?'

'No,' said Peter.

'Well then . . .'

'And if I'd talked in that strain you'd have told me I was bullshitting,' said Alun rather sourly.

'Well, you would have been, wouldn't you?' said Peter. 'You're not Malcolm.'

'Cheers.'

Afterwards Malcolm said he thought he had seen some people laughing at him. Again, he went on altogether as if he really had, granted some further temporary transformation of his character. 'You can laugh if you like,' he opened uncontroversially enough, not looking at anyone in particular. 'Pretty funny sight, a Welshman getting steamed up about Wales. Silly old bugger all in a tizzy about Wales going by the board. Specially funny of course to English people. Silly old Welsh bugger. But they'll be laughing on the other side of their faces before long. Because it's going to be their turn next. In fact it's already – '

That was all they gave him time for, not very much, not very offensive, not at all provocative, but it was enough for them to have fatally had a good look at him. Charlie had not taken in that anything much at all was happening till it was half over. Two or three or four men closed in on Malcolm, obscuring him from view. Voices were raised and some rapid movement seen. Malcolm went sideways over a table, an ordinary wooden one, and a glass or glasses dropped to the floor. The barman who had rebuked Peter threw up the flap of the counter with a crash and strolled forward advancing one shoulder at a time.

'Outside the lot of you,' he bawled. 'You too. Go on, you four. Out before I call the police.'

By now Charlie had reached Malcolm and found him bleeding from the nose. There was blood on his face and hand and jacket, not very much, but some.

'Let me clean him up, eh?'

'All right, but out straight after, see. The other two go now. That includes you, Fatso.'

There were no towels in the Gents, only a hot-air blower. Charlie did what he could with their handkerchiefs. The bleeding had almost stopped.

'I didn't say anything very terrible, did I?' asked Malcolm.

'Not that I heard.'

'So what was it all about?'

'They were rather a rough lot and they reckoned we were misbehaving on their patch.' Charlie decided against a satirical harangue on the demoralising effects of unemployment and inadequate leisure facilities. 'And we knew you meant no harm but they didn't, or they could say they didn't.'

'A bit unfair, chucking us out like that. It was them, those local fellows.'

'Just as well perhaps.'

'Of course I see it was no use arguing. You know, Charlie, I think I must be a bit tight. Probably hurt more if I wasn't, there is that. No thanks, I can manage.'

'Fine bloody pub-crawl we've had, haven't we?'

'Sorry.'

'Not your fault. I suppose Alun made good use of the time. Some of it, anyway.'

Their way out took them through the bar where they had spent most of their short time on the premises.

'I could tell what sort they were the moment they came in.'

'Men that age, you'd think they'd have learnt how to behave by this time.'

4 Peter

1

Peter's getting-up procedures were less taxing to the spirit than Charlie's or Malcolm's but they were no less rigid. They had stopped being what you hurried heedlessly through before you did anything of interest and had turned into a major event of his day, with him very much on his own, which was right for an oldster's day. Among such events it was by far the most strenuous performance. The section that really took it out of him was the actual donning of clothes, refined as this had been over the years, and its heaviest item was the opener, putting his socks on. At one time this had come after instead of before putting his underpants on, but he had noticed that that way round he kept tearing them with his toenails.

Those toenails had in themselves become a disproportion in his life. They tore the pants because they were sharp and jagged, and they had got like that because they had grown too long and broken off, and he had let them grow because these days cutting them was no joke at all. He could not do it in the house because there was no means of trapping the fragments and Muriel would be bound to come across a couple, especially with her bare feet, and that was obviously to be avoided. After experimenting with a camp-stool in the garage and falling off it a good deal he had settled on a garden seat under the rather fine flowering cherry. This restricted him to the warmer months, the wearing of an overcoat being of course ruled out by the degree of bending involved. But at least he could let the parings fly free, and fly they bloody well did, especially the ones that came crunching off his big toes, which were massive enough and moved fast enough to have brought down a sparrow on the wing, though so far this had not occurred.

The socks went on in the bathroom with the aid of a particular low table, height being critical. Heel on table, sock completely on as far as heel, toes on table, sock round heel and up. Quite recently he had at last found the kind of socks he wanted, short with no elastic round the top. They did his swollen ankles good, not by making them swell less but by not constricting them, and so leaving them looking less repulsive and frightening when he undressed at night. Pants on in the bedroom, heel and toe like the socks but at floor level, spot of talc round the scrotum, then trousers two mornings out of every three or so. On the third or so morning he would find chocolate, cream, jam or some combination of these from his bedtime snack smeared over the pair in use, and would have to return to the bathroom, specifically to its mirror for guidance in fixing the braces on the front of the fresh trousers, an area which needless to say had been well out of his direct view these many years.

There was nothing non-standard about the remainder of his dressing routine except perhaps for the use of the long shoe-horn, a rare and much-prized facility he had once mislaid for a whole miserable week, filling the gap as best he might with a silver-plated Georgian serving-spoon from Muriel's kitchen, where it had naturally had to be returned after each application. He had worn the same pair of featureless slipper-types for years now, hoping to die or become bedridden before they fell to pieces and forced him to go to one of these do-the-whole-thing-yourself shoe-shops which he understood were all they had these days.

The part of the course that involved the bathroom hand-basin was less demanding only than the first. The foam went on to his face in two ticks, the sweeps of his razor were bold and swift and he hardly did more with his toothbrush than spread paste over his gums. But even so some bending and stretching and arm-raising was unavoidable, enough to see to it that by the time he was as ready to face the world as he would ever be he was breathing fairly hard and pouring with sweat, especially from his scalp. At one period he had tried to reduce this effect by leaving large parts of himself undried after his bath, but after several weeks of non-stop cold symptoms had surmised a connection and desisted. He went downstairs carrying the sleeveless pullover he would draw carefully over his head when he had cooled off.

Where was Muriel? – this particular morning as every other morning a question to get settled right at the start. Not in her bedroom: its door had stood open and she was an early bird anyway. Not out in the car: he would have heard it. In the garden? Likely enough at the moment, with no rain falling: as she often said, a great deal needed doing in the third of an acre with only Mr Mayhew, who had once worked in the manufacture of metal boxes, coming in to do some of the rough on Tuesdays and Thursdays. At times like this, Peter recalled the brief period when he had magnanimously volunteered now and then to lend a hand himself, and on every occasion had been told off to shift as it might have been five hundred gallon-sized flowerpots from one end of the estate to the other. It was almost as if Muriel would sooner have been able to complain of not being helped than be helped. Well, well, there was no fathoming some people.

Yes, there she was on her knees near the far hedge, getting a place ready to put something into the ground or even actually putting it in. He could not see which from the dining-room windows nor would he have cared at any distance, having disliked gardens ever since having been expected to amuse himself in one otherwise than by pulling up the plants. It was one of his earliest memories (he must have been about four) and his parents' garden had admittedly been much smaller than this, but the lesson had stuck, indeed he had been elaborating it off and on ever since. Gardens, he had long ago perceived, were all about power, from overawing you with their magnificence (sneering at your penury) to rebuking your indolence, mean-mindedness, barbarity, etc. Houses were pretty bad too and in the same way, but there was mitigation there, with so many people having to live in them.

The house he lived in himself, this house, had immeasureably more than that to be said about it. Nowadays there were only two people in it constantly, not more than half a dozen had ever come to stay at once and a maximum of twenty or so might turn up for a party, but almost that number could have found beds and a couple of hundred somewhere to sit. In the dining-room, for instance, the twenty mentioned would have had space to breakfast simultaneously while as many more waited their turn on chairs round the walls. These were smothered with pictures, every single one of which Peter thought was absolutely terrible. Either it was not a picture of anything on earth or else it was nothing like what it was supposed to be a picture of. Over the years he had got as used to them as he could, considering new ones were constantly appearing. Muriel would go up to London and the day after her return the two blokes made of purple plasticine would have been replaced by an arrangement of wavy lines and blobs. A new rug or coffee-table might well have turned up at the same time. And there was nothing he could do about any of it, for as many guessed and very nearly as many had been told, Muriel had money, and the house and most of what was in it were hers. He still wondered occasionally how much difference it would have made if things had been the other way round.

His breakfast stood on a tray at the end of the dining-table, prepared and put there by Mrs Havard, who came in every weekday morning. As always it was half a grapefruit, cereal, toast and coffee in thermos flask. He went to work on the grapefruit with the serrated knife, separating the wedges and swearing once or twice as he encountered awkward partitions between them. Digging them out to eat was no walkover either. Some clung tenaciously to their compartments after being to all appearance cut free, others came only half way out, still joined on by a band of pith. He dealt with such cases by lifting the whole works into the air by the segment and waggling the main body of the fruit in circles until the bond parted and it crashed back on to or near its plate. How different from the accommodating spoonfuls of memory, emerging first go as perfect geometrical segments. The buggers were fighting back, he muttered to himself. Like everything else these days.

The struggle with the grapefruit, though troublesome, had not been really severe, and soon after it was settled he felt he had lost enough heat to make it all right for him to wear his pullover, which was draped over the back of the chair next to him. He muffed reaching for it and the thing slid eagerly to the floor. At the same time he caught a movement through the window and saw Muriel approaching the house. Hurriedly, he bent over in his chair, failed to make contact, got to his feet, crouched down, grabbed the pullover, put it on, sat down again, took three deep breaths. Then a pain, the pain, started up in the left side of his chest.

Try and time them, Dewi had said in a tone faintly suggesting that that would be as good a way as any of occupying himself. Peter uncovered his watch and kept his eyes fixed on it, hoping Muriel would not come into the room. Usually she did not at this stage, indeed he was given his breakfasts in here to be kept out of the way of something or other, but now and then she did, and when she did it was not always with the intention or effect of cheering him up. Describing the pain to Dewi he had mentioned a gripping, squeezing quality and Dewi had said that was characteristic, which was a great relief. He had said too that if things took a turn for the worse he was willing to consider prescribing some pills, adding in a similar spirit that while they would relieve the pain they would not improve his physical state in the smallest degree.

When the pain or series of pains began, a couple of years before, Dewi had asked him about possible sources of stress in his life. Stress? Yes, you know – tension, anxiety, irritation. He had said Muriel was not the easiest of women to get along with and Dewi had not quite managed not to grin, because of course from what the world saw he, Peter, was the difficult one. Well, difficult he might be, difficult he admitted, but not on Muriel's exalted level, surely to God. As to anxiety now, that was good. Fear was the true word for it, simple fear of her tongue, which nothing he had ever thought of would explain away, and specifically an ultimate fear that one day she would carry out her periodic threat to sell the house, which was inevitably in her name, and go back to Yorkshire on her own, leaving him to find a couple of rooms in Emanuel or somewhere. He acknowledged that there was not much dignity about any of this, but again it was hard to see a remedy.

After four minutes and twelve seconds the pain left off. Even before opening his diary he knew it continued the downward trend since Christmas, if that counted for anything. Better ring Dewi later, though, he thought, trying to drive other thoughts away. Well, tomorrow, then.

He had brought himself to start on the cereal, which by his preference was of a resolutely unauthentic type, penurious in things like natural fibre, when he heard the telephone ring in the hall and stop after a few seconds and then Muriel's voice, a wordless mumble from where he sat. After only a few more seconds this too stopped and her heavy footfalls approached the door but stopped just short of it. Peter took a further couple of deep breaths. He had not told her about his chest pains and what Dewi had said about them, because for one thing he doubted whether the news would cut much ice with her, in fact . . . Another thought to leave unexamined.

But when she had evidently changed her mind for the second time and come into the room he almost smiled. At the sight of her it was hard to believe that this not very large figure with the jaunty manner, sort of hemispherical haircut and (at the moment) green plastic knee-pads for gardening could make anyone afraid, except perhaps of being mildly bored. Although they were meeting for the first time that day she did not come over, let alone come over to kiss him. They had not touched each other for nearly ten years.

'William,' she announced, meaning their son, their only child, who by no intention of either had turned up in 1955.

'Oh . . . right.' He gripped the arms of his chair.

'No no, don't bestir yourself,' said Muriel, raising a hand; 'the connection is terminated. Just a tip-off that he'll be collecting some lunch here and might see his way afterwards to shifting a clod or two if the monsoon hasn't broken by then.'

'Oh, great. But it's not Saturday. Or Sunday. How – '

'It's his day off. Estate agents stay open all the time but individual employees have days off. Which has a bearing on the matter in hand in that the said William Thomas is employed by an estate agent.'

Peter nodded wordlessly. The facts had just dropped out of his sight for an instant, but long enough for her to get in.

'I suppose it's easy for people who don't have days on to forget that other people have days off,' she said with an air of illumination. 'I take it you'll be putting your nose in at the Bible later?'

'Yes, I think so, but I'll be – '

'I think so too. He, young William that is, declared his intention of arriving about one so if you roll in pissed at three you won't see a lot of him.'

'Okay, fine.'

'I wonder if you'd mind calling in at that garden centre place off Hatchery Road and picking up some vegetation for me. It's all ordered and ready. Would you mind doing that?'

'No, that's easy.'

'Because do say if you would mind.' Muriel looked gravely at him.

'No, I don't mind a bit. No problem.'

She looked at him a while longer, then, apparently satisfied, flashed a smile (in the sense that it went on and off fast) and clumped out.

He exhaled slowly. There, that had been all right; the smile had been quite well worth having. It was all how she was feeling at any given moment, he told himself, with some conviction for once. She was not too bad really.

He finished his breakfast and went along to the sitting-room, where by now Mrs Havard had been and gone. As usual she had moved every object that could fairly be moved, from matchboxes to sofas, as evidence of her assiduity. When he had as usual shifted everything back where it belonged he settled down with a technical journal and put in a spell of pretending to keep up with his branch of chemical engineering until it was time to be going along to the Bible.

2

Most of those whose marriages have turned out less than well, say, might have been considered to have their ideas of how or why but not to know much about when. According to himself Peter was an exception. If challenged he could have named at least the month and year in which he and Muriel had been making love one night and roughly halfway through in his estimation, what would have been halfway through, rather, she had asked him how much longer he was going to be. He had got out of bed, collected his clothes, dressed in the bathroom and driven over to the Norrises'. He and Charlie had sat up most of the night with a bottle of Scotch while Charlie went on telling him he had not been criminally selfish all his married life and it was not his fault if Muriel disliked it or was indifferent to it. But he had perhaps not managed to take those ideas on board, not quite, then or since.

Anyway, since that night things had accountably never been the same between the Thomases. What it had become inexact to call their lovemaking dwindled in both frequency and duration. After a few years of this it had dawned on Peter that, however strongly Muriel might have disliked it or however deeply indifferent to it she might have been, she expected him to go on going through the motions of providing it in token of still wanting it, and of course not so much it as her. A further decline set in, quite soon followed by the inception of the random verbal punch-ups, and that had been that, rubbed in by separate rooms, no hugs, no endearments. Even perfect love, he used to say to himself, was probably cast out by fear. With all this it was some consolation, though not much, to notice that not even the most colourful punch-ups had anything sexual in them, like references to lovers or what would have been jolliest of the lot, doubts cast on William's paternity, an enormous and surely significant omission.

Peter played back bits of this to himself while he made his way home from the Bible in the middle of a small spinney; he actually managed a new thought on the subject in general. Part of men's earlier average age at death than women's, perhaps a substantial part, might be traceable to wives driving husbands to coronaries single-handed by steadily winding them up with anxiety and rage. Put it to Dewi. But never mind Dewi for now. He focused on the Bible session just over: old Tudor Whittingham, old Owen Thomas, old Vaughan Mowbray and old Arnold Spurling, not to speak of old Garth Pumphrey, who had as good as chaired an impromptu Brains Trust on false teeth, giving unasked a full account of the events leading up to the final installation of his own current set — Peter's mouth tingled at the memory and he clapped a hand over it. But no Charlie, no Alun, no Malcolm. Boding ill, somehow, the last one.

William's smart Audi was thoughtfully parked so as not to block the way to the garage. The time was 1.23, specially selected so as not to do more than brush the fringe of lateness while still allowing mother and son some minutes alone together at the outset. He found them standing by the sitting-room window looking out at the garden and talking about something called mulch or mulching, or rather Muriel was talking about it and went on doing so till a little while after Peter had joined the party. She also remained arm in arm with William throughout, so that on the whole, any kind of Peter/William embrace seemed excluded. William had done what he could in the meantime with waves and cheerful grimaces.

In the end Peter touched his son on the shoulder. 'Hallo, Willie boy, how's it going?'

'Darling, you must have a drink,' Muriel insisted to William. 'Now what would you like?'

'Hallo Dad, fine thanks. Have you got a beer?'

'Sure. What about you, love?'

'Oh, er, anything for me. I don't care.'

'Oh, but you must have a preference. Gin and tonic? Vodka?'

'Is there any dry sherry?'

'I'm afraid not.' Peter never drank sherry himself and he could not remember the last time Muriel had asked for it.

'Oh, well don't bother then.'

'That's no way to talk,' said Peter in his best jocose style. 'Nothing's too much trouble around here. What about a spot of – '

'Is there any wine open?'

'No, but I can easily – '

'Oh, oh, never mind.'

'Come on, Mum, have a glass of wine,' said William.

'If you're going to take that tone,' said his mother, 'what is there for me to do but give in gracefully?'

And of course when Peter got back to the sitting-room with the drinks they were no longer there, they had gone out into the garden. They could have gone out and in half a dozen times while he was looking for something to take down to the basement to open the new case of Muscadet with, and carrying on from there. When he reached them they were strolling, still or again arm in arm, down along the left-hand edge of the lawn with William on the inside, so that to be next to him he would either have to haul the pair of them a good yard to their right or walk on the flower-bed. Neither seemed advisable in the circumstances and he positioned himself instead on Muriel's other side. At the foot of the garden they did not make an about-turn but a right wheel, and stayed in the same relative positions till they were back in the house. It was much the same at lunch: Muriel at the corner of the table, William beside her, Peter at the end on a diagonal from him. They were just sitting down when the telephone rang in the hall and Peter went to answer it.

At his grunt a woman's voice said, 'Is that you, Peter?'

He nearly dropped the handset. He had no breath.

'Mr Peter Thomas?'

'Yes. It's me.'

'Rhiannon here, Peter. Just to ask, are you coming to our party tonight at the Golf Club? Your old haunt. I sent you an invitation.'

'I hadn't really thought. I'm sorry.'

'Do come. It's our house-warming, only the house still isn't properly ready yet so we're having it at the Golf Club. Six-thirty onwards. We'd love you and Muriel to come.'

'I'm afraid we can't. I'm sorry.'

'Can you really not come?'

He wanted to lie but could not, nor, he found, did he know how to say what he felt. 'I just don't think it would be a good idea.'

'Peter, listen. You can't keep out of my way for ever, love. It's incredible we haven't run into each other already by this time. And you think: it'll be much better not out of the blue and with lots of people there, won't it? I can't remember if you've met our daughter Rosemary. She's down from Oxford. Please come.'

'All right. I mean thank you, yes I will. I don't know about Muriel.'

'You turn up anyway then. See you later.'

Peter went on sitting for a moment longer on the pseudo-Chippendale chair by the telephone on to which he had dropped at the first sound of Rhiannon's voice. From there he could see the bottle of Famous Grouse on the kitchen dresser and hesitated. Then he dragged himself to his feet, hurried back to the dining-room and said before he could think better of it, interrupting Muriel to do so,

'That was Rhiannon Weaver inviting us to a party tonight at the Golf Club. Six-thirty.'

'What a merry thought,' said Muriel. 'Just my cup of tea. Two hundred assorted Welsh people standing up talking at the tops of their voices. Right up my street. You go.'

'Yes, I think I will.'

'I wouldn't want to spoil the reunion of two old flames.'

'Six-thirty at the Golf Club did you say, Dad? I've got to be off anyhow about then and it's right on my way, the Club. I suppose there will be females present. Not aged a hundred and fifty I mean.'

'Their daughter for one,' said Peter.

'Great. I can go instead of you, Mum. I can take Dad down and he can get a minicab back. One more drunken-driving conviction evaded.'

'You must be pretty hard up for a bit of skirt if you think Holland Golf Club is likely country,' said Muriel.

'Pretty hard up for a bit of a lot of things is what you quite soon become out at Capel Mererid,' said William. 'Not boredom, though. No supply shortfalls there.'

Shortly before six-thirty Peter settled himself in the passenger-seat of the Audi. He felt what he had not felt for many years, the sensation of one about to sit an exam. William, serious, dark and already thinning at the temples, wearing a rather ugly tie his father had lent him, got behind the wheel. Peter was fond of him, at least liked him better than anybody else he knew, but was shy when alone with him because he found it hard to think of things to say to him that were not likely to bore him. This mattered much less than it would have done if he had been alone with him at all often or for long at a time. Anyway, he need not have worried on this occasion.

William set the car in motion. 'Seat-belt, Dad.'

'Sorry.'

'I can see you'd like to get out of it if you could. You know you're enormously fat, do you? Fatter than ever? No-joke fat? Well of course you do, you could hardly not. The booze I suppose mostly, is it? I'm not saying I blame you, mind.'

'That and the eats. Don't let what I ate for lunch fool you. I'm very good during the day, marvellous during the day, a lettuce-leaf here and half a sardine there, and then I'm sitting on my arse with the telly finished and I start stuffing myself. Cakes mostly. Profiteroles. Brandy-snaps. Anything with cream or jam or chocolate. Also cake, Genoa cake, Dundee cake with almonds. Seed cake with a glass of Malmsey. Like some Victorian female only this is one o'clock in the morning.'

'You can't be hungry, not then. Not really.'

'Well, it's partly giving up smoking. Four years now but then I still feel, you know, is this all there is for tonight? So you start eating. But it's also partly, partly I don't know what to call it. Scared as much as anything I mean. I hope that doesn't sound too much like piling on the agony.' When William said nothing Peter went on. 'Well, there's quite a good selection of things to be scared of when you get to my age, as you may well be able to imagine.'

'And not only then,' said William. 'Yes, I was reading the other day where the fellow said, Welshman too by God, he said carbohydrates, which is what we're talking about, they're tranquillising, just mildly. Well, that clears that up. But are you all right, Dad? You mustn't mind me saying this, but when I first saw you today I didn't think you were looking very well. Nothing wrong, is there? Silly not to tell me if there is.'

Peter told him straight away, sticking to physical facts, making not even the most indirect allusion to Muriel. When he had finished he felt a little better, but not much because of finding he was forced to listen to his own words as if he had been William, and they had sounded rather daunting like that. They drove in silence for a couple of minutes. Then William said,

'Mum still goes on those trips of hers to London, does she?'

'Oh yes, like mad. Every couple of months or so. In fact she's about due for one now.'

'Right, well when she goes, give me a ring and I'll pop down and we could have lunch or whatever you like. Just give me a ring. When Mum's in London.'

'Fine.'

'Or you could come up to me if you felt like it. Never been, have you? Not that there's much to see. There's this pad I share with one of the blokes at work. Miner's cottage it was, quite nice really, with a bit of garden at the back. And I'll tell you something about that garden. We've been there two years all but a few weeks and it hasn't had a fork in it the whole of that time. Don't you think that's interesting?'

Rhiannon was the first person Peter saw at the Golf Club when he went in by the side entrance from the car park and entered the large old-fashioned hall where non-members were entertained. She was standing in its opposite corner but seemed to have caught sight of him even before he saw her. At once she smiled with what looked like pure pleasure, pure affection, though how that could have been he had no idea, and hurried over towards him. He realised he had been afraid of not recognising her after so many years, but when she came in range of his glasses (supposed to be for reading only but kept on most of the time out of inertia) he saw her face had not changed at all – well, a few lines, a fullness under the chin, nothing really, of course her hair was probably a bit touched up. The eyes were the same. Surely she was not going to kiss him but she was, she did.

'This is William,' he said almost without knowing it. 'My son.' He realised something else, that William had not said a word about her, or about Alun either, when he had had the chance. He must know, know something anyway.

'Hallo, William. Rosemary's round the place somewhere.'

The voice was the same too, but he had noticed that already, on the telephone. He said something back and she asked about Muriel. The three talked for some minutes, had drinks, were joined by Rosemary. Peter took in very little: he was too busy looking furtively at Rhiannon and listening to her talking rather than following what she said. Now and then he tried and failed to explain to himself what he hoped to achieve (or perhaps avoid) while present. No sooner was the question sharpened for him by William steering Rosemary away than Alun came up and hailed him with his normal supernormal display of warmth. He was looking disagreeably fit, and well turned out: hair snowier than ever, new pearl-grey suit in some unfamiliar, doubtless fashionable cloth, pink carnation in buttonhole. The effect was in part that of an upper-second-rate actor, one of the sort you wondered about a bit, too, which had to be accidental. But it was fair to say that the comic side of this was almost endearing, Peter considered, nearer to it at least than anything he was likely to come up with himself.

'You have the good fortune,' said Alun with all his vivacity, 'or as some would no doubt call it, the misfortune to find me in a state of euphoria. One based moreover not on artificial stimulants but on sober fact. Two facts. Today I received a commission for seven half-hour television programmes, title to be agreed but something about Wales, what else, all right Peter, and more important, incomparably more important, I wrote a poem, well, got to the end of the first draft. It's been a long time. I don't know whether it's any good but the point is writing it, getting it written, finding you can still do it. Marvellous bloody feeling. Like finding you can still, er . . .'

He fell silent abruptly and with seeming finality, blinking at the floor. After a number of seconds he flung up his head in triumph. 'Sing in the choir, sing in the choir. You thought you'd, er . . .'Another pause followed, but a much shorter one than before. 'Forgotten the harmony, forgotten how the part went, but you've still got it, it's still there. Very much the . . . Ah, here we are, there you are, you old devils, you.'

He turned with rekindled enthusiasm to Charlie and Sophie, to Garth, to Siân Smith and Dorothy Morgan, not abating it even for Dorothy; euphoria had been the word all right. When the cries and embraces of meeting were over Dorothy led Rhiannon away in the direction of a grim-faced female who looked like a retired bouncer in drag and shorty silver wig. Somebody's mother, Peter guessed; it had always to be remembered that there were still quite a lot of people about who had mothers.

Garth, quite natty in his usual tweeds, was eulogising Alun's suit. 'Oh, lovely bit of garment you've got there, boy. Beautiful. Must have cost you a packet.' He reached out and turned a lapel over. 'Of course, I suppose having to look right for all your television appearances, this sort of thing comes off tax, does it?'

'I shouldn't be surprised. My accountant sees to all that. Anyway, what – '

'Do you know how long I've had this suit I'm wearing now?' Garth asked them all in a grim, challenging way. 'Thirty-seven years. You see, I've had a bit of sense, I've taken care of myself. Not like some, eh? Well, you're not as bad as these two, Alun, agreed, but you have let yourself go just a wee bit, come on, admit it now. Under here' – he tapped his chin – 'and here and – '

'I can't do anything about your terrible mind, Garth,' said Alun, grinning harder than before, 'I can't help your inability to notice anything that doesn't directly involve your pathetic self,' he continued, starting to shake with mirth, 'but when you start vaunting your supposed moral superiority, you bloody little cowshed mountebank,' and here he started laughing as he spoke, 'then at least I can tell you to shut your blathering trap before I slam your doubtless irreproachable dentures down your fucking throat.'

By now he and Garth had their arms round each other's shoulders, both of them bent in the middle and red in the face, roaring fit to bust, two old mates who had seen things so much in the same light for so long that they could be carried helplessly away together to a region of feeling no outsider could penetrate or understand. Charlie looked on with an unsettled smile, Peter without expression.

Alun was the first to come round. 'Well,' he said, breathing noisily and sniffing, 'that'll show the little bugger, what? Ah. Ah!' And he dashed off across the room to greet old Owen Thomas and his wife who had just come in the front entrance, near which there also stood a photographer.

'Oh dear, dear,' said Garth, 'there was a performance and no mistake. That boy's got a tongue to him, hasn't he? It's a treat to hear him use the language. God alive, I can't think when I last laughed like that.'

'How's Angharad?' asked Charlie.

'Oh, well enough, thank you, Charlie. Er, well enough.'

'I couldn't follow the bit about the cowshed,' said Peter when Garth had moved away.

'He's a vet, or was, at Capel Mererid. Sheep rather than cows, but you get the general gist. I thought everybody knew that. He doesn't give you a fair chance to forget it.'

'I knew. Well, after all, the mind's got to start going some time.'

'Not very nice, that just now, was it?' said Charlie. 'In fact not at all nice. It's odd, that was exactly what you've always wanted to say to him, you hoped somebody would one day and then when they do it's nothing like the treat you'd been banking on. Bloody . . . bloody little cowshed mountebank was it? M'm. There's trenchant, eh?'

'You think Garth got it?'

'No. If he told Angharad about it she would, but he probably hasn't told her anything for twenty years. No, if he'd got it, that would mean what he said to us about a treat and the rest of it would have had to be ironical and also played just right, and okay, perhaps you can never be absolutely sure a Welshman's not being ironical, not even that one, but playing something even approximately just right – Garth Pumphrey? No. What gets up my nose is Alun thinking he's got away with it. Like . . .'

'Or not caring if he has or not.'

'Correct. I don't think he'd have gone quite as far as that in the old days. Anyway, who cares? Let's get another drink.'

'Why not, it might be our last.'

'Cheers.'

3

Recalling his youthful self in this one respect, though not at all in any other, Peter spent some time trying without success to get Rhiannon on her own. Indeed even this much recall was faint: in those days he might well have brought matters to a head before very long by muttering a blunt directive to move elsewhere or, if it came to it, by seizing an arm and pulling fairly gently. Tonight he followed Rhiannon round tamely and, for the look of the thing, only some of the time. Dorothy Morgan appeared, stayed, went, reappeared, and while she was present and talking, in other words present, the best-case scenario, like Rhiannon and himself spontaneously taking to their heels, would have been no good because she would beyond question have come tearing after them. And when it was not Dorothy it was Percy and Dorothy, then Sophie and Siân again, then Alun briefly again, then old Tudor Whittingham and his wife and old Vaughan Mowbray's lady friend. Well, Peter kept telling himself, she was the hostess. When he saw Gwen approaching he gave up. She would have rumbled him in a moment and let him know about it in one taking-her-time look.

Glass in hand, hardly drunk at all, he stood or walked here and there a few paces at a time. The heavy furniture, dark panelled walls, faded Turkey carpet in a style once seen all over the place but now disappeared everywhere else, or so he thought, persuaded him that nothing here had changed. The hefty flat-fronted gas-fire at the back of the room presumably concealed an open hearth, but if so it had been concealing it as far back as he could remember, whenever that might have been. He worked on it while he went out to the Gents. Though smartened up a little, this too seemed much the same, even to the fetching-up noises coming from one of the cubicles. Everybody had been in their twenties then; well, round about thirty. Now, from round about seventy, all those years of maturity or the prime of life or whatever you called it looked like an interval between two bouts of vomiting. Approximately. Not his genre, more Charlie's.

He went back into the hall trying to recall being in it when he had been round about thirty. It was likely, it was as good as certain that on at least one such occasion, drinking with a mate in the corner there, where you always went if it was unoccupied, or waiting for his father in the bar itself, he had thought of Rhiannon, felt excited about her, looked forward impatiently to seeing her. No doubt, but it had all gone, as finally as his childhood. His eagle two at the sixteenth in 1948 was still with him, though, and the champagne he had stood afterwards in the bar. How awful, he thought.

By this time he had reached the small dining-room that opened off the hall and was also open to non-members, though it was chiefly valued after sundown as a flaking-out facility for members. It was empty and in darkness now. He reached towards the light-switch, then left it and squeezed along the edge of the bare dinner-table to the window. Outside all colour had faded, but there was still a clear view of part of the course, including the pine-woods on one side and, furthest off, the nearly straight line of the cliff-top beyond which on bright days a shimmer was reflected from the sea. Whatever he might have made of this view in the past it looked only bare and desolate to him now, and he had hardly taken a good look at it before retracing his steps and turning the light on after all. His eyes moved half-attentively over the roll of members dead in the two wars: three Thomases in the second, one a cousin from Marlowe Neath, the others unknown to him. He realised he was waiting for Rhiannon to come and join him here. Well, if that sort of thing had ever happened in his life it was certainly not going to do so now. Time to be off.

The throng in the hall had thinned out a little but not much. He bumped into one or two people on his way through, partly because of drink no doubt, his or theirs, more that he had still not really learnt to allow for his increased bulk after the historic escalation of 1984, when he had eliminated all controls at a stroke, bar a few quaint medieval relics like slimline tonic. But he got to the opposite end without knocking anybody down and went to the telephone. Yes, a minicab would be along in five to ten minutes, or so said a girl's voice that sounded almost demented with satisfaction at this prospect.

While he telephoned he had been aware of some disturbance, of raised voices, on the far side of the solid door that separated him from the party. On his return to it he saw that whatever had happened was just over. There was Rhiannon with her daughter watchful at her side, Alun explaining something with a good deal of head-shaking and hand-spreading, William in attendance too. Malcolm and Dorothy Morgan had their arms round Gwen, who seemed to be in tears, and were accompanying her, perhaps forcing her slightly, towards the side entrance of the Club. Everybody else in the room was making no bones about watching and starting to chatter excitedly.

Charlie turned to Peter and said, 'Quite a performance, eh? Pissed out of her mind, of course.'

'I was telephoning.'

'Your loss. It was all over in seconds but she got quite a lot in. Bloody this and fucking that, what would you, and selfish monster and windbag and hypocrite and broken-down Don Juan and phony Welshman. Nothing at all damaging.'

'The broken-down Don Juan part sounds a bit damaging in the circumstances.'

'Well not really, mixed in with all the other stuff. But the whole . . . I mean it was clear enough from the general tone and situation that there was or had been something going on. As it were.'

'Clear to Malcolm, would you say?'

'I don't know. That's his choice, isn't it? I warned him, didn't I, Alun that is, that bloody awful time we went down to Treville. You'd have thought he'd have picked up enough experience by this time.'

'He'll have forgotten it,' said Peter. 'A broken date, do you think?'

Charlie dismissed the question. 'That fucking old fool is going to do some real damage before he's finished. Hell-bent on it.'

'Good thing Gwen didn't actually, you know, say.'

'Yes, admirable self-restraint, what? Admirable buggery. She played it so she can say she didn't say anything any time she feels like it. It's called keeping your options open. Nay, stare not so. Peter, you don't mean you think when a woman loses control she loses control, do you?'

'It's not a settled view of mine, no.'

'Losing control is just another thing they do. Christ, here's another one that doesn't seem to have noticed much what's going on round him. Hey, I'd have given a few bob to be over there a moment ago, Alun saying he hadn't done what no one had said he'd done. Anyway, I think he can be trusted to carry off that part all right. I think I'm a bit pissed, too. You off?'

'I thought I'd just have a word first.'

Charlie glanced over at the Weavers and back at Peter. 'Good luck.'

As Peter joined the group Alun left it, still shaking his head slightly in bewilderment. Face to face with William again, Peter was fully aware for the first time of what his son had said to him in the car and what it meant. The rush of understanding erased from his mind anything he might have been going to say. The girl Rosemary glanced at him sharply, not sure whether he was to be tolerated or not. Rhiannon gave him a little nod and no more, as if acknowledging him at a funeral. He waited. It was all he could think of doing.

'I was just saying, Dad,' said William, 'that crabbed youth has got to make allowances for the impetuous excesses of age,' – sterling stuff, thought Peter, and much better than anything he could have run up on his own account.

'Stupid old cow, you mean,' said Rosemary with plain indignation. 'I wouldn't mind so much if she didn't think she was being interesting.' She looked over her shoulder with no better-disposed an expression. By now Alun was nowhere to be seen.

'I noticed she'd been knocking it back quite a bit recently.' Rhiannon said this in her factual way, then turned brisk. 'Peter, love, I haven't talked to you at all. Let's go off somewhere and have a gas. Quick before Dorothy comes back.'

'I'm away in a minute, Dad,' called William. 'Be in touch now, right? I mean you with me.'

'Yes. Thanks, Willie.'

Rhiannon finished mouthing and signalling to her daughter from a couple of yards off and hurried Peter to the front door, wheeling nimbly round the mother-person he had classified earlier. It was obvious that the old creature was dying to grab her and stop her doing whatever she wanted to do, but she just failed to bring herself to bear in time. He had explained about the minicab and been assured that it would be safer to wait outside. Neither had a hat or coat. As they went down the front steps she took his arm. It was a fine night, overcast but dry and mild and gone altogether dark in the few minutes since he had stood at the dining-room window.

There was plenty of light from the windows behind them, and the traffic was quite busy on the new multi-million-pound double-carriageway that curved round towards town.

'That was quick,' said Peter. 'Where are we going?'

'It wasn't awful leaving like that, was it? I had talked to everyone. It just seemed like such a good time to bugger off. I thought we could go and have a drink somewhere. Well, half a drink it had better be for me – I've had three glasses of wine already. Have you got a nice place you go when you want to be quiet?'

'I wish I had. Everywhere's so noisy these days.'

'I thought there's that place in Hatchery Road, the Italian joint, Mario's is it?'

'Oh, out to dinner, are we?'

'No, love, Alun's got this table at the Glendower later. I'll have to turn up to that, but we can have a gas before. You see, there's a little bar place at the back at whatever it's called where you haven't got to be going to eat. Er, Gwen knows them there. We'll talk about her and the rest of it another time. Actually it's not very nice really,' said Rhiannon, suddenly doubtful. 'I mean it's not very classy. Sort of cheap and cheerful, if you see what I mean.'

Peter saw what she meant almost before they entered Mario's, clearly a former shop converted some short while before at no great outlay of cash or imagination. The front part held a few rows of flimsy tables for four laid with very clean red-and-white check cloths and napkins and a central line of bottled sauces and mustards. Long sticks of bread or biscuit in red-striped transparent plastic lay on every side-plate. A plump, heavily-moustached waiter in a tartan jacket was serving, vocally and with great sweeps of his arm, plates of rather British-looking meat and veg to a quartet of silent youngsters. Their wary, first-date look made Peter feel a good hundred and fifty. He saw that Rhiannon was watching him to gauge his reactions, so he smiled and nodded brightly.

There hastened forward another plump man with a moustache and a notable jacket, one resembling an abbreviated dressing-gown. He too cut the air a good deal, proclaiming himself generally to be the proprietor, and of an Italian restaurant too. His greeting to Rhiannon fell short of kissing her hand but not by much. If he was not Italian himself by blood, which in this part of South Wales and in the catering trade he might quite well have been, he was the next best thing, even perhaps one better: a Welshman putting it on all-out. Peter got something different from him, the graver reception appropriate to a senator or international operatic tenor. 'Mario' or very possibly Mario led them through a curtain of hanging strips of shiny vari-coloured stuff into the back-of-the-shop part of the premises. Here, in a kind of boarding-house interior, a couple of groups of soberly-dressed middle-aged people were drinking reddish or yellowish liquors out of glasses with a band of sugar round the rim or chock-a-block with straws and stirrers. Rhiannon and Peter sat up at a walnut table with barley-sugar legs and found it most handy for their drinks when they came, white wine for her, slimline tonic for him: he wished he had done without his last one or two at the club.

'Not too awful, do you think?' whispered Rhiannon.

'You'll have to speak up if you want me to hear you – deafer by the day. No, it's fine, I could enjoy a drink in a coal-shed as long as there was no music.'

In fact for the first time in his life he felt he could have done with some to take the edge off the silence. It had been all right in the car, but there they had had the driver not to say anything much in front of. After three seconds Peter felt he was never going to speak again. Then he brainily remembered that, except of course for Muriel, mothers liked talking about children and approved of fathers who did too, so he started on William, which allowed him to work in a lot of the necessary crap about houses, neighbourhoods and such. Rhiannon came back along the same lines with bits of Rosemary. Then they got on to the party and she said in a special offhand voice,

'I reckon William quite took to Rosemary, didn't you? Stayed close, anyway.'

'I was impressed by her myself,' said Peter. He meant it, in fact the sudden oblique reminder of the youthful Rhiannon had almost made him catch his breath, but he had to admit it came out sounding like hell. 'She struck me as, as . . .'

'I told you she's going to be a barrister? Arguing in a law-court. She's always had a way with words. Like Alun, I suppose.' She gave him a cautious, measuring look she probably thought he missed. 'William got a girl, has he?'

'I don't really know. I think not at the moment. He has, you know, had girls.'

'Oh, and Rosemary's had boys. Well, I say *had*, I just assume.'

'That's all I can do with William, assume. He's perfectly normal and perfectly fit and he goes about with girls. He's also thirty. And there we are.'

'Yes, and he's sure of himself in a good way. I think that's enough really. To be going on with, I mean. From your point of view.'

'I suppose so.' He went on without thinking much, 'I'm pretty sure my old man had a much better idea of what I used to get up to than I have about my son.'

'I wonder. If he had I doubt if he was any better off in consequence, your dad. But you can't help comparing, I catch myself doing it all the time. And things are much better now. Infinitely better than they used to be.'

'You and Rosemary, you're pretty close, I expect, aren't you?' asked

Peter. Now he sounded sickly as well as fatuous. To improve matters he added, 'People say it's easier for mothers and daughters.'

'No great confidences, just a few little remarks she's dropped from time to time.'

'That make you think that . . . things have got better.'

'M'm. Yeah.'

That seemed to be that for the moment. Peter was not at all sure where this was leading but he could tell it was somewhere, if only from the look of slight tautness about the corners of Rhiannon's mouth that he had seen before. Then he noticed that she was goggling for his benefit at the nearest of their fellow-customers, who he was sure were too far off to hear them and not interested anyway. Oh Christ – Wales for ever, he thought: thirty years in London and further parts and when it came to *certain subjects* you still kept mum when strangers were present, or visible, so as to be on the safe side now, see. He smiled; after a moment of mild astonishment she did the same.

At this very juncture the Mario-figure came bustling up and brilliantly announced to the party in question, 'Your table is ready whenever you like,' making about thirty syllables of it. Just as obligingly they started to move at once.

Rhiannon had evidently used those few moments to decide it was all right for her to go ahead. Not before the diners had well and truly departed, she began, 'What I meant about comparing, mostly anyway, what they don't seem to have now is all that awful routine you had to go through every time. I don't say they actually do any more of, you know, *it*, or less of it, or it's any better or worse when they get there but at least they're spared that. Sometimes when I look back, for a moment I can't credit it. It was like following an instruction manual – well, that's what it *was*, for goodness' sake. Stage one, arm round; stage two, kissing; stage three, more kissing; stage four, hand up top, outside; stage five, same thing, inside; stage six, really rude, not there yet but on the horizon. At one stage per date, max. It's like what some tribe in Africa used to get up to to make it rain before they learnt better. Only this used to go on for months often. And usually never get there. Same for everyone and no exceptions. Or am I exaggerating, do you think?'

'No,' said Peter, who in the last half-minute had found out he had not forgotten everything after all. 'Not in the least. And there were terrible sorts of tips on how to get round the rules.'

'Oh, and we had ours on how not to let them get round the rules. Phew. Could it have been a class thing?'

'I don't know.'

'No, unless it was just the aristocracy did different, because there were plenty of girls from the valleys in Brook Hall – you remember, and they were just the same. A bit nastier about it they were, I used to think, some of them. More cynical. I am exaggerating because it wasn't as clear-cut as that, couldn't have been. But there wasn't much that didn't more or less fit in with it in the end. I remember thinking once or twice at first it might all be Welsh, because of the chapel and everything, but I soon found out it was English as well. In a big way. So then I thought, well if I thought about it at all I thought it must be British. Couldn't be French. Didn't know about the Irish. The last thing was, do you remember those books by an American chap called Oh-something? Charlie was very keen on him. And the Sahara came into it somehow.'

'O'Hara. And the book you mean is *Appointment in Samarra*. I used to have them all at one time. John O'Hara. Good God.'

'That's the chap, but I'm not sure it was that book. Anyway, I started reading whichever it was and I nearly jumped out of my skin, it was exactly the same. That side of life, I mean. And they were meant to be ordinary average people, not millionaires or actresses but not hillbillies either. There was this guy and the dame he fancied, and first time out nothing, he may have kissed her goodnight, I can't remember. Then second time out you were expecting it to be here we go, but it wasn't at all, it was so far and no further the whole way. It was a good deal quicker than it would have been here, but then it's a book, isn't it? But it was the *same . . . thing*. In *America*.'

Peter still had little idea of what was expected of him, if anything. 'Could you call it the old Victorian ideas on their way out?' he suggested, trying not to feel like an exam-paper and failing soon enough. 'How did we ever agree to go along with it?'

She nodded absently and squared up her cigarette-packet and matchbox alongside one of the ornamental grooves that ran the breadth of the table-top. 'Not making yourself cheap, that's what it was all in aid of. Anyway that's what it was called.'

'A charade, in fact.'

'In a way, yes, but it was not-a-charade as well. That was the whole trouble. One moment you said it very, well, cynically and then a second later you'd find you'd said it completely seriously. *Cheap*. I expect the chaps called it something too, didn't they, that whole system?'

'Probably. I think they mostly took it as just part of existence, something you had to put up with, like getting up in the dark to get the bus to go to university. And it was a comfort to know that everybody else was in the same boat. Or you thought they were, which was just as good.'

'Oh, we had that too. Tell me something now, Peter: say a chap's girl had said all right straight away, would that have made him think she was making herself cheap?'

'Not unless he was a shit – he'd have been delighted. After he'd got over his surprise. But then I suppose if she started going round – '

'*That's* right. You can't make yourself cheap just with one person. Still, mustn't take it too seriously. As well as awful bits there were funny bits too, weren't there?' But apparently no funny bits came to mind for the moment. She lit a cigarette and when she went on it was at a reduced speed. 'So I'm glad that whatever Rosemary gets up to or might be going to get up to she's not going to not make herself cheap. It took too much out of people, that way of carrying on. Made them concentrate on the wrong things. And it was easy enough to go off the track without that. And what I saw was only half of it. The chaps' half must have been much worse.'

'We behaved much worse,' said Peter. 'On average.'

'A lot of it, some of it anyway wasn't your fault. I know you think you treated me tremendously badly, love, but you didn't, not really.' For the first time he got a look straight from those grey eyes and now he did catch his breath. 'It's more it sounds bad before you go into what actually happened, which was just we had an affair, not a very long one, though it would have been longer if I'd thought to do different, and you started to be attracted by someone else and we broke up. And it was after that, don't forget, I found I had a bun in the oven, and you took care of things, and *after* that . . . You were in love with someone else. I couldn't have expected you to walk out of it and come back to me, how could I at that stage?'

'I wish I had.'

'That's another matter. I'm sorry, I know we seem to have got on to this rather fast, but it could be ages before we're on our own again when I've had four glasses of plonk. And these days you never know how much time you've got. I wanted to tell you this before anyone starts dying. Just, it was lovely.'

He put out his hand across the table and she took it. 'Yes, it was.'

'So you'd better try and realise that some of the other bits aren't quite as bad as you thought.'

Not much later they were standing in the street outside the Glendower, he with his arm around her waist, she leaning her head on his shoulder. In the minicab, which waited near by now to take him on home, they had held hands all the way but barely spoken.

After about a minute she said, 'Would you like to come in for a drink?'

'No, I'd better be getting back. Unless it would make it easier?'

'No, don't worry about that. Look, I hope you don't think anything I've been saying was to do with anything that happened at the party. Or anything else.'

'No, no trouble there, love. I didn't take in everything about you during our thing together, not as much as I should have done, but I did get that far. So no, I don't think that.'

'Good. There's no reason why we shouldn't go out to dinner, you know.'

'I'll be in touch.'

'Rosemary goes back on Thursday. After that.'

She gave him a quick kiss on the mouth and went. He hung about a little longer, walking to and fro on the pavement with his head turned down and his hands clasped behind his back, not seeing what his eyes were trained on. Then he straightened up and went over to the car and got in the back.

'Cwmgwyrdd now, is it?' asked the driver, an oldster wearing what looked like his grandson's recent cast-offs. 'What part do you want?'

'I'll tell you when we get nearer.'

'Well, it makes a difference to how I go, see, with them shutting the old bridge over the – '

'Just take me there, will you, by any reasonable route.'

The man's head, white and unshorn, slewed intolerably round. 'Are you feeling all right, sir?'

'I'll live. Now kindly do as you're told.'

'*Duw, Duw*, sorry I spoke. Not from round here, are you?'

'No, I'm from . . . from . . . .'

'If you ask me, all the proper Welshmen are leaving Wales.'

'I say, are they really? Well, that's splendid news, by George. Over and out.'

But then when they drove up and the house was in darkness he remembered that Muriel was in Cowbridge, dining and staying the night with English friends she had told him he obviously had no time for, so he was free for over twelve hours.

5 Rhiannon

1

The next morning Rhiannon and Rosemary sat at breakfast in the new house; Alun had only a moment before driven off for West Wales, there to see over a location for something or other. Through most of the carpetless, curtainless ground floor step-ladders stood, their summits linked by heavy old planks, in the midst of opened drums of paint and other applications, silently awaiting the return of the contracted decorators from wherever they had been these last weeks. It was possible to sit in part of the sitting-room, though it helped if you were quite tired out before you started, and to cook and eat in the kitchen. Here the poppies-on-white cotton curtains were up but, for instance, a couple of boxes of plates and saucers had yet to have their contents deployed on the dresser shelves. Nelly, the new black Labrador puppy, lay stretched out in her basket, idly chewing the side of it from time to time in preference to her purple plastic bone.

'Didn't I give you that mug?' asked Rosemary.

'When you were a tiny thing. It's really quite a nice piece of china.'

The vessel referred to was of a rounded many-sided shape that widened at the top, with gilt round the rim and on the built-up handle, apple-blossom portrayed on the sides and 'Mother' in florid cursive lettering. At the moment it held some tea made from lemon-flavoured powder and a slice of real lemon floating on top. Also before Rhiannon were a plate that had an orange and a banana on it and a bowl of tinned pineapple pieces.

Rosemary ran her eye over these materials. 'Is that all your breakfast, just what I see in front of you? Wouldn't you like me to scramble you some eggs?'

'Of course I would, but they're terribly bad for you, eggs. Full of that stuff, you know, gives you heart-attacks. Fatty stuff.'

'And what you've got there is supposed to be good for you, is that right?'

'Yes. Oranges and bananas are full of potassium, which is very important for your liver.'

'Who says so?'

'Dorothy. She knows a lot about it. She's read all sorts of books on it. She sort of keeps up with it.'

'You mean as if it were something like nuclear physics. Nothing to stop her, I suppose. Surely there can't be much potassium left in that,' said Rosemary, nodding at the bowl of pineapple.

'It must be a bit all right, though. It's still fruit.'

'Well yes, I quite see how you must feel your liver needs all the help it can get after a night on the tiles like you've just been on.'

'I wasn't awful, was I?'

'I've never known you awful. Good time had by all, I hope.'

'Well, I had a nice chat with Peter. I think I told you, he's always felt bad about what happened years ago.'

'As well he might,' said Rosemary, but gently.

'No need to go into it all now. Anyway we cleared one or two things up between us.'

'Good, now mind you get a proper lunch. Something cooked, not snacks.'

'No, it'll be a proper lunch all right. You can always rely on old Malcolm to take care of a thing like that. Rather too much so, in fact.'

'How do you mean, Mum?'

'Oh nothing really. I say, talk about living it up. Drinks with one boy-friend last night and a lunch-party and tour with another one today. Dirty little stop-out.'

Unseen, Rosemary smiled for a moment at her mother with no great amusement, even with some sadness, but said only, 'Go over my duties while you're gone.'

'The main thing is that creature there, obviously. Take her out every two hours. And some men are ringing at eleven about an estimate for the roof.'

'I'll get them to ring again later. What time will you be back?'

'I don't know. Could you tell them – '

'Tomorrow morning, then.'

'The thing is, we've already accepted another lot's estimate which is lower, and these ones need to be told we don't want them. So could you tell them? You'd just be passing on a message.'

'Whereas if they found they were talking to the party who'd actually taken the decision not to have them they might fly into a rage. I see. Yes of course. Anything else?'

'Not really. It doesn't seem much to keep you in half the day.'

'Never mind, there's plenty round here that needs putting straight.'

And that puppy to impress, to make sure of being remembered by on future visits, and very sensible too, thought Rhiannon, but revised her thought at the quiet speed with which Rosemary left the room to answer the telephone.

A tabloid newspaper lay open on the breakfast-table, folded back at the horoscope feature, which was quite good fun to read, not that there was anything at all in it, in astrology, whatever Dorothy might say. It was the style of this feature, the clear lay-out and central position of the television programmes, the young-marrieds strip and the twice-weekly political column by old Jimmy Gethin that years ago had given the paper the edge over its rivals as far as Rhiannon was concerned. She still took it even though poor old Jimmy's liver had packed up once for all in the meantime, whether for lack of potassium nobody had said. In fact he had been Alun's pal more than hers, and she had never read his column unless its first paragraph happened to catch her eye by promising an attack on one or other of the couple of far-left politicians whose activities she fitfully noticed. That was about as far as her interest in politics went, and she was not much better when it came to literature: she only paid attention when Alun's concerns came up and, to be quite honest, not very closely even then.

At university, under Gwen's and Dorothy's guidance, she had done her best to put this right by reading or trying to read books on the two subjects and also on art, where some of the pictures had been nice, though not by any means all. But it had never taken, and at about the time she left there she had given up the attempt with relief and shame at the same time. The shame had lasted; it still troubled her to remember the time she had been taken out by a rather small chap doing German Honours, and at the end of the evening he had said wonderingly, 'But you're not interested in anything at all.' She had had no answer then or since; the things that did interest her were too small and spread-over to add up to a subject you could sit an exam in. And that was that, but it would never do to feel all right about it, ever.

She heard Rosemary at the door, and guiltily stuffed back into the packet the cigarette she had started to take out. Pretending to be absorbed in the horoscopes she read that for Leo subjects (like herself) this would be a good day for clinching business deals provided they managed not to let rip with their famous roar.

'That was William. You know, William Thomas.'

'Oh yes,' said Rhiannon, trying to get the right amounts of interest and surprise in.

'It's his day off apparently, so I asked him if he'd like to come over. I hope that's all right.'

'Oh yes of course, good idea. That'll – ' She stopped herself from going on ' – give you something to do with yourself' and substituted ' – be nice' rather feebly and only just in time.

'More tea?'

'No thank you dear. I think I'll go on up now.'

'Give me a yell when you want me.'

In the bathroom Rhiannon hung up her good roomy man's-fit towelling dressing-gown, originally a birthday present to Alun, but after a week or two he had gone back to his Paris one in chartreuse watered silk. Her slippers, knitted by Dorothy in red wool with a green R on each like the colours of the flag, were on the tight side, especially over the left instep, and it tended to be a relief to get them off. The nightdress rather played safe by being just white cotton with broderie-anglaise trimming.

On the glass shelf beside the basin there sat a fresh plastic bottle of natural-herb shampoo with a cardboard thing round its neck. Six such things, she saw on reaching for her glasses, would if sent in get you an absolutely free hanging basket for indoor plants and greenery, so she carefully removed this one and stowed it away in the cabinet. These days almost any special offer found her wide open. Going in for them was a bit like betting on the Derby: you could lose for instance, like that set of chef's kitchen-knives (eight pork-pie seals and cheque for £8.55 incl p&p) that had stayed sharp for about twenty minutes.

She stepped into the shower, a glassed-in job featuring a massive control-dial calibrated and colour-coded like something on the bridge of a nuclear warship. Along with the central heating and parts of the kitchen it was understood to have been newly installed by the previous owner, a garage-proprietor who could not have had anything like his money's-worth out of it before driving his Volvo into a wall – dead of a coronary before he hit, they soothingly said. Rhiannon was still not really used to the shower and kept falling back on trial and error, though no longer seriously afraid of smothering herself with ice-water or saturated steam. The shampoo, which said it was mild enough for her to use it every day, went on, off, on again, staying on for the essential two minutes while she soaped herself, finally and thoroughly off before a burst of cold all over to tone up the skin.

As she stood on the self-drying mat she got going with the bath-towel while gauging the intensity of the sunlight coming through the frosted pane. Arriving at a decision she carefully pat-dried her legs and while they were still damp spread make-up from a tube evenly over them, thus among other things covering up any unattractive veins. A drop of Sure here and there, a dab of talcum top and bottom and then on with the dressing-gown and slippers and across the landing with a call down to Rosemary on the way.

Apart from a couple of bulging black sacks by the window and a frock and suit or so the bedroom was in order, centring on Rhiannon's wonderful old Victorian marble-stand dressing-table with the heavy oval free-standing mirror and a tall jug, itself painted with rose-buds, holding roses from the garden. Here she combed out her hair, telling herself as always how lucky she had been in this department, thick as ever, easy to manage, even now only needing a little touching up. She was still at it when Rosemary came in.

'What's that on your legs, Mum?'

'Sheer Genius. I mean that's what it's called, I noticed particularly. Max Factor. I got it for my face but it turned out too dark. Honey Touch it says as well. I suppose that's a colour, is it?'

'All right, but what's it doing on your legs?'

'Well, it was that or stockings, and the weather's too nice for stockings, I thought.'

'You realise they don't match your hands?'

'Yes of course I do, but men don't think of things like that. Not as a rule.'

Rosemary gave up the matter. During its discussion she had been sorting out the drier and now she began to wield it on her mother's hair, no great test of skill or devotion but pursued steadily enough. As she worked away with blower and comb she glanced round the room, taking particular notice of the female garments on display, but before she could say anything the door was barged aside and Nelly the puppy came running unskilfully in. She seemed not so much thankful at having found the two women as indulgently gratified by the joy and relief her arrival must bring them. After a quick circuit for form's sake she went straight under the bed, starting to growl furiously somewhere in the alto register.

'I should have shut her in downstairs,' said Rosemary.

'She's all right. She's got to learn her way round the house.'

'Wouldn't it be better if she learnt that after she's trained?'

'Well, it's all part of the training, learning not to go when she's up here.' Rosemary leaned over to see what the now emerged puppy was doing. 'You know she's got your slipper, do you?'

'That's all right,' said Rhiannon after checking that the Dorothy slippers were safely on her feet. 'She can have that one.'

'You can't just let her chew away at anything she happens to fancy. That's no way to train her.'

'It'll sort itself out.' Rhiannon considered telling her daughter that she might feel differently about such questions when she had had a couple of children of her own, but let it go. 'You can't watch them all the time. Right, that's fine, dear, thank you. I like it a little bit damp.'

'What, er, what outfit were you proposing to wear for this jaunt, Mum?'

'I thought the blue denim suit – yes, there.'

'M'm.' The accompanying nod was non-committal. 'What else?'

'There's a white cotton sports-shirt with long sleeves that come down out of the cuffs of the jacket. Then if it gets hot I can take the jacket off and roll the sleeves up. Only when he can't see my legs, of course.'

'Hey!' shouted Rosemary at Nelly, who in full view was carelessly lowering her hindquarters towards the carpet. 'Oogh! Urhh!' she added, scooping the puppy up and hurrying her out of the room.

'Don't forget to tell her – '

'I know, Mum, I know.'

Left alone, Rhiannon sat pushing her hair into place at the mirror. She wished very much she could look forward whole-heartedly to the coming excursion. The way Malcolm had sounded over the telephone when he invited her originally, and still more so his manner as he confirmed the arrangement at the Club the previous evening, had puzzled her, troubled her, nothing to do with his old awkwardness which had never been a problem. No, there was something, perhaps the way he had kept pausing as he talked, that had suggested to her that there might be going to be more to this half-day outing than met the eye. Still sitting, she crossed fingers on both hands.

The sound of her daughter's voice from below, duly raised in tones of unreserved triumph and admiration, got her moving again. By the time Rosemary came back to the bedroom she was in pants and bra at the dressing-table mirror putting on foundation.

'Just you think yourself lucky she didn't drop that lot up here is all I can say.'

'I will, I do. Thank you, dear.'

'Right, well now let's just take a look at this, this *suit* we've heard so much about, shall we? Tell me, you like it yourself, do you?'

'Well, I feel nice in it.'

'M'm.' Rosemary accepted the point. 'Any ideas about shoes at all?'

'I thought these,' – lace-ups in the same or much the same blue denim.

There was a bit of a hiccup over the shirt, with an alternative in frilled terracotta silk considered and briefly tried on, but in the end everything went through all right and, after a final squirt of Christmas-present cologne, Rhiannon trooped off downstairs carrying her linen-look sand-coloured shoulder-bag. She wore no jewellery, just her wedding ring.

In the kitchen again Rosemary made coffee and the contents of the bag were gone over in a comparatively relaxed spirit. Compact, spare handkerchief, purse with window showing essential telephone numbers on card, toothbrush – all passed in lenient silence. But then –

'What's *this* for God's sake?' asked Rosemary, sounding at the end of her tether.

'Plastic mac. Rolled up.'

'I'm not blind, you know. *Honestly*, Mum. *Christ*. Why haven't you got an umbrella?'

'I keep losing them. Leaving them in places.'

'There are ones that fold which you clearly haven't seen, and go in your bag and don't cost the earth.'

'Well, I haven't got one.'

'M'm. I suppose there's a hat to match, is there?'

'No, there's a hood attached to the collar that hangs over my eyes. I'll wear it all through lunch if you don't look out.'

Rosemary peered into the bag. 'Funny, I can't find any wellies here.'

'You wait, I'll fetch Dad's galoshes in a minute.'

'I'd better get you my umbrella.'

'No, I'll lose it. And there's no need to treat me as if I'm fourteen years old.'

'Oh yes there is, because that's all you are. When I was that age you were much older, but now you've gone back. You are fourteen years old. Aren't you?'

'M'm,' whined Rhiannon, cringing and trotting her feet on the floor.

The telephone rang. Rosemary was there first and asked who was calling. With a face of stone she passed her mother the handset. 'Gwen.'

'Hallo Gwen.'

'Rhiannon dear, this is old *Gwen*.' These words and the way they were spoken were enough to banish expectation that any sort of genuine apology or voicing of regret might be at hand. 'Thank you for a super party. I thoroughly enjoyed myself, in fact it rather seems a bit too thoroughly towards the end and got sort of carried away. Over the top I believe you're supposed to call it nowadays. I hope it wasn't too embarrassing for you.'

'That's all right.'

'I'm afraid I do tend to get ever so slightly cross with poor dear Alun from time to time over, well what the hell is it over, I suppose you'd have to call it *Wales* I'm sorry to say. The thing is that, you know, according to me there's a touch of the stage Welshman about him, he says so himself, fair play, but perhaps it's more than a touch – still, and he thinks I'm a dried up schoolmarm. Well, there we are, and it's all right until I drink too fast because I'm having a good time and Alun says something to do with I don't know what and then I find I've – '

'That's all right, dear. All forgotten.'

'Well . . . It wasn't very seemly, I'm afraid. Turning nasty in my drink. Alun about?'

'No, he's away all day today.'

'I'll talk to him again. It really was a fantastic party. I'll ring you later.'

'Good-bye, love.'

'There's lucky you've got a fine day for your excursion now. Young Malcolm's on pins. Cheers.'

Rosemary, who after some hesitation had stayed in earshot, gave her mother what could not but be an inquiring look and got a kind of mock-doleful one back.

'She got cross about something Dad said about Wales.'

'Oh I *see*. Golly, what a terrific help. Must have cost her a bomb to come clean like that.'

'Well it is quite, a help I mean. One of us had to work out a way of us going on being friends.'

'Had to? She's not nice enough to be a friend of yours.'

'She's not so bad. When it's been long enough that sort of thing stops mattering.'

'You let her down too lightly.'

'It's much too late to start letting people like Gwen down heavily. Let's go outside. Malcolm's obviously on his way.'

Rhiannon picked up her shoulder-bag. As they moved Rosemary put an arm round her waist.

'Don't you mind about, well, any of it?'

'What are you talking about, of course I bloody well mind. But that's all I do, I stop myself doing any more than that. Like brooding or going back or joining things up, no point in it. As long as I don't *know*. And this isn't knowing.'

'Mum, I wish you'd let me – '

'Let's not say any more about it now.'

The garden in front of the house was not large but it had the bright green grass often to be found in this part of the world and a few flowers in half-overgrown beds, including an unexpected treat in the shape of a large clump of Canterbury bells. Nelly crashed into the side of it, then doubled back up the path effortlessly surmounting the obstacle presented by each three-inch-deep step. A good view stretched almost due south, over woods and shadowed lawns down over an unseen cliff to a wide stretch of sand shining wetly in the sun and, about as far out at the moment as it ever went hereabouts, the sea with half a dozen small boats sailing. Some cloud was drifting near the horizon but not much and none of it dark. There was nothing ugly or dull anywhere.

'You are looking forward to this do, aren't you, Mum?'

'Oh yes. Well . . . yes.'

'What's the not-so-good part?'

'Well, he's . . . He's a very sweet chap without a nasty or unkind thought in his head but he's a bit wrapped up in himself. He's liable to say things when he hasn't thought how they'll affect other people, just because he wants to say them. Just sort of blurts them out.'

'Such as he's never loved anybody but you in all his life?'

'Sort of thing, yeah.'

'Well if it's no worse I don't think you have much to worry about. Surely you can manage that. You must have had plenty of practice.'

'Oh, come on, dear.'

Rosemary looked at her mother for a moment before she spoke again. 'Of course, I suppose he might embarrass you about Gwen and so on.'

'No, he understands about not doing things like that, and besides he won't think anything happened.'

'How do you mean, Mum?'

'She'll have made him believe her version.'

'*Made* him?'

'Yes, nothing to it with him if she sticks to it, and she will.'

'Well, I dare say you'd know.'

Turning to address the dog, who watched her with an air of stark terror, Rhiannon said, 'You're not coming today. I'm sorry, but you're not.'

'Oh my God,' said Rosemary. 'You don't seriously imagine she can understand you, I hope.'

'It wouldn't do to be too sure of that. Probably not now, but she'll understand everything like that by the time she's grown up, and there's no knowing when they start. All part of the training.'

'Well, she's your dog . . . Is this him now?'

'I think . . . Yes.'

'Mum, if you're going to go out looking as nice as you do now I'm afraid you'll just have to grit your teeth and face up to him saying he loves you. Now . . .'

Mother and daughter proceeded to stand to. Without waiting for orders Rosemary went and dragged the puppy out from the laurel bush she had bolted under and held her in her arms. Rhiannon turned and put her hair right by her reflection in a sitting-room window, then neatly snapped off the half-open yellow rose she had had her eye on all along but had left on the plant as long as possible. Finally the two moved a little apart from each other so as not to look too lined-up and organised.

When he had got out of his very shiny bright-blue car and at a second attempt shut its driver's door, Malcolm revealed himself to be wearing a hacking jacket in dark red, green and fawn checks that were too large by an incredibly small amount, cavalry-twill trousers he must have been uncommonly fond of, a pale green I'm-going-out-for-the-day-with-my-old-girl-friend cravat or ascot and, thank goodness, a plain shirt and ordinary brown lace-up shoes. Seen closer to, he proved to have an ample shaving-cut on his cheek, about like a boil on the end of his nose to him and not worth a second glance to anybody else. He carried a florist's plastic-wrapped bouquet of a good forty-quid's-worth of red roses and pink carnations which he handed over to Rhiannon fast and at arm's length.

'Lovely to see you,' he muttered, obviously discarding on the spot an earlier draft, and called 'Hallo' with unmeant abruptness to Rosemary, whom he had met more than once before but never for long, and had not bargained on seeing now. Then he took in the puppy and loosened up a little. 'Ah, now here's a splendid fellow and no mistake.'

'Hallo, Malcolm,' said Rosemary, 'female fellow actually,' and went on with exemplary stuff about how he would not have said that if he had been on the spot just earlier, the awful chewing, etc. Rhiannon fixed the yellow rose in his button-hole and passed the bouquet to Rosemary, who had set Nelly down on the grass as now to be considered defused.

'Put them in that pretty Wedgwood jug – they'll look marvellous in there – and find somewhere in the cool for them.' Rhiannon was too shy herself to embark on a full-treatment head-on thank you. 'We'll decide on a proper place when I get back. That won't be before five at the earliest – I've got one or two things to see to in town first.' The last bit was said looking over her daughter's shoulder.

2

Immediately upon getting into the car beside Malcolm, Rhiannon noticed a peaked cap in nearly the same pattern as his jacket folded up on the shelf in front of him. All she could do about that was hope he had already tried this and thought better of it, rather than that he was keeping it by him to spring on her later. Anyway she sighed comfortably, or tried to. There was a faint pleasant smell hanging about and the whole interior told of hours of tidying and cleaning. In a way she hardly understood, it was like something she remembered from years ago: she had complimented Malcolm on his clear neat handwriting and he had thanked her and said, well, he reckoned however boring or no-good what he wrote might be, at least whoever it was would be spared the extra chore of deciphering it. Like a lecturer's duty to be audible, he had said.

The first few minutes passed easily enough with chat about Rosemary, then Alun briefly, then Gwen no more briefly – Rhiannon's idea, that, to rub in that the subject was ordinary. The next few went even more easily with taking notice of the approaches to Courcey and after some delay the island itself. She had been along here quite recently with some of the crowd for a Sunday-lunchtime drink at the King Arthur just off the causeway, a brief or single drink as it had turned out, because the one huge bar had been full of fat young left-wing activists from a weekend school ordering things like blue curaçao with passion-fruit juice. But they were soon past there now and on to where she had not been for at least ten years, probably a good deal more.

To Rhiannon the greenery looked greener and also thicker than it had, the hill-tops perhaps not as high, but it was hard to notice when the whole place was so tremendously more crowded. Approaching Chaucer Bay down the west road they ran into traffic like a Saturday morning in town: cars, buses from Cardiff and – she was nearly sure – Hamburg, bikes and of course caravans, of which some hundreds were stationed in lines like those of a military cantonment across the whole width of the furze-covered slope that faced the bay.

'Sorry about this,' said Malcolm as they came to another halt. Far from sorry, he looked cheered up by the thought of how much worse matters would have to get before he had to decide or do anything.

'We've got plenty of time.' With a qualm she realised how much.

'I'm glad I allowed for it. But it is remarkable, eleven-thirty midweek and still in school term.'

Rhiannon mentioned the marvellous weather and said to herself that that was good old Malcolm for you: it would simply never have occurred to him to start going on about where did all the money come from was what some of us would have liked to know, and so this was what a recession meant, and the black economy and minimum-wage agreements and the closed shop and who ever cared a curse for the pensioners. Everybody else she could think of for the moment except Rosemary would have been well into that by now. And Alun unless there had been other people around too.

They moved on a few more yards and round a bend. Malcolm was keeping fussily closed up to the car in front, but she had plenty of room to see the shingly, littered way on to the beach through a gap in the cliff and the half-naked people hurrying along it, all loaded with food and drink containers, tents, boats, sports kits, games, anything and everything for children – plenty of them about, school term or no school term. When they drove past a minute later Rhiannon got a squint at the sort of village of plastic stalls and booths that had sprung up to screw the visitors in every available line, cosmetic, decorative, educational, you name it, some of them not so plastic, but surely . . . A beach-boutique on the beach? In South Wales? Now?

Then the lights changed and they started squeezing their way up the hill on the far side between the groups of young men straggling down from the car-park with no shirts on, satisfied with that being all right and not bothering about looking horrible, being it too for not bothering. From the top Rhiannon had a view of the whole of the long, wide expanse of sand scattered over with moving or still figures as she had never seen it before. Some had wandered along as far as Rundle Bay, which they would have to move back from when the tide came up or face a steep climb up to the road, all right in the day, she remembered, but not much fun after dark with a pushy chap trying to give you a hand.

'Seems a long time ago, doesn't it?'

For Malcolm, this bit of advanced thought-reading was uncanny. She gave him a special look of appreciation before saying, 'Yes, thank God.'

'What? I meant, you know, going on the beach and bathing and what-not the way everyone used to.'

'That's what I meant. Yes, everyone did use to, didn't they? Coming for a swim?' She speeded up before he could think he was being asked to come for a swim now. 'Coming out to Courcey with us, and you just went along without thinking. Like, well, like a lot of things then. I never really liked swimming.'

'As I remember you were pretty good at it.'

'Not bad, and of course it was lovely in the water once you'd survived going in, but awful being out. Hoping you looked wonderful with wet hair and feeling it standing out in the wind and starting to go like straw.'

'Surely, didn't girls wear caps in those days? Bathing caps I mean.'

'Only if you didn't mind your face going the size of a nut. It's amazing thinking of it now, I can hardly believe it. Sort of half sitting with your legs out to the side and smiling and trying to feel if half your bottom was out of your bathing-costume. And it wasn't just me either – Gwen was the same, Siân, Dorothy, everyone. We used to – '

'But you all seemed so absolutely marvellously . . .'

'Poised? You should have seen us. All that awful tanning. I remember a serious discussion in Brook Hall about how red in the face you could afford to let yourself get at a time. And what you did about the hair on your legs and arms. Choices to be weighed up there. Snags to all of them.'

'But I mean you did enjoy it,' said Malcolm anxiously. 'Parts of it.'

'Oh yes. You noticed things like your hair and what horrible stuff sand is but you didn't really take it in. You were wondering how it was going and what would happen next and whether you could handle it. We weren't poised really, just trying not to give anything away. Of course, I don't suppose it was all plain sailing for the chaps,' she wound up thoughtfully.

'No.' He took a vigilant look at the now-empty road ahead. 'No, it certainly wasn't,' he added.

After waiting for a moment she started again. 'It wasn't only going on the beach, not being poised. It was a big one, the beach, but it didn't really touch dancing.' When she saw Malcolm smiling and blinking uncertainly she went on, 'You know, going to a dance. With a band and partners and quicksteps and all that. Sticking together was the thing. Dorothy used to get us on parade in Brook and make sure we'd all been to the lav before we started so there'd be no sneaking away later. Then you'd stand in a bunch waiting to be asked for a dance and wanting to bite your nails and hoping the bra-strap you should have pinned was still behind your dress-strap. I was, anyway. Didn't you worry about things like that?'

'Yes, I suppose I must have done.'

She thought to herself she might have another try later. So far she had obviously not been going the right way about getting him to say he had gone through the same little agonies as she and all the others had, which might have helped him to see that it worked the other way round as well, that she in her way had been as embarrassed and incompetent as he in his. The idea was to show him that she was not the curious creature, something between Snow White and a wild animal, that he had seemed to take her for, but an actual friend of his, and by now quite an old one. Well, there was still a lot of time.

'Those days, you know,' he said now, with a hint of wisdom coming up. 'All I can say is I hope there were certain, shall I say mitigations.'

'Oh *yes* Malcolm, don't get the wrong idea. How awful, I was only – '

'Because this today, after all, we are, well, taking a stroll down *Memory Lane*.' He said this as if he thought he had just invented the expression, or at least was betting she had not come across it lately.

'That wasn't there before,' she said, so promptly that it took him a moment to see she meant something real, something in a field they were passing, a kind of cabin or pavilion with a factory-built look and talkative notices done in very aggressive lettering about things to eat in the basket or in the bag. There was a mass of tyre-tracks round it but nobody in range just then. Seen like that in the unexpected strong sunlight it seemed the sort of place you were meant to admire without wanting to go there, like a piece of a new housing project in Mexico.

'How vile,' said Malcolm with feeling. 'New to me too, I think. Just spring up behind your back. Same everywhere you go these days.'

That last phrase kept coming up in Rhiannon's hearing, often along with another one about it being a waste of breath. It seemed to hit them all sooner or later, even someone like honest old Malcolm who never wondered where all the money was coming from. Once he got into this one the conversation would at least stay out of harm's way a bit longer. But nothing followed, and when he went on it was in a new, dreamy sort of tone, not much of a good sign with him.

'They say people change over the years,' he began, and seemed set to end too for a while before hurrying on, 'And indeed it does often happen. You remember a fellow called Miles Garrod? Used to act a lot. Quite good he was. He played Marlow in *She Stoops to Conquer* in the Arts Theatre.'

'Oh yes,' lied Rhiannon. When it was not going to make a difference she always did that except with Alun; it seemed fussy and cocky not to and you were going to get the rest of it anyway. This was a general policy of hers. People sometimes wondered gratefully how it was that she had never heard any stories before.

'Well, you wouldn't recognise him now, Rhi, that I guarantee. I bumped into him just a few months ago, at a wedding in Caerhays. Or rather I didn't bump into him, praise be, a fellow said there's old Miles Garrod, I said where, the fellow said there, and there he was, totally different. A different person. Not specially old-looking or unprepossessing. Just altogether different. A different individual.'

Having shown that one who was in charge he could have afforded to throw in something about what Miles Garrod was up to these days, but no. Returning to the dreamy tone and unmistakably starting paragraph 2, Malcolm said, 'But some people haven't changed, or only imperceptibly. You, Rhiannon Weaver, you haven't changed, not you. You're still the same person as the one I knew, well, let's call it *then*, shall we?'

'What nonsense, I've put on at least – '

'No, no, basically you're quite unchanged. The way you move, your glance, everything. The first sight of you that very first evening . . .'

She let him run on, but stayed alert for any wandering off into dodgy territory. Sudden blurtings of the type mentioned to Rosemary could not be guarded against, only watched for.

' . . . last glimpse of you eight years ago . . .'

A bit longer than that, but he had put it down very firmly, and what of it anyway. Not far now, surely.

' . . . never more than a few minutes at a time . . .'

Well, there again she seemed to remember proper evenings, even a weekend visit or two, in fact, certainly one thorough enough to have included a couple of chats with Gwen about the forthcoming arrival of what had turned out to be Rosemary's elder sister in 1959, but if he preferred to see it like this, well, fine with her.

' . . . I was seeing you for the first time since *then*. Ah, when I used to read about people feeling the years dropping away I thought it was just a phrase, just a fancy. But it's what *happened*.' He looked at her a little bit wildly but quite briefly out of the corner of his eye. 'And I'd known all along it would. Don't ask me how,' he told her, to be on the safe side.

STOGUMBER 1 PETERSTOW 2½ the signpost said, and Peterstow was where they were scheduled to have lunch. How many minutes did that mean? Five? One and a quarter? Rhiannon crossed the fingers of her left hand. It was awful to think the thought in this way, but hopeless not to: if things got no dicier than at present, then no problem. They had got as far as they had pretty fast, true, and unassisted by drink, but he might have been encouraged by not having had to meet her eye any of the time because of driving, and he had not actually *said* anything yet and it might all blow over.

The car came to the crest in the road a hundred feet or so above Stogumber village and from the sea on their right, limitless now, to the dense greenery on their left nothing showed that time had gone by.

'I don't just mean of course you're unchanged on the outside,' said Malcolm, dashing what could never have been more than a faint hope. 'Anybody with half an eye can see that.' He paused and drew in his breath. 'I mean on the inside too. But then I don't think anybody changes there much, do you? On the inside?'

She tried to consider it. 'No, I shouldn't think so probably.'

'Now I know I've changed a lot on the outside. A decrepit old bloke is what I've become. No complaints but that's how it is.' He wagged his head from side to side as he sat behind the wheel.

'I'm not having that,' she said indignantly. 'Decrepit is the absolute opposite of what you are. You're in jolly good nick and fit-looking and you've kept your hair and everything. You could pass for, for a much younger man.'

It had never been Malcolm's way even to try to hide things like pleasure at compliments, and here was one department in which he had certainly not changed. Another was making it very easy for the other person to tell when a compliment was called for and roughly how it should go, and then still enjoying it when it came. 'Oh, honestly, Rhi,' he said now a couple of times, continuing quite soon, 'Anyway, I'm still pretty much the same on the inside.'

Dumbly-dumbly-dumbly-dum on the inside, she thought to herself, waiting to hear how, dumbly-dumbly-dumbly-dum on the outside, but crossing her fingers again. But then when it came it was fine, in the same style as before, covering rather more ground, not much though: incurable romantic – always tended to expect too much from life – rather envied practical man who just got on with things – triumph of hope over experience – incurable romantic – count your blessings – help us get through life – never really wanted to be one of the down-to-earth sort that just stuck to the job in hand – too old to change now, he maintained firmly. Matters took a slight turn for the worse after that with him saying how much he had been looking forward to today and how he still had his hopes for the future, but he stayed vague on that and quite soon stopped. The end of the beginning, with luck.

They were in and out of Stogumber itself in not much more time than it took to notice a jumble of flags, posters and stickers coloured lime-green, yellow, pinky-red and black and white. Then having turned up left along the further edge of the little valley they came to another signpost, one of a new sort in dark green with a picture of a wigwam on it and thin white print which was quite easy to read from close to. This lot said Peterstow 0.8 km, and no doubt if you went the way it pointed you got there in the end.

Rhiannon had been hoping and expecting to recognise the village when they came to it, but she failed to do so. There was a raised stretch of grass with some lumps of grey-white stone here and there, and an old drinking-fountain sort of built into the side of the slope, the remains at least of such a thing with a place where a chained cup might once have been joined on. Next to it she made out four or five names carved on a tablet and realised she was looking at a local war memorial. Here and there were hefty cottages in a darker stone or in a dark brick behind low white gates, and on the far corner a larger building done with beams and tiles. A sign said it was the Powys Arms and also mentioned old-fashioned things like finest ales and ciders. Although there were other cars about, it was still possible to park near the front door.

Malcolm did that, pulling on the hand-brake with a rasping flourish. 'Well,' he said, turning to Rhiannon and smiling at her with his eyes crinkled up – 'here we are.' He was behaving as though he had given her a costly present which only he in his sensitivity could have chosen for her, and looked very sweet and sitting up and begging for a smart clip round the ear.

'Marvellous,' she said.

He got out of his seat and came round to open her door, moving quite fast but not as fast as she did to forestall him. These days she never liked people 'helping' her out of or off things unless she could do a crone imitation with it, and not much even then. He arrived a second after she had got both feet to the ground, but in the nick of time to alert her against leaving behind the shoulder-bag she was just picking up. As they strolled towards the pub he put his hand round her elbow in case she started to fall over or tried to walk into a wall. She could just about recall him using this instant this-one's-mine-you-see indicator once or twice when he had taken her out in the old days. Actually this time it came in useful for stopping her from going ahead and heading into the pub just like that.

He glanced at her again and said, 'Hasn't changed a lot, has it?'

'Doesn't seem to have done.'

'Apart from the rebricking along under the roof there and taking the lean-to part into the main structure and paving over where the old well was. Not to mention the wall round the car-park. And wasn't there a hut in that corner?'

Rhiannon had no answer to that. She nodded her head slowly and mumbled to herself.

'And obviously the tables. Still, it is very much as it was. In essentials you might say.'

'M'm.'

'The rubbish-bins aren't very pretty but at least they're practical.'

After a last satisfied look around he made to steer her through the doorway, but again she was too quick for him, thinking that it – being too quick for a man – was not something she was often called upon to be any more. Inside, she looked round with a show of interest. Whether it was very much as it had been she had no idea, but anyway it was not crowded yet and not noisy. The only thing she noticed was the little brass rails or railings round the tops of some of the tables, to keep you on your toes when you – no, rubbish, she told herself, off a ship, ten to one, a point Malcolm might well be just going to clear up for her. He kept quiet on that, though, saying only that of course he had no idea whether the place was any good these days, a whopper if ever she had heard one.

The place, as regards food and drink, which he called victuals, was good enough, but with him there that counted as no more than a start. Of all the men she knew, he was right out in front the likeliest to be ignored at the bar, given a table the kitchen door banged into, brought his first course while later arrivals were drinking up their coffee, overcharged. However, he escaped without so much as a dab of butter on that cravat of his. By the end of lunch, sipping cautiously at a small glass of green Chartreuse, her treat drink, she felt quite relaxed. Parts of the action, like him finding a speck on a wineglass and waving it slowly to and fro to get it changed, or calling for a 'proper' pepper-mill and keeping on the lookout till it came, were telling-Rosemary material rather than good fun at the time, but the dialogue, or rather what he said, was unimprovable, boring almost to a fault. She forgot her misgivings as he took her through the histories of more people whose names meant nothing to her. They even got on to Wales, of all topics; well, friends in England had taken to going on a bit about England. When Malcolm said you got very unpopular for saying Wales was in a bad way, she thought at once of his nose and how he had had it bashed in the pub at Treville. It looked absolutely all right now, though of course no nearer his mouth than ever.

After finishing at last with Wales he said rightly that it was still early, called without too much urgency for more coffee and invited her to tell him about herself. So she told him a bit about Alun and the girls. She went carefully on them because of what Gwen had said, or rather not said when asked, about their own two boys now in their thirties. If Malcolm had something to get off his chest in that department he kept it to himself.

Although he was paying her polite attention it became pretty clear after a few minutes that she was on some sort of wrong tack.

'Would you like another sticky drink?' he offered, as soon as she stopped speaking.

'No thanks dear.'

'Well, from what you've been saying you're very much content with your life as it is now.'

'Oh yes. Much more than I was with my life as it was then.'

'Oh really?'

'Considering I had as good a time as anyone it's funny how often I catch myself being bloody glad to think, well whatever happens I haven't got to do *that* any more,' she said, 'going on the beach or going dancing or going out, going out to dinner that is,' and one or two more along the same lines until she noticed he was not listening much, smiling away and nodding now and then, his eyes on her face but in a kind of spread-over way.

For a man not to be listening to what she said had always struck her as a sound scheme whichever way you looked at it, and nowadays its corresponding drawback was greatly reduced. Whereas in the past such a man would have had that much more chance of noticing a patch of surplus powder or a pimple pit, failing sight in age would probably have ruled that out, unless of course he unsportingly put his glasses on, which Malcolm had not done. But it struck her now that the ear-shutting thing was part of not wanting her to have changed into just one of his mates, preferring her to stay on out of his ken, so to speak, where he could go in for whimsy-whamsy about her. That, seeing that, rather cramped her style for the time being.

While he was asking one of the waitresses for the bill another of them was putting it in front of him. 'Not too bad, I thought,' he said after calculating the tip for a couple of minutes in his head, on paper, and then in his head again.

'Oh, very good. Proper food.' She had not managed the prepared-by-someone-else gravy dinner she had rather been counting on, had had to pass up the beef curry because of the rice, had steered clear of the lamb ragout on account of possibly lurking tomato seeds and had settled for the chicken pie, the meat moist enough but the pastry definitely waxy, pappy almost, needless to say fatty, but as against that she had eaten up all her lettuce and watercress and some of the green pepper, which with a good squeeze of lemon had hardly tasted of catarrh at all.

Alone in the very nice Ladies she tried to relax as far as she could and took a few deep breaths before getting down to work on her falsies. While she was doing so she straightened to her full height, shook back her hair and did her best in the way of putting on an important, haughty expression. The general effect might have struck Malcolm as bursting with poise, but the idea was to give herself a head start, an improved chance of facing down anyone who might presume to come barging in and find the sudden sight of an old girl with her teeth in her hand somehow remarkable, or embarrassing, or in any way out of the ordinary, unless in the experience of very common persons. As it turned out, no sweat: the miniature of Dentu-Hold was safely in her bag well before a harmless little thing, in jeans anyway as it turned out, sidled in and vanished into the W.C. Rhiannon left in a flurry of self-assurance.

Outside, the sun had left the front of the building but the day was still bright and quite hot. Over near the car Malcolm was standing with his back almost turned, his head slightly on one side, just admiring the view by the look of him, and yet there was something calculated in his casualness that warned her of what was on the way. As she came up he edged into position by the passenger door. Yes, he was going to do it. At some figured-out moment he threw the door wide, stood extra upright with his chin in the air and did a tremendous juddering salute like a sergeant in an old movie. Feeling her cheeks turn hot she sketched a gracious Queen-Mum-type smile and lift of the hand and scurried into her seat. Performances like that were supposed to show how relaxed the two of you were together, but actually they brought out your awkwardness and almost your resentment of each other, or some of it. Well, at least Malcolm had not thought to bring that tweed cap into the act.

'So it seems I can safely assume you are not possessed by an over-whelming desire to immerse yourself in the ocean,' he said when they got moving.

'Yes indeed you can.'

'Nevertheless I take it you'd have no strong objection to a small sight-seeing trip to a part of the coast of the island?'

'Oh no, lovely idea. Whereabouts?'

'That will emerge in due time.'

They drove back to the coast road and moved south again into the more countrified area that had mostly farms and woods and an occasional large house inside a park. After they had skirted the boundary wall of one of these with its fancifully bricked-up gateway, Rhiannon began to pick up small landmarks: an old-fashioned milestone showing the distance to Carmarthen, Cardiff and 'Brecknock', the momentary sight of a castle among whose ruins, it had been said, there grew a flower found nowhere else but in the Pyrenees, a National Trust plaque about something, the gable of perhaps a barn with the torn irregular triangle of bleached poster still stuck there as always and finally, unmistakably, the sudden steep turning that led down to Pwll Glân and, further along, to Britain's Cove. It was obviously Pwll Glân that Malcolm was making for, the only bay with a Welsh name of the score all round that coast, if not the finest then, all would have agreed, the most unusual, and known to Rhiannon from plenty of visits in the past.

For the first couple of hundred yards the slope was so extreme that right of way on that narrow twisting road went automatically to people driving up, and twice Malcolm had to pull into the side and stop. The second time, on a right-angle bend, brought Rhiannon a view of the half-mile or so of flat before the beach itself and then of most of the bay, the low curving arm to the south, the long almost-straight stretch of sand and, on the far side, the tree-covered headland where the church was. The road took them to the foot of the escarpment and through the marshes, formerly salt, freshwater now for many years and grown over with reeds of a peculiar and beautiful pale orange-yellow. At the end they turned along the top of the shore, where shabby greenish plants were scattered, and drove finally into the extensive car-park, unseen from above, unexpected almost until reached, but a matter of course after that, full of familiar things like people eating and drinking and making a lot of noise while they walked about.

Malcolm lost no time in leading the way out of it and down crosswise towards the sea, to an empty part where the sand was strewn with unattractive seaweed and broken by patches of bare rock. By chance it was also just about the part where, one far-off night, Rhiannon and Dorothy had tried to catch flounders in the shallows, or rather not to hinder too much the two, possibly three, young men who were supposed to know how and, for all Rhiannon could remember, had succeeded. There had been nobody about then. There was nobody about now, not at least up this end towards the headland, nowhere to bathe, nowhere to sit or lie or throw a ball, nowhere for the kids to run to and fro. Not saying much, but keeping a close eye on her, Malcolm took them across a stretch of quite rugged rock on to the path that led up to the moss-stained wall of the churchyard.

On the far side of the gateway here no sound could be heard from the shore, just waves. They were on a narrow granite promontory less than a hundred yards long, with the sweep of Pwll Glân bay on their left as they faced out to sea and another bay on their right too small to have a name, more of a creek really, heaped with stones of various sizes and always empty – well, in the past Rhiannon had seen a couple of fishermen there, serious ones in oilskins and thigh-boots standing into the sea, but it would have been safe to say that nobody went there now for any reason.

There was room on the promontory for not much more than the church itself, three or four lines of graves and dozens of mature trees, sycamores mostly, tall and flourishing even in the salt air and at this season deeply shading the ground underneath. Nobody came here either in a manner of speaking, but the two of them were here today, and somebody else had been here not long before to take a bit of care of the graves and make the place seem not quite desolate, though hardly a single stone remained in one piece or uneroded. But some names and dates could still be read easily enough, Welsh names, English names, none that she saw later than 1920. The church was very thoroughly shut up and impossible to see into from anywhere at ground level.

'It's still a church,' said Malcolm, having let the matter rest for quite a long time. 'That's to say it hasn't been deconsecrated.'

'But they can't still be using it.'

'The last service was held here in 1959. Longer ago than half the people on that beach can remember.' He smiled and went on confidingly, 'I looked it up. Perhaps they think there might be something left here some day.'

'Who? What sort of thing do you mean?'

'Well . . . I don't know,' he said in a gentle tone. 'At the moment it's too far for anybody to come, you see. Too far by car, that is. How many years would it be since it wasn't too far to come on foot, with that climb for most of them to face after? Eighty-four in congregation the nave held, according to what I read.'

'Do you believe in it yourself, Malcolm?'

'It's very hard to answer that. In a way I suppose I do. I certainly hate to see it all disappearing. I used to think things would go on round here as long as anywhere in the kingdom, but do you know I doubt if they have?'

'Well, there's nothing to be done about it, that's for sure.' Rhiannon tried to sound gentle too. 'One thing, it's too far for vandals to come too, by the look of it.'

'Yes. Small mercies. I like to come here occasionally. It helps me . . . no, it's impossible to say it without sounding pompous. Anyway, it's a wonderful spot. Peaceful. Solitary.'

'A bit lonely, though. Windy too.'

'I'm terribly sorry, Rhi, are you absolutely – '

'No, no, I'm fine.' She looked about. 'It certainly has an atmosphere.'

'You remember coming here before?' he asked eagerly.

'Oh yes, of course.'

She would have added 'lots of times' but he hurried on. 'What about that terrible concrete hut, I think it was concrete, just where the road stopped? That's gone too now, of course. Ha, one's quite glad to see the back of some of what they pull down. It was the only place to eat, though.'

'That's right, and the lady washed up so loudly you couldn't hear yourself speak, and kept the key of the lav in her apron.'

'Do you remember having lunch there?'

'Oh yes,' she said in the same spirit as a moment earlier.

'We took what we were given – sausages and chips and OK sauce.'

'M'm. There was a hopeless cat there too, that when you stroked it, it looked at you as though you were barmy.'

'I'd forgotten about that. You drank Mackeson stout, didn't you? It was your regular tipple in those days.'

'So it was. You never seem to see it now.'

'And the two of us went for a stroll after.'

She felt she probably should have spoken then but she could not think how to say it, just smiled and waited and crossed her fingers in her head. He stepped a pace back from her before he went on, still with insistence,

'When we got up here we found there'd been a storm a night or two before and there were leaves and bits of twigs and branches and stuff all over the place, and the sea was still very rough. And we went right up to the end there where it jutted out over the water – just there, remember? – quite dangerous it was, I suppose, but we do these things in our youth, actually I think most of it's fallen away now. And I said, I know I'll never mean as much to you as you mean to me, anywhere near, and I'm not complaining, I said, but I want to tell you nobody will ever mean as much to me as you do, and I want you to remember that, I said. And you said you would, and I think perhaps you have, haven't you, Rhiannon?'

If it had been too early a moment ago to contract out of his recalling of that day, it was obviously much too late now. Not sure that she could have spoken in any case, she nodded.

'Wonderful. Oh, that is lovely.' The tautness departed from his manner. 'Well, an awful lot of things seem worth while after that, I can tell you. Thank you for remembering me, with so much else in your life.'

He sent her a smile of simple affection and indicated they should move. As they began strolling down the slight incline towards the gate he put his arm chummily round her waist.

'Yes, I'd got my pal Doug Johnson to lend me his car for the day. It was the first time I'd taken it out and I was a bit nervous, I hope it didn't show.'

'I didn't notice anything,' she said.

'We stopped for petrol and the surly bloke wouldn't change a fiver, remember?'

'Oh yes of course.' With the heat off, Rhiannon would have agreed that she remembered General Tate's landing at Fishguard.

'And we'd hardly gone ten yards after when that terrific cloudburst started and I had to stop because the windscreen-wiper wasn't working properly.'

'That's right.'

'Ah, now I think I can almost fix the date. The Australians were playing at Cardiff and in their – '

He stopped walking and stared ahead of him. She knew something awful had happened. Her eyes skidded away to a horizontal stone gone almost black and read helplessly of Thomas Godfrey Pritchard who departed this life 17th June 1867 and was sorely missed. When she looked at Malcolm again he was still staring, but at her now.

'Doug Johnson was away in France the whole of that summer,' he said, 'doing his teaching prac. He certainly wasn't around to lend his car to me or anyone else. So that must have been a different day altogether.'

'M'm.' She forced herself to go on looking at him.

'We must have taken the bus down. You couldn't have remembered it like that, the way you said you did.'

'No.'

'You don't remember any of it, do you? Not having lunch or walking up to St Mary's or what I said or anything.'

It was not to be got out of or away from. Coming on top of the little tensions of the day the unashamed intensity of his disappointment was too much for her. She hid her face, turned aside and started to cry.

He forgot his own feelings at once. 'What is it? What's the matter?'

'I'm so stupid, I'm so hopeless, no good to anybody, I just think of myself all the time, don't notice other people. It's not much to ask, remembering a lovely day out, but I can't even do that.' She had his arm round her now and was resting her forehead against his shoulder, though she still kept her hands over her eyes. 'Anybody who was any use would remember but I can't, but I wish I could, I wish I could.'

'Don't say such ridiculous things. You don't expect me to take them seriously, do you? It's sweet of you to worry about it just slipping your mind like that, but I didn't remember it very well myself, did I, confusing those two times? Anyway you remember coming down here? To Pwll Glân?'

'M'm.'

'And perhaps me bringing you? You know, sort of vaguely?'

'M'm.' Perhaps she did.

'Even this bit? Just . . .'

Suddenly it went impossible to say yes, even to this bit. 'Not . . .' She shook her head wretchedly. 'It's gone. Sorry.'

'I can't have you apologising to me, my dear Rhiannon. Honestly, now.' He gazed over the top of her head in the general direction of the land. 'Well, put it this way, the fact you minded so much about not remembering, that's worth as much to me as if you had remembered, very nearly.'

That set things back a bit, but in the end it was only the clearing-up shower. She got to work with her tissues and comb and he wandered about making suitable points like the church being *probably* twelfth century and having effigies of a member of the de Courcy family and his lady in the south wall of the chancel and a battlement round the top of the tower, exactly what she wanted to hear just then, no sarcasm. When he saw she was ready he gave the bay a final going-over.

'It was all houses there once, before the sea came up,' he said. 'A whole village.'

Rhiannon thought she had heard that the sea had once been over the marshes and then gone back, but that must have been another time. 'I suppose they can tell.'

'At low tide twice a year when the water's calm you're supposed to be able to see down to what were streets. Houses even. I think another church.'

'Do you still do your poetry?'

'You remember that.' He smiled with pleasure. 'Indeed I do, yes. And I mean to go on. I'm lucky enough to have a few things to get off my chest still.'

Before he could get on to what they were she found herself saying, with a sense of instant inspiration that amazed her, 'There used to be a lovely rose-garden with brick walls and, you know, pergolas along the paths belonging to some grand house somewhere. You could look round it in the afternoon. I don't know whether you still can.'

'Let's see, would that be Mansel Hall? Over by Swanset?'

No prizes for not rushing in this time. 'I'm not absolutely . . .'

'No, I know where you mean – er, now, Bryn House, that's it. Bryn House, of course. Local stone with brick facing. Not far from here. Anyway, you'd like to go there, would you?'

'M'm. Didn't we go there once before, one summer, not a very nice day?' The not very nice day had stuck in her mind all right, not actually raining but chilly and dark.

'I think so,' he said, as he more or less had to. 'Yes, I'm sure we did. Come on, let's go and have a look. Might bring all sorts of stuff back, you never know.'

'It may have just gone, the garden, like a lot of things.'

'Let's go there anyway.'

He spoke dreamily again, as if he felt that he or they had started on some semi-fated course, and glanced at her in a way that suggested the lip of the frying-pan was still not too far off. Well, she would have to let him say what he liked now. She reached out and took and squeezed his hand as they walked down to the churchyard gate and took it again on the far side, in comfort or apology or what she hoped would pass as understanding, or perhaps like one person letting another know that whatever it was they were facing they would face it together. He squeezed back but kept quiet after all until they were on their way inland through the marshes, and then for once in his life he talked about nothing in particular.

6 Malcolm, Muriel, Peter, Gwen, Alun, Rhiannon

1

'Bible and Crown Hotel, Tarquin Jones speaking.'

It was characteristic of Tarc to refer to his house in this way although, more likely because, the place was not and never had been a hotel in any bed-and-board sense, nor even called one by anybody until he came along. So much could be readily agreed but, as Charlie had once pointed out, or alleged, it was much less easy to say what characteristic of Tarc's it was characteristic of. And that was very Welsh, Garth had added without running into opposition.

At another time Malcolm would surely have been ready to consider such matters, especially the last, but not now. With strained clarity he gave his own name in full.

'Who?' – an unaspirated near-bellow with no fancy suggestion of actual failure to hear or recognise.

After an even clearer repetition Malcolm asked if Mr Alun Weaver was on the premises and met immediate total silence, relieved fairly soon by distant female squeals of pretended shock or surprise and what sounded like a referee's whistle indiscriminately blown. Malcolm waited. He took a couple of deep breaths and told himself he was not feeling at all on edge. After some minutes Alun came on the line with the kind of featureless utterance to be expected from someone wary of unscheduled telephone-calls.

Once more Malcolm introduced himself, going on to ask, 'Many in tonight?'

'They've mostly gone now. I was more or less just off myself as a matter of fact. Don't often come here at this time, you know.'

His tone held a question which Malcolm answered by saying, 'Rhiannon, er, mentioned where you were.'

'Oh did she? Oh I see.' This time Alun spoke with all the artless accept-ance of a man (perhaps Peter would have specified a Welshman) getting ready for a bit of fast footwork.

'Look, Alun, I was wondering whether you might care to drop in for a nightcap on your way home. No great piss-up or anything, just *un bach*.'

There was a faint sound of indrawn breath over the wire. 'Oh, well, now it's kind of you, boy, but it's getting late and I think if you don't mind . . .'

'Actually I'm on my own tonight. Gwen's been in a funny sort of mood, I don't know what's got into her. Not like her to pop out on the spur of the moment. Well, I say popped, she told me don't wait up for her.' This was rounded off by a light laugh at feminine capriciousness.

'Well now, that being so, the case is altered beyond all recognition. Of course I'll be delighted to alleviate your solitude. Taking off in about five minutes.'

The simple prospect of company made Malcolm feel better for a moment. He picked up his glass of whisky and water, not a habitual feature of his evenings, and carried it into the sitting-room. This was so full of unmasculine stuff, like loose covers and plates not meant for eating off, and so narrow in proportion to its quite moderate length that some visitors had taken it for Gwen's own little nook where she might have held tea-parties, very exclusive ones, but in fact there was nowhere else to go or be outside the kitchen but Malcolm's study, and even he never went there except for some serious reason.

Tonight a small masculine intrusion was noticeable in this sitting-room, not in the obvious form of the gramophone or record-player itself, which was of course common in gender, but of actual records fetched earlier from their white-painted deal cabinet in the study. The machine, called a Playbox, black with timid Chinesey edging in a sort of gold, now faded, had been pretty advanced for the mid-1960s. The records were from the same period or before, deleted reissues of micro-groove 'realisations' of even more firmly forgotten 78s made in the 1940s in a style said to have been current two or three decades longer ago still. Most of the performers were grouped under names like Doc Pettit and his Original Storyville Jazz Band, though individuals called Hunchback Mose and Clubfoot Red LeRoy were also to be seen, accompanied here and there by an unknown harmonica or unlisted jew's-harp.

Malcolm had been meaning to play some of these to himself as a means of recapturing more of the past, going on, so to speak, from where he had left off with Rhiannon earlier that day. He had put the project aside when Gwen said her piece and flounced out of the house; now, it seemed possible again. Only possible: first he must visit the bathroom, or rather the W.C., and check how matters stood in that department. They had not been too favourably disposed that morning, and once or twice he had had to fight quite hard not to let the thought of them overshadow the outing. His left ball had played up a bit as well, but he was learning to live with that.

He set down his drink and went upstairs and lo and behold it was all right. As he was finishing up he thought to himself that on this point at least he was two people really, a bloody old woman and worryguts and a marvellous ice-cold reasoning mechanism, and neither of them ever listened to the other. Actually a *real* split personality, one fellow completely separate from the other, would have had a lot to be said for it: every so often each of them could get away from himself a hundred per cent, guaranteed.

In the sitting-room again he at once switched the Playbox on and took out of its cover a recording attributed to Papa Boileau and his New Orleans Feetwarmers. They looked back at him from the sleeve photograph, a line of old men in dark suits and collars and ties, six, seven faces about as black as could be, sad and utterly private, no imaginable relation to those Malcolm was used to seeing on his television screen. He arranged the disc on the central spindle and in due time it plumped down on to the already rotating turntable where the pick-up arm, moving in a series of doddery jerks and overshoots, came and found its outermost groove. Through a roaring fuzz of needle-damage the sounds of 'Cakewalkin' Babies' emerged. Malcolm turned up the volume.

The stylus was worn and the playing-surface too, but this bothered him not at all, any more than he cared that the recording was poorish even for its era, the clarinet slightly flat, the cornet shaky in the upper register; he was gripped by the music from its first bars. As always he listened intently, trying to hear every note of every instrument, leaving himself when it came to it no time to reflect on the past or anything else. Too excited to sit down, he stood in front of the Playbox and shifted his weight from one foot to the other in time with the music. At appropriate stages he took a turn on an invisible banjo, beating out a steady equal four, did all any man could in the circumstances with a run of trombone smears and punctually signalled a couple of crashes on the Turkish cymbal. Precisely at the end of the number, which came without warning to the uninitiated, he went rigid and breathless, coming to life again at the start of 'Struttin' with some Barbecue'.

By now he was thoroughly sent, as he would have put it in the old days. He had heard that a barbecue had to do with cooking out of doors, but had always assumed that this here was a different use or even a different word, perhaps a corruption, and that 'some barbecue' meant a fine fancy woman and no mistake. Seeing such a one pass by, people would say in wonder and admiration, 'Now that's what I *call* a barbecue!' Malcolm had never strutted or, assuming to strut was to dance, danced in any fashion with such a woman, nor was he really pretending to now, just going off on a heel-and-toe shuffle round the small circuit of the room.

Breaking his stride when the doorbell pealed made him stagger. Until he saw that yes, he had pulled the curtains, he was afraid he might have been observed from outside – some treat for the neighbours, an oldster capering about on his own like a mad thing. He straightened his jacket, wiped his eyes, squared his shoulders and went out to the hall. Voices could be heard from the far side of the door.

When he opened it, two persons at once entered with all possible certainty of being expected. One of them was Garth Pumphrey, the other a taller, perhaps younger man Malcolm half-took at first to be a stranger. This second visitor had a full head of white hair, very neatly cut and combed, and a tanned skin. The combination gave him something of a look of a photographic negative, or perhaps just of an old cricketer; in any case his wide brown calm eyes made the negative idea worth forgetting. He turned his head when he caught the music from the sitting-room.

'Hold the door a minute, Malcolm,' said Garth – 'Peter's on his way now.'

'Oh, right.'

'You remember Percy, don't you, Malcolm?'

Of course he did immediately: Percy Morgan, builder, husband to Dorothy, to be seen from time to time dragging her out to the car after the end of a party, encountered less often, not for about a year indeed, up at the Bible. Garth's occasional usefulness with this sort of reminder was to be set to his credit, against his rather more frequent and famous senility-imputing introductions of Charlie to Alun, Alun to Malcolm, Malcolm to Tarc Jones, etc.

After a short interval marked by awkward standing-about in the hall Peter toiled up the garden path, groaning and muttering as he came, and the party moved into the sitting-room. The Feetwarmers sounded very loud in here – they had started on 'Wild Man Blues' by now – and Malcolm reduced them somewhat before offering drinks, wondering as he did so how far his just-over-half-bottle of Johnnie Walker would go among four – five, rather, which raised a point.

'Alun's coming, is he?' he asked Peter.

'Is he, I've no idea. I say, do you mind turning down that noise?'

'I thought you used to like that old New Orleans stuff – Jelly Roll Morton, George – '

'If I ever did I don't now. If you don't mind.'

Percy Morgan looked up from turning over some of the records when Malcolm approached.

'Have you any Basie or Ellington? Or conceivably Gil Evans? Thanks.' The thanks were for an offered glass of whisky and water. 'I can see it's no use asking for Coltrane or Kirk or anybody like that.'

'Not a damn bit of use, boy,' said Malcolm with slight hostile relish. 'And my Basies stop in 1939 and my Ellingtons about 1934. And no, no Gil Evans – I seem to recall a baritone man of that or a similar name playing with somebody like Don Redman, though you obviously don't mean him.'

He reached out to lower the volume as requested, but Percy Morgan held up a demurring hand and indicated that he should attend closely to the music. A clarinet solo was in progress. 'You wouldn't call that melodic invention, would you, seriously?' asked Percy at the end of the chorus.

'No. I wouldn't call it anything in particular. Except perhaps bloody marvellous.'

'He was just running up and down the arpeggio of the common chord

with a few passing-notes thrown in.' Not a vestige of complaint or dissatisfaction coloured Percy's tone. He seemed perfectly resigned, seeing it as
quite out of the question that the performance could ever have been
different.

'Was he now.' This time Malcolm did manage to turn down the sound.
'No doubt he was, I don't deny it.'

'Oh, don't turn it down, Malcolm,' said Garth in real protest. 'I love
these old Dixieland hits, they really swing, don't they?' He mimed a bit of
simplified drumming, hissing rhythmically through his teeth. 'Which lot is
this?' Malcolm passed him the sleeve. 'Oh yes. Papa . . . Oh yes. Have you
got any, any Glenn Miller discs?'

'I'm afraid not.'

'Any Artie Shaws?'

'No.'

Malcolm was as close as he usually came to being angry at the way his
quiet drink and unburdening chat with an old friend had been turned,
without anywhere near as much as a by-your-leave, into a jazz discussion
group. Not that he would in the least have minded the right sort of attention
being paid to his records: a respectful, if possible attentive, silence broken
only by a personnel inquiry or so and one or two – not over-frequent –
appreciative cries of 'Yeah!' He realised he had been half-hoping for this
sort of outcome ever since the three had arrived and longer than that in
the case of Alun. Yes, and where the hell was Alun?

He was on the doorstep a couple of minutes later with Charlie at his
side, crying out in loosely intelligible greeting and apology, pressing on his
host an unopened bottle of Black Label – like old times, except then it
would have been a flagon of John Upjohn Jones nut-brown.

'I hope you don't mind me bringing these boys along,' said Alun. 'Only
Tarc was calling stop-tap and they all seemed to feel like another.'

'I see. No, that's all right. Of course.'

Charlie crossed the threshold with real dignity. 'Or even him sending
them on ahead. Known as the advance-guard or covering-party tactic.'

'I'm sorry,' said Malcolm, 'I don't – '

'Ah, the old righteous sound!' cried Alun, hurrying over to the Playbox.
'Surely I know this one, don't I? Wasn't there a Louis version with, with
Johnny Dodds? On the back of, was it "Skip the Gutter"?'

'It was "Ory's Creole Trombone" actually.'

'*That's* right – on the old Parlophone 78, correct?'

'Correct,' said Malcolm, beginning to smile.

Alun set about vivaciously looking through the pile of records. Percy
Morgan glanced briefly and without hope at the rubric of every third or
fourth one he came to. Malcolm went off for more glasses. Charlie turned
to Peter and nodded to him in a pleased way, as though the two had not
met for some weeks.

'Cheer up,' said Charlie. 'Cheer up and enjoy the music.'

'I'm afraid the effort of cheering up sufficiently to enjoy this music would be beyond me.'

'What's wrong with this music more than any other?'

'Not much, I suppose. When I look back, you know, music's like chess or foreign coins or what, folk tales. Something that only interested me when practically everything else interested me as well.'

'I wouldn't have gone to the Bible in the first place if the Glendower hadn't been shut.'

'While they fit the new stove. You said.'

'Where are these bloody drinks?' Charlie gave a searching look round. 'And where's bloody Garth? I thought he was meant to be here.'

'He was and is. As you came in he was going up the stairs, in all probability on his way to the lavatory.'

'Hey, there's one very good thing about Garth,' said Charlie, including in this announcement Percy, who had finally given up on the records, and repeating it for Malcolm's benefit as he approached with the promised drinks. 'Mark me closely. Whenever you see, er . . . What?' He frowned and looked from face to face. 'Oh, whenever you see *Garth* you get the most wonderful feeling of security. You can relax. You know, m'm? – you *know* you're not going to suddenly run into Angharad. No chance of it. You can relax. Eh? And a very much more minor benefit of seeing *Angharad* . . . is knowing you're not going to suddenly run into *Garth*. Well.'

Peter had looked away sharply at this, but the other two at least showed they understood the reference, namely to the frequent observation or supposed fact that the Pumphreys never both appeared at once. It gave rise to regular good-natured speculation about the homicidal-maniac uncle or two-headed son who needed attention of some sort at all times. Anyway Charlie was on well-trodden ground.

'You know I was thinking about that pair the other day,' he went on. 'Now: if they were in a detective story there'd only be one of them. See what I mean? Only be one of them really. One of them would have knocked off the other years ago and now whichever one it was would be going round posing as the other. As well, I mean. Just some of the time. They're about the same height, aren't they?'

'Why only some of the time?' asked Malcolm, glancing at Percy, who shook his snowy head very slowly from side to side.

'What? Well, Christ, because the rest of the time he'd be going round being himself, wouldn't he? Or herself if it was Angharad, of course.'

'I don't seem to have given Alun a drink,' said Malcolm, and moved off.

Alun had that moment slid a record out of its sleeve and was peering at the label in a vigilant way but, without his glasses, surely in vain. 'Ah, *diolch yn fawr*, dear boy. I can't make out, I can't make out whether this is a remake or the original – '

'Could I just have a quick word?'

'Sir, a whole history.' He sighed briefly. 'I mean take as long as you like.'

'Thanks, Alun. I wanted to ask you . . . Well, something Gwen said gave me a really nasty shock.'

2

'Well, I treat the whole thing as a joke,' Muriel was saying. 'Which I can just about manage to do most of the time if I keep my teeth well and truly gritted. Take it easy, lass, I tell myself when the adrenalin starts to flow – you've seen it all before and you've come through without a scratch. Well anyway you've come through. Say it slowly and calmly: you're in Wales, land of song, land of smiles, and land of deceit. Taffy was a Welshman, Taffy was a thief all right, and by Christ boyo Taffy has been keeping up the old traditions indeed in a bloody big way oh yes now look you.' The last couple of dozen words were delivered in an accent that sounded as much like a West African one as anything else, Ghanaian, possibly, or Ibo. 'I thought counting the spoons was just an expression till I came to live down here. Nothing more than a colourful catch-phrase.'

Dimly recognising this as the end of a section, and even more dimly aware of having heard something rather like it before, Dorothy Morgan looked up. She had lost the initiative a minute or two earlier. Astonishingly, she had found herself out of immediate things to say about New Zealand, the adopted home of one of the Morgan sons, a whole country gloriously unknown to anyone she was ever likely to run into round here and in many other parts, serving her as a magic wand or spell for reducing great assemblies to silence. Now, she missed her chance of coming in with alternative unanswerable stuff on what Percy had said to the County Clerk, or what she remembered of a magazine article about DNA she had recently happened to read. It was not of course that she was actually listening to what Muriel was saying, just that the continuous sound of another voice distracted her, put her off even the unexacting task of knocking one of her starters into shape.

What Dorothy had looked up from was the stylish Scandinavian table, made of different sorts of wood, in Sophie's apparatus-packed kitchen. It, the table, was strewn with the debris accumulated in twelve hours of drinking wine, smoking cigarettes and not eating all manner of biscuits, sandwiches, portions of cheese, little plastic zeppelins of pâté. Muriel and Dorothy were the only two still present and active: Siân Smith was thought to be asleep somewhere upstairs and Sophie herself, never a keen partaker, had gone off to her sitting-room TV quite a while before, though at the moment she was in the hall on the telephone trying for the second or third time to get hold of the much-needed Percy.

'I think I may have told you about a long-service warrior I ran into in

Monmouth,' said Muriel now, sounding in no doubt whatever on the point. 'Twenty years up-country in the thick of it, doing something to do with reservoirs and pipes among the Welsh hill-tribes. Normally, of course, at home that's to say, Yorkshire people don't think a lot to Derbyshire folk, but it's different when you're abroad. Anyway he and I got on all right, and he was very knowledgeable about, you know, what makes Johnny Welshman tick. Quite fascinating. One day, he didn't explain how but I imagine it involved showing tolerance for local rituals and such, one day he found himself among those present when the village man of God preached a sermon in Welsh. Which no doubt would have meant plenty to you . . .'

Here Muriel made an audacious pause, confident that she could gauge Dorothy's coming-round time to a nicety, and resumed on the dot,

' . . . but, as far as he was concerned, the fellow might just as well have been rabbiting on in Apache. But one thing he did notice, did my chum. The fellow, the Welsh fellow, kept using a word that sounded like the English word truth. As in veracity, honesty and such. There'd be a flood of bongo-bongo chatter, and then, suddenly, truth, and then more monkey language. Apparently, when he asked afterwards, apparently it was, it had been, the English word he'd used. Why not use a Welsh word, he asked him. Well, he said,' and Muriel's accent shifted again to the Gulf of Guinea, 'there isn't a Welsh word with the same connotations and the *force* of the English word. And if that isn't funny enough for you, he said, there is a Welsh word *truth*, same word, spelt the same anyhow, and it means false-hood. Mumbo-jumbo. As you well know. Talk about coming out in the open. I've often meant to check that in a Welsh-English dictionary. After all there must be such things. Just a matter of knowing where to look.'

Sophie had come into the room in time to hear the last part of this. The sight of her went down remarkably well with Muriel, who liked holding the floor as much as anyone living but preferred a more normal audience, one that could safely be allowed a turn now and again. It would have been good if Dorothy had been listening, too, especially to the yarn just recounted, but then she had heard it, had had sound-waves bearing it strike her ear-drum, a couple of dozen times before, so there was a chance of its entering her mind by some route or other, perhaps bypassing the conscious part of it. As it was, talking to Dorothy, or rather in her presence, was a bit too close for comfort to being that type in the story who found himself shut up in a prison cell somewhere nasty with a mad murderous Arab for company, not a lot in the way of company because you very soon found that the only way of keeping him quiet was by staring him in the eye: take too long about blinking, let alone nod off, and you were for it. Muriel lit a cigarette in one continuous operation rather than as when addressing Dorothy — piecemeal, like somebody driving a car at the same time.

'Any luck with Percy?'

'Still no reply — it's not like him. I had Gwen on just before, phoning from that Eyetie joint in Hatchery Road.'

'Oh, Mario's, I know. What had she got to say for herself?'

'Fed up she was, according to her,' said Sophie, who had actually been prepared to pass on this information unprompted. 'Malcolm given her a big row.'

'No, really? That doesn't sound the gallant Malcolm's style at all. I can't imagine him giving any size of row to a cockle-stall proprietor.'

After a short pause, Sophie said, 'Well, you know. She asked if she could come up, so – '

'And how did you respond?'

'I thought why not, more the merrier.' Sophie glanced at Dorothy. 'Right?'

'Oh, every time. I couldn't agree more.'

'Maybe she'll have something to tell us about the great day trip.' Malcolm's excursion with Rhiannon had been speculated about earlier.

'Very possibly. I must say our Rhiannon has been *going it a bit* recently. She can hardly have recovered from her piss-up with my old man.'

This time Sophie paused a little longer. 'I always think, the way you feel about the Welsh, Muriel, it must be fantastic, you and Peter seeing absolutely eye to eye on a thing like that.'

'I must go,' said Muriel. 'Well actually not as much as you might think. It's perfectly possible to go a long way with somebody on some point or other and then suddenly find you and the other chap are literally rolling over and over on the bloody *floor* about it. Easiest thing in the world.' She picked up a nearly full bottle of Corvo Bianco with a slight clunk against an unopened tin of laver-bread (from Devon), got a no-thanks from Sophie and poured unstintingly for herself. 'But of course it doesn't go very deep with me. More a matter of being a little bit naughty among friends.' This, driven home at need with a where's-your-sense-of-humour gibe, was her standard retort to any Welsh person who might take exception to being categorised as a liar, cheat, dullard, bully, hypocrite, sneak, snob, layabout, toady, violator of siblings and anything else that might strike her fancy. 'Yes, I'm a long way from getting my official invitation to join the Peter Thomas Anti-Welsh Brotherhood, and not only on grounds of sex, which I dare say the chairman's prepared to waive these days. No, it'll take a – '

'Oh, and there's another way you don't qualify, Muriel,' said Sophie with a bright smile. 'Only Welsh people can join. Born Welsh. Peter must have told you, surely. I remember him going into it one time after Christmas dinner at Dorothy's. Very particular he was on the point. Two non-Welsh grandparents was too many, he said.'

After the sound of her name had triggered her dinosaurian reflexes, Dorothy lifted her head for the second time in ten minutes. The talk between Sophie and Muriel, animated to begin with, had lost its impetus and that too might have percolated through her nervous system. Behind the black-framed lenses her eyes steadied and focused. With majestic deliberation she drew in her breath. The other two struggled wildly to think of something to get in ahead with, but it was like trying to start a motor-bike in the path of a charging elephant.

'Of course you know in New Zealand they celebrate Christmas just the same as here,' she said, showing a notable sense of continuity. 'Roast turkey and plum pudding and mince pies in the middle of the antipodean winter.' She pronounced the penultimate word correctly and clearly, as she did every other, as she invariably did while she could speak at all. 'I mean summer. Imagine roast turkey and stuffing and hot mince pies in July. Howard and Angela have got some friends in Wanangui, that's in what they call North Island . . .'

'I think I'll try Percy again,' said Sophie.

3

'I'd just like an explanation,' said Malcolm. 'Just the merest hint of an explanation. That's all.'

'You're the feeblest creature God ever put breath into,' said Alun. 'Why any woman should have spent thirty-three minutes married to you, let alone thirty-three years, defies comprehension. You've no idea in the world of what pleases a woman: in other words' – he seemed to be choosing these with care – 'you're not only hopeless as an organiser of life in general, you're a crashingly boring companion into the bargain and needless to say, er, perennially deficient in the bedroom. Correct?'

'That about sums me up. Oh, I'm also cut off.'

'Cut off?'

'Cut off from real people in my own little pathetic fantasy world of dilettante Welshness, medievalism and poetry.' Malcolm drained his glass.

'*Poetry?* You ought to be ashamed of yourself, a great big hulking fellow like you. What are your other shortcomings?'

'That's all I can remember for the moment. And as I say I'd love to know the explanation. There'd been no row before, no upset, nothing. It's most odd. Anachronistic in fact. She hasn't spoken to me in that strain for God knows how long.'

'M'm.' Alun pursed his lips and blinked at the wall, as if reflecting upon one or two mere theoretical conceivabilities, preparing to eliminate them for form's sake. He said, 'She didn't happen to, er, mention anybody else, I suppose, *refer* to anybody who in any way might have . . . ?'

'Not a soul. I'd have remembered if she had.'

'Yes.' Now an expression of considerable relief appeared for an instant on Alun's face before he added quickly, 'That's a, that must be a considerable relief to you. Well, quite a relief.'

Malcolm nodded and sighed. His neck was aching and he wriggled his shoulders around to ease it. 'But of course what's bothering me, what I'm trying to work out is the connection between this and the way she flew off the handle at you. Which I may say I'm very sorry ever happened.'

'The . . . ?'

'Last night in the Golf Club,' said Malcolm, himself starting to blink slightly.

'Oh. Oh yes. Yes. Yes, I wondered when we'd get round to that. Yes, quite a little hatful of words, wasn't it? What did she say to you about it?'

'Well, I had to drag it out of her. But I wasn't going to let it pass.'

'Quite right, it doesn't do. Never. Anyway . . .'

'Well, she was tired, she'd had a few, she was a bit under the weather, and the rest of it was, quite frankly, Alun, I mean I'm being quite frank now, she was furious with you, no not furious, annoyed. Irritated. Some linguistic point which I must confess I didn't really – '

'Oh, I know. She grew up in Capel Mererid speaking Welsh and I didn't. I know. To be frank with you in return, Malcolm *bach*, she thinks I'm a fraud, and worse than being a fraud I peddle Wales to the Saxons, so of course I irritate her. No no, don't . . . We won't argue about it, it's not the topic under discussion. Talking of which . . .' Alun leant forward and said emphatically, but in a lowered voice, 'Don't take what she said at its face value, not any of it. There's something more basic at work there, and yes, you're right, it's connected with what she said to you this evening. Now, the whisky's in the front room.' He spoke to the purpose, in that he and Malcolm had retired to the kitchen for this part of their talk. 'Can I freshen that? Come on, it'll do you good.'

'Do you really think it will? All right, just a small one. Thank you.'

After getting up, Alun laid his hand gently on Malcolm's arm. 'It's all right, boy. I'll explain it to you now. It's not easy but it's all right.'

Malcolm sat on alone. He realised he must be drunk even if only slightly, a state unfamiliar to him for over thirty years, in fact about as long as he had been married to Gwen, until Alun had come back into his life. He felt confused but not dejectedly so, half reassured about Gwen, keeping Rhiannon at the back of his mind for later, not making any connections between the one woman and the other or what each might signify for him. Decent of Alun to come along and listen and, the chances seemed good, sort out what there was to be sorted out. And yet somewhere he felt an apprehension that faded away whenever he started trying to account for it and came creeping back again as soon as he stopped.

Since moving out to the kitchen he had intermittently heard a mumble of voices from the sitting-room, the music first faint then inaudible, once or twice Garth's laughter. Now Alun's voice was raised in some flight or other and more general laughter followed. No, he was not cracking a joke at his, Malcolm's expense – nonsense, paranoid even to think of it. And here he came straight away, not lingering, bustling responsibly back with the two drinks. All his movements were as lively as they had ever been.

Stern-faced, intent on seeing the thing through, he pulled his chair up to the table, which incidentally Malcolm had cleared earlier of most of the odds and ends of supper and earlier meals and nibbles Gwen had left there. He sat up specially straight in his own chair.

'Right,' said Alun in a military bark. 'Right. I'll give it to you in one word. Jealousy. Plain old-fashioned jealousy. Also envy, which isn't by any means the same thing, but no better. I was reading where someone made that point recently – envy's worse for a marriage than jealousy. Welsh writer too. Can't think who for now. Anyway. Something nice, something a little bit romantic has come your way, to wit, Rhiannon. Nothing like that has come her way, poor old Gwen's,' he said, staring quite hard at Malcolm. 'You have a nostalgic day out, you come back in triumph, she punishes you. Simple as that. Don't think hardly of her. Happens all the time wherever there are women. Like a reflex.'

'But I wasn't in triumph, I thought of that, I'm not a complete fool, I guarded against that. I said it was quite fun, food nothing much, bit chilly and so on and so on.'

Foreseeably, Alun had started shaking his head before the last was half over. 'Listen, you come back after that sort of jaunt anything short of minus your head and you come back in triumph, got it? That's how they all . . . oh Christ.'

'But you're saying she was just trying to hurt me.'

'Check.'

'But I wasn't trying to hurt her.'

A fervent groan suggested the hopelessness of any kind of answer to that one.

'But she . . .'

'She'll have forgotten she said it by tomorrow morning.'

'But I won't.'

'Yes you will, not by the morning but eventually, and the sooner the better. Repeat after me – no, you needn't literally but pay attention. She didn't mean what she said. She used words instead of howling and screaming. She was upset – rightly or wrongly doesn't matter. And you swallow it. That's an order.'

'Well, you'd know, I suppose.' Malcolm sighed again. 'All right, I'll do my best. Anyway, how's it meant to fit in with what she said to you?'

'M'm . . .' Alun had whisky in his mouth, in front of his teeth actually, and he held up a finger while he put it out of the way. 'More of the same, only pointing in the other direction. I mean seeing Rhiannon, probably seeing her talking to you, that did it. Gwen wanted to bash her but she couldn't bash her direct because they're old buddies and all that, so she got at her via me, not that she didn't get at me *con* bloody *amore*, what? No problem. Jealousy . . . and envy. More sort of direct envy in this case because it was one female's of another of roughly the same age and circumstances. Plain as the nose on your pikestaff. Happens every day.'

Garth's laughter was heard again faintly, or fairly faintly. Malcolm said, 'It sounds pretty devious to me.'

'Devious my eye. When you've – '

'Sorry, I think that should be tortuous.'

'All right, tortuous my eye then. Once you've – Christ – relinquished the perverse, pig-headed expectation that women should mean what they say and say what they mean except when they're actually lying, this sort of thing gets to be all in the day's work. Tortuous, or devious, *my . . . eye.* Couldn't be more obvious and straightforward.' Alun's voice softened. 'I know Gwen's different in all sorts of ways, but she's the same in some other ways and this is one of those. Agreed?'

'Yes,' said Malcolm after almost no hesitation. 'Of course you're right. It'll just take a bit of getting used to. Well. Thanks, Alun.'

'All part of the service, boy. Now don't mention it to her again, right? Go on as if it had never happened. And be nice to her – but your own experience and common sense'll guide you there. And hey,' he went on as they rose from the table, 'what did you get up to with Rhiannon on Courcey, you old monster? The bloody girl was treading on air when she got back.'

'Oh no,' said Malcolm, turning his face away.

'*Yes*, honest. Looked about twenty years younger. Now just you watch it, Jack, okay? Sardis and Bethesda have their eye on you, see. Christ,' said Alun with regard to the time. 'Just before I go, it's marvellous to hear some of that old stuff again. Let's have an evening of it on our own without all these philistines and Ornette Coleman fans like Peter. But I was going to say, there was one of that lot used to appeal to me particularly, a trumpeter with a French name, would it be Matt, Nat . . .'

'Natty Dominique, a great man. Yes, I've got quite a few tracks with him on. Fancy you remembering him.'

'Perhaps we could hear just a couple before I take off. Didn't he do a lot with George Lewis?'

'I think Dodds more.'

These last exchanges took place as the two were filing from kitchen to sitting-room, so naturally enough Malcolm missed Alun's transitory but enormous looks of release from tension, thanksgiving to tutelary powers, lubricious glee, etc. They found the Playbox inactive, though its ruby on-light still glowed, and Garth telling the others what he had done or seen on some occasion in the past. From the way he shut up at the sight of them it could be deduced that he had not only been talking for the sake of talking but for once knew it too. Peter sat with pursed-up non-specific displeasure. Charlie faced the blank screen of the television set, if not hoping it might spontaneously jump into life any second then merely happening to have his head pointed in that direction. Percy, half settled on the table where the gramophone was, half propped against it, indicated without word or movement that he was not with the others, in no way ill-disposed, just belonging to a different party close by, though about ready for his flight to be called. Nobody seemed to be drinking. After bringing them this far, vitality had given out.

'I thought we might have a last record,' said Alun. 'And perhaps a small one for the road.'

'You have one,' said Percy. 'Of either or both. Thank you for your hospitality, Malcolm. Now I think some of us could afford to be on our way, don't you? Peter, you've got transport . . .'

Garth drew himself up with a fierce exhalation of breath. 'I'm going to walk,' he said. 'Get some fresh air into my lungs.'

'Yes, well there's only Charlie to worry about and I'll take him home. I've got to go there anyway to pick up Dot.'

'You mean from our place?' asked Charlie, twisting round energetically in his seat. 'How do you know she's there?'

'Dorothy went to Sophie this morning for coffee and drinks.'

'I mean how do you know she's still there? Have you rung Sophie?'

'She went to Sophie for coffee and drinks,' said Percy, speaking slightly louder but without in any way changing his placid, matter-of-fact tone.

'But you haven't rung Sophie.' It seemed that Charlie wanted this or something similar put into the file.

'Shut up, Charlie,' said Alun.

'Look now, the sooner we're away,' explained Percy, 'the sooner we can get our heads down.'

They were away very soon after that, all of them, including Alun, who might perhaps have been expected to seize on this capital chance of hearing his couple of tracks undisturbed, but he went off with the others muttering something about having to make an early start in the morning. So, nearly but not quite sure that Alun had come up with the right answer to the Gwen problem, and with his head swimming just slightly, Malcolm poured himself a glass of almost colourless whisky and water and played himself a last record, not all agog and on his feet now but sunk in his uncomfortable little chair.

The choice was what had once been a previously unissued alternate master of 'Goober Dance' (featuring Natty Dominique, cornet). He kept the volume good and low for fear of provoking the retaliation, then or another time, of the reggae-loving butcher's assistant who lived on that side. When 'Goober Dance' finished Malcolm thought he might as well hear another couple of tracks, and fell asleep trying to think of Rhiannon but instead wishing Gwen would come home.

4

'I asked this friend of Angela's what it was,' said Dorothy, 'and she told me it was a Maori dish – you know, the people who went there in boats first of all. Very civilised people. They have all their own things. For instance . . .'

Seated at the far end of Sophie's kitchen table, her husband looked at his watch. 'Two minutes, darling,' he called.

'What happens in two minutes?' asked Peter next to him. 'I'm afire with curiosity.' Well, he was quite interested, and to tell the truth he felt awkward sitting there and saying nothing. He had not had to explain that his presence was part of a routine, the rest of which embraced going wherever he had last heard of Muriel in case she needed a lift home or elsewhere, this without prejudice to her right to leave at any time by taxi without informing him. Having to do that, and so perhaps saving him an hour's profitless drive, made her feel tied down. Tonight he was lucky, in the sense that she was still where she had gone earlier that day, though not visibly so at the moment.

'You'll see, if you're still around then,' said Percy, helpfully answering his question.

'It's more than likely. Finishing a chat with Gwen might take all night.'

'What? Oh, is that what Muriel's doing?'

'Isn't that what you gathered?'

'I didn't gather anything, Peter, I was busy here, as I still am, but it won't be for much longer. Yes, compared with some I consider myself a pretty lucky fellow, having such an easy-to-cope-with wife.'

Peter could think of nothing to say to that. He had been running into Percy for years and years without ever having had to notice anything in particular about him, and had left it a couple of seconds too late now to scan his face and posture for intimations of irony. Of course the fellow was a Welshman. While he was still considering the point without urgency the door slowly opened and Charlie came slowly in, staying near the threshold for a nimble exit if required.

'I think I'm going to bed,' he announced.

'Okay,' said Peter when no one else spoke.

Sophie, next to Dorothy and now as so often her official auditor, looked round. She said through or over some information about the financing of the New Zealander health service, 'Siân's in the little room.'

'What's she doing there?' asked Charlie in the slightly contentious style he had fallen into at Malcolm's.

'Well, sleeping's what she went there for.'

'Can't she do that at home?'

'She's got nothing to go home for any more. You know.'

'As long as nothing needs doing about her.'

'Just leave her,' said Sophie.

This exchange had caused Dorothy's discourse to falter severely, but the flow was soon reestablished. With a gallantly assumed smile Sophie turned back to her. Charlie wandered half-way down the room.

'Alun in cracking form,' he said.

Percy looked at him brightly and in silence. Peter grunted.

'Rising to the occasion. Just the sort of thing that brings out the best in him, convincing a chap like old Malcolm that any misgivings he may happen to have about his . . . personal life are quite without foundation. Tones him up. Mind you, I'd love to know what they actually said to each other, wouldn't you?'

'I think you're jumping to conclusions,' said Peter, his eyes flickering towards Percy.

'Maybe. A summons to the telephone followed by what about paying a call on old Malcolm, that notorious night-owl and reveller. M'm. I predict a catastrophe.'

During these last words of Charlie's, Percy had again looked at his watch and now moved at a moderate pace to a position immediately behind and above his wife.

'They've even kept their own cuisine,' said Dorothy. 'A friend of Angela's cooked a Maori dish for us one evening. It had raw – '

Still unhurriedly, Percy leaned forward, put his hands under her arms and hauled sharply upwards, using great but seemingly not excessive force. Dorothy shot to her feet as smartly as a nail responding to a claw-hammer.

'Here we go, darling,' said Percy, pulling and pushing while Sophie at first stood by, then followed their joint progress. After a short interval Peter and Charlie heard him in the hall saying, 'Piece of cake.' Then the front door shut.

'Quite impressive in its way,' said Charlie.

'I hadn't seen it before.'

'Quite impressive. Sometimes she moves under her own steam without waiting to be counted out. No doubt depending on how she feels.'

'Yes, I suppose it must boil down to that in the end.'

'I think I'm going to bed,' said Charlie to Sophie, who had come back into the room.

'You do that, love. Are you all right?'

'Absolutely fine. Yes, really.'

'I won't be too long. Siân's up there.'

'I'll be fine.' Charlie kissed his wife on the cheek and turned back for a moment to Peter with a distant sparkle. 'Be seeing you. Bit pissed now.'

He had hardly gone, and Peter had hardly had time to start wondering how to handle whatever it was he had to handle, before Muriel entered the kitchen, closely followed by Gwen, whom Peter had barely set eyes on since arriving. Both carried empty glasses and the way each moved brought out for the moment a striking physical resemblance: rather short in the leg and moving slowly and softly, shoulders bowed but head well up and forward, rather pointed nose questing for the wine-bottle. None of those immediately on view had any wine in it. Without verbal or other comment Sophie produced a full one, a litre flask of Emerald Riesling, from a carton next to her sentry-box-sized refrigerator. Sharing the work, Muriel twisted the in-situ cork off the corkscrew in no-nonsense fashion, her head enveloped in cigarette-smoke. Gwen attacked the foil round the neck of the new bottle with a fruit-knife. Neither spoke until liquor was pouring.

'Exit our Dorothy,' said Muriel. 'Not before time let it be added.'

'The sound of the front door shutting was music in our ears,' said Gwen.

Muriel settled herself in her previous place. 'Young Percy didn't exactly fall over himself coming to the bloody rescue, did he?'

'He probably felt like an hour off,' said Peter, who was still rather impressed with Percy's smooth, resolute action and, even more, envious of his air of seclusion in some adamantine sphere of his own. 'That seems very reasonable to me.'

The three women looked at him in silence, Sophie only for an instant while she made for the door, Gwen, seated, rather longer. Muriel's look came over the top of her glass and lasted till she had put it down on the table. Then she said,

'Well, Pete lad, now's your chance for a small break yourself. My friend Gwen and I are just about to settle down for a nice cosy little sisterly chat which I don't honestly see you contributing much to, so you could take off right away, couldn't you? No point in sticking around, eh?' She smiled, or drew back the corners of her mouth and raised her eyebrows.

He had been expecting to be asked to hang on while his wife had one more drink and then to have to hang on while she had one more after that. Under this arrangement he would have been open later on to a charge of having spoilt the drink(s) in question by a display of impatience – this no matter how hard and continuously he might have beamed at everyone in sight – with another in reserve about having dragged her away while she was enjoying herself. She was not an inveterate boozer but when she was on it there was a routine for that too. He was accordingly ill prepared for being ordered out of Sophie's house.

'Oh . . . that's all right,' he said. 'I can easily – '

'No, no, I wouldn't keep you up, old boy.' Muriel gave a waggish laugh. 'You look as if you could do with an early night. Granted it's not that early, but every little helps.'

After another tepid protest or two he was driven from the room. Gwen gave him a farewell twiddle of the fingers and stylised simper that made him feel quite sorry for Malcolm, but only in passing. In the hall cloakroom he reflected, as frequently before, that if the Thomases had a second car, which they or rather she could readily have afforded, then all this would never have arisen. *All* this? A drop out of the ocean. And of course there would still be times like tonight, with her too pissed, or about to become too pissed, to drive. Well, at times like that, when she actually needed him, she could ring him or . . . What was he talking about? Let herself in for feeling tied down and pass up a gilt-edged chance of buggering him about at the same time? He must be joking. He must also have got this far almost as frequently before.

Outside in the hall itself he nearly ran into Sophie wearing a turquoise-blue scarf over her head, which was just unexpected enough to make him say, 'Off somewhere, are you?' Now he remembered, he had heard the telephone tinkle a minute or two before.

'Yeah. Why?' Her normal intonation had never needed much sharpening in order to sound snappish.

'Charlie'll be all right, I suppose?'

'Why wouldn't he be?'

'Well . . .' Peter shifted his head about in a way intended to remind her that as an old friend he rather naturally knew something of her husband's nervous troubles.

'Should be safe enough, shouldn't he, with three people in the house?'

'Oh yes. Yes of course.'

'If you're worried you can stay around yourself.'

This time he moved his head in a different way, thinking perhaps she had been pulling his leg.

'I like a bit of time off too, you know, now and then.'

Before he could give his answer to that, if any, Sophie went back into the kitchen.

5

Gwen and Muriel looked up at the sound of the outside door shutting a second time.

'Peter in a funny mood,' said Sophie.

'You know I don't think drink agrees with him,' said Muriel. 'Never has.'

'Decent of the old boy,' said Gwen, 'to stick up for Percy like that. And shows a great breadth of sympathy too.'

'You'd think he'd realise there's others needs a break,' said Sophie, and went briskly on, 'I'm just off round to Rhiannon's for half an hour. Now you won't be rushing away yet awhile, will you? Stuff in the fridge if you want it,' she said further, though there was enough stuff on the table to keep both the other two chewing hard for a couple of hours. 'Stay if you like, mind, there's another bed in the – '

Muriel interrupted to say she would get a minicab and Gwen interrupted her to say she would drive her, and the two fought over it briefly until Sophie had actually left, though they each managed to get in their thanks for the party and their sendings of love to Rhiannon. After assuring herself that they were indeed alone Gwen turned to Muriel with an intent frown.

'What we were saying – a tin of a good brand with a spoonful of yogurt stirred in . . .'

'And a spot of chopped parsley . . .'

' . . . and they start asking you just which vegetables you've used, isn't there endive in this, can't I taste celeriac. And wanting to know *how* you did it, surely you melted them in butter and so on. I just tell them, the old way, m'm, it's the only proper way.'

Muriel laughed with more elation than might have been expected at a simple discussion of kitchen methods. 'Right, there's not much they can say to that. And of course when it comes to chicken or Scotch broth or whatever, well, what is it, it's cubes and booze, that's what it is, cubes and booze. A tin of oxtail soup and a cube and a tablespoon of whisky and that's it. Not only easier, incomparably easier. *Better*,' she said challengingly. 'Better all along the line.'

'When I look back,' said Gwen, resting her chin on a hand that also had a lighted cigarette in it and squinting towards a recent wine-stain on the tablecloth, 'and think of all that carry-on with the wretched stock-pot, never let it leave the stove, in with every scrap of the joint and you'd have thought a chicken carcass was worth ten times the chicken itself and . . . Do you know, Muriel, would you believe it, time was when I'd go along to the butcher and get bones for the dog, no dog, straight into the bloody pot with the beef-gristle. And for what? What possessed us?'

This time Muriel's response was affectionate as well as appreciative, or at least it sounded like it. In the usual run of things she and Gwen got on no better than all right even when she was not finding Gwen sly nor Gwen finding her loud or strange or both, but midnight could bring some display of amity. Part of this must have come from mere co-survival at the drinks table, as both had reflected before now. But not all; not this time, at least.

Gwen waited for a moment, then said more or less at random, 'After all, it's not as if anybody in the world's going to notice, let alone appreciate even the most obvious . . .'

'Don't make me laugh.'

'I mean they don't even *know*.'

'Of course they don't *know*, love. You can only know if you want to know, and they don't want to know. They have other claims on their valuable attention, as I imagine you must have noticed before.'

'I can't bear the way they – '

'What, them bestir themselves to notice how life's lived in their own home, what makes the bloody world go round? Not them. Why should they? They've won.'

By this stage there was little doubt that those now under discussion were not the same as those who asked Gwen just which vegetables she had used. Nevertheless whatever the two women most wanted to talk about had pretty clearly not yet been broached. Give it time, as they used to say in South Wales when an unlooked-for silence descended on the company. Gwen was the one who let it come, that being what you did if you were the one with the luck when everybody present had given it time.

'Of course she still is very striking, I quite see that, I wouldn't call her beautiful, I never thought she was beautiful, but she is very striking.' She left the name out not through any Cymric instinct of non-committal but because her thoughts were undeviatingly fixed on Rhiannon, as in fact they had been for some minutes past.

Perhaps Muriel's were too: she joined in promptly enough. 'Oh, agreed, with the benefit of a small fortune laid out on facials and massages and health farms and I don't know what all. Plus never having to do a hand's turn in the home.'

'Oh fair enough, but you don't get skin like that out of a tube. And that carriage, you're born with it or you're not. But as for – '

'Not so much as heave a plate on to the bloody rack.'

'It's when it comes to the what would you call it, the social side that I start, um, veering away from the consensus a bit. The conversational – '

'Airs and graces at her age.'

'I mean she's fine on the chit-chat level, nobody better for a good chinwag, oh, I'll give her that, it's just all rather run-of-the-mill. You know, humdrum. Of course, I'm not asking for a discussion of Wittgenstein over the coffee and gingernuts, nothing like that, but it's all very agreeable and chummy and then at the end you ask yourself what has she actually *said*. Nobody's demanding a coruscating shower of wit . . .'

This speech had given Muriel time to do some catching-up. 'Always found her a bit of a bore, quite frankly.'

'Well, I don't think I'd . . .'

'Look, wasn't she . . . didn't you . . . weren't you . . .'

'Wasn't I what, pet?'

'You know, at the . . . place along the road, the . . . *you* know, the poly is it?'

'The university,' said Gwen a little stuffily.

'Yeah, that's right, well weren't you there together about a hundred years ago, you and her?'

'As a matter of fact we were, yes, way back as you say.' Gwen tried to remember what sort of place Muriel had been at. Surely if it had been another university or any other proper seat of learning then Muriel would have impressed it upon her many times over. So it must have been a teachers' training college or some other lowly institution where they had envy dinned into them. She realised she felt pretty vague on the whole topic. 'If the matter is of the smallest interest.'

'Sorry, I was just wondering what sort of showing she made as a student, you know, from the academic point of view.'

'*Oh.*' In the interval, not long but extended by a couple of soft interpolated belches from Muriel, it had returned to Gwen's mind that the place in question had been a school of art named after one of the industrial towns in the North of England and presumably responsible, to some degree anyway, for Muriel's taste in pictures as seen in her house. This made Gwen feel comfortable enough to go on, 'Well, actually now you come to mention it, er, it is quite interesting. She went to all her lectures, well that's sensible if you're not too sure of your own capacity to shine, as it were, and did all her essays, good girl, and would probably have ended up with a pass degree which was all she was going for, if she hadn't . . .'

'Right. What was she, what was she studying?'

'She was reading – ' said Gwen with some weight on the word, then carried on all offhand, ' – biology main with botany subsidiary or the other way round, I can't remember. Some English in her first year I think.'

'Not a very distinguished career do I gather?'

'She was a conscientious student but she didn't seem to take any interest in her subjects the rest of the time. Did her work and that was that, then off out. No shortage of offers as you can imagine. She, er, she never took much part in the swapping of ideas, midnight discussion side of university life.'

Muriel made a backhand gesture putting off consideration of that side of life indefinitely. 'Popular enough with her teachers I dare say.'

'Well: if you mean by that there was any – '

'No no, nothing improper, I'm not suggesting that at all. A girl doesn't have to go anywhere near that far to make herself agreeable to her pastors and masters. Winning ways'll do it.'

'Well,' said Gwen again, and stopped. She wanted quite strongly to oppose what was being insinuated without much idea of why, except that the vertical furrows along Muriel's top lip struck her all of a sudden as most unattractive. They had shown up extra clear in the last half-minute, which was just about when Gwen had found she was no longer being borne along by the thrill of disloyalty. She had talked and drunk herself off the heights of her revolt, though that was not at all the same thing as saying she wanted to go home. And it was miles and miles away from saying she was beginning to grow reconciled to what had taken place, what had almost failed to take place, between herself and Alun. It had been *all her fault* – for not having learnt her lesson years before, for being drunk too early in the day to be allowed for, for chancing her arm with a contemptible sod like that. In the past she had never quite made up her mind whether Alun was on balance to be despised or to be regarded as some sort of engaging rogue. Well, if nothing else, the events of the early afternoon of the day in question, that of the unveiling at St Dogmael's, had settled that one for good and all. But no point in going over it again now, if ever.

Evidently it had been the right moment for Muriel too to take a break. Sitting hunched over the table, she was making patterns with a matchstick in the loose ash that half filled the roomy blue-glass ashtray in front of her and hissing quietly through her teeth, perhaps in search of a new topic, if so in vain, as soon appeared.

'It doesn't make any odds whether you're bright or stupid or anywhere in between,' she said. 'They don't care what you think, what you say, or what you're like at all.'

'They don't even notice.' Gwen reckoned she ought to be able to hold her own here.

'You thought so at first, mind you. At least I know I did. Tell us what you think, love — no go on, I really want to hear. And then when you did tell 'em, well it was quite a long time before I started noticing the glaze in their eyes. They were being good about you talking. You can say what you please because it doesn't matter what you say. It's like, I was reading about one of these Russian satellite places, was it Hungary, anyway wherever it was, what you say's neither here nor there just so long as you don't set about bloody *doing* anything, it might have been Poland. And then they wonder when you start screaming and chucking things at them. Hey, that's like, dead funny isn't it, I never thought of it like that before, but it's like when somebody like a dissident or a minority finds they can't get anywhere through the legal channels so they go round blowing up power-stations. Of course I don't hold with people actually literally doing that, but by Christ I promise you I know how they feel.'

'And then they're never angry back. *You* get angry but *they* don't on purpose, so as to show how silly and childish you are and how mature and marvellous they are. Objective too.'

'It's all right for them to be fed up first, don't forget, like when you're late or they're late. You might be cross when they're late when what they've been up to *matters*, see? When you've not batted an eyelid.'

'And they go off to the club as if they don't love it.' Gwen had started to enjoy herself. 'As if we *don't know*.'

'Why we bother to talk to them passes my comprehension.'

'Ever. I often wonder.'

'They're all shits,' said Muriel. 'And the ones who pretend not to be are the worst of the lot.'

'I suppose so. Sometimes I think we're a bit hard on them.'

'Serve the buggers right, I say.'

It was very quiet in Sophie's kitchen. Even in the 1980s South Wales still kept industrial hours: early to work if any, early home, early in the pub, early to bed. The tendency gave sitting up an extra relish. Muriel poured wine with a mention of one for the road, and Gwen accepted some with a cautionary hand lifted, as at every previous pouring. Then, as if struck by sudden inspiration, Muriel snatched up a cigarette and lit it.

'This may not be a very edifying way of carrying on,' she said judicially and with a demonstrative jerk of the hand, 'but it's a long sight more fun than anything my poor old female parent had a chance of getting up to in her declining years. No cars or parties or telly then. In those days you had your chair and your stick and your cat and that was it.'

'Oh come off it, Muriel,' said Gwen, sharply enough to make Muriel twitch a little. 'I met your mother a couple of times, and one of the times I remember she was waiting for somebody to come and pick her up and drive her somewhere to play bridge. And I'm not at all sure she hadn't got a gin and tonic in her hand while she waited. Stick and cat indeed.'

Apart from the twitch, soon suppressed, Muriel showed not the smallest discomfort or sign of regrouping at this contradiction. 'All right, she was lucky. Thousands weren't. I'm thinking of the days pre-war now, you understand. A different world in all sorts of ways. Altogether different attitudes.' Muriel was talking faster and with more concentration than before, like somebody determined to get through a number of remarks already in mind, more than one perhaps long in mind. 'About marriage for instance. Now we're supposed to think that that generation never discussed anything like that. Well that's probably right enough and they didn't *discuss* it, go into the bloody business in every mortal detail – but you see you can discuss a thing till you're black in the face and end up knowing less about it than when you started. Understanding it less, less well. My mother,' said Muriel forcefully and quickening up further – 'my mother used to talk about the unpleasant side of marriage. No she didn't, she didn't talk about it, she referred to it, that was how she referred to it when she did. Now just you try and imagine the kind of roasting you'd get if you called it that these days. From everybody. But I wonder how many women would disagree with you in their heart of hearts.'

When Muriel did let up, plainly not out of any shortage of material, Gwen looked encouraging and prepared to pay close attention. Whatever was to follow she would pass on to Rhiannon at the first opportunity, not only on intrinsic grounds but also to offset earlier treacheries. Besides, any informed account of relations between Muriel and Peter, long suspected of being bad enough to be interesting, would win no small kudos among the other wives.

Even at prevailing speeds of thought Gwen was quite ready when Muriel went on, in no less of a rush than before and just where she had left off, 'Because they never had time to get used to it, to adjust. It's supposed to come naturally and I expect it does for a very great many, it must do, but not for all. But it's no use saying anything because they don't notice, and then when they do notice they think it's just a female acting up or asserting herself or getting back at them for something else in the way everybody knows they do. So then it's either a huge set-to or hoping it'll be better next time, and funnily enough it always seems to turn out the same way, isn't that striking? And *then* . . . it gets to be too late, very natural that, just like when you're talking to someone and you don't know their name, and you hang on because you're hoping they're going to say it or you'll remember, and then before you know where you are it's too late to ask them. Well, when you've got that far it's no time at all to when it's really too late.

'Some people seem to manage quite okay to keep up with their old buddies after not seeing them for twenty years. Siân was telling me she's still in touch with a mate of hers who went to Toronto I couldn't tell you when but a hell of a long time ago.'

Gwen still said nothing. Very reluctantly, and feeling fed up as well, she saw that she would not after all be able to tell Rhiannon what Muriel had let out, could at most drop a hint or two along with a plea of amnesia. That amnesia might easily turn out to be genuine enough, and even the hint or two might stretch her morning self too far. It could be that Muriel had been half-rationally counting on something like that, trying out an unusual form of self-revelation, one that popped back into the box overnight. Certainly her last couple of sentences had been just the sort of thing you expected to hear on coming round from a fit of extreme apathy in the small hours. No harm in passing that on.

'Would you very kindly telephone for a minicab on my behalf,' said Muriel after a minute of complete silence. She spoke with rather better control than before from much further out. 'The number can be found in my handbag which is somewhere.'

More of the same, thought Gwen, picking up the handbag from within reach. But she made up her mind to be less bothered in future when Muriel seemed to her strange or loud, if she could remember the reason, of course.

6

'Was it baby Babs whose hideous crabs distressed Father Muldoon?
Oh no, it wasn't baby Babs, it was Mrs Rosenbloom . . .'

Alun sang quietly not out of any ordinary precaution, for he was alone at the wheel of his car, but to avoid giving way to anything in the nature of vulgar triumph. On leaving Malcolm's in a mood of heavily qualified satisfaction he had happened to find himself passing, or as good as passing, the house of an old friend. Until the party at the Golf Club they had not met for something like twenty years, met even then hardly long enough for him to tell her she was obviously in terrific fettle and how sorry he had been to hear about Griff. In his day Griff had been a successful and venturesome doctor, unstinting with the early pep pills, master of a sizable red-brick villa on the Beaufoy road. Alun had just had time to ask where she was living now – same place actually, good old Griff, trust him to see her right. Alun had notified himself, more or less as he turned into that road, that if a light happened to be showing there at this hour then he would pull in for a moment and give a toot, or perhaps better a quick ring, just on the off-chance. And there had been a light and the chance had come up.

To take a fresh step in that general direction so soon after nearly coming a cropper over a previous one, while not yet out of that danger in fact, might have seemed foolhardy to some. It certainly did to Alun, or had until the moment he was invited in for a couple of minutes. After that, and especially now he was driving away, it felt more like having successfully gone up in his own light aeroplane immediately after a bit of a spill. That of course made it no less foolhardy in the undertaking. No, well there it was.

At the age of twenty-six or so, having noticed that he was obviously not a particle more grown-up or less reckless than he had been at thirteen, he had been greatly relieved to come across a newspaper article by some fashionable psychologist saying that adolescence among human males could be a drawn-out process, lasting in some respects and cases until the age of twenty-five or even thirty. This assurance had given him intermittent hope and comfort of a sort until about ten years later, when it had come back to him in a moment of what had been, even for him, an outstanding act of goatish irresponsibility. Thereafter he had clung to the consolation that there was nothing he could do about it.

The house in Holland when he approached it had a light on in the sitting-room, a departure from his expectation that brought mild vexation cross-hatched with foreboding. The vexation went along the lines of here he was, having taken all this trouble to leave people to themselves, give them plenty of time to get themselves off to bed, faced now with God-knew-what hold-up before he could get himself off there after a hard day. The foreboding was less straightforward.

For Rhiannon to be still up and on her own much after eleven, never mind getting on for one o'clock in the morning, was unheard-of, imaginable only in bombshell situations, good news it might be, bad much more likely. Short of that, she would most probably have Rosemary with her, back from her evening out (or somewhere) with William Thomas, who seemed to have been around since first light or thereabouts. It was no trouble at all for Alun to picture the bloody girl looking up alertly this very moment at the sound of his engine, getting into position next to her mother as president of a two-woman court of inquiry into his recent activities and overall behaviour. Or it would be Rosemary on her own, no more alluring an option. Whereas other possibilities hardly bore thinking about: Gwen with an expanded edition of her grievances? Malcolm with a more accurate one of his? The police he ruled out unless a mistake had been made. An incident in Harriston in 1950 involving a woman probationary sergeant and a patrol van might well have seriously displeased them at the time, but at this date could surely be passed over as grounds for a midnight descent on a non-black.

These speculations and others went through Alun's head while he was still driving up to the house. When he got closer he saw there was a car parked outside it, one he was nearly sure he had seen not far away not long before. That was the best he could do: he knew well enough that car recognition was an important proficiency for one who led his sort of life after hours, but he had been neglecting it, was still dangerously unschooled in local detail. Moving on foot to the front door he let his neck go rubbery and his eyes uninquiring, getting ready to lurch into action as a drunk. Then he sort of remembered it was Rhiannon he would be hoping to fool and went ordinary again, in so far as he now could. After it was too late he started trying to think of a topic to take the initiative with.

When he walked springily into the sitting-room he was faced with Rhiannon in towelling dressing-gown over nightie and Sophie in day clothes; no Rosemary. Neither of the two present smiled very positively or spoke. Without thought, intent only on action, he moved over and kissed each of them in turn, then, as his brain began ticking over once more, he stepped back and gave Sophie a sequence of cheerful interrogative nods.

She responded at once. 'I had Dorothy, I was saying to Rhiannon, and then I had Muriel, she's probably still there. Really one of her nights. Bad as I've ever known her, she was. Cruel. You don't see her like it, you know, Rhi. Gwen dropped in and I left Muriel putting her through it. Just nipped out,' she ended, with a girls-together half-wink at her chum.

'I don't blame you,' said Alun warmly. Good old Soaph, he thought with more genuine warmth — never any need to worry there from the word go. Not really bright as you usually thought of it, but bright as a button when it came to anything that bore on the old ins and outs: the throwaway mention of Gwen was a typical touch. With a quick switch he added, 'Rosemary gone to bed, has she?'

'Just this moment,' said Rhiannon. 'I wonder you didn't bump into William as you drove up.'

'Oh, he just dropped her off like that, did he?'

'Well, yes.'

'I see.'

At no point could Alun have said what he meant by his last question. But whatever it might have been intended to convey — surprise, resignation, outrage, boredom, disappointment, fatherly concern, heartfelt co-masculine approval — he of all people had no business to be asking it in front of these two, or perhaps anywhere on earth. This dawned on him a bit at a time while he stood there taking in the information. Then he suddenly said,

'You know if by any chance this ridiculous weather carries on, we could probably do worse than go down to Birdarthur for a couple of days. Old

Dai the Books still keeps up his place on the cliff there. Sophie, you've stayed in that cottage, haven't you?'

'Oh, I'm included in this, am I?'

'Why not, there's two decent bedrooms and Charlie can leave Victor at the tiller for a spell. Not next week because I'm filming then. Dai's only ever there at weekends, he was telling me. I didn't manage to get him at the shop today . . .'

It would have been miraculous if he had, not having gone within a league of the place, tried it by telephone or even admitted Dai the Books to his thoughts more than a few seconds before pronouncing the name, though the facts were as stated. Anyway, with his talents for persuasion, which had less to do with direct pressure than with making something sound fun for long enough, he soon had Sophie's assent to the Birdarthur project with Charlie's thereby taken for granted. Rhiannon's had been taken for granted from the start.

'Well, I'm off,' said Alun finally. 'Don't break the party up on my account, now.'

'You needn't think you're going to get away like that, *was*,' said Rhiannon.

Into Thy hands, O Lord, thought Alun to himself. Although he often said where he was going, or might have been going, he never said where he had been, nor did Rhiannon ever ask until . . . unless . . .

'You take that creature out, outside, and then settle her down in her basket in the kitchen. And mind you wait and make sure before you let her back in.'

Enfeebled by the exertions of her day, Nelly had responded to Alun's arrival with no more than a couple of feeble thumps of her tail and a lunatic gleam out of the very corners of her eyes. Now, hearing herself referred to, she made a slovenly attempt to sit up and did a thorough squeaking yawn that would have been quite impressive in an animal of any size. He took her away as bidden, but in a style that emphasised his decency in doing so, his detachment from the whole concern. It was not that he disliked the puppy, rather the contrary: he just could not afford to let it be thought that he could be roped in any old time to minister to her needs. Why, next thing he knew he would be rushing back from Griff's or somewhere to give the bloody hound her tea!

7

When the door had shut behind Alun there were two releases of breath of which neither quite amounted to a sigh of relief. Sophie lowered herself to the floor, twisted her head about till it rested comfortably against the arm of the chair behind her and said she must be going. Rhiannon suggested more coffee, adding that it would only take a minute, and rearranged her legs under her on the sofa. They sat in a more or less habitable corner of the room with bare boards and half-decorated walls hardly out of reach.

Sophie had probably missed the coffee proposal altogether. 'You ought to get out more, you know, Rhi,' she said.

'Oh no. It's so lovely not having to after years of not wanting to and having to.'

'It'd be easier if you learnt to drive.'

'Not you too,' said Rhiannon, bouncing upright. 'I can drive as well as anybody if I haven't actually forgotten how. I drove a dry-cleaners' van for eighteen months in London when we were hard up. It's not I can't drive, it's I don't drive. There being no car except the one with Alun in it. Can't afford a second car, he says, at least he'd say if I brought it up again ever. He does all the shopping I can't do round the corner and if I want to go anywhere there's a minicab. Much cheaper than running another car ourselves. And no parking problem. He'd say that too. You try him.'

'Funny, he's never been one to pinch the pennies. I mean . . .' Sophie looked about her, but there was little evidence of lavishness except perhaps the only picture so far on display, a large Cydd Tomas over the fireplace, dated 1981 under the artist's signature and yet attractive enough – it very likely showed Dragon's Head from the sea – to be almost worth its place on that ground alone.

'Sure, no trouble there,' said Rhiannon, 'but it's nothing to do with that, the point is with him having the car nobody ever knows where he is, and me not having a car, everybody knows where I am, only that's not nearly so interesting. Take tonight, now.'

'M'm. Any idea where he'd been?'

'Not the faintest, have you?'

'I only hope it was somebody sensible.'

'Oh, me too.' Rhiannon paused before going on. 'How was Gwen really?'

'Oh. Coming round, I reckon. Still a bit shirty but going to be okay as long as he doesn't make any waves for a bit.'

'If only he had the sense to keep it in the family, sort of.'

'I know,' said Sophie, 'I couldn't agree with you more. Especially now he's down here. It's not like London down here.'

'Absolutely. It's silly of him in another way too. It lands up there are things we can't talk about, him and me. I don't mean important things, I mean unimportant things, but they're still quite important when you add them together. Who was there and how they seemed and what was said . . . At least it makes it harder.'

'M'm. Is he all right, Rhi, do you think?'

'All right?' repeated Rhiannon in alarm. 'How do you mean?'

'No, nothing, he just seems to have got a bit wild. You'd think he'd know by now not to take up with Gwen all of a sudden like that and then expect to get away with treating her like . . .'

'Take up with Gwen *again* all of a sudden like that, but it doesn't really make any – '

'Oh, I didn't realise they were – '

'Oh yes. Funny, I never thought he was very keen. In fact I wonder a bit who took up with who, either time. Of course it was more all right for her then, not being exactly the only pebble on the beach. She had other things in her life then.'

'Like Malcolm,' said Sophie.

'Yeah.'

That was all for the moment. Sophie sat with her arms round her knees, shapely sleek dark head towards the thick shaggy rug as if she was following a train of thought, not a thing she often gave any sign of doing. Rhiannon lit a cigarette, holding the flame as usual a couple of millimetres inwards from the tip. She had wondered a little at the time what had brought Sophie along to her so late, nearly too late to find her up. Something to do with Alun, it had soon emerged; saying she hoped he was settling down all right after the move from London, not saying what she could well have been thinking now, that she also hoped his recent goings-on did not mean she had lost her special bit of hold on him, however lumpy that bit might have looked to the outside world. For various reasons Rhiannon too hoped as much, but felt that here in Wales that was not the sort of thing you could really say. So with no particular intention she asked how Charlie was, rather less inquisitively than when she had asked after Gwen.

'That bugger knocks it back like a fool,' said Sophie without looking up.

'Yes, I thought . . .'

'I never realised how much he drank till the night he came home sober. A revelation, it was.'

'Not even nice at the time, I don't suppose.'

'What had happened that day I'll never know. Anyway it was a hell of a night after that. He made me sit up with him till he was asleep which wasn't till after two, and then it couldn't have been much after four he was cootched tight up to me, stiff as a board and breathing in and out, in and out as if he was doing it for a bet. And he wouldn't say what it was, what the matter was. I went on and on asking him but he wouldn't say. Next day he was paralytic by six, Victor said.'

'If he's going to make you sit up and all that, he really ought to say.'

'He's never said, except being alone makes it worse and the dark isn't good. I've given up trying to get him to try and say what it is. All he's ever said is it's nothing to do with anything and it doesn't mean anything. I'm fed up. He ought to say *something*. I mean about *something*. It gets depressing when a bloke never says anything. There's not as much difference as you might think between him pissed as a lizard and him passed out. Not when he's with me there's not. I quite like him, old Charlie, or I used to, and I miss him, sort of.'

Rhiannon took her time about finishing her cigarette. 'Sounds as if the two of you could do with a nice break. You will come to Birdarthur, won't you? You and I can have a proper gas. Alun'd like you to be there too. He's always complaining he never seems to see enough of you.'

Now Sophie did look up. 'Oh, he doesn't, no, does he really?'

'*Yes*, always going on about where's Sophie these days.'

'Oh no, really?'

'Won't do him any harm either to get away for a bit. Now there's a bloke who says something if you like. If only the silly little thing would learn to leave it at that.'

7   Alun

1

Soon after eight o'clock on a Tuesday morning Alun lifted the hatch at the rear of what he occasionally called the family car, or even our family car, though not in Rhiannon's hearing. The two were off to Birdarthur shortly. It had been agreed that Charlie and Sophie should follow them out the next day in time for lunch, with all four set to return late on the Friday. Alun's move to let the Cellan-Davieses know of the impending trip had consisted in full of ringing their number once the previous noon, a fore-doomed venture seeing that Gwen was expected at Siân Smith's for coffee, etc., and Malcolm strongly presumed to have left for the Bible, but it counted as not having been able to get hold of them. Peter had been told he really must come down, pick any time to suit himself, just turn up, and after a word or two about a bloody Welshman's invitation had conceded he might try. First categorically disowning any responsibility for anybody or anything, Tarc Jones had consented to write down the number of the people called Gomer who lived two along from the telephone-free abode of Dai the Books.

Alun had not so much lifted the hatch of his car as flung it boyishly upwards, which was something he would have done with no more and no less vivacity if he had thought he was being observed, and in that event whether by jobless school-leaver or high-ranking TV executive. First into the cargo-space went, in quick time, a carton of drinkables: twelve-year-old Scotch, classy spring water to put in it, gin, tonics, a rare bottle of Linie-Aquavit from Oslo, a much commoner bottle of Bailey's Irish Cream, ostensibly for Rhiannon, in fact no more than chiefly for her, one each of Asti Spumante and Golden Sweet Malaga absolutely solely for her, four large cold Special Brews in wet newspaper for him, and a spot of coffee liqueur and other muck he could not quite face simply throwing out of the house. Next he stowed a box of hand-picked groceries, featuring soused herring fillets, allegedly smoked oysters, German lumpfish roe and other dainties thought to be proper to accompany the aquavit. He laid on top of this a flat paper bag containing a new pullover in yellow cashmere and two sports shirts still in their packaging.

Trips, up to and including ones directed at funerals, had always heartened

Alun, livened him up in prospect, and not just because you never knew what you might run into even in Blaenau Ffestiniog. It was admittedly getting a touch late with him for breaking new ground, however cruelly he might ravage the old. In addition, this coming trip was not a fit occasion for any of that, and besides there was nothing under Birdarthur in the for-his-eyes-only address book. A big part of the thrill could probably be put down to nothing more than anticipating a journey by car, by no means an everyday experience in the South Wales of the 1930s and later, as he had been known to remind his London friends. But with all that said he got through the first part of the loading in fine breezy style, as also the second and duller part involving actual luggage and bedclothes and pillows assembled by Rhiannon after managing to get hold of Dai at the shop. The third part slowed him down.

This part began with a typewriter, not the one from his study upstairs, the noble Japanese office-pattern needless-to-say electric job, but the lowly Italian portable, an acoustic model, as he would express it when he had the energy. Another carton followed it, not nearly such a nice one as the one full of drink, containing books and papers. The books included the *Concise Oxford*, a collapsing Roget's *Thesaurus, Y Geiriadur Mawr* – The Big [Welsh-English/English-Welsh] Dictionary to him, a compilation notable for its *golygydd ymgynghorol* – the Rev Tydfil Meredith's *Courcey and Its Churches*, Sefton-Williams on Celtic mythology and the Brydan Complete Poems. Out of simulated personal need as well as feigned piety he took the last-mentioned volume with him everywhere he went within reason, pointless at best this trip perhaps with only Charlie and Sophie and possibly Peter to bowl over, but there it was. The papers in the carton consisted of typing paper and forty-six pages of a novel of whose existence only Rhiannon knew, together with a few notes.

Doing some more work on this novel was an unstated reason for going to Birdarthur, already present somewhere in his mind before he blurted out the suggestion a couple of weeks before. He had knocked off the dreaded forty-six in six days in the spring, when a little bastard in BBC radio had tardily cancelled the definitive talk on the Welsh nonconformist conscience he had engaged to prepare and record, and he had not looked at them since. Now, under the self-imposed pressure of a measured length of time in semi-confinement with no excuse for shirking, he was to apply himself to the hideous task of adding to them. As they stood, or with some minor surgery, they were supposed to be, he had striven to make them, his devout hope was that they were, the opening section of the only really serious piece of prose he had written since his schooldays. In more sanguine moods he softened this to his most serious, etc. But anyway a great deal, including the prospects for the whole undertaking, hung on whatever he would make of those forty-six in two or three hours' time.

No wonder then that his demeanour was staid as he settled the creative container into place. And yet he felt an obscure excitement, nothing to do with any literary burgeoning except very remotely, just an internal squaring-up to a tiny bit of a leap in the dark. 'I was ever a fighter,' he muttered defiantly, continuing in a milder tone, 'or perhaps more accurately ever a medium-range light bomber designed for night operations and low-level reconnaissance. Thank you.' He reckoned he had it about as near right by now as he was ever going to get it.

After that it was a cakewalk to shuttle the bloody puppy round to the char's daughter's, cancel the papers and fetch the ordinary suitcases and the rest of the gear out to the car. Last to go in were the heavy waterproofs and gumboots indispensable to the visitor to rural Wales at any season. The weather for the moment in fact was clear without being bright, though scattered showers were unadventurously forecast. Rhiannon turned up for the off at blokes' time as usual, wearing a dress with some sort of pattern, also shoes, or so Alun assumed. Likewise as usual on any journey she reached over and squeezed his hand when the wheels started turning.

On Courcey the roads were practically empty, flushed of visitors by a lightening revolution in taste or nuclear accident. Even the streets of Birdarthur itself were unobstructed, with no obvious tourists to be seen. Brydan Books, dimly viewed by Dai as a pillar of greed and also as unethical competition, held no customers for the moment, nor was any Continental bus stuck on the acute-angled turn up to St Cattwg's church, in whose shadow the poet slept. There was some activity in the approaches to the Brydan Arms, though that had been just as true at mid-morning when the place was still called the White Rose. With the end of its function as a port and the closure of the metal works and the silica quarry, Birdarthur had shown marks of unemployment, but none were visible now that the town had been designated or turned into an enterprise zone and the unemployment had gone away somewhere else.

Alun took them round the corner by the Brydan Burger Bar and into the road – unmade for centuries, metalled now to suit visiting traffic – that ran above the foreshore and the larger and deeper part of the bay. The tide was full, near the turn, the sea flat calm and ginger-beer grey touched with green and yellow. The sight of the sun going down here had been a special favourite of Brydan's, people were always saying, and indeed he had been well placed physically to witness it from his cottage near the start of the row facing the water, though how often he had been up to taking it in, even when technically conscious, was another question. After extensive refitment to mend the devastations of his tenure, the building had been converted into a museum and gift shop, especially gift shop, and the one next door a little later into a coffee shop and refreshment bar that, excusably in the circumstances, sold no strong drink. From the secured outer door of this a lone elderly female in a parachute jacket, of necessity an American, was turning away in bafflement just as the Weavers passed.

They passed along to the end of the line of cottages where there was a rough triangle of waste ground spread with refuse old and new. A cinder-path led on from here, signposted Brydan's Walk, though again local opinion doubted whether you would ever have got boyo to set foot on it, there being no pub or free-pound-note bloody counter at the other end. By prearrangement Alun sent Rhiannon on foot down the walk while he turned the car round and backed it after her for eighty yards or so, until the path was too narrow for him to go on. So he stopped there and more or less watched her unload all the stuff through the hatchway. Then he drove back to the triangle and parked arse-first up a muddy and precipitous lane and hurried to rejoin her.

'There must be an easier way of doing this,' he said, catching her up actively with the case of booze clasped in his arms, 'but I can't seem to think of one.'

'Oh, I can. You climbing over and out of the back and taking the whole lot out and carrying it to the cottage and putting it all away.'

'Strange the way things come back to one. Before we left I could hardly have told you which direction Dai's place was, and now we're here I haven't even had to hesitate.'

'Whereas I remembered this bit perfectly. Very strange.'

'Put those down and I'll come back for them, go on. Oh, all right, suffer then. What's for lunch?'

'Pork pie and baked beans.'

'Did you bring the mustard?'

'Yes, and Spanish onion and sweet pickle.'

'Little genius.'

They had reached Dai's place, not the prettiest or best-situated on this side of Birdarthur but by no means the dampest or the smelliest, a two-up-two-down affair with a sliver taken off one of the two up to form a narrow bathroom-lavatory, so narrow that only someone with thighs rather on the short side could have expected to use it in full comfort. Rhiannon went to and fro opening all the windows.

'No trouble round here guessing who was brought up in a bloody town,' said Alun. 'Say the word and I'll knock a hole in the kitchen wall for you.'

'You can take these out to the bin,' said Rhiannon, passing him a trayful of elderly foodstuffs. 'How long has anyone not been here?'

'Hey, some of these are all right, aren't they? What about this pot of – '

'You eat what you fancy.'

When he had checked in with the Gomers and established that no dollar-laden commissions had materialised in the last couple of hours, Alun cleared a space for his typewriter at one end of a smallish table by the front-room window. Doing this entailed shifting a number of uncommonly horrible china dogs and other creatures. Their surfaces were blurred, with a buggered-about look as though someone, perhaps under Muriel Thomas's influence, had caused a flame-thrower to play upon them at some stage of manufacture. Their colours were off too. He bundled them away in a cupboard, thinking it was a bit hard to have come all the way out to south-west Courcey and walk into a bunch of boldly innovative china dogs at the end of it.

To put off the evil hour he ran his eye over Dai the Books's books and soon saw there would be nothing worth even short-listing for removal. The works of Brydan, on the other hand, were present in all sorts of editions, rendering his own copy of the poems an even more superfluous piece of luggage than before. Like everybody else in middle South Wales over the age of thirty, not to speak of many further off, Dai had his Brydan connections. On the wall there was a framed blow-up of the famous almost pitch-dark photograph of the two of them he kept in his shop. He used to say he had had Brydan in there to lend him a hand once or twice in the school holidays – liked to think he had done a bit to help the lad out. In fact Brydan's main association had come rather later, when he used to drop in on his way to the station to steal a few pieces of new stock for subsequent resale, or rather sale, in that second-hand joint off Fleet Street. Alun shook his head at the memory. A great writer, he sometimes thought to himself and had often said in non-Welsh company, but in too many ways a sadly shabby human being.

Almost in the act of turning away from the shelves he caught sight of a strip of jacket he recognised, that enwrapping *The Blooms of Brydan*, a selection by Alun Weaver. Some alchemy, compounded of a nervy literary agent, a gullible publisher, a matter of coincidence with the date of Brydan's death and a historic review in *Time* magazine, had turned the produce of three weeks' work into a quite decent and lasting annuity: 5,000 last year in hardback in the USA alone and *Brydan's Wales* still very much alive. Whenever reminded of this Alun was tempted to think of himself as quite good at making money in his line, better than at pushing himself forward, not enough of a power man for that, too much of a sensual Celt. And in recent weeks he had been wondering rather about how he was doing, how he was making out as the organ-voice of Wales in Wales. Perhaps after all he had been more audible in England, where competing strains were fewer and less clamorous. He had never quite got over the paucity of his welcome home at Cambridge Street station. So be it: here squarely in front of him was a chance to do something about that all round.

He was sitting at the table looking out of the window at the seashore when Rhiannon came in wearing – well, he was nearly sure she had changed her clothes.

'Sorry, are you – '

'No, just wool-gathering. Can't think how that's got itself a bad name, can you? Pricey stuff, wool. Getting it for free, too.'

'I thought I'd just take a look round the town. I haven't set eyes on it for donkey's years.'

'Fine, see you later, love.'

'What did you make of Ingrid?'

'Ingrid?'

'Ingrid Jenkins or whatever she's called. You know, Norma's daughter.'

'Who's – of course, the char, the char's daughter. To be sure. Well.'

'M'm, what did you make of her?'

'I don't know, I don't know that I made anything of her. Seemed perfectly pleasant, I only saw her for a moment. Why, what should I have made of her?'

'Oh, nothing. Did she seem the sort to look after Nelly properly, did you think?'

'Christ, Nelly's the puppy, right? Yes, fine. Well, I mean the whole place looked respectable enough. Clean. Things like that. I mean . . .'

'Oh, good.' Rhiannon's manner changed. 'I couldn't have brought her here, could I?'

Alun thought he saw now where this conversation was designed to lead. 'No, no,' he said, frowning at the idea. 'No, out of the question.'

'You can't leave them on their own for a minute when they're that age. I'd have had to be taking her out the whole time or else stay indoors with her here. Or make you.'

'Cheers. No, of course. You couldn't have brought her along and have any kind of proper break yourself. Out of the question.'

'M'm. Are you going to look at that stuff of yours?'

'Just glance at it, you know.' He always kept her roughly abreast of what he was up to in the writing part of his life. About broadcasting, with the sudden excursions here and there it might require, he was sometimes less informative.

'Good luck, dear. Be about an hour.'

She was gone. Yes, what she had wanted was moral support for farming out the pooch. Normal and understandable. He made to pick up the horrendous buff envelope in front of him, then paused with a groan. There had been something crappy about what had gone before that. What the bugger had it been? Something to do with Ingrid. He had barely glanced at the girl – well, female, pushing forty he had supposed, smallish, pale; nothing else. So obviously there could be no question of . . .

He gave a muffled cry, then, remembering he was alone in the house, unmuffled it. His glance dropped to the floor at his side, to the carton of books there, to the scuffed green cover of the paperback *Thesaurus*. Absurdity, he subvocalised: stuff and nonsense, fiddle-de-dee, bosh, bunk, rats. *Ffwlbri*. Tell it to the Marines. *Credat Judaeus Apella*. If Rhiannon had been stirring the pond to catch him betraying an interest in this Ingrid, if she really thought he might have in mind getting off with the charwoman's daughter, then she was barmy. Unless that kind of suspicion, suspicion of stuff at that level, though unfounded in this case, was not unreasonable in general, was no longer unreasonable, in which case he was the barmy one. Was that the way it was going to take him – not willingness or ability but judgement, nous?

Several unalluring trains of thought presented themselves at this juncture. He found himself in pursuit of the one about anybody of any sense knowing when he was well off with Rhiannon. But he had not got any sense, or enough sense, or . . . But he had got this far a thousand times without ever having got any further. He hoped his unpreparedness for the Ingrid question had let his innocence show through, because if not there was nothing he could say about it; it was much too late for any of that, ever. Almost eagerly he picked up the envelope.

Before he had got as far as pulling the contents out his demeanour changed to a frenzied casualness. Head on one side, eyebrows raised and eyes almost shut, mouth turned down at the corners, he condescendingly turned back the flap, exposed the top half of the first sheet and allowed himself to let his glance wander over the typewritten lines there before he actually fell asleep as he sat. What he read woke him up with a start and set him doing what he had very, very nearly done a minute before: leap out of his chair and go glug-bloody-glug with the Scotch, not forgetting to top up his glass before returning whence he had come. There he slumped and stared out at the bay and tried to reason with himself.

Of course the first couple of sentences had reminded him of the opening passages of dozens of stories and novels by Welshmen, especially those written in the first half of the century. That was the whole point, to stress continuity, to set one's face against anything that could be called modernism and to show that the old subject, life in the local villages, in the peculiar South-Wales amalgam of town and country, had never gone away, in fact had a new ironical significance in these days of decline. Worth doing, agreed, but had he done it, any of it? Well, he might have. Like Socrates now, who when his time came (he remembered reading) had quite willingly and cheerfully drunk off the hemlock, he laid the typescript down on the table just like that and began at the beginning.

After five minutes or so he began to relax his rigid bomb-disposal posture. From time to time as he went on he winced sharply and made a correction, screwed up his face in pain or goggled in disbelief, but several times gave a provisional nod and even laughed once or twice without mirth. At the end of an hour Rhiannon came back and found him at the typewriter with four lines and a bit along the top of the paper. When he looked up she spoke.

'How did it go?'

He scowled ferociously at her and held his hands in the air with the fingers crossed. 'It may be remotely conceivable,' he stage-whispered with precise delivery, 'that not every single syllable is absolutely beyond all hope of redemption.'

'Oh, good.'

'No no no, not good, nothing more than a bare possibility. It needs a lot doing to it. But I thought I'd better press on while I felt like it, rather than go back and start tinkering. No, keep your distance, girl,' he said as she seemed about to close in and deal him a congratulatory hug. 'Later, if ever.'

'All right, though, isn't it?' She went on standing near the foot of the stairs. 'There's just . . .'

'What?' he asked ill-naturedly.

She made a crying face. 'Dorothy rang while you were taking Nelly to Ingrid's . . . and she asked us over for tonight . . . and I couldn't not tell her why we couldn't go . . . and then she asked if she and Percy could drive down tomorrow evening . . . and I couldn't tell her they mustn't . . . sorry . . .'

Having filled all the gaps in Rhiannon's speech with strong language or wordless howls, Alun waited till it was a theatrical certainty that there was no more to come and said, 'Is there more to come? Siân or Garth or old Owen Thomas or bloody fishface Eirwen Spurling or . . . Because if there is . . .'

'I couldn't help it, honest.'

'No, of course you couldn't, dull,' he said, embracing her. 'You'd need a tank division with close air support to fend off the bag in question. No, we'll manage. Think yourself lucky the work of words went all right this morning, mind. Now drink – gin and tonic coming up. Go on, *myn*, you're on holiday.'

He finished his paragraph in the few minutes it took her to put the lunch out in the kitchen. When they had eaten and, quite freely in his case, drunk, Rhiannon declared she would never have thought getting shot of the puppy would be so much like getting shut of the girls years ago and disappeared for a rest. Alun found on Dai's shelves a book of short stories about Cardiganshire life in the 1930s by a Welshman whose name he barely recognised – right up his street, especially at this stage – and an old Alistair McAlpine paperback about a raid on a Gestapo HQ in Holland, now a feature film, it said, and by the time he fell asleep in Dai's beaten-up armchair by the midget fireplace the colonel (Richard Burton) and the wing-commander (Trevor Howard) were already synchronising their watches for the drop. On awakening he fell asleep again with no trouble at all, but on reawakening took Rhiannon a cup of tea. Then he wrote a dozen lines of dialogue while she pottered about overhead, and then went out for a stroll.

The land and sea were quite boringly normal to look at, mousey grey at any sort of distance, but there were some yellow and slate-blue patches of sky that might once have meant something to the locals. They went along Brydan's Walk to the far end where it petered out among scruffy bushes and long pale grass, down a cliff path to the beach and back along the foreshore. A part of this was in the process of being flattened for something to be built on it. Half a dozen birds were wandering about near the water's edge, herons or oystercatchers; Brydan would have known which, or would have said. A few sailing dinghies heaved sluggishly in the harbour. At its corner they took a shallow flight of steps up to the main level and walked up the High Street with the name Birdarthur to be seen on shops, offices, posters, postcards wherever they looked. At the beginning of the narrow part, opposite what had been a bakery on their last visit, stood the pub, almost unchanged since longer than that except that it looked somehow newer. The sign, White's Hotel, was brilliant gold on navy-blue.

The inside looked much newer still and was not at all unchanged, so little so that Alun could have sworn he had never been in there in his life, but he was used to that by now and took comfort from the forbearance of the music, generic sleepy-lagoon muck full of swirls and tinkles. On a window-sill next to a fat potted plant there rested an object without a name in his vocabulary, a kind of video-screen on which streams of sparkling coloured light flowed through clouds and bands of steadier illumination. In some equally undefined but still horrible way a connection with the music seemed to be suggested. He would make a note of the phenomenon for putting into the *In Search of Wales* file, but first he sat Rhiannon down in a kind of medieval pew against the opposite wall and went to the bar. Here the order of white wine produced a glass of white wine instead of the stare of gloomy triumph that could once have been counted on in these parts, and he was asked which whisky he preferred instead of settling for what was planked in front of him, as fond memory would have it.

Rejoining Rhiannon he found an old man had settled himself on a padded stool facing her and was going on as if he was a great friend of them both by all means short of speech. Seen from in front he looked a really very old man, fit to give Alun himself a good four to five years, the precise model of the kind of sturdy, self-reliant Welshman who had tilled the neighbouring acres and fished the waters since time immemorial, and also one of the kinds of bloody *lossin* and berk he would dearly have liked to hit in the eye straight off with a jet of soda-water in the days before syphons went out. On his white head the fellow wore a white hat, though it was not obvious what this signified or how it had arisen.

Seating himself next to Rhiannon in the pew, Alun conversed with her for a few moments about the place and the people until he was sure that this was no previously undeclared uncle of hers. Then, telling himself he was buggered if he was going to be diverted, he brought out his ring-spine notebook and started on a pen-picture of the sparkling-light facility as intended.

If the white-hatted sod had missed anything that had taken place in front of him in the last couple of minutes it could not have been by much. He said now, in a bass voice that sounded to Alun like a close imitation of a dance-hall proprietor he used to know, 'Yes, well, you're a writer, aren't you?'

'Yes,' said Alun when Rhiannon had banged him in the ribs.

'Yes. Here after Brydan, are you?'

'What? Well no, not exactly.'

'A lot of them comes after Brydan. Brydan was a famous poet used to live here in Birdarthur. He used to come into this pub quite frequent, with Americans. He used to call it White's Club. Because it was like a club, he said. He was a Welshman, Brydan, but he wrote in English, see.'

'Yes, I know.' Alun's life was coming to consist more and more exclusively of being told at dictation speed what he knew.

'Brydan was a Welshman himself, but he wrote . . . his poetry . . . in the English language.'

'Indeed he did, in fact – '

'But he was a Welshman through and through. Don't you go thinking you can understand Brydan,' boomed the old sod, rocking back and forth slightly on his stool and smiling, but making it three parts plain he meant Alun rather than the world in general, 'that's *understand* Brydan, eh? – not being Welsh yourself.'

'For your information I am Welsh myself. I was born and brought up not twenty miles from here.'

'No, no, I say *not* being Welsh yourself you can't understand Brydan. It's Welsh people can, right? Appreciate. Appreciate is better. Yes, appreciate. Fully appreciate.'

'But . . .' Alun could think of nothing to say. His awareness that Rhiannon was sending him furtive hushing looks did nothing to loosen his tongue. Actually of course he could think of an enormous number of things to say, though none at all that would not make him seem to have lost some argument or other. 'But . . .'

'A writer, you say. For a paper, is it?'

'No. Yes. Sometimes.'

The sod seemed to think this a full and satisfactory answer, or at least one worth thinking over before moving on. He had got as far as stretching out a finger in Alun's direction when a young man with very short, almost colourless hair hurried in from the street and came over. As well as having pale hair he had a large face and was slightly moist about the nose and eyes. Looking at Alun and Rhiannon he lifted his head sidelong in consternation or apology.

'You're late, Grandad,' he said loudly. 'Tea'll be on the table now. On your way, Winston Churchill.' Without lowering his voice much he added, 'I hope he hasn't been too much of a pest.'

Alun could only think of saying, at the cost of some damage to his sense of justice, that he had had a most pleasant chat.

'No kidding?' The youngster looked more closely at him and his large face broke into a smile. 'Hey, I know you. Seen you on television, haven't I? What is it, the Welsh something, the Welsh side of things? Tell me now, that, what's he called, Bleddyn Edwards, is he a great mate of yours?'

'No, I don't think I've even – '

'Well, I'm no expert but it's perfectly obvious to me – he's not up to the job – you are. All the difference in the world,' said the young sod with an authority his alleged ancestor would have had to acknowledge. 'No comparison.'

'That's very nice of you.'

'Get away, marvellous to have met you. Good luck, and thanks for putting up with old buggerlugs here.'

'Well, that was all right,' said Alun as he and Rhiannon came out of the pub a little while later. 'Not like life at all.'

She squeezed his arm against her. 'Good boy for not going for that old fart.'

What with one thing and another he felt quite pleased with life for the rest of the evening. Pre-eminent among the things there featured prominently and foreseeably the provisional clearance, or seven out of ten, he had awarded the existing portion of *Coming Home* – the sterling anti-trendy title for the complete work he had somehow captured over the last hours. The elevated mood lasted long enough to prompt him to make love to Rhiannon when in due course they got into the surprisingly cosy little bed.

They stayed lying there for a few minutes with the light on uttering contented mild animal sounds as they had done at such times for thirty-four years. Something about the bedside lamp was setting up a bit of a hoarse sort of screaming noise, but it was quiet enough in general to hear the waves breaking on the beach, not all that far away because by now the tide had come in again nearly to the full.

'Lovely day it's been,' said Alun. 'I'd forgotten how nice it was here.'

'Jolly good about your work.'

He shushed her and made disclaiming faces but with less conviction than earlier. 'They haven't managed to bugger the place up totally yet.'

'You must be tremendously relieved, or a bit relieved rather. It must be all right to say that.'

'What? Oh yes, I'll have another look at it in the morning.'

'Do you good to stay in one place and put your feet up for a couple of days.'

'Yeah, well . . .'

'I thought you were looking a tiny bit peaky, you know, just one per cent. There's nothing worrying you, is there?'

'No.' He was not going to let on about bloody Gwen, not now, not with no exterior limit on the discussion. He would have to see if he could pick a spot like three minutes before the arrival of a television team. 'No, not a thing. Bar wondering how long they'll go on making Scotch the way that suits me.'

' . . . Good,' she said without much sense of relaxation.

After more silence, he said, 'What time are they due tomorrow?'

'Twelvish. Evidently Charlie doesn't want to start drinking too early.'

'Oh I see. Well I'd better get some shut-eye if I'm to do any good before they turn up.'

The thought of television had set going something he had left unexamined in the meantime: the identity of Bleddyn Edwards, said by the young sod in the pub to be inferior to him, Alun, but still mentionable in the same breath. The name was not unfamiliar, the face and everything else stayed out of view. What a pissy poser to be stuck with at this time of night. He fell asleep before he had got anywhere with it.

2

Alun went out early the next morning and got newspapers. On his return he stood facing the bay in pale sunlight, took some deep breaths and thought to himself, if a waft of industrial pollution had ever been perceptible here there was no question of any now. When other thoughts, to do with time and age and all that, started to occur to him he rather consciously went indoors to breakfast, a scheduled fatty's flare-up presenting two boiled eggs turned out on to fried bread and fried potatoes as well as bacon and tomatoes. While he ate it he worked animatedly at the *Times* crossword. 'You *fiend*,' he said, writing in a solution. 'Oh, you . . . you *swine*.'

At the typewriter afterwards he got through another half-page of dialogue, very rough, almost token. It had turned out hard for him to concentrate: he felt fit, the sun was shining on the water and Sophie and Charlie were on their way. Several times he glanced up from his table, fancying he heard or saw them. When they finally appeared he ran out on to the path with whoops of welcome, snatched their suitcases from them, chivvied them indoors. Some who knew him used to say that Alun never came nearer convincing you he meant it than when he was being glad to see you.

Like other enthusiastic hosts he had definite ideas about how the party was to be organised. Coffee and drinks went round in the front room while the Norrises' offerings – a fresh sewin picked up in Hatchery Road that morning, a 57% Islay malt whisky – were brought out and admired. The women were not hindered from going off on their own, for the moment only as far as the kitchen. Alun refilled Charlie's glass and said,

'I want you to do something special for me if you would.'

'I'll have you know I'm a respectable girl and never touch kinky stuff.'

'No, it's . . .' Alun had rehearsed this part but he still had to squeeze it out. 'The thing is, I've started a sort of novel, it's supposed to be a serious novel, a proper one, you know, with no ham or balls or flannel about it, look you to goodness boy *bach*, but it's hard for me to tell. So if you could just sort of glance through the first pages of the thing, not bothering about merit or the plenteous lack of it, but just seeing if . . .'

'If I can give it a free-from-bullshit certificate.'

'Exactly.'

'Well . . .' Charlie's glance was uneasy. His familiar battered look seemed intensified without actual bruising or laceration, as though he had been perseveringly beaten with padded cudgels. 'Unless I give you my honest – '

'I'm not asking for a bloody bunch of roses – of course you must speak as you find. Please, Charlie. Go on, you old bugger, you're the only one.'

'As long as you . . . All right. Where is it?'

'Here, but don't look at it now. In a few minutes I'll herd the females into the village, where booths and bazaars of hideous aspect and degraded purpose display wares of varied and arresting squalor. But – they are useless, and they are for sale. What merit more demands the female heart? I'll go up to White's and see you in about half an hour or three-quarters. If you run out of water there's plenty in the tap.'

Wearing among other things the new cashmere pullover Alun did much of what he had promised, but before making for White's he looked in at Brydan Books. He told himself that it could do no harm and that he had never much cared for sitting about in pubs on his tod. But as soon as he was fairly inside the shop he was recognised and plurally shaken hands with. Customers were introduced and all asked for his autograph, a copy of his old *Celtic Attitudes* miraculously appeared and received his uninhibited inscription, and an elderly lady in a Brydan Books, Birdarthur, Wales apron who had no other obvious connection with the trade was brought from the back of the premises simply in order to have sight of him. He left bearing a newish book on the Rebecca riots that nobody would take his money for and telling himself now that the whole concern was a lot of bloody nonsense.

The bar at White's Hotel was filling up, but he achieved the same seat as the previous evening. He looked round quite eagerly but in vain for the white-hatted sod, whom in his present mood he would have thoroughly enjoyed seeing off, doing so with a minumum of exertion, furthermore, like a whatever-it-was Black Belt. Just as he was starting to wonder whether it had been such a good idea to shut Charlie away like that with a bottle of whisky, in he came. His face seemed to have smoothed out slightly in the past hour or less, no doubt through assisted abatement of hangover. Nothing was to be read from his expression.

'Well, fire away,' said Alun briskly when they were settled with their drinks. 'Let's have it.'

'You did ask for my honest opinion . . .'

Alun's glance fell. 'Which you have now made clear enough. How much did you manage to struggle through?'

'I read twenty pages carefully, then skipped to the end.' Charlie spoke with a hesitancy unusual in him. 'I must emphasise that this is just my personal – '

'Spare me that if you will.'

'Sorry. Well now. I can see here and there what you're trying to do, and

I think it's worth doing, and . . . you've probably made the best attempt at it you can, but . . . I'm not sure if it can be done at all, very likely it can't in the 1980s I don't know. But you haven't done it, that's to say you weren't doing it in what I read.'

'What about the bullshit?'

'The whole tone of voice, the whole attitude is one that compels bullshit. If I say it's too much like Brydan I mean not just Brydan himself but a whole way of writing, and I suppose thinking, that concentrates on the writer and draws attention to the chap, towards him and away from the subject. Which I suppose needn't be Wales in a way except that it always *is*, and somehow or other it's impossible to be honest in it. Now I'm sure you've tried your hardest not to put in anything you didn't mean or you thought was playing to the gallery, but it all gets swallowed up and turns into the same thing.'

Alun was still looking down. 'Nothing to be salvaged?'

'Nothing I saw. I'm sorry.'

'You're saying I've got to the stage where I can't tell what's bullshit from what isn't bullshit any longer.'

'No. I don't think I am. I'm saying if you want to talk seriously about that place of yours and the people in it you'll have to approach the thing in a completely different way, as if you've never read a book in your life — well no, not that exactly, but . . .'

Before Charlie had spoken a word Alun felt as if he might have been going to faint, only never having fainted before he found it hard to tell. The feeling had passed after a few seconds, since when he had had a good half of his attention on keeping his head from wobbling about, another sensation new to him. He had also been distracted by suddenly remembering who Bleddyn Edwards was, namely a man who came on at the end of the six o'clock news on Taff TV and spent a couple of minutes trying to be comical about piquant Welsh happenings of the preceding twenty-four hours. Another man did this turn-and-turn-about with him at a slightly lower level of wit and sensitivity, a man called something like Howard Howell about thirty years younger than Alun Weaver and of less refined appearance but, all too plainly, confusible with him just the same. Cheers *yn fawr*. With quite enough competing for his notice he saw with brief amazement that Charlie had not yet touched his drink. Quietly, trying as hard as he could to make it sound right, Alun said,

'Well, it looks as though I'll have to junk what I've done and have a totally fresh stab at the whole affair. Simple as that. I do agree, one can get horribly inbred in Wales without realising it.'

Now Charlie did drink. 'Sorry, Alun,' he said again.

'Oh, come on, what are you talking about, you've just saved me several months at least of wasted work. Do you think I'd rather have been given the green light for a load of crap? In case you're wondering, the answer's no. Well, now we've got that out of the way we can get down to the serious business of the occasion. Knock that back and have another.'

'I'll make room for it first if you don't mind.'

Left alone in the pew, Alun relaxed and prepared to let his head do its worst, but it had cleared up now. Other things had not, though, not quite, and he sat there telling himself to stop swallowing like a fool and to breathe normally and to come out and admit he had had a sneaking suspicion all along that the stuff was bloody useless, so it ought to be a relief in a way to be told so in no uncertain terms.

Soon Charlie came back carrying two large whiskies. 'Well, the bog hasn't changed,' he said. 'Even to your pee hanging about instead of running away properly. Did I hear something about Percy and Dorothy coming down?'

Alun knew just what to say to that, but when he came to say it he found he could not get the words out, nor any others that he tried. He opened and shut his lips and blinked at Charlie.

'Are you feeling all right?'

Laying his hand flat across his upper chest Alun nodded vigorously and did some more swallowing. He kept trying to push words out with his breath. His head was perfectly stable as an object and clear inside, but he was beginning to feel a little frightened. Then, with an effort no different from the previous ones, he found himself saying, 'Yes, Charlie, to answer your question, Percy and Dorothy are indeed coming down, some time in the late afternoon or early evening if my information is to be relied upon. Hey. Bloody hell. What was that? Phew. Quite enough and to spare, thank you.'

'Can I get you anything?'

'It's here,' said Alun, grabbing his drink and taking a swift pull. The sights and sounds of the pub, really full now and noisy with pitched-up talk and laughter, rose about him as if for the first time. 'Well, whatever it was we don't want any more of it, right? – however popular a Weaver-suppressor might prove in certain quarters of Lower Glamorgan and beyond.'

'You've gone a bit pale. Or you had.'

'No wonder, with the rare and deadly *dorothea omniloquens ferox* poised to descent on our peaceful and happy community. Now there's one who could do with a few fits of silence visited upon them if you like. Can you remember, who was it who said about Macaulay's conversation . . .'

Charlie still had a look of concern and compunction and Alun worked on driving it away. By the time he had done so he had restored his own spirits too to the extent that, provided he kept the thought at arm's length, he could believe he was going to have a whole proper new crack at *Coming Home* after the holiday – keep the title and also the typescript, which was bound to have some material in it that could be rescued with a bit of imagination, or nerve. He continued satisfactorily through the pub session, another couple back at the cottage, and lunch off the pickled fish with plenty of gherkin and chopped onion, the whole firmly washed down with aquavit and Special Brew and tamped in place with Irish Cream. By a step of doubtful legitimacy the men thinned their glasses of the heavy liqueur with Scotch.

After that there was a natural break. The women went off for a walk, Rhiannon grumbling that she ought to have brought the puppy after all. Charlie threw himself by instalments up the stairs and was heard all over the building, and perhaps further, dropping on to the bed in the back room. Alun took to the armchair as on the previous afternoon and dreamt Mrs Thatcher had told him that without him her life would be a mere shell, an empty husk, before jerking awake to find the image of a bearded man mouthing at him (the sound having been turned down) and frenziedly drawing cartoons on the postcard-sized screen of the little Sony they had brought down with them.

Hardly a minute later the women were back from their walk, pink-cheeked, brisk of step, determined at any price to get the tea. He sat on and listened to them shouting and laughing to each other in the kitchen and the minor thumps and crashes they made as they shut cupboard doors or set up crockery. At one point Sophie burst out of the kitchen and ran up the noisy wooden stairs, calling over her shoulder to Rhiannon as she went. Her glance passed over Alun as if they were unacquainted guests at a hotel. The same happened in reverse when she charged down again with a packet of biscuits in her hand. He knew it was not done to annoy, to set up an offensive contrast with male lethargy: it was just an illustration, more vivid than some, of the old truth that women were drunk half the time without benefit of alcohol. (Children over the age of about two were of course drunk all the time when not asleep.) Queers aside, men above twenty-five or so were never drunk however pissed they might be. Rather the contrary, he said to himself, hearing now some widely separated foot-falls above his head.

When Charlie appeared he stared mutely at Alun in mingled appeal and reproach, as if covered with blood after a plucky lone fight against oppressors. So far from being in any such state he looked rather well, whatever that might mean applied to him. Comparatively, again, he had so far been restrained in his intake, not urging the rounds along in the pub, sitting behind an empty glass for long periods like ten minutes on end. If he went on like this he could just find himself still on his feet quite far into the night. Alun felt it might be done for his benefit and was touched.

Tea was brought in, with anchovy toast and Welsh cakes featured but not Sophie's biscuits, which she and Rhiannon had presumably wolfed in the kitchen. The meal was eaten, finished, cleared away and then nightmar-ishly reanimated when Dorothy arrived with Percy and brought out scones from a paper bag, strawberry jam, Devonshire cream and chocolate éclairs. After greeting all four in POW-reunion style she could likewise be seen to be well in arrears of her usual state at five on a weekday afternoon. This meant that she would also likewise stay around longer than usual, but on the other hand she would presumably take longer to become unbearable, and might always fall down dead before that stage was reached.

Not many people unacquainted with Wales or the Welsh would have found it the easiest thing in the world to reconcile Dorothy as she would be later with Dorothy as she behaved now, when the tea-things were removed for the second time and a bottle of white Rioja was brought from the kitchen. Far from clear at first, it seemed, about what was in the wind, she watched with a slight frown while Rhiannon took out the cork and poured three glasses. After some thought she picked up the bottle in a gingerly, furtive way and, head craned forward, read the label from beginning to end through her black-bounded spectacles. Then, carefully following the movements of the other two women, she lifted her glass, drank, and looked interested and rather tickled: so this was wine.

Alun watched all this in some professional distaste. He knew he overdid that side of life a bit himself, but in his case it was just high spirits, buggering about, derived from an only child's self-entertainment, whereas old Dot was seriously trying to create an effect. Well, hardly that, perhaps, at her time of life, in front of this mob; though the present carry-on would have had to be descended from the beginning of her career of piss-artistry, when she could still pretend she got sloshed out of not knowing about alcohol. Sort of a ritualised version.

'Let's go and pay our respects at Brydan's tomb,' said Sophie.

'It was more of a grave when I last saw it,' said Charlie. 'Of course they may have shifted him to a mausoleum since then. Or a cromlech, on account of him being Celtic and all.'

'Grave is fine with me,' said Alun.

Percy turned to Dorothy. 'Would you like to go, darling?'

'Lovely idea. It must be twenty years since I was last there. When I've finished this.'

'I think they shut the churchyard at six,' said Rhiannon.

The way she said it dispelled any lingering doubts about the unspontaneity of Sophie's suggestion. Alun would have loved to know whether the idea had come from her or Rhiannon in the first place – quite liked to, anyway. Whichever it was, Dorothy was hooked, about to be irresistibly sundered from the wine-bottle not only for the period of the respect-paying but later too. There were the shops that would be staying open late or late enough, shops no doubt marked down earlier as ones she could not in conscience pass by. (The chaps would be safely in the pub for that part.) With luck and further good generalship she might not be recoupled with the bottle for getting on for two hours. But after that . . .

As the company rose to leave there was talk of how they might as well be getting along if they were going, only a few minutes' walk and such while a couple of sets of facial signals were exchanged. Charlie wanted to know if Alun had anything to do with this obnoxious plan and Alun tried to indicate not. At his side, Percy watched Dorothy stoutly knocking back her drink in one so as not to keep the stage waiting. Sophie and Rhiannon left theirs. Rhiannon's glance at Alun admitted complicity and also managed to plead that it would have been no good trying to keep the wine away from Dorothy in the first place. Granted, and indeed he could just imagine her wonderment at happening upon the bottle in the refrigerator or, if things had gone that far, the gauche impetuosity with which she would have pressed upon her hostess the funny wine-bottle-shaped gift parcel she had nearly forgotten having shoved into her luggage at the last minute.

Defying local odds, the summer sun shone brightly up the gentle slope of the churchyard, which at this time of the year proved to stay open till seven, a pleasant spot with carefully-tended brilliant green turf between the graves. That of Brydan lay towards the end of a row of newish ones in the south-east corner. It was no different in arrangement from any of its neighbours: a stone, a grassy mound enclosed in a stone border, some fresh flowers in glass vases. The inscription was severely factual except for a single appropriate line from the writings. The nearby ground had been only a little marked by intruding feet, as if word had gone about that there was not much to be seen up in the churchyard.

The party stood apart from one another in silence, almost as if trying to show respect. Only Dorothy looked recognisably like someone standing by a grave in a film. At least Alun hoped so, feeling Charlie's eyes on him as he bowed his head and tried dutifully to think of Brydan, whom he had run into on several occasions and once spent most of an evening with. He had several times compared the poet's character to an onion: you success- ively peeled away layers of it, with frightful shit and quite decent old bloke alternating, until you got to the heart. The trouble was he could not at this stage remember, and certainly not decide off the cuff, which of the two you ended up with. There was something of the same difficulty with the works: talented charlatanry, or deeply flawed works of genius? Or perhaps they were just beside the point.

Imperiously giving a lead, Dorothy swung away and led off down towards the gate with Rhiannon and Sophie in attendance. To one side stood the low mound called Brydan's Knoll, formerly and less tastefully called Brydan's *twmp* or tump, though never much called any such thing outside print. The poet was half-heartedly feigned to have spent untold hours squatting on it and gazing over the town and the bay, well worth while perhaps if there had been nowhere else to see them from. Some support for the feigning was given by a passage in one of the late poems, and now the erstwhile *twmp* was sure of its place in the indexes of learned works as well as in guide-books.

Percy gave the spot a friendly wag of the hand. 'Rather agreeable up here, isn't it?'

'Somebody's fought the good fight,' said Alun, and went on quickly, 'Not letting them turn the whole thing into a tourist attraction. Full marks to that man.'

'Oh yes of course, I remember now, you were at school with Brydan, weren't you?'

'Well, there must be a thousand people who could – '

'Ah, but the personal link is there. It must give you a feeling of special intimacy when you read the poems. Adding, I mean, to your sense of kinship, being a poet yourself. Something to be profoundly grateful for. Aren't you aware, perhaps keenly aware, of a peculiar insight into the man's mind? Into his soul?'

'I don't know, I suppose so,' said Alun, resolutely not looking at Charlie on Percy's other side and far from being inclined to look at Percy.

'Oh, for God's sake, Alun, don't speak self-deprecatingly about a thing like that.' Percy intensified the mournful solemnity of his tone and expression, which managed to save him from being picked up and thrown over the lofty privet hedge they were passing just then. 'It's a miraculous privilege. Not your own doing.'

'No, I do see.'

'Because let's face it, you are Brydan's artistic heir. Not in any obvious, reminiscent way, but . . . Surely at least you're conscious of being part of the same stock, sprung from the same root?'

'Well, there's obviously something inescapable in the blood of every Welshman that unites him . . .' Alun tried not to panic as he heard his voice relentlessly modulating into the old practised tones. He let it die away.

Percy did not press him. 'Well, these things will be as they will be,' he said, steadfastly accepting the duty to move on now with the round of mundane affairs. 'See you in the pub later, then? Right.'

'Dry-ballocked bugger, that,' said Alun as he and Charlie watched Percy's tall white-haired figure hurrying down the hill to catch up with the women. 'I mean I assume he was taking the piss?'

'No idea.'

'For Christ's sake, Charlie, he must have been. Miraculous bloody privilege. He did it well, I grant you.'

'What about it? I've never seen enough of him to say, but there are plenty of people about who talk like that for real, or semi-real, as you may have observed. And not only in Wales, either.'

'What? It's probably something to do with being married to Dorothy. That must bring out any dormant piss-taking proclivity, don't you think?'

'I don't know.'

'And why's he so brown? I know he's a builder, but surely that doesn't have to mean he's on the site all the hours God sends. And it can't be Morocco because he'd have had to take Dorothy with him, and if she'd been there we'd have heard by now. Sun-lamp. But why?' Alun finished in chapel style, 'In God's name, my friends, why?'

Charlie shook his head without replying. The group of four ahead of them had reached a shopping street, with Percy walking on the inside. That was so he could block Dorothy off if she tried to go into an off-licence. It was to forestall that that he had joined the group a minute earlier. If she made a dash across the road his superior physique and condition would, from so near, enable him to overhaul her. Something deterred Alun from putting this rationale to Charlie, who presently spoke up.

'Mind you, the last bit of what he said was a bit too close for comfort, intentionally or not.'

'Oh, but – '

'I don't know what you think of Brydan's stuff these days, and I dare say you don't yourself, and I'm sure you'd deny indignantly or even sadly that you were his successor, but it's his influence that makes that stuff of yours you showed me so awful. Well, I don't say you're not capable of making it awful without assistance from anyone, but you see what I mean.'

Now Alun said nothing.

'I didn't put it strongly enough in the pub, but if you want *Closing Time* or *Coming Home* or whatever it's called to be any good at all, you must scour Brydan right out of it, so that not a single word reminds me of him even vaguely. Whatever you think of him, you must write as if you hated and despised him without reserve. You said you wanted my honest opinion, well, now you've got all of it.'

Alun said nothing to that either, but by then he and Charlie had come up with the others, who had halted on the pavement to gaze, none more intently than Percy, at a stationer's window. Actually it was that of a stationer in the extended sense, with not only writing materials and accessories visible there and in the shop behind but also framed photographs of local sights (including guess-who's cottage), mantelpiece ornaments including manufactured *objets trouvés*, mugs, ashtrays, scarves and teacloths with generally Welsh or specifically Birdarthur matter printed on them.

'Well, what of it?' asked Alun when everyone else seemed speechless at the sight. 'Somebody want to buy something?'

'We thought perhaps you might,' said Dorothy, smiling artlessly at him.

'Me? What, what the hell would I be buying at a little shithouse of a place like this?'

'Oh, all sorts of things.' She switched slightly to a humouring tone. 'What about a nice tea-towel to help you with all that washing-up you do?'

At a better time Alun would probably have recognised these remarks as attempts, tiresome no doubt but far from malicious, to egg him on, to bowl the local funny man an easy one, and he would probably have responded. But now he was silenced yet again, seeing Percy with an expectant look, Rhiannon's mind on a hot bath and putting her feet up, Sophie no more than ticking over, and Charlie of course there too. He made to walk on, but his way was barred.

'Or perhaps some typing paper. I noticed you'd been tip-tapping away.'

This found him his voice all right. 'You need a drink,' he very nearly snarled at Dorothy, adding just in time, 'We all do. Now for Christ's sake let's get moving. Come on, *move*.' Then he turned on Percy. 'And if you were thinking of asking me if I feel like dropping in at the cottage to commune with the shade of my poetical progenitor, my advice to you would be to relinquish the venture.'

There was some laughter at this, not much, but again just enough. Alun took a stealthy but far from nominal punch in the small of the back from Rhiannon for getting cross. Outside White's, Percy said he thought he would look round with the girls for a bit before joining the session.

'Having seen Dorothy safely on her homeward way,' said Alun after carrying the first two drinks over. 'Towards Dai's I mean.'

'Where there's enough booze to float a battleship,' said Charlie. 'A light cruiser anyway.'

'It wasn't my idea, you know, that cultural expedition.'

'Well, it's over now and no bones broken.'

'It did cross my mind that I might have been getting a spot of stick here and there for having turned the party out of doors.'

Charlie looked at him. 'Don't be ridiculous,' he said.

3

Most of the evening was all right as far as it went. When eating came to be discussed it was felt but not said that Dorothy might consider she ought to hold back a bit in a public place, while what was said was that of course Rhiannon must not be allowed to cook, so no sewin tonight. Either half-sensing the unsaid part or out of simple awkwardness, Dorothy argued for a takeaway. Alun objected that the food was certain to be vile anyway, but if you ate it on the spot at least you could insult them for it, not much of a point perhaps, sufficient though to carry that assembly. Off they sped in the twilight past the Brydan Burger Bar and up the hill, the six of them hardly filling Percy's Swedish limousine, which smelt unexpected but all right, rather like a cough-medicine factory.

When it was just too late the restaurant they chose turned out to have some sort of formal dinner going on in it, with toasts and speeches. Dorothy was subdued, talking barely half the time and making Alun reflect that they might have been too hard on her in the past and could afford to have her expire painlessly after all. The meal itself proved to be of no more than common-or-garden vileness, below the threshold of insult-incitement. Both Alun and Charlie were noted for grabbing the bill on these occasions, but tonight Percy got there first. The party spent almost the entire journey back arguing about what the place had been called. Or some of them did;

others – Rhiannon first, then Sophie and Charlie – fell asleep or relapsed into silence. Percy said nothing much either, driving at ferocious speed but with great concentration. And nobody seemed to feel like going on after Alun had asserted that Welsh cooking was nothing more or less than bad English cooking, or possibly just English cooking.

It might have been anything from New Zealander income-tax allowances to the future tense in colloquial Russian that Dorothy got going on in the pub; nobody could remember afterwards, nor cared to try. Whatever it was, she made up for lost time and went critical within a few minutes. Percy got her to her feet and Sophie gave him a hand. Together they urged her towards the door, a troublesome business among the crowded and slow-reacting peasantry.

'Quite comforting, really,' said Charlie. 'Makes me feel no end posh.'

'I'd better go along too or Sophie'll never get away,' said Alun. 'Should be fun to watch too.'

'Do you really think so?'

'I find the whole thing absolutely fascinating. Somebody who – '

'No accounting for taste, is there?'

'See you in a few minutes.'

Alun had taken it for granted that Dorothy was to be loaded with what speed was possible into the limousine and whisked back to town. So clearly had Percy, but it was not to be. First she insisted on fetching the cardigan she had left in the cottage. Dragged off that, she refused to leave without wishing her hostess good night, and short of disablement there was no obvious way to drag her off *that*. So the end of it was she led the other three back to Dai the Books's, beating off assistance the couple of times she stumbled on the uneven, unlit ground of Brydan's Walk. The moon was hidden behind the high ground on the landward side.

There was a light in the front room but no occupant, and no light upstairs. As asserted many times in the last few minutes, Rhiannon had gone to bed. Oddly in view of her previous firmness of purpose, Dorothy rather passed this over. With a preoccupied look she went out to the kitchen, came back with a bottle of Banat Riesling, looked slowly but briefly about for the corkscrew and went out again.

'You can get off back to the pub now, you two,' said Percy. 'I can handle the next stage. You really shouldn't have bothered to come this far.'

'Are you sure you can manage?'

'Oh yes, after another glass or two she should go torpid quite fast. Piece of cake.'

'Well, I'm going to have a quick one,' said Alun. There was not much chance of any real money's-worth but he would hang on a moment in case. 'That pub Scotch, it's all very well when you're not used to anything better.'

'Suit yourself.'

Percy, head bowed, had been edging along the bookshelves. Now he gave a satisfied grunt, straightened up and moved away carrying a paperback called, Alun saw, *Kiss the Blood off my Hands*. This he opened and began to read attentively while he established himself in the battered armchair with more contented noises. When Dorothy reappeared and handed him bottle and corkscrew in meek silence, he successfully eased apart the binding of his book and spread it flat on the arm of the chair so that he could continue to read during his operation on the bottle. In due course Dorothy sat down on a stray dining-chair next to the table and got stuck into a glass of wine. Her silence had attained a serene, meditative quality.

After a sample of this, Sophie turned to Alun. 'I think we ought to be getting along to Charlie – you know.'

'Yes, yes, let's be off.' He was quite keen to leave now there was no mileage in staying. 'Er – are you sure you'll be all right?'

'Yes, thank you, Alun,' said Percy, turning a page and looking up. 'Nice evening. See you soon.' Then, after just the right hammy interval, he half-called, 'Oh, Alun.'

'Yes?' said Alun without parting his jaws.

'Don't, er, don't forget what I said about Brydan now. And your heritage.'

'I won't, never fear.'

'See you stick to it, boy. Good night both.'

As soon as he and Sophie had taken five paces outside Alun said, not loudly but violently, 'That man is a *shit*. And a fucking *fool*. A *shit*, a *shit*, a *shit*.'

'What? What's the matter with him? What did he say?'

'Well, you heard him . . . It was what he said earlier. Anyway, never mind. He's just a *shit*.'

'What did he say earlier?'

'Oh for Christ's sake forget it, I can't start on all that now,' said Alun, angrily increasing his pace.

'What did he say about Brydan?'

'Never *mind*. It's not worth going into.'

She pulled him to a halt. 'It's not worth going into anything, is it, not with me,' she said at top speed and sounding pretty angry herself. 'You think I'm a fucking moron, don't you, Weaver? Always have done. Can't even be bloody bothered to pretend. Just another stop on your bloody milk-round. Another satisfied bloody customer. Well, thanks a million, mate.'

'Keep your voice – '

'And I thought you thought I was special. That's bloody foolish if you like.'

'You know very well I – '

'When you can't even put yourself out to give me the bloody time of day.'

Dodginess, a display of temperament from old Soaph was of course nothing new, nor its headlong onset. What was new was the last bit or the bit before and the tears under it. After no great struggle he got his arms round her.

'You silly little bag,' he said gently.

One thing led to another, or went some way there. Near where they stood there was a very serviceable little grassy hollow between Brydan's Walk and the edge of the cliff. He remembered it well, remembered it as if it had been yesterday without any memory at all of whether or not he had any time acquainted Sophie with the place. Leading her to it now and then coming across it by chance would need care, though for the moment that was looking ahead rather.

'What about a spot of num-num?'

'Don't talk so soft.'

'There's been not a drop of rain for weeks.'

'No.'

Matters had reached an interesting pass when the two heard a loud thump or crash in the middle distance, not so much loud when it reached them as obviously loud at source, clearly audible anyway above the sound of the waves quietly breaking on the beach below them. The disturbance had come from somewhere in the row of cottages, perhaps seventy or eighty yards from where they stood in shadow. As they looked in that direction, a light came on upstairs in one of them: Dai's, no question. After a quick glance at Sophie, Alun set off towards it.

'We ought to be getting along to – '

'Leave it for now,' he said urgently. 'Come on – Christ knows what's happened there.'

She hesitated a moment but followed him. They arrived back at the cottage not so very many minutes after leaving it. What had happened there was essentially simple and needed no thought to be found likely too: Dorothy had come out of the lavatory and fallen down the stairs, giving the noise added resonance by overturning a chair next to the front door with two empty suitcases on it. Far from being visibly hurt or in any way reduced by the experience, she seemed invigorated, toned up, though ready to agree she needed a drink.

When it was clear that all was well and nothing needed doing, Sophie said to Alun, 'We really must go back now to Charlie. He'll be wondering what the hell's kept us.'

Alun looked at his watch. 'You know, now I come think of it, by the time we get there it's hardly going to be worth it. Fifteen minutes, if that.'

'What time do they shut round here?' asked Percy, who had not also asked how Alun and Sophie had come to be in earshot of the great fall. 'Country hours are different, aren't they? Earlier.'

'Well, he'll be on his way back then.'

'He doesn't like the dark,' said Sophie. 'And it's very dark, that last bit.'

'If he gets into a tizzy he could ring up, couldn't he?' Alun had an air of cheerful puzzlement. 'I can't see what's so – '

'He can't ring here, only the neighbour,' put in Rhiannon. In her towelling dressing-gown and knitted slippers, she had been present all along. 'He wouldn't have that number.'

'It's only a few yards, for Christ's sake, and there are bound to be people – '

Dorothy had heard everything too, and had evidently taken some of it in. 'I'll stroll back with you,' she said, topping up her glass and draining it. 'I could do with a breath of fresh air. It gets quite stuffy in here, doesn't it, in the hot weather.'

'What about this neighbour?' asked Percy, after a longing glance at his book. 'If he really is a neighbour I could go there and ring the pub.'

Rhiannon explained and he went out after Dorothy and Sophie.

'I don't care for that fellow at all,' said Alun. 'Nasty piece of work, if you want my opinion. Malicious. Well, we had to get her out of the pub, you see, and then she wouldn't go in the car, kept saying she wanted to say good night to you, so we had to bring her along here. Then Sophie and I were just on our way to the pub when we heard the bang and saw your light go on, so we rushed back.'

It sounded absolutely terrible, and he wondered in passing whether everything he had ever said when he had anything at all to hide had sounded like that. Remarking affably that he supposed another one might well not kill him, he poured himself an unwanted drink. He saw that Rhiannon, on the chair lately occupied by Dorothy, was fiddling in a preoccupied way with a small irrelevant object like a shampoo sachet.

'What made you change your mind?' she asked.

'What about?'

'Going back for Charlie.'

'Oh, I just hadn't noticed the time before. Everything was a bit confused. Just popping up for a pee.'

While he was up there he thought about the things he could not say, all manner of them, most of them true, most of them already known but still unsayable. There had been a case for simulating concern for Charlie and going along with Sophie and Dorothy, but that would have looked to Rhiannon like evading her. Oh bugger, he thought wearily, and a stupendous yawn almost clove his skull in two. He wiped his eyes on lavatory paper and went down.

Although he knew well enough that inside those walls Rhiannon could hardly have blown her nose, let alone gone anywhere, without being heard all over the place, he was none the less disagreeably surprised to find her still sitting there. Then he thought of something and took himself to the chair he had sat on to do his typing.

'Amazing Dorothy managed to follow that conversation when you think how much she'd had. In the restaurant alone she must have – '

'Well, she'd have heard before about Charlie's troubles about being afraid of the dark and all that. Like most of his old friends must have done, including you.'

'Why including me particularly?'

'Because you're the only one that doesn't seem to care. Look at Percy off to telephone like that, no questions asked, and he hardly knows him compared with you.'

'I honestly can't see what all the fuss is about. Good God, if he's scared of the dark it's bright street lighting all the way to where the cars are, and after that, well even then it's not *dark*, and it's what, two hundred yards. Less.'

'Quite far enough if you're afraid. Remember how it was when you were a kid.'

'What? He's supposed to be a grown man. My observation tells me old Charlie makes a bloody good thing out of being scared of this and that. Gets himself picked up and shifted to and fro and generally feather-bedded wherever he happens to bloody be.'

'He may do that too, I hadn't thought of it.' Rhiannon put the sachet in the waist pocket of her dressing-gown. 'Did you show him that stuff of yours?'

'Yes, he thought it needed pretty hefty revision, which was much what I thought, you remember.'

'Yes,' she said. 'Good. I'm going to make a cup of tea.'

'Marvellous, I'd love some.'

Alun grabbed his whisky, telling himself he needed it after all, and started to relax, but he had not had time to do much of that before he heard the sound of voices approaching outside. For a moment he thought they were those of strangers, but he soon recognised Sophie's, then Dorothy's, in a tone he had never heard either use before. There was a third voice, a high-pitched whining or wailing that varied in intensity. When Alun realised it must be Charlie's voice he could hear he sat up straight and felt quite frightened. Rhiannon hurried in from the kitchen, opened the front door and stood on the step. Alun got to his feet and waited.

Charlie had turned a curious colour, that of a red-faced man gone very pale. His eyes were tightly screwed up and he was pressing hard with both hands on a grubby handkerchief that covered his mouth, in spite of which the wailing noise was quite loud at its loudest. Saying comforting things to him, Sophie and Dorothy got him into the armchair, and Rhiannon knelt down beside him and stroked his bald head. When he seemed comparatively settled, Sophie dashed upstairs and came down with a box of pills and gave him one. Alun stood about and tried to look generally ready for anything within reason. Dorothy, whose words of comfort far outdid the others' in range and inventiveness, was obviously having a whale of a time distinguishing herself in fields like responsibility, compassion, etc. So he said to himself. He also tried to consider fully the question of how much of this she would remember in the morning. But it was hard work driving off the thought that whatever Charlie might be going through, and however it had come about in detail, he, Alun, was to blame.

Now and then Charlie took the handkerchief away from his mouth and got out a word or two in a brief squeal before stuffing it back again. Several times he said he was sorry, twice perhaps that he had thought he was all right or could make it, and once, 'Get Victor.' That came just as Percy reappeared to announce no success with his call to the pub. He had hardly had time to take in the scene before Sophie bundled him off again whence he had come with instructions to telephone the Glendower.

Nothing surprising or of consequence happened after that for half an hour or so. Percy soon returned and said Victor was on his way. Charlie had two or three calmer and quieter spells but relapsed after each. Dorothy, sitting on the floor next to him, fell asleep or into a stupor, head down. Sophie told the others that when found he had been crouching by the corner of a wall at the edge of the part where the cars were, apparently unable to move. Rhiannon handed out cups of tea, not looking at Alun when she came round to him or at any other time. He just went on standing about.

Finally Victor arrived. He was wearing a dark jacket and trousers and a ribbed black shirt with a polo neck and his face, closely shaven, was quite expressionless. Looking neither to left nor right he walked straight across the room and held Charlie tight in his arms for a minute or so. Then he straightened up and ordered everyone else but Sophie from the room, taking a leather or plastic case about the size of a spectacle-case out of his pocket as he did so and starting to open it.

In the kitchen, where the ejected party found themselves with notable speed, Percy suggested to Dorothy that they would only be in the way if they hung about now and should slip out by the back door. When she had taken in the proposal and vetoed it, he readily produced *Kiss the Blood off my Hands* and settled down with it directly under the ceiling light. Now Rhiannon did look at Alun, only once and for a moment and telling him only what he knew already, but it was enough to make him suddenly interrupt his breathing. He knew there was nothing he could ever say or do that would change her mind. She had gone straight on with piling the cups in the sink and now went quietly outside, leaving the door half open behind her, perhaps to invite him to follow, more likely just because she had always been rather inclined to leave doors open. Alun decided it would be best to follow her. There was still nothing useful he could say but sooner or later he would have to say something.

There was no breeze, and the air seemed to him to be of exactly the same temperature as that in the kitchen. The moon had come round a corner of the hill and lit up those parts of the neighbouring ground that were not shadowed by small trees and straggling bushes, more or less everywhere Rhiannon might have been expected to be. He took a few indecisive steps up the garden path between huge clusters of weeds and rank grasses, halfway to a low fence beyond which the slope began to rise too steeply to be taken on without some serious reason. Nothing moved anywhere. He was trudging down the narrow strip at the side of the cottage when a larger wave than usual broke audibly down on the beach, and at the same time he noticed that Charlie's voice could no longer be heard, at least through the wall and then the front door. Alun stepped on to where he could see up and down Brydan's Walk: still nobody. After more hesitation he quietly lifted the latch and went in.

Victor and Sophie were talking in low tones, but they broke off now and looked up at him expectantly. Between them Charlie sat sprawled and apparently asleep.

'Is it all right to come in?' asked Alun.

Neither spoke in reply, but Victor nodded.

'He seems quite peaceful now, doesn't he?' Alun went nearer Charlie but still not very near. 'What have you – what have you done for him?'

'Largactil it's called,' said Victor in his clear tones and staring rather at Alun with his clear eyes. 'A powerful tranquilliser. Injected intramuscularly.'

'Really.'

'Yes really. Yes, you can learn how in two minutes. Charlie and I arranged that I should keep the stuff by me. He was afraid if he had it he'd start trying to inject himself when he was pissed. Very sensible of him.'

Alun had just enough wit not to ask why Sophie had not been deputed to keep the stuff by her. 'What was the matter with him?'

'He's not mad, if that's what you were wondering. An attack of depersonalisation. Panic brought on by being cut off from the possibility of immediate help and then self-renewing, as it were. Very frightening, I imagine. Well, we haven't got to imagine, have we?'

'Will he be all right now?'

At this point Victor suddenly stood up. 'Yes. Thank you. Is there anything else you'd like to know?'

'I feel responsible.'

'Yes,' said Victor warmly. 'M'm. You had heard about Charlie's dislike of being alone after dark and so forth.'

'Are you asking me? Not in detail, no.' Poofter, thought Alun shakily to himself. Ginger-beer. Brown-hatter. 'I mean I hadn't heard in detail.' Taxi-driver.

'But a bit, from what . . .' Victor's jerk of the head did no more than allude to Sophie. Nothing in his glance touched on her connection with Alun.

Finding himself expected to go on, Alun said, 'Yes, I'd heard enough. Enough to have a good idea I might fuck him up by leaving him to come back here on his own in the dark. I wanted to do that because I was angry with him for saying that something I'd written was no good, just copied from Brydan. Who does he think he is, I thought. I wanted to pay him out for . . .'

He stopped because neither of the others gave any sign of paying attention.

Victor turned his head and said with exaggerated suavity, 'Oh, yes, well, of course, absolutely, I do very much appreciate that. Now I suggest we get things moving.'

The first thing he or anyone else got moving was Dorothy and Percy, cordially and shortly thanked for their help and sent on their way, an unaccustomed mode of departure for them as some might have thought. Then Victor told Sophie she was to drive the Norris car while he travelled in the back with Charlie – who all this while had sat perfectly quiescent in the armchair – and would later arrange for the collection of his own car. Finally, at the front door, with Rhiannon now present, he said, rather less smoothly than earlier,

'Mr Weaver – we met, if you remember, at the restaurant owned by my brother and myself. I'm afraid I wasn't able to give you a very nice meal on that occasion, and I had been so much hoping to give you a better one. Well, I'm afraid various problems like supply and staff, and as you may have heard our new stove has had teething troubles – all that has rather got in the way. In fact I shouldn't advise you to venture into the place at all until further notice. We just can't offer you what you're used to in London. I'm sure you understand. *Nos da.*'

'It's the worst thing I've ever done,' said Alun a minute later. 'No need to tell me it doesn't make any difference but I'd like you to believe I realise it.'

'Oh, I don't know about that,' said Rhiannon. 'Do you mind sleeping in the spare room now it's free? That bed in the front's rather narrow and I want to get a good night's rest.'

After another minute he walked over to the table where his typewriter and papers still were, idiotically trying to do so in no particular way at all, took *Coming Home* out of its envelope and held it up to be torn in half, thumbs tip to tip, elbows lifted. Then he thought it could look good to make a present of a couple of pages of it to the next little non-paying bastard to write in for a contribution to a student magazine or an item to be auctioned for charity or something – anyway, you never knew. Having spared his own work he could see no overriding case for going ahead with his next project, the destruction of the Dai/Brydan photograph, which after all would not have been the original. Nor did he as intended finally push his copy of the Complete Poems in among the books on the shelves where he would never have to see it again. He would quite likely need it for reference the very next time he wrote a piece or prepared a talk or whatever you bloody well like that involved the master. He could always stop doing that, of course. But of course he never could.

8   Charlie

'It boils down to this as far as I'm concerned,' said Garth. 'Pink gin. Thank you, Arnold. – Oh yes: is a man for Wales or is he not? Simple as that.'

'With all respect, Garth, I'm afraid it isn't as simple as that,' said Malcolm. 'A man can be for Wales in such a way as subtly to denigrate the country, and that's what I'm sorry to say and rather surprised to have to say I thought Alun was doing. He – '

'Excuse me interrupting,' said a thickset man with a heavy moustache and the Turkish or even Assyrian facial appearance to be seen in some Welshmen, in fact a quantity surveyor from Newcastle Emlyn and old Arnold Spurling's guest. 'Didn't you use to be the English teacher at St Elizabeth Grammar? Years ago?'

'No,' said Malcolm rather curtly, as if he had been taken for a schoolmaster once too often. 'Not at any time.'

'Sorry if I've made a mistake,' said the guest, not sounding or looking at all satisfied that he had.

Malcolm went on with a touch of gameness, 'To write a newspaper article about the Eisteddfod in a humorous and entertaining style is one thing. To portray those taking part as figures of fun is quite another. In my submission.'

'I accept that,' said Garth. 'Certainly.'

'When did this . . . article appear?' inquired the guest.

'A couple of weeks back, possibly more. It was one of a – '

'But, I mean surely the Eisteddfod is an occasion for old friends to meet and exchange news and gossip.' The guest's lustrous dark eyes moved round the circle, canvassing support for this obvious view of the matter. 'I haven't been to one now for I don't know how long, but I used to attend quite regular, and in those days I was *constantly* running into people I hadn't seen at least since the previous year. *All the time.* Or were you thinking of the *Inter*national Eisteddfod?'

'No,' said Malcolm more curtly. At the same time he seemed bewildered.

'Tony Bainbridge,' said the guest straight away and shoved out his hand as he sat. 'I don't think you caught the name before.'

Malcolm gave his own name without impetuosity, especially at the second time of asking.

'Ah,' said Tony Bainbridge, narrowing his eyes now. 'M'm.'

He stopped short of actually arresting Malcolm, which Charlie, on the other side of Garth, had been half preparing for. One of Malcolm's troubles, and many others' too, was that he expected not only to follow conversations himself but that those around him should do the same, without any allowance for their being bored, mad, deaf, thick, or drunk without having been seen by him personally to set about becoming so. There he was now, as Charlie watched, looking furtively at Tony Bainbridge's glass, considering, looking at his own, wondering. And this after sixty-odd years in Wales, or just on the planet.

Before the silence had stretched too far Arnold Spurling reappeared with six drinks on a tray. The sixth went to Peter, who had said nothing since arriving, though he had snorted a couple of times when the Eisteddfod came into the conversation. The Bible had not been open all that long but, with the low cloud and heavy rain outside, the twilight seemed to be closing in already. Never mind that by the calendar it was still summer, the local weather had always had its own ideas on that.

Charlie had not found much to say for himself either. Today was only the second time he had left home unaccompanied since returning from Birdarthur a fortnight previously. For over half of that period, home had meant the Glendower, a sofa-bed in the flat there and the close proximity of Victor. What had happened on the evening in question was far from clear and without any detail in Charlie's memory, but he was quite decided that Sophie had not been there when he needed her. He also remembered, however, having taken a bad gamble on his own account, having thought he could manage without her, and he bore her no resentment. Nevertheless, rebuilding his confidence in her would take time. He wondered now and then how much time.

'I heard,' said Garth, lowering his voice but not quite talking behind his hand – 'I heard you'd had a little spot of trouble down at Birdarthur.'

'Just a bit of a dizzy spell. Nothing to worry about, Dewi said.' Dewi had said several times over that Charlie's case was not uncommon and that actually he had nothing to be afraid of after all. 'Got to take things easy for a bit.' This was to explain his restricted movements.

'Has he given you anything for it?'

What you would have to have the matter with you before Dewi would consider it necessary to give you something for it was a good question; not he but an unnamed friend of Victor's had been the true supplier, once upon a time, of the Largactil and syringe. It was a far cry from the days of Griff, who was said to have had half the infant population of Lower Glamorgan groggy with opium as a matter of course in furtherance of soothing their chests in a hard winter. But then Griff had belonged to the vanished breed who saw it as part of their job to make their patients feel better.

Garth interrupted this rather Peter-like train of thought by asking, 'Had he anything to suggest about your weight problem?'

'Dewi, you mean? No, not a word. I was reading a – '

'Still, I imagine you'll be making arrangements off your own bat, as it were.'

'What?'

'Thing like that, dizzy spell or whatever you call it, that's a warning. Nature's warning. Reminding you you won't be able to go on in your old ways for ever. Did you know that being just *half a stone* over weight measurably reduces your life-expectancy? Seven pounds. Seven pounds avoirdupois. My metabolism . . . my good luck . . . your metabolism . . . your bad luck . . . poor Roger Andrews . . . fat . . . sugar . . . salt . . .'

Others had been known to find Garth's homilies bothersome, even offensive; never Charlie. Just a part, an insignificant part of the great fabric. Life was first boredom, then more boredom, as long as it was going your way, at least. Charlie made these and other representations to himself while Garth quacked indefatigably on. In a comfortable half-listening state he let the whisky do its work on him and ran over in his mind the bomb-proof security of his next few hours: more drinks here; safe conduct to the Glendower in the charge of Peter, who knew the story; Victor eventually driving him home; Victor assuring him that Sophie would not leave him alone in the house. At the moment Peter too seemed content to let matters proceed while they showed no clear signs of worsening. Beyond Garth, who had now veered into autobiography, the other three pursued some Welsh topic.

So it trickled along until Alun arrived. He too had somehow failed to come up to scratch that evening in Birdarthur as Charlie recalled, or more as Victor had once or twice implied to him – well no one with a titter of wit had ever relied on him for more than the way to the Gents.

Having passed over the stranger, Alun's glance returned and stayed. Charlie saw with placid horror that Tony Bainbridge was smiling with his lips pushed up so that his moustache was squashed between them and his nose. His eyes were half closed again too.

'Hallo, Alun,' he said with awful quiet confidence, chin raised.

After a count of three Alun went into an equally awful but very watchable sequence of slow-motion Grand Guignol, from incredulity that came to border on naked fear through dawning recognition to joyful God-praising acceptance with double handshake. 'Who the fuck are you?' he asked at this stage, but it was clear to all present that he quite likely did remember and given a moment might even have come up with the name. 'What is it, thirty years?'

'Oh, not that. Fifteen more like.'

'Oh. Tell me, where are you based now?'

Tony Bainbridge told him that and more besides, receiving information in return. The others sat in silence, cautiously shifting position in their chairs as if a sound-recording was in progress.

'Now you had, what, two girls you had, wasn't it?'

'Spot on.' Alun gave a respectful nod. 'One married, one at Oxford.'

'Oxford. There. Well, that's what time does, no question. It goes by.'

'I'm afraid I can't – '

'So you've got a girl at Oxford. I haven't. I haven't got anybody. What are you drinking, Alun?'

'No, my shout.'

At this point the door opened and Tarc Jones advanced into the saloon lounge. He wore the heavy cardigan that, for all anyone knew, he never took off, and carried an unfolded sheet of paper printed in green, evidently an official form of some sort. This he planked down on the table some of them were sitting round, in front of Peter as it happened. There was silence while he stared accusingly from face to face.

'So this – this is the kind of slough into which our democracy has declined,' he said with much bitterness and gigantic quotation-marks where needed. 'Have any of you any idea of what had just reached me through Her Majesty's mails?'

Evidently none of them had. Garth did a slow wink at Tony Bainbridge to let him know that he was not really expected to be able to throw any light on the question.

'The Lower Glamorgan Water Authority,' went on Tarc without mending his pace at all, 'desires to be informed within 28 days, date as postmark, how many rooms in this establishment possess water facilities, of what nature these are in each case and their main uses and the approximate volume in gallons per day of water so utilised. For external appliances see back. Approximate. There I detect and welcome a ray of sanity and a spark of common human consideration. They might well have required measurement to three places of decimals. No. No. They drew back from that. Approximately is good enough. To the nearest gill is deemed to suffice.'

His listeners, even Alun, seemed completely demoralised by this show. Nothing was attempted or said while Tarc glanced this way and that and crouched forward over the table.

'Power,' he said in a whisper that was like a puma snarling. 'That's what it's all about. Some little jack-in-office is having the time of his life, drawing up forms and chucking them round the parish and generally trying to put the fear of God into the rest of us. How am I to deal with it, I ask you? What am I to do?'

Now Alun twisted round in his seat to look at him. 'What are you to do? If you really don't know what to do then God help you. But I'll tell you what you don't do, so at least you'll know that much for next time, all right? You don't go on as if they've told you they're coming round to take you to a gas-chamber and you don't hold the floor for half an hour with a bloody music-hall monologue when you could just be boring us stiff about the price of booze like anybody else. That's what you don't do, see.'

As well as visibly infuriating Tarc this caught him off balance. With a jerky movement he snatched up his paper from the table and started asking Alun how he dared, what he meant by it, who he thought he was talking to and similar questions. He, Tarc, sounded uninterested in the answers and also, compared with previous form, altogether under-directed. But he came back strongly towards the end. While he spoke and during what followed he doggedly, almost obsessively scooped away with a middle finger at the resistant deposit in the corner of one eye.

'I don't have to take that shit from anyone,' he said with returning assurance. 'Least of all from a second-rate bloody ersatz Brydan.'

Afterwards Charlie always wondered in what measure Tarc understood and intended this remark. The grin of anticipation with which Alun heard him out remained in place.

'Just to take you up on who I think I'm talking to. Not just a miserable idiot but the kind of idiot who's ruining Wales.' Charlie had heard Alun pronounce two or three different kinds of men to be that kind of idiot. 'Turning it into a charade, an act, a place full of leeks and laver-bread and chapels and wonderful old characters who speak their own highly idiosyncratic and often curiously crude kind of language. Tourists sometimes – '

'He's having you on, Tarc,' said Garth. 'Pay no attention. Fellow's idea of a joke.'

Tarc ignored him. 'Out,' he said, extending arm and forefinger horizontally to demonstrate his meaning. 'Out, the bloody lot of you. Off you go now. Go on. Now.'

'Take it easy, Tarc, for Christ's sake. I don't know what's got into him. Have a drink.'

'The bloody lot of you. Starting with you, Squire Weaver. And this also applies furthermore and notwithstanding to you, Professor pissy pernickety thick as two planks Cellan-Davies. And you, little Garth, on your way, brother. And this pair of bloody soaks by here.' This seemed most unfairly to mean Peter and Charlie. 'And you, Spurling and whatever your name is. No, sorry, I withdraw that, no fault of yours, sir, but you'll oblige me by leaving too. If you'll be so good.'

Garth made one last effort. 'Can't we just – '

'*Out*. If you're not gone in two minutes I'll send my lads in and then you'll know all about it. And you can take this squash-club pathetic bullshit with you. Every bloody scrap of it – I'll burn anything you leave, I promise you. I've been dying to get rid of you buggers for years and now's my chance. On second thoughts one of you can come back in the morning and pick up the junk then. That's if you think it's worth the bother. Now get moving, the lot of you. Two minutes, mind.'

Under his louring eye they filed out and assembled ridiculously in the passage that led to the front door, embellished as it was with speckled greenery and dismal old photographs and littered with the remains of packages that might have held footwear or clothing. Here tongues broke loose.

'That was a disgraceful piece of behaviour,' said Malcolm. 'On your part, Alun. Quite indefensible. You're supposed to know better.'

'I'm sorry, I just can't stand that kind of posturing,' said Alun.

'Whereas other kinds you've no rooted objection to,' said Peter. 'Anyway, thanks for destroying our pub for us.'

'I'll have a word with Tarc tomorrow,' said Garth.

'We're off,' said Arnold Spurling with decision, and he and Tony Bainbridge left at once and were not soon to be found in those parts again. At the same time a great general roar of laughter sounded from the bar and Charlie saw Doris the barmaid at the hatch peering at them through her upswept glasses.

'It's shocking that an educated man should descend to downright verbal brawling,' said Malcolm.

'I said I was sorry.'

'Oh, that's all right then,' said Peter.

'Tell you what,' said Garth: 'it's early yet to pack it in and we could all do with a drink and what shall I say, a pause for consideration. Why not come up to my place? It's only just round the corner. Angharad's away seeing her mother,' he added. 'Ninety-one, she is.'

There was a pause there and then, for consideration of Angharad, perhaps, or her mother. Eventually Alun said with a touch of defiance,

'Yes. Why not? I certainly fancy a drop. Thank you, Garth.'

'What about you, Peter?' asked Charlie. 'Unless you feel you . . .'

'No. Let's go along. Why not indeed.'

'I ought to be getting back,' said Malcolm.

'Oh for heaven's sake,' said Garth. 'Never even seen the inside of the Pumphrey domain, have you?'

'Go on, move, you old pests,' bawled Tarc's voice from up the passage, booming and resounding in a frightening way. 'Outside, the pack of you, you're making me nervous.'

Without a rearward glance they hurried out into the rainy, windy gloom where what light there was came mostly from shops and houses and reflections in the roadway. Charlie had a close impression of heavy bodies piling into cars, the lights of the cars coming on suddenly, loud grunts and door-slamming and the whinnying of starters. Now was a time for the years to roll back. But no, they stayed where they were. Beside him, Peter gave a whistling sigh and pushed the car into gear.

'You all right, Charlie?'

'Full of fun.'

'Well bugger me.'

'Absolutely.'

They said no more for the moment. Charlie's mind drifted off to one side. The ancient sanctuary of the Old Gods, he thought. No: when the primeval fastness of the Ancients is, is menaced by unknown powers, its guardian, the giant Tarc (bass) comes before them with a moving plea for counsel ('*Ach, was muss ich?*'). In response, the most illustrious of the Ancients, Alun (baritone), haughtily rebukes Tarc for his presumption ('*Vergessen nun Sie*'). A stormy exchange between the two, which the fool Garth (counter-tenor) tries vainly to quieten, introduces an elegiac portrayal of desolation and defeat. In a climactic . . . In a ritualistic monologue of great power and beauty ('*Heraus Sie alles sofortig*'), Tarc invokes his immemorial right to banish the Ancients from their refuge, ordains and salutes their passing one by one and compels the removal of their age-old trophies. The Act closes with an Ancients' chorus of . . .

'Wake up. We're there. I think.'

The Pumphrey house, which Charlie could not remember ever having seen before, was unlit within. There were slippery wet leaves on the flags of the garden path and he nearly stumbled over the trailing stem of a rose-bush or something similar. The two clambered up half a dozen rounded stone steps to a Victorian Perpendicular porch with stained glass to be faintly seen. Charlie stamped his feet rhythmically on the tiled floor.

'Is this right?' he asked. 'If it is, where's Garth?'

'I think he took a lift with Malcolm. Even he isn't going to walk it in this, I mean Garth.'

'Oh well, there we are then. Be here till midnight. Well no, er, eh? Unless Garth doesn't know the way either. Brilliant of you knowing. I suppose this *is* right, is it. It certainly feels right, it's giving me the shivers before I've even crossed the bloody threshold. Like a house of the dead.'

Peter pulled his raincoat more closely round him. 'Here they are. And Alun. Do you think he's mad, by the way?'

'No, just fed up because . . . I'll talk to you later.'

At once upon entering, Garth turned on the lights, first startlingly over-head in the porch, then two in the hall. Both of these seemed of low wattage, not doing much to cheer up the heavy parental or even grandpa-rental furniture or help to identify the wide-mounted engravings that covered large parts of the walls. Charlie noticed a cylindrical stand full of superannuated umbrellas and walking-sticks. When everyone was indoors Garth switched off the porch light, switched on a staircase light to indicate the lavatory on the landing, switched it off again and led them into a room at the back of the house.

It was cold in here, in a settled way that suggested it had not been warm for some time. Garth activated a small mobile electric fire, from which a smell of scorching dust soon began to issue and loud clangs were heard from time to time as the metal warmed up. Some large armchairs and a sofa were theoretically available, but none looked very inviting. The party clustered round the sideboard of some unpolished black wood on whose top a number of bottles and glasses were arranged.

This display had attracted Charlie's attention on entering and almost immediately thereafter his disquiet as well: all the liquor-bottles, which included, he saw, ones containing port and sherry as well as gin, Scotch, brandy and vodka, had optic measures like those used in pubs fitted to their necks. Then he brightened up again at the thought that Angharad would not have been the first or the last wife to try to limit her husband's drinking, heavy-handed as this particular scheme might appear. No cash-register was on view and when his turn came Garth served him a double whisky and passed on without delay. Water came out of a half-empty plastic bottle beaded on the inside with air-bubbles of unknown antiquity.

'Welcome to my humble abode,' said Garth as soon as they all had drinks. When nobody said what a nice place they thought he had or anything else, he went on, 'Rather sad to think it took a dust-up at the Bible to get the gang of you along here. I don't think we need be too despairing about that, by the way. I'll pop round in the morning and see how the land lies.'

Whether or not his words had any cheering effect, resentment of Alun's conduct seemed to have cooled or petered out in apathetic acceptance; anyway, no more was expressed. After a few minutes Charlie glanced at Peter and led the way towards a grand piano which showed every mark of having been *in situ* since about the time of the death of Brahms. Photographs of various sizes stood along its lid or hung from the wall behind it.

'God, what a shower,' said Charlie, moving on from the likeness of one staring bearded fellow in a high-collared jacket to another. 'They can't be Garth's or Angharad's parents or uncles et cetera – too far back.'

'In their comparative youth perhaps. That would be quite far back.'

'Oh, but not . . . Look at this old bitch here. Are those ostrich feathers, would you say? What would that make it? Not even the Boer War, more like the Zulu wars in when, the 1880s?'

'Well . . .'

'You know, I don't think this lot are anything to do with the Pumphreys. I think they must have come with the house, like the carpets and the curtains. And the furniture too by the look of it. There's something . . . Don't you get a funny feeling in here?'

'How do you mean, Charlie?'

'I can't see any sign of anybody actually living here. No bits of possessions. Of course it could be this room's just kept for visitors. Not such a ridiculously antediluvian idea in these parts, after all. But it's more like a time I remember when a bloke from round here called Lionel Williams, perhaps you came across him, anyway he took me home once in Kinver Hill for a nightcap after the pub, and it was quite a bit like this. Very much like this. It turned out, I'd naturally assumed it was, you know, the marital domicile, but it turned out his wife had divorced him, oh, fifteen years before and he'd gone on living in the house as a lodger, her house it was. And it was very much like this, the atmosphere. Imagine that. You don't suppose it could have happened here by any chance, do you, Garth living here as, er, as Angharad's lodger?'

'No I don't,' said Peter rather sharply. 'That's absurd.'

'What? Well, of course it is. Not meant to be a tremendously serious suggestion. But it was very odd at Lionel's that time, you know. The atmosphere.'

Drink in hand, Charlie moved from the piano-top to the dozen or so photographs on the wall. Over by the sideboard Alun had coaxed a rather reluctant smile from Malcolm and got a falsetto squawk of laughter out of Garth. Willingness to amuse Garth was to Charlie a sign of great humility. Or perhaps above-average vanity. Nevertheless he was glad of Alun's presence and of the others' too. There was no such thing as a good room to be shut up alone in, though the one at Birdarthur where he had read Alun's typescript had been not too bad, tolerable enough to have given him false confidence in himself. This one here could never do that. He pulled himself up and passed over an elongated coloured print of a desert sunset or dawn, complete with camels, palms and pyramid, that he would have laid a thousand quid he had seen a clone of in seaside lodgings in Porthcawl fifty years before. What he came to next made him stop and stare.

'By Christ, what's this? Hey, I could have done her a bit of no good in days gone by. Proper little bugger too, you can see with that mouth. Nobody made that one do what she didn't want to do. Ever. Who the hell would that be?'

He noticed now that Peter had sat down on a nearby sofa and was looking at the floor. 'That would be Angharad. I never thought . . . It never occurred to me . . .'

'What?'

'Angharad as she was before her illness.'

Charlie lowered himself beside Peter and put his drink on a small polygonal table of Oriental suggestion. The leather or synthetic material of the cushion-cover at once struck cold, even damp, to the backs of his thighs. 'What?'

'Serves me right for coming here. It doesn't do her justice, what you see there. Not to what she was when I first saw her. It was her I left Rhiannon for, not Muriel – Muriel was later. I didn't want to give Rhiannon up . . .'

Peter's face had grown dark red and he was pressing his hand against his chest. He breathed in and out noisily a couple of times, as if he was going to cry.

'Can I get you something?' asked Charlie.

'If you could just sit back, that's right, so they can't see me,' Quite briskly Peter took out a small tubular bottle and from it a white pill. 'Could you just sit with me, it'll go off in a little while.'

Not swallowing the pill, keeping it under his tongue, Peter held himself rigid in his seat with his eyes shut. Now and then he winced sharply, once so sharply and with such a screwing-up of his face that Charlie thought he was going to die the next moment. Charlie also stayed still, with his hand ready in case Peter should want to hold it, and listened for any pause in the others' talk or any stir of interest, though he had no ideas about what to do in that event. The electric fire hummed away. It was not really so long before Peter's colour improved and he began to breathe more normally. After another minute he opened his eyes, smiled a little without parting his lips, as he always did now to keep his teeth out of sight, and sipped his drink. This was whisky and water, lately his preferred tipple in place of the old gin (which he had said he thought made him depressed) and slimline (bound to retain some baneful calories however rigorously pruned).

'Well, that's it for this time round. Where was I?'

'What? Well, you were on about Angharad. Are you sure you want to – '

'Yes, I'm all right. Thanks for sitting there, Charlie. Yes. Angharad said – please let me tell you this – she insisted I had to give Rhiannon up completely if I wanted ever to see her again. She was the insisting type, as you astutely perceived from that photograph. Well, a girl like that, you can understand it in a way, and understand it even better if you allow for the bloke being a selfish shit who's rather thrilled to be the object of it. Then not so very long afterwards Angharad was doing some more insisting, but what she was insisting on this time was that I shouldn't see her any more. Some other fellow had . . . well . . .'

When he broke off and gazed at his empty glass, Charlie said, 'Can I get you another?'

'No. Don't go, Charlie. Can I finish yours? Just for this minute.'

'You're not to regard it as a precedent, mind.'

'Thanks. Then, of course, I should have gone back to Rhiannon, or tried to. But I couldn't face her. A bit hard to understand now, perhaps. And there was cowardly stuff about my job which is much easier to understand, I'm sorry to say. It's all so obvious really, but I'd met Muriel by then. She was a friend of Angharad's, if you can credit such a thing.

'All this was well before Angharad got ill. Cancer of the womb it was, or that was what it boiled down to in the end. Quite rare at twenty-nine. They took out the whole works, gave her a total pelvic clearance I believe it was called. Plays hell with the hormonal system and the rest of it, or it can. I didn't see anything of her for four or five years, and when she did turn up she looked within shouting distance of how she looks now.

'So there we are. They didn't know a hell of a lot about these things in those days. I don't say they know much more about them now, but then they thought that kind of thing was brought about by excessive sexual indulgence, as they would have phrased it. Or anyway helped on by it.

Well, even then I could see it would have been altogether too funny for words if I'd done all the damage myself, but I could have done my bit, along with one or two others. Yes. No doubt that's something you dismiss from your mind if you've got any sense, and also if you happen not to have grown up with a lot of bloody Methodists and Calvinists and Calvinistic Methodists.

'Anyway, thanks for listening, Charlie. At least I suppose a lot of it you hadn't heard before.'

'Some of it, yes. Everybody was wondering but there were things nobody knew.'

'People always say you can't keep a secret in Wales, but there's no problem if it's nasty enough. They know all too well what they're like, what talkers they are. And hypocrisy's good too. Comes into its own, you might say.'

'But Muriel knew.'

Peter actually laughed. 'Oh yes. When I look back, me marrying her is about the hardest thing to believe of all. Next to her marrying me. She was keen, of course. She wasn't quite a virgin but near enough not to count. She may even have thought she honestly didn't mind coming third to Angharad and Rhiannon. If so the scales fell from her eyes with . . .'

'Prodigious precipitation.'

'And comprehensiveness. And irreversibility. And everything else. Well, it's done me good to get that off my chest.' Peter was breathing naturally now and just with this mention of his chest he finally removed his hand from it. 'How long I can expect it to last is another matter. Oh, God, there I go – moan, moan, moan. It is a time for the recharging of glasses.'

As they got up thankfully from the sofa Charlie asked, 'How much of the story does Rhiannon know?'

'All of it, I should think. Well, not everything I've told you. I haven't discussed it with her since.'

'No, I can see how you wouldn't.'

Charlie tried to set it all in order in his mind. He told himself he could not be expected to manage the whole thing straight away. There was quite enough for an old josser to take in in one evening. Whatever the time might be he was beginning to feel like moving on – after another here he would suggest to Peter that they should drift along to the Glendower for a bite and a swallow. The fire had failed to warm the room appreciably and a headachy reek of damp had emerged, with a touch of stale flower-water thrown in. But if Garth was not living in the house then where was he living? Or could he really be a lodger after all?

Peter and Charlie came up to hear Garth saying, 'Well, whose shout is it, then?'

As if by pre-arrangement first Alun and Malcolm, then Charlie and Peter looked at each other. It fell to Malcolm, as sometimes in the past, to say what everyone else was thinking and not saying.

'Sorry, Garth, I'm not with you. How do you mean, shout? We're not in the pub now.'

'No, boy, of course not, of course not,' said Garth, laying his hand reassuringly on Malcolm's arm. 'Just with the prices things are these days we simply can't afford unrestricted hospitality. Of course we'd like to, but we can't. So?' He sent round an interrogative glance.

'All right, if it's shouts we're on to, I'll shout first.' Alun still looked very much astonished.

'Good for you. Double Scotch, is it?' Garth tipped the bottle twice while the rest of the company paid close attention. 'Right. Help yourself to water or soda.'

'You don't mean to say they're free? Oh, goody bloody goody, what?'

Garth nodded without speaking, his eyes on a pocket calculator that had appeared on the sideboard before him.

'Mind you don't forget to add on the cost of the first round.'

At this Garth moved the calculator aside, though not far. 'I regard that as distinctly uncalled for, Alun,' he said in a sorrowful tone. 'If not downright gratuitous. Those first drinks were not a *round* in any sense of the word. They were my freely offered hospitality. Good God, man, do you take me for some kind of Scrooge?'

Instantly Alun choked on his large first sip of whisky and water. Coughing with marked violence he shakily clunked his glass back on the sideboard, strolled a pace or two and went down sprawling with most of his top half across one of the sofas and his legs spread out on the thin carpet. This seemed even for him an unusually thorough imitation of a man collapsing with rage or revulsion. So at least Charlie considered. Since he was the nearest he stooped down over the sofa. Peter followed him.

Alun was breathing loudly and deeply through his mouth in the guttural equivalent of a snore. His eyes were wide open and to all appearance focusing, though not on Charlie or Peter, nor on Garth when he too bent over him. In a low voice but quite distinctly he said a couple of meaningless words and his mouth moved. Then his eyelids drooped and he stopped doing anything at all.

'I think that's it,' said Garth.

'What?' Charlie felt utterly bewildered.

'I think he's dead,' said Garth, continuing none the less to loosen Alun's tie and unbutton the neck of his shirt. 'Yes, I'm afraid he's gone.'

After a few moments Peter asked where the telephone was and on being directed went out into the hall, closely followed by Malcolm. Charlie helped Garth get Alun into a more or less natural position lying on the sofa. By now he seemed quite unmistakably dead.

After less than a minute Peter came back into the room. 'On their way,' he said. 'Malcolm's trying to find Rhiannon. Well now. Well indeed.' He stood uncertainly by the door.

'Have a drink.' Garth sat and continued to sit on the arm of the sofa beside Alun. 'And Charlie. On the house. There's an irony for you if you like. Go on, help yourselves.'

'What was it? Any ideas on what it was?' Charlie looked over at Alun's body from where he had instinctively moved to, the furthest possible corner of the sideboard. 'Was. Christ.'

'Heart. Or stroke. Perhaps not heart because he didn't seem to be in any particular pain as far as I could see. Of course it was only those few seconds. But they don't usually go off just like that, not with heart, not as a rule.'

Charlie missed Alun's being able to say, I suppose you mean sheep and bloody bullocks don't. Not as a rule. His glass was empty and he poured himself a treble, or another treble.

'Do you know if he'd had any funny turns recently?' asked Garth. 'Or headaches or . . .'

There had been something a couple of weeks back, but Charlie could not call it to mind. He shook his head. Malcolm came in and said he had not been able to find Rhiannon or learn where she was. If the others agreed he proposed to travel down to the hospital in the ambulance and go on trying to reach her from there. Before they could even think of any other option the ambulance arrived. Its crew declined to pronounce Alun dead but they would not say he was alive either. With almost too much speed they had him on to a stretcher, out of the house and away. Malcolm had said good night briefly and hurried after them.

'To think not ten minutes ago he was standing there as alive as you and me,' said Garth. 'A breath of fresh air is quenched for ever.'

Charlie responded. He wanted very much to get Peter away and to leave himself, but as things were they could hardly go stalking out just yet. Peter, he guessed, felt this too. So they hung on, keeping to the same spot by the sideboard as before.

'Good little drinker he was,' said Garth. 'You can say that without fear of contradiction. Good little pourer too.'

'He what?'

'He kept pouring. Drinks. He was always one who was calling for more drinks. Very characteristic almost his last words were ordering up more drinks. He'd have liked that.'

Whereas absolutely his last words were pissing on you for asking for money for drinks in, according to you, your own house, which he'd probably have liked even more, thought Charlie. Then he relented a little: Garth had just refilled the glasses without question. But, again, it would have taken some strength of character to ask who was going to cough up now Alun had defaulted. 'Do you think whatever it was could have been brought on by that row with Tarc?'

'No.' Garth fingered his chin. 'No, I don't. No, that sort of thing only happens in films. No, he had it coming. In fact that's the one great comfort of the whole sad tale. There wasn't a damn thing he or anyone else could have done about it. Not a thing.'

'Oh, fabulous,' said Peter, breaking a long silence. 'Well, that certainly softens the blow and no mistake. Blessing in disguise, really, looked at in that light.' He paused to allow the mantle of solemnity to become resettled, no doubt hoping to be excused from making any definitive pronouncement in farewell. 'We'll be off, then,' he said weightily. 'If that's all right with you. Thank you for the drinks.'

Garth gave a sonorous sigh and clasped both Peter's hands in his own. With sudden awful clarity Charlie foresaw he was going to call upon them to salute the passing of a great Welshman. But before another word was said there was a low sound from outside the room, hardly a sound, more like a tremor. Whatever it was Garth turned his head, dropped Peter's hands and compared his watch with the wall-clock, an instrument unnoticed until now, disquieting in appearance but only to a minor degree, about right for the billiard-room or butler's pantry in Castle Dracula. The three waited as if for an explosion until the door opened and Angharad was to be seen.

What with one thing and another Charlie found it really hard not to give a shudder or a groan of dread and despair at the sight of her. She wore unnameable dark garments high at the neck and long in the cuff, topped by a waterproof of some sort which she very slowly unbuttoned, took off and draped over one arm as events proceeded. Her general aspect reminded Charlie, after a moment's utter blankness, of the photographs he had been looking at not long before, perhaps even an individual one. By the look of her eyes and mouth she had aged perceptibly since last seen. At no time did she send the least glance in his or Peter's direction.

'You're back early, love,' said Garth, smiling at her.

Angharad said crisply in her out-of-keeping voice, that of a woman half her age or less, 'There was no point in hanging about – it was quite obvious she didn't know me. If you remember, it's been coming on for some time. I told her clearly and repeatedly who I was, kept saying my name, going on I was her daughter, and she heard me but she didn't take it in. No idea in the world. So I came away. That woman, Mrs Jeffreys is it, she was seeing to her perfectly well, and I wanted to watch that Great-Gardens-of-England programme, which you really do need colour for and she's only got black and white. Not that I could have concentrated on it properly anyway.' She too looked at the time and added, 'I did telephone, but the line was engaged.'

'Yes, well . . .'

'So we're having a party, are we?'

'Not exactly.' No relish or any other tinge of ill will could be heard in Garth's tone. 'Alun Weaver fell down dead just about where you're standing now, it would have been, well when you rang you'd have run into Peter dialling 999. And . . . there we are.'

'Ah.' She acknowledged the objection and continued, 'More like a wake, then.'

'Sort of.'

Charlie wished Malcolm had been present to list some of the ways in which what had just been taking place could not fairly be said to have constituted a wake. He watched Angharad while, the removal of her outer piece of clothing now accomplished, she stood between him and the door pulling her cuffs down over the backs of her mottled hands and casting her eye over the sideboard top, perhaps in quest of the cash Garth should have taken off his patrons. Finally she gave this up and turned towards him again. 'Well,' she said with an upward, munching movement of her jaws, 'I'll be getting on,' and made to leave the room.

'I'll be going for my usual,' said Garth with a kind of wink at her in his inflection.

Five-mile jog? Aberystwyth BA (Hons)? Chicken and chips? Without staying to consider, Charlie got Peter out through the hall and on to the porch as soon as the coast was clear. The rain had packed up and there was a great tapping and plopping as what had already fallen dripped off the trees and the eaves of the houses. With the sky mostly clear now there was if anything more light than when they had arrived.

'Charlie,' said Peter as they stood at the top of the steps. 'I simply – '

'Yes, I know. Listen: I'm too drunk to drive and you're too, er, drunk to drive. As you may or may not have noticed there's a pub on the top corner where we turned off. However gruesome its appointments it must sell drink and possess a telephone. While you're working on a very large whisky I'll mobilise Victor. Then sandwiches and our own bottle in the flat at the Glendower and your car fetched. How about that, Major?'

'Oh . . . fine. I mean coming on top of . . .'

'Of course. Tell me later. Left at the gate, then eighty yards or so along to the corner. Not more.'

9 Peter

1

'That was William,' said Peter. 'Not dressed yet. He says we're to go on and he'll see us at the church.'

'Hardly a bolt from the blue.' Muriel was moving a hat about on her head in front of her dressing-table. 'I can't remember having this out of the cupboard since the day the lad took his degree.' She turned lingeringly away from her reflection. 'Well, what do you think, then?'

Peter thought in general that most people seeing the two of them as a married couple would wonder what cruel fate had landed such a comparatively presentable female, still slim and well taken care of as to skin and hair, with such a bloated, beaten-up old slob. More to the purpose, he thought that the subtle fore-and-aft groove or corrugation in the crown of the hat gave it a slightly sat-on look. But that was not called for either. He concentrated his attention. 'Fine,' he said, widening his eyes and giving a succession of little nods. 'Fine.'

'Or there's this one. I'm not sure I've ever even had it on till now since the bloody shop.'

It was like a sturdy cake-frill in pale pink with a reinforced gauze or netting top. He nodded at it more slowly and judicially, finding no words.

'Which do you think is better?'

After a moment of the usual attempted clairvoyance he reminded himself sharply that the day might have come when, in defiance of all history, she was asking him what he thought because she wanted to know. Still no help. Trying not to smirk at his own cunning, he said, 'I suppose some of the women will be wearing hats, will they? I thought even for weddings it had more or less faded away. Of course I'm not much of a – '

'Oh, it's a dead duck in England, wearing hats. Never see them in London.'

'Well then . . .'

'Ah, but we're not in England.'

'I'm sure it would be perfectly all right. Nobody would object.'

'Well, I don't want to offend the native wives by flouting ancestral taboos.'

He had thought that line quite funny on its first appearance about the time of Suez. 'I don't think you need worry.'

Rather to his regret she took off the cake-frill piece and laid it on the dressing-table. 'How do I look without it? Go on.'

'All right,' he said soberly. 'You look all right.' Yes, she had been going to do that all along.

'Good. That's settled that. Well, we'd better be getting . . .'

'Oh, we've got a bit of time yet.'

'There's a case for being in position when you're expected to be.'

To hear this sentiment on Muriel's lips marginally astonished Peter, but he said nothing more than, 'Okay, well I'll go and bring the car round. You come down when you're ready.'

As he almost ran down the stairs he affirmed internally that he must put top priority on pulling himself together. If he went on in that kind of strain, going off at tangents, giving brilliant imitations of a man who really wanted his wife to look her best and things like that, he would soon come to grief. From the moment early in the year when William had announced his intention to marry Rosemary Weaver, Peter had been given a new lease of life. Every time he thought of it he felt as if he had been reading a communiqué announcing a catastrophic defeat of the shits.

In the hall now, moving with exemplary speed for one of his weight and condition, he climbed up on the pseudo-Chippendale chair by the telephone and swung about just in time to fart with a kind of gulping sound into an enormous green and mauve face, rendered in a mixture of paint and filth, that hung from the side of the stairway. On descending, much elated, he spotted the necessary bottle of Famous Grouse in its place on the dresser in the kitchen. Spotting it was all that was needed. Without bothering about surely on this day of all days, etc., he took just one small quick nip and then just one more small quick nip. Irrelevantly, he remembered Charlie once informing him that ghillies or crofters or some such persons in the Scottish Highlands would drink regularly, as a matter of routine, a tumbler of whisky before setting out on the day's round, so at least Charlie had said as he put down a similar quantity to see him through their twenty-minute car-journey to a lawyers' piss-up in Welsh St Hilarys.

It was a fine bright morning in early March of the sort much more often recalled in these parts than actually met with, the air calm and mild along the whole of the coastal plain and inshore waters. On days like this gardeners recently in London, but not gardeners alone, would say how much further forward everything in Wales seemed to be: daffodils, rhododendrons, azaleas, even the sticky-buds on the chestnuts were two or three weeks ahead of what you saw in the London parks and squares. Low in the sky still, the sun made long shadows, casting a light no stronger than that on a summer's evening, clear but not vivid, with a softness that would be gone by May. Cwmgwyrdd gleamed gently in the sunshine, and Peter, who had noticed the good weather, felt for a few moments that it was not such a hopelessly bad place to live as he let himself into the garage.

'Am I all right?' he asked Muriel when she came down into the hall.

'Quite suitable for the occasion.'

'I was thinking really of stains, you know, custard, chocolate, that kind of thing. There's not much else I can do anything about at this stage.'

'No, all clear. Tie could be tighter.'

Tightening it, he looked her over summarily and said, 'Much better without the hat, no doubt about it.'

They got into the car and drove towards town. He considered their exchange in the hall and some bits, at any rate, of the one in the bedroom just before. They had talked like that a good deal in past weeks, with studious normality, like an English couple in a socialist country, fearful of being eavesdropped upon, conspiring to be dull together. But there was a lot underneath that. When she asked him about the hats she had not looked at him, not really, not properly, any more than he had looked at her when he answered. His enjoyment of parts of the charade was real enough but had something hysterical in it. Time to play safe now.

'They couldn't have wished for a better day,' said Muriel.

'No rain forecast before tomorrow.'

'I think it's warm enough to sit out.'

'We'll have to see how it goes.'

And this little piggy cried wee, wee, wee all the way home. A run-through, thought Peter suddenly. A series of rehearsals for being parents-in-law, the very image or images of a decent, comfortable and above all ordinary old couple rather unexpectedly turned back into part of a family some time after anything of that sort had perceptibly lapsed. And of course merely to put on an in-law style when it seemed called for would be very slipshod and insecure; something more fundamental was required. To adapt the concept of the couple in Eastern Europe, this was the period of pre-drop training. On his mind's television screen Peter could see an MI6 man, one of the fashionable aloof but hot-eyed sort, saying he would have them thinking, feeling, dreaming like Darby and Joan before they were through. And yes, the new style of talk, which was really only new in quantity, in proportion, had begun to be noticeable just about when or after William had told them he and Rosemary were going to get married.

'Well, now the day's here at last the whole thing seems to have happened rather suddenly,' said Muriel.

'Yes, I suppose it does in a way.'

'And isn't it extraordinary, we've hardly discussed it at all.'

'No, there wasn't a hell of a lot to discuss, really, was there?'

'And now it's too late, whatever conclusion we might come to.'

For Peter, that exactly defined a signal superiority of this day over its predecessors. He said nevertheless, and not in pursuance of any intention of playing safe, 'Oh, I wouldn't be too sure of that. You'll agree we're still in Wales.'

'What are you talking about?'

'There were some people called Ungoed-Thomas over in Caerhays, related to a cousin of my father's I think. Anyway, there was a daughter there called Gladys, a couple of years older than me. Now Gladys had got hold of an American, can't think how she managed that in Caerhays in those days, but she had – this would have been 1937 or so. Well, it got to the point where Gladys was going to marry her American, and indeed it was all fixed up, ready to go. Haven't told you this story before, have I? No, so the night before the wedding a call comes from Gladys and my parents nip on the train for Caerhays – you could do that in those days. I wish I'd gone too. Would they use their influence to stop Gladys's mam stopping the wedding.'

'And did they?'

'Yes. Marvellous, those two being on the progressive – '

'What could she have done anyway, the old girl? How could she have stopped it?'

'I agree she couldn't have stopped it indefinitely, even in Caerhays in 1937, but she could have caused a large upset instead of just a small one. What was interesting was her reason for being against the American. He was an American.'

'I heard you.'

'No, I mean that was the reason. Why the old girl was against him, according to her anyway. Not that it isn't a pretty serious charge in general, but in fact this one was hilariously proper. Name of Foster, Ralph Foster. Funny how you remember things that are nothing to do with you. Professor of physics at Yale University he was. God knows what he'd find to do in Caerhays in 1987, let alone 1937. He was so proper he fell down dead of excitement at a baseball game not many years later, but Gladys was well settled in the States by then.'

After saying she heard him, Muriel had begun wriggling her torso over the back of her seat, arm extended from the shoulder towards a blue-and-white box of tissues on the rear shelf. Having captured it she pushed herself forwards again by degrees, almost rolling over laterally when the car took a fair-sized curve, and twisted round into her original position just as he finished with the baseball game. 'I'm listening,' she said.

'That's it.'

'What?' She pulled down the shade over the top part of the windscreen in front of her and stared at her reflection in the oblong of mirror there while she picked repeatedly at the tissues. 'What, what's interesting about that?'

'Well. Scene from Welsh life. I thought you liked them. Caption, in Wales you never know.'

'You mean if I could think of something like that I'd try to put a stop to William marrying what's-her-name, Rosemary, if there was just something I could come up with. Otherwise what's the point?'

'Oh, no. No, no. Of course you're as pleased as I am. Still, she was born in London, and I've noticed you've been getting really quite noticeably Welsh in your old age. I was staggered, quite frankly, when you said just now it was a good thing to be seen in your place on time. You couldn't hope for anything more Welsh than that, not off the cuff. Chapel you'd think we was going to.'

Beside him Muriel suddenly opened her mouth as wide as possible consistent with keeping her lips stretched over her teeth, perhaps in unspoken comment but more likely so as to get those parts of her face lined up for the application of the tissue she had now managed to wrest from its box. She still said nothing.

'Oh, er, what line would you have taken if we had discussed the marriage before today?'

'Nothing very much,' she said, going on peering, 'And after all there's no sense arguing about it now.'

Well no, no more than five minutes ago, and he had not really expected to hear how much she felt like killing him at the idea of a son of hers and her only child marrying the daughter of a woman her own husband would rather have married, and that just for a start. But he realised that asking the question had been the latest spurt of the dangerous euphoria that had again possessed him. Take it *easy*, for God's sake. *Watch* it.

After doing something undetectable to her mouth she put the tissue away and said, 'You've got quite saucy these last months. You know, cheeky.' She spoke in a tone of measured approbation more suitable to telling him he had shown signs of becoming well read or kind to animals.

And interfering with the body after death more than cursorily to pay him out for being pleased at something that displeased her. 'Yes, I probably have been a bit full of beans seeing William looking so happy.'

'It's not just that. It started before that. It was in full swing by Christmas.'

'Was it really? I can't think of anything to explain it,' he said without trying to at all.

If Muriel could think of something she kept it bottled up. They drove in silence over the old bridge, repaired now, past the roofless smelt-houses, through St Advent, past Victoria Station, up the Strand, past the Trevor Knudsen Fine Arts Museum, Marks & Spencer, the Glendower, the Royal Foundation of Wales, the cricket and rugby ground and the university and round by the hospital towards Holland.

'Peter,' said Muriel when they were a couple of minutes from the church: 'I'm selling the house.'

'What?'

'This time I mean it. Now William's settled, that's my last reason or excuse gone for hanging on any longer round here. Yes, it's back to Middlesborough for me, and if you care to come along too there'll be a bed for you at the end of the road. Now it could so be, sooner than shift to sunny Yorkshire or Cleveland or whatever it's called these days you'd prefer to go it alone here, under your own steam as it were. Well, I dare say that can be arranged. Entirely up to you.'

So much for the parade of cosy domesticity. Muriel had spoken with all her usual matter-of-factness, even perhaps a little more. It occurred to Peter that the presence of William and his best man as first arranged would have made no real difference; she would have seen to it that he got the lot, or enough, some time or other before entering the church. This was now just round the corner and the early guests were on their way to it. He caught sight of old Owen Thomas and his family getting out of their car.

'There's no more to say,' she began again. 'These people may be good, they may be bad, and I'll not say I'm not fond of one or two of them, but they're not *my* people, and I mean to do something about that while I've still time. So I'm checking out. The house goes on the market first thing Monday morning. And that's that. Okay? Understood? No appeals, no conditions, no stays of execution, no compromises, no practical alternatives. Final. Now I may be completely wrong again and you've been bursting to get shut of the place since whenever, but if I'm not wrong I'll give you one piece of advice. Start getting used to the idea right away. If I were you I'd go left here and park in the Holland Court car-park.'

'Go and . . .'

'Nobody uses it much this time of day.'

So it turned out, but Muriel had barely had time to take up groom's-mother station at Peter's side before they were fairly among old Tudor Whittingham and his wife and son and daughter and son-in-law and two grandchildren and married sister and niece whom he hoped it was all right for him to have brought along only they were staying with them. There was more, much more, all the way to the church and on the broad asphalted walk surrounding it. Some, like Percy and Dorothy, Malcolm and Gwen, old Vaughan Mowbray and his arthritic lady-friend, a few dimly remembered figures from university, industry, Golf Club, various youngsters identifiably or presumably connected with William, came and went; others, like Garth, Siân Smith, Arnold and toffee-nose Eirwen Spurling and two quite independent funereally-dressed couples, unknown, silent and demoralising, came and stayed around. No family of either parent were to be seen. Muriel's of course were all in England, and evidently staying there; Peter had two brothers living, but these days he hardly knew as much as where.

Grimly, with an air of putting down any nonsense about celebration, an attendant removed the two of them and escorted them inside – at the last moment Peter spotted Rhiannon coming in at the churchyard gate and waved, but was not sure if she saw. The small delay provoked the man into an impatient jerk of the head, a bit of a risk in view of the glossy pudding-basin wig he wore on it. His general bearing suggested that he thought he had come to a funeral. If he did he was not deviating all that far from the spirit of a good slice of the congregation, who stared pessimistically at the groom's parents as they passed, on full alert for hiccup or tell-tale stumble. They reached the front pew without offence, though, shuffling in beside Charlie and Sophie.

As far as he could remember, Peter had never been in here before. Enough sun came through the unstained parts of the stained glass to make the place look bright and very clean, like new, in fact. The light-coloured woodwork seemed familiar, personal to him in some way, and presently he realised that it reminded him of the kind of furniture, said to have been Scandinavian in inspiration, that had been fashionable when he and Muriel got married.

Having reached him by a side route, thoughts of that time and what had followed it, up to and including today, proved impossible to drive off. They were not so much thoughts as a confusion of memories and feelings. The memories were powerful but misty and spread over, with Angharad and Rhiannon in them as well as Muriel and a mass of all-but-forgotten faces and places he could not have named. Of his feelings the two foremost ones were remorse and self-pity. Well as he knew them both, he had never learnt how to deal with them, and he stood and sat in his place now vainly trying to see past them to his son's marriage ceremony, which he had been looking forward to a dozen times a day since first hearing it was to come about, and which he had determined to take in and value minute by minute. Instead, what was happening in front of him took the short cut and went straight into the past to blend in with everything else. As usual in these last years.

He went through most of the service in a state similar in important respects to boredom. At the same time, screened off as he was from the centre of the picture he still managed to catch on to details at the edges. So he heard the congregation singing – no choir, naturally, because somebody was on holiday or had just thought of something better to do – and found it puny, thickened by men singing the air, some of them an octave low half the time, the whole performance to be defended only as far as it showed any English present how wrong they would have been to expect anything out of the ordinary from singing Welshmen in the flesh as opposed to on television. Or so he might have said if he could have been bothered. Charlie stood out quite a bit from the mess, in tune and probably accurate with the bass in the hymns and making a good shot in the psalm – much more testing. Peter found he could remember him years ago sneaking off to practices with some secular choir in Harriston or Emanuel, promising to be back by half-nine at latest to sink propitiatory pints.

He noticed that the ceremony was performed by two or more clerics and that they wore embroidered vestments of some white material, not cotton. Parts of the service were chanted. Peter had started to welcome these touches of High as likely to affront some parts of the congregation when he saw that a subordinate figure he had mistaken for an effeminate boy was actually a female, a young woman, not a bad-looking one either. Oh

Christ. He had come to think that almost the whole point of Wales these days was that you were going to be spared that kind of thing, for the time being at least. He was overcome by a great weariness, a longing to be done with everything, but in a couple of moments that too passed. Then right at the end, when William and his bride were supposedly being blessed, he found Muriel's hand groping for his and made out a tear-track on her averted cheek. He put this down as all part of the performance, but it was impossible not to grasp her hand, and to be on the safe side he at once ran up a well-disposed look in case she should turn her head, though this soon turned out not to be needed.

2

The organ sounded out with Mendelssohn: there in the loft was one man (or of course woman now, bugger it) who had not taken the day off. As he passed down the aisle William glanced towards his parents. Without seeming to do anything at all with any part of his face he conveyed unmistakably to Peter a cheerfully hangdog confession of surrender but of surrender none the less; Peter wondered suddenly what he thought his mother thought of his marriage and his wife. Rhiannon gave a smile, too friendly to be called impersonal and yet still not personal. It was time to move. Those still in their pews stared at Peter as before, with no hint of having been appeased by what had taken place in the meantime.

'Well, I reckon we done the young couple very tasteful,' said Charlie. 'I don't know about you, I wouldn't presume to presume, but I could do with a drink.'

These words, or the manner in which they were spoken, made Peter look at him for a moment. He said, 'Yes, me too.'

Charlie grinned briefly. 'Bad as that, eh? It's these bloody new sleeping-pills of Dewi's. Finest thing out, he says, no systemic effects, you know, like actually getting the system off to sleep. Well, we'll get if off tonight all right. Look, if you want to slip away later we could have a couple down at the Glendower. I'll be there in any case. Just one stipulation. Don't bring Garth. On this happy day . . . this day of typically Welsh family feeling and good fellowship . . . our thoughts naturally turn . . . to stringing up Garth Pumphrey, FRCVS, outside the Bible. Jesus, there he is.'

'Somebody's got to say all those things.'

'Oh no they haven't. Well wait a minute, perhaps they have. There's an awful lot of filling-in to be done in life, isn't there?'

'Anyway he has one great virtue, young Garth, as you pointed out some time ago. When he's around you know for a certainty you're not going to run into Angharad.'

'When did I say that? I hope at least I said it lightly. I'm sorry, Peter.'

'Nonsense, you were quite right. You spoke better than you knew. And never more applicable than today.'

'I suppose so.' Charlie looked seriously at his feet as they halted in the porch. 'She'd have been nothing but a . . .' He started on another word and stopped.

'Skeleton at the feast, yes. Oh dear. Once again, very well put. You know, it's a funny thing . . .'

'What is? I think I can – '

'Just, ever since that evening at Garth's I've had the – '

'I'll see you down at the house. But . . .'

They were being borne onwards and outwards into the sunshine among hurrying or resisting bodies and there was not going to be much more of this conversation. Sophie and Dorothy were near, Sophie not looking at anyone, silent, possibly tearful, Dorothy clutching a leather handbag that might have held a baby's cricket-bat and pads and wearing something of which it could be said with certainty only that it was lime-green and that she had made it herself. Charlie backed Peter into a minor angle of the stonework and gave a muted yelp as his ankle hit a boot-scraper.

'Er . . . there's something it would be good if you'd say to Rhiannon if you get a chance to talk to her alone.'

'Yes?' said Peter, pretty sure he knew what it was, his mind still on the events at Garth's.

'You know Victor and I are doing the reception, well for one reason and another we want to charge her the full rate on paper, so to speak, but she'll get a rebate in the post next month which she needn't acknowledge, okay?'

'Oh, marvellous,' said Peter, laughing a good deal at the imaginative poverty of his guess. 'Absolutely spiffing.'

'I mean Victor, we thought it might come better from you. If you would.'

'I'll make a point of it.'

'Cheers. See you there.' Charlie reached for a passing lapel and was gone.

Alone for a space, Peter had time to look without much engrossment at the dozens of people hanging about on the well-kept lawn and paths, searching for one another with heads raised or drifting uncertainly away, William standing with friends of his, Rosemary with friends of hers, younger couples being pulled this way and that by children, older couples consisting usually of a more or less apathetic old boy and vigilant, questing old girl with glasses and hat – yes, hat, nothing to do with the wedding as like as not, just part of the uniform – , solitaries wondering what on earth had possessed them to come, Rhiannon in grey with white collar and cuffs along by the gate next to Alun's very fat and unsmiling brother who had come down from London to give the bride away, and hemmed in by Breconshire aunts and cousins and such, but at the moment speaking hesitantly into a microphone held out by a squat man in a white raincoat while a photographer circled round her – all this, as far as it went, Peter contemplated, until a well-known voice was heard.

'Tell us now, when's the baby coming then?' Although Garth's voice was quite well known in some quarters he sounded at the moment more like a Welsh comedian than usual.

'There isn't one, I mean not yet as far as I know,' said Peter, wishing he could drop easily into character like Charlie and the others.

'Awh! Reely! Well, there's posh for you.'

'There's *swank*,' corrected Tudor Whittingham at Garth's side. Tudor had somehow managed to shed his followers for the time being and kept looking round to make sure they stayed shed. His amazing lack of surplus flesh allowed full visibility to the spare, narrow frame that had stood him in such good stead as a squash player in the remote past. Its narrowness was extended upwards to his skull, which all generations had pronounced inadequate for an adequate amount of brain without compression of some sort. He had been Tudor Totem-Bonce in the form above Peter at the Grammar.

'Posh or swank, same difference,' said Garth. Then his manner changed abruptly and he went on to Peter at reduced volume, 'Tarc was saying last night he hoped you'd come in today for a bit if you had the time. You haven't been in much since poor Alun went, have you?' He rolled a mournful bardic eye at Peter.

'No. No, I suppose I haven't.'

'No, well we miss you there, Peter. I know Tarc does particularly. He feels rotten about that evening still, throwing us all out neck and crop. It's not that he feels responsible at all for . . . what happened later; I think I've talked him out of that. It's more that it grieves him that he and Alun parted for the last time on such bad terms. Was that your impression, Tudor?'

'No question. No question whatever.'

'Of course he never seriously meant we should take all our gear away. Temper, that was. He as good as admitted it when I went round the next morning. Perhaps I told you.'

Addressing Peter, but obviously reproaching Garth for the omission as well, Tudor said, 'I thought it was a lovely service and the young people looked absolutely radiant and I hope they'll be very happy.'

'Oh yes. Oh yes.' Garth intimated that between him and Peter that side of things was taken for granted. 'Yes, old Tarc really respected poor Alun. I reckon everybody did. Mind you, there's not a man who's ever walked this earth who didn't give those around him something to put up with. But taking him for all in all he was the best of fellows really, wasn't he?'

Somebody has to say it, thought Peter. 'Yes, I suppose he was.' The words drew a look of puzzled incredulity from Tudor.

'Actually,' Garth went on, 'actually not everybody did respect him if the truth were told. Remember that article in the *Western Mail*, that so-called appreciation? Nasty. Curmudgeonly is what I'd call it. Thoroughly curmudgeonly. Oh, and did you see that reference in a *Times* review, was it, the other day? Oh yes – wait a minute.' His hand moved towards his breast pocket but stopped before it got there. 'No, I've filed it. Er . . . he could be called a follower of Brydan if that were not taken to imply a certain degree of strength and vital . . . something. Very nasty. I'll get it copied and send it you.'

Tudor said with some determination, 'William and Rosemary going away for a bit, are they?'

Though ready and willing with a reply Peter never gave it, being instantly hiked off to be photographed. He hoped Tudor thought he was getting his money's-worth out of having dumped his family.

There was a line-up in the sunshine with backs to the church wall. Peter had been for sidling into his place at the end next to Muriel, but embraces were called for, not of course with the unsmiling brother, who unsmilingly nodded and that was that, nor with Muriel. She smiled, though, but not for long, which was just as well. He was not going to start digging all that over. There was one thing to be said at any rate: neither he nor anyone else could have done anything about it, probably ever. Who had used almost those very words to him not so long ago, and about what or whom?

For some minutes three or four photographers, one a woman or girl, all showing in their clothing and hair structure what some might have seen as an unhealthy disrespect for stuff like weddings, huddled the six principals together with no result, spread them apart again, brought some forward, waved others away with sudden backhand sweeps. Nor was it lost on Peter that advances in science meant they took ten times as many photographs as would once have been found necessary and shaped up to take twice that number. It was easier for them like that, he inferred, more fun too, licitly buggering a set of strangers about. Quite understandable. Do it himself if he had the chance.

Eventually the consensus emerged that it would be unnecessary or perhaps futile to prolong the photographic session, which faded away without anything being said on either side. Soon afterwards removal to the Weaver house was set going, a matter of a couple of hundred yards on foot. As if the manoeuvre had been organised beforehand Muriel drifted across, thrust one arm through William's and the other round Rosemary's waist and seemed to swing them both through a semicircle towards the gate. With an advance six or more abreast pretty well ruled out, Peter found himself in a second rank between Alun's brother, said on their very brief first meeting the previous night to be called Duncan, and his suddenly manifest wife, who had glasses and a hat with the best of them and very red lips and abnormally long teeth thrown in.

On the far side of the gateway Rhiannon was with an aunt or cousin or so and Peter was stuck, irremovably as it turned out, with these in-laws of hers. He had always thought of himself as a cool head in a situation like that, not for the life of him to be driven into speaking first. Nevertheless after four minutes of total silence, the last three of them spent standing in a row at no particular point on the pavement, there he was asking the wife whether she and, er, Duncan proposed staying over until the following day or whether, on the other hand, they would be returning to London that same evening.

She turned to face him hungrily. 'Oh, we've got to get back, no two ways about it,' she said in an accent from somewhere not very nice in England. 'I tell you, it took all of everybody's time getting him to come away for just the one night.'

'Business responsibilities, I suppose.' Peter dimly remembered something about a finance company or building society.

'You're joking. They're a thing of the past, they are, it's getting on for four years now,' she said with gloomy relish. 'No, it's just he won't be moved if he can help it. What he's doing now, Mr Thomas, he's giving them a chance to get settled where we're going, you see, so he can just sneak in there without any of them saying anything to him.'

'Quite,' said Peter, turning his eyes but not his head towards Duncan, who was making rhythmical puffing noises and rocking to and fro where he stood.

'Or so he thinks to himself. He doesn't like being spoken to because people expect him to say things back. That's why he doesn't look very friendly. I tell him he wants to wear a hearing-aid, everybody knows better than try and talk to a person wearing one of them, but he won't. Just draw attention, he says.' She turned back her gold-inwoven cuff. 'Christ, that's long enough to get your grandmother and Mrs Brown settled.' Facing her husband now, she said in a tremendously loud voice with a lot of facial activity, out of sight from Peter but audible enough in her speech, 'We'd better get moving, Dad. They'll be wondering where we've got to. Come on, old boy. There.'

She did plenty of pointing into the middle distance while she was saying this. Duncan nodded and got moving. The three of them crossed the road to the corner of the lane that led to their destination.

'I don't know why I still shout at him like that. Just habit. The nerves have gone, you see, both sides, so whatever you do he'll never hear anything. Virus, I think they said. Oh yes. Rhiannon did tell you, did she?' Duncan's wife mispronounced the name without any suggestion that it was unfamiliar to her. 'I mean she did mention it.'

Like enough, indeed. 'Yes,' said Peter.

'There's not a fat lot he can get up to if you follow me. He can't face learning the lip-reading and that sign language, everyone does it different, he says, no rhyme nor reason to it. There's the subtitles though, on TV. He likes his food all right, as you can see from his . . .' She paused for the first time but went on firmly, 'You know I feel a pig dragging him all this way and running him into all these people he doesn't know, but I'd go potty if I didn't get a break once in a while.'

'Of course you must,' he made himself say. 'That's quite reasonable and normal.'

At Rhiannon's front gate they halted again, Duncan prompted by his wife's hand on his shoulder. She said, 'Take my advice, Mr Thomas, and don't go deaf. Well, it's been nice talking to you. He's a lovely boy, that William. Now you go off and enjoy yourself. We'll be along in a minute.' Duncan gave a not quite unsmiling nod of farewell and thanks for not having said anything to him.

Inside the house the first person Peter saw was Gwen, her head at an offensive angle as she listened to whatever some tall, dignified old ninny in an injudicious green suit might have been trying to tell her; a cousin of Malcolm's, perhaps. It was easy to imagine her frowning and leering interestedly over the account of the conversation with Duncan's wife she was never going to be given. Peter looked round for Charlie, failed to spot him and made for the bar, a trestle table with a really seriously snowy white tablecloth spread over it and loaded with bottles, an astonishingly high proportion of which seemed to hold soft drinks; not all of them, however. The ruddy-faced girlish youngster from the cocktail bar at the Glendower was doling out the stuff, with great efficiency as it proved. Another class of youngster sat round-shouldered on a folding metal chair against the wall. His face was not at all ruddy and his collar was undone. Good going for the time of day, thought Peter.

His only slightly delayed arrival had in fact given time for a large part of the crowd to get settled here or there, dozens of them in the garden all exclaiming at the warmth of the day and knocking back their drinks at a speed that, if maintained, would quite quickly stretch them out in the herbaceous border. He observed the scene from the step outside the french window and very soon picked up Muriel's rear view by her stooped head and clumping gait. With a couple of William's presumed friends, who stood not less than thirteen foot tall between them, she was strolling along the edge of the lawn and, just as he noticed her, she half turned to run a superior eye over what was growing – nothing very much, perhaps – in the nearby bed. She let her gaze linger, making quite sure things were as bad as they had looked at first glance, then snatched it apologetically away, both in a style he felt sure he would have recognised with an inward yell of loathing at ten times the range. Seeing it, seeing it unseen, catching the old bitch out even on such a puny scale, was as good as a stiff one.

He was turning away to refill his glass, which in the last minute had mysteriously emptied itself, when he caught sight of Rhiannon not far off, nearer than Muriel had been. She was one of a group of a dozen women and some men apparently in a single noisy conversation, glances switching from one speaker to another, all briskly absorbed. Sophie was among them, Siân too, and a couple more he knew by sight, but who were the others? Well, for God's sake, who do you think they are, you bloody old fool – *friends of hers*, see, he notified himself carefully. What else would they be?

But why should it need realising? Because he had forgotten, if he had ever begun to understand, how small a part people played in others' lives and how little they knew about them, even if they saw them every day. Between Alun's death and this morning he had thought many times, several times anyway, about Rhiannon and her life, about how she managed for company with Sophie, Siân, Gwen, Dorothy, Muriel for Christ's sake – none of them exactly her type, he had thought since much longer ago – and no doubt with more besides, her daughters, London friends. What he was looking at gave him some idea. Not much even now. He would have said he had forgotten about love too, but just for the moment he would have had to admit there had been a few weeks once when somebody else had played a very large part in his life and he had known a great deal about her, until the rest of the world came swimming back.

He had to wait a minute or two at the bar, where Victor now presided, while a wave of refills was dealt with. In the interval he saw a man with a moustache nudge a man with a wholly different moustache and pass the word about himself, a word that must have left out the information that he was the sort of old buffer you could just go up to and say hallo to like that and, you know, that would be fine. Before it came to his turn, Victor reached over someone's shoulder and passed him a major Scotch and water with a flourish that said any possible Alun-related bygones were indeed bygones, and oh by the way don't forget that little message to Rhiannon. The unruddy youngster had departed but he was soon accosted by a different one in the shape of the bridegroom.

'Dad, where have you been hiding?'

'Out in the open. Too big to be seen.'

'Come on, come and meet the blokes.'

The blokes were not far away, about five strides from the drink, in fact, and Peter felt he did pretty well with them, considering. He was touched and impressed by the unobtrusive production William put into this event, letting him feel he was meeting all or most of them while nursing him through with a couple of talkative reliables. After a time William said to him, with no fear of being overheard in the ambient uproar,

'She's a marvellous girl, you know. Or do you know? She says she's hardly seen anything of you over these weeks, I mean before today.'

'Yes, well, there sort of hasn't been a hell of a lot of, er . . .'

'No. Anyway she is. I expect you've heard it said that it's absolutely marvellous when somebody's very difficult to get to know and to get on with at first, and then when you do get to know them it's somehow much better than, well, if it hadn't been like that. Eh?'

'Yes. I mean I have heard it said.'

'So have I, and I suppose it might be right, but I must say personally it sounds pretty fair balls to me. Anyway, the point is that's exactly how it wasn't with Rosemary and me. Absolutely no snags or problems of any kind at any stage right from the start. My God, I've just realised it was love at first sight. Doesn't that sound ridiculous?'

'No,' said Peter.

There was a short pause while William took a considered sip of champagne instead of alluding to his parents' marriage, then or now. 'Anyway, she's a marvellous girl. You'd better find her quick if you're going to. We're nipping off right after the speeches. Don't want to get caught up with all these drunken bastards.'

'No, you certainly don't want to do that.'

'I think I might be a bit pissed myself actually. Look, we'll see you as soon as we get back. Really we will. I'm sorry I haven't done anything about it before when I said I was going to, just before I first met Rosemary, do you remember?'

'Oh, was that that day?'

'That was rather the point I'm afraid, meeting Rosemary I mean. It sort of drove everything else out.'

'Yes, I know the feeling. Well, I expect you're – '

'How are you, Dad? I've hardly seen you all this time.'

'I'm all right. I'm better. Those pains I mentioned seem to have, well, I'm keeping my fingers crossed.'

'I gather you were there then, well, when he went off.'

'Yes. It's an awful thing to say in a way, but I absolutely sailed through that bit.'

'Must have been a shock at the time, though. Pretty horrible.'

'It was a rather raw occasion all round.'

William extended his arm with military smartness to present his glass to the circling champagne-bottle. 'Well, at least I shan't have him to deal with.'

'He didn't need a lot of dealing with. Not if you weren't married to him.'

'Well, yeah. Frightful shit, wasn't he? I hardly knew him, of course.'

'I suppose so. The longer I go on the harder it gets to say that about anybody. Himmler, well certainly. Eichmann, that type of chap. Of course he did leave a certain amount to be desired in the way of friendship, Alun, I mean. Bloody Welshman, you see.'

'You really are okay, then? There's really nothing wrong?' asked William, looking hard at his father.

Peter returned the look. 'Nothing whatever, I promise you. Now you're quite right, I'd better track down your wife while there's still time. Have a word before you go finally.'

'Last time I saw her she was in the garden with my mother-in-law. Jesus Christ.'

By now they had moved to the dining-room, where there was an extensive spread of cold ham, veal-and-ham pie, English-style sausages and Continental-style sausage. Also on view were bowls of unadventurous salad and, more to the purpose, an array of pickled onions in three colours, pickled walnuts, pickled gherkins in two sizes, pickled beetroot, four kinds of chutney, three kinds of mustard, six kinds of bottled sauce, in other words a meal plumb in the middle of the genuine Welsh tradition, remarkably complete too barring only the omission of tinned fruit. Banks of sandwiches and uncountable cheeses stood in reserve and most flat surfaces within normal reach carried at least one opened bottle of Victor's special-price red or ditto white. Either or both of these would go down a treat after a few quick glasses of champagne and four or five large gin-and-tonics and in company with salami, mustard pickle, garlic bread, corona-sized spring onions and watercress. Victor himself stood at the head of the table dealing out plates and cutlery and trying to awaken some sense of order in the talkative rout that had started shambling up to be fed.

After pushing past and through them Peter made his way as indicated to the garden. The general drift towards food had reached back as far as here and the last few figures were slowly converging on the french window. Rosemary was one, but he sent her no more than a glance of apology before almost clutching Rhiannon at her side.

'Can I talk to you privately? I've got a message for you.'

'Nothing awful, is it?'

'No, not in the least. I just want to talk to you for a couple of minutes.'

When they had moved thirty or forty yards away from the house she turned and faced him, smiling but still uneasy.

'Charlie asked me to tell you he and Victor are charging the full price for today but you'll get a refund they don't want to acknowledge.'

She waited a moment and then said, 'Oh. What's that in aid of?'

'I can't imagine. Something to do with the office, probably. Some fiddle or other. I've no idea.'

'Oh. That's not all, is it?'

'No, it isn't, there's another message. This one's from Alun. No, it's all right – not awful at all, I promise you.' When she just stood very still he went on, 'Immediately before he died, in those few seconds, he said something, only a couple of words, but quite clearly. He said, "Little thing". Charlie must have heard too but I doubt whether he understood, but I feel I did. Alun was thinking of you, he was speaking to you.' Peter wanted to take her hand, but lacked confidence to do so. 'He was sending you his love before he died.'

'Might have been,' said Rhiannon. 'Perhaps he was. He used to call me . . .' Her mouth and chin moved in a way that recalled her youthful self to him more sharply and unexpectedly than anything he had yet seen. Then her eyes steadied on him. 'That's still not all, is it?'

'It's all I've got about him, but if you wouldn't mind just . . .'

'Hang on a minute. Stay there.'

He watched her hurrying back up the lawn to where Rosemary and another young woman still stood near the windows. After a moment he realised this must appear inquisitive of him and quickly turned his head away. The movement brought his eyes to a triangle of grass the sun had missed and left apparently still damp with dew. Beyond it, in the sunlight, a dishevelled brownish butterfly was clinging to the boundary fence and stirring feebly. Much further off, woodland flecked with thin greenery ran from one side to the other and out of sight.

When Rhiannon came back she said, staring over Peter's shoulder and speaking in a monotone, 'Thank you for telling me that. Don't mind if we don't say any more now. Can't really talk about him properly yet. But it was nice of you to tell me.'

She waited again and it dawned on him that he had almost no idea of how to start or where he wanted to get to. 'You are staying on here, aren't you, are you? Or are you . . .'

'Yes, for a bit anyway. I'll probably have to find somewhere smaller in the end. Round here, though. Rosemary and William'll be moving to London, but I don't – '

'Really? When? He hasn't said anything about it to me.'

'Perhaps he doesn't know yet. In the autumn. It's for the Bar, you see, for Rosemary.' Rhiannon's expression appealed to Peter not to question her about the Bar.

'Of course. But wouldn't it make sense for you to move there too? You've lived there for so many years.'

'Not now I'm back here. Now I'm here again I want to stay. You probably think that sounds silly – I've heard you go on about the awful – '

'It may sound silly but it isn't. You can't explain it.'

'Not to anybody who isn't Welsh you can't, or even talk about it.'

'Not to the Welsh either. Not to them, of all people. Wales is a subject that can't be talked about. Unless you're making a collection of dishonesty and self-deception and sentimental bullshit. That's all you ever hear.'

She said hopefully, 'But it makes sense when you think about it, to yourself. It's all right then.'

'Yes it is. Indeed it is, but only then.'

'M'm. So you think it's quite sensible on the whole to hang on. You would if you were me.'

He hesitated. She was looking at him in another special way of hers, affectionate, attentive, troubled, the way she had looked at him just before he told her that final abject lie, that there was nothing wrong between them and she was still the only one for him. Over her shoulder now he saw Rosemary, no doubt under orders, step out and head off the nearer approach of one of the hatted females from indoors, stacked lunch-plate at chest level. In sudden agitation he asked himself how long it would take a particular hatless female to miss him and Rhiannon from the party and scurry to find and fuck up. He said in something of a rush,

'Well, that's really what I wanted to talk to you about. Muriel says William getting married means she can leave Wales as she's always wanted, or does now, I don't know, and go back to Yorkshire. When she said that, she hadn't heard he was off to London either or she'd certainly have mentioned it. Well, I'll have to go too, to Yorkshire. I don't want to, I don't want to leave any more than you do, I've lived here all my life. And it's more than that, as you say. But I just can't think of anything else to do. The house and everything else all belong to her and I haven't got a bean. A pension that would keep me in corn-flakes. It doesn't sound very high-minded, I know, but it's a bit of a struggle being high-minded when you're hard up and pushing seventy.'

'But you wouldn't be able to stand it,' she said in open dismay.

'I'll have to. It's not sort of uniformly appalling. Some of the time we struggle along more or less all right. Six of one and half a dozen of the other.'

'Oh, really? Funny, I've never known anything to be that. It's just a thing people say.'

'To sound decent. Yes.'

Rhiannon shook her head impatiently to recall herself to the point. 'She'll change her mind. It's a big step at her age.'

'No she won't. Not after saying it the way she did, with dates and things. I know her. Take it from me, there's nothing for it.' He said with great emphasis and finality, 'I hate everything about it, but I'll have to go.'

'But you can't. I mean I thought we were going to start seeing each other again. You'd said you'd ring me up but you never did.'

'I did mean to but when it came to it I couldn't face it. Me, not you.'

'But I thought by about now you might be thinking it would be all right to. With the children getting married and everything. To each other, I mean. I was so hoping you would.'

'After everything I've done? After the way I treated you?'

'Yes. It was losing you I minded. The other didn't matter really, not after a bit. Didn't I tell you that time, we'd been to the Golf Club party? You can't have been listening. God alive, perhaps I didn't really say it. Anyway, I meant to tell you you'll always be . . . I can't say it now either. It used to be so easy. Now, it's like talking about Wales.'

Slowly, to give her time to back off if she felt like it, and furtively, so that Rosemary and the others should not see, Peter reached out his hand. Rhiannon gripped it. Furtively again, he looked at her and saw that she was trying to look at him. Yes, she had changed: not the direct confident glance now.

'Let me try. Though you might well not think so,' he said with care, 'and there was certainly a time when I forgot it myself, I've always loved you and I do to this day. I'm sorry it sounds ridiculous because I'm so fat and horrible, and not at all nice or even any fun, but I mean it. I only wish it was worth more.'

'Ring me up. This time.' With her back half-turned she said, 'I'm sorry, but I can't talk any more now.'

'I've got so much to tell you.'

He again watched her retreating, moving hardly any faster than earlier, certainly not running. One of her distinctions from other females had always been that she only ran to catch buses and such, not to let the world know about her wild free spirit or alternatively the coruscating wave of emotion that for the moment enfolded her. At her approach Rosemary released a foolish-looking black dog whose collar she had been holding. It jumped up at her in an ungainly fashion, half fell over itself on landing and followed her into the house.

Peter did the same at a greater distance, feeling very much drunker than he had ever felt in his life before, or something. By the time he got to the food most of it had been swept away, the main body of it at least, but back-ups were still in place. He found the sandwiches excellent, especially the cheese-and-pickle and the egg-and-tomato, more especially still with plenty of Vin Rouge de Pays to help them past his teeth, and he silently undertook never again to underrate Victor, as he was conscious of having done in days gone by. But he commented aloud on the merit of the sandwiches.

'First-rate sandwiches these,' he said. 'Especially the egg-and-pickle.'

'Don't seem to have come to those yet myself,' said Garth.

Peter had started on Dundee cake and Founders Reserve port when the word came that the speeches would begin in five minutes. Instantly, as intended, all those with elderly bladders, or as many as were capable of responding, made for the toilets. Others went or were there too. From among a small crowd round the one outside the kitchen Peter identified Percy Morgan.

'Marvellously happy occasion,' he told him.

'Oh, I should just about think it is, boy.' Percy was perhaps a little startled to hear this from Peter about anything. 'Seems very nice, your new daughter-in-law. I've seen a bit of her, you know, with her mother. No nonsense about her, oh no by George. Never took to the father, I tell you frankly. Never much cared, myself, for people who laid it on thick about the Welsh heritage and all that. I don't know whether you agree with me, Peter, but as I see it that kind of thing is, well it can be a trifle embarrassing, you know, if it's overdone.'

'Oh absolutely, I was saying just now – '

'I'll stay for the speeches, of course, and then I think I'll be cutting along. It certainly takes you back, this lot, eh?'

'You mean the – '

'Well, queueing up for a piss. Takes you back to nights out after rugger. Takes me back, anyway. She went off it in a week flat after one chat with Dewi.'

There had been so little apparent pause between this remark and the previous one that Peter wondered whether he might have passed out on his feet for a few seconds. 'Oh yes,' he said, doing his best to smile encouragingly.

'Liver,' said Percy. 'Another couple of months the way she was going and – ' he passed the edge of his hand across his throat and gave a loud palatal exhalation. 'Of course, her being off it, I'm glad for her, but it leaves me a bit up in the air. I used to be the bloke with this impossible wife who was bloody magnificent about her, that was what I did, so what do I do now she's possible again all of a sudden?'

'Yes, I can see that. I think I'll try upstairs.'

Upstairs Peter found waiting Siân Smith, Duncan Weaver and another man he was nearly sure he was supposed to know, had even perhaps invited. It seemed to him reasonable, and also enterprising, to go up a further flight to the top floor. Here a passage ran the width of the building, at the far end of which he was just in time to glimpse a half-naked white-haired female with a garment or two over her arm dashing across and out of sight. A door shut and a bolt clicked. After a moment another door opened and the face of old Vaughan Mowbray peered out and turned in his direction, and after another moment, occupied by mutual astonishment, drew back again. On the whole Peter felt he might as well go back to the floor below.

He found the situation there unchanged, except that Siân had moved over to the landing window and was leaning across the sill, presumably in quest of fresh air. He presumed otherwise when he was near enough to pick up the noises she was making. Duncan Weaver also had his eyes on her, more casually though; with his deafness he had no call to shift from the fresh-air presumption. Simultaneously the second fart of Peter's day rang out – from Duncan it had to be, unless the other man's start, glare and forceful rattling at the door-handle were the work of a consummate actor. Peter contemplated briefly the strangeness of a world without sound.

There was still a queue near the kitchen, though with different people in it, but now he came to think of it there was a little cloak-room place by the front door which he had not yet tried. In mid-transit he was again perfectly placed to catch old Arnold Spurling and the best man quite turbulently hustling the Levantine-moustached Tony Bainbridge along the hall and out of the house. Before the fellow was lost to view Peter saw him mouthing curses and shaking his fist in an old-fashioned way.

The speeches came and went. Drinking continued until suddenly there was nothing to put in your glass, not even wine. Victor was having the whole lot collected, stowed in cartons, carried out to a small off-white van. One moment Peter was in a group, the next alone with Rosemary – Rosemary Thomas, as she now was and as he addressed her a couple of times.

'I gather you're going to be seeing something of my mother,' she said. Her ears had fuller lobes than Rhiannon's.

'Am I? I mean of course I am, but how do you know?'

'She told me.' Rosemary looked him in the eye and said not altogether seriously, but quite seriously enough, 'Now you behave yourself, right?'

'What? How do you mean?'

'I mean don't misbehave.'

'What? How could I do that?'

'Any pal of Alun's could find a way. On today's showing – no problem. No, I mean severely misbehave. Like let her down. If you do, William and I will kill you, okay? Oh Peter, I don't think you've met Catriona Semple, also reading law at Oxford. Catriona, this is my father-in-law.'

10   Malcolm

'How's she getting on up there?'

Gwen turned one of the neatly-written pages. 'Oh, having a whale of a time, it appears. Dinner-parties every night, house never empty, weekends in the country. Country? What country?'

'It's quite a big place, actually, the size of here. She must still know a great many people locally, some of them pretty well off I shouldn't be surprised, even in these days of industrial havoc.'

'Muriel never kept up with them much as far as I heard. Anyway, there she is. The theatre, what's she talking about? In Middlesborough? It can't be the theatre as *civilised folk* think of it. Racing? Is there a course somewhere in that region?'

'Sorry, no idea,' said Malcolm, smiling and spreading his hands. 'Not my department.'

'No, I realise that, no, I just thought you might happen to know. Whippet-racing perhaps she means.'

'Well, it's good to hear that she seems to be doing reasonably well.'

'It says something for her pride that she exerts herself to give that impression.'

'I'm afraid I'm not quite with you.'

'If you want my opinion, she's protesting too much. Life's not turning out to be much fun, how could it in a hole like that, but she's buggered if she's going to let anyone think she's made a mistake. Very roughly.'

'Maybe, I suppose.' Malcolm tried to sound about half convinced. 'What does she say about Peter?'

'Nothing very much. She's surer than ever she was right to make the break when she did, exactly what she said before, er, oh and if you see Peter tell the lazy sod to drop her a line. Underplaying it there, you see.'

'She must miss him a lot in spite of everything.'

'It's not him she misses, for Christ's sake, it's having a husband as a social seal of quality. And then, well, she doesn't like him not being there in another way, because he still belongs to her really. Some women don't like parting with anything on their inventory even when they've no further use for same.'

'You're amazing, the way you see things. I'd never have been able to penetrate that far into her motives.' He missed the sharp look these remarks drew from Gwen and went tentatively on, 'But you don't visualise her coming back.'

She gave a restrained sigh and said, 'Peter's more likely to go there than she is to admit she was wrong in letters nine feet high, and that's it. Mind if I take first knock in the bathroom?'

'You go ahead.'

Left alone, Malcolm poured a last cup of tea and lit his daily cigarette. Putting aside the *Western Mail* for later he noticed a section headed 'Welsh News', a mere quarter of a page or less, and that in the daily newspaper of the capital of the Principality. That, he considered, was coming out into the open with a vengeance. But it was hard to go on feeling indignant for very long, especially after having just spent a good ten minutes reading about a police scandal in South London and not much less on the prospects for England's cricketers on their Australian tour.

As strongly as ever before, the conversational dealings at his breakfast-table had reminded Malcolm of those at another, the one at 221B Baker Street. There, as here, the first party regularly offered well-meaning provisional explanations of bits of human behaviour and the second party exposed their naivety, ignorance, over-simplification, non-virtuous unworldliness. But there, unlike here, the exposures were sometimes softened with a favourite-pupil tolerance or even varied with an occasional cry of 'Excellent!' or 'One for you, Watson!' Nor was it recorded of Holmes that half of what he said came in aural italics or bold or sanserif. Had Gwen started piling this on recently? Or had she only started doing it so's-you'd-notice recently? Well, they had been married a long time.

He picked up Muriel's letter. The firm, spacious hand, which he could not remember having seen before, impressed him and made him wish, vaguely and momentarily, that she had made more of herself than she had. Scorning the small change of inquiries after health or other sociability, the text launched itself *in medias res* with a fully dramatised but not very lucid account of some visit to somebody somewhere. The more factual stuff came later. Among it Malcolm noticed a piece of information, or supposed information, that Gwen had not passed on: in alliance with two friends and the daughter of one of them, Muriel proposed to open and run what she called a coffee-shop in a suburban shopping-centre. The way she talked about it sounded to him quite unlike part of a brave or overdone attempt to hide boredom and loneliness, whatever bloody Sherlock might say.

Malcolm cleared the table, loaded the dishwasher and set it going. Of late the steady humming it made had been reinforced by an irregular drumming and it shuddered violently every few seconds. With no one repairing anything any more the best plan was probably to let it run until it blew itself up. *Western Mail* in hand he strolled to the cloakroom. Some delay, but no real bother there, in fact all was well – as far as he knew.

No, all was well. He had started telling people who asked him how he was keeping that he was all right as far as he knew, and then stopped when he realised that that was as much as was meant by just saying you were all right. As if it mattered.

Gwen had about finished at her dressing-table, squirting anti-static fluid on her tinted lenses and preparing to follow with the impregnated cloth. He thought the movements of her hands made them look slightly fat.

'All right if I take the car? You'll be looking in at the Bible, will you?'

'Might as well, I thought.'

'If Peter's there you could give him Muriel's message, perhaps.'

'Eh? Oh yes. Actually he hasn't been in for a week or two.'

'One can't help wondering . . .' She sat facing him on the oblong padded stool, her spectacles held up to the light. 'Has he ever said if he hands over any cash for his bed and board? Makes any contribution to the household?'

'Well no. Nobody's asked him, not even Garth. Putting up at Rhiannon's for a bit is what it's called.'

'For quite a bit – what is it, three months? Fascinating. In Wales. Under the same roof as an unprotected female in Wales. And her a widow too. You'd think you were in the twentieth century.'

'Good luck to them is what I say.'

'Oh, do you really? It's certainly what I say. I also say it to or with reference to the representatives of the younger generation. I imagine the lad can practise his trade no less profitably in London than hereabouts. Anything to get out of this dump.'

'You can call it that if you like,' said Malcolm. 'Personally I feel that any place where two people can manage to fall in love can't be as bad as all that.'

'Meaning who? Meaning who?'

'Well – William and Rosemary.'

'Ah. Well, of course. Malcolm dear, I was just – I meant that's how William might think of it, as a dump to get out of. I'm very nicely set up here, thank you.' And she smiled at him.

'Sorry,' said Malcolm. He had forgotten to include sonic inverted commas in his run-through of Gwen's special voice-effects.

She got to her feet after that and brushed down her chequered front. 'Well. Give my love to Charlie.'

'I will if he's there. He hasn't been in for a bit either.'

'I'm worried about Charlie, I really am. That evening at Dorothy's, you noticed nothing out of the way but I thought he looked awful. Awful.'

One of Gwen's things was not only to know better in general but to know better than you did about the people you were supposed to know better than she did in particular. Or so it had more than once seemed to Malcolm, who now said, 'He told me he hadn't been sleeping well for a year or more.'

'Right, I'm off. Smarty-pants Eirwen could do with some critical comments on the exhibition of alternative Welsh culture at the Dafydd ap Gwilym Arts Centre' – some system of tonal notation would obviously have to be developed to handle stuff like that – 'and then it's coffee and perhaps a glass of lemonade at Siân's. See you.'

Malcolm went and brushed his teeth in a glancing style, an even less demanding exercise than formerly, now that the lower-jaw one with a hole in it had fallen to pieces on a mouthful of ham at the wedding in the spring. While he shaved he thought about the fact that since the moment when he had brought her the news of Alun's death Gwen had not mentioned him in any way. At first he had put this down to shock or other temporary state, but it had long since been too late for that. For months he had been able to close a conversation with her by an oblique reference, or would find he had done so, not that he had much use for such a weapon. What kind of punishment or self-punishment her silence was meant to inflict he had very little idea, but if she had wanted to remove any doubts he might have been trying to hang on to about whether she had had some sort of affair with Alun – well, she had pulled that off in fine style. He had not quite lost the hope that one day a casual pronouncement of the name would touch off an equally casual allusion to that affair, and he could tell her that that was of no consequence and never had been. But he judged it very unlikely. And it was odd how a taboo on a single, less than all-important subject had seemingly turned out to impose a blackout on so much else.

When he had finished in the bathroom Malcolm fetched his jazz records from the sitting-room, where they had been lying about for ages, and put them back in the white cabinet in his study on the first floor. Before settling down at his work-table he glanced out of the window. What he could see of the sky past various roofs was overcast, promising rain, real Welsh autumn weather. He had an hour or more, before leaving for the Bible, to work on his translation of a long poem by Cynddelw Mawr ap Madog Wladaidd (*c.* 1320–?1388), *Heledd Cariad* – more of an adaptation, actually, for among other adjustments he had altered the physical characteristics of the central figure to correspond with Rhiannon's. If she had found love with Peter he was glad, because he had nothing to give her himself. But she had given him something. The poem, his poem, was going to be the best tribute he could pay to the only woman who had ever cried for him.